TORN BLOOD

TEHILLIM 137:5–6

אִם אֶשְׁכָּחֵךְ יְרוּשָׁלִָם תִּשְׁכַּח יְמִינִי
תִּדְבַּק לְשׁוֹנִי
לְחִכִּי אִם לֹא אֶזְכְּרֵכִי אִם לֹא
אַעֲלֶה אֶת יְרוּשָׁלִַם עַל רֹאשׁ שִׂמְחָתִי

PSALMS 137:5–6

If I forget you, O Jerusalem,
May my right hand forget her skill.
May my tongue cleave to the roof of my mouth,
If I do not remember you,
If I do not exalt Jerusalem
Above my chief joy.

TORN BLOOD

DAVID J. BAIN

Bo Iti Press, LLC
PO Box 1045
Jackson, WY 83001
www.BoItiPress.com

ISBN-13: 978-0-9881710-0-8 (paperback)
ISBN-13: 978-0-9881710-1-5 (ebook: ePub)
ISBN-13: 978-0-9881710-2-2 (ebook: Kindle / mobi)

Library of Congress Control Number: 2013906864

Printed in the United States of America

Special photo-effects added by RD Studio
Map by RD Studio
Book design by DesignForBooks.com

Find out more at

www.TornBlood.com

Some tales are tall

Some . . . true.

Hidden in antiquity

as passing years bury their light.

Dig deep, roots appear

seemingly without life

yet nourishing all that grows from them.

This is such a tale.

RELATIVE SIZE OF ISRAEL TO THE UNITED STATES

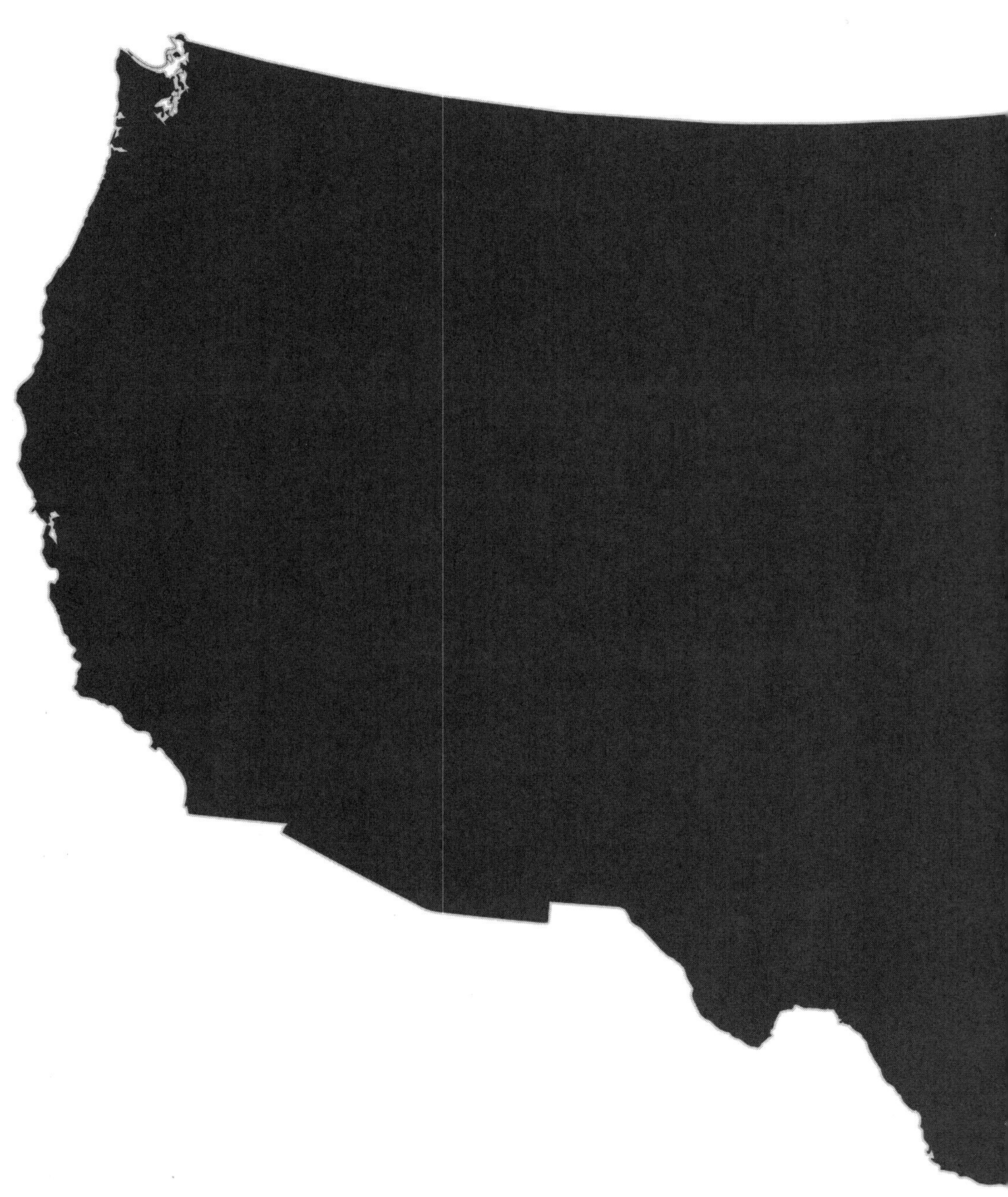

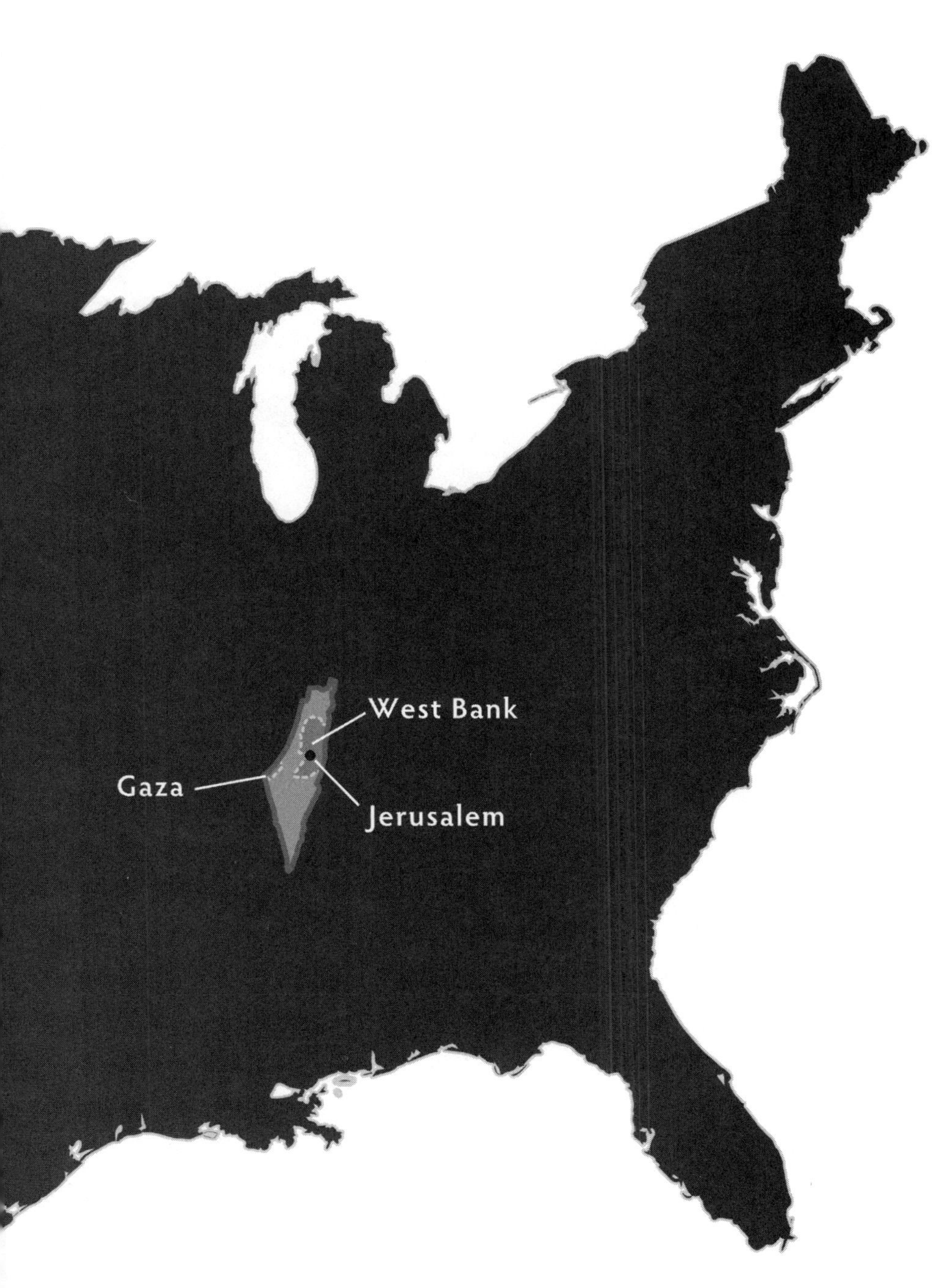
West Bank
Gaza
Jerusalem

Disclaimer

Torn Blood is a work of fiction. All references to real people, events, establishments, organizations, or locales are intended only to provide a sense of authenticity, and are used fictitiously. All other characters, and all incidents and dialogue, are drawn from the author's imagination and are not to be construed as real. Any devices or weapons used in *Torn Blood* may or may not exist as depicted but are used solely for plot purposes.

Most government organizations mentioned in *Torn Blood* are authentic organizations in their respective governments. These real-world agencies have been used solely as a plot device to further the dramatic impact of the story. None of these agencies have been involved, in any way, with the events portrayed in *Torn Blood.*

There are more than one billion people of the Muslim faith in the world. The overwhelming majority embrace peaceful coexistence. *Torn Blood's* antagonists are terrorists—not militants—terrorists; radical Jihadists. Some estimate a mere one percent of all Muslims are radical Jihadists. That means, as you read these words, there are 1,000,000 men, women, and children (yes children are used, such is blind hatred) who are sworn to wage war on every other human being who will not conform to their interpretation of god. So committed are these individuals to Jihad, armed struggle, they count it god's blessing to forfeit their lives in the pursuit of purifying and extending their faith by killing all who refuse to agree.

It is imperative to remember that the overwhelming majority of Muslims, ninety-nine percent by some estimates, are peace-loving men, women, and children whom any community is richly blessed to have as neighbors and friends. *Torn Blood* deals with a tiny subset that follows the path of hatred which expresses itself in violence. Only by acknowledging this evil can it be dealt with. By ignoring its existence we open ourselves to catastrophe that will make 9/11 look like a September stroll in the park. *Torn Blood* is fictional. The hatred portrayed in *Torn Blood* is as real as the evening news.

—David J. Bain

Acknowledgements

To a young Israeli dynamo, Channi Sagal, for your research and attention to follow-up questions, seemingly without end, I am indebted. Ken Harthum, your expertise helped bring life to an event I pray will never become reality.

Gabe Robinson, thank you for commitment balanced by knowledge and wisdom far beyond your years. Melissa, your perspective and observations made me look deeper. Thank you Kathleen Erickson for your steady and insightful proofreading.

To the one whose life manifests the meaning of the word love spoken about so eloquently in 1st Corinthians. Doris, you are the living example that a life of faith is possible. It is because of you this story has been written, for without your faith in whatever meager abilities I might have stumbled upon there would be no words, no story. Thank you my love, we did it.

PROLOGUE

Tuesday 11 September 2007

STEPNOGORSK SCIENTIFIC AND TECHNICAL INSTITUTE FOR MICROBIOLOGY, NORTHERN KAZAKHSTAN

Behind the lectern, in the stark windowless room, Dr. Vikesha Nikitin, pausing to look at the chosen, understood what God must feel; he was about to bestow life and death.

He forged ahead with the scripted remarks. "A bacterium of the genus bacillus anthracis was isolated. Of the three types—inhalational, gastrointestinal, and cutaneous—only inhalational affords maximal battlefield outcomes. Existing strains effected a mortality rate approaching forty-five percent. Research identified, and then isolated, a variant strain which demonstrated an eighty-six percent mortality rate. Endospores were purified and the spore preparation was coated with an excipient which carries the pathogen, or in colloquial terms, the germs. Some at the U.S. Defense Intelligence Agency heard rumors of this strain but we managed to keep the Americans guessing as to its existence."

A member of the select audience arose, waited to be recognized, and then spoke. "There were rumors of the Jefferson Project in the U. S."

"Ah yes, the Jefferson Project in Nevada. We provided faulty specimens from preliminary studies; such are the demands of existing treaties. The U.S. Defense Threat Reduction Agency did some work attempting to isolate our variant. In fact, they were close to its discovery but with strategically placed assistance we were able to limit their success and divert attention to other activities. Our operatives were aware of DTRA's activities and capabilities. One must be vigilant when pioneering efficacious methods for realizing one's goals," the doctor replied.

"Most impressive," the questioner responded, and then sat down.

"Are there other questions?"

From the back of the room a solitary figure with a salt and pepper beard arose. "You speak to the strength of different strains which all agree are lethal, but I am not a scientist, can you tell me how anthrax works?"

"In inhalational anthrax, spores enter the subject's lungs where they germinate and multiply in the alveoli—"

"Alveoli? I am not familiar with this word."

"Alveoli are the final branches of the respiratory tree, which act as primary gas exchange units of the lungs. Infection then spreads to lymph nodes and once in the bloodstream releases toxins, resulting in internal bleeding and finally destruction of tissue."

"Yes, yes, that is all good, but still you speak as a scientist. Which is good, we need scientific expertise, but I do not understand what would be observed when this weapon is used if one were so unfortunate to be in the midst of this." Nervous laughter rippled inside the room.

"Within twenty-four to thirty-six hours after initial exposure to the bacterium, subjects would develop cold or flu-like symptoms: headache, fever, sweating, cough, shortness of breath, chest pain. During the next twenty-four to forty-eight hours a rapid physiological decline results with increased fever, severe shortness of breath, shock, and finally death. Eighty-six percent of subjects who contract this strain will die twenty-four to forty-eight hours after the onset of initial symptoms, and this rate will not vary even with early treatment."

"Won't Zionists simply put on gas masks to avoid exposure?"

"This would be ineffectual for two reasons. First, the spores have been bio-engineered to pass through currently manufactured masks while also being large enough to remain in the lungs when one exhales. It is a beautifully delicate balance since spores must stay in the lungs to effect disease. This singular requirement demanded great patience and technological skill to accomplish. The second reason is that the anthrax will be dispersed as airborne particles, invisible to the naked eye with no discernible scent, detectable only through the use of specialized equipment. This is substantially different than what we observed when the Aimes strain was sent through the mail on the East Coast of the United States in 2001, which was a trial by friends intended to test deployment and defenses. The quantity of material we are dealing with and its delivery system will not avail itself to being placed in envelopes," Nikitin said, then smiled. "Though authorities may be aware of the situation—Jews have proven themselves to be worthy adversaries—by the time the anthrax is released it will be too late for remediation. We alone developed antibiotics for our variant. The array of treatment antibiotics—fluoroquinolones, ciprofloxacin, doxycycline, erythromycin, vancomycin, and penicillin—are of sporadic efficacy and thus of no strategic value. Other questions?" the doctor finished.

"Spores from anthrax do not disappear," another voice pointed out. "I have been informed they reside in the soil for decades. Too many souls have waited, some for over sixty years, to return to the land of their birth. We must be able to repopulate Palestinian land without further delay. This is a major concern that could change all of our plans."

Rising from her chair near the front of the room to her full glorious height, with unapologetic freckles, and fiery red hair cascading to her shoulders, a woman focused her attention on the speaker as every male eye focused on her. "Vikesha, I'd like to speak to this concern."

"I would be most pleased Aleksandra."

As she moved catlike to the lectern, throbbing eyes followed every move. When she reached the dais, Dr. Nikitin introduced Dr. Feedorov.

"Thank you, Vikesha. Our team has been responsible for the development of this strain. One of the greatest challenges faced, from a weaponization perspective, was, as you have pointed out, the lifespan of the virus once released into the environment. Research documents that spores remain viable, and capable of interacting with living organisms wherever conditions permit, for decades. Though some degradation occurs, spores remain active and lethal. We have addressed the issue by bonding rod-shaped gram-positive bacterium with our modified anthrax spores and sealing them in a vacuum to halt reproduction. These bacteria begin to reproduce only upon exposure to nitrogen, oxygen, argon, and carbon dioxide, or, as you would know it, air, at which point they begin attacking anthrax spores that have not begun to replicate inside living organisms, rendering them ineffectual within forty-eight hours. Thus we are able to neutralize enemy forces while ensuring this weapon's effective life is limited to forty-eight hours."

"You are saying two days after anthrax is released anyone can enter this area?"

"Precisely, if there are no other questions?" When none arose Dr. Aleksandra Feedorov returned to her seat, every male eye enslaved to each of her steps.

Dr. Nikitin waited for his colleague to be seated and attention returned to the lectern. "After the strain was stabilized, a vaccine for our variant was isolated by independent teams of Biopreparat scientists. Researchers worked seven years transforming the administration of the vaccine from subcutaneous injections to aerosol immunizations. I will not go into the great difficulties involved in such a task. Suffice to say they were monumental. While other countries discovered limitations in such methodologies, we have been successful in our implementations. The microbial properties of the cell-free filtrates, that is, the vaccine which contains only modified bacillus anthracis to create immunity, were disseminated using highly concentrated, fine-dispersal aerosolization, which yielded results that have yet to be realized in any theater of operation by any other country."

"Including the eagle?" asked one of the listeners.

"The United States, capabilities are sometimes overrated," replied the speaker, a hint of a smile rising on his face.

"How effective is this methodology for immunization, doctor?" questioned one of the visitors.

"Dr. Taysir—" Dr. Nikitin addressed the audience member.

"No names, please, one must never use names. There are too many ears and we would be forced to look elsewhere," Dr. Taysir said.

"Friend, you are here because this is the only place to find not only bio-solutions but also counteragents," replied Vikesha Nikitin.

Removing his glasses by the rims, Dr. Taysir glanced down, seemingly lost in thought, before returning the bifocals to his head and securing them behind his ears. Focusing his attention back to the speaker he continued: "There are many paths one may choose my friend. Though some are longer, they eventually lead to the same destination."

"True, but mutually beneficial goals bring the greatest good."

"*Na'am,* Yes," Dr. Taysir replied. "Of this I am certain; now about the efficacy of aerosol immunization, doctor."

"Multiple immunizations utilizing subcutaneous injections are standard for anthrax. Six are required, given two weeks apart, then additional boosters at six, twelve, and eighteen months with annual boosters thereafter. Our models indicate a successful immunization rate of ninety-four percent with a single aerosol vaccination, a follow-up at twelve months, and thereafter every five years. The aerosolization of the variant vaccine improves its efficacy while decreasing the number of immunizations required for protection."

"Has this technology been adequately tested?"

"All research methodologies have been thoroughly vetted. We began with computer models, proceeded to cellular studies, advancing to animal experimentation on multiple species, and after all trials demonstrated success we completed trials with volunteers."

This was met by subdued snickering. Many at the conference had longstanding arrangements for their enemies. It was all the more pleasurable to get rid of impediments while allowing them to serve a greater purpose. Somehow it elevated what the unenlightened might call barbarous to noble.

"We produced a strain with a modified molecular structure which increased its efficacy, or, as you would understand, made it more lethal. Remember the final molecular structure of the vaccine could not be completed until the bacterium was stabilized. Once this was done, volunteers were immunized utilizing aerosol protocols."

"Then the aerosol will protect our people?"

"We have completed rigorous testing protocols. After 10,000 test incidents, we have conclusively demonstrated that aerosol application of the vaccine is efficacious."

"I am most pleased with what we have heard today. We are one step closer to ending an injustice our people have endured for too many years," Dr. Taysir said.

There was a collective nod as thoughts of a final and lasting victory danced through the conference members' minds. In the back of the room, Imam Marwan's soul smiled.

CHAPTER

1

Thursday February 21 2008

United States Embassy, Consular Section, 71 Ha-Yarkon Street, Tel Aviv

Dialing her well-used phone, Lynda Touree smiled into the vacant stare of the weary presence before her while awaiting her boss's familiar snarl.

"What now?" the phone's receiver demanded, civility being a luxury seldom afforded.

"Mr. Cantwell, Addison Deverell is standing in front of my desk."

"And I am being interrupted because?"

"He is reporting for duty sir."

"Duty, no one's listed as arriving for a month, unless you failed to get me papers."

"Sir, all arrival credentials are in your possession."

"Then who, as I so kindly asked, is this interruption?"

"Mr. Deverell's papers indicate he's our new consular officer, sir. He is due twenty-one days from today."

"Three weeks, one month, no difference. Not due today—don't bother me today."

"Sir, you know mission protocol states once a consular department officer proffers assignment papers they must be accepted by the deputy administrator."

"How about handing him a map of Gaza and a compass, that ought to keep him out of my hair for three weeks."

"You don't mean that."

"Don't bet on it."

There was a pause on the line. "Sir, Mr. Deverell?"

"I'll get to him when I get to him." Slamming down the phone's receiver, Deputy Administrator Cantwell could be heard cursing through the meager door that separated his office from the rest of humanity at the back of the embassy.

Smiling, Lynda looked up, "Welcome to the U.S. Embassy, Mr. Deverell. I believe Mr. Cantwell would like you to have a seat until he can welcome you to Israel. You'll want to hang on to these," Lynda said holding out his assignment papers. "Mr. Cantwell needs to personally accept them."

Retreating to the back wall, where four overstuffed chairs formed a protective semi-circle, Addison wondered when he'd be free to disappear into Israel to uncover what he came three weeks before his reporting date to find.

Later that afternoon

The phone's ring invaded Addison's thoughts. He strained to overhear *Ms. Lynda Touree*, as her desk's nameplate announced, speaking with the wild man from the inner sanctum.

"Yes, Mr. Cantwell," she paused. "Yes sir, he's still waiting, patiently I might add." She listened intently. "I'll call and see who's available." After several silent moments she said, "I'll let you know, sir."

Lynda looked across to Addison and smiled, hitting her phone's receiver button, entering numbers with the dexterity of practiced fingers.

"Liddy, who do we have available for escort?" She listened for a moment, then said, "How about consulate?" More silence, then "how long has he been with us?" Again silence, "credentials?" After several nods of Lynda's head she said, "thanks hon," hit disconnect and dialed consulate's inside line. "Marcie, hi hon, this is Lynda at the DA's office Tel Aviv . . . Fine and you? I'm looking for one of your escorts, Hafiz IbnMansur. Will you put me through?" a momentary pause then, "Do you know when he's expected?" Another brief silence followed by, "please have him call me soon as he arrives. It is most pressing. Thanks, hon." With that she hung up and dialed the inner sanctum.

"What now?"

"No one is available locally for Mr. Deverell. I located someone down at consulate in East Jerusalem who should do nicely: Hafiz IbnMansur, he's their guide for in-country tours and orientations." Lynda fell silent listening intently, finally volunteering, "mostly visiting VIPs, but he has escorted several State people and been with consulate over ten years." After a brief pause she continued, "He's away from his desk, doing some volunteer work with Elizabeth Daniels of Messianic Jews International."

"Daniels!" Cantwell bellowed through the door. "I ran into that fanatic at a meet and greet when I first arrived. Damn near started a riot toe to toe with Muslim and Jewish clerics. I don't want that troublemaker—"

"As I said, Mr. IbnMansur is performing volunteer work but is expected back shortly." Listening, Lynda then responded, "No, I don't know what shortly means, I will inform you the moment he calls." With that she hung up her phone. She winked at Addison. "Patience, it's a long career path you have chosen and it seems that begins today. Are you hungry?"

Addison nodded.

In no time he was tearing into a ham and cheese on rye and washing it down with an ice-cold cola while he sat imprisoned in his overstuffed chair.

As he ate, a lone janitor at the end of the hall finished dust mopping the floor. Going to the utility closet she exchanged her dirty dust mop head for a clean one, put on her coat, and headed for security check. Passing Lynda's desk she said, "See you tomorrow, Lynda."

"Getting out early Yasmina? Hot date?"

"Father would have thoughts on that. A cousin is with child and soon to be delivered. She asks for help so I'll stop by on the way home."

"Aren't you the kind one. See you tomorrow."

After clearing security Yasmina stopped by her cousin's then walked home. Diplomatic Security Service, on routine surveillance, noted her early departure and the visit. Lynda Touree would be questioned the next day; Yasmina was assigned to her area.

Later that evening, Yasmina's cousin's husband paid a visit to a café PMIJ members were known to patronize.

The ringing of the phone jolted Addison to consciousness after the food, warmth of the room, and jet-lag had caught up with him. He stretched and attempted to focus on Lynda's phone conversation. As she hung up he busied himself with the paper he had picked up at Ben Gurion. His Hebrew skills were coming along but reading right to left still felt awkward. It would come with time, he knew, if he could just report and get out of here. Becoming lost in a story, he barely noticed the phone ring again nor Lynda's conversation. When his mind surfaced from the Hebrew characters, he heard Lynda say, ". . . within the hour, I appreciate that."

Lynda dialed an extension and waited while listening to the receiver before saying, "Mr. Cantwell, Mr. IbnMansur at consulate just called. He has received clearance and will be up within the hour to discuss your needs. Call if you have questions." As soon as she cradled the handset on its base, her phone rang and Addison could hear Sid Cantwell's voice through his closed door.

"Why in the devil didn't you put consulate through to me?"

"Your line was busy, sir.'

"And you couldn't walk the fifteen lousy steps to my office?"

"You told me yesterday not to interrupt you this afternoon since you would be reviewing the Status Report for Washington."

"Yesterday—yesterday was before young mister what's-his-name showed up unannounced."

"Addison Deverell is the young man's name. You might as well learn it now because he's going to be with us for quite some time."

"Don't remind me."

"You just like scaring people."

"What did he say?"

"Who is that, sir?"

"Touree!"

"Mr. IbnMansur asked what our need was. He was most polite, unlike others I know."

"And?"

"And, he said he would need to talk with you personally, had been given clearance to do so and would be up within the hour, exactly what I said in my message."

"Just make sure you only let him in and not Deverell as well."

Hanging up, Lynda went back to her computer.

What have I gotten myself into? Addison wondered. He dove back into the *Yedioth Ahronoth* newspaper, the safest harbor he could find.

~

"Mr. Deverell . . . Mr. Deverell?" Addison started as he felt a woman's hand on his shoulder. He struggled to orientate himself. The clock on the wall read 5:17. An Arabic man came into view over the woman's right shoulder.

"You drifted off," Lynda Touree said. "Considering how long you've been kept waiting it was most sensible. Someone has come for you." With that the Arabic man stepped forward while Lynda said, "Mr. IbnMansur will be your escort for the next few days."

Handing the man a clipboard, Lynda said, "Just the usual: Sign right there beneath Mr. Cantwell's signature."

Taking a pen from his jacket pocket with his left hand he scribbled on the page then handed it back to Lynda.

She gave him a copy. "You'll want to hang onto this."

Addison stood, dropping the half-crumpled newspaper on the floor and extended his hand to this stranger whose name he wasn't sure he had heard correctly. Grabbing his hand the intruder shook it perfunctorily, saying, "Quickly, collect luggage—follow me."

~

Sunlight glistened off the mirrored surfaces of the random array of skyscrapers as it followed its daily path toward the sea. Its reflected glory embraced shorter buildings as they maintained their silent witness to Tel Aviv's earlier years. The first Jewish city built since biblical times was far removed from its founding in 1909 as Ahuzat Bayit, when it had been established on sand dunes by sixty families as a low-cost alternative to the more expensive Arab town of Jaffa. Renamed Tel Aviv one year later, it never looked back.

After the sun set, the city began its metamorphose from a metropolis of commerce to nightlife mecca. Family men and women withdrew to the suburbs of Ramat Ha-Sharon, Giv'atayim, and Bnei Brak, as the nocturnal transformation took until just after 10 P.M. when the young and beautiful left their lairs in a nightly ritual of wanton and abandoned carousing.

Addison watched as Hafiz careened between countless cars, squeezing past fenders, oblivious to the near misses as he charged through traffic with little more than a grunt every now and then.

"Would it be impolite for me to ask where you're taking me?"

"No." Hafiz spat out, followed by another jarring lane change and then silence.

"Well?" Addison asked.

"Going to Intercontinental David."

"And?" Addison pressed.

"Embassy has standing reservations. If lucky we get suite with couple bedrooms, not so lucky, a room, and two double beds."

"What do you mean we?" Addison asked.

"We, you and me," Hafiz said.

"I don't need company," Addison shot back. "Just drop me by a decent hotel and I'll find my way back to the embassy when I'm rested."

"Sorry," Hafiz said. "As of now, we're joined. Where you go, Hafiz goes. Never lost a Junior F.S.O., and with your boss's reputation, don't feel like starting now."

"Don't you live in Jerusalem?" Addison asked.

"East Jerusalem," Hafiz's responded. "You eavesdrop on Lynda?"

"Then why stay in Tel Aviv with me?"

"Because that's what I'm paid to do. Forget everything you learned in orientation and training at State in U.S. of A. This world has no equal. You'd be swallowed up and never surface again—ever. It's my job to see that doesn't happen, at least for the next few days."

"Look, we'll just keep this between you and me. I don't need a sitter."

"Like hell you don't," Hafiz snarled. "You have American written all over you. There are people who will slice your throat open for that fancy watch on wrist."

"America tries to help around the world, and what's wrong with my watch? It was a graduation gift."

"Not everybody wants to be helped. Tomorrow you'll get different watch and keep graduation memento from those who would deprive you of future memories. Addison, you're nobody. You have an advanced degree and will spend long days pushing papers for impatient, ungrateful people all demanding more than you have to give. Maybe, after years of sacrifice, you'll rise high enough to make a tiny difference that will never be anything because important decisions are made by political brokers at nation-state level, not career diplomats. To start life's work you showed up ahead of schedule. Don't think that nice man you tried to report to takes an interruption to his world kindly. Our time together is costing your government money it didn't intend to spend, but the damage you could do outweighs the cost, so you get me as your date. You pay attention, follow every instruction, or I'll lock you in a back room in East Jerusalem. I have a brother who doesn't so much like Americans and would love to visit with you. I could retrieve you just in time to deliver you to deputy administrator who won't be too concerned how you enjoyed time." Hafiz's jaw muscles clenched and unclenched. His arms were taut as individual muscles pulsed while he maintained a stranglehold on the steering wheel.

"What do you want me to say?" Addison replied. "I just wanted to make a difference. This is my first duty station."

"What is decision?"

"You won't have any problems. I'll follow directions."

"Israel has been simmering and boiling over for thousands of years," Hafiz said. "My assignment is to show you some of country and how to survive when I'm not around. We've got just enough time to do that but remember this isn't like any other place on earth.

Things aren't what they seem. Be cautious, watch back. Maybe if lucky you might tell grandchildren about first days in Israel."

The jet lag, day's wait, and dressing down, along with his bondage to this stranger, leveled Addison. He needed to get to the hotel, pull the sheets over his head, and lose himself in a dream that wouldn't assail him.

CHAPTER

2

1982

al-Quds (Jerusalem) & Abu Dis, West Bank

In 1982, Aadil Gamal was the largest baby born at Al-Makassed Hospital, al-Quds. Aadil's mother, Zahira, confined to a wheelchair for three months before the blessed event, required a Caesarean Section to deliver her 28" long, 16.7 pound behemoth.

1¼ miles from the southeast outskirts of al-Quds, lies Abu Dis, an Arab town of 11,000 souls. Two months after Aadil Gamal's two-fisted entry into the world, Khalil Ahmad fought his sickly way into existence in a stonemason's modest dwelling. Khalil's birth occasioned no notice, just another Arab baby, born with the assistance of a midwife. In childhood, Khalil was malnourished and suffered from rickets. Work was not easy to come by for Khalil's dad, even as a skilled stonemason, in the political turmoil that was Israel. As some are destined for greatness, Khalil was ordained to be a slight boy growing into a slight man. Slight men do not make good stonemasons.

June 2007

The early morning sun was warm on Khalil's face as he sat sipping sweet tea outside the Harr Qahwa Café, enjoying the comings and goings of those more industrious. The time was near for Aadil to barrel down the street and sweep him up in their latest adventure. Aadil never developed the proper respect for relaxing and watching the morning unfold. With his arrival they would be off on today's quest with no time to enjoy the simple pleasures of being.

He couldn't remember a time Aadil wasn't moving. The big oaf was always chasing work. At ninety pounds lighter and seven inches shorter, Khalil had resigned himself to seeing things Aadil's way. It had been that way since first grade at Abu Dis Elementary when Aadil stepped in to save him from a beating, but one of these days he would be the champion.

CHAPTER

3

Monday October 15 2007

Wilsonville School District, Wilsonville, Oregon

Janelle's lithe figure strode across the lot, belying her fifty-four years, as she made the accustomed trip from her parking space into the district office. Stopping by the mailroom for personal correspondence, she greeted familiar faces and then headed to her office and the start of another week.

"Morning, Dr. Henning," came the languid greeting as she entered her outer office.

"Rough weekend, Stanley?" Janelle inquired of her middle-aged executive assistant.

"Baby ran a fever all weekend and I got the night shift. It broke around three this morning."

"Now you know what mothers go through." She handed him her vanilla latte. "Would you heat this for me? I've got mail and some papers to deal with before the staff meeting at nine." With that she swept into her office ready for the day's onslaught.

As she scanned her mail Stanley came in with the steaming latte. "Not much in general mail but here's one that missed routing to your box. Thought you'd want to open it," he said, handing her an envelope. “Not often I see anything from the Ukraine. We have something going on there?”

“Not that I know of,” Janelle said, taking the envelope. Glancing at it she placed it on the stack she'd brought from the mailroom. “Need to concentrate, Stanley,” she said, dismissing him so she could prepare for her meeting. The envelope would wait with all the other demands on her time. After fifteen minutes of frenzied preparation Janelle left her cooling latte to keep its vigil on the desk as she made her way to another staff meeting.

Returning to her office from the quasi-productive meeting, Janelle sat at her desk and checked her voicemail. As the droning demands for her time continued she glanced over the stack of personal mail. The letter from the Ukraine was relegated to the bottom of the pile as she skimmed through the rest of the stack looking for anything that demanded immediate attention. When she finished listening to her telephone messages she concentrated on the mail. After making quick notes on several for routing to Stanley she was left with the letter from the Ukraine in her hand. What is this about, she wondered as she opened the envelope.

Just then her inside line rang. Picking it up she heard Jerry's familiar voice. “How would you like a free lunch?”

“Jerry, you know how Mondays are,” Janelle responded, not wanting to deal with him right now.

“Sorry, this is business. I have to cover new security guidelines with all administrators as per Superintendent Kasnow's order from the twelfth.”

“Won't there be a meeting for this, Jerry?”

“If I were the doubting type I might begin to suspect you don't want to see me.”

“What can I say? Last Monday's holiday put me a day behind and I am in the middle of three bear projects with more around the corner. When you add existing directives that don't allow anyone to stay late it's nearly impossible to get everything done. Sorry, but social lunches with the Chief of Security sometimes just don't fit in," she said, annoyed at the time his call was costing her.

"Sweetie," Jerry began.

"Hey, we talked about familiar names at work," Janelle scolded him.

"Okay, Dr. Henning, like I said, all administrators have to be briefed on new procedures. I have to go to lunch; you have to go to lunch, so why not get this done so I can sign you off and go on to the next willing administrator?" Jerry said, annoyance creeping into his voice.

"Fine, be a dear and pick up a small container of low-fat yogurt, vanilla if they have it, from the cafeteria and we'll meet in the west conference room," Janelle said trying to soften her tone.

"Hey, I didn't think we wanted familiar names," Jerry replied, a smile back in his voice.

With that Janelle hung up. Stanley opened her door, peeked in, and said, "You've got five minutes to make it to Dr. Kasnow's office."

"Is it that time?" Janelle said trying not to show the rising frustration in her voice.

"You've got four minutes and fifty-five seconds now, boss," Stanley said leaving the door open and returning to his desk.

With that Janelle grabbed files from her desk and scooted out the door, heels clicking down the corridor. The letter from the Ukraine waited on her desk.

CHAPTER

4

Friday February 22 2008

Tel Aviv

Awakening gradually, the night's rest-infusing energy beginning to replace sheer exhaustion from the long flight crowned by his welcome to the embassy the day before, Addison felt himself resurfacing. Grabbing the plush hotel bathrobe from the camel leather chair by the bed he slipped into the waiting slippers and padded off to the opulent bathroom.

The rich, cream-colored, travertine flooring was warm under his slippers. A Jerusalem Limestone steam shower and matching tub with burnished brass fixtures awaited his pleasure. Addison's immediate need required neither. *This is a far cry from dorm housing,* he thought. Utilitarian unisex drab was how he remembered it.

Relieving himself he went to the sink where warm water cascaded from the burnished faucet as he washed his hands with the hotel's scented beauty bar. Toothbrushes, toothpaste, mouth rinse, along with four crystal glasses, waited on the polished granite counter. Declining their gracious invitation he dried his hands on a luxuriantly soft hand towel, preferring to avail himself of enticements he had sensed on his way in.

Leaving the bathroom, Addison inhaled the aroma of freshly brewed Arabica coffee waiting on a handcrafted maple and ebony side table sitting against one of the suite's wainscoted walls. Next to it were magnificent pastries, the largest he'd ever seen, fresh and warm, arrayed enticingly on a gilt-edged heated platter. Adjacent to these temptresses resided an exquisite etched crystal bowl filled with grapes, pomegranates, figs, plums, nectarines, bananas, and melons of more varieties than he could name. The final contributor to this gastronomical windfall was a carafe of chilled juice in a silver ice bucket on a side table. Addison's stomach growled in anticipation.

Pouring a steaming cup of coffee Addison set it on the side table then filled and downed a leaded crystal glass of juice. The ambrosia crimson-orange combination continued to lift yesterday's cloud. Placing a huge cream cheese Danish on a linen napkin embossed with the letters ICD, he picked up his coffee and pastry and made his way back to the bed. As he bit into the Danish, he thought, *now this is the Israel I've read about.*

Setting the coffee and what remained of his pastry on the nightstand, Addison propped oversized pillows against the headboard and climbed back into bed. He inhaled a sip of the steaming brew and focused on the giant plasma television hanging from the wall above the side table, vaguely remembering the bellman's boast of 250 international channels and a 5.1 digital surround system with six discreet concealed speakers he'd been too tired to care about as he was shown the room.

"You will also find the hotel's extensive, interactive Israel travelogues waiting on your HD window to the world," the bellhop had said in perfect English. After turning down the bed and laying out a bathrobe and slippers, he had left the room, quietly locking the door behind him. Addison had fallen asleep moments later.

As he drained the last of his coffee, the morning sun shone through oversized windows, embracing the bed and Addison in its glow. He was going through the events of the last twenty-four hours when the door to his bedroom flew open. There stood his minder. A feeling of restraint entered with him.

"You slept well?"

"Best night's rest I've had in Israel."

"But it was your first night in our country, was it not?"

"It was. Perhaps my attempt at levity needs some work," Addison said, making a mental note to avoid humor.

"Today will be day to rest and adjust to Israel. The journey of last two days must have been tiring and your welcome to the embassy was not, I suspect, what you had hoped for."

No kidding, thought Addison. Perhaps this was going to turn out all right after all.

"You enjoy coffee?" Hafiz said looking at the empty cup on the nightstand. "It is special blend. I took the liberty of making it for your pleasure. I also ordered fruit, pastries, and hotel's special juice blend from room service."

"You have been busy, not to mention kind. Thank you, it was delicious."

"I was quiet in preparations, not desiring to disturb sleep. It's an ability mastered over many years. I knew the coffee's aroma would awaken you when you had sufficient rest. I wanted to ease the way past yesterday's circumstances."

"Consider them eased."

"Have you been to the windows?"

"I've been to many," Addison answered, forgetting his decision to avoid levity.

"Come, come, you must see," Hafiz said walking to the window overlooking the hotel's magnificent pool and the Mediterranean.

Looking down on the beach Addison saw tiny gulls landing on the sand in search of tourist-strewn bits of food. People crisscrossed the shore bundled against the crisp February morning surrounded by the gulls. From his vantage point fifteen stories up, Addison could see the sea vanish into the horizon.

"Get dressed; the best breakfast of your life awaits. No food is like the delicacies in Israel. Arabic and Jewish dishes that fill one's heart with joy," Hafiz said.

"What was it I just had?"

"That was just to awaken taste buds. Come, dress. Hafiz will show you what true Israeli breakfast is." With that he left Addison standing at the window. At last Addison shuffled in the direction of his suitcase.

CHAPTER

5

Mid-November 2007

Nablus, West Bank

For as long as he could remember, Nasir Ghafour resolutely looked toward his future. At twenty-two his black curly hair and swarthy skin could foreshadow him as Jewish or Arabic, depending on who was looking. His five foot eleven frame confirmed youthful vigor awaiting disciplined conditioning to reach its masculine potential.

Yearning to join the intifada after graduating from An-Najah National University, Nasir understood throwing rocks only brought Israeli reprisals. He was reminded of his longing that morning in the mosque. When mid-morning prayers ended he delayed approaching the young visiting cleric, holding back until they were alone. "Imam, your words this day challenged my soul."

"What words spoke to you, my brother?" Imam al Bari said.

"Your words about the difference between bringing disorder, and shaping a future."

"I am pleased. Many hear but do not understand."

"I have one question I have carried within but do not know where to seek an answer. You are god's voice. Perhaps he will answer my soul."

"What are you called by, my brother?"

"My given name is Nasir."

"What brings you such distress Nasir?"

"Too long have infidels ruled our land. I promised father I would finish university before becoming a part of our glorious struggle. My promise has been fulfilled, now I look to the future. So many talk of bringing change, but your words this day have shown me all efforts are not the same—that many end in futility. Can you help me find those making a difference? I am ready to fight for the liberation of Palestine."

Fourteen days later an emaciated man with a dirty, unkempt beard walked up to Nasir as he was leaving morning prayers. Handing him a folded paper, he hurried away. Nasir puzzled after the rapidly disappearing form, then at the creased page in his hand, finally realizing the mystery could be solved by unfolding it. *'18 November, 2:00 P.M., al-Eizariya, Tomb of Lazarus'* was scribbled in barely legible script. Tomorrow the mystery would be revealed.

Arriving early the next day, Nasir waited outside Lazarus' tomb until after dark. No one arose that day. On his way home he brooded. He was young, intelligent, and strong; that must count for something. Now was his moment to make a difference.

Week by week messages arrived, always from someone new, for him to go to still another destination, and week by week no one appeared to show the slightest interest that he had.

While it had been imparted, by Imam al Bari**,** on each visit to the mosque, that leaders were pleased and for him to be prepared, no action came. To question meant to be excluded, so he persevered, finally enrolling in graduate school to fill his time, without understanding why he was never chosen to act on behalf of the cause he yearned to embrace.

Reaching this week's destination, Nasir sat down outside an outdoor café and concentrated on his *Knafeh Nabulsiyye*. A stranger, an old man grey in color and countenance, with a glass tumbler of tea asked to join him. Since there were other empty tables, Nasir wanted to blurt out he was waiting for someone, but his mouth, full of warm sweet pastry, forestalled words. So he chewed and attempted to swallow as the stranger sat down.

The outsider sipped his tea, seemingly oblivious to Nasir's presence. After a gulp of coffee washed down his sticky mouthful, Nasir, looking at this old man sitting opposite him, asked, "Do we know one another?"

"I have message."

Nasir wanted to shout 'out with it old man,' but instead offered his companion a piece of his Knafeh Nabulsiyye and waited for him to speak. His patience was rewarded by indifference. Nasir never understood the ways of old men he had seen so often in animated discussions, and he did not understand this one, so he concentrated on his pastry. He looked down, closing his eyes, savoring the texture and taste of his pastry. When he looked up the messenger was gone. Scanning the immediate area he saw the old grey form hurrying down the street. He shot up, determined to catch him. The old geezer proved a great deal more agile than seemed possible, eluding Nasir as he darted in and out of shops and alleys. Exhausted, Nasir gave up the chase and, not knowing what else to do, returned to his snack.

He was ready to quit. But quit what? He'd never done anything. It was not heard of to volunteer, to be welcomed—he thought he had been welcomed—then never given anything to do. He sat down and finished his Nabulsiyye, thankful that café owners never seemed in a rush to do anything, including removing uneaten food.

Taking the final bite he moved his plate to the center of the table to make room for school books. Studies were his refuge, the one thing he was gifted at. In moving his plate a folded paper revealed itself. Examining its contents he read: '*Jenin, 2:15 P.M.*' He looked at his watch, 1:40. Jenin was twenty-seven miles away. He had no car and thirty-five minutes to get there. Commitment and fear battled but his desire for glory overcame doubt and he bolted from his chair wondering if the Israelis and their mobile checkpoints would deny his chance in the sun.

Riding in the back of an oil-belching, grime-encrusted pickup truck, sandwiched between wooden crates of reeking chickens, was not the image Nasir had in mind when he'd volunteered to work for the greater glory of *Allāh*. His arrival in Jenin left him rank with chicken excrement, sore from the potholed ride, and nauseous from the stench of chickens and the remainder of his Knafeh Nabulsiyye, sitting as a lump, in the pit of his stomach.

Nasir wanted to go home and shower, but even though miserable and crawling with filth he knew he couldn't. Finding a ride anywhere covered with dank chicken feathers and fowl crap sealed his fate. Then there was his commitment to the *Palestine Mujahideen Islamic Jihad*. He wanted to please god and knew those in the PMIJ, wiser than he, were pointing the way. He was determined future generations would speak his name with pride as a hero among heroes, who overcame the descendants of pigs and monkeys, ridding Palestine of the infidels.

Nasir brushed sticky feathers from his face and glanced at his watch. Praise Allāh, there were two minutes before his appointed meeting. Looking around he noticed people staring. Stretching cramped legs, he watched his newfound chicken foes depart in their grimy transport, oblivious to their imminent fate.

Nasir realized, as he looked down at himself, that his present unkempt state masked his identity as a university student. Most people, he observed, did not appear anxious to get close to him. A freedom never before felt surged within him: Gone was any concern about being robbed. Many believed university students wealthy and lazy, thus they gained little sympathy or help when bothering to report crimes to the authorities.

Nasir began surveying his surroundings when it dawned on him he didn't know where he was supposed to meet his contact. No matter how many times he re-read the note neither contact name nor location materialized on the tersely worded message. His gaze darted to every new face that came into view.

Feeling his pocket for money, he wasn't sure he trusted his street skills, but if he left the least that would happen was he would never be contacted again. At worst, he might meet Allāh sooner than planned without the benefit of seventy-two perpetual virgins. Though out of ideas, he knew he couldn't leave—so he stayed.

As the afternoon waned Nasir abandoned his aimless search and found an inviting bench in a town park. Sitting, the weight of his world pressed upon him. As he kept his solitary vigil others approached his bench throughout the fading afternoon, but always veered off. The chickens had been better friends than he realized: No curious voices asked questions he could not answer. But how would he meet his contact? *Where are you* he wondered as people of varying ages headed for his bench then changed direction at the last minute. Opening his backpack, he pulled out a book.

Hours later, as night descended, Nasir left his sanctuary in search of food. He approached a stand with six green and white nylon web chairs strewn around two white plastic tables. "Peace be upon you," he said.

"And peace be upon you. How can I be of assistance, sir?" the zit-scarred, sixteen-year-old food stand proprietor said.

"What do you have that is not made of chicken for a hungry traveler?" Nasir asked.

"Sir, I have wonderful kebabs. Lamb to which I have added fresh local vegetables, sir," the boy said.

"And what would a lamb kebab with a tumbler of mint tea cost?"

"Sir, as a special price to you, since the hour is late and I wish to sell the remainder of what was prepared for today's business, I will sell you two kebabs and mint tea for the price of 1½ Jordan dinars. It is a most attractive price, much less than I normally charge."

"That is generous. I accept your offer."

"Sir, good, very good. I will bring this fine meal to you straight away."

As Nasir tore into the lamb, the food vendor attempted to engage him in conversation. "I have not seen you on our street before."

Nasir kept eating. After finishing a kebab and finding the boy in no hurry to leave, he responded, "I am from al-Quds and have found myself in need of lodging. Do you know of a place I might stay?"

There is a hostel only 1,000 meters away that would have a bed and a shower, all for a reasonable price.

"I am most grateful," Nasir said. "Would you be so kind to provide directions?"

After finishing his meal, Nasir followed the boy's directions to a building where he found a crude painted sign that read 'Jenin

International Youth Hostel' on the ground leaning against a side wall. Its red Arabic letters faded into a dingy yellow background. The building, a mud brick single-story structure in the poorer part of this ancient town, had seen better days. Nasir learned later that two young Americans had stayed in the owner's spare back bedroom some time ago, so the owner felt he could advertise his modest dwelling as an international hostel, keeping to himself, of course, the origins of his lodgers.

Sunrise found Nasir sleeping in a worn but clean bed. A shower the night before had removed yesterday's filth, enabling him to rest comfortably. The owner's offer to have Nasir's garments washed by his wife for no additional charge was a kindness he could not refuse. Nasir awoke rested, his laundered clothes folded on a chair by the bed.

"Good morning, my friend, how was your rest?" the proprietor asked, stopping in front of Nasir's open doorway as he stirred.

"Yesterday's trip left me in need of both a shower and a comfortable bed. You have provided both. Many thanks for cleaning my garments."

"My wife is a good woman. How is it you came to be so soiled?"

"I was in need of immediate transportation from al-Quds, and a farmer transporting chickens was the only available ride."

"Then you have business in Jenin?"

"I came to meet a friend."

"And what is your friend's name? I might know of him."

"I must be going or I will be late."

"But I might be of help. I have lived here from birth."

"These are dangerous times. Someday we may speak of such things."

The owner understood. "Breakfast is prepared if you are hungry."

After dressing he devoured fresh fruit, oatmeal, and sweet coffee. Life did not seem as bleak as it had a few short hours ago.

"Your kindness is appreciated. Please thank your wife for me." Paying for the lodging and food, Nasir set out to find his contact.

The day, bright with hope, disintegrated into aimless wandering. He passed through much of the town hoping someone, anyone, would motion or signal him. He avoided old men sitting around their hookahs with time on their hands for gossip and questions he couldn't answer. A sea of blank faces bustled past, oblivious of his existence. Nasir found himself back on the park bench with his books. If he was contacted, fine, but no one, not even the PMIJ, could expect someone to contact a phantom without face or name.

That night he was back at the hostel.

The next day Nasir wandered past shops throughout Jenin. None of the busy residents questioned his presence in their midst thanks to the demands of commerce. He skirted past old men bundled up outside cafes with coffee and hookahs, with their opinions and questions on everything, keeping to those whose hectic lives prohibited curiosity.

Passing a group of antiquated seniors he failed to recognize wandering past the day before, he heard "*As Salam a' alaykum,* hello," from one of the more animate old men. Not about to get involved with a group whose life energy was expended in gossip about other people's business, Nasir increased his pace.

"Young man, I am speaking with you," shouted their leader.

Caught, he knew that to continue would bring more attention. Turning, he said, "*Salam*, hi, were you speaking to me?"

"Who else would I be speaking to in such a loud voice?"

"Forgive me, *abba;* my mind is on other things." Nasir considered running but discarded the thought.

"I see words fail you. Let us begin with your given name, mine is Haroun."

Nasir stared back.

"Do we need a *PALFA* officer to aid your memory, young man?"

"It's Nasir."

"And what brings you to Jenin, Nasir?"

"An-Najah University."

"How does a university located in Nablus bring a young man to Jenin?"

"For an assignment entrusted to me."

"And what is this assignment that makes one forget the ways of respect, young Nasir?"

"I have sworn secrecy. Such are intrigues of academic life."

"Surely telling old men in a city over twenty miles from the university—"

"Could jeopardize studies with a professor who controls my future."

"We could be of assistance, young Nasir. You walk our streets and it is old men that know things about these streets," Haroun said.

"Helping those younger is all we can do since we are too old to fight the Zionists," another added.

"Well?" the third one said.

What could he say that would satisfy them, leaving him free to meet his contact? "Perhaps what I seek is best seen through eyes of wisdom, but it must be agreed I can only speak in generalities. If Professor Khoury were to suspect I had spoken to any others, years of study could be lost, and shame brought to my family."

"Old men like to talk, young Nasir; it is what we have. But there are secrets buried in each heart that death itself could not tear from us; we will hold your words to ourselves."

"I need a moment to frame my words, for none can answer with precision when words are left to chance." *Nasir, you can do this. Just give them something they can answer then take notes to show the importance of their words.*

The old men waited in silence for Nasir to begin.

Nasir tried to project intense thought. The responses on their grizzled faces were hard to read, but who could know with all the hashish they must have smoked over the years. He took a deep breath, "You found me wandering Jenin."

"This we know."

"My journey has shown me what lives in Jenin today, but Professor Khoury asks what came before."

"I suspect he wants you to see apart from the prism of books you have studied."

"Why would books' truth not be sufficient?"

"Words surrender to their creator's bias."

"Professor Khoury teaches truth and would fail me were I to embrace less."

"Truth sometimes appears different in the sun than in the shade. How far into the past do you seek to see Jenin?"

"Jews claim Palestinian land. Uncovering the root of their Zionist lies would please more than the professor."

"Have a seat, young Nasir," Haroun said. "You have much to see and have come to those with vision."

Nasir was thankful the old were pleased to hear their own voices. They asked few questions of him. He pulled a notepad and pen from his backpack, ready to write.

Haroun began, "Ancient traditions of Jenin trace back to the early Bronze Age. Though its original name has been lost to antiquity, Jenin is thought to have been built on the ancient site of Ein Ganim, known as the Fountain of Gardens, for its abundant water. Since most tribes were migratory back then, knowledge of specific ethnic groups claiming Ein Ganim has been lost to time."

"Why would this be, Haroun?"

"People were hunters and gatherers. Earliest tribal history was passed verbally from one generation to the next, not written as it is today. Warfare between neighboring peoples sometimes vanquished the losing side or eliminated it. When writing started to appear, oral traditions began to wane. Ein Ganim was recorded as having been allotted to the sons of Issachar, one of the twelve tribes of Hebrews, when they invaded what they called their promised land after their exodus from Egypt some 3,408 years ago, around 1401 B.C. These sons of Issachar gave their conquered city to the Gershonite Levites. The Levites were Hebrew priests and evidently Issachar's sons felt the need to treat the emissaries of their god hospitably. But who can know the way of the Jews? Is stolen land given to priests any less stolen?"

Nasir stopped writing. "Bronze Age tales are no more reliable than antediluvian claims of a pre-flood earth. They can't be proven."

"Truly spoken, young Nasir, but traditions exist in our body of knowledge that has been passed down through the ages. Is this not more than you had?"

"What I seek is the recent history of Jenin."

"Then let us go to those days my companions and I have experienced. For all our lifetime Ein Ganim has been known as Jenin. In Israel's war of independence in 1948, Jenin was captured by Iraqi and Transjordanian troops. What a glorious victory, but sadly the Israelis captured Jenin on the first day of the 1967 Six Day War. Through international political pressure in 1996, the Zionists returned Jenin to its rightful owners in keeping with the Oslo Accords."

"But Haroun, you have forgotten the U.N. resolution in 1947?" one of the other men interrupted.

"Ah yes, we cannot forget 181. No one living then disputes the passing of U.N. Partition Plan for Palestine, Resolution 181, in November 1947 against Arab will, which ended the British Mandate in Palestine and signaled the renewal of *jihad,* struggle, for Palestinians. We were but twenty years old when those dark days descended upon us. Before the resolution was even passed, the Jews commenced their attacks against the British and peace-loving Palestinians. It's no wonder the British wanted out. Our leaders assured those of us carrying the fight to the Zionists that the problem would be taken care of when the British were gone. The following May the Israelis declared statehood on the fourteenth of the month. It was pronounced from the Tel Aviv Art Museum by David Ben Gurion, the infidel's first Prime Minister, as if stolen land had the right to a prime minister. All three of us took part in those glorious moments of promise when Syria, Iraq, Egypt, Transjordan, and Lebanon vowed to show the Jews they had worn out their welcome as we struggled to defend our homeland in what good and noble hearts called a war of extermination. Our ancestors from Egypt, Jordan, and Syria would have been proud."

"But I'm Palestinian," Nasir said, "and it's Palestinian rights to this land—"

"Ah yes, Palestinian, a most useful people. Where one begins determines whose land it is. All land changes hands over time. The land perseveres and each of us becomes the dust of the land we fight and die for. Zionists claim al-Quds as their eternal capital, but what of the Jebusites who called al-Quds Jebus when David and his band of invaders conquered the city and named it *Yerushaláyim*? And who, if truth is allowed among friends, did the Jebusites take the city from?

"But now, young Nasir, is the time for Palestinians, and if being Palestinian secures this land for me and you, ridding it of Zionists, then Palestinian I will be and Palestinian you can nobly be. Our battle is not of might; Israelis have proven their ability each time we have tried to expel them. They grow stronger while our women, disabled, and children are used as living bombs to our eternal shame. Our battle is founded in faith—god will prevail."

"Send them back to Europe," Nasir said. "Hitler is long gone but his greatest evil was the softness his failed remedy left in the world's heart, which now believes only Arab land can rectify the suffering these vermin brought upon themselves."

"So much hatred in one so young, it's an evil that will make you stumble. I have spoken of the long road of history. It is through time and patience we shall overcome and, young Nasir, we will prevail. My friends and I are old, our fighting is behind us. We live out our days because Allāh wills it. I think we won't see a Palestine cleansed of infidels, but you, with your university education and the ways of those educated, will bring about that which has been our dream for a lifetime."

Nasir knew he could go. He put his notepad and pen away. He looked into Haroun's aged eyes. "If we do not meet again, *abba,* remember the struggle continues, *ma'a salama*, goodbye."

"Remember my words about hatred, young Nasir. The fight must continue until glorious victory, but to hate is to lose yourself and *jihad*. Hatred has driven too many good men to their death."

Walking away, Nasir knew failing age could cause sons of Islam to forget what every true Muslim knew. Two states existed in the world: *Dar al-Islam*, the house of peace, where Islam prevailed, and *Dar al-Harb,* the house of war, which existed everywhere Dar al-Islam did not prevail. As long as one Jew blighted the soil of Palestine, Dar al-Harb remained. He had learned truth at the university, which no enfeebled mind could steal from him. He headed for the park.

As the days passed, Jenin delighted Nasir: the Mediterranean homes that dotted the town, its vibrant shopping center offering, in its open-air stands all types of fresh produce and fruits along with merchandise of every sort and kind. He had never visited this pleasant city, and though searching for a face that would return his glance, he embraced this more as an adventure than the serious business he was about.

As the days turned into each other, Nasir resolved to stay until money ran out. He didn't know if he would be contacted but he knew he must remain until forced to leave.

As Nasir entered the hostel one evening, the owner said, "You seem to have no job, my friend. Sometimes I work at the market and today Abdullah, who delivers vegetables, asked if I knew of a strong young man who could assist in bringing vegetables from the fields to market. I thought you might have interest."

"Thank you for your great kindness in thinking of me. It is true I could use work. I have been waiting for a friend, but it seems he has been delayed and money is getting low. How many days do you think my help would be needed?"

"I believe Abdullah mentioned three or four. I was told it pays seven Jordanian dinars a day and everything helps, does it not?"

"I am most grateful. I can watch for my friend and help to bring vegetables from the field. Why not do well when opportunity presents itself."

"Then it's settled. I will wake you for morning prayer and after breakfast take you to the fields before going to the market."

Work started early but prayers came before work. It surprised Nasir how he had become accustomed to rising late, but knew he had neglected morning prayers. It was good to be faithful again, so he arose the first time his name was called.

After prayer and breakfast of pita bread dipped in *mouhammara* with sweet tea and fruit Nasir walked toward the fields. Upon arriving, he was greeted by row upon row of plastic-covered greenhouses, and was put to work loading waiting baskets filled with freshly picked vegetables into an ancient two-wheeled wooden cart with an automobile axle and tires. He accompanied his new field boss, Abdullah, to the market, riding behind what passed for a donkey. The nineteen-year-old beast of burden was more a grandfather than working animal and slowed to a crawl when going uphill.

"Nasir, be a good man jump out and help tired old Himaar pull his burden."

After unloading their bounty at various vegetable stands in Jenin, the pair returned to the field and Nasir found himself digging potatoes, picking broad beans, and cutting tomatoes, cucumbers and lettuce, as well as harvesting cauliflower and squash. When the baskets were full the cart was again loaded and Nasir, Abdullah, and Himaar were off to the market once more.

The owner of the farm turned out to be a fair man. Nasir was not afraid of work and got along with Abdullah and the others in the garden. He returned to the hostel dirty and tired but feeling elated. It had been a long time since he'd worked with his hands and it felt good to have money in his pocket he had earned.

The next three days were consumed by physical labor, with no thoughts of an unknown contact. At the end of the last day, Nasir accepted his daily wage along with an extra five Jordanian dinars from the field owner. "You are good worker, Nasir."

"When you are paid to do a job then it is right to work hard, that way everyone prospers."

"I have only a few men for my small field, but upon any of them leaving I would be most happy to have you work for me every day."

"I am honored, but I will be leaving Jenin to continue my education." Nasir kept to himself that he didn't graduate from the university to become a field hand. "May your days be filled with peace and prosperity reward your efforts."

As they left the field, Abdullah called out from behind Nasir. When he caught up they walked together, talking about weather and football and those things which the newly acquainted speak of.

Nearing Jenin's outskirts Nasir said, "We'll have to get together again on my next visit to Jenin." Though he had no intention of coming to Jenin again or looking up Abdullah, respect must be observed.

"That would be most enjoyable."

Nasir turned to his left, moving toward the hostel, Abdullah called out to him, "Let us meet after third prayer at the food stand next to the great mosque in the Square. I will buy mint tea."

Not wanting to affront this simple man with his kind gesture, Nasir agreed. He would be at prayers and liked mint tea—who did not—so why not show himself to be friendly? "I would be most honored," he called back and continued walking toward the hostel's waiting shower to donate his daily portion of field dirt.

The next day after 11:53 A.M. prayers Nasir took one of two remaining chairs by the food stand where he had eaten his first meal in Jenin. He watched fellow worshippers stream out of the mosque heading for family and friends on their day of rest. Out of the throng Nasir spotted Abdullah. When he approached, Nasir stood, a sign of respect, and waited for him to be seated before taking his seat again.

"It is a good day to be alive, is it not?" Abdullah said, enjoying the sixty-three degree sunshine.

"Yes, it is, especially when reclaiming Palestine is so near," Nasir responded, remembering why he came to Jenin.

Abdullah ordered mint tea and *basboosa* for them both. "You will enjoy the basboosa here. I know the cart vendor and his secret is that his mother makes everything from scratch, as only an Arab mother can. The tart will melt in your mouth. Is your mother also a fine cook, my friend?"

"My mother is not alive."

"Killed by the Zionist pigs?"

"In childbirth."

"I am sorry."

"It was a long time ago. My father re-married when I was fourteen but she is not so good in the kitchen. I think my father married her for other reasons."

"Ah yes, the ways of life. You are from Nablus. What brings you to Jenin at this time of the year when you should be in studies?" Abdullah asked as the basboosa and tea was served. He dove into the syrup-soaked tart with gusto.

Nasir's mind raced as he took a bite, stalling for time, his mind anywhere but on the pastry. He had told everyone he was from al-Quds. "You must have misunderstood," Nasir said. "I am from al-Quds."

"My friend you are not. You are from Nablus."

Nasir continued eating, not wanting to deny the truth but afraid of his lie.

"What brings you to Jenin?" Abdullah asked again.

"I have come to find a friend."

"What is the name of your friend," Abdullah asked, appearing to enjoy this game.

"I cannot speak of the matter. I do not know if he would be pleased if I mentioned his name."

"Your friend's name is Abdullah."

Nasir froze. He could not process Abdullah's words.

"There have been many eyes upon you. It had to be shown if you would persevere. Many volunteer but lack the will to endure. It has become necessary to determine the heart of those who would serve Allāh's cause. You have done well, my friend."

"You are the one I have been waiting for? I have gone so many places only to find no one there. This past week left me fearful my desire to serve would never be rewarded."

"All that you've experienced was to prove commitment. I don't know the task to be placed upon you but it must be important to require all you have been through. Enjoy this moment, my brother; it is your time to enter the battle."

As Nasir reveled in the moment, wondering what would happen next, a dark grey Fiat Punto stopped across the street, its motor running. Abdullah motioned to the stopped car, "It's time to go."

Excitement permeated the air.

"Walk normally, don't draw attention to yourself. Move to the far side of the grey vehicle, get in the back seat. It will be shown you what comes next. If ever our paths cross again, we've never met."

Nasir's heart pounded. He left his basboosa with a single bite taken and compelled one measured step after the other to the waiting car. The back door was held open. Nasir climbed into the dark interior of the abyss, the left rear seat occupied, two presences in front. The one holding the door climbed into the seat beside Nasir, closing it with a solid thump, trapping him in the middle. He couldn't see through the darkened windows. His breath labored. The car pulled into the traffic.

Surrounded by silent menace, Nasir was handed a pair of sunglasses, he put them on. As the car drove from Jenin, its destination unknown, malevolence permeated the air as the weight of commitment sat as a stone on his heart.

The car continued its travel though towns Nasir did not recognize. The driver said 'Israeli patrol' several times as the presence to the left of him ordered him to 'remain on course.' Nasir lost track of time and direction as the vehicle seemed to turn back on itself. Even street sounds were muted. *What kind of car was he in?*

Finally coming to a stop, a blast of the car's horn caused a door in front of them to roll open. They entered the unknown—the door closed behind them. All got out. Nasir found himself in a cavernous garage. Lifting his hand to remove his sunglasses, his gesture was greeted by a shake of one escort's head. He dropped his hand. Someone grabbed the back of his right arm and started leading him into another part of the building. Twelve stairs, he counted them, and they were on a landing with a door. A single knock, the door opened. He was thrust into a darkened room.

The sunglasses were removed by one of his handlers. Nasir's eyes began to focus. The room's sole illumination came from a single bulb hanging above his head near the front of the room. It lit little more than the spot where it hung, leaving the room's edges to bleed into darkness. The back corners hid others Nasir couldn't make out. The room was scarred by gunfire and signs of a bomb blast, the floor littered and dirty. No one had lived here for a long time.

"Nasir Ghafour, welcome," came a familiar voice from the front of the room. Walking toward him, Professor Khoury came into the light.

Nasir embraced his beloved professor in the traditional manner: three kisses, one on his left cheek, then right, then left, in respect. This man, his mentor, had opened his heart to the history of Palestine.

"Professor, I am pleased to see you."

"You have been through a good deal, but the way of resistance requires vigilance. I am here to help you along that path in our struggle."

"I have been ready for a long time."

"I know your eagerness to serve; you have done well, now for your first assignment. You went through elementary grades with Aadil Gamal and Khalil Ahmad, did you not?"

"Yes, I know them both. We are friends. I should say they are the friends of everyone. I see them from time to time, but since I started at the university I have lost contact. We do not embrace the same things in life."

"That is what we have heard. You are to become their friend again. This should be easy. I understand they make a unique pair in their pursuit of employment."

"I have observed Aadil is more interested in work than Khalil."

"*Nam*, yes, but the constant closing of checkpoints provides for our needs. They both have families and families need to eat, yes?"

"What would you have me do professor?"

"Continue in school. If anything changes in your life, Israeli spies will know and you will find yourself down at Moriah Police Station."

"But I have been gone from classes for many days in Jenin."

"You have attended class every day. I have seen to the attendance record myself. Your classmates will say they have seen you each day. You are a member of PMIJ and will find many open doors."

"I am beginning to understand."

"A messenger will come to you each day—"

"Where will I meet this person?"

"They will come while you go about your day, as in the past. When you find Aadil and Khalil, buy them sweet tea, discuss old times. Aadil will not want to take time, until you tell him you have heard of work you cannot do yourself because you are in school. Aadil is your friend. He is a simple man and does not understand important matters in life, but he understands his need for work. When you have made contact, a messenger will give you a name, a different one every day or so, that needs work done. You will pass these names on to your friends. They will be paid well and in cash each day."

"Then what is required of me?"

"Patience, remember what is needed will be revealed. This task may not seem important but it is something you alone can do. What you hear and see must remain with you. Never reveal yourself to anyone, no matter the cost. The Israelis have their methods, but whatever you give them betrays those in the struggle. My life is in your hands; you must protect it. Be wise and if you are careful you will live a long life and see your children and grandchildren in a free Palestine."

"It is my deepest desire, my reason for life."

"I know this or you would not be here." Handing him an envelope the professor said, "Inside you will find sufficient funds for a week. When it is spent more will be provided. Use it only for your time with Khalil and Aadil."

An escort stepped up to Nasir, handing him the sunglasses. Putting them on, he was led back down the stairs to the car. Fifteen minutes later he was let out not far from his parent's house. The sedan sped away. He removed the sunglasses and put them in his pocket, they were a link that he was on his way.

~

"What is your opinion professor," came a voice from the back of the room.

"I have known Nasir many years. He remains an idealist but is determined and committed. I would trust him with my life."

"You have," replied his interrogator. "Thank you, professor, peace be upon you."

The professor was let out of the room and made his way back to Nablus.

"Do we proceed, Nuri?"

"We proceed." Nuri al-Massalha rose and each man present stood in respect to their leader. The time was at hand.

CHAPTER

6

Sunday 9 December 2007

South of Aleppo, Syria

Scanning all points of the compass, Nuri probed for anything out of place, randomly backtracking to ensure no one was following. Never before had so much been at stake. No one must follow as he made his way into northwest Syria.

The weather, in the mid-fifties, made the journey close to pleasant, but other matters kept him from enjoying the day on his way to Aleppo. He'd stayed overnight in a safe house and after morning prayers had set out on the final leg of the journey. His destination: a mosque south of the city. If Allāh was with him he would gain everything he had waited a lifetime for.

As he arrived, mid-afternoon prayers were being called. Nuri joined the worshippers and made his way to the mosque. Once the prayers concluded, he went to an inside door and knocked softly.

The door opened a crack. The man inside was huge, towering above Nuri, his massive head covered with a turban. There was a sash around the middle of his *jubbah* and the largest curved knife Nuri had ever seen fixed in a scabbard on his sash. Nuri had never seen this one before.

"Name?"

"Nuri al-Massalha."

Opening the door, the giant stepped aside, "Come." Passing through several doors inside the newly built mosque, they climbed to the second floor. Rich woven tapestries adorned the walls interspersed with carved reliefs in exotic wood panels depicting Muslim conquests from long-lost glories. His escort stopped at an ornately carved door and knocked. Nuri recognized the voice inside bidding them enter. "Stay," came the singular command from his guide—Nuri stayed. After a minute his menacing escort returned and opened the door. Nuri entered the room.

Rising from an inlaid ivory chair, a salt and pepper bearded man approached Nuri with open arms.

"Imam, it is good to see you," Nuri said, kissing Imam Marwan in the traditional manner of respect.

"Your journey was pleasant?"

"Most agreeable."

"Please sit, you must be tired. No one followed?"

"The skills you taught ensured my journey was not detected."

"Then all is well. Let us get to the heart of this business that brings you here."

"I have waited for this moment, imam."

"The meeting in Stepnogorsk went well. Our friends have delivered all promised supplies."

"Everything is ready?" Nuri asked.

"All is in readiness. We have acquired agents for the initial phase of the plan. Within one day of your signal selected volunteers throughout Gaza and areas we control in the West Bank will be exposed. Then it will be just a matter of days. It would not look good to have poor, sick Palestinians dying of a treatable disease at such a critical moment in our ongoing negotiations with the Zionists."

"We've much to be thankful for imam."

"As vaccine will not be available in the quantities needed, we shall require assistance. Since the Israelis have already vaccinated their population, it would be inhumane to deny Palestinians the same protection. The Jews will have little interest in helping but will be most concerned to be seen caring before the world."

"So protecting our people will proceed with little oversight by the Israelis?"

"The Israelis will closely watch the operation, Nuri, but public outcry will work in our favor. Once numbers of those infected begin to escalate, friends will be ready to move and you will be afforded the opportunity to implement the transfer. Ensure that those chosen are reliable."

"I will handle this task myself; there can be no other."

"You have learned well, my son."

"When will word be given, imam?"

"I remain in direct control. Accept orders from no one else. When you receive word, act at once. Timing is everything. If you need transportation you know your contacts."

"No others know?"

"I have spent my life laying a foundation of great trust for this moment. Those chosen have been given only what is needed. All understand the necessity for secrecy and have pledged their fidelity and lives." Rising, the imam started pacing. "It has been agreed friends will conduct war games when the time is right and will be ready to address old grievances. When destruction rains over al-Quds that will be their signal, forty-eight hours must pass, then the attack. As god's warriors arrive in the Zionist stronghold, the way, after too many tears, will have been prepared."

'Won't war games alert the Israelis?"

"Is this not delightful?" the imam said, resting on the edge of his desk facing Nuri, "to see the combined might of Allāh's glorious warriors and be powerless to change their long overdue fate. It has been given to you to understand that providentially the Zionists' action, if successful, will ensure our victory."

Wondering if he understood, Nuri looked upon his mentor. "If an enemy missile strikes we will not reach altitude."

Rising and returning behind his desk, the imam sat down and looked at Nuri. "That is the joy, the beauty, my son. All of Israel's might, that has compelled people of peace to wage *jihad* for survival these past sixty years, will be brought to its knees. We have learned their methods and capabilities over these sixty years, paying for each discovery with Arab blood. In armed struggle only a thermobaric missile can incinerate anthrax so we increased the quantity to compensate for the amount burned. If the minaret catwalk is attacked, the enemy's missile will disperse the anthrax spores into the atmosphere. Such foolish action would destroy the minaret, providing justification before the world for Arab wrath, so close is the minaret to the *al-Haram Ash-Sharif*, Noble Sanctuary. If our shell launches, the Zionist's missile will scatter our gift throughout the skies of al-Quds."

"And if both fail I will trigger the launch."

"Nuri, my son, all outcomes have been weighed. The delight is the Israelis will see something coming but will fall back on previous days, utilizing old strategies. It is then we will deliver the blow into their heart and only after their defeat will the few that remain understand. Then it will be seen if the Great Satan, or Europe, or indeed, the whole of the U.N., desires these vermin. My conviction is the world will find, as they did during Hitler's noble attempt to rid mankind of this scourge, no country wants them, and the few that survive will never raise their evil heads in any society they scurry to."

Nuri drew strength from the familiar voice heard so many times when he sat, one of many, listening to this man of god.

The imam picked up the phone and spoke into the receiver. Within minutes a side door opened and a tray with tea and pita bread with *Mouhammara* was placed on the desk. "It is time to refresh ourselves, Nuri."

Both men enjoyed the bread, cheese, and dip, washing it down with tea.

"You will be provided an untraceable cell phone and funds for expenses. Should any need arise, contact no one else but me. Jaafar will provide the number. Memorize then destroy it. The number provided will be monitored twenty-four hours a day. Call, then hang up after it answers. Say nothing, I will return the call within one half hour day or night.

"I understand."

"If the call is not returned, or anyone but me calls, the operation has been compromised, hang up, and destroy the phone. You know where to go. The phone has been modified so incoming and outgoing numbers won't be recorded. If you are taken into custody, you understand what is required."

"Yes."

"We have one final matter. Nuri, our people must be protected before the anthrax is released. They must not be hurt."

"If time allows, Allāh willing, this will be done, but we must not lose the moment to strike the final blow into the heart of our enemy."

"Nuri, do you know how many souls there are in Gaza and the West Bank?"

Nuri's nostrils began to flare. "Supreme causes do not count souls." He knew words must be measured. Life depended on what was said, even to this trusted mentor. Nuri cared little for his life compared to the importance of his glorious goal. His sole need was for victory, and for that he must stay alive.

"How many, Nuri?"

"There are over four million, imam."

"At the last census there were just under 2,500,000 Palestinians living in the West Bank, 1,500,000 abiding in Gaza, and 230,000 in al-Quds. Nuri, *shaheeds*, suicide bombers, have been a vital part of our struggle. They have prevailed against infidels where our armies have failed, but a wholesale slaughter of over four million worshippers of Allāh is not acceptable. Do not proceed until you are sure Palestinian lives are protected. Some will be lost, that is the price our people pay for freedom, but we must care for our children and preserve life the best we can."

Nuri felt his face begin to burn. "If it is Allāh's will."

"I have just given Allāh's will." Imam Marwan lifted his right hand. Jaafar entered the room and approached his leader, bending his immense head to listen while the imam whispered in his ear. Rising to his feet, the imam signaled the meeting was over. Nuri arose as well. "Nuri, I am sure you will make wise choices when you carry out Allāh's will. It would be most unwise to defy him."

Bidding his teacher goodbye, Nuri followed Jaafar from the room.

"You must be about Allāh's business," Jaafar said, leading him through the mosque. Silently, two Arabs fell into place, one in front, the other behind Nuri and Jaafar; each with sheathed knives at their waists. Nuri forced throbbing nerves under control. *I must not fail so close to victory.* He knew survival depended upon these next few moments.

Taking the stairs to the first floor, Nuri did not exit the building as he had come in but continued, with his escorts, into the basement. The unadorned stone walls echoed their steps across the limestone floor in the cavernous labyrinth. Coming to the end of the hall, his escorts remained outside while he followed Jaafar into the windowless room. Nuri knew it well. How many others had he extracted information or a confession from in this room?

"What is this?" Nuri asked Jaafar.

"The imam has said you must not proceed until our brothers are protected against the anthrax. We would become a curse in the land if you do not save from harm those lives whom are yours to care for."

"It is my operation," Nuri said, control threatening to flee. "Why should mere lives matter when final victory is within grasp?"

"It is Allāh's operation. Nuri al-Massalha, you will swear before Allāh that you will not launch the final attack before our brothers in al-Quds, Gaza, and the West Bank are protected."

"And if I do not swear?"

"Then I alone will leave this room alive."

Silently, Nuri stood before this giant, his breath coming in short bursts, his head throbbing. Was this the day to die?

"What say you, al-Massalha?"

Blind hatred ached for release no matter the cost, but the annihilation of his hated enemy was within his grasp. He must not forsake that for anyone or anything, including the pleasure of watching this swine in Arab clothes die a slow death when the knife from his scabbard was slammed into his vulnerable belly.

"It is . . . as you wish."

"It is not my wish but what, by Allāh, must be done. Do you swear before Allāh?"

Trembling, mouth twitching, Nuri knew what must be said. "By Allāh, all Palestinians will be protected before the anthrax is released on the infidels, or it will not be released."

"You have chosen wisely."

Jaafar went to a cabinet along the wall, and opening a door, retrieved an envelope and a cell phone. "These are yours."

Nuri opened the envelope. It was full of American dollars. He placed the envelope inside his robe along with the phone.

"There was to be a number."

"It is inside the envelope. You know what to do after committing it to memory."

Jaafar went to the door and knocked. Nuri heard the door's lock release; he had not heard it being locked. He must be more careful in the future. No words passed between them as he was led out of the mosque. He memorized the phone number before arriving at the basement steps. Placing the paper in a sand-filled ashtray Nuri pulled a match from his pocket, struck it, and watched the flames incinerate the paper. He set his face toward al-Quds.

CHAPTER

7

Wednesday December 19 2007

Wilsonville, Oregon

September 11th 2001 was six years gone and seemed a continent away, yet it permeated the fabric of life in Oregon. The air, once crisp and clean, was overcast with suspicion. Anything unforeseen, unexpected, caused a moment's pause no matter its innocence. Janelle didn't know what she felt, but life was not the same.

It had been more than nine weeks since the letter from the Ukraine appeared. It was the farthest thing from Janelle's mind when she unlocked her door, grateful the tyranny of the urgent was behind her, anticipating a nightly routine that brought solace and closure to each day. Noting the camellia's encroaching branches on the porch, Janelle made a mental note to put it on the calendar for pruning in March before spring growth, and then she entered her sanctuary. Setting the mail and her purse on the vestibule table she hung her coat in the hall closet and positioned her handbag in its allotted space.

Retrieving the mail, she walked across the foyer's polished marble floor and placed it by the phone on the table next to her overstuffed chaise longue, the one piece of furniture Blade had not purloined in the divorce. It had been her favorite then and somehow had avoided the stench of his presence that clung to every memory of him.

Sitting on its edge she checked the day's voicemail, deleting marketing calls with little conscious attention. Messages were never left. The beeps of their intrusions were marked by silences as automatic dialers hung up when no one answered their unwanted incursions. Only their numbers on Caller ID, when not blocked, gave them away. *Don't they ever give up?*

As she listened to the last message a faltering accent arose from the phone's speaker. The alien voice identified itself as Tatyana Sloviovich and professed to have important information. Then it asked, in broken English, for a return call. Haltingly a local number was provided. Caller ID showed the number to be the local Phoenix Inn & Suites. *What marketers won't try,* Janelle thought, erasing the message.

Janelle arose from the chaise. Going to the kitchen she took a bottle of Pinot Gris, chilled to a perfect fifty degrees, from the wine fridge, and opened it. Pouring a glass, she began to relax. It delighted her senses with its bouquet of white peach and citrus fruits as each day's stress evaporated in the warmth of its fermented grapes. With life moving faster than the days that strived to contain them, her nightly glass of the Northwest vintner's art was one of life's joys.

The next evening Janelle was sheltered in her chaise longue beginning to relax when her phone rang. She glanced at the handset's display; it was from the Phoenix Inn & Suites. *I'll take care of this*, she thought, reclaiming her daytime persona. She placed her glass of wine on the table and took the phone from its cradle. "Yes," she answered coldly.

She listened briefly. "I don't want whatever you are attempting to sell. Please put this number on your 'Do Not Call' list. Have I been clear that I do not want to receive any more calls?"

The caller hesitated. "Not understand."

"What part of do not call this number again isn't clear?"

The confused voice said, "I no sell something. Send letter before. Have come from Odessa to speak to Janelle Henning, very important. No charge, to sell. Please I speak to Miss Henning?"

"This is Doctor Henning," Janelle shot back.

"Please, Miss—ahh—Dr. Henning. Name is Tatyana Sloviovich. I send letter. You receive?"

Janelle was too irritated to remember any letter and remained silent.

"It was from Ukraine. I send over two months ago to you work."

Searching her memory Janelle finally remembered the odd letter from the Ukraine Stanley had given her. "If I received such a letter at my office I disposed of it."

"I came from Ukraine to speak important matter."

"Important matter?" *How do I get rid of this disturbance?*

"Must fix eyes on, then I tell," Tatyana replied.

"Fix your eyes on me?" Janelle's mind raced to assimilate this disquieting demand. "I don't know who you are or where you're from. In this country strangers don't get what they want by calling on the phone, no matter their pretext," Janelle spat out, nascent fear on the edges of her words.

"I don't understand all you say, in home country—"

"Where might that be?" Janelle interrupted.

"I say before. I am from Ukraine, was part of SSR."

"The Ukraine, you have the wrong person. I've never been there nor do I know anyone from that part of the world," Janelle said, knowing she should have already hung up. No telling what this person wanted. The only thing she knew: It wasn't her problem.

"Please just few minutes of time, then I go away," Tatyana begged.

"You're going now," Janelle half-shouted, slamming the phone down.

Janelle's heart pounded as fear, having already conquered her emotions, wrestled for control of her mind. Inhaling deeply she remembered to center. She willed calm and tranquility as a chant came softly to her lips Aum . . . Aum . . . Aum . . . When that failed Janelle grabbed her wine and let it begin its ministrations to her anxious soul.

The phone remained silent. Janelle finished her wine, telling herself the intrusion had been a marketing call gone bad. She headed for a hot bath. Home was her remaining sanctuary.

CHAPTER

8

First Week of January 2008

Abu Dis, West Bank

Nasir looked for Aadil and Khalil for three days. He gave up trying to determine where they would show up, always just missing them no matter what strategy he employed in his search. Why was nothing easy in his struggle with the Zionist occupiers? The fourth morning of his pursuit he settled down at the Harr Qahwa Café and resolved to stay put until they came across him.

As soon as he took his first sip of coffee he saw Khalil. "Khalil, over here."

"Nasir, my friend, it has been much time since seeing you."

"Please sit, I will get breakfast," Nasir said speaking to the café owner, "coffee, and *kataif* for my friend."

"Coffee and kataif, I am most grateful. The border is closed too many days for me to afford both coffee and kataif."

"How have you been, my friend?"

"It's day to day. Sometimes there is work, sometimes not. There seems no end to it all, but somehow Allāh provides. And you?"

"I have graduated and now take advanced courses."

"More schooling, what is the purpose of that?"

"I study for my Master's degree. That way when Palestine is free

I will work for the government with a good job and a future for my wife and children."

"You have a wife and children?"

"No, no, it is the family I plan to have someday. They must be supported, and I take classes now so I will be able to take good care of them when I do marry and have children."

"It is fine that you study. Maybe someday, when you have a good job in the government, you will find something for Khalil and Aadil."

The coffee and nut & cheese stuffed pancakes along with a pitcher of syrup was delivered to the table. Khalil soaked his kataif and started devouring the savory treat.

"How is Aadil these days?" Nasir asked, surprised such a slight man could eat with such zeal.

"He is forever on the move," Khalil said between mouthfuls. "I must start the day when the sun has just risen to sit and enjoy morning coffee. Once the big oaf comes there is no sitting, no enjoying. Just getting, and going, and finding work."

"I have been offered work, but it would hinder my studies so I cannot take it. Do you know of anyone who would be interested in jobs, jobs that pay well?"

"Did you not just hear when I said, Aadil and I seek work every day? We are good workers. What work have you been offered?"

"It varies, different days, different jobs. Some days moving—"

"We do moving. Aadil is as strong as an ox."

"Sometimes it's helping in the bakery. It is through friends at the university. I could ask if they have work for you and Aadil."

Just then the one-man tornado came rushing up to the café, "Khalil, time to go."

"Aadil, sit, say hello to Nasir."

"Nasir, nice to see you. Let's go," Aadil said, reaching for Khalil's shoulder.

"Wait. Nasir is telling about a job."

"Job?"

"Yes, job. He's still in school but friends have jobs he cannot do and asked if we want to work."

"We're forever looking for work."

"Aadil, sit. I will buy you coffee and we can talk."

"No time for talk, must find work."

"I will go back to the university and speak with my friends. It may be a few days before they have work. Where can I reach you?"

"Khalil is at café every morning. You can reach him here. We go." He grabbed for Khalil's shoulder again. Chewing the last of his kataif, Khalil nimbly slipped out of Aadil's way and followed him up the street.

Two days later Nasir followed the noise near the café and found Aadil and Khalil making their way up the road. "Aadil, Khalil," he shouted.

Turning in the direction of his voice they hurried upon him.

"I have found a good job for you. Can you start today?"

"Not today. We have promised to help collect trash."

"Here," Nasir said. He tried to hand Aadil a sheet of paper. Khalil snatched it and looked it over. "The baker Ferran has several days' work. See him tonight and he'll tell you when he needs you for work."

"Is good pay?" Khalil asked

"It pays well."

"Khalil, we must go. Is good you help, Nasir. Jobs are hard to find and family needs us to work." With that they headed out to collect trash.

During the next five weeks Khalil was treated to coffee, mint tea, and treats as Nasir gave them work all over Abu Dis, al-Quds and RamAllāh. Khalil savored the quiet morning moments, especially when accompanied by kataif or basboosa. Aadil was content with steady work.

CHAPTER

9

Monday January 7 2008

Wilsonville, Oregon

Janelle's sanctuary was beginning to crumble as messages continued to make unwanted incursions onto her phone. Disconcerted by the calls and their possible meaning, her once steel-edged will was slowly eroding by the unrelenting trespasses.

She considered changing her number but dismissed the idea. Sloviovich had already obtained one unlisted number—what would changing it accomplish? She couldn't tell anyone at work. What would she say? A grandmotherly voice was calling and wouldn't stop? How did she know? She'd never seen the intruder. It could be anyone, someone younger, or more dangerous. Her mind kept returning to the question of why. What could anyone want with her?

Janelle sat at the kitchen table reading the day's mail, her chaise longue too close to the phone—no longer safe. The phone's ringing cut through her defenses. She sat, immobile, prisoner to its ring. She waited for the answering machine's outgoing message.

"Dr. Henning is Tatyana Sloviovich. Answer phone. I need to tell something you must know. Pick up phone, pick up phone."

Janelle's nerves constricted, her breathing was held captive, waiting for the call to end. Seconds seemed minutes, until she heard the phone's electronic click; breathing returned. She walked to the phone and reached for the delete button instead hitting play out of nervous carelessness. Listening to the message again she could not understand why she had been targeted. *What is so important, Sloviovich?*

Janelle remembered the last time she had received unexpected news. Blade came to her while she was applying makeup for an evening out together. "Janelle, we've been after this for a while now."

Turning her face to him she asked, "Isn't that good?"

"Don't you ever wonder what we're capable of?"

"I think we're doing pretty well. I'm the first in my family to get a doctorate and my job with the school district is challenging and fulfilling. And you're at the top of your career. I don't care for your constant travel to New York and Washington, but it's what you do so we live with it. Is there something I'm missing here?"

"Not that, I meant personally."

"What are you talking about? Life is not perfect but we have a good life, Blade. Don't you think so?"

"It's not that—"

"What then?"

"I need more than we have. Remember how it was when we started? There were mountains to climb and climb them we did, but now . . . there are no mountains."

"Get a hold of yourself. We're both in our mid-forties. We have our health, a loving son, and each other."

"That's just it. We may love each other but it's not enough. I want to climb mountains again."

"What does that mean, Blade?"

What that meant was her losing a fulfilling life and a man she loved so he could go climbing. What the bastard forgot to mention was the twenty-six year old mount he was scaling in Washington and would marry within two weeks of their divorce. Would it have been a sacrilege to allow the joy of loving and being secure in that love? After that, Janelle vowed never to be blindsided again. She didn't know what Tatyana Sloviovich, if that's who was really calling her, wanted and she didn't plan to find out. There was no room in her life for surprises.

CHAPTER

10

Late January 2008

Wilsonville, Oregon

The phone's ring startled Janelle; dread once again invaded her mind. Looking at Caller ID she relaxed and picked up the receiver. "Mom, hello, how are you?"

"Hi, sweetie, what say we get together this week?" Rebecca Henning asked her daughter.

"It's always good to see you mom. Is anything special up?"

"Why, sweetheart?"

"Because we had lunch the week before last."

"And?"

"Mom, we've kept our once a month schedule as long as I can remember and you're just not one to change routines. How do you think I became so ordered?"

"Well it's about time for a little spontaneity. The simple fact of the matter is I was thinking about you and decided I wanted to see you."

"Just like that?"

"Just like that, call it a mother's prerogative."

"Great, my calendar is always open for you. When's good?" With the strange woman's escalating intrusions, Janelle was curious if she sensed something, call it intuition. She'd never seen her mother break routine without reason. If something was up she'd see at lunch.

Lunch trade at the Olive Garden in Lake Oswego was normally brisk. Janelle, arriving first, was pleasantly surprised when she was shown to a table without waiting. Rebecca was escorted to her daughter's table. The waiter remained to take a drink order. Janelle sipped on a glass of sparkling mineral water.

"Been waiting long, sweetie?" Rebecca asked, sitting down.

"Barely able to get a drink, I've enough sparkling water for both of us."

"Unlike you I don't have to go back to work, and since you're going to drop me off at the Mall where I'll meet Dad, I'd like something with a bit more body. Waiter, I'd like a Limón cello lemonade, and while you're here," Rebecca said, turning to Janelle, "the usual, sweetie?"

Janelle nodded.

"Good, we'll have the Pasta e Fagioli soup with breadsticks and salad with the house dressing. But, bring my drink first, thanks." The waiter jotted down the order and left.

"Looks like you're in a celebratory mood, mother."

"I'm happy whenever my daughter takes time from her busy schedule to see me. Now why has my heart been heavy when thinking about you lately?"

"Wow, how do I answer that?"

"Truthfully?"

"Mother, when have you ever known me to be less than honest?"

"You mean discounting growing up?"

"All children shade the truth when growing up. A mother as perfect as you knows that."

"And compliments do not an answer make."

"I can't answer why your heart is heavy. I get up each day and accomplish the tasks set before me. Did I mention I heard from your grandson last night?"

"I'm pleased he is communicating with one of us. You might remind him he has a grandmother and a grandfather who would not be displeased were he to call once in a while, even if it needs to be collect. How is he doing?"

"He's ready to graduate close to the top of his class."

"Not the top student?"

"You wouldn't believe the cutthroat competition he ran into. I didn't raise him to backstab just to succeed, so you should be proud he's done so well. He's excited about his first assignment and in two weeks I'll be flying back to see him graduate, though he called it something else. Not much of a ceremony from what he says, but all the same, I'm going."

"Tell him how proud grandpa and I are."

"I will, mom."

"And tell him to call."

Just then the waiter brought Rebecca's Limón cello lemonade along with the salad and bread sticks.

"So much for getting my drink before our meal," Rebecca said.

"It's lunchtime mom; they're serving a lot of tables," Janelle said, dishing salad onto her plate and taking a bread stick.

Taking the hint, Rebecca took a sip of her lemonade and did the same. The soup arrived and conversation took second to enjoying the delicious food.

"How is Dad doing?" Janelle asked, attempting to control the direction of the after-lunch conversation.

Placing her soup spoon down and blotting her lips with a napkin, a grin came to Rebecca's face. "He's your dad, what else can I say? His latest passion is golfing. Be prepared to be inundated with facts and information about golf the next time you come for dinner."

"How in the world did my sedentary dad get interested in golf?"

"I blame cable television. He blames me. Ever since retirement your father has altogether too much time on his hands. When he got tired of puttering in the shop with wood projects he turned his attention outdoors. Miguel threatened to quit unless I kept your dad from the yard and garden, so I suggested he might enjoy some

TV. Now what harm could a seventy-eight-year-old man get into watching television? First it was watching golf, then off to the golf course and lessons, then clubs and a bag, and now golf, golf, golf every time he opens his mouth. Did you know they have an entire channel just for golf?"

"Mom, you know Dad's exuberant personality. It'll burn itself out."

"He's talking about selling the house and buying a home on the golf course."

"You can afford it."

"Not you, too, I told him if he wanted to live on the golf course he'd better be willing to move there alone."

"Don't even joke about that. I know what divorce feels like. Besides, it's part of Dad's charm—when he likes something he really likes it."

"And when my heart becomes heavy thinking about you I have to know why. Sweetie, I just feel something is going on and it might help to talk."

"Why would you say something is going on?"

"Three weeks ago I received several calls from a woman claiming to be from the Ukraine."

Janelle leaned forward, "What did she want?"

"She wanted—no—demanded, to talk with you. Her name was Tatyana Sloviovich; she made several calls and was very insistent, so Dad contacted a couple of his friends back in Washington and they gathered some information."

"What did they turn up?"

"Has this person called you?"

"What did they say, mom?"

"Evidently she worked for the government in Odessa, Ukraine, and retired last year. A month or so ago, she left the Ukraine, under a B2 visitor's VISA. She wasn't required to tell anyone, at least officially, where she planned to visit or why she was coming to the U.S. Dad learned, under the VISA's terms, her stay is good for six months, so she'll be compelled to return home in four to four and a half months or be here illegally; not that anyone would consider breaking immigration laws important today. Finally, Dad got on the phone when she called one day and told her to never call again or he would contact the authorities. The calls stopped."

"I've received several calls from the Phoenix Inn. The caller identified herself as Tatyana Sloviovich, but why would she call you, Mom?"

Rebecca could feel the conversation beginning to close in on her. She couldn't answer without breaking a promise to someone whom she could never ask forgiveness of. "I can't say why she called, but I think you should come and stay with Dad and me for a couple of weeks."

"Mom, it's just someone over the phone. Besides, you know what Dad says, "Hennings take care of our own problems."

"Sweetie, staying with Dad and me a few days is prudent. We don't know who this woman is or even if she's alone. I didn't provide any information and yet somehow she managed to get your unlisted number. What else can she do?"

"Easy, mom, there have just been a few calls and I let her know I'm not interested in what she is selling."

"The calls have stopped?"

"Not exactly, she seems persistent, but like you said, her time here is limited. I don't see the need to uproot my schedule just because of a few calls from what appears to be an old woman."

"What if she's not an old woman?"

"Mom, don't make this worse than it is. I have been concerned and, in truth, I still am, but a rash decision is not the solution to any problem."

"My practical daughter, you know the things stalkers can do."

"I never said she was stalking me. I've received a few calls and dealt with them. At first I thought it was aggressive marketing turned belligerent. I don't know what to think now."

Rebecca knew this was no sales call. "I would feel much better if you came and stayed for a couple of weeks.

"Mom, I love you but the district schedule is what you should worry about doing me in, not some old woman. Things are hectic at work and I just don't need the extra half hour commute each way from your place to work. If it makes you feel better, remember I live in a gated community and my doors have dead bolts and security cameras, not to mention the security patrols. I'm safer than you, but then if anyone tries to break in your place Dad can clobber him with a golf club."

"Don't you make light of this. I am still your mother and I reserve the right to worry whenever I choose. It's just my fate you turned out stubborn like your dad. Call, every night."

"I'll try to but don't worry—since Blade left I've had to deal with aggressive men and even a woman or two at work who thought I would make the perfect date. I'm not defenseless. If the phone calls escalate I'll take whatever steps necessary—including staying with you—but I don't think it's wise to make more of this than it is."

"Just remember your Dad and I are here."

"I'll remember, now no worrying."

As Rebecca rode beside her daughter to the mall, she prayed Sloviovich's secret would leave the country with her.

CHAPTER

11

February 2008, Early Afternoon

Office of the Honorable Dr. Azim Al-Haroun, Palestine Minister of Health RamAllāh, West Bank

"Four days ago reports began coming in from Primary Health Care Centers in the West Bank and Gaza noting escalating cases of rubeola. I assigned investigative teams. They examined three hundred thirty-nine individuals who were symptomatic. Patient records were reviewed, secondary examinations performed, and new blood work-ups run. Three hundred thirty-seven cases were positive for rubeola," Dr. BintZagr began.

"Are we looking at a measles epidemic, Kadira?" Dr. Al-Haroun asked.

"Too soon to know it at this time."

"Reasoning?"

"First, current numbers infected are insignificant compared to the population. Second, Israelis are going to want to make that call. We have fewer than one hundred doses of MMR vaccine, with 4,045,839 doses required for first-round immunizations, so like it or not we'll need help and unless the Israelis are on board it will take longer than we have to make the case internationally."

"So we wait for additional information?"

"That's not easy to say. A sudden appearance of three hundred thirty-seven cases of rubeola raises concerns. Measles are usually confined to scattered occurrences in the West Bank or Gaza, six, seven cases at time. Never more than three hundred cases, or outbreaks in both the West Bank and Gaza. Our last health minister placed urgent health care needs ahead of a general population vaccination program; considering the status of negotiations there wasn't any other choice."

"How many have received MMR vaccinations?" Dr. Al-Haroun asked.

"That's what concerns me. We've held limited clinics over the past few years, but many records were lost because of hostilities. I'd guess the number vaccinated is about eighteen percent of the population."

"Not just children, the entire populace?"

"Everyone."

"Contact Dr. Kiva, Israel Ministry of Health, apprise him of our situation. Give five percent as the number of Palestinians that have received both rounds of MMR vaccinations. I will contact Dr. Giacobbe at World Health."

As Kadira BintZagr entered her office, the emblazoned lettering on her door, *Palestine Ministry of Health, Chief Epidemiology Division*, escaped her usual notice. She left a message for Dr. Kiva and waited. At 5:32 P.M. she answered the phone on its first ring.

"Dr. Kiva, how good of you to return my call. We have all the markings of a serious problem on our hands so I'll get right to the point. In the past four days three hundred thirty-seven cases of rubeola were reported in Gaza and the West Bank. This was confirmed by teams I sent out. Our numbers continue to escalate. The majority of our adult population has not been immunized and is exposed to serious risk."

"What percentage of your people has received both rounds of MMR?"

"Our numbers, as you know, are not exact, doctor. Dr. Al-Haroun gave me a figure of five percent."

Which means it's more like twenty percent, Daniel Kiva thought to himself. "What are your reserves?"

"Fewer than one hundred doses."

"What is it I can do for you?"

"We need 4,045,839 doses of MMR vaccine to vaccinate everyone, since our records are too problematic to leave anyone but those pregnant and under a year old out. Even if the cases don't continue escalating, our population is at risk until Palestine is immunized."

"First, total your figures. I need exact numbers. Second, contact WHO."

"Dr. Al-Haroun is contacting the World Health Organization."

"You'll need them. Let me pull something up on my computer . . . . Ah, there it is. Worldwide there are fewer than one million doses available."

"Fewer than one million?"

"Numbers change but I should be in the ballpark. Globally, total stockpiles are larger than those figures since every country maintains reserves. The U.S. has a six-month reserve. France and Great Britain and a few others have three-month reserves, but no one tabulates their reserves when reporting stocks on hand."

"Why?"

"Despite all the grand gestures at world citizenship it's still a hard world, and each country takes care of its own. My bet would be WHO will turn it over to UNICEF. If anyone has access to the amounts you need they will, but don't expect much. Your numbers are beyond even the rosiest projections."

"We have a problem."

"Let's not give up just yet. This may or may not develop into a full-blown epidemic, although the numbers are troubling. Give me some time, say until tomorrow, since it's too late to move on anything tonight, and we'll see what we can come up with. By the way, you have the funds for this?"

"We'll find the money, there is no other choice. Thank you, doctor." Kadira did not trust this Jew, aware of what his country had done to her land and her people, but there was no other choice: They needed help and they needed it now.

CHAPTER

12

Early the Next Morning

Apartment of Dr. Kadira BintZagr
Palestine Ministry of Health, Chief Epidemiology Division
RamAllāh, West Bank

The night passed fitfully. Kadira awoke at four A.M. With sleep impossible, she called her driver, dressed, and went to her office. Staring at overnight figures, Kadira's heart sank. Six hundred and forty-two new cases reported, with several Primary Health Care Centers' figures still to be reported. She awakened Dr. Al-Haroun.

The day brought field reports of increasing numbers of sick and continuous, unrelenting attempts to locate the necessary vaccine while fielding calls from divergent ministries, with offers of concern but no vaccine. She was running out of the thing she needed most: time.

In mid-afternoon the phone rang. Her secretary came over the phone's intercom, "Dr. Kiva from the Israel Ministry of Health is on the line, doctor."

Picking up the phone, she said, "Our numbers of infected are exploding."

"How many?"

"Six hundred forty-two overnight with an additional seven hundred nineteen through two P.M. Our total is one thousand six hundred ninety-eight cases."

"Doctor, it appears you have an epidemic on your hands."

"Tell me something I don't know. What you have turned up, Dr. Kiva?"

"Have you ascertained the actual number of doses needed?"

"4,045,839 is my best estimate, and that's not inflated, doctor."

"I've come up with 345,000 doses with delivery next week."

"A week for less than one tenth of our need?"

"The vaccines are scattered around the globe and will take a week just to collect and get to you. I've also received an interesting call, a feeler from the Russians."

"What are the Russians offering?"

"You're going to have to hear this one in person."

"I'm not authorized to meet with you. My call is under the authority of the Minister of Health."

"Up to you, I'm willing to meet. Let me know so I can have the required travel permits issued. I'll be in my office for another three hours."

"Thank you, doctor. I'll call within the hour."

One hour and fifty-one minutes later Drs. Al-Haroun and Kadira BintZagr walked into Dr. Daniel Kiva's office at the Israel Ministry of Health. Formalities were short and to the point.

"I talked with every contact cultivated over the past twenty-seven years. In addition, my subordinates called everyone they could think of. All we could locate were the 345,000 doses I spoke of earlier. Supply is just not there."

"You're a doctor, we're doctors. Politics aside, our people need help or many will die," Dr. BintZagr said.

"I am cognizant of political realities, and I agree that in this room sit three doctors. As a doctor, I promise you we looked everywhere. Just before my earlier call to you, Dr. BintZagr, I received an unexpected call from the Deputy Minister of Public Health and Medical Industry of the Russian Federation, Dr. Aksana Galina Ivanovich. I've never met the woman, but what she said is intriguing."

"We're listening," said Dr. Al-Haroun.

"The Russians have been experimenting with aerosol vaccinations for the past several years. There has been some research by others, most notably the Americans, French, and British, but their investigations have been comparatively rudimentary. We knew there had been limited success with research, but until today no one has demonstrated large-scale success in field trials with the aerosolization of vaccines, including, we thought, the Russians. Today Dr. Ivanovich informed me they have completed successful trials on more than ten thousand subjects in a facility called Stepnogorsk."

"What are the Russians offering?"

"Nothing specific, Dr. Ivanovich provided the barest of details and said you could contact her office if you're interested."

"This is a matter for the President's office. I will relay all the information you have provided," Dr. Al-Haroun said.

Dr. Kiva reached across the desk and handed Dr. Al-Haroun a folded sheet of paper "Here is the contact information, best of luck."

CHAPTER

13

February 2008

Office of the Honorable Faqih Wardam, President of Palestine RamAllāh, West Bank

"The President will see you now," announced the corpulent secretary with a sweep of her flaccid arm toward the ten-foot-tall carved mahogany doors. As they opened, Drs. Al-Haroun and Kadira BintZagr entered the office of President Wardam. One Palestinian Freedom Army soldier stood guard in each corner of the cavernous room, with two more stationed by the doors, having pushed the symbols of Palestinian power shut behind the doctors.

Crossing the office to the elaborate desk, both doctors greeted the president and all three sat down. "Mr. President, there has been an outbreak of measles in both the West Bank and Gaza. We also just learned of cases occurring in eastern al-Quds. Few people have been vaccinated."

"Come now Azim, measles is not a scourge. Why, I had measles as a child, and as you can see I am still very much alive."

"You're right, Mr. President, many have contracted measles as children, but contracting rubeola as a child is not the same as what could happen to our adult population if this respiratory infection runs its course."

"And that is?"

"Dr. BintZagr has been gathering information, I'll let her answer."

"Mr. President, worldwide there were six hundred and ten thousand deaths from rubeola in 2002, the latest year we have statistics on. Rubeola, or measles as it is commonly known, can lead to ear infections, pneumonia, encephalitis—"

"Encephalitis?"

"Inflammation of the brain, which can lead to seizures, coma, and death, also deafness and mental retardation. Adult measles is capable of permanent damage. It's also known to cause miscarriages. Those who don't miscarry may pass on significant congenital defects to their babies. Mr. President, among those never vaccinated there is a ninety percent chance of infection on contact with a carrier."

"How many have contracted measles, Azim?"

"Yesterday at 2:00 P.M. the figures were one thousand six hundred and ninety-eight. When we left for your office four thousand eight hundred and six cases had been reported."

"It escalates that rapidly?"

"When it's an epidemic it does."

"What should our course of action be?"

"With the exception of those pregnant and infants under one year of age, who must be quarantined to isolate them from contact with the disease, we need to vaccinate every Palestinian man, woman, and child, even those who have been vaccinated, since our records are too incomplete to rely on."

"Not quarantine those infected?"

"Thousands are incubating the disease as we speak. Numbers will soon be too large to count. The incubation period, the time it takes someone to exhibit symptoms from initial exposure, can range from seven to eighteen days after contact with an infected person. During this period, rubeola is contagious five days before the appearance of a rash and, this is important, rubeola may be contracted by breathing air where any infected person has been, up to two hours after the infected person is gone. We can't isolate our entire population, but it's possible to isolate pregnant women and those less than twelve months of age who are too young to receive vaccine. It's the best we can do."

"What is being done for those already sick?"

"Dr. BintZagr," Azim Al-Haroun said, looking to his subordinate.

"Bed rest, hydration, vitamin A, which lessens the severity of the disease. Teams from my office and the Palestinian Red Crescent Society are showing families how to care for their sick. PRCS is contacting other Red Crescent societies for needed vitamin A. Without it, mortalities and those permanently injured could cripple our population."

"Have you contacted the World Health Organization?"

"I called for help. World Health turned our request over to UNICEF, which said little of the vaccine is available, maybe some for children but not for adults. The amount offered was not even enough for our children," Dr. Al-Haroun answered.

"But children infect adults. To break the cycle should not all be immunized?"

"Apparently it doesn't matter. Rules weren't made for Palestine. They sympathize, but can't break their organization charter. They asked for a count of children so their committee could meet then tell us what help is available. Palestinian children will be infected; adults will die by then."

"I want three reports sent to my office each day, an in-depth summary each morning with overnight statistics and briefs at least twice a day on the continuing status of this emergency. Akil Farook will be my liaison. He'll be available at all hours. If you need me, General Farook will get you through, no matter where I am, any hour, day, or night." He pressed the phone's intercom button.

"Yes, Mr. President," came the sagging voice of the secretary.

"Rihana, I want Dr. Al-Haroun to have General Farook's phone numbers, both office and cell. He will pick them up on his way out. Also call the General and tell him to come to my office immediately." He hung up then looked at his friend. "What else do you need?"

"Mr. President, we had less than one hundred doses of MMR vaccine but who could we give them to with a riot possible for those not chosen? Dr. BintZagr contacted the Israeli Minister of Health. He located 345,000 doses from various countries, but it will take a week to deliver."

"The Israelis, so helpful, wouldn't appear compassionate to have Palestinians decimated by a virus modern medicine has wiped out in their country," the President said. "What are the numbers?"

"We need 4,045,839 doses of MMR vaccine along with syringes to administer the vaccine."

"If we don't have sufficient vaccine for the population and none is available internationally, how do you propose we proceed, Mr. Minister of Health?"

"In trying to locate vaccine, Dr. Kiva, Israel Minister of Health, received a call from Deputy Minister of Public Health and Medical Industry of the Russian Federation, Dr. Aksana Galina Ivanovich. She said they have completed successful trials of aerosol vaccination at a biotechnical facility in northern Kazakhstan. Dr. Ivanovich told Dr. Kiva if we were interested to call. I have the number."

"Aerosol vaccination seems pretty far-fetched. You're convinced it's real science?"

"I am a doctor, not a research scientist, but without another source for the vaccine there is no other choice."

"We may have to trust the Russians with our most precious resource, Palestinian lives. This does not make for happiness."

"That is why you are president."

"What did the Russians say exactly?"

"Mr. President, I didn't talk with Dr. Ivanovich. She talked with Dr. Kiva and he passed on the barest of information, which I just gave you. Russians have proven a friend in the past, and they know of our need."

"A friend yes, but one that looks to their own interests. There seems no other choice, so we'll call. Use my phone, its number is blocked. Place the call on speaker, but don't reveal where you are calling from or that I'm present."

He turned the speaker toward them. His secretary's voice came over the intercom, "Mr. President, General Farook is here."

"Send him in."

"Akil, come, sit. You know Drs. Al-Haroun and BintZagr from the Ministry of Health. We have a vital call to make. I want you to sit with us and listen, but do not speak. I have a most important assignment I will brief you on later. Doctor, place the call."

The Minister of Health pulled out the slip of paper and dialed.

"*Zdravstvuite*, hello, this is Dr. Ivanovich."

Outside the President's office, Rihana was recording every word through a concealed microphone in the president's ornately carved desk.

"This is Dr. Al-Haroun, Palestine Minister of Health. Doctor, I will get to the point. We are facing an epidemic. We have a need for 4,045,839 doses of MMR vaccine. 345,000 have been located, but they are a week away and we need them today. Dr. Kiva at the Israel Ministry of Health told me you spoke with him yesterday. The purpose of my call is to determine if Russia can provide humanitarian assistance to my people that will save great suffering and the loss of many lives."

"Russian researchers have been successful in developing aerosol immunizations. I know is fantastic but Mother Russia triumphs where others fail. The benefits will prove inestimable for mankind. This achievement had to come, hand in hand, with formulation of vaccines that could be administered through aerosolization. We have succeeded there as well."

"Doctor, forgive my directness, but this matter is the most important health issue Palestine has ever faced. Do I understand correctly, you have perfected MMR vaccine for aerosolization?"

"Good, doctor, *da*, yes."

"Yes, you . . . you've perfected?"

"We have completed extensive field trials with the greatest of successes. I send results for you to study."

"Doctor, it's vaccine that will save my people. Technical papers I welcome, but we need the medicine first."

"How many, and I need exact numbers, to be vaccinated?"

"4,045,839 dosages. Have you produced such numbers?"

The room became still.

"Did you say 4,045,839 doses are needed?"

"Yes, that number will vaccinate all our people in Palestine, Gaza, and eastern al-Quds."

"Our current inventory shows just over five million doses."

"Five million MMR doses?"

"Yes, that is our inventory."

"I am overwhelmed with joy."

"We are indebted to you—"

"How could this be?" Dr. BintZagr cut in.

"Doctor, methodology of vaccination and vaccine is greatest medical achievement of twenty-first century. Extensive trials were conducted but, in order to gain acceptance, it must be demonstrated that aerosol vaccine is as efficacious and safe as subcutaneous injections. By providing vaccine, and aerosol applicators, we prove, where even Americans are not able to discredit or deny."

"Dr. Ivanovich, I am away from my office. I need my staff to make final arrangements. Will you be available in one hour?"

"I wait for your call, we have much to discuss."

"Thank you, thank you with all of heart. Goodbye."

"*Do svidaniya*, goodbye."

There was silence in the room as Azim hung up the phone.

"I don't know how to understand this aerosol vaccination, Azim."

"Allāh has shown the way. It is our only path, Mr. President."

"Yes, faith leads us. But in bringing medicine to Palestine Azim, you did not mention payment. The Russians like their rubles," the president said.

"The matter of money did not cross my mind, Mr. President. Funds must be found. Any other course is unimaginable and would endanger Palestine's future."

"There are sources we have relied on. If the Russians prove greedy, we will expand our circle of friends for help. This is one need we cannot ignore."

"Thank you, Mr. President."

"General," President Wardam said, turning to General Farook, "Dr. Al-Haroun informed me of an outbreak of measles which I am confident your subordinates have brought to your attention. Numbers, though low, are escalating. We don't have sufficient vaccine to immunize even a fraction of our people. The call you heard we pray will result in enough vaccine to prevent a full-scale epidemic. Drs. Al-Haroun and BintZagr will provide you three status reports each day. You will represent me; do not assign this to another. Make yourself available twenty-four hours a day should the doctors need to contact you. Keep me apprised of the situation. Additionally, if Dr. Al-Haroun needs to speak with or see me, no matter the hour, arrange it. This is most urgent and, as much as possible, is to remain among the four of us. I don't want to alarm our people."

"I understand, Mr. President. Everything will be taken care of," the General said.

"One other thing Akil, do your best to ensure that Gaza cooperates. The PMIJ can cause problems, but everyone there will need to be immunized."

"You can count on me, Mr. President."

After briefing General Farook in his office, the doctors returned to the Ministry of Health. Dr. Al-Haroun dialed Moscow while Dr. BintZagr turned on the tape recorder.

"*Zdravstvuite*, this is Dr. Al-Haroun from Palestine Ministry of Health."

"Your Russian is good. Hello to you."

"Many apologies but I did not inquire on costs. You know we are a poor country which has benefited from the generosity of the Russian people many times in the past. The world itself cannot contain the gratitude in our hearts. If not for Russia, Palestine would not stand as a nation today, *spasibo*, thank you."

"For Mother Russia you are welcome. We doctors do what we can while politicians make decisions that affect our nation. I will pass on kind thoughts to Vladimir. He is a close friend and will welcome your words."

"What about costs, doctor?"

"Mother Russia has struggled so we understand plight of oppressed people. To purchase vaccine and technology would cost hundreds of millions of rubles, but we know this is not possible nor is what Russia, a friend to Palestine, wants. For assistance we ask your country to pay cost of transportation of vaccine and immunization tents that are required. Also cost of medical technicians to administer vaccine. I cannot provide exact figures, but my word is Palestine will only pay the costs Russia incurs. I have also been instructed to say Finance Minister will work out payment schedule that meets Palestine's needs while getting vaccine to your people."

"I am overwhelmed by this generosity. Such magnanimous kindness will be remembered."

"There is one benefit I haven't mentioned. As you know, MMR vaccinations are followed up by a second vaccination in three to four years in case those receiving the initial vaccine didn't develop immunity from the vaccination. Our restructured vaccine does not require a second vaccination. We have identified no cases in which the initial vaccination was not one hundred percent successful in producing immunity."

"Words fail me, doctor."

"Our doctors will require free access to monitor program and conduct follow-up examinations so we can verify, scientifically, what has been achieved. We will provide complete lists of all personnel so Palestine security will know who we are sending. Let me relay to proper authority what we have discussed today and I will get back to you with final arrangements."

"Because of the imminent nature of our need, when do you anticipate I will hear from you?"

"Is matter of hours, we are aware of your need. When letters of agreement are drawn they will be presented by Ambassador Demyan to Ambassador Abd-Yusuf. Signing of papers is then in Palestine's hands. Soon as agreement is signed we'll obtain permission from Israelis to fly all personnel and materials to Ben Gurion."

"Israelis will demand to search and transport personnel and vaccine into Palestine; they trust no one. After Zionists observe all is in order vaccinations can begin."

"Unless Israelis hinder us we should be in Palestine within two days."

Azim sat amazed at the power of Allāh, blessed be his name, to once again rescue his people from peril.

That night Rihana stopped for vegetables on her way home from work as she did several times each week. By the time she finished picking out tomatoes, green onions, and lettuce, micro-chips of the day's conversations in President Wardam' office had been dispatched to Gaza and Sayed Amal Wasim.

CHAPTER

14

February 2008

Lod Airport
Outside Tel Aviv

On July 11, 1948, Lydda Airport, which was constructed twelve years earlier, was captured by the Israel Defense Force in their war of independence and renamed Lod International Airport for the nearby town of Lod. The airport was divided into a civilian airport and an IAF base. After the death of Israel's first Prime Minister in 1974, the civilian facility was renamed Ben Gurion International Airport in his honor, while the adjoining Israeli Air Force base kept Lod as its name.

Within twenty-four hours of the MMR Accord being signed by the governments of Russia and the Palestinian Authority, an Antonov AN-72 touched down at Ben Gurion International Airport and taxied to the IAF base of Lod, which sits parallel to Ben Gurion's shortest runway.

Inside the AN-72, thirty Biopreparat-trained doctors and thirty Russian Ministry of Health nurses looked from one to another while waiting to disembark along with five tons of medical tents, vaccine, aerosolizers, and miscellaneous medical equipment.

A solemn officer boarded the airplane. Standing silently at attention, with a clipboard in her right hand, she waited until all eyes were upon her. "*Shalom*, welcome to *Eretz Yisra'el*, the land of Israel. I am Captain Kefira Beider of 123 Squadron. Yisra'el has made arrangements for a trouble-free stopover. Passports will be checked inside the terminal. Have them ready for inspection when you deplane. Refreshments and food have been prepared for your enjoyment and are waiting in the terminal with comfortable seating. After security procedures are complete you will board helicopters for a short flight to the Ramalla government compound. I will now call your individual names. When you hear your name, answer, and take all personal baggage and exit plane. Officers are waiting to escort you to processing. Sevastian Eltsin."

"Da."

"Raisa Gorlacha."

"Da."

"Luba Petriova . . . , Luba Petriova."

"Da."

"Gavril Steparkov . . ." Kefira Beider knew this would be a long day.

Ten hours later every passenger, all luggage, medical equipment, and every infusion bag of vaccine had undergone three separate, painstaking thorough, security inspections, including electronic, infra-red, and biological scans. Combined IDF experts were assigned to conduct meticulous detailed inspections of these travelers and their unique cargo. They were unable, in the time available, to ascertain the exact chemical composition down to parts per million of the MMR vaccine being transported through their country, but they were convinced it was MMR vaccine and that nothing heading for Ramalla contained any explosive or biological agents which could be used against Eretz Yisra'el.

The weary Russian doctors and nurses were beginning to wonder if they would make it out of Israel that day when Captain Beider entered the passenger lounge with two other Israeli officers and announced, "All checks have been finalized. Three S-70A helicopters are waiting for boarding. All luggage has been loaded along with equipment and vaccine for direct transport to the Ramalla government compound on a separate helicopter as there is no room for baggage with passengers. We will divide into three groups. Twenty people, please line up in front of me."

"Quickly, twenty people here," commanded Lt. Yaron. The remaining twenty lined up in front of Lt. Goldwasser.

"Follow me," Captain Beider said as she charged out the door to the waiting helicopters.

Each group of doctors and nurses raced to keep up with their officer. As they neared the transports the three officers split off to their assigned helicopters. Captain Beider yelled over the roar of the rotors to her group, "Keep heads down. When seated I will show you how to secure harnesses so no one falls out." The doctors and nurses followed every word they could hear—life depended on getting it right.

After the officers made sure every passenger was secured in the five-point harnesses, they closed the doors and escaped the prop-wash as the helicopters strained to be free. Ground crews pulled wheel blocks from the restive beasts and quickly backed away as each one in turn slipped the earth's unwelcome confines. Rising slowly at first, the helos, emancipated by 3,400 thundering horses, leapt skyward. The combat takeoffs left more than one Russian stomach sitting on the tarmac wishing it had not partaken so freely of the lavish assortment of foods and sweets the Israelis so delighted in sharing with visitors. Inside the cockpits several Israeli pilots could be seen smiling.

Forty-five minutes later the Russians and all their equipment were the guests of PALFA, Palestinian Freedom Army. The S-70A made their way home to Hatzerim by way of Lod.

CHAPTER

15

Monday February 4 2008

Wilsonville, Oregon

Four days passed with no contact from the stranger. The phone's silence brought hope the tempest had been weathered, but Janelle's daily habits, though clothed in familiar garments, were unwilling to release their apprehension. Arriving home, she unlocked her mailbox and glanced through bills and junk mail then hurried to the porch. As she reached for the storm door her heart began racing. Wedged ominously between the storm and front door an envelope from the Phoenix Inn lay in wait. The motel's address on Boones Ferry Road was so close. Her fingers felt numb as she removed the envelope and entered her sanctuary. Locking herself in she banished the offender to the edge of the vestibule table. What now? There was no plan. What did this violation mean? *Perhaps the stranger got my address with my unlisted phone number. She could have. One is not harder to get than the other, is it?*

Routine always redeemed whatever life threw at her. She would deal with the offender later. An envelope can't open itself. Wine and a few moments to think, and reason would prevail.

Janelle set the remainder of the mail on the vestibule table away from the trespasser and sat her purse on the mail. She turned to the hall closet, took off her coat and hung it carefully, meticulously, then placed her purse on its shelf.

The vestibule table's lower shelf, mirroring the half moon shape of the top, stood six inches above the floor where it attached to the table's three fluted legs. On its polished surface the silk burgundy rose bouquet stood slightly askew. Janelle's eyes, searching for something to occupy her thoughts, spotted the off-center spray. Carefully, with exacting precision, she centered it. Even when life precipitated a momentary detour, there was comfort in order. *Must not let an old friend flee because an interruption threatens. After Blade's betrayal this is nothing. After Blade, no obstacle will undo me.*

Janelle retrieved the mail from the vestibule table, exiling the intruder to solitary confinement on the table's edge. Glancing down at the carefully positioned flowers, Janelle, satisfied, continued to the kitchen, dropping the mail on the chaise table. Opening the wine refrigerator she removed a glass and the Pinot Gris, her senses anticipating its intrinsic essence as she filled the glass.

Blade had accustomed her to the pleasures of fine wine, and she wasn't about to let his miserable failure as a human being diminish one of the few good things he brought into her life. Though successful in his professional extortions, Janelle thought, with a momentary surge of bile creeping up her throat, his newer, younger model wouldn't do any better in the long haul than she had. Did that please her? She couldn't tell, but why waste time on him? Indeed, why allow Blade any part of her when thoughts of him changed nothing and didn't help decide what she should do with this invasion from Russia. *No, one must be precise; she is from the Ukraine, which makes her Ukrainian. The Cold War ended; must stay within known facts. The only way to prevail is reasoned logic.*

Janelle walked to the chaise with her glass, took a sip, and set the wine on the table. She picked up the mail, the Phoenix Inn & Suites envelope conspicuous in its absence, *time for that later*, she thought, sinking into the overstuffed chaise longue. It embraced her in its comfort as its protective soft leather warmed to her body. Along with the wine, its sensuous feel soothed her, shielding her from the letter, lying in wait.

Going through each piece of mail, she knew there was just one whose presence demanded attention: bills to be paid, catalogs of things unwanted couldn't distract her. Janelle understood the subterfuge of momentary diversion was futile. How does one will the absence of thought? The more she attempted to distance herself from the envelope, the more it invaded every thought, destroying her nightly ritual.

Finally, forced from her cocoon, she finished the wine and filed each piece of mail in its place. Glancing toward the vestibule table, she returned to the kitchen and poured a second glass of wine, then inhaled half the glass. *Have to be careful, mustn't lose control. What was it Blade spat out? That my problem was always being in control. My control never kept him from pursuing his goals. How could something good be turned into a thing that sounded so ugly? Why did he intrude . . . now? It had been too many years; she was over thoughts of him and his bimbo wife. Must be one unwelcome intrusion invading another.*

Janelle understood the battle was lost and what must be done. She walked over to the envelope waiting on the vestibule table. Burning it would change nothing. There would just be another to replace it, then another and another. It seemed to take on a life of its own lying there. *What do you contain?* As she reached down Janelle was surprised by the trembling in her fingers. *Come now, old girl, it's just an envelope.* Janelle took hold of its edge and lifted it warily. She put it back down. Going to the chaise table she retrieved her letter opener and returned to her bête noire.

Taking the envelope, she walked past the chaise, and went to the kitchen table. She placed the interloper next to the letter opener, taking care not to let either touch. Pulling out a chair she sat down. *This is the place to deal with unwanted intrusions. If it proves threatening, I'll call Jerry, no matter how much he misunderstands. If not, I'll see what must be done to end this.*

As she slit the envelope's throat, she anticipated evil. "Why can't people just leave others alone?" she murmured, waiting for something to happen. When nothing did, she placed the letter opener on the table and stared at the envelope. There was no rush to view its contents, no hurry to unlock its malevolence. Silently, she observed its exterior, hoping a clue to its contents might be revealed.

What are you waiting for? Exhaling, she opened the top of the envelope. Looming inside was a single folded sheet of paper. *It's just paper.* Trembling fingers entered the envelope, pulling the page from its lair.

Placing the sheet on the table, she made no move to unfold it. Minutes crawled past; her nemesis waited with her. With dread and curiosity she accepted what must be faced and unfolded the letter. Twenty-five words confronted her. She read them again and again, 'Must see you. Important, you have to know. Call number below, ask speak Tatyana Sloviovich. Will meet anytime, anywhere, but must see soon. Tatyana Sloviovich.' Underneath was a number she would never call.

CHAPTER

16

Wednesday February 6 2008

Wilsonville, Oregon

Wednesdays were errand days. Janelle stopped on her way home from work for groceries and whatever needed to be dropped off or picked up from the week before. This mid-week ritual freed weekends for an occasional ski trip to Mount Hood Meadows in the fall and winter, or kayaking in the Deschutes, Calapooia, or Clackamas rivers during the spring and summer. These adventures brought her the joy of the outdoors she didn't find at work, and helped her keep fit, as did bicycling around Portland whenever weather permitted and sometimes when it didn't. Trips to the Oregon Coast from Astoria to Cannon Beach and Newport to points south, any weekend she could get away, provided life's true joy. The Oregon Coast held a special place in her heart. She explored miles of coastline and quaint art galleries. The ocean's spirit, being alone with the crash of waves against shoreline, purified her soul and clarified her thoughts.

After dropping off laundry at The Cleanery in the Village on Main Street, Janelle found a parking spot outside Harvest Grains Bakery. As she opened the bakery door, the tantalizing aroma of fresh baked bread conquered her senses and bid her enter. After years of loyal patronage, she was family.

"Buonasera, Dr. Henning. What's your pleasure today?" the fleshy baker asked.

"My usual plus apple bread."

"I'm a sorry, doctor, but the apple bread we sold all out of them, no more than thirty minutes ago."

"And you didn't save me a loaf, Guido?"

"We try to save some loaves for special customers like you, but last ten customers also come here long time and each asks for apple bread. Don't know why today it's got to be apple bread, but as I say, it's all gone. You tell Guido when you come back and I protect a loaf for you with my life."

"I don't want your life, Guido. Who would create your delightful breads? What do you recommend?"

"I try new recipe just today. It's cranberry-almond. Everyone who tries it wants more. I think you like."

"Then make it one loaf of cranberry almond."

"You want in addition to your usual loaf of 14-grain bread?"

"Of course."

"And all the bread sliced medium just the way you like."

After signing the charge slip Janelle glanced toward the windows facing the mall's parking lot. An oddly dressed old woman, coming from the bus stop on the other side of the mall, caught her eye. She appeared to be headed for the bakery. Janelle felt the blood drain from her face. The woman's pace increased. Grabbing her bread, Janelle hurried out of Harvest Grains and headed for her car. She heard her name being called in halting English, and recognized the voice on the phone. Janelle felt dizzy as she reached her car. Yanking open the door, she tossed the bread onto the passenger's seat then jumped in and started the car. Barreling back out of the parking space, she slammed the transmission into drive, leaving the stalker hurrying after her as she sped away. Laying under the bread was her weekly grocery list half crumpled, forgotten, as thoughts of escape forbade stopping for anything but home.

All the next day Janelle's mind returned to her mall, her bakery. *How could she know unless she was stalking me, tracking my weekly stops? Why Tatyana Sloviovich, why me?* Time after time she forced her mind back on work only to return to the mall and an encounter she seemed hopeless to escape.

The parking lot was almost empty when Janelle went to her car a quarter hour after quitting time. She tried to exile thoughts of yesterday's encounter but her mind refused. *Where will the stranger show up next?* Her familiar route was a labyrinth of shadowy forms as she peered around at every stop for a lurking presence—even the usual drug-enslaved beggars at traffic lights sent off alarms.

Then it came to her: Abandoning her grocery list yesterday wasn't fear but her inner guide showing the way. Routine must be discarded if she were to prevail. Thursday was better than Wednesdays for errands anyways. One day closer to the weekend. She saw the crumpled list on the passenger's seat and would fill it on her way home and that was that.

Checking each aisle for any sight of the stalker—why tempt the gods—Janelle hurried through the store. When she arrived home, no letter from Tatyana awaited. As she approached her front door, her porch light came to life, startling her. No silhouette could be seen lying in wait. *Was the camellia swaying? Get a hold of yourself.* A slight breeze assured her frayed nerves it was just the wind and camellia branches that needed pruning. Balancing the groceries and mail against the doorjamb she inserted her key in the lock, opening the front door. As Janelle pulled the groceries to herself a presence appeared from nowhere beside her on the porch.

Janelle tried to scream. No sound wrenched itself from her constricted throat. Holding her groceries and mail defensively, she searched for a way out. Panic washed over her as she attempted to escape through the door, slamming it in the invader's face, but saw, to her horror, the key—still in the lock. She attempted to rip it from the door.

Tatyana closed in. "Please, not be frightened, need to talk."

"You!" Janelle shrieked, fear and anger fusing. "Get Away From Me, Get Away Now!"

"Just few moments . . . Please few moments . . . I have come so far . . . just few minute."

The plaintiveness of Tatyana's voice broke through to an unguarded sliver of trust deep within Janelle. Her panic began to abate; this was an old woman begging for a moment of time, but pent-up emotion could not completely dismiss the intruder as a threat to every part of her existence. Nostrils flaring, breath quivering in short blasts, Janelle's entire being riveted on the woman.

In the momentary silence Tatyana began pouring out her story on the porch. "I was charge of *Dom Rebyonka*, baby house. Fifty-one years ago child come through Dom Rebyonka removed from parents because illegal associations against Motherland. Supposed to no more hear from family but over years father, mother come asking information, bringing letters. Parents sent to labor camp but brother comes still asking for news, any news, about Shayndel Laila."

Janelle looked on with mounting terror—this ranting woman was insane. As Tatyana pressed on, Janelle wondered why this lunatic was confronting her. "WHY ME?" she screamed. *Am I losing my mind as well?* "STOP, I DON'T KNOW YOU. YOU DON'T KNOW ME. I HAVE BEEN CHASED AND PURSUED RELENTLESSLY. THIS ENDS HERE: NOW!"

"Shayndel," Tatyana whispered. The word bounced off Janelle as nonsense.

Tatyana stepped toward Janelle. Caught off guard, Janelle retreated, dropping her grocery bag onto the entry floor. Primal fear arose as the lifelong pacifist attempted to hurl this threat from her world. As Janelle moved forward to grab Tatyana, she stepped on the side of a can from the bag of groceries. It shot across the room, taking Janelle's balance with it, she flailed in the air, trying to grab anything to catch her falling body. Her plunging hand grasped the strap of Tatyana's bag, tearing it from the old woman and dislodging its contents as it hit the polished marble tiles.

Struggling to get up, Janelle's shoe slammed into Tatyana's bag launching it across the floor into the vestibule table. A music box, hidden under the upturned edge of Tatyana's bag, started to play. The notes pierced Janelle's soul, suspended in a realm between fear and wonder. As the notes played, Janelle's heart was transported to a world she never knew existed. The notes surrounded and mesmerized. Invading her as they made their way to a heart—but not her heart—the heart of a child, as Janelle was captured by a haunting melody she had never heard yet somehow knew every note to.

It was then Janelle saw the music box, the source of this melody that pierced her soul. Slowly, reverently, she crawled to this object of wonder, not daring to touch it lest the music stop.

She heard a foreign voice, exquisite in its untrained timbre *"Laila, Laila, feigelach reien zeier gezang . . . Laila, Laila, chalomos, dein numen zei riefen tzee zeech."* Where was this from she wondered as she listened to its continuing refrain *"Laila, Laila, dee levonah shein geit oif."*

As she sat on the floor Janelle heard with her heart. Whose voice? Whose words? She had never been at a place where logic failed and stood as an obstacle to understanding. Janelle would give everything she owned to reveal the mystery of words she discovered coming from her own mouth.

When the music box wound down, questions were born that pleaded for answers. Words were spoken, apologies made, in a fog of profound bewilderment where answers were not understood, native tongues and worlds separating one woman from the other.

For the first time in her life, Janelle's mind failed her. She could not understand the quintessence of notes that inhabited her soul but she knew—finally—Tatyana was not her enemy.

The conflict and fatigue of past weeks were etched on Tatyana's face and slumping shoulders. She saw frailty where before she had only known fear. Janelle needed answers but saw the old woman's need of rest. She called a cab—Janelle couldn't drive under the weight of this moment. While waiting, efforts to explain fell victim to a language she didn't understand, the confusion of the moment, and a tired soul so far from home. Then the cab; then she was gone, with promises to rest, and then talk.

Sleep came in fragments. Forcing herself to remain in bed, confusion plagued Janelle's thoughts. At last rising from the chaos, Janelle knew she couldn't face work, or questions that battled one another in their demands to be answered. Calling in she took the day off. A call to Stanley ensured everything would be taken care of.

Dressing casually, she grabbed a backpack and went out for a vanilla latte. Calling the Phoenix Inn she learned Tatyana had asked not to be disturbed. *Poor dear, the ordeal has been so hard on her.* That settled her plan. A couple of days would give each the needed calm to hear the other's words and give her time to contact Mark in Eugene, he would have someone who spoke Ukrainian. Watching all the thirty-somethings hurry off to work after getting their morning caffeine fix, she realized twenty-four hours before she had been a part of that world. *What is my world now? Where do I belong? Who am I a part of?*

Unmindful of the latte, she sat near a window and pulled out a notepad. She tried forming questions. Thoughts bullied their way past each other, her mind still too confused to make sense of competing voices. Putting the notepad away she turned to watch people come and go. When she was a child, mom or dad would dash into a store for a few items, leaving her alone in the car. She made a game of watching those passing, the people, all different in looks, dress, and manner of walking. Would the next be a man, woman, boy, girl? There were four choices back then, it seemed a safer world. Couldn't leave a child alone in a car today. It had been forty-five years since a little girl had bothered to notice; the woman took the time to notice now.

The day needed to be restorative. Janelle knew just where to go.

Returning home she left a message for Tatyana then packed a bag. Logging onto the internet she booked a room at the White Heron Inn. Dialing her folks on the cell phone as she merged on I-5, their answering machine pickedup, "Hi, just me. With everything that's been happening the past few weeks I decided to take a couple of days off and head for Cannon Beach. I'll be staying at the White Heron. I should be back tomorrow or Sunday. I'll have my cell with me if you need to call. Everything is fine. I mean I think it's fine. We'll talk when I get back. Love ya, bye."

Janelle merged onto OR-217 and then US-26 on her way to the Coast. Packed in the weekend bag, a music box made the journey with her.

~

It was overcast and forty-four degrees when Janelle pulled up in front of the White Heron. Winter was putting forth its last efforts to hang on as spring prepared for its annual incursion. It was the perfect weather to ensure the seashore wouldn't be crowded. Bundled warmly, Janelle stopped long enough to check-in and then headed to the beach.

The whitecap's spray misted over her as frenzied thoughts began to hush. She became lost in the majesty of the ocean at hightide, the waves a reminder of how insignificant individual concerns can be. Something inside stirred as she was enfolded in their timeless movement.

Janelle spent hours meandering from beach to galleries featuring creations the world would never notice. Those moments, hers alone to savor, resplendent in their serenity, were twinkling milliseconds that infused hope and washed confusion away. It was here she came after Blade left.

~

Janelle arrived home late Sunday evening. There had been no calls, no interruptions. The evocative music box's notes were a part of her now, ingrained into the fabric of her being. *Now I'm ready to learn the mystery of the box, tomorrow after work.*

Monday was calm for a Monday. Stanley confirmed her wisdom in hiring him: Everything was under control and taken care of. The meetings and appointments kept Janelle occupied, but in those moments when she wasn't dealing with pressing demands, her mind wandered to Tatyana and what she would hear. Mark still hadn't returned the call she left at the Language Lab on Saturday.

Stopping at the Phoenix Inn & Suites, Janelle glanced at the slip of paper then climbed the stairs. A flood of emotions pressed into her. When she reached the second floor her mouth was dry. Her pulse beat faster with each step. There was no reason to fear, but was she prepared for all she would learn?

Stopping at Tatyana's door, Janelle rechecked the room number, took a breath, then knocked. No answer. She knocked again—no response. Struggling to control unstable emotions she went down to the registration desk. “Hi, I’m looking for Tatyana Sloviovich. I was just up to her room and no one was there. By any chance do you know where she’s at?”

“Waiting for a bus last time I heard. Some friend she needed to see. At least I think that’s what she said. She has an interesting way with English.”

“I’m the friend she wanted to see.”

“If the bus hasn’t come by you should find her on one of the benches.”

Turning, Janelle headed for the door. “Thanks,” she said over her shoulder. The clerk responded but she was already outside, scanning for Tatyana. There was a bench in front of the office; no one was there. Looking across the street, she saw a couple of teenagers intertwining their lips while waiting for the bus, but Tatyana eluded her. “Come on; don’t disappear now, she said in an effort to make Tatyana appear: It failed. There were so many questions. *Where would I be if I were waiting for a bus to my place?* Looking across the parking lot, Janelle spotted a bench she’d missed. Someone was sitting on it, their back to her. “Tatyana, let that be you,” Janelle whispered as she approached the bench.

Sitting on the bench Tatyana awaited the bus.

“I’m so glad I found you. There are so many questions I have and—” Tatyana ignored her. Janelle came around the front of the bench and sat beside her. Tatyana’s head was resting on her chest and Janelle realized how tiring this trip must have been for someone her age. “Please, let me take you to dinner, Portland has some wonderful restaurants; it will make you feel better. I know someone who speaks Ukrainian so we can understand each other.”

Tatyana’s head remained on her chest. Finally—the stillness—Janelle saw the stillness. She placed her hand gently on Tatyana’s shoulder, then leaning over, listened to her heart, finally feeling for a pulse. The silence of death shrouded this stranger who opened a door only to leave before Janelle could enter. She removed her hand from the still form beside her, tears trickling down her cheeks. Janelle had learned the spectacle of death as a child, but this, this was different. As a child there had been no questions, just unbearable loss. Now questions birthed grief because answers had died with this stranger she would never know.

Janelle arose from the bench. Walking to the car, she dialed 911 on her cell phone. "A woman on the bench in front of 37669 SW Boones Ferry Road needs an ambulance." The operator asked what the medical emergency was. Janelle hung up and turned her cell's power off. Pulling onto Boones Ferry Road, she heard the wailing moan of a siren in the distance.

The next days were lost to Janelle as she went over again and again the little that made its way to her memory from that chaotic night. Trying to cobble together fragments of words and unclear emotions left Janelle no closer to understanding than before Tatyana had entered her world. Notes from a simple music box drew her close, but to what? The unfairness of it all pierced her soul. Grief turned to anger, and then anguish, of all she didn't know, would never understand. Janelle puzzled over every remembered word, but Tatyana's pronouncements were lost in the haze of a moment and emotions she scarcely understood. Time did not heal, it wounded.

Work was salvation. The more challenges budget cuts demanded, the more conflicting agendas special interest groups politicked for, the greater effort Janelle was compelled to expend. This was her contribution. The school district needed her and she needed them to make sense of an increasingly meaningless world.

Unlocking the door after another exhausting day, Janelle went through her nightly ritual: mail on the vestibule table, coat in the closet, and purse on its shelf. Retrieve the mail, move it onto the chaise table, and then the wine refrigerator. She was ready to scream. *When did life become a weight to be endured? So what if I'm good at my job. You're supposed to be good at what you do. Each day is so ordered; would life cease if it weren't?*

Janelle filled her glass, drained it and filled it again before putting the bottle back on the shelf in the wine fridge as her nightly buzz kicked in. *Must be careful, wouldn't do for a Henning to become a lush.*

Janelle sat on the edge of the chaise and lifted her music box from the table. She studied its simple form, pondering the mysteries it contained. The case was six inches long, four inches wide and tall. The olivewood box, long since having lost any sheen from a finish applied decades before, had carved pomegranates on its front and sides. A wood-framed beveled glass top was attached with a brass piano hinge, offering a view of its working mechanism. A bedplate of grey metal cradled a brass cylinder whose tiny studded pins struck the tuned teeth of the horizontal brass comb as it rotated, producing notes that seared her soul. On one end of the box was a hole with a brass sleeve inset in the wood where the windup key was inserted to tension the spring motor. Beneath the sleeve inset, on the bottom edge of the box, a horizontal brass lever turned the enigmatic notes on and off. Incomprehensible solace washed over and through her when she turned it on binding her to a place never known, an existence she felt a part of, somewhere. Carefully winding the music box, she lay back on the chaise. Turning it on she opened the top to hear each note sweetly, distinctly, caressing its edges as it rested upon her. Tears formed and slid without shame down her cheeks, dropping off her chin and onto her chest as a part of her she never knew existed responded to notes forged into her soul.

Lying still, absorbing the notes, she glanced at the vestibule table. *Something's not right. What am I seeing? The roses . . . they're crooked.* As she tried to lose herself in the evocative notes, the flowers refused to release their hold on her. Turning off the music she got up from the chaise and placed the box on the table. She took another drink of wine. Going to the vestibule table, Janelle bent over and centered the flowers. *Must be slipping to have missed that. Now I can get back to*—the phone's jangling interrupted her thoughts.

Going to the phone, she saw it was her parents' number. "Hi, how are you?"

"Beginning to miss my beautiful daughter."

"Oh, Dad, first Mom and now you, it hasn't been that long since I was out. Our regular schedule makes it due about next week."

"Well if you want to put it that way."

"That's not what I meant and you know it."

"Sweetheart, Mom shared a few things with me and I get the impression you're going through a rough time right now. You do remember that's what parents are for?"

"Well, Dad, things have been, let's say, interesting, but I didn't want to bring you or Mom into the mix because I don't know what the mix involves. I'm working through some things and when I know enough to be able to define what those things are I promise you and Mom will be a part of the conversation."

"Are we going to see you next week?"

"You can count on it. Tell you what; I'll share everything I can at dinner."

"We'll have it at home, just the three of us."

"Sounds great Dad, I appreciate your call and concern. I'm a big girl but I love that you still care."

"How can I stop?"

"Give Mom my love. Tell her I'll call next week to set a time."

Hanging up she glanced back at the vestibule table; the roses still appeared, ever so slightly, crooked, *can't have that.* Going to the table she got down on both knees in front of it. "I'll show you." She placed the flowers just so then gave the arrangement a final appraisal—they were still askew.

She glanced at the table and something on the floor, peeking out from under the bottom shelf, caught her eye. *What's this?* When she tugged at it, her fingers slipped off the stuck object. Setting the burgundy roses on the floor, she stood up and lifted the table off to the side. As she looked down, an accordion folder stared up at her. She scooted it away from the table with her foot and returned the table to its proper place. Back on her knees she repositioned the flowers, ensuring the table and arrangement was placed according to the pattern in her mind. Satisfied, she got up.

Looking down at the overstuffed folder, she made no effort to pick it up. She knew everything in her townhouse and this didn't belong. Reaching down with one hand, she was surprised by its weight. Taking hold with both hands, she lifted the curiosity.

She walked over to kitchen table and set the tightly packed expansion folder down. Going to her wine she placed it on the kitchen table next to the folder, then pulled out a chair, and sat down.

Turning the button and tie folder over she saw lettering in a language she didn't understand. When she untied the string, the expandable envelope seemed to double in size. She began pulling out papers. After two minutes Janelle decided she needed a box so that none of the documents, now in a stack several inches tall, would fall on the floor. Getting one from the utility closet she resumed placing the papers in it, being careful not to drop anything.

Glancing over the documents, as she removed them from the folder, she noted what appeared to be three different languages. She wasn't ready to decipher anything yet. Order must first be rescued from chaos. Janelle pulled three boxes from the closet then separated the stacks into what she concluded were their respective languages. She was content to be surrendered to the process, her curiosity diverted to create order that could be studied and once studied understood. First define, then organize, then discover.

~

Picking up the phone's receiver, Janelle glanced down at her address book and dialed the University of Oregon. On the third ring her call was answered. "Language Lab."

"This is Dr. Janelle Henning is Dr. Landon there?"

"One moment please." As Janelle waited she ordered her thoughts.

"Janelle, been expecting your call. One of the grad students told me you called on Saturday but didn't leave a message."

Things have been chaotic and there was no way to succinctly parse my words in a message without speaking directly with you."

"Sounds serious, how can I help?"

"Mark, I need a favor, maybe a big one. I have some papers I need translated."

"That's not a problem. Just drop the papers by and I'll get them looked at. What language are we talking about?"

"That's just it, Mark, I don't know for certain, though I have my suspicions."

"That shouldn't prove insurmountable. I am paid to be the expert."

"One thing, Mark, these are personal, maybe incredibly personal. It's too involved to go into. I can't know until I get them translated, but if they are, whatever they contain must be protected at all costs."

"We talking some juicy stuff here, Janelle?"

"I don't know, but I need absolute privacy whatever they contain."

"If it falls outside my expertise I'll find someone discreet to do the translating. What's your guess on the languages?"

"I would conjecture Ukrainian and either Jewish or Yiddish. The third one is in French."

"I can handle the Jewish and Yiddish. My French isn't bad either and Carol Ivar would be the go-to gal for Ukrainian. And, just so you won't worry, she can be the soul of discretion. How soon you need these?"

"Don't even ask. It's one of those moments where life itself, as I've come to know it, may be changed."

"Get them over to me and I'll work on them between classes. Carol owes me so I'm sure she'll be able to get right after them as well. Obviously, the more pages there are the longer it will take but it sounds pretty serious so, of course, I'll help."

"It is, and you're my official hero. I'll bring them over after work tomorrow. Are you still at the same office?"

"Same old overcrowded cubbyhole. Make it after five; I'll be back from class by then. I'll tell security to expect you."

"Thanks Mark. I can't express how much this means."

"See you tomorrow."

~

Over a week later Janelle's outside line rang. "Dr. Henning."

"Hi, gorgeous."

"You have the most interesting salutation, Dr. Landon."

"I also have three separate translations, all finished, and typed. If they are about you, I think your life is about to get interesting."

"When can I pick them up, Mark?"

"Don't have to. I'm heading north as we speak for a weekend conference at Portland State. I can swing off I-5 and bring them to my lady's doorstep. I'll be by in the next twenty minutes."

"Mark."

"Yes."

"Could you leave everything in your car and call? I'll come out to you."

"I understand. See you in a few."

Friday nights normally felt secure like the embrace of her chaise longue. Another week concluded with the weekend to relax and unwind. Janelle didn't know how sheltered she would feel on Monday considering the box waiting on the floor next to her table containing translations of papers which had announced their appearance under the vestibule table. Would they contain a story of beginnings or would the papers only deepen a mystery?

As she sat at the kitchen table the open box of papers waited on the floor beside her. Janelle reached down and removed the top folder. Placing it on the table she took a sip of wine. Though her French was rusty, she decided to follow the source document, referring to Mark's translation only to verify.

Toulon Bureau des Adoptions, 94–96 place Monsenergue, 83000 Toulon Provence-Alpes-Cote d'Azur, France, under authority International Social Services, Paris Branch 1239 Rue de la Choisy, Region Iie-de-France, Paris.

Contracting Agency: Bordeaux Adoption Services. Janelle read and re-read every word. Date stamped 17 February 1957. Shayndel Laila Yochanan, age 3, minor female under SSR Politick Adoption Medical Services Authority. Reason for placement: Politick insurrection. SSR Agency: Dom Rebyonka, Odessa Ukraine SSR.

Date of adoption 29 April 1957.

Adoptive parents:

Janelle glanced away from the page, and got up from the table. Her heart pounding, *do not allow the name of Layton to be on this page. Let it be another child, a horrendous mistake made by a debilitated old woman. Please, if anyone cares, not Layton.* Taking her glass she drank deeply then walked away from the table and paced the room. *What if everything I've known in life has been built on a lie? A lie from those I trusted.* Truth demanded she know even if it separated her from everything she had grown up believing.

She walked back to the table and sat down, placing her glass in front of her. Her chair wasn't adjusted correctly, she slid it back and forth, scooting it here, and then there, finally satisfied it was in the perfect position. Lifting the papers and placing them on end, she tapped their front edge on the table, straightening the tiny stack, then laid them just so in front of her. Nope, still out of perpendicular alignment to the table's edge. She nudged them into exact alignment. Looking down at the papers, she searched for her place; Date of adoption 29 April 1957. Adoptive parents: Garrett and Dana Layton. Janelle winced. There sat the names of her biological parents. *How could this mistake have been made? Why did you come into my world, Tatyana Sloviovich? For this you tracked me down?* But she knew the journey she was on demanded completion no matter where it led. Taking a deep breath and slowly exhaling, she continued reading.

At two A.M., bleary-eyed and exhausted enough to permit sleep, Janelle stumbled to her bedroom. Every page had been read. Her thoughts were spinning, confused. Tomorrow she would go over it all again. People, places, and events had transpired that were epic, heart-wrenching, and life-changing. *So much for the boring life of a divorced educator*, she thought as she lay down.

After tossing for two hours, Janelle arose from the bed and the battle within. Pulling a blanket from the closet she lay down on the chaise longue. The comfortable chair's soft leather caressing her, Janelle, at last, drifted off to sleep.

Arising mid-morning she felt numb and battered. Cobwebs clouded her mind as a headache pounded within. Trudging to the bathroom, she turned the burner on under the teakettle on her way through the kitchen. As she splashed water on her face, last night's discoveries began rushing back. Taking two acetaminophen, she went to the kitchen and spooned latte mix in a cup. *Good start to the day,* Janelle told herself. Pausing, she glanced over the assembled mess that passed for a kitchen. *This is not the way today is going to begin,* she thought. Dumping the faux latte back in its container, she turned off the stove then gathered fresh clothes from her bedroom. After she'd showered, fixed her hair, and applied makeup, the clouds started to lift. Standing back Janelle inspected her handiwork in the mirror. *Not bad for fifty-four.*

Leaving the stacks of papers, she grabbed her coat and purse and ventured into the world. After grabbing Friday's *Portland Tribune* from the green rack outside Starbucks, Janelle ordered her usual breakfast and sat down with her paper, a vanilla latte, and bagel. Life would go on.

CHAPTER

17

February 2008

RamAllāh, West Bank

Akil delighted in his new assignment. The fool politician never understood the slightest notion of subordination and respect; otherwise he never would have assigned a command General of Palestine the job of being a liaison, nothing more than a low-level go-between, for an insignificant outbreak of a disease most children survive as easily as a cold. But fools play into the hands of those Allāh has commissioned to rid their land of infidels.

So humbly, he, Akil Fateen Abdullah Farook, had accepted this task with the mock humility any true Muslim would see through; blinded by his own importance the traitor saw nothing he did not want to see. Akil prayed that when the moment was at hand he would be allowed the honor of seeing the imposter receive his just reward.

Akil found it useful to maintain two apartments since rising to the rank of General: one in RamAllāh, the other in Gaza City. The Gaza apartment was maintained by friends lest the imposter wonder why the Palestine Mujahideen Islamic Jihad would allow a Palestinian Freedom Army General an apartment in their controlled area. Both residences' exteriors were modest in appearance but lavish and secure inside, equipped and staffed so he could not be denied a home whenever the Israelis enacted one of their insufferable border closings.

After spending the night in Gaza City, Akil arose at his customary 5:00 A.M., showered, and dressed. Upon entering the kitchen, he found his aide already at work.

"Good morning, sir," Lieutenant Ansari Amin said, handing the General his morning coffee, brewed double strength, double sugar, no cream. The caffeine jolt helped to dispel an increasingly foggy mind each day brought as age continued its unrelenting advance.

Following the General to the library, Lt. Amin locked the door, went to a sideboard desk arrayed with multiple monitors, and scanned the screens for any activity, though such checks were merely routine. Automatic sensors would have alerted outside sentries within a second if anyone were foolish enough to attempt trespassing the restricted zone that surrounded the General's residence.

Akil Farook surveyed his handsomely appointed room and took a deep swallow of coffee, burning his tongue on the steaming brew. He slammed the cup on the corner of his desk. Rubbing his tongue across his teeth, he regained focus and removed a book from the shelf, titled *Strategy and Tactics in the American Civil War,* which had been mandatory reading while attending the National War College of the infidels as an International Fellow. The Americans foolishly believed that by training those professing a desire to coexist with the Zionists they would build leaders who shared their perverted values and love affair with the Jews.

The Americans, he knew, could not be defeated militarily, possessing as they did advanced weapons systems—about which he could glean only the most basic information and strategic training—that were clearly superior to his country's feeble weapon systems and forces. The Achilles heel he found by observing Americans—so many lowered their guard, thinking him to be a friend—was that they did not possess the will to endure a generational war, while Arabs had been fighting generational wars since the temporary defeat of the Caliphate. American partisan political divide condemned them to bickering and hurling invectives unless victory was assured and rapidly obtained. In the end, they would destroy themselves, when the fools, if they understood what they possessed, could be masters of the world. Allāh makes a way.

Looking at the cover of the worthless treatise on Civil War battle strategies, Akil opened the well-worn volume and extracted a cell phone from its hollow middle. Turning it on, he dialed a coded number, let it ring one time, then turned the phone off and placed it back in the book. He returned the volume to its place on the shelf. "Time to go, Ansari," the General said.

Leaving the house with Lt. Amin, the General informed his driver he was in the mood for fresh fruit. The driver took them to his commander's favorite fruit and vegetable stand then departed as the General and his aide entered the market. Passing through a back curtain, they exited the building and entered a waiting rusted four-door sedan with darkened windows. From there, a ten-minute ride ended at an industrial building where a door was rolled shut behind them.

Exiting the car, they entered the nondescript building through a narrow passageway and passed through several rooms, crossing into an adjacent building. Going down a long corridor, they entered a room at its end. Inside, Palestine Freedom Army General Akil Farook greeted his PMIJ counterpart, Sayeed Amal Wasim, with open arms. "Akil, is good to see you," Sayeed said as the two men embraced, brushing each other's cheeks.

"As it is to see you, my friend, we must deal with matters at hand. Has every unit arrived?" asked the General.

"All is in order. The journey, though long and at times perilous, was successful. Allāh provided protection through every danger. Enough anthrax vaccine has arrived to protect all our people."

"Where was it taken, Sayeed?"

"It has been stored in a safe house close to the government compound. Our old friend, Nuri al-Massalha, will visit your office this afternoon; ensure his name does not appear on any of the registries. He will provide the location of the safe house for your drivers. It is to be stored in RamAllāh this day under the eyes of the imposter where the Zionists delivered the measles vaccine and doctors for our unfortunate outbreak."

"Who will prepare the vaccines?"

"You are to provide Drs. Yerik and Oleg the opportunity to inspect all supplies and equipment tonight. They know what to do. They will need three uninterrupted hours."

"And the anthrax?"

"Nuri and our contact in Syria alone know where it is secured, but I am assured, my friend, it's in Nuri's control."

"My playing nursemaid for an unfortunate measles outbreak brings it rewards," Akil said. "Who would have believed a childhood disease could prove so useful."

Each could feel destiny's soft lips upon theirs as these two battle-hardened warriors parted. The time was at hand.

Later that afternoon

"General," droned Rihana, her head barely nodding, "you may go in." The doors opened. General Farook entered the inner chamber of Palestine's declared leader.

"Akil, is good news you bring?"

The General sat down and waited to speak until the doors were closed. "Yes, Mr. President. All vaccines and equipment have arrived. The Russians are secretive and have requested sufficient time to inspect and set up their equipment without oversight."

"Will this delay the vaccinations?"

"They request two doctors to inspect and calibrate all equipment. The remainder of the Russians will be traveling with Dr. BintZagr's staff and PRCS's doctors to set up the vaccination tents in the West Bank, Gaza, and eastern al-Quds."

"There's no harm in allowing privacy, my friend. The Israelis have finished their inspections and the Russians work will take place in our compound. I have no concern. Do you agree?"

"One concern—the Israelis," General Farook said. "A demand came across my desk late last night. The Zionists insisted on unrestricted access to all immunization tents. I referred them to Dr. Ivanovich since it's the Russians equipment and medicine. This morning I received a call from the Russian Federation Ambassador Demyan's office telling me the occupiers have changed their mind and would communicate any further concerns about the immunization program through his office. The Russians agreed to inspections before and after inoculations each day. They limited sampling during the immunizations so as not interrupt the immunization process. It appears the Jews are concerned with international opinion. Olmert is a practical man. Evidently, interfering in a humanitarian crisis might not look good. I think the Jews will behave themselves, and if they do not, the Russians will handle it."

"Everything seems to be moving toward a positive outcome, Akil."

"We have reason for hope," the General said, a smile on his face. He stood and left for his office.

By evening, the anthrax vaccine was concealed inside the corner of the warehouse where the MMR vaccine had been delivered the day before.

The following morning, after both vaccines had been combined into sterile bags, the emptied infusion bags were incinerated in a furnace deep in Area A.

By the end of the day, thirty immunization tents were set up throughout the West Bank, Gaza and al-Quds.

Secret Israeli recordings of the immunization process showed the vaccination of Palestinians proceeded in an ordered and professional manner. Morning and evening inspections inside the medical tents found nothing unusual. Every lab test confirmed the presence of MMR vaccine.

Office of General Akil Farook
Palestine Government Compound
RamAllāh, West Bank

Lieutenant Ansari Amin's phone rang.

"General Farook's office."

"General Farook please. This is Dr. Al-Haroun."

"One moment doctor."

"General, Dr. Al-Haroun on line one."

"Doctor, all is well?"

"All is well. The vaccinations will end this afternoon. All our people except children under twelve months and those pregnant will have received MMR vaccine. We'll need to vaccinate the children when they reach one year old as well as the pregnant women after they've given birth.

"When will the Russians be ready to leave, doctor?"

"They will be our guests one more night while all tents and equipment are disassembled. The Israelis will need to be contacted."

"I will call the President for permission to contact the Israelis for the transportation of doctors, nurses, and equipment. We could escort them to the Qulandia Checkpoint, but with international press involved, I think the Jews will find helicopters to Ben Gurion more in keeping with the image they like to project."

"I will call when all vaccinations are completed."

"Thank you, doctor."

CHAPTER

18

February 2008

Yechida Meyuchedet Le'Lochama Be'Terror (Ya'Ma'M) Headquarters Office of Colonel Aaron Samech, Henza Military Detachment Commander North Tel Aviv

"Colonel, we've been picking up random chatter about anthrax."

"What about it, Captain?"

"Several reports from the street suggest something is in the works."

"Our population has been vaccinated for anthrax. Why discuss this?"

"This might involve a new strain cooked up in Kazakhstan no one but the Russians have the vaccine for."

"Those rumors are old, Captain Ashtor. No one has ever verified them."

"Colonel, the Russian doctors who just vaccinated the Palestinians were from Biopreparat, which oversees the Stepnogorsk weapons facility in northern Kazakhstan."

"We know. Biopreparat's cover was a pharmaceutical company, while its mission was bioweapons. We must remember Biopreparat produces vaccines at several facilities, so it's best not to jump to conclusions until we see connections."

"Sir, the timeline is troubling. Chatter increased from multiple sources just when the Russians were next door vaccinating the Palestinian Arabs. When we attempted to pin down sources for the chatter, everything dried up. Even old rumors sometimes contain a kernel of truth, Colonel. Something doesn't feel right."

"Everything going through Lod was searched by men I trust with my life. Nothing but MMR vaccine was detected. Dr. Kiva's team took samples every day during the Russians visit to the West Bank, and their lab checked every sample. So what did I miss, Captain?"

"Bear with me, Colonel. Nothing was missed in the original procedure, but after receiving reports of continuing chatter I dispatched Estreicher to the Ministry of Health. She reviewed their records. Daily checks determined the presence of the MMR vaccine, but no one at the Ministry of Health checked for any other vaccines."

"You know Kanatjan Alibekov?"

"He defected to the U.S. several years back. Was head of the Russian bioweapons program. Americans debriefed him and learned the scope of their program in spite of the Russians being a signatory of the Biological Weapons Convention in 1972 banning all bioweapons development."

"Good, Captain. He wrote a book about his life under his Americanized name, Ken Alibek. My point is, everyone knows about Russia's bioweapons facilities, and many experts have visited. It's hard to conduct secretive research with the world watching."

"After Alibekov wrote *Biohazard*, the reading public learned some of what U.S. intelligence agencies knew from debriefing him. What concerns me is no group I've found was granted access to every part of Stepnogorsk."

"Yes, yes Captain, and all this plays into the rumors of anthrax being smuggled into Eretz Yisra'el, but can MMR be combined with anthrax vaccine since without anthrax vaccine any anthrax attack would also kill millions of Arabs?"

"I don't know, but more importantly, Dr. Kiva's staff didn't know."

"Then, Michael, who knows this?"

"The Russians?"

"Let's talk with the Minister of Health."

The next morning

Daniel Kiva picked up his ringing phone.

"Dr. Kiva, this is Colonel Samech. Sgt. Estreicher talked with Dr. Koret about tests conducted on samples from Russian vaccine. The doctor reported her tests confirmed the presence of MMR vaccine. Is this so?"

"Those were the parameters we were given, Colonel."

"Who gave them?"

"Our orders came from the Prime Minister's office, Vice Prime Minister Dobrin to be precise."

"He instructed you not to check for anything but MMR vaccine?"

"What he said, Colonel was to verify the presence of the measles vaccine. Your people searched all incoming vaccines and equipment; therefore, I saw no imperative not to do as instructed."

"You saved samples?"

"Most were consumed in our testing protocols, but sample archival is our customary procedure."

"Good. I'll send someone to pick up the remaining samples. We need to carry out additional tests."

"I'm afraid, as of this moment, that is not possible, Colonel."

"I am Ya'Ma'M. Why is this not possible?"

"That you are, Colonel, but without a release from the Vice Prime Minister, my hands are tied."

"I'll tie more than hands," Aaron Samech mumbled under his breath.

"What was that?"

"Nothing, I will have written authorization with me when I come tomorrow."

"I look forward to our meeting."

CHAPTER

19

The Next Day

Israel Ministry of Health
Office of Dr. Daniel Kiva
2 Ben Tabai Street
Yerushaláyim, Yisra'el

"Colonel Samech and Captain Ashtor to see Dr. Kiva," Michael Ashtor said to the young receptionist sitting behind the desk.

"The doctor has been expecting you. Please, go right in," she said, buzzing the pair into the Health Minister's office.

"Colonel Samech?" Daniel Kiva said, rising from behind his desk and extending his hand.

"This is my aide Captain Ashtor."

All three shook hands. "Please, gentlemen, be seated. Colonel, I trust you understand my request for written authorization was based on instructions received in a directive from the Vice Prime Minister's office. The situation with the Russians was, to say the least, out of the ordinary; therefore detailed instructions covered every phase of the operation. You have the required release?"

Captain Ashtor extracted a manila folder from his briefcase and passed it to the Colonel. After opening the folder, Colonel Samech removed a single sheet and handed it across the desk to Dr. Kiva. "You will find everything in order. I also understand this was the first time Russians came through Yisra'el en route to Judea and

Samaria which is one reason for caution. Understand the job I've been given allows you to sit here and conduct business each day. Many people don't want Yisra'el to survive. If I don't do my job, maybe they get their wish."

"Colonel, I appreciate all you and your officers do each day to keep Yisra'el safe. I spent time in covert ops when in the IDF, so I understand some of what you must deal with, but I assure you my instructions were specific and they applied to everyone. If there are any issues that need resolution, the Vice Prime Minister's office, having issued the order, is the accountable authority."

"It's solved. I'd like to see the vaccine now."

"Of course, come with me." Daniel Kiva escorted the two officers to the bio-tech laboratory. As they entered, a man in a lab coat approached the group. "I'd like you to meet the laboratory director Dr. Da'uud," Dr. Kiva said.

"You're Arabic?"

"I am of Arabic descent, Colonel. I am also an Israeli citizen."

The Colonel nodded. "I just seek to understand."

"Dr. Kiva asked me to pull all extant samples from last week's testing on the MMR vaccine. Unfortunately, I haven't been able to find any."

"Were they logged, Quasim?" Dr. Kiva asked.

"Logged and filed. When I pulled their pouches, they were empty. None of the samples were listed on the daily pull sheets, and a review of staff turned up no one requisitioning samples for evaluation."

"Doctor, how are samples stored, and how many have access to them?" Captain Ashtor asked.

"As we are accustomed to storing contagious pathogenic bacterium and viruses, strict procedures must be followed whenever anything is requisitioned. A senior member of staff must sign off when any Level I biological sample is accessed, and all personnel are required to be in biohazard suits whenever handling any infectious substance. An alarm and flashing light are engaged and doors automatically lock. No one can wander into a lab when such viruses are being worked with. All doctors and research scientists assigned to the Ministry of Health have been cleared for access and are aware of and compliant with all procedures," Dr. Da'uud replied.

"Would MMR vaccine be classified Level I?" asked Captain Ashtor.

"No."

"So it's a good story, but the procedures you've described don't apply to MMR vaccine."

"Not entirely. The samples were considered high value because of their origin. Russian sympathies are not unknown. Anyone with access to the lab could have requisitioned them, but standard operating procedure requires they be signed out and all approved protocols followed when working with samples."

"It seems they weren't. Dr. Kiva, do you have procedures to locate the samples before I order a lockdown and have your staff confined to the premises while we investigate?" Colonel Samech said.

"Colonel, give me until the end of the day. We're serious about following protocols. One of our people could have checked out the samples intending to complete the paperwork and then put it in general storage. There are innumerable places they could still be stored, and several staff are not here at the moment. I'd like the opportunity to contact everyone and conduct our own search before we allow anyone in to try to locate the samples. We store dangerous pathogens which require extreme vigilance, and we are, I assure you, better equipped to search than you."

"This is acceptable, but we need the samples."

"You will have our fullest cooperation, Colonel."

Later that afternoon

Israel Ministry of Health

Bio-Tech Laboratory

Daniel Kiva picked up the receiver on the ringing phone. "Dr. Kiva, this is Quasim Da'uud."

"Quasim, what have you learned?"

"It's not good. Dr. Etalon's research assistant ran tests on the MMR samples into the morning hours the night before last on Dr. Etalon's instructions. She thought the doctor had checked the vaccine out and so did not complete required paperwork. The fault was lack of communication between the two. I have addressed the issue with both of them and will issue a written advisory so this does not take place again."

"Such things happen, but you have taken the appropriate steps to ensure it doesn't occur again. Prepare the remainder of the vaccine for transport to Ya'Ma'M and all will be taken care of."

"There's no vaccine."

"What do you mean?"

"The test consumed the remainder of the vaccine."

"What about the storage pouch?"

"It was incinerated: standard procedure when all materials are used up."

"Okay. You don't happen to want to relay this to Colonel Samech?"

"I don't even want to think about the man."

Hanging up, Daniel Kiva pressed the intercom's button. "Rivkah, would you get Colonel Samech on the phone please?"

Two minutes later Dr. Kiva's phone rang. "I have the Colonel on the line, sir."

"Colonel . . ." The conversation went better than expected. Apparently, the thought of going through some of the most dangerous biological scourges known to man had tempered the single-minded resolve he had expected; in any case, whatever Ya'Ma'M wanted the samples for was lost.

Three days later

Israel Ministry of Health

Bio-Tech Laboratory

"Quasim, I located something that might be of interest," Dr. Etalon said, entering Dr. Da'uud's office and placing a storage pouch on his desk.

"What is it, Ze'ev?"

"Near as I can figure, one of the nozzle tips used during the aerosol vaccinations. Can't imagine how the Russians didn't notice its absence."

"Where did you find this?"

"It was sitting untagged in general storage when I ran across it. Ever since the screw-up on the MMR vaccine, I've spent my spare time looking for any errant samples that might have passed unnoticed. When I came across this I couldn't figure out what it was but decided to ask Gideon Bina since his team collected the samples from the Russians, I figured it was the best shot I was going to get. He said it looked like an aerosolizer nozzle from the Russians equipment, but he hadn't removed it and no one from his team would admit to having borrowed it either. Yet, here it is."

"So you'd go on the record that this belongs to the Russians?"

"Well, not officially, or we'd be obligated to return it. But it's some type of nozzle. When I asked Gideon to size it up he wouldn't commit to anything, but one of his research assistants said it was the spitting image of a tip from an aerosolizer she observed being changed while she was in one of the immunization tents taking samples. I figure if MMR vaccine shows up on the surface we have ourselves a winner."

"You tested it?"

"Not on your life, good buddy. I've been spanked enough for one week. I haven't so much as opened it. Figure with Kiva and Ya'Ma'M so interested in it I'd turn it over to you and keep my job."

"This is good. Maybe now we can redeem ourselves to Dr. Kiva."

"I'll have the incident report on your desk within the hour."

"I'll call Dr. Kiva as soon as it arrives, thanks."

"No problem," Dr. Etalon said, whistling softly as he returned to his office.

One hour and twenty minutes later, Quasim Da'uud was on his way to Dr. Kiva's office with the finished report from Ze'ev Etalon, along with his own report on the matter and the storage pouch containing what could be his redemption.

Two hours after that, three reports—one from Dr. Etalon, one from Dr. Da'uud, and the third from Dr. Kiva—were on their way under armed escort to Ya'Ma'M headquarters, accompanied by the suspected aerosolizer nozzle secured in a bio-hazard pouch.

CHAPTER

20

February 2008

Yechida Meyuchedet Le'Lochama Be'Terror (Ya'Ma'M) Headquarters Office of Colonel Aaron Samech, Henza Military Detachment Commander North Tel Aviv

The phone rang. Its tone alerted Michael that the Colonel was on the line. "Captain Ashtor," he answered in his practiced manner, cultivated to portray the professional respect his commander demanded.

"Ashtor, my office, now." He was on his feet and headed for the door.

Michael passed the Colonel's secretary and knocked once—never twice—on the solid door.

"Enter," boomed a voice from within the closed door. He entered. "Sit." Michael sat.

He waited until the Colonel was ready to divulge the reason he had been summoned. While Colonel Samech finished signing papers, a duty that soured his baseline irritation with life, Michael ran through the current list of reasons he could have been sent for. "Coffee?" The Colonel's voice cut through his thoughts, appearing to ask if the Captain wanted coffee. Hitting the intercom button, the Colonel snorted, "Ozora, bring coffee." It was not a matter of whether Michael wanted coffee or not. He was about to drink a cup.

After Michael had taken his cup of the diluted mud the Colonel considered coffee, he continued to covertly study the clear plastic-sealed pouch on his commander's desk he'd spotted when first sitting down. The Colonel's meticulous habits, everything in place—always—made it an easy task to spot anything new. The Colonel picked up the object. "Do you know what this is, Michael?"

"No, sir, I haven't studied it."

"You mean other than your repeated glances since sitting down." The Colonel handed it to the Captain. "Do not open pouch, but you may inspect it."

Taking the pouch, Michael turned it over.

"Well, Captain?"

"It appears to be some type of nozzle, sir."

"And why would I have interest in a nozzle, Captain?" The Colonel was now in true form, asking questions Michael knew he already had the answers to. It was a favored interrogation tactic he had seen deployed many times.

Michael was aware he was in risky waters. A guess had to be undergirded with logic his boss would accept, or Samech would eviscerate his answer. He knew the Colonel's focus had not left the Russian vaccine; he volunteered, "The Russians?" The less said the better. *Let the old bird connect the dots*, he thought as he lobbed the grenade back in the Colonel's court.

"Good, Michael. We need to test it, someone who understands its importance. An expert who can tell us what we need to know. You know someone? And not the Ministry of Health—they've already proven unacceptable."

Michael was convinced Samech wanted to find anthrax so he could launch into action. If there was nothing on the nozzle, he needed someone respected enough that the Colonel wouldn't question the results. He was accustomed to anticipating what would be demanded of him, knowing that the more prepared he was, the better his chances for survival. Having a network of resources to cover spontaneous demands from his commander was part of the job. Michael was ready.

Pretending to consider the matter, Michael knew he must wait the requisite amount of time for maximum impact but no longer lest he provoke his commander's impatience. "Whatever is, or is not, on the nozzle, Colonel, we need an expert with the training and expertise to identify, with absolute certainty, what we have."

"I knew this before I called you. I'm waiting."

Remain calm, Michael told himself, *just a moment longer*. "The expert I would most trust is Dr. Yochanan at the Golda Meir Bio-Technical Research Laboratory, Hadassah."

"Dr. Yochanan, a possibility, why him?"

"To begin with, he was highly decorated in the 1982 Lebanon War for showing bravery worthy of a son of Yisra'el." *That's a good opening, he thought. Get the old warrior where he lives.* "Many lives were saved as a result of his efforts. Second, Dr. Yochanan is the leading forensic toxicologist in Yisra'el. He is a respected expert sought by many of our European neighbors."

It didn't get better than this, relying on his network for information that might never have occurred to him. "As a respected doctor and scholar, if he doesn't find anthrax, it's not there. Finally, his laboratory on Mount Scopus is state-of-the-art and can determine, down to parts per million, any anthrax that had contact with the nozzle."

"Good logic Michael. Check on the doctor's security clearance."

Michael began arising. "Stay, use my phone, call now," Samech said.

Within ten minutes Michael knew Dr. Yochanan held a Top Secret clearance. Within fifteen minutes he and the Colonel were headed toward Jerusalem and Mount Scopus.

The meeting with the doctor was brief. Dr. Yochanan promised to have the results within twenty-four hours. Michael observed that the Colonel seemed to function as a human being with the doctor. He filed it away for review at a later time. Understanding his commander was essential for promotion, and Michael Ashtor had no plans to remain a Captain. Field grade command was the key to the political ambitions he had his sights on.

0300 hours the next day

Loud jangling tore into dead sleep as Michael Ashtor's roused brain attempted to identify the source of the relentless invasion bombarding its senses. Through the fog of sleep, embedded neurons registered the invader as the phone. Groggily, he patted around on the nightstand, too tired to curse. Unable to stop the unremitting assault, he opened his eyes just enough to locate the blurred outline of his tormentor, but neither eye cooperated enough to focus in the darkened room. Each eye demanded to be left in peace while his brain struggled to direct bodily defenses to silence the noise that still assailed him. The misery continued until his hand, at last, found a familiar object beneath its grasp. As he attempted to lift the handset, it fell to the floor and was forgotten. His arm dropped listlessly on the nightstand. He was back asleep before the voice of Colonel Samech could be heard shouting through the phone's receiver.

The door to his bedroom burst open. The Colonel was yelling, "Captain . . . Captain . . . we go to Mount Scopus." He started to awake in the car while the Colonel careened between the lines on the road as if demons were chasing them. Michael rolled the passenger's window down, letting the brisk morning air wake him. He began to fear for his life while he barreled toward Jerusalem with a madman. He didn't provoke the Colonel with any questions about why they were out in the middle of the night headed toward Mount Scopus lest he divert his attention and send them to an early interment.

The Colonel slammed to a stop, half in a handicapped parking spot, in front of Hadassah Medical Center. Two waiting Israel National Police officers escorted the pair toward the Golda Meir Bio-Technical Research Laboratory. One of their escorts had a brief exchange on a field radio. When they approached the lab a policeman unlocked and opened the door. The four men proceeded into the building. It was at that precise moment it dawned on Michael's still foggy mind: *This is not good.*

They wove through empty corridors until they came to an unmarked steel grey door with its tiny rectangular window radiating meager light as it attempted to chase darkness from the hall.

As they went through the door, Dr. Yochanan looked up from a computer screen he had been studying and walked toward them.

"Thank you. I'll call when we're done," the doctor told their escorts. Exiting the lab they locked the door. Their steps could be heard receding down the hall.

"What is the news that must be told in person?" Colonel Samech asked in his usual abrupt manner.

"Good morning, Colonel . . . Captain. How good of you to come at this hour. I trust the traffic was light."

"Of course it was light; there was no one but us. You called in the middle of the night."

"I'll be leaving for London in a few hours to attend a regional medical conference I cannot get out of. The reason you're here at this hour is because of what my tests revealed."

"Which would be?" demanded the Colonel.

"You will know presently, Colonel. I need to explain my results in a specified order to ensure there are no misunderstandings. The more you demand a simple declarative statement, without accompanying background, the longer it will take me to address the results of the tests."

Captain Michael Ashtor fought the smile that attempted to climb onto his face. He had never witnessed the Colonel being so adroitly handled.

"It's late. You talk, we'll listen. I didn't mean to hurry you. I just need to understand what you found."

"Testing protocols were implemented to determine all specific substances on the nozzle. Since I knew MMR vaccine should have been present, I began by identifying those viruses. MMR vaccine consists of three separate live attenuated viruses: measles, mumps, and rubella. I excised scrapings from the nozzle and immersed them in a modified saline solution. The solution was then divided into equal parts so each test could be carried out three times."

"Is it normal to test three times?"

"No, Colonel, tests are usually repeated one time. I wanted no statistical chance of error in the results, due to the serious nature of this matter. DNA was extracted from the vaccine and amplified using a process called polymerase chain reaction. The resulting DNA fragments were then sequenced. I found, as would be suspected, DNA sequences representing the genomes of the three viruses in the MMR vaccine. I also found a mystery DNA sequence which didn't match the genomes of the MMR viruses."

"You're saying there was MMR vaccine present on the nozzle, doctor?"

"Yes, Captain. It was genetically modified from commercially produced MMR vaccine, but due to the nature of the aerosol vaccination methodologies employed I expected variant anomalies which would be attributed to the deviations required for the aerosolization process, but its markers showed the constituent viruses for measles, mumps, and rubella."

"You said there was something else, a mystery vaccine. Did you determine its makeup?"

"In this case the detective work was simple because I knew what was suspected. I sequenced the mystery component and searched it against the list of sequenced eubacterial genomes for bacillus anthracis. What I discovered was a heretofore unknown DNA vaccine for bacillus anthracis or, as you would know it, anthrax. It has all the markers of anthrax vaccine, but its DNA sequence is different than anything I've ever seen. The specific sequence of this vaccine officially does not exist. I checked with colleagues in America at the Centers for Disease Control and National Institute of Allergy and Infectious Diseases. I also contacted World Health. None had seen anything like I described, but all three requested samples for study. That, of course, is a matter for the Ministry of Health."

"So what you have said is—the measles vaccine was combined with anthrax vaccine, doctor."

"That, Colonel, is the least of what I have said. The anthrax vaccine I found is unlike any other vaccine in existence, and it appears it has been used to vaccinate the Palestinian Arab population of Judea, including Yerushaláyim, Samaria, and Gaza. If the anthrax this vaccine was prepared for is unleashed on Yisra'el, our population would be decimated."

CHAPTER

21

February 2008

Wilsonville, Oregon

The boxes on the kitchen table held voices demanding to be heard, but each spoke only for itself. Janelle knew those voices must be interwoven if any were ever to be heard.

She began with what she knew. When she came into the world in 1954, Janelle Layton was given no middle name. As she grew older, she often wondered why, but after the Christmas of 1963, when her life changed forever, there was no one to ask. There was a party to celebrate the success of dad's business. Clients gathered at the best restaurant in Rockford, Illinois. Food was extravagant, drinks plentiful. On her parents' way home, their car went off the icy, eighteen-below-zero, road. Inside the car, Dana Layton was killed instantly. Her husband, Garrett, held on for three days, giving Janelle just long enough to hope, before dying on Christmas Eve. His blood alcohol level had been twice the legal limit.

The funeral was a frightening, sad affair. In front of her at the church, in two closed caskets, were her mom and dad. Her mother's sister and husband had flown in from Oregon for the funeral. Afterward, they went to Janelle's house with her and asked if she wanted to go home and live with them. At first she was too numb to respond. What could a nine-year-old say? When the Last Will & Testament was read two days later, her parents' wishes were clear. She was to live with her aunt and uncle. There was little she could do. No one else wanted her.

The first few months of life in Oregon were confusing. She'd left her friends behind in Rockford, and her parents in the cold Illinois ground. Then she began to see her mother in her aunt, the mannerisms and beauty remarkable in their similarity. Without understanding why, she found herself referring to Aunt Rebecca as mom. Adoption was discussed. She couldn't understand the concept—what child does?—she knew the love she carried within for a mother now resided in her aunt. The child worried that this somehow denied her love for a mother who was gone and would never return, but she felt what she felt and, after her tenth birthday, she became Janelle Henning. She never regretted her decision. When she thought of parents, Rebecca and Edmond Henning came to her heart.

Now, it seemed, the Laytons' and Hennings' only claim was on her heart. She had not been born in Rockford, Illinois, but in Odessa, Ukraine, SSR. Not the daughter of Garrett and Dana Layton but of Yossel and Liba Yochanan.

Knowing she would need the internet for details she still didn't understand, she walked to her study. Opening the closet door, Janelle pulled out a folding table and clicked each leg in place. She then set the table at a right angle to the computer table, ensuring she'd have the needed space to organize papers waiting in boxes on the kitchen table. Walking back into the kitchen, she carried each box to her office.

Looking at the stacks of paper, she began the sorting process by arranging papers into a rough timeline. She had to guess at some dates, but forged ahead and ended up with four uneven stacks.

One represented, approximately, the first three years of Shayndel's—no—her life. In those pages the history of her birth family found a voice. The second contained adoption papers from France. This was the shortest in length. The third stack contained items dated after her adoption: letters and cards from birth parents and a brother—how illusory that felt, a brother—and correspondence written after she was in the United States.

The fourth were papers from Tatyana, along with anything that didn't fit into the first three stacks. *Don't know I'd submit an organizational plan based on this protocol, but for a rough sort, not too bad,* she thought.

Picking up the first page from the stack, Janelle dove into the collected words. Born Shayndel Laila Yochanan nine kilometers west of Nikolayev, Ukraine, Soviet Socialist Republic, 1954, to Dr. Yossel Yochanan and his wife Liba. *Liba, what a pretty name.*

Yossel, a medical doctor, spent three years trying to survive brutal guards and the inhumane cold of a labor camp in Siberia when Joseph Stalin's paranoid state of mind convinced him doctors—all doctors—were conspiring against him. Yossel appeared to have been released from the Gulag after Stalin's death on March 5, 1953. Janelle read online articles of the rumors that Stalin had been poisoned, and yet, ironically, the doctors who attended him were routinely locked away in labor camps. The doctors called in near the end had never attended Stalin, and arrived too late to do anything but watch him slowly and painfully die.

Janelle picked up a letter. It read: Shayndel, My Dear Daughter, I prayed for your birth. Tevel is G-d's blessing, but my heart cried for a daughter. You were my miracle after pápa's return from three long years of separation. Many did not survive where he was sent, but pápa promised he would come back and he did. They said pápa conspired against the leader of all the Soviet Union, but who are we that a simple doctor could conspire against such a man?

One month after pápa returned home I knew, in the way of a woman, that you were inside. Yossel called me silly, not accepting I was pregnant until the second month of my morning sickness, and even then he said I could not know a daughter was growing inside. But I knew, my daughter, I knew.

Will you ever learn I brought you into this world? How I longed and prayed for you before you took your first breath? Will my words ever find you? Even if no, they must be written. When you gaze in the mirror, will it be my face you see? My heart you feel beating? What will life bring that I cannot shield you from or hold you when tears of pain rip through your soul as they have mine.

Janelle paused. It had never occurred to her she had the right to embrace hurt in her life. When pain surfaced, she had been taught to never succumb, never surrender to the grief that longed to be embraced and dealt with—it was a sign of weakness. Yet words, written so long ago spoke to her heart. She continued reading.

How will you see life with my love not there to guide you? It is well and good for Tevel; he has pápa to guide him into manhood, and I will be there, too. The part of him that belongs to me will know tenderness and caring. That is how it is when a mama's love is held within a son's heart.

But, my precious one, whose arms will you reach out to when only a mama's love can comfort? I need you to know and carry this truth in your heart: I would have given life itself to keep you. The authorities came with horrible, ugly words. That Jews forever caused problems. Never wanted to be a part of our country? Not a part? This is the place of my birth. This is where you and your brother were born. Where pápa and pápa's pápa were born, right here in our village. No one listened. They came from the city to our village with words of anger. They did not come to hear.

When we tried to make *aliyah* to Yisra'el, to leave the ugly words behind and go to the land *HaShem*, G-d, gave Abraham, Isaac, and Jacob—they said no, that our desire to leave proved their words true. We must be taught never to betray Motherland. They took me to Odessa to doctor, but I said my Yossel is doctor, I don't need another doctor. Motherland had their own doctor, and when I returned home, no more children could I bring into life.

I never saw pápa cry before, no matter what was done to him. When I came back from Odessa he wept. He said his tears were for children I would never have.

We hoped and prayed to be left alone. Our village needed a doctor and pápa is a good doctor, but when we rejoiced on your third birthday men with anger in their hearts came back telling us you must leave Motherland. But how can you leave so young, without mama and pápa? They said when you grow up you would bring more Jewish babies into the land and that must not happen. Pápa and I begged to go with you, but angry men would not listen. They said village needs doctor. If they didn't take you others, angrier than them, would come.

I didn't want to live, but orders were not to kill, only to take. Pápa said Tevel needs a mama and he needs me always. Neighbor has gun but I never shoot one, so how could I protect you from angry men? Pápa says even if these men go away others come till they get what they want. Pápa gave me a drink the day you were taken. I did not want this drink but can't say no to pápa. I could not hold you or even say goodbye and then you were gone.

The next days I could not wake fully, everything muddy, unclear. I never said goodbye and is not possible now.

Hands trembling, Janelle put the page down. How was it possible to have been loved so deeply and never have known? To be taken from a home—her home—where she was treasured? How could anyone do this?

The two undergraduate classes she'd taken in modern history did little more than cover the holocaust focusing on the Nazi's conquest for supremacy but that happened to Jews and other perceived enemies of Germany—a world distant from her time and heritage—why pay attention? Janelle typed '*pogrom*' on her keyboard and saw, for the first time, the inhumane organized persecutions, and massacre of Jewish people throughout the ages. She knew of Hitler, of course, but grew ill as she read that Hitler was but one, throughout the centuries, whose hatred had spurred atrocities against Jews, against her people. She was sickened when she read of Jews' expulsion from England in 1290 by Edward I and that in fourteen hundred and ninety-two, as she learned in grade school, while Columbus sailed the ocean blue King Ferdinand and Queen Isabella banished every Jew from Spain who refused to convert to Christianity.

Janelle immersed herself in the translated pages as the years of her life, her childhood in Rockford, Illinois, and then Milwaukie, Oregon, surrendered to faded professions written on yellowed and cracking paper, sent from a tiny village she'd never heard of, words that had to be translated to even be understood.

Postcards and letters testified to trips made to Dom Rebyonka, the state-run orphanage Yossel and Liba learned she had been taken to. The pattern ever the same: In the spring and fall Yossel and Liba would travel to Odessa and ask for word on their daughter, each time to be told there was no information on Shayndel. She had been adopted by a loving American family, but the adoption records were sealed and no one knew where she was. America U.S.A. was such a big country.

There were cryptic notes on every letter and card her mother then brother left, each visit logged by an uncaring bureaucracy. Nothing could be mailed, only delivered in person after threats of reprisal for burdening the system. Janelle learned that Soviet policy required all correspondence be retained. Year by year, her file grew as her parents' visits were documented by letters and postcards.

Janelle found a gap of two years. No visits were recorded or letters added to her file for 1968 or 1969. Remembering an entry from Tatyana's stack, she shuffled through the papers. There a cryptic note stated: Yossel & Liba Yochanan assigned by the NKVD Main Directorate for Corrective Labor Camps for the years 1968 through 1969, released February 1970.

Janelle got up from the papers and walked into the living room, her mind swimming. She looked around her townhouse at the accumulation of fifty plus years of living and wondered, for the first time, what it meant. She ached to see her son, on the East Coast beginning a career of his own. She had never suffered loss of freedom for the sake of a loved one. What would she do if she were to lose her son? What choices would she make if his life were stripped from her as it had been for her mother and father in the Ukraine? How could she answer such questions?

Going back to her papers Janelle sat down, picked up another letter, and started reading.

My Dearest Shayndel, the Lord answered my heart's cry. Pápa and I go back to Dom Rebyonka after too many times of being told not to come anymore. Dom Rebyonka's director retired and we found a kind person who was there when you arrived. She told us the Motherland saves letters but we had to promise not to make, what she called, waves. What is this make waves I asked pápa and he told me the lady will take our letters and tell us if she ever learns where you have been taken but that we must only come once a year. If we don't agree, police could be called, and we might never come back from the labor camp. Pápa agreed and I respect pápa's wishes, but I don't like coming just once a year.

Pápa said the woman's face speaks trust. It's not easy to trust someone when a part of you has been taken, but there is no choice, pápa said, and so we'll come back next year and every year after until I look into your beautiful eyes.

You're now sixteen years old. Every year on your birthday, pápa, Tevel, and I, thank *HaShem,* G–d, for your life. We ask Him to watch over and protect you, my daughter. Your birthday is the special day when HaShem brought you into this world. I clean house, set best dishes on table and cook your favorite, *varenykey,* just the way you like with cheese mixed into the potatoes and sour cream with fried onions to cover them steaming hot from the water. Do you remember how you used to love them fried the next day, the dough browned and hot from the skillet? We eat many things, so many blessings, but varenykey is for one special day.

Shayndel, you're becoming a woman. You know I was married at fifteen. At sixteen Tevel was born. He had colic, and couldn't stop crying, but mama, your gran-mama, was there to show me how to help your brother. Pápa was a new doctor then and so busy helping others, but even he did not know how to help Tevel. Some things only a mama knows. There is so much I want to teach you but thoughts on paper say so little. How is it possible to put what I hold in my heart into words?'

Janelle couldn't go on.

The afternoon wore into the evening. Janelle returned to the chronicle of a mother's love that spanned her life. She came across a letter missed the night before that brought time to a halt.

My Precious Daughter: For many years I have held on to something not mine to keep but I have reasons. When my heart is shattered with no hope for healing I go to a special place and wrapped in a blanket, your gran-mamma made for you, is my treasure. I remove the blanket covering, and ever so gently wind it up. I sit down and listen while each note sings to my soul. Tears come, my daughter, but tears that wash away pain longing to see you brings. This treasure, a music box pápa saved to buy just for you.

When I went into labor we thought you would come in no little time. Tevel had been in hurry to come into world so pápa and I thought you would come just like your brother. I started labor at eight in the morning but though contractions continued to get closer and closer you would not come until you were ready. Eight in morning became noon and still you weren't closer to being born. Noon turned into six and labor continued. At nine-thirty I thought time for you had come but just as I began to push you said no again and waited for your time. At eleven pápa began to worry. As eleven-thirty came you decided the time was right. At five minutes before midnight you made your way squalling into world.

We named you Shayndel because you were our beautiful daughter. Shayndel means beautiful in Yiddish. But we did not give you middle name when you were born. It is custom in family to see how child embraces life and then to give middle name that has meaning.

You were our night baby. Born at night you slept during the day. At night you wanted not sleep but life. Pápa had to work during the day and I tried to keep you quiet, but babies do not know quiet.

So pápa, after one long night when you woke him many times, said to me, "Mama, there can be only one middle name for our Shayndel."

'"What is this name, pápa?" I asked.

He picked you up, holding you above him, looking in your face and said to you, "Shayndel, from this moment your middle name is Laila, for night. You like? Is fine name."

Maybe you didn't like it so much because you spit-up on pápa, but Laila is what pápa says and Laila is your name.

You continued to stay up at night but pápa had to work, a family needs to eat. He said maybe he should go to his pápa and mamma's in next village until you started to sleep at night. I didn't want pápa to leave so he stayed. There was a song on the radio pápa heard when visiting a patient.

Its name was Laila, Laila. The song wasn't new. It had been written before you born but pápa never heard it before. After pápa heard the song he looked for a music box that played Laila, Laila. One day he came home and in his medical bag was a music box for you. That night when he tried to sleep you were awake and making noise as usual. Pápa got the music box and set it on the table by the drawer in our cabinet where we made a nice bed for you to sleep. You continued to fuss but pápa didn't pay attention. He wound the music box and opened its lid, then turned it on. At first you continued to fuss but little by little you quieted down, then your tiny head settled onto the pillow, your eyes closed, and sleep, beautiful sleep, came. Of course you woke up four more times that night but two times I fed you and two times I just rocked you, but each time I rewound the music box and you drifted off to sleep with your song playing.

I learned each word and every night at bedtime, with the music box playing, I sang: *"Laila, Laila birds rest their singing. Laila, Laila dreams call your name. Laila, Laila moonlight is rising. Sleep my child, new-day to-be claimed."*

Each night you heard your song but I couldn't take the music box to Dom Rebyonka after you were taken because I needed it; but this was wrong. It was for you that pápa bought it and so tomorrow when we go to Odessa your music box goes with us. This was the one thing I had, in all of world that was part of you and part of me. I now see you'll always be a part of me and the music box belongs with you.

Janelle could not see the pages. Tears flowed down already tear-stained cheeks. Time, order, restraint, no longer her masters; a lifetime of emotion was released.

Finally, she gathered the papers, placing them in boxes then setting them on the closet shelf. She knew there would be a time to read again of a childhood unremembered. How that childhood changed an adult life she couldn't know. There would be time to learn and time to understand, but for this day her heart had all it could hold.

The next day

MILWAUKIE, OREGON

Janelle pulled to a stop in front of the home she had known since childhood. Dinner was the last thing on her mind as she made her way toward the door. On awaking that morning, her nerves started their assault; as dinnertime approached, her emotions began to bleed. She thought about cancelling, wanting any excuse to beg off, but knew she had to face questions that crowded out everything else.

As she walked into the family room dad was there, always the first to greet her. Coming over he wrapped his arms around her in a loving bear hug.

"It's so good to see you," he said.

Almost imperceptibly, without meaning to, Janelle held back returning his hug. Was that hurt in his eyes? He said nothing. "It's good to see you, too, Dad." Going into the kitchen, Janelle observed her mother hard at work preparing another delicious meal. "Hi, Mom, don't you think it's time Dad started cooking the meals? By my count you're enough ahead to last for the rest of your life."

"That's a great idea, but I am used to good food and if I allowed Dad in the kitchen I'm afraid those days would be over. You remember his tomato snow peas."

"Don't remind me."

"Hey, I'm standing right here you know. Besides, I thought they were great."

"Well, dear, they might have been had you understood what three tablespoons of garlic salt would do to one can of tomatoes mixed with a can of peas."

"Say what you will, but I have noticed, for someone who never cooks, I eat quite well."

"And that will continue, my dear, as long as you take me out to dinner when I need a break."

Conversation turned to golf during dinner. Edmond explained the joy of his new passion: differences between woods and irons and strategies to master his new love he had cobbled together from the Golf Channel and the resident experts on the links he favored. After dishes were cleaned up, everyone went into the family room where they all settled into their favorite chairs they'd laid claim to too many years ago to remember.

"So tell me what has happened to your Russian lady, Janelle?" Rebecca asked.

"Ukrainian, mom, she was Ukrainian."

"Was?"

"She died."

"Just like that?"

"Pretty much, she was sitting on a bench outside the Phoenix Inn & Suites and her heart gave out, or maybe it was a stroke, don't know. I didn't stay around."

"You were there?"

"Yes."

"Janelle, it's obvious you have something inside that is eating away at you. Now might be the time to let it out," Edmond said.

"Edmond, if Janelle doesn't feel like talking then we should respect her wishes."

"Rebecca, my love, we've known for a long time this conversation might come. It appears it's going to happen whether we like it or not. Why not just let it out, Janelle?"

"Okay, just one question. Were Dana and Garrett Layton my biological parents?"

"What kind of question is that? Of course they were your parents," Rebecca said.

"Mom, you and Dad are my parents. You were there through illnesses and when I was scared in the night. I remember Mom and Dad Layton and I love them, but it was your arms I ran to growing up and nothing will ever change that or my love for you. But I need to know if Dana and Garrett are my birth parents."

"Why, Janelle Henning, I have never once told you anything untrue, and I do not like your inference I would do so now."

"Mom, you haven't answered my question. Remember it was from you and Dad I learned to appreciate truth and understand no question was off limits if asked in love. Do I need to get a DNA test to have my question answered?"

"You would need me to participate in that test, and I can guarantee you that will not happen. If, after all these years, you don't trust me I've nothing more to say."

"Your anger and refusal speaks eloquently, mom."

"Rebecca, it's time."

"Edmond, I don't need you to tell me anything about time. It wasn't your sister."

"Mom, I met Tatyana. I tried to avoid her. I was running scared, fearing the worst, but she would not relent. She opened a door in my life I would have never believed could be opened. I need your honesty more than I ever have. After trying to maintain control through whatever life has dished out, I have come to understand I've never had control over anything."

Tears misted the corners of Rebecca's eyes as this quiet, reserved woman began trembling. Edmond got up and brought a box of tissues to her, then sat down by the side of the only woman he had ever loved.

"You don't need DNA. I'll tell you what you want to know." She paused, dabbing the corners of her eyes. "Edmond, would you get me something to drink?"

"Janelle, you care for anything, sweetheart," Edmond asked, getting up.

"No thanks, Dad."

He went to the bar in the corner of the family room, placed four ice cubes in a tumbler and filled the glass with twelve-year-old Scotch. He then retrieved a snifter and half filled it with brandy. Walking back across the room, he handed the Scotch to Rebecca. She took a swallow and coughed as the alcohol burned its way down her throat. He returned to his chair as she cleared her throat and took another drink.

"Janelle, in all these years I have kept the truth from you only one time. I understand this may give you license to begin doubting everything I say, but that would destroy our relationship and I hope you will understand there were reasons I could not speak."

Janelle's emotions raged within. She wanted to jump out of the chair, run from the home she had grown up in. She knew that must not happen. Instead, she focused on her mother's words.

"I don't know what you remember of your mother. I've not spoken of her often because those times I tried were too hard for you and for me. Somehow, as a child, in the midst of anguish and loss, you understood your mother and I were two parts of a whole. You came here addressing me as Aunt Rebecca, yet within weeks I became mom. Did you ever wonder why that happened?"

"I just thought of that the other day. What I have been learning has caused me to think about things I've spent a lifetime avoiding."

"Janelle, your mother and I were twins."

"But you had different birth dates."

"Dana, always in a hurry, was born just before midnight. I stubborn, then as now, waited till after midnight to join my sister in this world.

Janelle's eyes widened. She held onto every word.

"Not identical twins, fraternal. Though there were physical differences, we shared the same spirit in our deepest soul. When you came, in the innocence of your nine-year-old heart, you understood, intrinsically, your mom was a part of me and I of her. It happens, at times, between twins. With the miles and years that separated our lives, I had lost touch with the bond that existed in the cores of Dana's and my souls, each with the other. When you started calling me Mom I remembered . . . and understood . . . and loved you as I know Dana loved you."

"But that doesn't explain why you wouldn't tell me she was not my biological mother. Mom, even if you didn't want to tell me as a child, it's been a long time since childhood. There were so many times, such close moments, you could have told me."

"Could I have? Thank you for knowing what I could have done. It wasn't only Dana who couldn't bear children; I shared the same curse. You don't know what that means. Two sisters and neither can bring a child into this world. Your father is the most precious and understanding man I've ever known, Janelle. He knew I couldn't bear children before we married. Though wanting a family, he married me knowing that. All these years later he has never told me—not even once—in look or word, that I am less a woman because I could not give him a son . . . a daughter. The gift of a loving, understanding husband is not one Dana received." Rebecca took a sip of Scotch, fighting emotions never allowed to surface. Silence claimed the room.

"Mind if I have that drink now, Dad?"

"I'll get it, sweetheart."

"I know where it is," Janelle said, getting up. She went to the bar and poured herself a glass of Pinot Gris and returned to her seat.

Grateful for a moment to rein in unfamiliar emotions, Rebecca continued, "Garrett swore to your mother that children didn't matter, but as the years passed with Dana unable to bear a child, his heart changed. So they looked for someone to bring into their lives to love. It should have been a simple thing before the days of abortion, but they found no child to love, to raise, not one, not anywhere, in this entire country. They tried—how they tried. Dana, the practical one, broadened her search to Canada, then overseas. That's when they learned Jewish children were available for adoption through an agency in France. It was less than ten years after World War II, when the full impact of the Holocaust was reverberating around the world with the revelations from the Nuremburg trials, so your being Jewish ennobled their quest. But, in truth, you were loved because you filled that place in their hearts only a child can fill. Garrett's single provision to Dana, his one immutable condition, was that you never be told you were adopted."

"Why, mom?"

"I never knew. He made Dana swear and vowed he would leave if ever she broke that promise. Your mother ached for a child and would have gone to Hell to have you, so she agreed. She made me promise I would never reveal what I knew. Knowing the pain she endured before you came to her, I would have promised anything." Bringing the glass of Scotch near her lips, she swirled the cubes in the glass for a moment before taking a sip.

Janelle, adrift in a fog of words, didn't speak lest any words silence what she had to hear.

"After Dana was killed, I could not break my word and she could not release my vow. Since my pledge was to my sister, Edmond agreed to support whatever I needed to do. When you first called me mom, I understood Dana's heart. I would have died rather than betray what I had promised, because I couldn't risk being less a part of you, and if I would have admitted you were not Dana's natural child, I feared that would happen sooner or later. As you grew older, the promise remained; what had been done was done. I could not have known of the Russian, but even if I had, I was compelled to act as I have."

"Mom, is any part of life freely chosen? Not the day of our birth or the day of our death unless we abandon all hope. In between, life rushes past and we try to keep up. Into this mix is what I've always known is my bedrock, and that is family. Blade threw me life's biggest curve because I never saw it coming, and with him gone life changed, but his leaving did not destroy family: We endured. Would I be more of a daughter if I were born to you? The law doesn't think so, but what about my heart, what does it say? I can't answer all of the questions right now; it's a bigger issue than I knew existed two months ago. What I can say is that love never ends. I love Mom and Dad Layton. They brought me to this country and I became their daughter. I love both of you more than words can express, and my love is not diminished because of my love for Mom and Dad Layton. I have now learned there are two people whose love brought me into this world. Their names are Yossel and Liba Yochanan, and I've discovered a love I don't understand but know to be real. I used to believe I knew where life was taking me, all part of my master plan, but I am learning how foolish expectations can be. I don't know what life will bring, but with family it will be okay."

Janelle got up and walked over to her mother and sat beside her on the oversized chair. Taking her hands, Janelle kissed them lightly. "Mom, I need your love more than I ever have. There will never be a day you are not a part of me." Tears trickled down their cheeks as mother and daughter held each other.

"I'm so sorry I couldn't tell you, Janelle," Rebecca's trembling voice whispered.

"I know, mom."

Edmond looked on as the hearts of his two loves embraced in mutual need. He had never been more in love with the woman he married or the daughter he had raised. He knew his daughter was living a moment she never expected. The one thing he could not know is where that moment would take her.

CHAPTER

22

Last Week of February 2008

Intercontinental David Hotel
Tel Aviv

Addison sat propped against the pillows on his bed, chomping away, wondering what to do with himself. He'd spent yesterday afternoon in the pool, one of the few places he could go with Hafiz's blessing. Whenever he tried to stray by venturing onto the adjoining beach, Hafiz materialized, promising soon they would explore. His dictates were wearing thin.

Barging into Addison's room, Hafiz announced, "Today we see Tel Aviv."

"When are we going to Jerusalem?"

"I say Tel Aviv and you say Yerushaláyim? Do Americans always want what they don't have?"

"Okay, where in Tel Aviv are we going?" Addison asked between bites of Danish.

"Many places. No time to talk. Time to go, see, do. Much to learn." Hafiz shot from the room, calling over his shoulder, "Get dressed."

Not long after, Addison scanned the changing vista as Hafiz drove. "I'm not seeing ancient buildings Hafiz."

"Not surprising. Many places in Israel have great age, but Tel Aviv is not yet a hundred years old."

"So much for antiquities. Where in Tel Aviv we going?"

"Start with Dizengoff Square."

"Because?"

"Other than it's an iconic town square in the heart of Tel Aviv, it's where *Yisraelis* gather. You keep saying you want to talk with Yisraelis, so today talk with anyone you want." Hafiz returned his focus to defeating traffic.

Addison eyed the side of Hafiz's face suspiciously. "We'll see."

Dizengoff Square, named after the first mayor of Tel Aviv, Meir Dizengoff, was built in 1934, fourteen years before Israel was declared a nation. It was a major gathering center in Tel Aviv. When it was redesigned in 1978 to its current split level configuration, with traffic passing underneath and the square elevated above, fewer Israelis came to its plaza, fountain, and benches. The majority went nine hundred and eighty-four feet past the square to Israel's first mall, the Dizengoff Center, which grew to more than four hundred and twenty stores, food courts, and kiosks. The center, with its 20,000 weekday and 45,000 weekend customers, was a place Hafiz neglected to mention to Addison.

This," Hafiz said triumphantly, "is Dizengoff Square."

Addison's first sight of it came as they drove underneath looking for a parking space. "Here's a surprise. We have underpasses in America."

"Is not the underpass we came to see but what's on top of the underpass. It's where Yisraelis gather. You want to talk with Yisraelis, Dizengoff is where to begin."

Walking up the ramp, Addison saw one person coming down. When he reached the top fewer than a dozen people lingered.

"Well look at that," Hafiz said, wonder creeping in his words. "Must be too early in the day, but this way we don't have to fight to get to Agam's Fountain."

"You forgot to mention the blue plastic benches we won't have to fight the crowds for a seat on."

"You lead the way, Addison, and talk to whoever you want."

"Let's see, how about the guy in the wheelchair over there with the drooping head? Might be a fount of information, if he's not dead. Or how about the child playing by her mother's feet with the ribbon? Could go up with a hearty shalom. I'm sure mom won't mind two strange men starting a conversation with her. Good one, Hafiz, you got me, and I can talk to any Israeli I want."

"Do all Americans give up so easily? Day is pleasant and Ebenezer over there in the wheelchair will be waking from his nap in a little while with more stories from days in *Haganah* than you have time to listen to before reporting to the embassy. Sit, embrace the moment. People will pass and unhurried words will be spoken. You must learn, as I have, when there is a crowd, individuals are not heard. You want to see, to hear, come to places like this, not where everyone is too busy to have time for life."

Addison resigned himself to sit and let time pass. At least it wasn't raining. People meandered alone and in pairs around and through the waning afternoon, sometimes sitting on a bench across the plaza, other times walking the square's perimeter again and again, lost in thought. At last someone sat at the opposite end of Addison's bench. Hafiz motioned for him to speak. In finding his voice, Addison found Hafiz had been right as first one then another opened themselves up to him. Their first words were always the same after he greeted them, "You're from America." Did he have a U.S.A. tattoo showing? Still they didn't leave and seemed as fascinated by America as he was by Israel, these strangers embracing a stranger. They freely talked and left him with pieces of paper with names and numbers scrawled on them; he had no number to give in return. Along with their words, there was joy in their eyes; no, more than joy, contentment. He glanced over at Hafiz, whose silence astonished him—was there contentment within him as well?

Ebenezer woke late and was wheeled away. His stories would wait Hafiz said, and Addison knew where to come to hear them.

The spirit he saw was that which he had seen glimpses of in some returning from Iraq and Afghanistan: the contentment of purpose. This day would end, but maybe his journey had finally begun.

The next day the Eretz Israel Museum was on the agenda. Willing to give Hafiz the beginning of trust, Addison withheld comment. On stepping through the museum's door, he was drawn into a fascinating world of archaeological and historical exhibits. The thought occurred to him Hafiz might be introducing him to Israel in his own way.

"Time is different here than in America, with its rushing and doing. We look back 3,000 years and understand tomorrow will come," Hafiz said.

The following day 'Tell Qasile' excavations opened a door to ancient people, but Addison needed to become a part of Israel's panorama, not just observe it.

The Tel Aviv Arts Museum ignited a passion Addison was unaware he possessed, with its display of priceless art from Israeli as well as other world class artists. Marveling at the sheer genius a master artist's brush strokes could infuse a canvas with, Addison innately understood the honor it was to share the passion and grace each sublime masterpiece bestowed upon its viewer.

He continued to entreat Hafiz to let him take in the nightlife and bars in swinging Tel Aviv. "Hafiz," Addison framed his appeal, "I need to observe Tel Aviv's nightlife. In no other way will I be able to see how Israelis unwind and connect."

"A United States Foreign Service Officer must be careful how he connects. Remember who you represent."

"But you live here. I'm just trying to get to know your country, and yet you exclude a vital part of its life. It doesn't make sense."

"Makes sense to me. Do I go to bars and drink? No. Yet somehow I'm Yisraeli. Want go to bar, get drunk, wait till you're back at the embassy, then go every night."

In spite of more defeats than victories, Addison realized his understanding of Israel was beginning to change. What seemed like random visits to tourist attractions revealed a vibrancy he first experienced at Dizengoff Square.

The Batey Haosef Museum opened his eyes to the Israeli Defense Forces he once thought could never equal the might of the U.S. Armed Forces. Now, man for man, he was not so sure.

The Palmach History Museum chronicled aspects of Israel's founding he'd never heard, despite six years of studies in international affairs in college. *Why was so much of the panorama of this tiny, scrappy nation left out of my studies that claimed to focus on its history?* He had no answer but intended to find one.

Addison began a campaign to see Jerusalem.

Hafiz's answer was a fast-paced schedule as he kept Addison busy in Tel Aviv. Days were filled as Hafiz never deviated from his goal. In spite of his desire to see Jerusalem, Addison realized he was being provided an introduction to Israel he suspected few Americans would ever get.

"Perhaps now," Hafiz told him, "at least one American will not blame Israel for responding to the relentless attacks that threatens our soul."

Addison began to understand peace could never be ushered in by partisan divide as, line upon line, the age-old story continued to be written.

"Tomorrow we say goodbye to Tel Aviv, so make sure in the morning your bags are packed. Our destination is Yerushaláyim."

"Jerusalem? This isn't a joke, right? I ask, beg, and plead to go to Jerusalem and we go everywhere but there and—"

"If you want, there are other places in Tel Aviv we can go."

"Don't even think about it. I've been waiting for this moment."

"That's good; Yerushaláyim is the heart and soul of Yisra'el.

~

As they bounced along the unpaved road, Hafiz glanced at Addison, "Your thirst for ancient sites is to be quenched."

"What thirst?"

"I have volunteered you at the Bethsaida Excavation Project. It's closed for the season but Dr. Kolatch is on site."

"What about Jerusalem?"

"Yerushaláyim is after Bethsaida."

"Who's Dr. Kolatch?" Addison asked, beginning to become interested in spite of himself.

"She works for Israel Antiquities Authority. She agreed to let you assist. Some dirty work maybe, yes, but you get to explore an ancient dig."

As the car came to a dusty stop a quarter of a mile off the unpaved road, a pair of eighteen-foot-tall unadorned stone columns shot up before them at a ninety-degree angle from the raw earth. They stood twelve feet apart, matching sentinels over the ancient rock-strewn site where multiple trenches, dug parallel to one another on the elevated mound, added their silent witness to ancient civilizations that had once lived here. A long blast on the horn brought movement from inside a nondescript, tan, sixty-foot-long trailer that served as the site's office.

A raven-haired middle-aged woman emerged from the trailer. Her skin, neither dark nor swarthy, as would be expected from those having spent their lives digging through ancient civilizations in a quest for knowledge, was pallid, resembling the ashen complexion of a Goth. Her athletic body was firm, each stride evincing purpose and determination.

"Welcome to Bethsaida Excavation Project, Mr. Deverell," Dr. Lilith Kolatch said, extending her hand.

Shaking her hand, Addison was surprised by its coldness.

"You have received permission from the kibbutz for Mr. Deverell's lodging?" asked Hafiz.

"They are most pleased to have his company," Lilith Kolatch responded.

"There something I don't know?" asked Addison.

"Mr. IbnMansur has told me you have an interest in Israel's past, Mr. Deverell—"

"Please, call me Addison."

"So I have made arrangements for you to spend two days with me. You can be my assistant, which is not offered lightly," Dr. Kolatch concluded. "Mr. IbnMansur, do you not have somewhere to go? Mr. Deverell and I will get along admirably."

"Come, get suitcase. I will be back tomorrow evening, then onto Yerushaláyim," Hafiz said.

Returning from the car with his suitcase, Addison was directed to leave it just inside the trailer.

"Did I sense a little friction between you and Hafiz," Addison asked on returning from the trailer.

"Mr. IbnMansur and I have worked together through the years."

"But he works at the U.S. Consulate and you work for the Israel Antiquities Authority. At least that's what Hafiz said."

"Yisra'el is a small country, paths often cross. Mr. IbnMansur is an Israeli citizen but also an Arab. One must never forget that. Tell me Mr. Deverell—"

"You really can call me Addison."

"Mr. Deverell, academicians have not yet learned the practice of supposed familiarity with those we've just met. Though my given name is Lilith, it is not suitable for you to address me by it. I will remain Dr. Kolatch to you, and you, Mr. Deverell to me. Should we ever develop a personal relationship this might change, but considering the worlds that separate us, I do not see any possibility of that occurring."

Addison stood staring at this stranger who was offended by his attempt to be friendly. So far he'd succeeded in alienating everyone in Israel, with the possible exception of the embassy receptionist, and maybe she was just being kind.

"Tell me what you understand of archaeology, Mr. Deverell," Dr. Kolatch said evenly, displaying no sign of anger.

"You find a mound and dig with the hope of finding artifacts. Whatever you find goes to a museum for the rest of us to enjoy."

"Quite succinct Mr. Deverell, it also displays a non-existent understanding of a complex science. Though a two-day stopover is insufficient to acquaint you with what has been a life's work. I grew to love archaeology from earliest childhood because of a mother who cared for the historical record over fairy tales created for political objectives which opened the door for true service to Israel. Through this noble science, mankind is able to separate fact from myth and better understand the social development of man's evolution. If I can instill a modicum of knowledge with which you can view your world, our time together will have been well spent."

"Okay then, what's your science all about?" Addison asked to get the subject off him.

"Archaeology in Yisra'el provides a silent, unassailable witness to the people groups that inhabited Eretz Yisra'el long before one so-called Palestinian laid claim to a single inch of its soil.

Scientifically, antiquity proves Jewish people have a title claim to this land. Were it not for fool politicians, there would be no current debacle that threatens our existence, but what can be expected when men are in charge."

Feeling helpless to stop this moving train of Israeli feminism, Addison pressed on. "So archeologically speaking, the Palestinians didn't pre-date the Hebrews?" He was pleased he remembered Jews used to be called Hebrews.

"Palestinians, where are the ancestors of this people group? They do not exist as a separate genus. Evidence exists for other races in the Middle East: Egyptians, Yehudim—"

"Yehudim?"

"Jewish people, Mr. Deverell, my people. Archaeological evidence of Persians, Assyrians, and Arabs exists, but not one paper of recognized critical scholarship has ever isolated an ethnicity categorized as Palestinian. If you refer to Egyptians, Yehudim, Persians, or Syrians, then progenitor genera groups can be traced, but do not speak to me of Palestinians. I am a scientist and have no time for fairy tales."

"I guess somebody forgot to tell the world that," Addison said, instantly wishing he had not.

"Mr. Deverell, I realize nation-states base their foreign policy on the foundation of partisan political will and perceived national interest. I will not argue that the plight of some, kept in deplorable refugee camps by Arab political will, is heartrending, even though Arab nations have the ability, by virtue of their vast land mass and humanitarian obligation, to ameliorate this tragic human suffering. What I will not countenance is that the solution to this forced subjugation and deprivation in refugee camps has anything to do with my people giving up our heritage. What could not be won in war after war is now demanded in concession in spite of no archaeological evidence that would support such surrender. I would demand we Jews give up our claim to a land that is not, by right, ours if such an archaeological record existed, but it does not. Continuing scientific discoveries prove what my heart tells me, which is our right to remain on this land as long as there are stars in the sky and one Israeli left to defend our land."

No words came as the passion of Lilith Kolatch's words confronted Addison. "Maybe there's more to this . . ." he tried to say, finally giving up. Lilith Kolatch, he suspected, would not have heard his words anyway. "So what is your science all about?" Addison asked, hoping to get back on the topic of the Tell he wanted to explore.

"Strict criteria are utilized to ascertain whether a specific area is worth investigating. Many excavation sites do not, in fact, involve a Tell. Most areas' indigenous residents know the locations of nearby ancient mounds because they are self-evident and knowledge of them has been passed down from previous generations. In fact, the word Tell means a hill or mound. What any specific mound does not reveal is whether it is worth excavating. It comes down to a combination of factors, none of which I have time to elaborate on today."

"Can you tell me one or two of the reasons?"

"Mr. Deverell, they are complex considerations which involve not only archaeologists and anthropologists but political as well as local leaders. Each site is different, and no one explanation, however desirable, accurately explains these site-specific factors. Even when a precise location is given provisional approval, before a shovel is put into the ground, the presence or absence of archaeological artifacts must be confirmed. If I spoke of synthetic apertures or ground-penetrating radar, of archaeometric investigations by neutron activation and X-Ray fluorescence analyses, I would need to devote more time than you or I have available. So I will answer any specific question you have, but for a rudimentary grounding on archaeology I recommend Western Galilee College."

"Maybe I had better stick to international relations and leave archaeology to you."

"Precisely. Let us go to the office and I will show you some wonderful artifacts recently unearthed from the Hellenistic–Roman period. We have several items from the Iron Age I am sure will interest you."

"Now you're talking."

The afternoon flew by. Both mentor and student were absorbed in priceless artifacts museums spend millions of dollars of donors' bequests to acquire.

Putting down a bronze Menorah dated from ca 450 B.C., Dr. Kolatch told Addison, "It's late, and tomorrow I'll show you where the artifacts you have seen today were found. They are from several different levels. It's time to get these where they'll be safe."

"Where is that?"

"Beit Yagal Museum, it's in the Kibbutz Ginosur where we'll spend the night. It's not wise to be out too late in this region. The kibbutz is expecting us."

As Dr. Kolatch locked the perimeter gate and set the alarms, Addison took his suitcase to her jeep. Waiting at the vehicle, he scanned the horizon. It was then the Sea of Galilee came into view. *This land is full of surprises*, he thought. Mentor and student headed for the safety of the kibbutz.

The next day peace flourished between scholar and emerging diplomat. Addison's enthusiasm for archaeology appeared to disarm Lilith Kolatch's baseline disdain of people. She showed him the dig, allowing Addison to carefully remove overburden under her direct supervision.

Hafiz's ever-present intrusion slipped Addison's mind. He enjoyed the moment and Dr. Kolatch's ability to make ancient artifacts speak clearly and boldly.

Too soon Bethsaida was behind him as he sped toward Jerusalem with Hafiz. Something within him stirred. He couldn't pin it down, but the excavation, the antiquity of the artifacts, awakened something he'd never experienced; he felt excitement melding with tension. He glanced over at Hafiz, whose solitary attention, as usual, was focused on passing the latest impediment to his progress. Addison decided to leave well enough alone and look for the Bedouins with their camels he'd read about. He scanned the unfolding countryside.

As rain started falling, tiny rivulets formed on the windshield and meandered across the glass, only to be cleared by the steady arc of wiper blades whose sole charge was to ensure visibility in Hafiz's unrelenting progress toward Israel's capital.

Addison could tell they had entered a city of some size, but increasing rain obscured the high-rises and two, three, and four story buildings.

Hafiz smiled when Addison asked if they were close to Jerusalem. "This is Yerushaláyim. Did you not see the signs posted at the highway exit in three languages?" Hafiz asked, grinning.

"No. What happened to the ancient walls and the Dome of the Rock?" He knew he would not have missed those.

"We find hotel and then we see ancient city of King David."

"How many days will that take?" Addison said, tired of his constant chaperone.

Hafiz looked straight ahead.

Turning his attention to the changing city scenery, Addison strained to observe everything, finally spotting an ancient edifice as Hafiz pulled up to a curb and stopped. "Now this is more like it," Addison said, looking at the rectangular stone structure.

Large, rough, chiseled stone blocks, with no visible mortar lines, rose five stories into the evening air. Each story had three unadorned windows placed evenly along one end of the rectangular stone building, while six unembellished windows graced each floor uniformly along its length except for the top floor, which had an interior wide enough for only one row of rooms, with the remainder occupied by a roof deck covering the front two-thirds of the floor.

A rectangular yellow neon sign with black lettering was attached to the end of the building just under the front edge of the fifth floor deck with its silent invitation: HOTEL. To its left, on top of the fifth story flat roof, stood a bent television antenna, the hotel's acquiescence, along with the sign, to modernity. Plain canvas awnings stood at the ready above each first-floor window, while rollup blinds, visible through the windows, held the promise of shielding the afternoon sun from the remaining rooms.

'This is our hotel," Hafiz said.

"You can stay in such a place?" Addison wondered out loud.

"Everything is not always as it seems."

"This is incredible. I can see the Crusader's tool marks on the stones."

"That would make this building a recent addition to Yerushaláyim." He set Addison's suitcase on the ground. "Antiquity in Yisra'el is different from your country, where history is measured by the decade. In Yisra'el we measure by the thousands of years. So you can see crusader's tool marks on stone?"

"Yes, look here," Addison said, pointing to chisel marks on a stone block.

"Yes, I see, but remember all is not as appears. The stone cutter's mark was made only recently. This building was built in 1936. It's how much of modern Yisra'el was built. With sweat and calloused hands of immigrants returned home from the Diaspora that carved life from our ancient land," Hafiz said softly.

"I didn't think an Arab would feel that way," Addison said.

"I am Yisraeli. I was born in Yisra'el, as were my father and my father's father. The man that built this was Yisraeli, and I respect what Yisraelis have accomplished."

CHAPTER

23

First Week of March 2008

Yerushaláyim

Change pervaded the air. Gentleness infused Hafiz. He and Addison meandered rain-washed streets filled with outdoor cafes and shops. Around them people were sitting, strolling, and talking, some in small circles, others ambling in animated celebration of life.

"The joy, I don't understand. American television shows fighting, bombing."

"I've seen that over a lifetime. American, European news needs conflict. Not people enjoying life, each other. They cover evil when it visits, not the good. Some even stage conflict for never-satisfied cameras. They hire a few Palestinians always in need of money, get a couple of tires and gasoline, and its fire makes a convincing scene when screams are heard in a language few Americans or Europeans understand. That is sometimes the way with reporting outside of Eretz Yisra'el; inside we celebrate living."

"So much to learn."

"You have time."

They wandered through the brisk evening air with no apparent destination. Hafiz seemed content, greeting friends and embracing others' greetings. Addison wondered if those he saw were Jewish or Arabic, surprised he couldn't tell.

"I thought Arabs and Jews dressed differently."

"Some do. Addison, my friends are Yisraelis. It's not a conflict for those who chose to stay in Yisra'el in 1948. Problems came from those who left and have been kept from their homeland by enemies trying to drive Jews from Yisra'el."

"Hafiz, you've shown me Jewish sites I never knew existed. But I need to understand what they represent away from the glare of your watching over my shoulder, controlling the moment. If I can then maybe I'll find the source of the conflict between Arabs and Jews."

"You're not ready."

"Then you know?"

"I do."

"It's the reason I came here."

"I thought you came here to represent America. You'll be much too busy processing papers to change Yisra'el."

"Hafiz."

"Addison, what you want is something you must experience, a rite of passage. You think you're the first? Many come seeking answers. When you see Yisra'el's heart, you'll know. Until then, no words can explain."

Hafiz's cell phone rang. Street noise kept Addison from hearing his end of the conversation, which was over before it began. Hafiz placed the phone back in his pocket and looked at Addison. "A friend calls for help."

"Where are we going?"

"My friend is shy. She doesn't so much trust people she's never met. Besides, it might be late when I'm done. Come, I'll take you back to the hotel. The owner has many stories that will continue the journey you're on. You're ready for a night alone."

"You mean I'm just changing keepers."

"You can learn much from Tody, it's up to you."

~

The sun rose in a cloudless sky heading for sixty-nine degrees. Addison awoke refreshed and alive. After a light breakfast of matzoh applesauce pancakes with cinnamon and honey along with coffee at a nearby sidewalk café, he was ready to explore. Addison saw Hafiz walking toward him looking relaxed, a smile on his face. A dark-haired woman appeared to be walking beside him.

Mid-twenties, he guessed, a head shorter than Hafiz. She possessed lustrous, curly black hair, perfectly formed almond eyes. A clear olive complexion was complimented by full round lips. Walking confidently, her athletic build perfectly proportioned to attract a man or carry a child.

"Morning, Addison. I trust the Yerushaláyim air gave you good night's rest, yes?"

"Never slept better, the hotel is perfect. After you left, Tody, the owner, stayed up with me till after midnight, telling stories of Jerusalem. Did you know his grandfather built the hotel? He quarried Jerusalem stone, brought the stones here in a horse-drawn wagon, and stone by stone built the hotel. They have lived here five generations, five. That's way before 1948, yet in school we were taught most Jews came here in 1948."

"Have you forgotten what you saw at the Palmach?"

"I remember the Palmach, but when Tody showed me pictures of his family, I got it."

"May I introduce my friend?" Hafiz asked.

Addison focused on the stunning, olive-skinned beauty standing to the side and just behind his keeper. He had been with Hafiz too long to have dismissed someone so obviously worth his attention.

"Addison, this is Elizabeth Daniels. Elizabeth this is my American protégé, Addison Deverell."

"I'm pleased to meet you Addison," Elizabeth said.

Staring at Elizabeth Addison remained silent.

"You have no words, my friend?" Hafiz said, a grin plastered across his face. "We sit?"

"Forgive me, of course," Addison said, standing. I've forgotten my manners.

"I've been asked to show you around Yerushaláyim and think you'll find there is much of interest to see."

"I asked Elizabeth to be your guide until you return to Tel Aviv. Deputy Administrator Cantwell ordered that someone is to be with you which I committed to in writing. Elizabeth knows Yerushaláyim and was approved by Lynda Touree. You'll learn much from her."

"Where are you going?"

"I have another assignment that cannot be delayed."

"Wow, practically on my own. Who knew? I appreciate all you have done. Well, most everything."

"I'm in and out of embassy, we'll see each other. I know your introduction to Yisra'el wasn't on tourist brochures, but with time maybe you'll understand."

"Have you told him yet, Hafiz?" the woman said,

"Told me?"

"Time was not right, Elizabeth."

"Addison, you don't want to think every Arab is like Hafiz. Do and you'll get your head handed to you. Hafiz is a Christian, and he doesn't think or feel like the majority of Yisraeli Arabs."

"But what about the Arabs we saw last night?"

"They were believers in *'Īsā*," Hafiz said. "Most Arabs consider me dead. From what I hear, if you love 'Īsā in America, people don't care. Some might think you're weak-minded. Here faith in a Jewish Messiah can be a death sentence for an Arab. Each of us who comes to faith truly believes."

"Addison," Elizabeth said, "I know you've seen some of Yisra'el, but sometimes a little knowledge can be dangerous. Much remains ahead, but by the time we're through you'll have seen the heart of Yerushaláyim."

"I just need to throw one thing out. The fact that you two believe in this 'Īsā, by the way never heard the name before—"

"'Īsā is Arabic, in Greek it's Jesus," Hafiz said.

"Him, yeah, I've heard of Jesus. Those manners I mentioned keep me from what I might otherwise say. A lot of damage has been done by closed-minded bigots calling themselves Christians where I come from."

"Has 'Īsā ever hurt you?" Hafiz asked.

"Look, I'll do my time with Elizabeth, but no preaching. We got along just fine, Hafiz, and I didn't need to know what you believed. If this 'Īsā brings something into your world you think you need, great, but I have gotten along for twenty-five years sticking to things I can see and touch."

"Touch?" Elizabeth said.

"Yeah, touch, as in something tangible."

"Like love?"

"Love? What does love have to do with this?"

"Can you touch or see love? Pour it in a bottle, weigh it on a scale? In any way measure it?"

"And?"

"You said you believe what you can see and touch. Love is found in the human heart, yet it has changed the course of history."

"Just for background, I've never been in love, so I'm not an expert on the subject. Personally, I think it has more to do with pheromones."

"Sometimes things are not what they seem, Addison," Elizabeth said.

"That's the second time I've heard that in the last two days, and no doubt I'll learn something, but let's keep the lessons germane to the issue, which is Jerusalem and the Arab-Jew conflict."

"Nothing is more relevant to this subject than 'Īsā or, as He's known in Hebrew, *Y'shua*."

"Are you done now? Can we go on to something else?"

"Addison, I must go. Sorry to leave in the middle of a disagreement. Don't be hard on Elizabeth; you might discover things in front of you, not noticed," Hafiz said, standing up and extending his hand.

"I'll try to make nice, Hafiz," Addison said, standing and shaking his hand.

Hafiz hurried away. Addison watched him for a few moments then sat back down.

Elizabeth looked across the table and wondered what she had gotten herself into. "Ready to explore?"

CHAPTER

24

Second Week of March 2008

Abu Dis, West Bank

To Khalil it was fate that he had acquired a taste for the finer things in life like relaxing with morning coffee when who comes along seeking friendship but Nasir. University had to be hard with no one from growing-up years to share quiet moments with. Khalil understood it was his duty to be there for friendship with Nasir not to mention to partake in mint tea, kataif, and mouth-watering basboosa. It was noble Nasir always paid, this makes his friend's reward all the better for showing such kindness.

Even Aadil seemed more relaxed. The big oaf at least stopped to say hello. Oh, not to Khalil. Does a person say hello to his coat in the morning? He puts it on and together they face the day. It's something to take with him but not to acknowledge, unless it can't be found. Aadil's greetings were always for Nasir, never Khalil, but then Nasir was the giver of jobs.

University must be a busy place for there to be so many jobs needing to be done, and no one with the time to do them. This was good for him and Khalil. Their families now had food to eat and warm clothes for wearing. Of course, there were thoughts Khalil tried not to allow in, though sometimes they came anyway: What would happen if the jobs stopped? Aadil, the big galoot, would not think of such things; he was too full of each day. It had been a month, two months since their days had been spent seeking and finding work, with coffee and treats only now and then.

A good job would be every day in the same place. Nasir's jobs were for a day, maybe two, and then they must get another. Aadil and Khalil needed a job six days a week. Grandparents, mother, father, sisters, brothers, even lazy cousins must eat, but one day they would find a good job. Maybe Nasir knew of such a job. Maybe he would ask—someday. But, for now, Khalil knew he must not ask; it might anger the giver of jobs.

"Good morning," Nasir said, finding Khalil lost in thought nursing his coffee at the Harr Qahwa Café.

"I was thinking of you, Nasir. It's a beautiful day, yes?"

"Indeed it is, Khalil. I hope your thoughts were pleasant ones. Have you seen Aadil this morning?"

"Is the sound of a train coming in your ears? Aadil comes, everyone hears."

"I have a special job today. It's for an important man. When Aadil comes I will tell you both. Would you care for something to go with your coffee?"

"Nasir, you are a true gentleman. I was just thinking how sweet bread rings and fruit would bring out the flavor of the coffee. Can I order some for you as well?"

"Just coffee."

"Waiter . . . waiter, come quickly, paying customer needs food."

Khalil slathered both sides of his *ka'kat* with a copious quantity of olive oil paste, which seemed to decrease any resistance his throat offered as the bread raced ahead of mouthfuls of fruit.

Nasir kept his cup well away from the rapidly disappearing food, preferring his coffee without stray bits of bread or fruit. As he continued watching this Neanderthal appetite, he heard the other half of the team squalling his way up the street. Boisterous greetings ricocheted off the buildings as Aadil came upon him, nearly knocking him off his chair as his maw of a hand planted itself on his back in greeting.

"Nasir, how good to see you, my friend."

"Morning, Aadil. That you didn't knock me out of my chair is a pleasant start to the day."

"Nasir, you're funny, I wouldn't hurt my friend. Khalil, did you get job for today?"

Keeping a watchful eye on Aadil's hands to dodge any sudden movement toward him, Khalil turned his attention from the remaining crumbs on his plate and took a quick swallow of coffee, washing down his greasy throat. "Nasir has some kind of special job that must wait until you got here."

"I'm here. What's the job, Nasir?"

"Would you care for some breakfast first?"

"Ate at home now is time for work."

"Lieutenant Ansari Amin has some clean-up he wants you to do around the Government Compound in RamAllāh. It should take a week or two."

"That's good, but I don't know this person. How do I find him?"

"The Lieutenant is the chief aide to General Farook."

"I don't know General Farook. Why would a General want Khalil and me?"

"I guess he's heard you're good workers and has jobs he needs done."

"How do we find this important man?"

"Take this," Nasir said, handing Aadil a slip of paper. "Give it to one of the sentries at the main gate of the Government Compound in RamAllāh. The Lieutenant will explain your duties and pay you. Do not lose it or you won't be able to work."

Khalil took the paper from Aadil and looked at it intently. It contained their names and was signed by Lieutenant Ansari Amin. Too full to think, he stuffed the paper in his pocket. Work was work.

Arriving at their destination, they were met at the main gate by two serious-looking sentries, weapons at the ready. "What's your business?" one of them barked.

Retrieving the paper from his pocket, Khalil said, "Aadil Gamal and Khalil Ahmad here for work." He held out the slip of paper.

A guard stepped forward and snatched the paper from him, reading it then handing it to his partner. Spirited bickering ensued between the guards, then a cell phone was pulled from a pocket and a three-way conversation followed over the phone. Both guards nodded their heads at different points to the unseen voice until the first guard wrested control of the phone and hung up. Returning the slip to Khalil, he said, "Both of you stand over there beside the shack. Someone will be down later."

They waited. Ten minutes turned into an hour, and an hour turned into three, with Aadil and Khalil sometimes standing, other times sitting on the ground. Both became hungry, but Khalil didn't want to give the soldiers anything to be mad at. Just when Khalil's bladder was about to burst, a Lieutenant approached the two guards from the inside of the compound, carrying a cloth sack. A brief conversation ended with one of the guards pointing in their direction.

Finally, the Lieutenant walked over to the pair, "You have been waiting too long. Are you hungry?" Khalil nodded vigorously. "Follow me," the Lieutenant said, turning and entering the compound. Inside they were shown a restroom which they used, then were taken to a covered courtyard where a few tables with attached benches were scattered about. Their host picked one and motioned for them to sit. He removed bread, meat, cheese, and fruit from the bag, along with two bottles of tea. "This should satisfy your hunger. Do you have your work authorization?"

Khalil was about to say no then remembered the note, pulling it from his pocket and handing it to the Lieutenant.

"I'll be back. By the way, I wouldn't wander about. You don't want to be taken for PMIJ."

Finishing lunch with the threat of being shot was new for the duo, even in Palestine. After lunch, they made sure at least one part of their bodies touched the bench at all times while they waited. They searched each new face as it wandered past in hopes of finding someone to rescue them from their imprisonment. The hours passed and workers filed from the compound, heading home. They began to imagine spending the night on their picnic bench. Just when hope was making its final retreat, their escort emerged from the unknown faces exiting the compound and rescued them.

"I see you're still here. This is pleasing. It is good to follow directions. You ready to go home?"

Aadil stood. "We were told there was work, but all was sitting and not working."

The Lieutenant pulled an envelope from his pocket and handed it to Aadil. "I think this will cover your time today." Handing Khalil back the note he had taken from him earlier, Lt. Amin escorted them to the front gate. "Be here at 0700 hours in the morning and keep this work authorization with you. We have much to accomplish."

Outside the gate, Khalil snatched the envelope from Aadil and tore it open. There were one hundred Jordanian dinars, more than they could earn in a week. They would be back, they certainly would be back.

The next morning, Aadil and Khalil arrived at the Government Compound's front gate at 6:30 A.M. They watched others arriving for work. "Aadil . . . Aadil, is that Lieutenant Amin? That is the Lieutenant, Aadil. Why didn't he stop?"

"How do I know, Khalil? Maybe he didn't see us."

"Not see you? How do you pass a horse and not see it?"

"It doesn't matter. We're early so we wait."

"You know sometimes, Aadil, you amaze me. You're forever in a rush when I try to enjoy the morning. It's hurry, hurry, hurry, but we see the Lieutenant for work, he goes right by, suddenly you're not in a hurry. What is with you?"

"Khalil, we got paid. Yesterday we waited all day and foolish Lieutenant gave us many times what hard work brings. What he says, we'll do. Who knows, maybe he'll give us more money, but if not, we're already paid for a week. So don't mention money, but be quick to take what he offers."

"Good, Aadil. Where did you learn to think like that?"

"Maybe I listen to you at times."

The morning unfolded like the day before. Aadil and Khalil were content to while away the time. They took turns guessing what type of vehicle would drive up to the gate next: truck, car, or jeep. The fact that neither knew much about cars, trucks, or jeeps didn't lessen their joy in the game.

Lunch arrived in the same cloth sack it had the day before, after one of the guards returned from eating. Khalil named the pair Groucho and Chico. He loved the Marx brothers from old films sometimes shown around Abu Dis. Khalil was convinced Chico, Harpo, Groucho, and Zeppo were Arab. Who else could be so funny? Not that he understood their words, but the brothers' slapstick antics brought gales of laughter, sending him to the floor with glee. Even so, Khalil made sure not to address the guards as Groucho or Chico; they might not understand.

The afternoon faded into evening, and when a light rain began falling, Groucho and Chico let them sit inside the guard shack. It was a new wood and glass shed that had been trucked in to provide shelter when weather conditions required it. Few guards chose to occupy it since the previous shed had been destroyed by a PMIJ mortar shell. Aadil and Khalil were blissfully ignorant of that fact and were delighted to get in from the rain where chairs and heat provided comfort and warmth. Life could not get better.

At the sentries' shift change, Chico came to the shed and handed Khalil an envelope. "You are to return at 7:00 A.M."

"We can go?"

"You can go. Remember, 7:00 A.M. don't be late."

Walking from the compound, Khalil opened the envelope and another one hundred Jordanian dinars stared back at him. "We're going to be rich, Aadil."

"Not to count turkeys before they roost. Tomorrow maybe they ask for money back."

The next few days found the pair sitting more than walking and walking more than working. They were given notes to carry to the strangest of places, each time with specific and ever-changing instructions. 'Don't open . . . keep in hand, don't put in pocket.' Aadil and Khalil played the game, finding themselves all over the Government Compound and in RamAllāh running errands, doing a little clean-up, and carrying notes between various offices and individuals. Each night an envelope with one hundred Jordanian dinars was given them. Hidden eyes observed their every move, each step recorded and reported to Lieutenant Amin. Khalil and Aadil followed all instructions and passed the examination that could have cost their lives had they failed.

The last night of courier duties, Lieutenant Amin called them into his office. "I heard you could be counted on, and over these past two weeks you have proven yourselves worthy of such praise. I've included a little extra in tonight's envelope. It is my way of thanking you. Have either of you ever fired a weapon?"

"You mean like gun or rifle?" Aadil said.

"Precisely."

"We don't touch guns."

"Would you like to?"

"You want us to shoot?"

"Exactly."

"At somebody?

"No—no shooting anyone. You've both done well, and as a favor, well, every young man wants to fire a rifle."

"You mean we don't have to shoot anyone, just fire gun?"

"That's correct."

"Where do we go for gun firing?" Khalil said.

Lt. Amin picked up his phone. "Please ask Sgt. Dabir to requisition two Kalashnikovs from the armory and stop by my office. I have two eager shooters I want taken to the range." Listening, he nodded his head and said, "Thank you," then hung up. "The Sergeant will be by shortly. He'll bring you back when you're done."

Over the next forty-five minutes Aadil and Khalil were introduced to Russian-made rifles. After a crash course on gun safety to ensure Sgt. Dabir wouldn't get shot, he set up targets. "Who's first?"

"Khalil, you go," Aadil said.

Taking the rifle, Khalil lifted it to his shoulder.

"Is your safety off?" the Sergeant instructed.

"It's off."

"Good, remember to look down the sight at the target and squeeze, don't jerk, the trigger." Khalil squeezed and discovered a talent for the AK-47.

Retrieving the target, Sgt. Dabir observed that the center of the bull's-eye was obliterated. "And this was your first time shooting?"

"First time."

"The Lieutenant might want you for his personal guard."

"I don't want to shoot for living, only fun if it's a target. I couldn't shoot a person."

"Just the same, you're a natural. Okay, Aadil, let's see what you've got."

Aadil picked up the rifle. It looked like a toy in his hands.

"Put the butt end of the rifle stock on your shoulder, just like Khalil did."

Aadil snugged the rifle stock against his shoulder.

"Now flip the safety off. Good. Look down the sight, that's right, this right here," Sgt. Dabir said, pointing to the sight. "Look at the target and squeeze, don't jerk, the trigger."

Aadil's finger was stuck between the trigger guard and trigger. He pulled it free and got it stuck again.

"What's the problem?"

"The big oaf's finger won't fit in the rifle."

"My finger keeps getting stuck. Maybe rifle is tiny for Khalil. Got bigger rifle?"

"In all my years instructing I've never seen anyone unable to fire their rifle."

"You have now," Khalil said.

On their way to the Lieutenant's office, Sgt. Dabir called and briefed the Lieutenant. Leaving them in Lt. Amin's waiting room, he said, "Good luck. You ever want to become a sniper, Khalil, I can be found in the compound. You wouldn't have to worry about providing for your family."

"Not without Aadil. Who is to watch out for him if I'm not there?"

Five minutes later they were let into Lt. Amin's office. "Dabir tells me you are a marksman, Khalil."

"Shooting the rifle was fun, but without Aadil I don't want to be sniper."

"Your loyalty is admirable, but I have no intention of splitting you two up."

"Lieutenant."

"Yes, Khalil."

"You mentioned money and extra gift before we went to shoot the rifles."

"That I did, it's right here," he said, pulling an envelope from his center desk drawer and handing it to Aadil.

It was all Khalil could do not to tear it from Aadil. "If you need messages carried we, all the time, are ready."

"I will remember, Khalil. Goodbye. My secretary will escort you out."

On their way out of the compound they wanted to bid farewell to Groucho and Chico, but both had gone for the night.

Once outside the gate, Khalil grabbed the envelope and tore it open. "Aadil, it's five hundred dinars . . . five hundred."

"Lieutenant is nice man but not so good with money. Khalil, you think maybe we don't have land from Israelis because of how things are run?"

"What do you mean?"

"We're able to work. I am strong and you're not bad for little friend, but Lieutenant hires us to do things a child could do. They didn't need grown men. If that's the way our government runs, maybe it's no wonder we still don't have our own land."

"Aadil, Aadil. If the government wants us to take notes from one place to another, why should we say it's a job for children? We have many dinars because of carrying notes."

"I want to work for my money."

"You got your wish, Lieutenant said job is over. How about we rest tomorrow?"

"No rest, it's not Friday. Khalil, our families need food, we must work."

"Aadil, we have more money than we've ever seen."

"Maybe Nasir has job. If not, we go around and see who needs help like before Nasir gave work."

"One of these days, Aadil, you're going to push me too far. Can we at least stop for basboosa?"

Nasir just missed the duo leaving the Government Compound. He knew where they would be with five hundred dinars in their pocket if Khalil had anything to say about it. He headed for the Harr Qahwa Café.

"Khalil, Aadil, may I join you?"

"Nasir, my friend, is good to see you. We were big success with Lieutenant Amin. Just finished working for him and he gave us a big bonus in thanks for a job well done."

"I was told you are good workers."

"But we didn't work," Aadil said. "Take message here, take message there. A little clean-up but most was just messages. Don't know why the Lieutenant was happy with all the money he paid us."

"Aadil, many things are beyond understanding, but if each of us does what we can Palestine benefits. Are you ready for a new job?"

"Yes, always our family needs our work."

"This is the last job I have for you. It's also the most important. But the time is short. We must leave now."

"Now? Now is evening. Now is time to go home to family."

"You can do so if that's your wish, Khalil, but people are waiting to meet you who have come a long way. They have a job that could make it possible for you to never work again and tonight is their last night in Palestine."

"Not work? Ever?"

"That's right."

"Who do we have to kill?"

Nasir led them to a waiting car.

"Aadil," Khalil said in a whisper. "Can you see out the windows?"

"No, Khalil. Why do I have to see out window? I'm not driving."

"Aadil, I can't see out window either. Can't see where we're going."

"Why does it matter? Nasir is in front seat. He's taking us to talk about big job."

"But we can't see where we're going."

"You don't want job, Khalil?"

"Of course I want job where we'd never have to work again."

"Then do what you always say you want to do."

"What do I say I want to do, Aadil?"

"Relax, you always want to relax. We'll soon be there and see about the job."

After several minutes, the car stopped outside a dilapidated building. Nasir opened the rear door after Khalil tried to let himself out but found no door handle. The driver opened the other rear door and Aadil exited the car.

"Follow me and please be careful. The building is abandoned, and there are pieces of debris strewn about. I don't want you to hurt yourself."

"This is place for getting job?"

"Khalil, you complain maybe job won't be given," Aadil said.

Following Nasir, they wound their way through the building then went down a flight of stairs into an unlit basement. They stepped over mangled chair parts and other office furniture that had been twisted into surreal shapes by unseen forces, making their way by flashlight to a metal door. Nasir knocked once; the door opened.

As they entered the room, the flashlight was switched off. Their eyes adjusted enough to survey the area around them.

There were three chairs in the room, but no one moved to sit down. "Nasir, why did we come here? This place is a dump, there's no job here," Khalil said.

"I work with others trying to free Palestine from the occupiers. Our struggle has been going on for generations, but in recent months, after decades of sacrifice, efforts have begun to pay off—"

"That's good, but what do Aadil and I have to do with this struggle? We just try to feed our family."

"You two are known all over the Palestine, Gaza, and al-Quds doing odd jobs. I have watched the Israelis barely pay attention to you in your travels."

"You watched Aadil and me?"

"Yes, as did others more important than me, people with the ability to help you. Would you like to live away from all the fighting? No border closings, searches, or being stopped by Israeli patrols, a place where you and your families can live in peace?"

"We were born here. How do we live in such a place? No one wants us," Aadil said.

"Aadil and me going to live away from bombs and shooting? You know such a place?" Khalil said.

"Yes, in Syria. Would you like to live in Syria if it could be arranged?"

"Syria? Some parts are nice, others not so nice. Where you have in mind?" Khalil asked.

"A peaceful area in northern Syria near the Turkish border outside of Aleppo."

"We're not Syrian. How would we live in Syria?"

"There are friends, important friends that can arrange for not only you but your families to live in Syria for the rest of your lives."

"Aadil, what do you say?"

"We don't even have money for this country and who can know what is needed for Aleppo."

"It may not seem possible, but there's a job that could pay enough to support you and your families for the rest of your lives and even purchase homes for each of you. But it involves risk."

"What risks, Nasir?" asked Khalil.

"You know Elizabeth Daniels, don't you?"

"Elizabeth is good person, sometimes helps with jobs. Has even given us money when there were no job because borders closed, but you said risks."

"You take risks every day going to find work. We all do. Think how many of our people have been wounded or killed by the occupiers—"

"They are sometimes killed too."

"They are owed death. Our land has been stolen and we are subjected to humiliation every day of our lives."

"Not all are bad. Elizabeth is Jewish but has been kind to Aadil and me."

"You take one person out of ten thousand and tell me for that one person we should live like slaves on our own land? This is not about one person; it's about millions who have been denied our birthright to live on our own land."

"Aadil and I just want to make a living. We can't change the world. Each day we get up and work. Angry words are spoken by others, but anger is not ours to own. You have been to university; we never get there except to clean up if given job. But I know this, Elizabeth is good to Aadil and me; she is a human being, not an enemy. If you have job to hate Elizabeth, we're not able to do. Elizabeth is our friend."

"Hatred is not why you are here. Your hearts aren't capable of that. The question I have been given to ask is if you want to move to Syria with enough money to live there the rest of your lives with your family."

"We don't have to hurt friends?"

"No, though some risk is required. But with that risk is a life-changing reward, for you and your families."

"Can we sit down? Chairs have no one to sit in them yet we stand," Khalil said.

Nasir moved two chairs together. "Of course, please have a seat." Taking the third chair, he placed it facing theirs and sat down.

"What is needed to live in Syria?"

"An American arrived in Palestine to work at the embassy in Tel Aviv. He has been watched for some time now. We believe he will be touring Palestine sometime in the next few days. If he does, we want you to escort him to a safe house where he will not be hurt."

"Americans are not liked in Palestine. Why would he come where he could be hurt?"

"Americans are arrogant. They think the world belongs to them. This man's life will be in extreme danger by some of our people who hate the Great Satan, and those I work with don't want this. There's no telling what Israel and United States would do if harm came to an American diplomat in our territory. Once the United States understands the great service we have rendered in protecting one of their embassy staff, they will reward us and we will use that reward to further our just cause. We can then take part of that reward and share it with you and Aadil."

"How much do you think they will give for such help?" Khalil asked.

"The United States is a wealthy nation. They will be indebted for our kind help and the great risks such help requires. Because you and Aadil get around without drawing attention to yourselves, you are the perfect choice to help the American. Enemies of this struggle will pay you no attention. With your portion of the reward you will be welcome in Aleppo to live away from the fighting you have known all your lives. Think of how your family will feel to live at peace."

"Aadil and I will be heroes for such great help."

"Yes, but you must never tell anyone, because enemies would not thank you for helping an American. Every day, for the rest of your lives, you will live in peace and spend your years enjoying the wonder of Allāh's blessings."

"Why did you ask about Elizabeth? What does she have to do with the American?"

"She is escorting the American around al-Quds. He had another escort who was called away. She was seen with the American last night and again this morning. Word has come he desires to see Palestine. It is there we fear for his life. If they go into Arab land you can escort them. Not to do so could put them at risk. Elizabeth Daniels is Jewish, with an American, on Arab land. You understand the danger both face."

"How can we know where to find them?"

"I will be with you. It comes down to a simple matter of trust. Do you trust me?"

"I don't have reason to mistrust you, but everything you said is unknown to Aadil and me. We want to help but must know harm will not come to Elizabeth."

"Nasir, why did you choose Khalil and me for this? Many others want to leave fighting and live in peace," Aadil asked.

"Allāh has given you life for this day. You both are friends to Elizabeth Daniels. She now is with the American, but enemies of peace would kill this American just when Israel, under Prime Minister Olmert, is ready to return our land we have fought for. Palestine's enemies could set back the cause of peace for the next fifty years. It must not happen. Are you ready to fulfill the destiny you were born for?"

"We are ready."

"Allāh be praised."

CHAPTER

25

The Next Day

Jerusalem

As the sun dawned on another Jerusalem day, the brisk six A.M. air lingered near forty-five degrees. Scattered clouds held the promise of rain. Expectant café and shop owners were sweeping sidewalks throughout the old and new city in preparation for another workday where the demands of commerce prevailed in the city whose soul resided in the eternal.

Addison, not accustomed to rising early, stumbled into the Palatin lobby, where an ebullient Elizabeth Daniels met him, ready to take on the day. "Where do you want to start?" she asked.

"Coffee, I need caffeine."

"First, passport and visa, you must have them to travel."

Addison's face displayed a blank expression while his brain scrambled to make sense of the request. Elizabeth's words finally found their way to the correct hemisphere of his brain and he realized what was being asked. Retrieving papers from his pocket, he handed them to Elizabeth.

Looking them over, Elizabeth said, "Good, your diplomatic passport and visa are in order. Make sure to keep them with you. Yisraeli authorities can ask for them any time, and it would not be so good for seeing Yerushaláyim if you don't have them." Handing the papers back, she turned then took off. Her disappearing form finally registered in Addison's clouded brain as she charged through the front door. Failing to grasp, in his sleep-induced stupor, that he could crawl back to his room and surrender to his inviting still-warm bed, he tore after her.

He found himself at a near sprint as Elizabeth turned from Agripas Street onto Ha-melehk George Street.

Adrenaline coursed through Addison, awakening his mind for the challenge. Elizabeth forged ahead with seeming transcendent energy while the New City rushed past them. Addison saw neighborhoods come into view then disappear. He continued in dogged pursuit of his guide. After more than a mile, the Old City Walls arose to his left.

Elizabeth increased her pace.

Finally, at a near run, he caught up with her, breathing in deep gulps, "Does . . . the word . . . coffee . . . resemble . . . marathon?"

"No."

"Then can . . . we stop . . . for that coffee . . . I mentioned?" He paused to catch his breath, gasping deep gulps of air while trying not to sound winded. "Having passed a dozen coffee shops, I take it you're particular about coffee."

"I go too fast?"

"I can keep up, but what I can't do is learn anything while racing past everything."

"I have one café I want, a little ways. We see more of Yerushaláyim, yes?"

Forty-five minutes later on Emek Refaim street, Addison saw a crimson red canvas awning, about twenty feet long eight feet above the sidewalk. Its canvas was stretched taut over a rectangular metal frame secured to the building at its base then angling upwards at a forty-five degree angle where it joined the building. A black cord ran its length horizontally twelve inches above its bottom edge. Below the cord, stitched in white letters on the red canvas, the words Café Hafuch adorned its front. Inside the storefront glass walls, past an observant guard, nondescript round maple tables were scattered with four hard maple chairs around each table. Behind a polished tan laminate counter stood the ubiquitous coffee machines Addison had seen at more than a dozen coffee shops Elizabeth had passed in her quest to patronize this specific coffee shop.

When he opened the café door, fingers of aroma curled into his expectant nostrils as the need for caffeine drove him forward. Addison followed Elizabeth to the counter where a rapid-fire Hebrew exchange between Elizabeth and the barista ensued. Elizabeth removed money from her wallet and passed it across the counter, took her receipt, and headed for a table. Following her, Addison pulled out a chair across from Elizabeth and sat down.

"I like to kick start my day with a Mocha Latte," Addison informed his benefactress, wondering what had been ordered but not about to ask.

"Israeli coffee is stronger and sweeter than dishwater Americans call coffee. We get beans from Italy. Italians understand how coffee is meant to taste."

"Americans love coffee. In fact, the biggest coffee shop chain in the world started near my neck of the woods in the state of Washington. You may have heard of them, Starbucks."

"Americans drink, give or take, sixteen gallons of coffee a year. Israelis drink thirty gallons. Starbucks opened coffee shops in Eretz Yisra'el; Starbucks closed coffee shops in Eretz Yisra'el. Israelis have their own taste for coffee."

Along with their coffee, two platters of a triangular pastry with a flaky, golden brown crust was served, four on each plate. After bowing her head momentarily, Elizabeth took a drink of her coffee then proceeded to lift and reduce one of the pastries by one-third in a single bite.

Delicacy, Addison concluded, did not seem a trait Elizabeth Daniels strove for. "What are those?" Addison asked, pointing to the pastries, before Elizabeth could fill her mouth again.

"*Burekas.*"

"That's helpful."

"It's sephardic pastry made from thin layers of dough stuffed with feta cheese and spinach."

"You remember this is breakfast?"

"It has eggs. You'll enjoy."

Bacon and eggs with toast being Addison's foundational understanding of breakfast, his taste buds discovered another culinary joy in this interesting land after a first tentative bite. He finished off his plate and headed to the counter to order another. On returning to the table with his treasure, he sat down, chomped off half a *bureka*, and took a gulp of coffee. "I'm still not getting it. What's so special about this coffee?"

Light rain started falling outside. Elizabeth began, "All *hafuch*—"

"Hafuch, isn't that the name of this place?"

"It's also the word for espresso and frothed milk from cappuccinos to lattes."

"Okay."

"Coffee is good everywhere in Israel. That's not why we came here. Glance around, what do you see?" Elizabeth asked.

"Small coffee shop, nondescript maple tables, chairs, and standard coffee machines. Nice stone flooring though."

"Last year, a woman named Rosana Eshkol was to be wed. She met future husband when only nine. Over the years they fell in love, both kept pure for each other—"

"That's a waste."

"They were teased by friends. Yisra'el much like America, but both knew what was important and they waited. On warm spring evening night before wedding, Dr. Rafele Eshkol, chief Emergency Medicine, *Magen David Adom*, walked short distance from home with her daughter Rosana; was here they came. Maybe they sat at table that stood where we sit, maybe another. With promise of life in hearts they came for Hafuch and sharing; time to reflect, look forward. Momma wanted special moment alone with daughter away from family and friends who had come from America and Russia for this blessed occasion. They spoke matters of the heart, newness of life to come. What one shares with daughter on eve of wedding."

Addison shifted in his seat wondering where this was headed.

"Fourteen year old boy from Gaza, just beginning life, burst through door. Inside his jacket were nine pounds of explosives. When guard ran toward this son of Ishmael, he drew weapon and fired, point blank range, killing the teenager. Boy's finger relaxed on button he held depressed in his hand. Horrific explosion ripped through café and every living soul in it. The blast was felt more than mile away." Sadness overcame Elizabeth's eyes.

"This coffee shop was bombed just last year?"

Elizabeth nodded. "Seven people inside café died instantly. One week later, one of two people taking walk outside of café died. Three days later, after telling authorities the little she remembered, the other expired."

"That's the reason you ran this marathon to bring me here?"

"Is question? I don't understand."

"I want to see Jerusalem, not be killed by its lunatic fringe. Why bring me here?"

"To know Yerushaláyim's heart you have to experience her people. Is not places you need to see Addison, is Yerushaláyim's spirit. Once you see her soul then you'll understand."

"Let me get this straight. When I understand the natives, and how they annihilate one another, then, and only then, will I understand what makes Israel tick. How does sitting in a café a year after a bombing teach me anything?"

"To understand truth you need to see its layers. Truth is never found on the surface. Dr. Eshkol pioneered procedures for emergency treatment of bombing victims. All over Yisra'el she trained doctors and nurses how to respond. Hundreds of lives, both Jewish and Arab, were saved because of her efforts. She carried a pager and was there to lead rescue efforts when a bombing occurred anywhere near Yerushaláyim. When she didn't respond, knowing where she lived, people feared the worst. Her cell phone was found, crushed from the sheer force of the blast, on the sixth floor roof of a nearby construction site."

Addison remained silent.

"Rafele Eshkol was cherished; her life affected so many. She was buried in the soil of land she loved, encased in a *Tachrichim*, pure linen shroud, and lowered by somber men in black rekel trench coats and black hats: the Ultra-Orthodox who come to each bombing and carefully, reverently, remove the remains of Jewish men, women, and children whom hate, in the mask of shaheeds, suicide bombers, have destroyed. They had seen so much death but this was different—this was a cherished friend. Tears fell without shame from eyes that had ceased crying for all the pain they had beheld.

"Beside her lay Rosana. As Rosana was lowered into her grave the man she was to join in marriage that day slipped between black-coated figures and released a single white rose with two gold wedding bands tied to its stem with a satin ribbon from a wedding gown that would never be worn. He stood, too numb to cry, watching as it rested upon the descending tachrichim containing his life's love. It was her special flower: in Hebrew Rosana means graceful rose."

"How do you . . . ?"

"Rosana was my friend."

"I'm sorry for your friend's sake. I can't begin to understand that type of loss."

"Many papers carried this story, even from your country. Most times they do not. When we are attacked by other nations, we have prevailed. HaShem provides. Against overwhelming odds we have been victorious. But touching this . . . this evil, how does any country overcome? When a military checkpoint or a bus is targeted by shaheeds, I understand. I hate violence but comprehend how evil attempts to disrupt a country to defeat a perceived enemy. But when coffee café is targeted there's no disruption of country. Coffee café is not necessary. It's a target to crush the hearts of people. To kill and destroy for sake of killing."

"You talk about different targets. Are you saying there are different kinds of suicide bombings?"

"Hatred has many expressions."

CHAPTER

26

March 2008

Yerushaláyim

In the world of antique shops, Hamsa Gallery offered few treasures serious collectors would find compelling, though the gallery attracted a wide diversity of shoppers. Observant locals might have detected frequent visits from world travelers, but since there were too many shops to pay attention to Hamsa continued to serve a diverse clientele in unnoticed anonymity.

Hafiz entered the store without greeting its proprietor. He glanced from item to item while making his way to the back of the establishment. With a belying nonchalance, he scanned the back, then the entrance, and slipped behind a curtain. Proceeding past a second curtain to a locked steel door encased in concrete and structural steel that was covered by wood, he entered a five-digit code on the keypad concealed in the doorframe. While silent tumblers engaged, the door swung part way open, and he entered a vestibule. Hafiz descended three flights of stairs as the door closed and locked behind him. At the bottom of the stairs he was met by another door, and placed his right index finger into a hole concealed in the middle of a carving on the right side of the doorjamb. A biometric scanner read his fingerprint while a retina analyzer cross-checked his identity from a database located in the underground complex he sought entrance to. Verification complete, the computer notified guards behind the hardened carbon-steel door of his request for entrance. A confirmation keystroke, within the required ten seconds, initiated a series of clicks as bolts disengaged from the massive steel doorjamb. Hafiz remained stationary on a mat. It vibrated after verifying his weight, releasing the door to complete its opening cycle. He then pushed on the fifteen hundred pound hydraulically assisted door; it opened then automatically shut behind him after he passed through the entrance.

Two armed guards were stationed behind a heat-treated counter enclosed in thick ballistic glass and steel. Multiple monitors showed the shop thirty feet above them as well as every square foot in this underground lair. Passing them, Hafiz proceeded deep into the confines of the complex to the office of his area commander.

"Shalom," Ira Ramot said.

"*Shalom aleichem*, peace be upon you," Hafiz responded. Flopping down on a comfortable chair, he waited to see who else would show up. The specialists assembled would signal the basic scope of the operation.

Over the next few hours, scores of unit team leaders and members filtered into the cavernous underground complex from different Jerusalem shops each masking their true business, with each arrival adding to the mystery about their upcoming operation. Government buildings were routinely spied on, so Israel had long employed clandestine ways to assemble operational teams. The side benefit was each shop turned a profit and anyone watching a shop could be surveilled.

Everyone he knew in Shabak and many he'd never seen continued to arrive, filling several rooms. Hafiz formulated and discarded multiple operational objectives as, tired of sitting, he got up to wander through the complex.

At last word went out to assemble in the main conference room. On entering the room, which seated five hundred, Hafiz settled in the last row near the middle of the room—all the better to observe everyone. Whatever this was, it was big.

After fifteen minutes, every seat was filled, with folding chairs having been added to handle the overflow. Intense rambling conversation dominated the elite force. Guesses were rampant about the unprecedented meeting.

Commander Ramot entered the room from a front side door and stepped onto the dais located in the front of the room. Approaching the lectern, he waited for silence. Talking stopped. "Yisra'el is facing its greatest challenge. As you look around, you may notice many unfamiliar faces. Were there time I would introduce some of the greatest from *Sherut ha-Bitachon ha-Klali* who have preceded those of us now serving, but time is not a friend so I thank, from the bottom of my heart, those who have come out of retirement in response to our country's call. Everyone here will be deployed on the single greatest mission Yisra'el has faced since the founding of our nation."

Just then the front side door opened. General Oz's executive officer stepped through the doorway and held it open as he bellowed, "Attention!"

Everyone jumped to their feet. IDF's Deputy Liaison to Shabak, Brigadier General Sagiv Oz, entered the room. Going to a seat on the dais behind Commander Ramot, he said, "Be seated. Please continue, Commander."

"General Oz's presence indicates the seriousness of this evening's gathering. After the General finishes speaking, unit commanders will meet for a final briefing, then all unit officers will meet with their unit commanders." Turning toward the General, he said, "General Oz."

The General stood; everyone jumped to attention again. Stepping to the lectern, he adjusted the microphone. At five foot six, he appeared unassuming, but raw sinew, nerve, and lightening responses had sent seven enemy souls to the next life who had dismissed him as an easy kill. No one who knew him doubted his right to lead.

"Be seated." He waited for everyone to sit. "Operatives have picked up chatter that a strain of anthrax the Russians cooked up in Northern Kazakhstan is in close proximity to Eretz Yisra'el, perhaps inside our boundaries. All of you are aware of the measles outbreak among the Palestinians. Global reserves of vaccine were insufficient. World opinion and humanitarian concerns compelled our allowing international aid, which came in the form of a new aerosol vaccine and vaccination technology the Russians were eager to try on the Palestinians. With the Russians barely gone from Lod, information surfaced indicating that in addition to measles vaccine, anthrax vaccine was given to our Palestinian neighbors. Security for the vaccination program was rigorous but, evidently, not rigorous enough. After the vaccinations were complete, an unknown variant of anthrax vaccine was detected on a piece of equipment our Russian friends left unattended."

The impact of his statement reverberated throughout the room.

Oz waited for quiet then resumed. "Markers for this strain tested unlike anything ever seen. The vaccine was identified at Golda Meir Bio-Technical Research Laboratory with final verification from Israel Institute for Biological Research in Ness Ziona." The General's face reflected the gravity of every word.

"The Arabs have never possessed a weapon they haven't deployed. With Ahmadinejad's ratcheting of tensions under the thumb of Iran's Grand Ayatollah, we remain focused on Iranian ambition, along with their puppet Syria. Iranian nuclear ambition is an ongoing concern. Our most recent intel is while the world is watching that hen house, the foxes have plans to come in under the radar and attempt their goal of resurrecting the Caliphate over Yisra'el through their puppet Syria and its funding of the PMIJ which we know has its roots in Iran. The current situation looks to have all the marks of such an operation. Somebody paid off the Russians for their recent humanitarian efforts in Judea, Samaria, and Gaza and it wasn't our PA neighbors. Iranian petrol rials have been used against Yisra'el before and will be again." Pausing, he took a bottle from the lectern shelf opened it and took a deep drink. He sat it back on its shelf.

"Within the last eight hours, satellite imaging has recorded military activity determined to be the early stages of joint military exercises between Syria and Jordan, with a few Iranian Quds Force troops thrown in to direct their vassals. There's also been concomitant activity from Egypt near the Sinai, possibly intended to divert attention. Satellites are tracking activity along with our drone fleet. Many of you are involved, day to day, with our Palestinian neighbors and understand our continued focus on their every move. We obtained confirmation that Palestinians, under what is now believed to have been a planned measles epidemic, have been vaccinated with an anthrax vaccine no nation has declared under existing biological treaties. On the heels of this vaccination program, intelligence reports an unknown quantity of anthrax from Kazakhstan is headed for Yisra'el's heart. If its lethality is as rumored, this strain could inflict considerable damage, including overwhelming Magen David Adom and disrupting all of Eretz Yisra'el. This we know: All Palestinians—and I mean all 4,045,839 of our Arab friends in Judea, Samaria, East Yerushaláyim, and Gaza—have been vaccinated for an anthrax strain that has not been officially identified as existing. The only exceptions were babies under one year of age and pregnant women. In Yerushaláyim, we have 593,274 Jewish men, women, and children. Not one of these has been vaccinated for this variant of anthrax. Wait, let me correct that, we have a dozen undercover agents who were vaccinated."

General Oz turned and looked from his executive officer, Major Weiss, to those assembled, scanning the faces before him.

"Intelligence indicates this anthrax will be inhalational but deployment methods haven't been determined. IAF assures me it won't be by plane. Your sole mission—find the anthrax. If you turn up unconnected information, route it through unit commanders, but remain on task. Our eternal capital is once again the prize death alone will take from the hearts of our enemies. If we fail Eretz Yisra'el could cease to exist, then what land would there be in the world for our people?"

Minds and hearts went to death camps. Each had been raised in the shadow of Auschwitz-Birkenau, Belzec, and Treblinka. Each person's national and individual identity had been forged by lives that were bound to these camps where family and friends were slaughtered for the crime of being Jewish. The room became still as warriors wrestled with their impossible mission.

Oz waited for the right moment . . . "I will take questions."

"General, has the terror threat status level been elevated?"

"No. If *mehablim,* terrorists, suspect our search for anthrax, it could force their hand. The longer everything appears normal, the better our odds for mission objective."

"What about evacuation, sir?"

"No movement from any government branch other than planned, scheduled business. The population won't be told. With eyes in every part of Yisra'el, any exodus would alert the mehablim."

"Then who has been briefed, sir?"

"The highest levels of government."

"What about military command?"

"Senior ranking commanders are in direct talks with the Prime Minister and President of the Supreme Court. Look around you; assume that only those in this room possess this information. If word is received anyone has breached the information blackout, they will regret it. Does everyone understand?"

"Yes sir," came a machine gun of replies.

"General, you mentioned intel. Can you tell us how much traffic we have picked up?"

"Some of our Arab agents have been deep undercover for more than a decade and have only picked up whispers. Special Ops concludes this is more tightly controlled than any operation they've encountered, which means control from outside Yisra'el, but whispers always surface. A Russian operative verified the source of the anthrax and vaccine. Someone in the Kremlin apparently wanted the information locked up, and our operative was eliminated—dead from plutonium poisoning in England. The Brits are still on this, so for now, we wait and see. When the time is right we'll act, but for today we have other business."

Removing the water bottle, the General took a drink then set it back down on the shelf inside the lectern and continued. "Whoever controls this has limited operational command to a few people. *Mossad* uncovered information that an imam in Syria is rolled up in this, but funding looks to be from Iran. However, links to anyone specific have yet to be verified. Deep undercover operatives are out in force and committed to results. Next question."

"You mentioned equipment the Russians left behind. Sir, the Russians aren't sloppy. Nothing is just left behind. What's your assessment?"

"You're right, the Russians are too careful to be that careless. The piece of equipment found was a nozzle from an aerosolizer. We started with the premise it was planted. After it was tested and turned up positive for anthrax vaccine, we had undercover officers who were vaccinated with Palestinian Arabs in for blood tests. These confirmed the nozzle was legitimate. We had a chat with some Ministry of Health doctors. One finally admitted to 'borrowing' a spare nozzle when inspecting vaccination tents. At the end of the conversation, she understood an international incident could have been caused if the Russians hadn't wanted us to have that nozzle. Then again, she'll likely receive a commendation if we make it through this intact. Who's next?"

"Why favor us with a warning, General?"

"That subject has been tossed around and is still open to speculation. Nearest we figure, someone in the Russian camp wanted us to know and provided the opportunity for the nozzle's discovery. Cat and mouse, they drop a hint, sit back, and enjoy the game. Maybe someone wasn't happy and wanted to change the odds, we may never know." Looking around, General Oz pointed to a commander with his hand raised.

"General, I don't understand how a joint Arab exercise plays into this."

"The answer is straightforward but has some interesting possibilities. We learned that a strain of anthrax with estimates of an eighty to eighty-five percent kill rate if not treated within hours of exposure had been cooked up by Russian covert bioweapons research. The information was turned over a year ago, but until the past few weeks it was believed the Russians would maintain physical possession. When you violate multiple international treaties, it's not bright to be handing out samples. Besides, once transferred outside Russian control, all bets are off. It doesn't escape notice that any consignment could be used anywhere, including against the country providing the bioweapon, and the Russians have had problems with radical Muslims in the recent past."

The General grabbed the nearly empty bottle of water, and finished it in two gulps then placed it back on the shelf. "The release of this strain of anthrax and resulting casualties could trigger massive chaos and breakdown of order in Yerushaláyim. Martial law would be declared, but still problems arise. When you add enemy troops surrounding our borders, the dreams of Arab hegemony may prove irresistible to our neighbors.

"While command and control would be transferred outside the affected area, a biological attack could be a tipping point with Yerushaláyim, the beginning of concentric circles that end up enveloping all of Yisra'el. The IDF is monitoring troop movement, and we'll match any troop escalation by calling up reserves, but remember the mindset on the street cannot always be controlled. The Border Police are also monitoring all borders so we can concentrate on our mission, which is to find the anthrax, next question."

"General, how do neighboring war games figure into our objectives?"

"If we are successful, intel predicts our neighbors will stand down. If we fail, enemies may be emboldened and the results could end differently."

"You said Jordan and Egypt were involved in war games. I thought existing treaties put a damper on their aspirations against us."

"After Sadat signed the peace accord with Yisra'el, he was assassinated. Because Mubarak didn't annul the treaty, he was compelled to deal with insurrection within Egypt and came down on the Muslim Brotherhood. We've observed a resurgence of the Brotherhood in Egypt and Jordan, where it's gaining influence. King Abdullah II struggles with factions aligned with the Brotherhood, and though we don't anticipate trouble coming directly from him or his people, the fact of their participation in the ramp up of war games, concurrent with the threat of anthrax, signals his position is weakened enough to cooperate with whatever enemies of Yisra'el have in mind. It wouldn't be a stretch to see power change in Jordan from moderate to fundamental radical."

"General, what are our restrictions?"

He scanned the faces before him. "My answer is off the record—understood?"

Hearts quickened.

"This is for Yisra'el's life. Leave no evidence, none. If you do you're on your own but do what must be done. If some innocents are sacrificed, that is the cost we bear; just find the anthrax—Find the anthrax!—FIND THE ANTHRAX!!"

The room remained silent. Major Weiss stood, a warrior's guttural cry on his lips. By ones, twos, fives the massed combatants arose, adding their voices to the growing roar of assent. The challenge was staggering, but resolve ran through each heart, binding them to one another and Yisra'el no matter the cost.

CHAPTER

27

March 2008

Old City Jerusalem

"Why are we avoiding everything that resembles public transportation?" Addison asked as cabs and buses sped by.

"You want to see Yerushaláyim, need to walk. Old City is made for feet, not for cars."

"Then could we slow down so I have time to read some of those street signs and you can regale me with your vast knowledge of all things Jerusalem."

"I stop when something important comes along."

"Mind sharing where we're going?"

"We start maybe *Coenaculum*."

"You are aware I speak English."

"Coenaculum is Latin for Upper Room, site of Last Supper. Also at different entrance is David's Tomb. Since both are in the same building, we see together. You know of Last Supper?"

"Surprisingly, even though most of my education centered on provable facts, I did manage to read something about the Last Supper in mythology class."

"You say myth if you like, but I don't understand how such a fable is born. Y'shua met with twelve disciples for dinner. Within twenty-four hours, Y'shua crucified by Romans. One disciple commits suicide, leaving eleven. The remaining eleven go into hiding. How did news of this supper reach people's ears?"

"I believe it's in the Bible."

"It's there, but that doesn't answer my question. If Y'shua is a myth, how does a single meal for one killed, another who killed himself, and remaining followers, who were afraid of their own shadows, reach every corner of the world?"

"Who said they were afraid?"

"Bible says Y'shua was arrested by authorities after praying in garden named Gethsemane. Only two disciples, John and Peter, followed Y'shua into a courtyard outside the temple, where he was taken by those authorities, but when Peter was accused of being with Y'shua, he denied even knowing him three times. Which, in case it has been too long since mythology class, or you overlooked the part where Y'shua said Peter would deny knowing him three times—before it happened. The disciples ran and hid, shaking like leaves, behind closed doors after Y'shua was crucified. It was women who first went to Y'shua's tomb, where he was laid after his crucifixion, looking for his body, but no body was found, just resurrected Y'shua. Reading bits of the Bible is like eating crumbs that fall from a table. You may think you're eating nourishing food but end up starving. You've never read the Bible but somehow know what it says."

"I read the Bible. Okay so only parts of it, but it never made much sense."

"Not hard to understand, since you don't want it to make sense. Besides, Bible's own words say natural mind can't understand things of God—"

"Oh, so that means if my mind were unnatural I would understand? Hate to point this out, but where I come from, unnatural, at least when it relates to a person's mind, describes someone who is mentally ill."

"It means God can't be found by looking under rocks, but by looking to see who formed the rocks."

"It's called evolution."

"And you say I have faith. Scientists are still looking for how life came from non-life, since they don't believe Pasteur, who proved spontaneous generation of life isn't possible."

"So what's your point this time?"

"If the Bible is correct, you will be judged by what it contains, so it's in your best interest to read it before you decide to reject it. Men don't like directions when traveling, but without them many get lost. Your soul depends on these directions. It's worth a look before rejecting."

"Tell you what, stop with the preaching and I promise I'll study the Bible when I start work at the Embassy."

"Study, not just glance?"

"Just finished my Master's in International Relations, not to mention eleven months at the State Department learning how to be so diplomatic. I know the difference between glancing at something and studying it. I will study the Bible if that will get you off my back about your Y'shua, I give you my word."

"You're not so diplomatic."

"I can be."

"Okay, I won't mention your soul's depravity or need for God unless you ask a question, but you study the Bible when you're back in the embassy. Bible is different from what you think, but it takes reading and reflection to see just how different. Is good you study."

"Not really. I already knew I had to study the *Tanakh*. Some of your countrymen are overzealous in their beliefs, so as a diplomat, I have to study the Jewish Bible. It's not considered kosher to step on the locals' religious feet. Since that covers the Old Testament, which is the biggest part of the Bible, I figure I can be generous and sail though the New Testament as well if that will keep our discussions off my, so-called, personal need for your savior, and on the subject at hand."

"Your eternal soul is the subject at hand, but no one can feed someone who thinks they're full, even when they're starving. I'll keep my word."

"Thank you. But just so we don't get off track here, my guess would be I don't have much choice to avoid the standard religious sites, but I still want to see the West Bank and talk with Palestinians who are free to speak their mind."

As they walked through the crowd by the Zion Gate, two Arabs appeared to be bearing down on them. The first had an enormous head, thick meaty neck, barrel chest, and arms bigger than Addison's thighs. His shorter companion, with the banty gait of a rooster, followed closely behind pecking his way toward them at an alarming rate. As they closed in, twenty feet, now fifteen, the hair on the back of Addison's neck bristled. Ten feet now, Addison searched for an escape. As he scanned unfamiliar surroundings, he glanced at Elizabeth's face. She had a grin from ear to ear.

"Elizabeth is good to see you this fine day," the rooster said.

"Khalil, shalom, Aadil, *Ma shelomkha*. How are you?" Elizabeth said, still smiling. "What brings you to Zion Gate?"

"It's always work. We have job this morning, but now it's done so we go to find others that need help. Who is friend?" Khalil said, looking toward Addison.

"This is Addison Deverell," Elizabeth said. Turning to Addison, she said, "Addison, these are my friends, Khalil Ahmad and Aadil Gamal."

"I am pleased to meet you," Addison said, extending his hand.

"From the look on your face, relieved is a better word," Elizabeth said.

"What brings you here on this fine day?" Khalil said.

"We have come to see David's tomb and the Coenaculum."

"Ah, *Dāwūd*, a fine prophet of our faith."

"You're welcome to go with us."

"Is time for going and working, families need us to work," Aadil said. He took off with Khalil by his side.

"The big one's not too social," Addison said.

"His family is large, many depend upon him. Sometimes it's hard when others make trouble and checkpoints are closed. His mind stays on finding work."

Making their way through Zion Gate, they navigated around workers repairing the gate before stopping on Hativat Etsyoni Street. Addison examined the gate and observed the restoration, hopeful his focus would prevent another onslaught about all things

Jesus. Bullet holes scarred the adjacent walls. "Repairmen forget the spackle?"

"In 1948 War of Independence, Jewish Palmach Har'el forces captured Zion gate and broke through into the Jewish Quarter for two days. They needed additional troops to hold the Zion gate, and completely take the Jewish Quarter. The Arab Legion arrived in Yerushaláyim and attacked. Our forces were outnumbered; we fell back. The bullet holes are left to remind us of the cost paid for Yerushaláyim."

"Arabs won that one, so much for invincible Israelis."

"We are a tiny nation, smaller in size than your state of Maine. All of Yisra'el could fit into your United States over four hundred seventy three times, yet in 1967 we reclaimed all of Yerushaláyim."

"Well, except for the Temple Mount."

"We win there too, but in fourth day of battle Moshe Dayan, Defense Minister at the time, made a decision to let Arabs keep the mount. Not all in Yisra'el agreed with decision."

"Considering everything they told me at State about the importance of the Temple Mount, why in the world would anyone return control to the Arabs after it had been won in battle?"

"Minister Dayan thought the mount's importance was as an historical site. He was a Zionist, which means not so religious but secular in views. Giving control to the Arab *Waqf* caused great damage to the site. Many times they've allowed excavations that destroy Jewish history even to this day. They also think we're weak because of giving back after winning."

"So, basically, the story is ongoing conflict."

"Yisraelis don't want a fight. We just want our home and are forced to defend ourselves to keep it."

"And yet tourists stream in from all over the world. You'd think, with all the fighting and growing numbers of people attending college, this sightseer's mecca would lose some of its appeal as reason replaces myth."

"Education is not a barrier to truth, only for those who use it as an excuse to stop thinking. Yisra'el's appeal is God's presence in land."

"Too bad you promised not to hammer me about that."

"I promised not to remind you how much you need HaShem. I didn't promise to exclude HaShem from sites we see. Remove God's presence from Yerushaláyim, there is nothing to see but old ruins."

Following the stream of tourists, they proceeded across Khativat Etsyoni then down Har Zion Street. Pausing in front of the Franciscan Monastery's faded double, metal doors, black lettering on white label tape caught Addison's eye. The lower sign read, *Custodia Terrae Sanctae* (custody of the Holy Land). Pausing, Addison turned to Elizabeth, a smirk on his face.

"Is something funny?"

"You'd think the Brothers could have at least splurged for a painted sign. Kinda dispels the myth being perpetuated, doesn't it?"

"I don't understand."

"You're selling an image here and someone uses a label printer on the door? I can't quite see Moses coming down from the mountain with commandments printed off a label maker pasted on the stone tablets."

"Moses never made it into Yisra'el much less Yerushaláyim. Besides, it's just a back door. You want a gold plaque?"

"Well now that—"

Turning right, Elizabeth took off. The sprint resumed.

Not this time, Addison thought, tearing after her. The street narrowed as buildings and randomly planted trees with encircling stone borders encroached on the shrinking stone lane. A hundred feet away, the Dormition Abbey sat astride the lane. Going left at the fork in the lane, which bordered the Abbey, Elizabeth came to a stop in front of a fourteen-foot-tall bronze statue of King David. Waiting for the obligatory diatribe tying David to antiquated beliefs, Addison studied the impressive piece of art. With no speech forthcoming, he wasn't about to provide an opening, so he remained quiet.

Sixty-five feet beyond the statue, the lane ended. An ancient stone building spanned the street with adjoining buildings, at right angles, lining both sides of the lane. Elizabeth turned left. "We go to the Coenaculum." Passing through an arched stone entrance, Elizabeth went up metal stairs in an inside courtyard, through an entrance hall, then outside down a sloped wooden ramp that emptied onto a stone passageway leading to a plain stone arch entry. Following Elizabeth, Addison found himself in a cavernous, rectangular Gothic room.

"This is site where the Last Supper is celebrated," she said in a hushed tone near Addison's ear, the hard stone surfaces amplifying and echoing every sound.

The high ribbed vaulted ceiling was held up by columns placed throughout the chamber. Addison's eyes came to rest on a solitary column topped by what appeared to be some type of bird. "What's that supposed to be?" he asked.

"It's a capital of carved pelicans feeding their young with their own blood."

"You get all that from this column, or did someone tell you that what's happening here?"

"Pliny the Elder, who lived in the first century, wrote that a pelican would, if necessary, feed its young with its blood, even sacrificing its own life, which became a symbol of Y'shua sacrificing himself on the cross for a church looking to proclaim its faith."

"The fact that pelicans prefer feeding their young fish didn't stop Pliny from his observations?" Addison asked.

"No and it didn't keep Franciscan monks from adding this to column's capital when Coenaculum was built around 1335," Elizabeth said.

"Wait, you said 1335? So that means the place where the last supper was held, what, around 33–34 A.D., was built almost thirteen hundred years after the supper took place? So faith and math are on opposite ends of the spectrum?"

"Addison, I didn't say this is where the Last Supper took place. I said this is the site it's celebrated to have taken place. Yerushaláyim is built on the ruins of its many conquests. The current sites are representative of earlier buildings. Every Easter, many believers walk the Via Dolorosa, the way of the cross, which is held to be the path Y'shua walked carrying his cross. We know the street level in Y'shua's day was twenty-five feet below Yerushaláyim's current street level. If you search for doubt, that is all you'll ever find."

Addison had to admit there was something about the room. With its cut rectangular golden-tan stones, plastered ceilings, and largely plastered walls, it didn't seem a part of the meager lives that passed through its ancient confines, whenever it was built. Its ceiling, soaring above his head, imbued the room with a presence while bestowing upon its inhabitants a sense of smallness, insignificance. He observed an Ottoman stained-glass window with an Arabic inscription above a doorway, as well as an alcove (a *mihrab,* Elizabeth called it) pointing the way to Mecca. *These Jews don't seem interested in eradicating other beliefs.*

"So many civilizations touch each other here," Elizabeth said. "This room has had many owners over the years. It was a church, synagogue, and mosque. Each new conqueror rebuilt it according to his beliefs. Many buildings in Yerushaláyim share this. Remember, time is measured differently in Yisra'el than America. This is also where the church believes the Holy Spirit was first given to followers of Y'shua."

"Kind of a twofer?" Addison said, back in control of unfamiliar emotions. "I knew I should have paid better attention in mythology class."

"Bible says that during Y'shua's life, God, the Holy Spirit, had not come to dwell in followers of Y'shua. After Y'shua ascended to heaven, Holy Spirit came to believers. Today when someone accepts Y'shua as Lord, Holy Spirit dwells within to guide the believer, sometimes as hushed voice, other times a raging lion, but always as a witness to believers to manifest God in their life. Of course, we have a choice whether to listen or not. This room is part of the church's beginning, its legacy."

Addison began to notice the faces filtering through the Upper Room. Some showed mild curiosity, taking in yet another attraction before moving on, others boredom. Moving from face to face, he became caught up in the transparency of expressions, as one here, another there appeared enraptured by the moment. There seemed no single reference point that tied these faces together, but something emanated from each that spoke of a thing he could not identify. He felt like an intruder trespassing on an intimate moment between . . . what? He didn't know but, for a fleeting moment, he wanted to. Observing him, Elizabeth bowed her head. When the moment passed, Addison settled on Elizabeth's downturned face but couldn't understand her stillness.

"It's time for King David's Tomb," Elizabeth said. Addison followed her out and down stone stairs to a courtyard below. As he followed, she wove through a labyrinth of interconnecting outside passageways that looked more like a service entrance. When they passed a ripe pile of trash, Addison spoke up. "This is where tourists go to see David's tomb?"

"No, we head to its rear entrance. Front entrance was a few meters from where we entered the Coenaculum—"

"So I get the discount tour?"

"The back entrance is not far. I have something I want to do."

They approached the nondescript stone-block rear entrance. Blue handrails led up two semicircular stone steps, ending with rectangular sill at the doorway. An inset sign on the right of the building, above the handrail, was made of twelve tiles, set four across and three high. Centered black lettering on a pale blue background announced *'King David's Tomb'* in English. Above that, in Hebrew, '*tomb king David.*' A dark blue border, filled with intricate white filigree scrolling, bound the tile edges together. Eager to continue exploring, Addison found Elizabeth lost in conversation with a white-haired woman sitting on a bench next to the left handrail. She handed the woman five shekels, receiving in exchange a three-inch votive candle in a tin metal base.

Following Elizabeth up the steps through the doorway, Addison found himself inside a rough-cut rectangular stone room. A six-foot-long half-moon shaped niche was carved into the rock wall on the left side of the entrance, three feet up from the floor. Inside the niche, two stone shelves ran its length, the upper set back nine inches from the edge of the lower. Myriad candles, copies of the one Elizabeth bought, nearly filled the shelves, their glow softening the hard surfaces of the unadorned room.

"This is Candle Room."

"Inventive. Is there a purpose other than supplementing incomes of less skilled seniors?"

"Money wasn't for the candle. Money was given as an offering. Many need help, both Yisraeli Jews and Yisraeli Arabs. Each does what they can. Abigail, the woman I got the candle from, makes candles for *Tzaddik*, those we consider righteous. Money goes to help those who don't like help so much." Going up to the niche, Elizabeth bowed her head in momentary silence. Looking up, she took the candle and lit its wick on another candle, then placed it on the lower shelf to join the others.

She proceeded into the building. Addison caught up with her as she passed a raised rectangular courtyard. Turning, Elizabeth said, "The candle was for my grandfather. Tzaddik are our righteous dead, we remember them on the anniversary of their death."

"How long—"

"Grandfather was in Yom Kippur War. He died months after from injuries, but we remember."

"Not to dispel the moment, but Jews seem to make a national pastime of remembering."

"We live in a sea of hatred. Throughout history, people of all nations, including your country, have stood by while Jewish lives were taken."

"Hey, America has done pretty good as far as Israel is concerned."

"Many times, yes, it has been a friend, sometimes a stranger. When you are here long enough, maybe you'll see through Yisraeli eyes. We encourage friends, but we prepare, depend on God, not others. The sadness is, many are beginning to forget HaShem."

They entered David's tomb in the basement of the Crusader church, proceeding into a low rectangular antechamber with piers and vaulting.

Quiescence, born in reverence, infused their surroundings. Raucous sounds would have been as irreverent as shorts or low-cut blouses. Warnings were dispensed by the keepers of the shrine because of the dearth of respect witnessed over the years from those whose societies did not apprehend that some things do not change.

As they walked past two windows inset into a stone-block wall, sunlight seeped into the ancient chamber. They proceeded to an arched end wall covered with green and blue painted mosaic tiles of varying shades with tiny specks of red dotting floral designs. In the wall's center resided a time-worn, wood-casement doorway displaying drips from too many coats of dried pale green paint. The singular word, *Men*, was centered on the lintel in Hebrew and English. While they waited for the room to clear, Elizabeth spoke in a whisper with the keeper. He gestured toward a box affixed to the wall that held several *kippot* to cover the heads of men entering the shrine. Addison knew what was expected and placed one on his head while Elizabeth tied a scarf on hers. Finally, the room cleared and they were allowed into the men's side of the tomb of King David by the keeper whose bearing was a silent reminder of the respect due this venerated place.

Along the front of the chamber, a two and a half foot tall black iron railing ran the length of the room. A perpendicular wood fence, resting on braced wheels, two feet taller than the railing, divided the room in half, running from the railing to the back wall, the top eighteen inches made of lattice. One side was for men, the other women; an exception had been made for Elizabeth and she was allowed in the men's side with Addison. Addison assumed this was the reason they were alone in the room. Behind the railing, on a covered platform, a stone cenotaph placed by the Crusaders, draped in a blue velvet cloth with gold lettering, rested in a niche blackened by countless pilgrim's candles, lit when young and old came to mystically connect to the reality of their faith.

Above the cenotaph, secured to the back wall, hung a Sefer Torah scroll in a hexagonal bronze container with a crown-shaped lid, its luster tarnished with age. At the far end of the room, an arch inset in the wall surrounded a tiny window, allowing light from the outside hall to pierce the confines of the semi-darkness.

Laboring for breath, Addison felt the walls constricting. Gone was the desire to study faces around him. Reverence that seemed a part of the air he breathed turned combative, assaulting his senses. He needed to get out. Escaping from the room, he tossed his kippa in the box.

Elizabeth caught up to him as he got outside, "In a hurry?"

"I needed air."

"There was air inside."

"Don't tell me some voodoo was working on me."

"Something happened, but not voodoo."

"It has been awhile since breakfast. I just need something to eat."

"You need something food will not fill, but we'll find a café."

As Addison attempted to enjoy the food another appetite assailed him. The diminutive table barely separated him from Elizabeth, close enough to reach out, touch, but she might as well have been twice removed. He would never be allowed to caress her olive-toned silken cheeks or full sensuous lips, whose essence enticed while they forbade closeness. *A rose by any other name*, he thought: wild with fierce thorns, but even those could not arrest desire. Elizabeth glanced over, a provocative smile emerging from intoxicating lips. Addison was beginning to think a deity might indeed exist, but from Addison's viewpoint he looked to be sadistic. He returned to his food where he would not be denied satisfaction.

Nasir adjusted the earphone on his directional voice-activated microphone. This was a great day to be a spy recording his target's conversations while he moved throughout the Old City following the Jew girl. He had been kept from following the American until his minder, IbnMansur, departed. Someone in charge wasn't willing to allow him to prove himself against the acclaimed man. There were stories during watch changes, when twelve-hour shifts made mouths loose, about those who had tangled with IbnMansur. Nasir feared no man but was content to postpone their meeting. The day and his concealed equipment made him feel he was a spy, finally part of the *intifada*.

Toting a cloth bag swollen with enough food to sate a horse, Mudawar arrived for his watch. His free hand, holding pita stuffed with falafel, made a continuous circuit to his mouth.

"You be careful. If that food causes you to lose our targets, Nuri will have you for dinner."

"Hey, they eat, I eat. I won't lose them."

"See that you don't. Everything is ready whenever Nuri gives word."

"I'm standing by when Nuri is ready."

"I have to report today's travels. I'll call tomorrow with our location."

"Is good, *ma'assalama*," go in peace."

After grilled lamb, fava bean spread on flatbread, cheese and fruit, washed down with ice-cold pomegranate juice at the outdoor café near Zion Gate, Elizabeth and Addison made their way through the winding streets of the Armenian Quarter and out through the Jaffa Gate, where they boarded Egged #99 bus. The red double-decker, long a tourist favorite, looked like it had missed an exit from London and ended up in Jerusalem. They ascended the stairs to the top deck, sitting on the first seats they found in the open air.

A nondescript Arab, picking the last morsels of pita from his teeth with a well-used toothpick, boarded behind them and made his way to a lower deck seat, one of thousands of Arabs out for the day in the city of peace.

Eight stops and forty minutes later, Addison followed Elizabeth off in front of *Yad VaShem*. Just before the bus continued on its route to Giv'at Ram University, Mudawar exited the bus but did not trail them inside the museum, preferring instead to wait in the warmth of the sunshine on this pleasant spring day. He had no interest in Jewish myths.

Addison came up beside Elizabeth as she started down the long wooden bridge at the foot of Mount Herzl. "This is called *Har Hazikaron*."

"English?"

"Mount of Memory. The hill was named after Theodor Herzl."

"I know this one. He was the Austrian guy—"

"Hungarian."

"Whatever, the Hungarian guy who organized the first Zionist Congress and pushed for the return of Jews to Israel."

"You surprise—"

"Hey, what can I say, some things just stick in the old grey matter."

Addison and Elizabeth descended into the museum.

"Yad VaShem, also known as the Holocaust Museum, was built to remember six million Jewish lives slaughtered from 1933 to 1945," Elizabeth said.

"So what do we see first?"

"What we see first? Did you understand what I just said; six million Jewish men, women, children exterminated? Not to mention thousands who were used in all kinds of horrific experiments because some did not see Jews as human beings. Not human beings. And you ask what we see first?"

"I wasn't even born then. What am I supposed to feel about something so removed from my world?"

"You came early to Yisra'el to understand. Maybe understanding begins with an event that shapes Jewish lives, because, for Yisraelis, Yad VaShem is part of our soul. Our first Prime Minister, David Ben Gurion said, 'Our past is not just behind us, it is in our very being.' To know Jewish hearts you must understand this isn't just a place for tourists to view and then go on to the next site; it's part of the foundation that shapes how we know all of life. Each year we observe a national memorial day, *Yom HaShoa*, Holocaust Remembrance Day, for all of Yisra'el to remember what this means. Look deeply, Addison Deverell, you might begin to see what you came to Yisra'el for."

"From what I've seen so far, you spend too much time looking into the past. Here's a thought—life goes on."

"For life to go on we remember our past. Your country was attacked and it changed life in America. Now many don't seem to like your president because it's up to him to go about the hard task of preventing future attacks while many want to forget and think of the present. He understands what must be done more than those who choose to ignore your country's real needs. For us, if we forget, there may be no second chance to remember. What would you feel if your neighbors continued to say they will wipe you from the face of the earth? That their dream is to drive you and all your relatives into the sea? This looking back—remembering—allows us to keep looking forward so that our children and children's children never face what our people faced, not just under Hitler, as Yad VaShem remembers, but in pogroms throughout the ages wherever we tried to make a life. That's why we remember and will never be driven from land again, no matter the cost."

Addison thought he knew what waited when he descended into Yad VaShem, until confronted by the callous, vile inhumanity the museum bore witness to. He labored through photos, mementos, and exhibits, searching for hope in vestiges of relics that belonged with families, not as execrable witnesses to collective evil.

This testament to atrocity confronted him in the rawness of its primeval horror. How could mankind do what was so clearly depicted? Would not the vilest depravity of humanity's heart constrain such acts? This was visceral, malevolent, too immoral to be contemplated, much less systematically executed.

His head felt light, the room slowly turned around on itself, tears formed unchecked by control he no longer possessed. Moment by moment he continued to sink into an abyss no mind could conceive, as malevolence continued its barrage, challenging what he understood of life, humanity.

He felt tied to these inhabitants forever imprisoned within these walls; a bond of aberrant fascination? Could any human being view this travesty and not be sickened? For the first time he wasn't sure of anything, as each step, each picture, each exhibit compelled another. The assault on his senses made him ache. He could no longer sort the images bombarding his soul.

Then his eyes focused as light seemed to penetrate his eyes. He saw past the presented abominations, beneath facades that prevented true vision. He looked into the hearts of these strangers from another time, piercing their humanity, unlike any he imagined—living breathing beings who cherished life.

As he turned the corner, a free-standing serpentine wall confronted him, stretching into the distance. Eight feet high and surely four times that length, its undulating curves grew from the stark grey concrete it stood upon. Face after forlorn face in different-sized black and white photographs, some yellowed and cracking, others pristine, crowded each other as they pulled him into an unalterable moment.

One pair of eyes caught his, refusing to release him. He pulled away to look at others yet was drawn back to a waif of a boy—thirteen—fourteen, so gaunt he could not be sure. How can you tell a skeleton's age? He was dressed plainly, with dark, deep-set, luminescent eyes that bespoke sadness yet radiated serenity, calmness, in the eye of his storm, looking far older, more sagacious, than his years should have allowed. He had shining dark hair with natural curl, his head bent to the side, asking, 'Can you see me . . . really?'

Who are you? What happened in your life to end up here? Was there pain in these eyes that held his? He could not escape, nor understand. Had he seen them before, but where? Or were they a part of him waiting to be discovered in this place, at this time?

Looking away brought no release; his soul impelled him back. Then it began—*how could you have been evil? An enemy to be destroyed?*—the flicker of questions fanning into a flame he neither apprehended nor controlled. *How could anyone . . . anything have done this evil?* The room swirled as his heart raced and head throbbed. Hatred, seething and pounding within, was born.

Elizabeth watched in silence. A smile rose to her lips in a place of remembrance where smiles do not easily come.

Addison wrenched away from the piercing eyes that held his. Exhaling slowly, he retreated from the wall, struggling to understand. He needed air.

CHAPTER

28

Tuesday 11 March 2008, Early Morning

JERUSALEM

Nasir followed the boisterous greetings ricocheting off the stone buildings as Aadil and Khalil made their way toward Jerusalem in search of another day's work. "Aadil . . . Khalil," Nasir called out.

Turning, Khalil spotted his meal ticket and tugged his friend's sleeve. "Aadil, it is Nasir. We will get good job today."

Coming up to the pair, Nasir handed Khalil an envelope. "This is from Lt. Amin—"

"Lieutenant Amin," Khalil said, peeking into the envelope, "Haven't seen him for many days. How is our good friend the Lieutenant?"

"He is well. There's payment for one week's work at his usual generous rate."

"We were just going to al-Quds to see about work. You're lucky to find us."

"Not lucky; you've been under surveillance—"

"Surv . . . survell . . . what is this word you say?" Khalil asked.

"Others have been watching you."

"Watching? Why watching?"

"You are part of something important for Palestine that few others can do. Those much smarter than myself—"

"There are others smarter than you?"

"Many my friend, this struggle has been going on since before we were born. Generations have joined our cause. For you to do your part when needed, those in charge must know where you are at all times, so they observe as you travel about your day. How would I have found you in all this great area if someone had not told me where to look? This is good because those watching are friends who want to help, but remember when you are given something to do you must do it."

"If you had not found Aadil and Khalil, envelope with full week's pay might not have come to us, so it's good you found us. What you want us to do?"

"We are to spend the day together. I expect sometime today you will be asked to perform a simple task."

"How will we know when that is, Nasir?"

"I'll tell you."

"Why not tell us now, and then we go do."

"I don't know now."

"You don't know now?"

"I don't."

"Then when will you know?"

"I don't know when I'll know."

"Then how will you know that you know?"

"I will receive a message."

"How will anyone find you to give this message? You got someone watching you too?"

"Perhaps, but I will receive a call on my cell phone with instructions."

"You have a cell phone?"

"Yes, of course."

"Can I see? Aadil and I never have money for cell phone but see many people walking along yak, yak, yakking. Funny to see sometimes when someone is talking into the air and then bursts out laughing. Maybe sometimes crazy people are like that."

Pulling out his cell phone Nasir handed it to Khalil. "Don't touch any buttons. No one else must use it."

"It's pretty, Nasir, all black and shiny. Maybe someday Aadil and I will get a shiny phone, but then who would we talk with since no one in family has such a phone."

"If we come across any Israeli checkpoints, I will not go through with you."

"Why? You don't want to be seen with Aadil and me?"

"Enough with the questions, I know little has been revealed, but you wouldn't understand anyway. Even I don't know everything. I'm telling you what I've been told. For whatever reason, it wouldn't be okay for us to be seen together in certain places. When we approach an area and I'm not around, don't call out for me or worse yet try to find me. I'll show up. If anyone—anyone—asks if we are together, we aren't. You must follow every instruction or homes in Syria, away from all the fighting, will never happen. Today is a time to visit and enjoy the day. On top of that, you're being paid."

"Pay is good, but I could enjoy the morning much more with some kataif and syrup."

"When we find a café, you will have your kataif."

"You are a true friend."

By mid-afternoon, Khalil struggled to walk, having far exceeded his weekly quotient of sweets. After receiving a call, Nasir hurried the pair through back streets on their urgent mission.

"Why the hurry Nasir, the day is warm and my belly doesn't want to run. Maybe you get us cab if we need to be someplace in hurry."

"We're close, Khalil. Remember, your job is to keep up." They continued their pace.

Finally Nasir slowed, and then stopped. Looking at the pair to ensure they were paying attention, he said, "Elizabeth Daniels is nearby guiding the American around al-Quds. I'll show you where in a moment. He has asked to go into the West Bank but Elizabeth doesn't want to. When you meet, offer to go with them. You must keep the American from Gaza and the interior of the West Bank except Abu Dis, without telling them. If possible, use wisdom."

"But what if they talk about Gaza or the West Bank, not Abu Dis? What do we say? Gee, Elizabeth and new American friend, there sure is good kataif in Abu Dis or basboosa just waiting for Khalil to eat. Then Elizabeth would say kataif and basboosa is also waiting at many stands in al-Quds," Khalil said.

"For the past two days the American has brought up the West Bank to Elizabeth. When he learns you're from Abu Dis, he will ask your help. Americans always want their own way. If Gaza comes up, just tell the American you can't get into Gaza, but don't say anything unless he brings it up."

"What is our reason to show Abu Dis, not Gaza City, or RamAllāh?" Aadil asked.

"Israeli checkpoints make it impossible to get the American into Gaza. Abu Dis is closer and is easier to get into."

"But what about the separation wall?"

"You two go through every day. American can get through like our people if he wants to see our towns, but don't get caught by the Israelis. The American has a diplomatic passport. His trip would be cut short but you would end up at Moriah Police Station. Besides, it's safer for the American in Abu Dis."

"Sometimes Abu Dis isn't safe. Why are we all in a rush to show the American a place where there could be danger?" Aadil asked.

"Aadil, Americans think they have answers for all of life. This one won't take no from Elizabeth; I myself have listened to his words with a device friends provided for such listening. He is determined to go even if he must go alone. This is where you and Khalil can help. If you don't, someone from PMIJ might and you know what could happen. Peace that PALFA has worked for will be lost, along with the American's and Elizabeth's head if she is with him. Remember, she is Jewish—"

"She is a friend," Aadil said.

"But also a Jew and an occupier, PMIJ does not care she is your friend. She would not live, and then Israelis and Americans would storm in with Palestinian lives lost. You can prevent this. When you see the American, I must be elsewhere but will join you at the right moment and show you a refuge. The American will be safe, and then it's just a matter of time before the Americans reward your help. They have a great sea of money for such help, and both of you, along with your families, will move near Aleppo with nice homes away from all the fighting with enough American dollars to live in peace."

"I don't know about living in Aleppo. I've never been there, Nasir. It's too much for me, but I know about friends and Elizabeth is my friend, so I will help," Aadil said.

"Nasir, when you say to Aadil and me that we to go Aleppo, I think it must be a dream. The more I think, the more I want for this dream to be true. Aadil and I will do what you say, but if something happens—"

"Nothing will—"

"If something happens, you see family gets to Aleppo? We never have peace, and I want peace for my family."

"You'll make it there."

CHAPTER

29

Tuesday March 11 2008, Afternoon

Sabbiyah Café, Ben-Yehuda Pedestrian Mall Old City Jerusalem

"I don't get it. I've been dragged to every Jewish and Christian site you and Hafiz could think of. There's just two days before I have to report for duty, and still you ignore me when I ask to go where Palestinians and Jews live," Addison said.

"Where do you think we've been since we met? Yerushaláyim is the heart of where Jews live. You've talked to many Jewish people."

"Yes and each one steered the subject to my personal need for a savior. I thought Jews had their own religion."

"We do. Can I help it my friends know Y'shua? Besides, you don't want to go into the West Bank. You may not like Palestinian answers to some questions," Elizabeth said.

"Stop saying that. I came to Israel early to understand what undergirds the Jewish-Arab divide. I have traipsed behind Hafiz, and you've only let me talk to handpicked friends. But I want to see and talk with Palestinians, and with or without your help that's exactly what I intend to do. I've learned a lot, more than I would have thought possible, but even your Bible says there is a time and a season for all things."

"Very good, you find that all by yourself?"

"I picked up a couple of verses here and there. Tried that one on a date once, didn't work. Point is no more diversions. How can I understand this puzzle unless I see the pieces for myself? I'm still an American and the one choice you have is whether you want to help."

"It's dangerous—"

"Then make it safer."

"*As Salam a' alaykum*, hello," Khalil said, walking up to the table.

"Khalil, shalom," Elizabeth said. "Aadil, shalom. What are you two doing here?"

"We're here for a job but it doesn't start until later," Aadil said.

"Hello, important American person," Khalil said.

"I am far from important."

Elizabeth smiled.

"Everyone knows our friend is with important American," Khalil said.

"How?"

"How do crocodiles know someone is swimming in river? Sabbiyah Café is good choice for food. Would you like us to sit with you awhile, Elizabeth? We have time before next job," Khalil said.

"Forgive my manners, of course you can—"

Khalil was seated before Aadil could get his chair pulled out

"—sit down," Elizabeth said.

"Please continue conversation. We don't mind. Waiter, is there waiter here? Customer needs sweet tea for dry throat," Khalil said.

"Would you like something to eat?" Elizabeth asked.

"Food is never turned away, but I am full from good breakfast and lunch. I will remember when I am able to show kindness by receiving gracious offer. What is conversation Aadil and me stumble into the middle of?"

"Let's put the question before your friends. They might have a unique perspective on the issue. I mean they're Palestinian, right?" Addison said.

"What is question to have Khalil and I give answer?" Aadil said.

"All right," Elizabeth said, "Addison wants to go into the West Bank. He will be working in Yisra'el for some time to come and—"

"And I want to talk with Palestinians so I can understand the conflict between you and the Jews," Addison said.

"You want to go into the West Bank?" Aadil asked.

"How can I understand the conflict's foundation unless I see the root of the issue by directly discoursing with those embroiled in this struggle?" Addison said.

"What is question, Elizabeth?" Aadil said.

"You don't understand English?" Addison said.

"You understand Arabic, *kalb*?"

Elizabeth's lips pursed as she shot an anxious glance at Aadil. Addison had not yet learned the Arabic word for dog.

"Language was not my major in college, so no, I don't speak Arabic. Since English is the universal language I wanted to ascertain your proficiency with English to determine if I needed to translate through Elizabeth," Addison said.

"Sometimes we work for Americans, sometimes Australians, even British. All speak English, but much is different. I understand enough, if you speak clearly. So why do you want go into the West Bank?" Aadil said.

"Because that's where Palestinians are."

"Khalil and I are Palestinian. What you want know?"

"I want to speak with many Palestinians, to understand their perspectives—"

"What they think about how things are," Elizabeth said.

"You don't want to go into the West Bank," Aadil said. "In West Bank some people might want to deny you your life. They're not so fond of Americans."

"I don't get it. America sends millions of dollars in aid to Palestine."

"They also send tens of millions of U.S. dollars to Israel, along with weapons that end up killing our people. Khalil and I don't hate anyone. We make a living most everywhere and work for Israelis, Palestinians, Americans, anybody. We don't care, our families must eat, but there could be danger in the West Bank even if we went with you. Besides, there is no way to get there for you."

"How about a bus or a cab?"

"Busses and cabs don't go from Israel into the West Bank. To enter the West Bank you must go through Erez Crossing. Israelis stop you from entering on their side and even if you got through, Palestinian police or PALFA would stop you on the other. Even detain you unless you're on an official trip, which, unless I'm wrong, isn't the case."

"Then how do I get to Palestinians? I'm not the bad guy here; I just want to know what they think."

"There may be a way to get into Abu Dis but you must stay with Aadil and me. Only by keeping close will there be chance you don't talk to dangerous people that keep you from ever leaving."

"Khalil, I don't think this is good. You know what could happen," Elizabeth said.

"It could happen here but hatred lives everywhere. Between Aadil and me we can show some of our land and American Addison would have a chance to see our people. You must pay for time, American Addison; we have family that needs our work. What is payment for us to take you to meet genuine Palestinians?"

"How about $50.00 a day?" Addison said.

"That's $50.00 a day for Khalil and $50.00 a day for me?"

"I can do that, $100.00 a day for both of you."

"Plus expenses?"

"You sure you've never been to America?"

"You pay for café when it's time for food so all pay goes for family."

"Agreed, you coming, Elizabeth?"

"I promised Hafiz I'd stay with you."

"Let's go," said Addison.

"It's not let's go, sun will be setting. Night isn't when you want to see Abu Dis. We'll meet tomorrow, and then you can speak with Palestinians. See you here at seven in the morning," Khalil said.

"Whoa, I want to meet Palestinians, but they need to be out of bed first. What's say we meet at 10 A.M.?"

"Day is half gone by then. We meet at eight for breakfast. Is good to start day with food," Khalil said.

CHAPTER

30

Wednesday March 12 2008

Sabbiyah Café, Ben-Yehuda Pedestrian Mall Old City Jerusalem

Walking from the café after witnessing an hour of continuous eating, Addison asked, "You feel a little queasy?"

"Pleasantly full, thank you very much. Breakfast is most important meal of day, blessings upon you for such generosity. Aadil is forever in hurry while I half-starve, but today there was great abundance. I am good until lunch."

"We must speak of today," Aadil said, coming up beside Addison. "It's like no other. This talk you desire could cost more than breakfast and the American dollars you pay us."

"Look, I've been over this with everyone. Since coming to Israel, I've wanted to understand this hatred between Arabs and Jews, and it won't come from books. At first it seemed a smart career move, understanding root causes, but as I have begun to see this land, it has become something more. Everyone is so busy putting out fires no one stops to ask who started them or why. Maybe it won't end up mattering, but it does to me. Everywhere I go people tell me what I don't want. Today is about what I do want, whatever happens. I've tried to hear as much of the Israeli side as my keepers would allow. Now it's time for whatever I can get from the Palestinian side."

"Khalil and I know many in Abu Dis. It's where we grew up. But others, not from here, with pasts lived in shadows, have moved in. No families, friends, or ties to Abu Dis. You need to—"

"I get it. Some natives are hostile. The satanic American will be in their midst. You're right, something could happen. Aadil, stripped down to its core, life has to be more than drawing breath. If I'm ever to make a difference, the time for sightseeing is over," Addison said, digging into his stride and pushing forward.

Khalil sidled next to Aadil, keeping an eye on Elizabeth as she caught up with Addison. Under his breath he said, "You want American to stop? You forget our families?"

"I remember."

"Then why beg him to stay in Israel?"

"American has to weigh own path; I won't be responsible. I must know I didn't shape his destiny, only served as a guide for his choices."

Paved roads gave way to narrow lanes as Aadil and Khalil took the lead ahead of Addison and Elizabeth. They continued toward the Separation Security Barrier, which, in this part of the barrier, was a twenty-six-foot tall concrete wall isolating Abu Dis.

Their parting instructions from Nasir that morning were to avoid drawing attention when Israeli patrols rolled past on their continual security checks. Nothing must keep them from Abu Dis.

The barrier wall rose into the morning sun, monolithic and foreboding, dividing, and separating. Graffiti was scrawled haphazardly on the concrete canvas. Crude protests began to appear when the fence was started in June 2002, next to forceful drawings depicting the passion of a political divide whose roots were birthed in long-forgotten faith.

A row of nine booths, open along one side to display merchandise, were joined end on end bordering the lane several meters from the wall. Aadil and Khalil entered one booth where men's clothing was displayed on outdoor racks with folded garments inside on wooden boxes that served as tables. Aadil and Khalil disappeared.

Walking to the booth, Addison saw Khalil inside, motioning. He entered, and Elizabeth followed him.

Khalil turned and headed for a back flap, slipping out before Addison could catch up. Addison, a few steps behind, found himself outside under a tarp which ran the length of the shops. Flaps closed off both ends of the joined booths. In front of him sat a brown nylon tent with a rough tan and burgundy Persian carpet, a *kilim*, covering its floor. Plain wooden chairs were arranged around a circular table with a *hookah* sitting in its middle. Aadil and Khalil were already seated. The stale odor of tobacco pervaded the air, carpet, and tent, closing in the space.

"Please to be seated," a female voice said in Arabic from behind a side flap in the tent Addison had missed.

"She said to be seated," Khalil said.

Sitting opposite his escorts, Addison strained to see the source of the voice as Elizabeth sat down next to him. In a flurry of Arabic, Khalil spoke through the sidewall to the incorporeal voice. The tent flap parted, and a woman, with only her eyes visible beneath her *burqa*, came to the table with tumblers of sweet tea on a black lacquered tray. She placed a tumbler in front of each of them, and returned to her sanctuary.

"Look, we just finished breakfast. If we're going to get into Abu Dis, we can't stop every hour for refreshments," Addison said.

"Want to go through break in wall now?" Aadil said. "How long you think before you'd be shot? Maybe throat cut? Clothes tell everyone you're an American. Think many Palestinians will talk with an American? What about five minutes after you're spotted and nice man from neighborhood runs to PMIJ and informs them. People are poor, and Palestine Mujahideen Islamic Jihad pays money for such information. You think it's worth their life to talk to you when neighbor reports them, American Addison? Maybe you want to spill your own blood, but they want to keep theirs."

"I see, I'm an American, so the only time your warring political factions allow conversation is when millions of U.S. dollars are on the table. And that's not hypocritical?"

"It's how things are. You hear a few stories and think you know about Palestinians—"

"No, no, no. I want to learn."

"Then first learn to live. We're here to get clothes for you and Elizabeth; Jews are even less popular than Americans. Elizabeth has helped our people many times, she is a friend, but others maybe don't know that. Back room is not just for tea but out of view of people passing on the road while you dress to have a chance of talking with Palestinians," Aadil said.

"What about Fatima?"

"Who's Fatima?" Aadil said.

"The woman covered in a bed sheet listening to every word."

"Her name isn't Fatima. In our culture only husbands, fathers, and close family members call women by their first names. The bed sheet is called a burqa and it's important to our customs. Finally, she only speaks Arabic. I found those safe for you to be around. She will get clothes so you don't have to go up front. Which brings to mind, whatever I say—you must do. Don't argue, question, or even wait, but immediately do. This isn't for you to decide. It's not just your life, but Elizabeth's and ours that could be lost. Understand?" Aadil said.

"What is it with ultimatums?"

"You didn't answer. We go back now."

"Wait a minute . . . okay, fine."

"You listen?"

"Big choice."

"Good, when we leave here, don't speak. Maybe a quiet whisper to Elizabeth or Khalil and me if important, but no one else must hear. When meeting anyone you are mute. When there are safe people to talk with, then you can speak, but not unless I say it's okay. This is important."

In the next half hour Addison was grateful for the enclosed alcove. He stripped naked and was dressed from underwear to *kafiyyeh,* head scarf, in questionable but clean clothing that reflected the garb of the impoverished Palestinian masses his handlers tried to effect he was. Now all he had to worry about was getting shot by the Palestinians or Jews—maybe both. He was hoping for a mirror to see what had just cost him seventy-five bucks, but mirrors didn't appear to be fashionable in this boutique.

Fatima stood looking him over.

"Okay, so could I pass for your brother," he said, expecting silence.

"My brother prefers European clothes," Elizabeth said.

"Elizabeth, is that you under those drapes?"

"Be happy you're not a woman. I also have a skirt and blouse under my burqa. My clothes weigh ten pounds."

Stepping outside the shop, Addison expected to be discovered by Palestinians or Israelis, he wasn't sure which. It appeared the foundation makeup Elizabeth smeared over his face, neck, and hands did its job; no one paid attention to the mute as his group headed for Abu Dis.

The security barrier fence loomed larger with each step. Addison looked up at its twenty-six-foot height. Each section was ten-feet wide and joined monolithically to the section on either side.

Spotting a two-and-a-half-foot-wide opening in the wall, Addison whispered, "This should be easy."

"What should be easy?" Aadil said.

"That," Addison said, pointing to the opening in the wall manned by a single Israeli Border Guard.

"We can't go there."

"What are you talking about? We can just get on the end of the line and walk through."

"Elizabeth, you bring mirror?"

"What does—" Addison started to say.

"Look at yourself—you look Palestinian. Checkpoint identification is required. You have Palestinian identification I don't know about? Can you answer questions in Arabic? Your American Passport will get you to Kishle Police Station in a hurry. End of trip for Abu Dis and big trouble for me and Khalil."

He followed as Aadil steered a wide berth around the checkpoint. Addison didn't see the second Border Guard off to the side scanning the checkpoint while cradling her Galil assault rifle.

Twenty minutes later Addison decided to catch up with Khalil. "Don't mean to cast any doubts on our wonderful plan, but since we can't use the one opening I've seen, how we going to get over this wall?"

"Little ways down is an ancient stone wall the Israelis left in place and connected to their barrier. Israelis are big on antiquities, you'll see."

Following a gradual bend in the twenty-six-foot-high concrete barrier wall, a twelve-foot-wide stacked stone wall intersected its behemoth cousin. Smaller stones and concrete blocks scattered around its base served as makeshift stairs for those wishing to avoid checkpoints. Two eight-inch-square concrete beams had been placed horizontally on top of the ancient six foot stone wall, allowing a gap in their middle between the beam ends. On top of the beams, a vertical concrete slab jutted up an additional four feet. Inset metal fasteners locked the beams, concrete slab, and the barrier wall together. The twenty-six-foot-tall security barrier fence resumed its flow at the end of the ancient stone and concrete barrier wall, disappearing into the distance.

They stopped several feet from the breach. "Since the Israelis went to the effort to build the wall, why leave openings?" Addison whispered.

"Barrier wall is not to keep Palestinian Arabs from going to Yerushaláyim," Elizabeth said.

"Could have fooled me."

"It's here to keep shaheeds, suicide bombers, from attacking my people and to cut down on rocket launches. There are many places to cross, like this one, everyone knows about. They're more difficult to cross but quicker than official *machsoms*, checkpoints that can take a long time. Border Patrol keeps an eye on these breaches and catches many who want to harm others. Palestinian Arabs need these openings, so they don't like shaheeds to use them and get the passages shut down which forces everyone through machsoms."

"So we're being watched, right now?"

"It's one reason you don't want to make any quick gestures, Palestinian," Khalil said, looking at Addison and grinning ear to ear.

Aadil looked at Addison. "This is your last chance to go back. Once you cross barrier you're in a different world."

"If I back down now I'll never get back up."

"Khalil first, Elizabeth next, then Addison," Aadil said. Everyone complied. Threading his way up the scattered rocks and concrete blocks, Khalil pressed through the narrow gap with ease. Elizabeth followed, her burqa no impediment. Addison feared future Deverell generations might be in jeopardy when he squeezed through the tight opening. On the Palestinian side, assorted concrete blocks served as stairs, taking them to a dirt path running by the side of the wall. Incredibly, Aadil was on the ground before Addison could turn to watch the fun of him getting through the concrete beams. Khalil kept walking, quickly leading the group away from the wall, past scattered one and two-story residences and, within minutes, into the marketplace, where hundreds of Palestinians carried out the daily tasks of commerce.

Addison wanted to stop everyone to hear their story. Looking around he forced his own silence. Elizabeth was mute beside him. Walking through the marketplace, Khalil and Aadil made up for Addison's and Elizabeth's silence by greeting everyone they saw. Loud staccato bursts of Arabic were followed by hugging and cheek kissing. Fruits and nuts and pastries made a continual pilgrimage to Khalil's mouth.

When gestures were at last made in Addison's direction, heads shook in a way that required no interpretation, some indicating their decision more emphatically than others. Aadil and Khalil continued their journey past assorted stalls while Addison, surrounded by an invisible barrier of silence, took in the increasingly surreal scene.

Again and again, when gestured to, each motion signaled a resolute shunning.

In a hostile land, dressed in clothes he suspected fooled no one, beside a woman dressed like a bondservant from the Middle Ages, with no clue as to what was being said: *Yeah,* Addison thought, *this is going to work.*

Ninety interminable minutes later, Aadil motioned them to follow. Twisting and turning in the maze of alleys and paths, Addison was lost. His keepers made their way to a dilapidated shack. Through its open door a bouquet of mouth-watering aromas wafted outward.

Inside, Khalil held open a curtain as his stomach could be heard licking its lips. He motioned toward the rear, letting the curtain close after they passed. Along the back wall, a painted white plywood counter, thirty inches off the floor, was attached to the sidewall and was held up, along its front edge, by rusting metal pipes with flanged ends. Six discolored green plastic chairs were stacked on themselves in the corner against the wall. Addison opened his mouth to speak; Aadil shook his head.

Two girls, no older than eleven, in matching cotton blouses and long skirts, came through the opening in the curtain carrying plates, napkins, and juice in tumblers. Arranging them on the counter, they pulled four chairs from the stack then placed them by the counter and left. They returned with platters of meats, cheese, fruit, and pita bread, along with hummus in small bowls. After placing the food on the counter, they bowed their heads as they spoke in the direction of Aadil then left.

After everyone was seated, Aadil said, "Speak softly. Others must not hear."

"Why won't anyone talk to me? I just want to know what they think," Addison whispered.

"We talked about this. People are afraid. Chairman Arafat's Preventative Security Force was charged with the safety of the people. He died; many in the Preventative Security Force now take money and do other's bidding; no one can know who to trust," Aadil said. He took pita bread, tore off a huge piece, and dipped it into hummus before thrusting it in his mouth.

"So what's the plan?"Addison said.

Aadil finished chewing, lifted his tumbler, and washed everything down with half the tumbler's juice. "First lunch, then we see others. Maybe elsewhere some will talk. Must understand if no one agrees we go back and you find another way to gain understanding."

"Great."

After lunch was paid for, they headed from the derelict café. Tightly spaced wood stalls gave way to single-story stone buildings where pottery makers and metal-smiths, whose tin-glazed creations were commingled with carpenter's handcrafted superb pieces, each hoped would be sold in al-Quds, where everything brought higher profits. Neither Aadil nor Khalil greeted these hard-working craftsmen; families must be fed and interruptions were not welcomed. "Stay," Aadil ordered. He approached a blacksmith's apprentice taking a break from the heat of the forge. The familiar greeting was subdued; there was no brushing of cheeks when Aadil engaged the teenager. On motioning to Addison, the now familiar shaking of head signaled another rejection.

The teen shouted inside the shop. An ox of a man emerged, head bent low to clear the door's lintel. A sledgehammer swallowed in his massive paw, his forearms bulging with power. Rapid-fire Arabic flew as Aadil, dwarfed by this being, held his ground, trying to quell increasingly loud words.

Finally, Aadil turned, shouting, "Is time to go," which seemed to upset the living creature more. Raising his huge arm, meaty fingers choked the sledgehammer while veins pulsed in his neck. A growing torrent of guttural sounds spewed from his mouth, gaining momentum with each percussive burst. Workers began putting down tools, converging around the uproar.

Khalil was one step ahead, Elizabeth and Addison on his heels, Aadil bringing up the rear. Within minutes, a maze of streets put distance between them and the fuming blacksmith.

Close behind, two nondescript onlookers, with distinctive checkered neck scarves and Kalashnikov rifles strapped to their backs, tracked their way through the maze of streets, following their prey as they had all day.

"There is one other place some may talk," Aadil said.

"You mean without wanting my head?"

"We go to place for sitting, conversation. Maybe friends there won't feel anger," Aadil said, heading for the heart of Abu Dis.

Coming upon the town center, Addison saw a flat rectangular area just over fifty feet long and half that wide where hard-packed dirt competed with clumps of weeds, papers, bottles, and cans for dominance. On the far end, a food vendor had stationed a green and yellow cart. Strewn blocks of concrete served as tables and chairs. Along the side closest to them three benches of peeling paint tried to cover splintering wood whose rusted metal pipe frames were cemented into the ground. A single gnarled olive tree, its branches serving more to ensnare passers-by than provide shade, stood ten feet from the benches, testimony that an orchard had once graced what now masqueraded as a park. A lone attendant, dragging a large black plastic sack on the ground, mumbled to himself as he wielded a three-foot-long faded yellow broom handle with a sharpened sixteen-penny nail protruding from its end, spearing the rubbish of others less concerned with this patch of dirt than he. Several grey-haired men, oblivious to their surroundings, sat on the benches, deep in animated conversation, none of which Addison could understand.

Observing from a safe distance, he watched while Khalil was welcomed by the aged philosophers as a long-lost brother. Kisses and hugs abounded. Khalil slapped backs in greetings as he kissed his way through everyone. He and Aadil joined the spirited banter of obvious friends. After a seemingly endless exchange, Khalil pointed to Addison. He waited for shaking of heads, but the conversation, somehow, continued. No one shouted, nor left; friendly sounds continued.

After existing stories finished and new ones were swapped, Khalil headed their way, talking with two of his bearded friends, one on each side.

"Addison, these are friends, Habib and Umar."

"Khalil, I don't speak Arabic."

"Is good, Habib and Umar both speak American."

"There's so much to ask. Don't know where to start. How do you feel about America?"

"Thought you wanted to know about Israelis," Khalil said.

"Okay, let's start—"

Umar cut in, a percussive staccato whisper, urgent in its Arabic.

Words crashed in low voices between Khalil, Habib, and Umar, and then stopped abruptly. Habib and Umar began walking away.

"What's going on?"

"Look toward the far end of the park by the food cart."

Addison observed two men, rifles cradled in their arms, looking in his direction. Both were dressed nondescriptly save black and white checkered scarves tied around their necks. Aadil came over as the benches were being abandoned by the old men who scattered in different directions, none toward the food cart.

"Time to go," Aadil said. Walking single file, they passed back into the labyrinth of lanes and alleys that surrounded the town square. After switching back several times and catching no sight of anyone pursuing them, Addison began enjoying the intrigue of it all. Aadil stopped; Addison was sorry the excitement was over. He approached Aadil to find out what happened next. Aadil's jaw was set, his face somber. Following his gaze to the end of the alley Addison saw two men wearing checkered scarves heading towards them; each had a rifle pointing in their direction.

"Don't get behind," Aadil spat out, taking off faster than Addison thought the man could move. As they darted down side streets, the scarves seemed to guess their every move. Before they reached a cross street, they were cut off. Addison finally realized there were more than two men with rifles. *What's going on here?*

Aadil came to a dead stop. Trying to control his gasping breath he scanned three hundred and sixty degrees. No scarves came into view; his breathing started to return to normal.

The sound of a rifle bolt being slammed backward as a breech opened and a cartridge fed into a firing chamber assaulted their ears. The bolt closed with metallic certainty; Addison's stomach constricted.

"Move!" was all he heard. Addison took off at a dead run after Aadil. Elizabeth was just ahead, stumbling, tripping as she tried to run in her monstrous outfit. Addison came up behind Elizabeth and screamed, "Stop." He threw her over his shoulder, fireman style, struggling for balance. For once, Elizabeth kept her mouth shut. As he struggled to catch up, blood engorged his thighs as adrenaline granted the burst of strength needed.

His eyes scanned as he ran: two scarves, fifty feet, and closing. He wheeled to his right and went through the side yard of the nearest house.

A young child played outside. He rushed past the now screaming toddler as a three-foot fence attempted to deny his escape. He slammed into it, unable to lift Elizabeth over.

"Aadil," Addison screamed, arrested by the fence.

Turning, Aadil rushed back and grabbed Elizabeth like a rag doll. He tossed her on his shoulder and took off.

Right behind, Addison cleared the fence, then, turning back, grabbed Khalil's belt and the back of his shirt, helping him scramble over. Dodging their way through an adjoining yard strewn with tires and a rusted engine block oozing yellow-grey pus from multiple cracks, they charged through the unlocked backdoor. Frantic shouting attacked them as they continued through the tiny structure onto the street.

Aadil took a sharp left with Khalil and Addison right behind him. Nasir appeared, statue-like, flanked by one man on each side of him with rifles pointed their direction. Nasir lowered his rifle to Addison's chest staring directly into his eyes. All three mujahideen were wearing checkered scarves. Nasir's rifle motioned to a stone building at the end of the alley; Aadil headed for it. When he went inside, he was enveloped in darkness. Khalil and Addison followed. Nasir, staying outside, closed the door—the darkness became a shroud. Elizabeth slipped from Aadil's shoulder. Eyes were useless, none could see. Breathing was labored as each listened to the sounds of their new world. Gradually, their eyes began adjusting. What could be seen of the room, in distorted shadows, appeared bare.

What was . . . there? Were their ears playing tricks? A shuffling gait? None could be sure. "Is somebody . . ."

Addison's heart pounded, gaining volume with each beat, his breathing a whistling wind in his ears.

A solitary bulb faltered to life, weakly illuminating an anemic circle beneath it. Silhouettes of men holding rifles pointed at them registered in the gloom. Nuri al-Massalha's voice cut through the darkness. "I am pleased you could join us, Mr. Deverell. I have looked forward to this meeting, visa and passport infidel."

CHAPTER

31

Thursday 13 March 2008

Abu Dis, West Bank

Stripped of her burqa, Elizabeth slumped against the wall in the corner of the room, her eyes shut as she feigned sleep on the floor of her prison, a torn threadbare cotton blanket her covering.

Addison, under the oblivious guard of Aadil and Khalil, was trussed in a side room where a game of cards kept his keepers amused, more Khalil, ahead at the moment, than Aadil.

Nasir, having left to ensure final transportation to al-Ubeidiya, promised to return within the hour.

Looking toward Elizabeth, one of the armed guards, Mudawar, turned to his companion, Rafiq, and said, "Now watch a man."

"You stay away from the woman," Rafiq said. "Remember what Nuri—"

"Nuri's not here," Mudawar said, swaggering his way across the room, feral eyes fixed on his prey. "Get up, Jew." Elizabeth struggled to stand, hands bound in front, unyielding flex-cuffs constraining movement. Angrily, Mudawar yanked his quarry to her feet, her blanket bunching on the floor next to her burqa. The edges of her cuffs cut into sore wrists as the predator's scent radiated from him. Wincing, Elizabeth remained silent, eyes cast down.

Jerking his knife from its leather sheath, Mudawar cut through the center binding of the restraints, uncoupling her hands.

Slowly, barely touching the cloth, he ran the razor-edged tip of his seven inch blade over her left breast, pausing at the top button of her cotton blouse. Making a flicking motion, he freed it from its material. The blade traced a line to the next button; a flick of his wrist sent another button to the floor. Proceeding down the blouse, each button fell prey to his sharp blade while the room surrendered to primal lust. From the back, a voice trembled, "Next."

Leering, Mudawar grabbed the middle of Elizabeth's now uncovered bra, severing its halves. Fabric barely covered breasts every mujahideen eye lusted to see. Returning his knife to its sheath, he inserted it part way then pulled it out, then back in again. Mudawar's pupils dilated as his breathing exploded in staccato bursts. Elizabeth continued looking down, refusing to acknowledge the moment. Grabbing her hair, Mudawar jerked her head backward, forcing her to look at him. Elizabeth's eyes remained down, silence her only defense. Pulling his hand back, Mudawar released its power viciously slapping her. Elizabeth's head shot backward, hitting the wall. A moan escaped.

In the next room, Aadil, aroused from his game, paused . . . listening.

"Your turn, play card from pile or draw," said Khalil.

"You hear?"

"What's to hear?"

"Sounded like Elizabeth."

"Elizabeth has strong voice, she calls we hear. Now play card so I can finish beating you."

Grabbing Elizabeth, Mudawar wrestled her to the floor, yanking at her skirt. She fought to land a knee in his groin. He savagely smashed her nose, blood spurted. Elizabeth screamed.

Aadil's head shot up. "That's Elizabeth," he said, jumping from the crate he was sitting on. Khalil followed. Rushing into the next room, they saw Mudawar on top of Elizabeth, blood spattered on them both. She fought savagely, breaking nails as she raked them across Mudawar's face. Drawing back, he smashed his fist into her face, knocking her backwards. More blood flew.

Aadil covered the distance between them in five steps. His hand came crashing down, encircling Mudawar's neck, he yanked—hard. Mudawar flew across the room, missing mujahideen as they scrambled out of the way. Crumpling to the floor, his right leg jerked spasmodically, his neck at an ugly angle, gurgling sounds trickling from his throat.

Mujahideen eyes looked dazed, wondering who the enemy was.

Taking Elizabeth's blanket, Aadil ripped it in thirds. He bent over her, trying to stem the flow of blood, "Khalil, water."

Half filling a bucket with cold water from a utility sink, Khalil set it down by Elizabeth.

Aadil plunged the remnant of the bloody blanket into the water, rinsing it, then went back to dabbing her face.

Khalil took a remnant and spread it over Elizabeth's nakedness as best he could.

Alternating pressure to stem the flow of blood from her broken nose, Aadil continued patting the blood from Elizabeth's battered face, rinsing then re-rinsing the cloth in the scarlet water as the bleeding started to clot. Turning to Khalil, he said, "Check on Addison."

Khalil went to the prisoner.

Mudawar's gurgling stopped along with the shallow rising and falling of his chest. Rafiq, on his knees beside his friend, continued beseeching Allāh the Merciful for Mudawar's life as his struggle ended with one last frail breath. Watching Khalil leave, Rafiq fastened his eyes on the murderer. Mujahideen warriors do not kill mujahideen warriors. If the Jew was raped, what was that compared to rape suffered over a lifetime from the Jews? Their calling was to end the violence of Jews, and now his friend, with whom he had struggled together against infidels, was murdered by a brother. *How does such a thing happen? For a stinking Jew? This will not stand. This will not wait for Nuri.* Rising, he looked down at his friend and drew his Tokarev from its holster. He pulled back the slide then released it, chambering a round.

On his knees, Aadil continued to pat Elizabeth's face with the cool water, not knowing what else to do. "Never to be this way," he muttered. "Just protect then reward to live in peace with family."

He did not hear the Tokarev's round being chambered. He did not hear it explode as the bullet leapt from the pistol into his arm. One moment he was tending Elizabeth's swelling face, the next his arm jerked violently to the side, causing him to lose balance, nearly crushing Elizabeth as he fell. He stared as blood drenched his arm, its cause not registering. Then pain—searing, burning pain—from the bullet punching its way through his bicep, splitting his humerus before exiting through his quivering triceps.

The crack of the pistol's discharge echoed through the side room. Fear invaded Khalil's heart. Somehow, he knew, Mudawar had evened the score with Aadil. Running back to the main room, he saw Aadil on the floor, arm spurting blood. Looking across from him, he saw Rafiq standing by Mudawar, who was lying motionless. Rafiq's weapon pointed at Aadil. Khalil heard the gun . . . click—misfire.

Rafiq fumbled with his pistol's magazine, wrenching it from the gun and dropping it to the floor. As Rafiq reached for another magazine, Khalil looked for something—anything. Propped against the wall, he spotted two Kalashnikovs fifteen feet away, his only hope. Sprinting to the rifles, Khalil had one in his hands before anyone made a move to stop him. Locating the safety, he flipped it up and chambered a round. Khalil screamed, "DO NOT DO THIS!"

Pulling a magazine from his belt, Rafiq slammed it into the Tokarev. He chambered a round.

"My brother, do not hurt my friend," Khalil shouted.

"Mine is dead at his hand—"

"Nasir does not want—"

"Nasir wants? Mudawar's dead . . . for a Jew?" Lifting the pistol, he took aim on Aadil, who was lost in shock.

Lifting the rifle to his side, Khalil pointed the barrel at Rafiq—he started shaking.

Rafiq crushed the trigger. A bullet ricocheted off the floor, missing its mark. A second found the side of Elizabeth's thigh, grazing it. A whimper made its way through her lips.

Taking a step forward, Rafiq took aim again.

"No!"Khalil screamed. Slamming his eyes shut, he squeezed the trigger. The AK47 smashed against his rib cage; he shrieked in pain. The rifle heaved as bullets spewed from its mouth. The first three found their mark; Rafiq's body shuddered under their impact. Entering his abdominal wall, they tore through his abdominal aorta, splitting it open. Missing his left and right kidneys, they slowed infinitesimally as they raced to his spinal column, shattering the third and fourth vertebrae before continuing their carnage—severing his spinal cord—before bursting out his back, taking muscle, bone, and skin with them. Paralyzed, Rafiq's legs collapsed, driving him to the unforgiving stone floor. Blood filled his abdominal cavity as Rafiq raced from consciousness to death.

Panic stormed through the mujahideen. Fear stole every mind as duty was abandoned in a frenzied race for survival.

Then silence claimed the room as Elizabeth, Khalil, and Aadil were lost in pain and confusion.

Khalil struggled toward his friend. "You're bleeding."

"First Elizabeth."

Elizabeth's slowly coagulating blood flowed from her broken nose past her concave cheek and off her chin as she forced shallow breaths through her mouth.

"Elizabeth, you can breathe?"

Looking toward Khalil, she faintly nodded.

Khalil lifted the bloody bucket to get fresh water for Aadil. He screamed in agony. "Aadil, you lift bucket, side burns like knives stabbing from stupid rifle."

As he staggered to his feet, waves of nausea washed over Aadil. Grasping the bucket handle with his good hand, he lifted, surprised by its weight as he forced himself to take one step after another to the sink. Slowly placing the bucket on the sink's lip, he grasped its edge and emptied the bloody water into the sink. He rinsed the blood he could with one hand then filled the bucket before making the exhausting journey back to Elizabeth and setting the water by her side. "Elizabeth, I need help," Aadil said, handing her the blanket. "Wring out cloth."

Elizabeth handed the wrung-out remnant to Khalil. He turned to Aadil.

"No, Elizabeth first."

Khalil carefully wiped Elizabeth's face, then her leg. He rinsed the cloth in the water, and Elizabeth again wrung it out. He wrapped her thigh with a remnant, tucking its end in on itself. "Bullet grazed leg, cloth protects," Khalil said.

"No bullet in my leg?" Elizabeth said, her voice nasal, stopped up. Khalil smiled.

"Is something funny?"

"Voice not yours."

"Maybe I should break your nose so we talk alike?"

"Aadil needs looking at," Khalil said. He turned and began checking Aadil. "Hurting?"

"Throbbing," Aadil said.

"Bone sticks from arm; you need doctor."

Taking the remaining piece of the blanket, Khalil washed the edges of the wound then tore the cloth into three pieces, screaming after each tear. He folded two pieces, placing them on each end of Aadil's wound, and then wrapped the third piece around them tucking it underneath the makeshift bandage. "Don't move arm, it doesn't look good."

"It feels like it looks, we need to go before others return," Aadil said.

"Can't rush, ribs feels like a blade stabbing every time I move."

Going over to Mudawar, Khalil relieved him of his knife and sheath, shoving them into his boot top.

"What is with visiting? You forget we need to go?"

"I'm thinking here."

"Think faster."

Elizabeth struggled to her feet. Nose raw, cheek throbbing, leg and fingers sore. She slipped on her burqa, keeping the dense fabric from her face.

"Time to go," Aadil said.

"Forgetting someone?" Elizabeth asked.

Khalil and Aadil glanced at each other then around the room, a puzzled look on their faces.

"Addison?" Elizabeth said.

"Addison," both Khalil and Aadil said at the same time. Aadil beat Khalil, nursing his ribs, to the side room. Looking up at them from the floor, Addison attempted to speak though the gag in his mouth. Elizabeth limped into the room. Together, they cut his bindings.

"Where are we going?" Elizabeth asked.

"Wait, I realize you believe in your god," Addison said, "and whatever happens is all good, but I seem to be missing something. You're asking these two for directions? Or did it just appear they led us into this? And I paid them each fifty bucks. Does it take a hundred to avoid being hog-tied by maniacal terrorists on the tour?"

"It wasn't supposed to go like this, only to protect you. Much to say, but if we hang around we may not finish. Friends will be back and I think they won't be happy with Khalil and me," Aadil said.

"You want to strike out alone," Elizabeth said, "your call, America, but we need to move or some bad things will happen. No one knows Abu Dis like Khalil and Aadil. Besides, in case you didn't notice, they're about to be pretty high on PMIJ's wanted list, so I choose to trust them. Where to, guys?"

"Medical center, doctor friend is there," Aadil said.

"What about weapons, Aadil?" Khalil said

"They cause too much harm. Not for us, Khalil."

They limped toward freedom.

CHAPTER

32

Early March 2008

Wilsonville, Oregon

In the days following the dinner, Rebecca kept in close contact with Janelle. The passage of time assured her the customary rhythm and flow that had served mother and daughter for so many years had not been abandoned. Rebecca returned to her Garden Society and pinochle soirées, while Janelle's days were expended on the endless demands of the Wilsonville School District. Nights and weekends were consumed with the letters and cards Tatyana brought into her life. The music box linked her to a time and place she could neither escape nor understand. The letters opened a door to a world that bade her enter but provided no passage from words on paper to the lives unveiled in those words. Janelle sent inquiries to the Bordeaux Adoption Services in Paris and the SSR Politick Adoption Medical Services in Moscow; neither responded. By her third letter she realized no one ever would.

Methodically, painstakingly, she pieced together the chronology of letters and cards that came, always, from Liba until 1972. In February of that year, letters from her mother stopped. She guessed why, but it took a private detective to confirm that Liba had died in an automobile accident. The irony was not lost on Janelle. She felt the loss even though she was bereft of any memory of this woman or even her place in this stranger's world, save letters, cards, and a solitary music box.

In 1972, her brother Tevel had started writing. Masculine logic pervaded his words to a sister he would, he seemed to understand, never see. It seemed difficult, writing to a sister scarcely remembered. Gradually, Tevel's letters became more eloquent, manifesting his growing education as he followed their father into medicine. *Not bad for a family the government tried to destroy.*

Picking up a letter dated Friday, 12 September 1980, Janelle read: "Dearest Shayndel: This letter finds me ready to leave the only home I have ever known. A Christian ministry is helping me to emigrate from Russia to Yisra'el. They have worked on my aliyah for two years. I received word from Moscow yesterday that my return to our ancient homeland has been approved. I must be ready to leave on Monday the 15th. Though the authorities are letting me go, they make things hard with so little time to make arrangements for such a move. What they do not understand is that I have been ready for this trip all my life. Can you see the smile that covers my face? At the clinic where I work, other doctors agreed to take my patients. Many good people live in this the country of my birth in spite of the few who embrace hatred. Goodness lives in their hearts even with no way for them to understand what goes through a Jewish soul returning to a land longed for all of life.

"I will deliver this letter to Dom Rebyonka in the morning, but in going to my homeland, I do not know if I will be allowed to come back, and the authorities at Dom Rebyonka will not accept a letter that is mailed, again with the hardness of heart.

"I want you know I love you and pray my words and those of mama will reach you. Pápa could never write, though he tried many times. His love was too deep to put on paper. He ended up pouring out his soul before God to release all that was in his heart.

"Somehow, even if authorities do not allow me back into country, I will get letters to Dom Rebyonka. Maybe there's not much to say, but letters keep you alive in my heart. Sometimes I wonder if you are real, if memories were part of a dream, but then I remember mama, she knew, she knew. I will find ways to write and someday, merciful God willing, we will be looking upon each other's face. Words grow heavy now, so I must close, but my love for you remains forever. With kindest regards, your brother, Tevel."

Janelle placed the letter on the table, wondering what these words that may have cost Tatyana her life, would change. Who could she speak to of this? What would she say?

A detective agency she hired to search Israel for Tevel closed the barely open door that separated her from a family. The report came back: 'No doctor named Tevel Yochanan is licensed in Israel. We have investigated all official licensing records. With additional funding, an Israeli investigator could be contracted. Please advise.' She could not bring herself to search for the grave of a brother she never knew; it would shut a door she could not close.

Finally, Janelle placed each letter and card in their respective boxes and put the boxes in her closet. A heart with nowhere to go can only bear so much. The demands of life forced her attention from these strangers she ached to embrace. Sorrow of what might have been remained, but life makes its own demands. She stopped going to the closet.

CHAPTER

33

Thursday 13 March 2008

Abu Dis, West Bank

Alarm pervaded every molecule of air as Aadil led their way through narrow lanes past shops once familiar, now ominous, foreboding.

At last, the familiar green and yellow sign on the compound wall appeared—Al-Arab Medical Center. The gate was locked. The gate was never locked. Khalil pressed the buzzer—they waited. Their plan was to get back through the separation wall to al-Quds, but first they needed help. No one answered. Khalil buzzed again . . . silence. He laid into the number 5 button, not ready to give up.

An irritated voice startled him just when he was about to give up.

"What is all this buzzing?" the gate's speaker asked.

"Basimah, is that you?" said Khalil.

"This is Alzena. Basimah isn't here. Who is buzzing during lunchtime?"

"Medical clinic now closes for lunch? I'm Khalil Ahmad. I come with friends. We need to see Dr. Tahsin."

"What do you want with doctor?"

"This is a medical clinic, we have injuries, and we need help, let us in."

"Must check first."

"I have money."

"You have money—for Alzena?" The gate buzzed open. They walked across the compound to the main door. The waiting room was empty. This wasn't good; it always overflowed with patients waiting to be seen. A short stout woman, barely visible behind the counter, eyed the group. Spotting the American, she fled to the back without waiting for her payoff. Within seconds, Dr. Abir Tahsin approached the counter. "Aadil, what in the world?" she said, looking at Aadil's bandaged arm.

"Friends decide they're not friends," Khalil said. "My ribs hurt and Elizabeth has broken nose."

"What about the American trying to dress like what? A Palestinian?"

"Not hurt."

"Figures, follow me." She headed toward the back. Alzena stayed near the counter, "You too Alzena."

Going to a closed door, the doctor pushed it open. "Everyone in here." When Alzena got to the door, the doctor whispered in her ear. Alzena headed back to the front. "Khalil, prop yourself against the wall until I can look at you. If your ribs are bruised or broken, trying to sit wouldn't be fun. Everyone but Aadil find a seat. On the exam table, big guy. Now, what happened?"

Aadil and Khalil both started talking.

"Stop, Aadil speak first."

For the next five minutes Aadil then Khalil filled in the basics of their injuries while the doctor cut the crude bandages off Aadil, treating his wound as she listened.

"Aadil, I've disinfected your arm so it shouldn't turn gangrenous, get infected. The bullet went through your arm but shattered your humerus; it needs to be surgically set in a hospital."

"Humerus?"

"The largest bone in your arm. Considering it's protruding through your skin and I don't have the facilities or training to operate, X-Rays would be useless. Move it wrong, bump it, and you could sever your brachial artery, basilic, or cephalic vein—those are the big veins carrying blood in your arm."

"Is it bad?" Aadil said.

"Beyond bad, Al-Makassed has a good orthopedic department, but getting there, I would imagine, is the problem." Proceeding to the cabinet, she said, "I'm going to bandage your arm and put it in a sling. Then I want you to leave it alone. If circumstances demand, remove the sling from your arm, not your arm from the sling. The less you move your arm, the better the chance you'll use it again."

"Why would I move it? Break is bad."

"PMIJ is out in force, and from what I've heard, you four are the reason. Size alone makes you stick out, Aadil. Add a broken arm in a sling; you're a walking neon sign.

"We have to get back to al-Quds. Our friend—"

"No, only information on your injuries, that way I don't have to include anything else in the daily report. I'm likely going to have visitors anyway." Dr. Tahsin finished taping Aadil's arm and secured it in a sling after giving him an injection to relieve pain.

"Now, Khalil, let's see how things look with you."

"Ribs hurt, doc," Khalil said.

Dr. Tahsin gently inspected his ribs, lightly pushing on them. Khalil's guttural moans reverberated through his closed mouth.

Going to the door, Dr. Tahsin opened it and shouted, "Shafiq, bring a wheelchair." Within seconds, a wheelchair could be heard approaching while whistling bounced off the tile floors and concrete block walls.

Pushing the wheelchair into the room, its young driver said, "Who's my victim?"

"This one's not a race. Ribs may be fractured, so nice and easy on your way to X-Ray, Shafiq," Dr. Tahsin said.

"Doc, it's always nice and easy. Can't help it I'm young and fast."

"Ease into the chair, Khalil. Don't help, Shafiq. Khalil needs to lower himself." After three groans, two moans, and one scream, Khalil was on his way to X-Ray.

Glancing over at the American and Aadil, Dr. Tahsin said, "Face the wall. I need to examine Elizabeth."

"Doctor wants us to face the wall," Aadil said in English. "Elizabeth needs to be examined."

Turning to Elizabeth, Dr. Tahsin said, "Let me help you out of that." Together they lifted the burqa. "Someone didn't like you. Here, let's get you seated on the exam table."

"Tried to rape me, Aadil left him—"

"I can't know, dear. Whatever you tell me I have to report, and I don't think that's what you want," Abir Tahsin said, sadness filling her face. "At least we have extra clothing."

The door flew open and Alzena motioned from the doorway. "Excuse me for a moment," Dr. Tahsin said. Alzena spoke in a hushed tone. After receiving instructions, Alzena left, closing the door after her. Dr. Tahsin locked it. Turning to the American and Aadil, she said, "Come with me, make no sound." Going out a back exit, Addison followed Aadil. Dr. Tahsin returned within two minutes.

Elizabeth looked at her with alarm. "It's taken care of, don't be afraid. But we must finish. I fear others will come for a thorough search. That was just someone known to collaborate with the PMIJ hoping for a discovery that would bring a reward. He has been turned away—so few want to risk infectious disease—but others will come." After examining and cleaning Elizabeth's face, Dr. Tahsin placed her hands on each side of her nose. "Your cheekbones and nose are broken. I can handle your nose but your cheekbones will require surgery. This is going to hurt . . . a lot. You ready?"

"Nothing for pain?"

"Can't wait for it to take effect."

Taking a deep breath, Elizabeth nodded. Blinding pain staggered her. She felt herself falling, losing consciousness, as spots danced in and out of her vision. The acrid smell of ammonia hammered her nostrils, bringing her back to awareness of Dr. Tahsin holding her up. Both sides of her nose throbbed with unimaginable intensity. Something cool swabbed her arm as the odor of alcohol made its way to her battered nostrils.

"This will help," Dr. Tahsin said.

Elizabeth felt a sting when the needle for the analgesic injection entered her arm.

"There will be some dizziness, but the pain should be manageable enough to travel. Now, let's look at that leg," Dr. Tahsin said, cutting the bandage off. "You're fortunate the wound is superficial." Cutting a length of gauze, she soaked it in warm water, and after squirting antibacterial soap on it, she washed the wound, rinsing it with additional water-soaked gauze. Grabbing a plastic bottle of povidone-iodine, Dr. Tahsin squeezed it over the wound, tinting the skin reddish-orange as she used the gauze to confine the antiseptic to the wound. Opening a cabinet drawer, she pulled out sterile gauze and adhesive tape and had it on Elizabeth's leg within seconds. "What's next?"

"Fingers?" Elizabeth said.

"Examined them when you lost consciousness," Dr. Tahsin said, "three nails are broken below the quick on your right hand, two on your left. They will be sore for awhile, but they'll heal."

Walking to a cabinet, she unlocked a door and retrieved a large bottle with elongated pink pills. She took a small brown plastic bottle from a nearby shelf and filled it from the larger bottle. "Here," she said, handing Elizabeth the pills, "these will help. Don't take more than one every eight hours unless the pain becomes unbearable. It's vicodin. Might leave you constipated, but that's the least of your worries. There's enough for you and Aadil. There's none for Khalil, he needs to remain aware of his ribs, or he could further injure them." Putting the large bottle on the shelf she locked the cabinet, went to a chest of drawers and opening the bottom drawer, pulled out a blouse and a skirt. "Try these. Might look frumpy, but there's no blood on them. Now, let's get you in them then back in your burqa."

Three minutes later Shafiq entered with Khalil in the wheelchair. An oversized envelope was on Khalil's lap. Shafiq handed it to the doctor. Switching on the X-Ray viewbox, she extracted the film and pushed it under the clip. "Shafiq, would you go the back way into hydrotherapy. Inside the auxiliary storage room, you'll find two patients. Please escort them back here." Turning to the X-Rays, she studied them carefully. "Khalil, you have fractured ribs."

"How many?"

"Lower two, maybe three, right side."

"So fractured means broken?"

"That it does."

"I get cast and friends sign it."

"Afraid not."

"No cast?"

"Nope."

"But I have broken bones and everyone knows when bones are broken a cast is given."

"Not with ribs."

"Why not with ribs? How will anyone know I suffer injury?"

"May not want them to. When you were in X-Ray, someone came snooping to see if any of you had been here. Advertising your injury could prove unwise. I'll tape your side to help immobilize the ribs. Other than being careful, no pulling, no strain on them, there's not much else to do. You'll heal in time but hurt till you do."

"Then pain medicine. You have something for pain?"

"Nope."

"What is nope? You want Khalil to suffer?"

"Pretty much, if I give you pain pills you could further injure your ribs. With active pain receptors you'll treat those ribs like a long lost relative with money."

"All my relatives want money from me."

"And don't laugh, perform a pulling motion, or stress your ribs. If it's any comfort, should you get in a tense situation, the adrenal glands produce hormones that will give you a boost in energy and keep your mind off the pain . . . at first."

Shafiq entered the room with Aadil and Addison in tow.

"Hey, Aadil, I got broken bones. What you think of that?"

"I think you all need to get away before the PMIJ shows up," Dr. Tahsin said.

"Doctor, will you be okay?" Elizabeth said.

"Our work is to heal whoever comes. I don't know what you've gotten into, but there are many good souls here. No one will say words that will close this clinic; we have too much need. Blessings upon you for asking. Shafiq, look out the back and if it's clear, show them the way out of the compound. Remember, Aadil, your arm needs surgery or you may lose the use of it."

"One question doc."

"What's that, Khalil?"

"Why was clinic locked during day, no patients waiting?"

"Ask the PMIJ. Two mujahideen came by earlier with orders to lock the gate."

"You're a good type person."

"I try."

Following Shafiq to the compound's wall, the shipmates were set adrift from their temporary mooring.

Keeping to the shadows, they pushed their way through unmarked back roads where few were out in the waning afternoon. Aadil knew shelter must be found before dark or there would be no escape. This night, PMIJ would be out in force.

"Anyone know where we're going?" Khalil said.

"Friends with store are close," Elizabeth said.

"And they'll risk being caught?" Addison said.

"Friends are Christian. Brother and sister. No Muslim is going to risk being caught by the PMIJ; a Christian might," Elizabeth said.

"Who is this Christian who would risk life for American and us?" Aadil said.

"The grocer, Sammon, and his sister, Salwa."

"I know this grocer. He used to give us work before Aadil and me became so popular with jobs from Nasir."

On the lookout for PMIJ, Khalil took the lead through the backstreets as they made their way to the grocer.

"You there," came a loud voice behind them. Everyone stopped. They surveyed the area; it looked deserted. "Addison, disappear," Aadil whispered. Addison bolted behind a stack of wooden crates twenty feet distant, crouching down.

Changing direction, the other three began walking away from the crates.

"I said stop," the voice yelled. Everyone stopped—again, searching for the disembodied voice. From a side alley, two men, canes in hand, hurried up the street toward them.

"*Mutaween,*" Khalil murmured.

"What is woman's name?" one of the men asked.

"Her name Jamiliah," Khalil said.

"Is your wife?"

"No."

"Sister?"

"No."

"What about you?" he said, turning to Aadil.

Aadil stared, his breathing low and controlled every sense alive.

"Is she wife or sister? This question is simple."

"No."

Turning to Elizabeth, the man said, "Your burqa is pleasing, but you know the commands of being in public without someone proper." Drawing his cane over his head, he brought it down on Elizabeth's back: THWACK!

"Are there no words, no cry from a whore that comes in public with those she is not related to? Where are you from, tramp?"

In perfect Arabic, Elizabeth said, "RamAllāh." She fought to control her breathing as pain shot through her, each breath stabbing into her face, her back now inflamed. The pain's shock tempered a response that could have exposed her to these cleric police.

"Who is your father, so this disgrace can be reported?"

"Father's name is Hakimi. Asliraf Hakimi."

"I have heard this name. What is your father's business in RamAllāh?"

"He is Vice-Minister of Planning for Palestine."

"Your family is Hakimi?" the second religious policeman said.

"Na'am, yes, and father will be troubled when he learns a secret mission entrusted to his daughter and two faithful servants has resulted in my being caned and accused with such vile words."

"Your father sends a servant whose arm is injured?"

"The injury is recent and mission important, such is loyalty."

"We are mutaween and our loyalty is before Allāh to seek out those who do not act in accordance with decency and the holy *Qur'an*."

"Do not the prophet's words speak to knowledge before action?"

"My friend is zealous," said the second policeman. "Infidels influence our young, so we must be vigilant. Please understand we sought the right. Go with our blessings and wishes for great peace."

Turning to Khalil and Aadil, Elizabeth said, "Let us be about father's business." Elizabeth fell into line just behind them as the three began walking away.

Watching from the crates, Addison wondered what all the fuss was about as the lunatics with canes hurried away in the opposite direction, talking feverishly in a high-pitched squeal he couldn't understand.

When the men were out of sight, Addison, deciding to skip questions, rejoined his companions. They resumed their journey, keeping alert for more than PMIJ.

Arriving at the store, they found it locked. As they walked its perimeter in the fading light, nothing moved inside the crude stone structure. A few groceries sat enticingly inside the walled-off front of the shop, calling to stomachs that had not eaten for too long. Going to the back door, Khalil pulled out a loose stone. Reaching into the stone's cavity, his searching fingers found a key. When he inserted it into the back door's padlock, it snapped open. Khalil returned the key and stone, then they went in.

Shutting the door, Aadil slid the bolt closed. He glanced over the room. "We need to know what's here. Everyone look."

The three men searched while Elizabeth removed her burqa, dropping it by the wall. "Find anything good?" she asked when they finished scouring the room

"Three fifty-pound sacks of grain along with a couple sacks of chicken feed," Aadil said

"Found a couple cans of beans," Khalil said. "Cans are bulging on top."

"What did you find, Addison?" Elizabeth said.

"We got water. There's a sink and toilet in the corner.

"Sometimes food in a can bulges but it's still good. Let me see," Addison said.

Khalil handed him the can of beans.

"Doesn't look so bad."

"Can't know until we open it," Khalil said. "Where is the opener?"

"We don't have opener," Aadil said. "We find grain, food for chicken, and cans, but no opener."

"Khalil has a knife," Addison said.

"Where'd you get knife, Khalil?" Aadil said.

"Borrowed it from Mudawar, he didn't object." Setting a can on the floor he took the knife from its sheath, bringing the blade tip down on the top of the can. Pain pierced his side as the knife bounced off the can. Khalil dropped the knife on the floor beside the can. "Aadil?"

"I can't hold can and open it."

"Oh yeah, your arm."

"Let me have it," Addison said. "I'm the only healthy one here."

Grabbing the knife, he positioned the can on the floor. He pushed the tip down on the top of the can . . . nothing. "Guess your cans are a little thicker than in the States." He lifted the knife six inches and brought it down—it bounced off. "Okay, you little punk." Lifting the blade to his shoulder, he slammed it into the can. Slimy green and black pieces of beans exploded, bathing his face, neck and chest, the putrefying stench was noxious. Addison began gagging. Jumping up, he ran to the utility sink, turned on the water, and placed his head under the faucet, spitting out pieces of rotten beans that had made their way into his mouth.

After a couple of minutes, Elizabeth walked over to the sink. "Here," she said, picking up a box of soap from the floor under the sink and sprinkling a few granules on his hair. "Now scrub. I'll look for a towel. If not, use the burqa to dry."

Returning in a few minutes, she announced her find. "Found some towels near the door to the front. Let's see how you look."

Addison lifted his head. Water cascaded down his shirt; he was cleaner than he'd been in days.

"Here, dry yourself," she said, handing him a towel.

The smell of lye rose from the soap residue, but it was better than decomposing beans. Removing the towel from his head, Addison sniffed the air. "The stench is still here."

Khalil pointed to the exploded can still lying on the floor in a puddle of blackened goo.

"Great, now I get to clean that."

"You made the mess. Besides, we're all injured."

Addison took the lye-soaked towel and an empty plastic pickle bucket Elizabeth found and filled it with soapy water. Then he set about cleaning the splattered bean slime. Ten minutes later, he finished soaping and rinsing the rough plank floor. The smell of lye pervaded the room.

"I'm hungry," Khalil announced.

"We're all hungry," Aadil said.

"I'm not," Addison said.

"You already had beans," Khalil said.

"Addison, see if door to the front opens," Aadil said.

Turning the knob, Addison could hear it opening, but a keyed deadbolt kept the heavy door from budging. "Don't suppose we have a key?"

No one spoke.

"Let's see if we can get some rest. We can't chance being seen outside," Elizabeth said. "In the morning, Sammon and Salwa will be here."

Addison arranged the sacks of grain and feed into mattresses. Towels served as blankets while Elizabeth's burqa kept her warm. *Not the Intercontinental David,* he thought, *but better than trying to sleep on floor planks.*

The night crawled by, each sound threatening discovery. Sunrise broke through the room's solitary window on troubled restless dreams.

"Where is Sammon?" Khalil said. "Business cannot be run like this."

"Patience," Elizabeth said.

Hours passed, but sounds of commerce remained absent. Outside, all was still with the exception of solitary travelers passing.

"Something is wrong for friend not to open business," Aadil said.

"I heard few pass the shop last night, but with shopkeepers at home what else is to be expected," Khalil said.

"This is just one shop of many but there are no sounds of others at their business," Elizabeth said. "We'll just have to wait here it's too dangerous outside."

"Since we have to wait Addison, I have a question," Khalil said.

"And I have a question for you: Who was chasing me and why?"

Khalil glanced from Addison to Aadil. "Why would you be chased?"

"They knew my name, Khalil."

"Many do not like Americans, and to find you in their city—"

"Khalil, the jihad leader not only intercepted us but herded us into a specific building."

"We were there and chased as well."

"They were waiting for me, and if not for your injuries I'd be asking questions that have been going through my mind since we escaped. Like how I ended up hog-tied while you and Aadil played cards. And, even with your injuries, was it me or Elizabeth who caused you to act, which ended up in our being here?"

Khalil scrambled to get the conversation to a safer place. "You asked who is chasing us, but if it was you alone that was being chased, American, we would have slept in our own beds this past night while you would have remained captured. Only Palestine Mujahideen Islamic Jihad wears black and white checkered scarves we saw on those chasing us."

"Okay, I'll accept PMIJ was after me, but in State Department training—you've heard of the United States Department of State with millions of dollars in intelligence assets—I was told PMIJ controlled Gaza and PALFA the West Bank, and that both groups are fighting for sole power. Unless I read the map wrong, Abu Dis is not in Gaza."

"Is it too late to get your money for training back?" Khalil said.

"You telling me there isn't conflict between the two groups?"

"They would kill each other for the power to rule all of Palestine."

"So how can PMIJ be in the West Bank with PALFA?"

"Addison," Khalil began, warming to his subject, "each group is in control of different areas, this you have right, but PALFA takes money from America and Western nations. Money has its own demands, and peace with Israel is the demand no true Muslim can accept. PALFA was forced to declare that peace with Israel was their goal when speaking to those giving money. When interviewed by the Arab press, they promise to drive the Jews into the sea. PMIJ's money comes from Muslim nations. I don't know which ones, but their demands concerning Israel never mention peace. The result of each side's choice is PMIJ has more support from the people while PALFA looks to the West for more money and weapons, sometimes to use on its own people. The Palestinian Freedom Army controls much of the West Bank, but Abu Dis is an area where PMIJ has great support. Many PALFA soldiers agree with the PMIJ and so overlook their presence. Neither side wants a fight until the time is right, but on that day brothers will find who is stronger as more of my people die, which is a reason Aadil and I agreed to escort you, so our families can live in peace."

Addison turned Khalil's words—*agreed to escort you, so our families can live in peace*—over in his mind. He wasn't ready for the conversation he knew must come when he had gleaned more information, so for now he kept his silence.

"None of this helps us today. If Sammon isn't coming, we have to make our way to al-Quds. So what are our options? I mean, it's not like it's *Yawm al-Jumu'ah*, with many in the mosque," Aadil said.

"What's Yawm al-Jumu'ah?" Addison asked.

"Friday, you say Friday? Let's see, yesterday was? Was yesterday Thursday?"

"Nam, yesterday was Thursday," Khalil said.

"So today is Friday," Aadil said.

"It's Day of Assembly. Everyone knows that," Khalil said.

"I still don't know what you're talking about," Addison said.

"Assembly, like everyone gathers in church and no one works," Elizabeth said.

"Wouldn't know about that."

"Christians go to church, we go to mosque," Aadil said.

"Great, so your friend is not coming and we have another day to enjoy his hospitality," Addison said, heading back to his grain mattress. The air turned sour.

The morning passed into afternoon. Each of them understood venturing outside for food would end in capture.

By mid-afternoon Addison couldn't withhold the questions that plagued him any longer. He walked over to Aadil and sat down on a crate. "I have a question for you and your sidekick."

"What is sidekick?"

"Never mind, why did you take me hostage?"

The question pulled Elizabeth from prayer.

"We didn't take you hostage," Aadil said as he glanced at Khalil then returned his gaze to Addison. "We protected you. Things didn't work out like they were supposed to."

"How did your actions protect me?"

"All of life I'm strong, but never good with books and learning. Relatives all depend on me and Khalil to bring food, pay for needed items. Good jobs go to those with degrees, those who know people. All we know is hard work and family, but we never ask for help. Many times border is closed because some of our people don't want Jews in Palestine. I only want to work, and every day must hustle for different jobs so family doesn't go hungry. Friend from long ago days showed up and helped in finding work. More money than we ever saw for what a child could do, but money buys things family needs so we go on with work that is no work from friend."

"What's all this got to do with me?"

"Friend tells Khalil and me of plan to make money for family. That by protecting important American, much money would be paid for help. Everyone knows America is rich beyond words, and money to protect American would provide for Khalil and me to live in Syria for the rest of our lives away from everyday trouble."

"Wait, how did Syria get into this?"

"Outside of Aleppo Syria is a village, a nice village, away from danger. There is heat, running water inside, and yard for children to play. Friend from childhood days says if we help him, one home would be for Khalil's family and one for mine, with money to live on the rest of our lives. I have seen violence for a lifetime, and just want to live in peace." Aadil's eyes held the sadness of his world as he started rocking back and forth. "I never meant for you to become a prisoner, or Elizabeth to be hurt. Is shame of life that friend harmed because of me. Elizabeth, I know you say your god gives forgiveness, but how do I forgive such a thing?"

Elizabeth's shoulders slumped as tears trickled down her swollen, bruised face.

"Remember how I tried to talk you out of going to Abu Dis? I'm Arab. I said, talk with me, with Khalil, but you wanted to go into Abu Dis anyway because we're not Arabs with voices you wanted to hear. Americans don't listen. Khalil and I were told, by childhood friend, if we protect you then reward would come our way, but friend disappeared when evil happened and now we are hunted."

Walking over, Elizabeth wrapped her arms around Aadil's oversized head. No words came as she stood cradling his head. Floodgates opened as Aadil bathed Elizabeth's arms with deep, racking, sobs.

Addison stared at the floor, wondering if he could trust those who held his life in their power. Getting up, he turned and walked to his makeshift bed and lay down, back to the room, knowing sleep wouldn't come. Maybe, though, somehow he could figure a way out of this mess.

~

The setting sun attempted to break through the dirt on the anemic window that bound the storage room to the world. Addison tired of chasing plans that couldn't work arose and joined the group. Sitting on a crate, he looked at Khalil. "Earlier you mentioned a question."

"What is reason to talk with Palestinians in Abu Dis?"

"How do I tell you so you'll understand?"

"Words are nice."

"Sometimes yes, sometimes no. In college I had a professor who brought life into his classes. Ancient history was juxtaposed—"

"Juxta what?"

"He tied the roots of current events to ancient history, showing their links. Professor Zared bridged ancient battles to modern political movements in the Middle East with a knowledge and love of history that lived and breathed. Over the years, I was privileged to attend his classes. His knowledge and passion set my course to follow in his footsteps. Each summer he led a different group of students to various parts of the Middle East to introduce them to the one area of the world he loved more than all others. I had to work summers so I couldn't make it my first three years in college, but I resolved, no matter what, to go the summer before my senior year. Back on campus the first week of fall semester for my junior year, I needed to get up to speed on what was happening at school so I logged onto the university magazine, *Flux*. Professor Zared's picture covered the screen under the magazine's banner. As I looked at his black and white photo, across the bottom, in bold letters, *In Memoriam* with a Star of David assaulted my eyes. I never knew he was Jewish. I clicked on the picture, and his story came up."

Khalil wondered what this had to do with Palestinians in Abu Dis.

Addison continued, "The previous month, while leading his annual summer studies in Middle Eastern history, Professor Zared had brought his students to the Nabatean Arch in Bosra Syria. The trip was cleared; Syrian authorities knew he was there. He brought students and scholarship to the areas he visited as other scholars visited after him, such was his reputation. A group of men, later thought to be members of the Palestine Mujahideen Islamic Jihad, confronted Professor Zared and separated him from his students. They were armed with rifles, and a solitary sword. The terrorists forced Professor Zared to kneel on the stones in front of the arch.

'This is what happens to Jews who violate Arabic ruins,' their leader screamed then brought his sword down on Professor Zared's neck, the article reported. It took three blows to sever his head from his body. A female student said they were forced to watch. The story went on to say two of the students could not enroll in Fall classes. Two other students refused to be interviewed. No one was ever arrested even though the Syrian government issued a press release condemning the murder, promising to pursue all leads. I guess it's no surprise that the summer trips stopped. The thing was the professor led the trip on his own dime."

"What is this dime?" Khalil asked.

"It means he paid for his travel and expenses without reimbursement—being paid back—by the university. I guess when you love something . . . ."

"I am sorry for your professor. There is too much violence, which is why we seek to go to Aleppo. I think Syria is better for Arabs than Jews."

"I never believed anyone looked for the terrorists. This was one man. But I couldn't accept his being Jewish mattered, and that, for what it's worth, is one reason I wanted to talk with Palestinians myself. I had to know what could bring such hatred for a man of learning and peace. Professor Zared was kind to all, teaching understanding for every person. His legacy, the university held a candlelight vigil at the student union with one minute of silence. A lousy minute of silence for a life? That's it? I switched majors—the courses I was taking. I was still determined to work for peace, but the State Department seemed a logical choice. Because I was near the top of my class, I made it into graduate school and finished with a Master's in International Affairs. The State Department accepted me, and I jumped at the chance for an assignment to Israel when it became available. So now you know my history."

"But how does talking with Palestinians answer your questions?"

"The Middle East has simmered in non-stop wars throughout its history, but since 1948 Israel has been the recurring flash point for a hatred of Jews the world over. If I can find the root of this hatred, then I know it can be conquered, and not just in Israel. Professor Zared taught me that. It is Palestinians, living with Jews, who hold the key.

"What if this knowing brings you to your professor's end?"

"It's a little too late to think of that now."

"Addison, you ask questions that cannot be answered by words. The hatred is too deep, the answer too distant," Elizabeth said. "You're also looking in the wrong direction."

"Then point me in the right one."

"You must see it for yourself."

"That's what I've been trying to do."

"And look where it has brought you."

Each made their way back to their grain mattresses. It was going to be another long night.

~

Unlocking the front door, Sammon handed the keys to Salwa and began carrying in filled baskets from their morning stops at produce stands. The delivery truck had made it into the central warehouse Thursday, and providing no one lost their order, bulghur wheat, canned chickpeas, coriander, along with other spices and staples, as well as cold-pressed olive oil—they were completely out of—should be delivered by late morning. Salwa placed the keys inside the front drawer under the counter and picked up her broom to begin sweeping the rough plank floor.

"You know, it's amazing how I sweep before leaving every night and come back to dust covering the floor. It would be 'Īsā's gift to have door fixed at bottom so dirt from all of street does not make its home in our shop," Salwa said.

"Yes, yes I know of this," Sammon said, setting a basket of eggs on the counter. "You speak these words each time you sweep. But what would there be to do before customers arrive if not for floor to sweep?"

"You mean except for cleaning shelves, dusting all cans, stocking shelves with morning produce, and making your tea? It would not hurt to fix door, a simple board, and much less dirt would greet my broom each morning."

"Unlock door to back. I need the toilet."

"At least that's one thing you don't want me to do for you . . . yet."

"Open, open, nature calls."

Grabbing the keys from the counter drawer, Salwa unlocked the dead bolt then returned to her sweeping.

Sammon hurried to the toilet. Looking around things were out of place. Grain sacks had been moved and the towels were on the grain sacks with odd lumps under them. Quickly zipping his pants, he hurried to the front.

"Salwa, Salwa, come here quickly. Be quiet about it, woman."

Leaning her broom against the wall, she walked toward him. "Yes, brother, what is it?"

"Sshh whisper, there are people sleeping in back room."

"What do you mean, there are people sleeping in back? This is not a hotel. Why would people sleep here?"

"How can I know? Go see, and then ask. If they don't have guns maybe they tell us."

Tip toeing to the door, Salwa stuck her head in the back and looked from grain-filled mattress to mattress. Something moved. Petrified, Salwa couldn't budge. Khalil's face emerged from beneath a towel.

"Salwa," he said, beginning to stretch then recoiling from the pain in his ribs, "is good you are here."

Hearing the familiar voice, Sammon moved around Salwa just as Aadil emerged from under his towel. "Aadil?"

"Sammon."

Waking from the fuss, Elizabeth emerged from her burqa cocoon.

"Elizabeth, what happened to your face?" Salwa said.

Pushing the burqa off her, Elizabeth got up. "There is much to talk about, but first, please shut the door to the front."

"We must leave door partially open for customers, but few arrive early since we haven't had full shelves for three weeks. We have time for talk," Sammon said.

"All are hungry. What food do you have?" Elizabeth said. "We can pay after we get back to Yerushaláyim."

"I bought fresh eggs on our way to work this morning, also tomatoes, and vegetables," Salwa said, going to the front and retrieving eggs and tomatoes. She returned to the front, coming back with a two-burner hotplate and a large skillet. It was plugged in and simmering freshly diced tomatoes and eggs within minutes. The aroma of the cooking food awakened Addison.

"Do I smell food?" Addison said.

"Who is this?" Sammon asked.

As breakfast was cooking and coffee began perking preliminary information about the wanted American was being dispensed. By the time breakfast was cooked, Elizabeth began, between mouthfuls of egg-tomato omelet, to explain how being Christians brought uninvited fugitives, running from the PMIJ, to their store. "There was no other place if we are to live."

"But this American you say does not share our faith," Salwa said in Arabic. "It's one thing for you, Khalil, and Aadil, but what good can any American bring to our people?"

Whenever anyone walked past the shop Sammon rushed to the front only to return.

"I did not choose; there was no one else. Could it be God has given this moment and how we walk in it will confirm our faith?" Elizabeth said.

"All things are possible, though not easy, but when has following 'Īsā been easy?" Salwa finally said. "We'll keep the door to the back room locked. By now word has gone out so eyes will be looking; you know how it is with rewards offered by PMIJ. Today's delivery is to the alley in back, so for once I am grateful for the extra work. Few will come today since it takes a day after supplies arrive for the word to spread, and by that time we will have thought of how the Lord would have us go forward. Noise must not come from this room; if you talk, do so in whispers. I will ask Sammon to cover the window with butcher's paper and tonight we will see what Īsā will bring, Elizabeth."

"Yes, my sister."

"Your time would best be spent talking with Īsā. We need His help as never before."

"I have been in prayer since meeting the American."

The bloating in Addison's stomach, from having scarfed food on an empty stomach, made him queasy. He settled uneasily on his mattress.

Aadil tried to think through diminishing choices.

Khalil savored his belly's fullness and trusted good would come of this day.

Elizabeth, deep in prayer, beseeched God for the only plan she had—a miracle.

Sammon kept vigil in the front of the store, switching prayers from 'Īsā to Allāh that no one would find the intruders who carried a death sentence for any caught harboring them.

Salwa praised the Lord as she finished preparing for customers, ready to be surprised by God's next move.

The morning passed uneventfully. Several customers inquired about the central warehouse delivery and were told to check back the next day. They purchased a few vegetables, promising to return. At 1:15 a horn sounded at the rear of the store. Exiting the front, Sammon walked around the outside to the back. "Hamal, you're right on time," Sammon said as the beefy man climbed out of the cab.

"Sammon, why don't you use the back door? No matter, I need toilet, quick open door."

"You cannot come in."

"Why cannot I come in?"

"The door is locked. Over Yawm al-Jumu'ah toilet runs over and back room smells like Jews live there."

"I need relief."

"Is no problem, I already asked next door and Utt says go in back. The door is unlocked, toilet in same place as my shop."

"You're a friend. Goods are set out in back; just roll door open," Hamal said, hurrying next door.

Sammon opened the back of the truck and began unloading and carting the boxes to the front of the store.

After several minutes, Hamal reappeared. "I feel like a new man. Why don't you have magazines like Utt? It is nice to have something to read."

"After I get smelly toilet fixed then I'll think about magazines, but smell comes first."

"You finished unloading?"

"All is done. See you next time."

"What about signing for delivery?"

"Already signed, and on your front seat."

"You're a good man. See you next delivery, with toilet fixed by then?"

"Yes, yes, all will smell nice."

Few customers dropped by that afternoon. Sammon kept busy thinking about their visitors. Elizabeth was one of two Jews he liked. Aadil and Khalil were lifelong friends. But he knew—everybody knew—word had gone from the mosque of the American, and he must not challenge PMIJ. Life was simpler before Salwa came to stay and before her god came with her. How does a sister not follow the god of their family? Tonight he would pray, when the business of the day did not disrupt him. Then he would know what to do.

Salwa finished arranging cans and five-pound burlap bags of wheat and barley filled from the large bags in the rear. Standing back, she looked over the neatly arranged goods. Walking over to her brother, she said, "Sammon."

"Yes."

"I finished everything and business is slow. I'll go to the back and talk quietly. Maybe we'll find a way for friends and American to get back to al-Quds."

"Is good, they cannot stay here. The danger is too great. Earlier this morning a customer said the imam spoke heated words about them after prayers. The whole world seeks after them."

"Lock the door behind me."

After she went through the door, Salwa heard the lock engage behind her. She motioned to Elizabeth and Khalil; they came over and sat down on crates.

"How are things out there?" Elizabeth asked.

"Quiet at the shop until tomorrow when word of the goods goes out. Imam speaks of you this day at mosque, many angry words. We have to find a way for you to al-Quds."

Addison came up and sat on the edge of a bag of grain. "What's she saying?"

"Salwa, could you speak in English so American can understand?"

"They don't know if you're still in Abu Dis but want everyone to be on the lookout," Salwa finished.

"Any ideas how we can get to Jerusalem?" Addison asked.

"No."

"Great."

"Sammon is a smart man and knows many people. He has been thinking all day."

"We can only hope and trust in the Lord," Elizabeth said. "Salwa, would you tell Addison how you came to live in Abu Dis?"

"Home was in al-Eizariya, just few miles from here. I lived with my husband, Gadil. Our law says anyone can believe what they want, and so because of neighbors who belonged to Christian church; both Gadil and I accepted 'Īsā as Lord and Savior. Though law says every belief okay, many neighbors don't know law. We have fine shop, much like Sammon's, but bigger. It was broken into many times, after we became Christians. Neighbors say we're not wanted, that 'Īsā was prophet and not god, that Allāh alone must be worshipped. When Gadil goes to police they won't take report. We did what Bible says and turn the other cheek. We loved our neighbors but neighbors didn't love us. Store spraypainted by people, calling Gadil and me names, bad, hurtful names. One night someone left a note on our door saying to accept Allāh or leave home, but there was no place to go to so we stayed. One morning when opening our store mutaween showed up. They surrounded us then pulled Gadil and me into alley, and began hitting canes on us. Gadil tried to shield me. The more they hit, the angrier they became. Shouting *Allāuh Akbar* and hitting, hitting, hitting. I woke up, sometime later, how long I don't know. I was dizzy and sore from cane hitting me many times. Gadil was on top of me. I couldn't move my face to the ground. I called for help. No one heard. I pray to 'Īsā but still no one comes. I told Gadil to move that I cannot breathe, he did not answer. I tried pulling, scraping my cheek on hard stone causing bleeding. I pull and rest, pull and rest. Gadil was heavy and quiet on my back; I can't see him and fall asleep again. As night came I awoke. Gadil is still silent. I was so tired. Finally, I remember nothing. Then the cold causes shaking and I hear morning sounds. Why has no one come? Why is Gadil not moving?"

Salwa's upper lip quivered, sadness filling her face. Addison was not sure he wanted to hear any more.

"It was the longest time before I pulled myself from under Gadil. I did not need to look; I knew his stillness could only be one thing. But I am his wife, this is the man I caressed and held in my arms, the one I prayed to be with for all of eternity, and I have to know. He was on his face, so I pushed then pulled and with more strength than I know I have, at last, turn him over. No! No! God above no! This is not the face of my beloved. This is face of death . . . ugliness. His handsome features were black with open gashes. I did not recognize this person. This isn't Gadil; this is evil done upon my Gadil. Staggering into the store, everything was gone. I was dizzy and weak but shelves of food, medicine, knitted goods all gone. I went to the sink and ran water, sticking my head under its freezing coldness. It was fire, burning, I screamed. Even our mirror was gone. I couldn't see what was done, but parts of scabs washed from face and sticky hair. I left my head under the water for long time. Finally going to the back of the store, I lay on floor. Three days later I woke up in the clinic. I was there two weeks as salve was applied and a tube ran clear liquid into my arm. I carry scars on my back."

"Didn't anyone report this to the police?" Addison asked.

"Mutaween are police, cleric police. No one challenges them. When I made it back to store, Gadil was gone. I never found out where. No one would speak to me. I tried to go home, but Gadil's family said I am cursed and that heretics don't have a home with family. But where do I go, I say. All of store is gone, I have nothing. I saw things from our store in their home. They say I can go to *Jahannam*, Hell; I am dead person to them. Mutaween put out decree that no one in al-Eizariya can take me in. Sammon lived in Abu Dis, but even there mutaween warned him. He was told no one, not even brother, can hire me, so I work and he does not hire me but gives money for personal needs."

"What did your brother's wife say about you moving in?"

"Sammon never had wife. There were just the two of us, not like other families with many children. Sammon worked for father in store then mother got sick. Clinic said it was stroke and father stops all else to take care of her. Sammon runs store. Mother lived for eight years after stroke but only thing that comes from her mouth is a single word: no.

'How are you, mother?'

'No.'

'Would you like me to read to you?'

'No.'

'I love you, mother. Do you love me?'

'No.'

"Day by day father took care of mother. I helped with bathing and cooking, but all else father does, says is his right. Then mother, so quiet and peaceful, dies and father grieves more than I ever know is possible with all of life taken from heart. Three months after mother's death, father still grieving too deeply. One morning, Sammon went into the kitchen, father is sitting at the table, eyes staring, chest not rising, or falling. Father joined mother. After burial, Sammon found no wife to marry him. Young wives want young husbands and old wives do not give children. So now I am with Sammon, but if something happens to him I do not know what will happen to me. That is how I met Elizabeth."

"Elizabeth? How do you fit into this?"

"Arabic women who become Christians are often left out on streets to beg when close family dies. Mutaween punish anyone helping them because they deserted Islam, so many end up starving. An organization I am part of, Messianic Jews International, has set up relief homes throughout Judea and Samaria. PALFA signed agreements with MJI to allow help," Elizabeth said. "We use the acronym MJI in Judea and Samaria since Palestinian officials refused to sign an agreement allowing help for their people if the word Jews was used."

"Let me get this straight. You help their people and they dictate what you call yourself?

"It's our only way to help."

"Why do they even allow it?"

"PALFA demands a percentage of every shekel spent. They think it makes them look religiously tolerant before the international community."

"While lining their pockets, aren't you just enabling the government to steal?"

"Governments don't steal. It's people within governments that take money."

"And there's a difference?"

"Would you let women and children starve to make a point? We need to ensure all Salwas have a place to go. After a spouse's death, when there are no grown sons, someone shows up with papers saying all property has been sold and they are on street. We seek to fulfill our command to love in all circumstances."

Too much was coming in. Taking a walk always focused him, but the only place to walk was filled with people whose sole reason for breathing was to capture or kill him. He surrendered to the grain sack, and lay down his spinning head.

The afternoon passed into evening.

~

"Salwa, I think I have plan. I must go to see if it's good. Finish closing store but don't leave. I'll return."

"Be careful, my brother. It will soon be past the time to travel safely."

Pre-occupied, Sammon walked out

Four hours later he was back. "Salwa, I found a truck. They'll be here soon. Tell everyone in back to get ready to go."

Excitedly, Salwa went into the back. Waving everyone to her, she said, "I have good news. Gather your things. There will be a truck to take everyone to al-Quds."

"How did you find this truck?' Addison asked.

"How will we travel so late?" Elizabeth asked.

"Please, no questions. It was Sammon who made arrangements from many friends. All he said was for everyone to get ready and a truck would come."

Excitement and fear competed in every heart. Was this miracle possible? Elizabeth wanted to believe, but there were so many obstacles. If the truck showed up it would be a matter of minutes before they were at a machsom, checkpoint, and inside Yisra'el. *Please, Lord, protect this truck. Bless those you have sent to take us from danger.*

Within minutes, a single beep was heard outside the back door; excitement rose.

"Coming through," Sammon said, unbolting the back door. He pulled on the door. It refused to budge. "Come on," he said, "don't hold me back now."

"Sammon," Khalil said.

"Yes."

"Not to question, but could back door still have padlock on it?"

"I never leave outside lock on door when in store."

"Remember delivery man?"

"Of course, I locked the door to prevent entry. What am I thinking?" Sammon went out the front and soon sounds of a padlock being removed could be heard. The door opened. Just behind Sammon sat the back end of a dilapidated 2½ ton truck. An olive green canopy was stretched up and over the bed on metal ribs, with two flaps covering the end of the bed. Turning toward the truck, Sammon spoke to someone inside. Both end flaps were pulled back and tied off. Two men climbed down from the bed.

"Time to go," Sammon said, motioning to the group. "Makeen and Ommar will help you." Elizabeth, taking her burqa, went to the truck bed and Ommar threw it inside. As she tried to climb up, Makeen effortlessly lifted her into the truck.

Addison needed no help.

"Careful when lifting, ribs broken," Khalil said.

Makeen got on one side, Ommar the other. "What is your name, little man?" Ommar asked.

"Khalil Ahmad."

"We'll be careful Khalil."

Making a seat between their arms, they lifted.

Gritting his teeth, Khalil didn't utter a sound.

"You sit like Khalil then we lift you onto truck," Makeen said to Aadil. He sat between their interlocked arms and they lifted him onto the bed where a third helper grabbed his good arm and helped pull him onto the truck bed.

Both men climbed into the back and untied the flaps, letting them drop, closing off the back of the truck.

"Everyone must be quiet. No noise until we get to destination," Makeen said.

"You take us to machsom?" Elizabeth asked.

"We have to use back roads to avoid detection. American and Jew, get on floor, we cover with tarps. If stopped, be silent, do not move, you must not be found, understand?" Makeen said, looking at Addison and Elizabeth.

Adrenaline kept Elizabeth from screaming from the pain as her face was covered by a heavy tarp beside Addison. After a sharp metallic rap on the truck's side, the engine attempted to start. It coughed, chugged, and choked through five backfires before limping to life and wheezing away from the store.

Elizabeth began to pray.

Addison's thoughts were lost in how he was going to explain this to the wild man from the inner sanctum. His career was no doubt over.

Aadil wondered what would happen to Khalil and him. He knew PMIJ's power. *Who would hire us now? Maybe Americans will help; we helped American.*

The bumpy road soon focused all thoughts on the current moment as they were jerked and bounced around pothole-strewn back streets. The manual transmission alternated from a screaming high pitch when the driver continued to accelerate past each gear's range to the grinding, mashing anguish of gear teeth forced into the next gear. After a few minutes of the torturous ride, with Aadil and Khalil being thrown onto the floor on top of Addison and Elizabeth, all sense of direction was lost.

Finally, the truck slowed and stopped. This was different. It wasn't a lurch to a halt followed by rapid acceleration but a gradual slowing that brought them to a complete stop. The truck's horn beeped once. There were sounds of metal doors being rolled open. Indistinct voices could be heard in rapid-fire speech. Elizabeth tried to hear, but distance and the tarp muffled sound. The truck remained running; the cab door opened, someone got out. Animated conversation rose and fell while each captive in the truck's bed strained to hear.

Someone climbed in the cab; the door slammed. Grinding gears signaled their old driver was back. After grinding the transmission into submission he found first gear, and they inched forward. Street sounds disappeared, replaced by silence. The engine shut down and metal doors were rolled closed. Five minutes passed into ten. Sporadic whispers wafted past, too faint to be understood.

An exchange is being finalized to avoid repercussions from groups that would have an opinion about how every aspect of this is handled, Elizabeth thought. Was that English she heard, a good sign? If only she could make out their words. She knew they must not burst from their confinement. Others had been shot, in the last moment of captivity, because someone got spooked and bolted at the moment of freedom.

Minutes, taking on the weight of days, ticked past. Bam! Something hit the hollow side of the truck bed, startling already frayed nerves.

Makeen and Ommar opened the closed flaps, then folded and tied them back. "Get down," Makeen ordered. "We will help."

In just over two minutes, all four were off the truck and inside a cavernous warehouse.

"Where are we?" Elizabeth asked.

"Follow close," Makeen said, producing a flashlight and walking toward a side exit as shadows stood their ground, flanking them in the gloom on both sides. They followed with uncertain steps. "Almost there." Going through a side door, they found themselves outside in the brisk evening cold, heading for the next building and more shadows, silent, lurking. They entered a stone building at the end of an alley. The door closed behind them. Makeen led them to the center of the room; he stopped. A solitary bulb, hanging seven feet above the floor, labored to dispel the darkness.

"Hey, Aadil, this is something. Room looks just like one we've seen before," Khalil said.

CHAPTER

34

Saturday 15 March 2008, Early Morning Hours

Abu Dis, West Bank

A steel barrel jammed against the back of Addison's neck.

"*Ahlan wa sahlan*, welcome," came a voice from behind him.

He tried glancing back.

"Eyes forward. Is there need for death this night? I have awaited this reunion with great anticipation," the steel voice continued. "Your disappearance caused great concern. This night will help you understand the futility of resistance.

"Aadil, how you and your clown companion disappointed us, so much time spent proving fidelity, and yet it is a different path you have chosen. And Miss Elizabeth, what joy to have you back with us. It was most unfortunate one of my brothers became so amorous. I can imagine what your beauty was like before your unfortunate accident. Rest assured, your chastity will follow you to your god. I have special plans, and this time Nasir will not be leaving, so all will be looked after. *Leila sa'eeda*, good night." The door could be heard opening. The sound of footsteps receded.

Makeen approached Addison with flex cuffs. "Hands in front," he said in English. "Nice watch." He unsnapped its band and dropped it on the stone floor driving his heel into it. The sound of shattering glass and metal battered Addison's ears: He didn't protest. Makeen tightened the flex cuffs around Addison's wrists. Elizabeth then Khalil was cuffed. Khalil didn't cry out, his fear greater than the pain.

"Aadil my friend why did you choose so wrong?" Makeen said. "Now you must embrace the fate of others." Going to his equipment bag, he pulled out a set of leg irons with a nine-inch chain and tightened each iron on Aadil's wrists. "Your arm does not look so good, my friend. Are those streaks infection? But I am no doctor. If you prove worthy, your arm will live with no pressure on it. If you decide to lash out, for all the good it would do, the slightest yank on the chain will turn your mind from such foolishness."

Aadil, Elizabeth, and Khalil were herded to the far wall and forced onto the cold floor; three AK-104s eager for blood, rested on sand bags, their sights centered on them. Watchful eyes commenced the vigil on which their lives depended. "Try to get up, you won't make it," a shadow declared from the darkness.

Two forms closed behind Addison. A fist smashed into the back of his head, knocking him onto his shattered watch, bloodying his face. He cried out; his cheekbone broken.

"Bad things happen to those trespassing Arab land." His arms were grabbed and he was jerked then shoved toward the open doorway. "Why have you violated Palestinian sovereignty?"

Addison remained silent.

A rifle barrel's hard steel struck the back of his ribs, forcing him forward. "You do not speak when I command words?"

Stumbling through the open door, Addison was back outside in the darkness. The door closed.

Elizabeth struggled to escape the screams that pierced the closed door, drowning her prayers. Her only reprieve; the silence that followed Addison's shrieks as he was pulled back from unconsciousness. As the night wore on, the screams became weaker and mercifully finally dissolved into silence.

~

Sleeping fitfully, each hostage, lost in solitary thoughts, was aware of a body being dragged into their midst and left on the cold stone floor. The darkness of their prison, with the feeble light turned off, permitted no sight. Listening for breath too shallow to be heard robbed Elizabeth of hope as she awaited the day's light. It came slowly. Unable to see Addison in the shadows, she whispered his name, knowing that doing so could bring pain. There was no response. The daylight arrived through grimy windows, casting everything in shadows. Looking, Elizabeth saw—*Oh God.* His face swollen, eyes tightly closed slits. His right cheek concave, covered with caked, dried, blood, his jaw at an ugly angle. There were no place cuts and gashes did not intersect. Hideous streaks of deep purple with yellow and blood-blackened bruises. Addison's upper torso was folded over his lower body, his left leg twisted at a hideous angle, and right shoulder dislocated. Looking away she fought nausea. Forcing her eyes back, she had to know if he was alive. Looking, straining, *oh Father, you are the Lord of life; do not let this man die*. Distance and shadows refused to divulge God's answer.

"I need toilet," Khalil said, waking. "Is that food I smell? Breakfast would be nice."

"You think this is a restaurant? No food for traitors."

"Still need the toilet."

"We're eating, but we have time for American beauty treatment if you interrupt meal one more time. After we're done, then is time for toilet."

After the mujahideen ate, each hostage was escorted to a hole in the floor that passed for a toilet.

"How about privacy?" Elizabeth said.

"Swine don't need privacy."

Elizabeth concluded her business in silence.

Ommar walked over to the American still splayed on the floor. He pulled the cap from the hypodermic needle he was holding and jabbed the needle through clothing into the hip muscle as instructed. Pushing with steady pressure, he emptied the half filled syringe. The hostage didn't move. Ommar didn't give a damn; he'd done his job. If the American somehow clung to life, the shot would make sure he didn't wake until he was inside the cistern.

~

Nasir had gone over the information on the refueler trucks until he knew more about them than Nuri. Every refueler going through Israeli checkpoints had their manifest checked. The weight of fuel was compared with the weight of the refueler truck. Tanks were opened and fuel levels verified against the manifest. Additional roving inspections by Border Police verified delivery refueling stations listed on each manifest had received the volumes listed. No refueler wanted to run afoul of Israeli authorities and face fines or worse because of discrepancies in records.

Under Nuri's direction, a single liter here, another there, was bought and stored in a hundred different locations. Never enough to bring suspicion but enough, when added to the refueling trucks after their human cargo had been delivered, to account for the weight of four hostages sealed in separate trucks along with the oxygen tanks and masks to keep them alive.

Each refueler truck was ready to receive its passenger. Hidden compartments used to conceal the prisoners had been welded into each tank, assuring that the guards at enemy checkpoints wouldn't discover their illicit cargos. By the time the four refuelers finished delivering their load, the hostages would be in the bowels of al-Ubeidiya.

Aadil, Elizabeth, and Khalil were told to scream at any checkpoint they desired. Each was shown a wireless switch that operated tiny doors inside the tanks. At their first sound, the switch would be flipped, flooding their walled-off box with gasoline. All vowed silence. All kept their vow. Addison, unconscious, remained unaware.

CHAPTER

35

Sunday 16 March 2008

Sammon's Store
Abu Dis, West Bank

The day dawned like all others. Salwa grabbed her broom, clearing the store of the previous night's dirt. Many customers would come this day to purchase goods delivered yesterday. Salwa had not felt this alive since before Gadil's murder. There was a glow to the morning as she thought of her friends and even the heathen American safe from harm. How would she respond when the news was told to her? She must not seem too joyful; Americans do not bring happiness. She thanked 'Īsā that He had given such a brother who would risk his life to save those to whom he owed nothing. Walking over to Sammon, she said, "You are growing in the Lord more and more each day." Sammon remained quiet, but he had never been one for mornings, so she left her precious brother to himself and kept busy preparing the store for business.

Ketifa came early. No sooner was the door unlocked for business than she entered and said, "How about the American, right here in Abu Dis."

"American, what about an American?" Salwa said.

"Don't you play coy with me Salwa. Why, it's all over."

Salwa wanted to scream, *no groceries until you tell me everything*, but instead she said, "There will be many customers this morning from yesterday's delivery. See what you want before others arrive and buy it all."

"Aren't you the shy one, after all you and Sammon have done."

Three whirling dervishes descended on the store. "Ketifa," one of them said, "we knew if anyone would beat us to store it would be you. Salwa, we are so proud. I think now the mutaween may have second thoughts."

Before Salwa could ask a question, the four women were tearing through the store, grabbing needed items as they raced to beat others. Like locust descending, regulars and those she had never seen before stripped every shelf bare in the first four hours, every customer bearing words of praise for Salwa or Sammon. A sinking feeling came over Salwa every time she looked at her brother, but the busyness of the morning kept words from being exchanged. The last customer paid for her purchase and left the store.

Sammon turned to Salwa, "I must go out. It may be possible to get another delivery from the warehouse with so much business, but I have to see to this in person. I will return soon." He left Salwa to wrestle with her growing fear.

Two hours later, Sammon was back. "Is good news, delivery will come later this day. We have many friends I did not know, and it seems many want to shop here. If things continue we may even buy shop next door and expand."

"Sammon."

"You do not know this thing you think you know."

"Tell me so I can understand. What are these words I hear about the American?"

"What is this you expect? I had no place for this man. It was Elizabeth's fault to come here. PMIJ were everywhere when I left yesterday. Three times they stopped and questioned me, and three times I lied. Lied to our own people. What god is there who asks you to lie to your own people? The fourth time I was questioned, the truth came from my lips."

"Do you know what you have done? They trusted us."

"Americans bring pain to our people—"

"But we are people of God."

"You and the Jew have your god, a god for women. Did you think I could abandon the god of my father and father's father? Yesterday I was faithful to my god, and today's business shows his pleasure."

Salwa looked on this brother she had been raised with, her heart ripped in pieces.

"I am the man of this family, and you will do what I say or there will be no place for you."

"Will you send me out for following God?"

"Sister, I love you and promised father to care for you. Love any god you wish, but never again speak to me of this god. Now I go to the mosque. For too long my prayers have been absent."

CHAPTER

36

United States Embassy, Consular Section
71 Ha-Yarkon Street, Tel Aviv

Day One
Monday March 17, 2008

His hated nemesis struggled to intrude. "Not now," Sid Cantwell growled at the inanimate object, letting the call go to voicemail. Unbelievably, it rang again. "Touree, I'm busy," he bellowed through the door. Someone knocked. He lifted his head, a lion ready for prey. The door opened and Lynda's face blighted the doorway.

"Before you start with me, DS is here and doesn't look in the mood to come back when it's convenient," Lynda told her boss.

"No problem. Washington rarely cares if reports are on time. They ask, just tell them Diplomatic Security stopped by for a chat. Got anyone else who wants to join in Touree?"

Going around her, Keane Bodine, Regional Security Officer, invaded the room. "We've got a problem."

"You forget how the door closes?" Cantwell said to his secretary.

"Come on in, Lynda. You're involved. You'll understand, Sid," Keane said, taking a chair and motioning to her.

"Okay, so where's the fire?"

"Picked this up off the internet this morning," he said, handing Sid a solitary page.

Taking it from him, Sid Cantwell read:

Dated: 17 March 2008.

Israel Standard Time (UTC+2): 0300 hours.

Posting URL: http://www.palestinianliberation/dar/alharb.sy

Body of Text: American dollars for American Addison. Is worth 1/10th Usāmah bin Muhammad bin 'Awad bin Lādin for return, breathing?

Click on link for instructions.

Link page: Congratulations for concern of American found trespassing Arab land. Return twenty-four hours, not more, not less, for instructions.

Link page URL identification: http://www.pmij.sy

Laying the paper on his disk, Sid asked, "Who else in the mission outside security knows about this?"

"You mean other than Ambassador Walker? I told Lynda, just before you invited me in, Sid."

"Prior to me?"

"Hell, she does most of your work, other than barking at everyone. Besides, she's in this up to her eyeballs since she arranged for Deverell's escort."

"Mr. Bodine, I cleared Mr. IbnMansur through channels."

"Relax, Lynda, we've been inside and out of this thing. He's Shabak and not part of the problem."

"'He is?" Lynda said.

"Ninety percent of locals, at least the ones who regularly show up for work, are Israeli internal security. They don't get near sensitive areas and we get a lot of stuff in the pipeline through them."

"Touree, wasn't IbnMansur assigned to remain with Deverell until he reported for duty?"

"That was Mr. IbnMansur's assignment until he was called away last week, Mr. Cantwell, and before you start I cleared it with you and have your signature on file, knowing you'd forget."

"Touree, you forge more of my signatures than I sign."

"If you're not happy, Mr. Cantwell, I've been approached by other departments."

"I'll take Lynda any time you get tired of her, Sid. Half of my backlog would be cleared in no time," Keane said.

"Fat chance, I'm the deputy administrator; Touree goes nowhere. So, Keane, do we, in fact, know terrorists have our boy?"

"We know two things. One, IbnMansur doesn't have him."

"Because?"

"We woke the man earlier this morning than he appeared to like and he was emphatic that Deverell wasn't with him."

"And two?"

"He said Deverell was being watched by Elizabeth Daniels and Daniels looks to be a guest of the PMIJ."

"He told you all that?"

"I can be charming when needed."

"So why would a consulate employee, considering his ties to Israeli internal security, walk away from an assignment?"

"One week ago, IbnMansur was recalled by Shabak on what, we weren't supposed to know, was a search for enough weapons-grade inhalational anthrax to overwhelm the Israeli health care system and dispatch up to 600,000 of their citizens, give or take."

"And this is the first I hear of it?"

"Israelis aren't big on sharing."

"Unless we're dealing with multiple targets, we have only one city of sufficient Jewish population to make use of a weapon of that magnitude," Sid declared. "Jerusalem has around 594,000 Jews, but there are over two million Arabs in the West Bank and Gaza, so what good would it do?"

"What about other cities that might be in contention?" Keane asked.

"In terms of population, Tel Aviv has 391,000; Rishon LeZion in the central Israeli coastal plain over 222,000; and Ashdod, in the South on the Mediterranean coast over 204,000. The only other sizeable cities would be Petah Tivka, 185,000 and Netyana, at around 175,000."

"Of course, if we include the metropolitan area, Tel Aviv with Gush Dan add up to over three million combined, which puts it ahead of Jerusalem, but the population mix is heterogeneous with Jaffa conjoined at the hip, so we were at a loss to figure out where they planned to use it. Doesn't compute they would piecemeal this, carry out several isolated attacks—too demanding to launch successfully. Would require multiple rockets to explode at altitude, with difficult wind velocities for optimal dispersion unless you've got a plane, and the IAF is too good for that. Any plane approaching Israeli airspace wouldn't make it to their coastline," Keane said.

"Gaza would be my guess for launching multiple rockets."

"You'd guess wrong, Sid. If they were in Gaza they'd have to be undercover and you can't launch from inside a building. With the eyes Israel has in Gaza, nothing the size of the required rockets would get more than two blocks especially with the Israelis on alert. In drones alone Israel has overlapping coverage 24/7, not to mention human intelligence."

"Then how do Qassams make it through if drones and covert ops surveil everything?" Linda asked.

"Forget Qassams, no way to aim them and they don't explode until they hit the ground; for anthrax dispersal you need precise coordinates and detonation at elevation."

"The subject of anthrax has more of my attention, Keane, than a delivery system. What good is it if more Arabs die than Jews? You ruled out both Jerusalem and Tel Aviv because of the Arab populations living in close proximity," Sid said.

"Bright and early this morning, after the posting of Deverell's kidnapping note, I ended up at the Ministry of Foreign Affairs. The Israelis appeared to want help but wouldn't admit why. We needed help as well but they dug in and wouldn't give up anything of strategic value. After laying out that unless we were brought into the loop we'd go it alone with whatever response necessary to secure our consular officer, it took all of fifteen minutes for Shabak to show up and provide a deep briefing. So, for the moment, we believe we know as much as they do. You remember the measles outbreak in the West Bank last month?"

"Hard to miss with the Russians all over the place," Sid said.

What we didn't know is that along with MMR vaccine, every Arab in Gaza and the West Bank was immunized against anthrax. Amazing how you can get them to all turn out for vaccinations like that. You'd think it was a Bar Mitzvah for an Orthodox rabbi's son in Gaza. I digress. The Russians had a new aerosol immunization technology. We thought they were just tapping a willing control group to test their technology, benefactors that they are, but it seems they learned how to combine anthrax and MMR vaccine. Beauty is, by the time the Israelis found out, the Russians had left Dodge, so they couldn't get answers . . . talk about denied culpability. And we're not talking your garden variety anthrax vaccine. Kanatjan Alibekov, when he defected to our side a few years back, as Undersecretary of the Soviet Biological Weapons program—"

"Aren't we under a treaty signed with the Soviets back in the seventies?" Lynda said.

"Yeah, one of Nixon's pet projects. The Russians signed, we signed, and before the ink was dry the Russians went to town creating a massive biological weapons program hidden up in Kazakhstan. Out of Biopreparat, as the entity was known, came, among other things, a strain of anthrax no one else has. The other thing no one else has; vaccine for this strain."

"How much anthrax we dealing with?" Sid asked.

"Rumored to be over nine and a half kilograms, close to twenty-one pounds."

"Inhalational, right?"

"Preferred form for weaponization, greater dispersal."

"Translate that into volume. What it would take to get it up in the air?"

"Any Qassam 2 or 3 could carry it, but they don't have guidance systems, would burn up as much anthrax as they dispersed, and can't explode at elevation."

"So that means we don't know how they plan on launching the package."

"We know one thing."

"What's that?"

"They have something in mind. With the breakup of the Soviet Union, Russia is at a unique place in her history but I look for the central government to pull things back together."

"Which translates to what?"

"Jihadists have one shot for glory. Whoever got the anthrax, the door's been closed. There's too much notoriety while their biological weapons facilities are now trying to position themselves as legitimate drug manufacturers. Who'd have guessed, capitalism is alive and well. Once the bear consolidates its power no terror group will come within a billion rubles of getting Russia's biological weapons again. Keep in mind the Russians had their own bouts with Muslim terrorism. You got anything cold to drink, Lynda? All this talking has given me a dry throat."

"How's some iced tea sound?"

"Any juice?"

"Peach, apple, pomegranate?"

"Pomegranate, it's not so sweet."

"Mr. Cantwell, what can I get for you?"

"Pomegranate."

"Be right back."

"Keane, I don't get pulling Touree into this. I know she's got clearance and invited IbnMansur to the party, but that was my call so what's her need to know here?"

"Routine stopped the moment I entered your office. Consular officers are to carry on as usual, but all other assets must be made available. We are on twenty-four hour alert status until we stand down, all leaves cancelled, all personnel confined to the mission. You're going to need Lynda. Sid, you're too old to carry on like you did a few years back. Every action is going to be reviewed and parsed for intent, much less execution, by every sub-committee the House and Senate can find a reason for creating, so you'll need your A-game. Be grateful you have Lynda."

"What about non-essential personnel, Keane?"

"The last thing the Israelis want is a mass exodus from Ben Gurion; Washington agrees. We spook these guys and anything's possible. It must appear business as usual. Besides, we still have the sub-basement safe rooms."

"Official alert status?"

"The playing field is outside the embassy. Officially, status remains as is with the provisions we talked about and, no surprise here, all information is classified. We don't need this thing rippling though the embassy or consulate in Jerusalem."

"That may prove a challenge with everyone confined to the mission."

"That's your job, Mr. Assistant Director."

Opening the door, Lynda came in with a tray of strawberry smoothies. "Pomegranate was out. Didn't think you'd want me calling the kitchen, with the time that would take, so I got strawberry smoothies, but not too sweet, Mr. Bodine." She placed the drinks on the edge of the desk by each man, took a glass, and sat down.

"Thanks, Lynda. So what do you need, Keane?"

"A copy of Deverell's paperwork, starting with the Assignment Notice of Appointment. Everything between then, up to and including today. What, when, where. Time in, time out, everything. Every contact, call, even if you were taking a crap and thinking about him."

"We got all that, Lynda?"

"Yes sir, all but the times you might have thought about him on the toilet."

"Washington tells me he was fresh out of training, so at least I won't have to backtrack ten years."

"Why is that, Mr. Bodine?"

"No skeletons to dig up Lynda, he had just completed rigorous background checks when hired. Which leaves his time here, and most of that has been covered by IbnMansur. I haven't seen the full report, but he's Shabak and they're not known for consorting with terrorists. That leaves Elizabeth Daniels, his Jerusalem guide after IbnMansur was called back to Shabak. Considering she's Jewish and appears to be a hostage, I wouldn't put odds on meeting her."

"IbnMansur hired Daniels? No wonder our consular affairs officer is in trouble. She came close to starting a religious war when

I was at my first meet and greet with the local religious leaders. Had to remove her before she restarted the Crusades."

"I doubt she'll get in what's left of your hair again, Sid."

"Which still leaves us with who tracked Deverell's arrival," Sid said.

"Could be his early arrival and wandering affected their plans. Makes sense they wouldn't move until Shabak was out of the way. We'll find the source. After you have compiled the information, I need you to deliver it to me, Sid, and yeah, I know that's why you have your indentured slave here, but this one has to come direct and I don't need to tell you the Secretary and then the President will read everything. Word is the President's interested in how an American Conselor Officer, on first assignment, ended up in the hands of terrorists instead of at the United States Embassy. Don't cover any tracks. I've got friends in direct contact with the man; he's as straight as they come. He demands truthful information, then a solution, not someone to roast in one of his Texas barbeques, you're lucky on that."

"Are we dealing with PMIJ or one of their proxies?"

"All information points to the real deal. The URL link in their love note didn't happen accidentally. They want us to know. And yes, we checked it out; the URLs are legitimate, though the contact address is suspect."

"Why's that?"

"It's our address: 71 Ha-Yarkon Street."

"Nice touch."

"None of this means a direct PMIJ connection inside the Embassy. We're too thorough in screening, but someone who knew someone will be our guy."

"Okay, but if Deverell has been a hostage for nearly a week, why haven't we heard anything before today?

"Hasn't been a week Sid. When IbnMansur was recalled, he hired Elizabeth Daniels. This was about a week before Deverell was due at the embassy, and with all of Jerusalem's tourist sites, IbnMansur figured she'd keep him busy. That fact, added to Deverell's age and being single with, according to IbnMansur, a stunning escort, he didn't figure Deverell would wander too far.

After I talked to IbnMansur this morning he did some checking and the last anyone saw of Deverell and Ms. Daniels was with two Palestinians as they were headed toward Abu Dis on March 12th. My guess is they were taken hostage shortly thereafter. And no, the two Palestinians aren't PMIJ. They're well-known for hustling jobs and had no terrorist connections. My sources figured they were hired for protection."

"Hope they came cheap considering their skills as guards. So Keane why do we care, other than the appearance of looking for Deverell? With all the places they could hide him, let the Jews find their terrorists and promote them to an Israeli prison or the harem in the sky, and Deverell will be pulled up in the same net. It's a given we won't pay ransom unless the target is high value, and that's not the case here."

"The ransom demand at five million isn't all that startling, Sid. My take, the demand is a smokescreen. Deverell is with the anthrax, or shortly will be."

"Why would the PMIJ marry our FSO with their anthrax unless he was an insurance policy to keep the Israelis from dismantling them on first sight?"

"That occurred to the Israelis as well. Bottom line is, they get a shot and FSO, or no, they're taking it. The Israelis want that anthrax before it's launched; it's the only way to contain it, so unless Deverell's astride a rocket at launch, he's shot through and through. Back in '67 during the Six Day War, the USS Liberty was stationed off the Sinai Peninsula in international waters. The ship was assigned to NSA, collecting electronic intelligence and passing it along to the Arabs. Of course, nothing was ever proven. What is known is that the IAF blasted a 39-foot-wide by 24-foot high hole amidship, forcing the Liberty to limp back to Malta for temporary repairs. This happened under the Johnson Administration, and he was as hard-boiled as they come. There were all kinds of apologies from the Israelis about the tragic mistake that killed thirty-four Americans while wounding one hundred and seventy-three more. Israelis even forked over several million in reparations, which rumor has it came from the Johnson Administration and Congress through back channels. The one thing that hasn't changed since, and that every Administration understands, is that when it comes to their survival, no one is off the table for Israel. That and the fact we need them more for stability in the region than they need us."

"They don't seem to have been all that successful at times."

"They're our canary in the coal mine. Pays to keep birdie alive, especially when that coal mine is a powder keg waiting to blow the Middle East apart."

"Keane, I still don't get it. Why would terrorists think someone fresh out of training would make a strategic asset? His dad a major Republican donor?"

"We could fill encyclopedias with what the terrorists don't know, but they seem to think an American Foreign Service Officer, any American Foreign Service Officer, is high value."

"A consular officer and not a full ambassador, they're morons."

"Granted, but morons who appear to have a strain of inhalational anthrax none of us has been vaccinated against."

"Speak for yourself. I've had all my series."

"Yeah, and you've been vaccinated against measles, which will do you about as much good. Think of the Aimes strain that showed up in envelopes on the East Coast between September and October 2001, on steroids. Any immunity previous vaccinations provided has been wiped out, and it appears the local Arabs around Jerusalem are the only ones protected."

"Well, at least we've got thirty-six miles between here and Jerusalem if they hit there. Anthrax shouldn't travel that far."

"Wouldn't bet my life on it Sid. At least we've got the safe rooms. I've got to go, others need cheering up. Need that report ASAP."

CHAPTER

37

United States Embassy, Consular Section
71 Ha-Yarkon Street, Tel Aviv

Day Two
Tuesday March 18, 2008

Keane barely slowed as he barged through the Assistant Director's door. Sitting down, he slid a solitary page across the table. "Read."

"Coffee?" Sid asked.

"Read."

Dated: 18 March 2008.

Israel Standard Time (UTC+2): 0301 hours.

Posting URL: http://www.palestinianliberation/dar/alharb.sy

Body of Text: American enablers of Zionism, because correct response, American Addison breathes. How long, you choose. Five million U.S. dollars in five hundred dollar bills, non-sequential numbering. Delivered to Area A town. Click link for instructions.

Link page: Is good, Zionist lovers. Return to site in twenty-four hours for instructions.

Link page URL identification: www.pmij.sy

"What response? We didn't do anything."

"We checked in on time."

"How do they know?"

"You need to become acquainted with the internet, Sid. Simple tracking software records every visit."

"Yeah, I'll do that with all the free time I have. Next item, I thought ransom was off the table, Keane."

"It is."

"Someone forget to tell the bad guys?"

"Washington made a decision."

"This I've gotta hear."

"No ransom. It's policy and it won't be changed."

"So far, so good."

"They've authorized the money, though, to catch the kidnappers."

"Which is different from paying ransom how?"

"They get caught."

"In a PA controlled area?"

"Look, I've been on so many video conferences with Washington since yesterday, I'm thinking of hiring a press secretary. A contingent of Israelis descended on them last night and convinced State the kidnapping is hooked up to the anthrax."

"Is it?"

"Who the hell knows? That's their story. So Washington came to the brilliant decision they won't pay ransom but will put the money out there as bait to capture the bad guys along with the anthrax."

"I think I've read this book."

"There's more, Sid."

"Such as?"

"What follows was specifically cleared. It's for you alone, which doesn't include Lynda. Any questions?"

"That's clear. What've you got?"

"The money is being flown in from a specialized lab, one of two in existence. This gets a little technical and I don't understand it myself, so bear with me. Bowieite is a rhodium-iridium-platinum sulfide mineral that is being applied to the ransom currency with High Impact Power Magnetron Sputtering utilizing HIPIMS plasma, a partially ionized gas. At least that's what the science geeks grilled me on until I memorized it. During this process, the currency is sprayed by a weighted liquid. The Bowieite is attracted to its surface, where a microscopic coating is left when dried. The Bowieite radiates electromagnetic waves in a specific part of the spectrum that, not only can be picked up at great distances by specialized equipment but, has a half life of 10,000 years. Oh yeah, and it's invisible to any equipment used to inspect it."

"Sounds like something that could be used for any ransom situation."

"Not when you consider the exorbitant costs involved. Officially, the process has not been perfected. The decision was made at the highest levels that Deverell represents a strategic high value asset to the United States government, so the procedures were employed."

"A probationary consular officer?"

"A United States foreign service officer kidnapped in a highly visible public manner that threatens the existence of a host country. Unless his kidnappers are tracked and eliminated, and I mean every last one of them, it would be open season for any disenfranchised group. No diplomat, in any country, would be safe."

"The nature of diplomacy requires intimate and ongoing contact with foreign nationals in their country. We'd have to change diplomacy's foundations."

"Now you understand why Deverell just became so special, but no one in the Israeli government knows about this."

"So why was Israel all over our paying the ransom?"

"One more hook in the water, see what's caught."

"The five hundred dollar bills should be a concern."

"Why's that Sid?"

"They were removed from circulation forty years ago."

"Starting in 1969 to be precise, but not for the Federal Reserve. Besides they have an added advantage."

"Such as?"

"They won't need to be treated for drug residue like current denominations. Seems it ensures Bowieite will be the only thing detected."

"I still don't get handing over that amount."

"Sid remember its half life?"

"Yeah 10,000 years, a little bit of an overkill considering the seventy to eighty years most of us are given."

"Of course but it will allow that money to be tracked no matter whose hands it passes through which will give us a depth of knowledge of where the money flows as well as acquirable targets along the way. At home we accrue money to make our lives more comfortable, the latest toys, whatever. Money for jihadists is to further their cause and being able to track that five million will give many times that amount in information on their movements because to move they need money and lots of it."

"So Deverell is just part of the bait."

"Keep in mind he volunteered—"

"Anything else?"

"For what it's worth, the Israelis have called up every retired covert ops guy still ambulatory. Big surprise, they're at their highest alert level."

"That sure won't warn the terrorists."

"Whatever is going down is imminent, so the Israeli alert would be expected. PMIJ doesn't seem to care how many Israelis are involved. In fact, they might be enjoying the show, one other thing."

"There's more?"

"At 1500 hours yesterday, the nations of Jordan, Egypt, Syria and Lebanon began War Games near their borders with Israel. There was an immediate protest to the U.N. by the Israeli Ministry of Foreign Affairs."

"And?"

"Arabs claimed it was scheduled last fall."

"Was it?"

"Got a source at the U.N., she didn't find paperwork filed on it."

"Big surprise."

"The Arab League lodged an immediate protest, claiming the U.N. was notified about the War Games last fall and if the U.N. failed to file the documents, they would pursue a committee investigation on Zionist influence in the U.N. that kept the paperwork from being recorded."

"Sorry I asked."

"Interesting thing, though."

"What's that?"

"As part of my initial assignment to Israel, I studied all the wars since '48. Time after time, events looked bleak, but every time something happened and the Israelis prevailed."

"Something happened? Is that a new battlefield strategy? What does that mean, something happened?"

"That' just it, Sid, it was always different, but Israel shouldn't have survived declaring independence yet all these wars later here we are. Maybe it's nothing; just don't count Israel out. Someone seems to want their survival."

"Well, when you meet up with him or her, let me know."

"Or you can just sit back and enjoy the show. I've got a video conference in a half hour. Get some sleep. Lynda can hold down the fort; this thing has a ways to play out."

CHAPTER

38

Wednesday 19 March 2008

al-Ubeidiya, West Bank

The Ubeidiya Formation, containing a myriad of primeval dry cisterns, occasionally attracted paleontological interest. Only the largest cisterns, residing sixty or more feet below ground, appeared on any geologic maps where stratigraphic contour lines were drawn of selected deep strata. The shallower cisterns were content to remain anonymous and undisturbed, save for enterprising locals who sometimes found great utility in hiding things from the Israelis.

One specific mujahid leader grew up aware of these hideaways and claimed, as did most Palestinian Arabs, de facto ownership of what had, more than one time in history, been Jewish land.

Outside al-Ubeidiya, a town of 10,753 souls, five and one-half miles from where the grocer acted nobly, assuring himself Allāh's favor, Nuri al-Massalha set about writing the final chapter of a story birthed from the death of his father a lifetime ago, as he made his way through the vertical rock fissure and descended ninety-four wooden steps to the heart of his lair fifty-one feet below the surface. With only one way in and, most importantly, one way out, his twenty-five armed, testosterone-driven mujahideen, along with local guards, were all aware of the consequences of another escape. With his wings clipped Nuri doubted the American could attempt to flee with or without the traitors or the Jew.

On arriving at the bottom step, Nasir awaited. "*Marhaba*, welcome, all is prepared."

"The bomb-maker?"

"He has arrived and, according to his words, is ready for tonight."

"Why is he not here to greet me? Words were passed of the time I would arrive."

"I relayed those words. He appears to be a man of great self-worth. I was not greeted when I went to welcome him as he arrived with his assistants."

"He would show wisdom not to forget respect where it is due. Our guests?"

"Secure in the northern pit. Their injuries and darkness of their surroundings testify to the futility of any attempt to escape. Local volunteers are posted should they challenge their lodging."

"You have done well. Has everyone arrived for tonight?"

"In ones and twos, as instructed; all twenty-four mujahideen have arrived over a three-day period to avoid notice."

"The time is at hand. I have final preparations to complete. I will make myself available to receive the bomb-maker in my quarters in thirty minutes. It would not be in his interests to fail to embrace respect a second time."

"He will come."

Central Meeting Alcove
later that night

Nuri advanced to the front of the eighteen by forty-foot alcove off the main cave that had been divided in half and set up as a meeting area by the addition of wall and end curtains, overhead lights, and a hanging white linen tablecloth attached to the front wall, tensioned between four poles into a screen. Two rectangular, eight by two-and-a-half-foot folding tables, placed end to end, occupied a plywood stage in front of and below the screen, with folding chairs on the dais for the bomb-maker and his two assistants. Twenty-four scuffed polypropylene chairs with steel frames were arranged in pairs in two rows on the nearly flat floor of the cave in front of the platform. A single chair sat by itself behind them with another single chair near the rear curtain.

Stepping up on the nine-inch tall stage, Nuri awaited silence. Conversation ceased. He looked from face to face, and then began. "This day we assemble for a cause generations have sought and been denied. Less than seven miles from this spot, each of you will embrace the freedom our people have too long been denied. Brothers from every nation of god and even those from *Jannah*, Paradise, have looked on as each of you was chosen for this moment sixty years in coming. Failure is not a mujahideen word, even if success takes us from this life into Allāh's glorious presence."

"The virgins, don't forget the virgins," one man said, his pimply face witness to his never having experienced the joy of a woman's embrace.

Smiling, Nuri betrayed no contempt for any motive other than destruction of the detestable Jews. "Yes, the joys of eternal bliss, but to win these you must act with courage and honor. Cowards and unbelievers do not share in god's promises." He paused to give his words weight. "What is done in these next three days will determine the fate of our people. Two days will be for training, the third for rest and prayer, and then we will attain what preceding generations have only held in their dreams. Many have launched Qassams, set off IEDs. Our shaheeds are known the world over, yet infidels remain on Arab land. There are other ways you will learn this night and tomorrow, ways to victory using our combined strength which evil itself cannot thwart. Few, in all of Islam, understood what must be done to break from old paths, past defeats. Our calling demanded a man of understanding and skill. After much prayer and searching, one has arisen to train each of you in ways the Zionists will not overcome. Our land, our future, resides within you. Do not think on former days. Listen with minds and hearts; though we have much to learn, the world stands to be gained."

Looking down on the bomb-maker sitting in front of him, Nuri said, "Fakhir, my brothers are your brothers. We are ready for your wisdom."

Standing, the bomb-maker came around the end of the platform and stepped up beside Nuri, where the lesser of the two, Fakhir, greeted his leader with three kisses on his cheeks. Satisfied, Nuri yielded his position, stepping off the dais and walking to the back of the room as every mujahideen's gaze followed him. Without glancing back, he slipped out through the curtain.

The bomb-maker's assistants used the moment to open four wooden crates that rested on the back edge of the stage. All was ready. Fakhir looked from mujahid to mujahid, demanding attention at the center of the stage, the place he was born to inhabit.

"*Masaa'al-kheir,*" good evening, "I am Fakhir Saleem al-Din. No doubt many have heard of my work. I am the third generation called to the noble profession of bomb-making. While my father and my father's father were limited in what they were able to achieve, the Great Satan has done the soldiers of god a service in micronizing components to allow the use of traditional materials combined with state of the art devices that extend their reach and power with the promise to bring down the most infamous military in all the world, the Zionist army. In these next two days, you will learn how to connect devices that will bring an end to the occupation, as other brothers join in removing the Jewish scourge from the land of our ancestors."

Rising, one of the mujahideen said, "There are others? This glory was to be ours alone."

"Perhaps I speak to things not revealed. I have accepted but one task, however complex, and have no direct knowledge of other actions to be undertaken, but words, like hope, gather wings and fly where they will. It has come to my ears that yours will not be the only voice heard, but I cannot speak to such matters; I can but dream."

Looking around the room, Fakhir was satisfied that all had surrendered to his will; these were warriors worthy of the honor of his calling. "It is not chance each of you has been seated next to a specific mujahid. From this moment, you and your brother mujahid are a team—all teams were chosen by Nuri al-Massalha personally. We are charged with five critical objectives. Each team will be assigned a primary objective that will be accomplished in a specific order and time. Do not be concerned if you struggle to learn. When we are done you will know all that is required and be able to complete your task during the challenges on the field of valor."

"Where this will take place?" Nasir asked. "We know it's near. Wisdom demands it be on occupied land."

"Our target is *Burj Daūd*, what infidels call the Tower of David."

"Burj Daūd in al-Quds? Jews crawl over every inch of their precious tourist attraction. Our only claim to this tower Ottomans built is the crescent moon on top of the minaret."

"In three days all will change. You have much to learn, so we cannot linger on each point. After all has been made known, I will answer questions. My brothers, every element has been prayed over to ensure victory. Sadiq and Nadim will now hand each team a cell phone."

Fakhir's assistants handed out a cell phone to each team.

"Sadiq, the projector, Nadim, lights." A huge picture of the DiDaTel p3500 flip phone came into focus on the linen screen behind the speaker, the open phone's major parts labeled. "What do you hold in your hand?" Silence echoed through the cave. "Come now, surely someone can speak."

"A cell phone master bomb-maker, many of us have such a phone."

"These phones will thwart the Israelis and their billions of shekels spent on keeping our peace-loving people subjugated. None have been altered. It's what we do with them, how they are to be connected, that brings us victory."

Over the next six hours, every part of the DiDaTel p3500, Fakhir's wiring harnesses, and how all wires must be connected was drilled into the mujahideen by Fakhir and his assistants, so many times and in so many different ways that the slowest mujahid could have taught the lessons to any feeble-minded *jihadist* who had never set eyes on a cell phone. When the presentation was complete, vacuous mujahideen eyes stared at Fakhir, testifying to their need for rest.

"It is late, my brothers, but we have ground we must walk together this night. Nourishment will come soon and each will find prepared delicacies worthy of warriors, but first let us give heed to our five operational objectives; success and glorious victory live in them. Once you have embraced these, a feast awaits."

Two hours later, ravenous and brain-dead mujahideen were released from their mental indoctrination.

After the meal, as the mujahideen settled in from their too short break with sated bellies, Nuri slipped into the back of the room and sat down while Fakhir took his place on the dais. "Before nourishment we explored five operational elements. Which is first?" Silence greeted his words. "This ends now. I have come a vast distance at great peril and crossed many enemy lines to be here. I possess glorious knowledge to bestow, but silence imperils your calling. I need to know what you keep hold of, so when I ask questions I expect answers. Is that understood, my brothers?"

"Na'am," echoed throughout the room.

"Good. Which element is first?"

"Securing hostages."

"Securing hostages to the tower."

"Securing—"

"Na'am, yes, good. You were paying attention. What is the second element?"

"I know bomb-maker," came an excited voice.

"Well, what is it?"

"Securing the launch—"

"Tube," another broke in.

"I become impressed, but when a brother begins to speak let him finish. There will be other times for you to speak. The third element?"

Competing voices shouted over each other. "Antenna."

"Timer," came from the back.

"Such zeal, I am pleased. Let us stay with the third element."

"Antenna."

"Good. The fourth?"

"It is wiring connections, bomb-maker," Nasir said.

"What is the last element we must deal with?"

"Timer."

"Na'am, yes, now we can proceed. You will take hostages to Burj Daūd. My joy is what will be done on the minaret catwalk. The greatest of skill was demanded to assure success: details pored over, every possibility considered for the tiniest flaw. All actions require the simplest of connections, that when made are impossible to defeat. Leader al-Massalha, would you care to tell our brave warriors why this specific target was chosen out of all *Isrā'īl*?"

Nuri stood, making no move to the front of the room, compelling all mujahideen to rise and turn to face him, demonstrating, once again, his command of these men. "Burg Daūd minaret is the highest point in the Old City and serves our launch purposes best, as it establishes, one final time, that all of al-Quds is Arab possession, not just the 1967 boundary line. Sixteen hundred feet away is the Dome of the Rock on the al-Haram Ash-Sharif, our Noble Sanctuary, and one place even the Zionist army, depraved as they are, would dare not touch in a counter-offensive to disable the launch."

"What are we to launch?"

"This is the reason the bomb-maker has come to us. He will teach how a single fireworks shell, filled with twenty-one pounds of anthrax, will usher in the final birth pangs that will deliver Arab land to its rightful owners. There will be small arms fire resistance, but to stop our launch demands a missile capable of destroying all twenty-one pounds of the anthrax. Not only is the cost too great, considering the destruction of the tower and surrounding buildings, but the exploding missile itself would deliver the anthrax to the winds above al-Quds while the resulting destruction of our holy places would bring the wrath of the Arab world. While you have been here preparing for your destiny, countries from Jordan to Lebanon are taking final steps to amass along every border with Isrā'īl to engage in War Games. Brothers, when the signal is given, they will join in driving the sons and daughters of pigs and monkeys from sacred Arab land."

The room became still. This day of all other days, destiny became their champion. Nuri left the room.

One by one, each mujahideen's gaze returned to the front. "Be seated," the bomb-maker said, looking into each face. He saw determination building in those before him. He waited for the juncture of time and inner fire. "Two will guard the exhibition hall, and four the minaret base and tower entrance. Ten will provide counterfire while two mujahideen secure each hostage and set up armaments while the catwalk is exposed to Israeli fire. This is your calling and fate." Fakhir looked down, the faces of the warriors before him rapt in anticipation. "You will be protected. I have secured world-class bullet-resistant vests from friends in Iran. They are made of inverted, triangular tungsten, carbide ceramic disks encased within fiber composite laminate to protect against high ballistic performance of enemy weapons." Blank faces stared back at him. "Brothers, you will have bullet-resistant vests and helmets to protect you from Israeli fire."

"Bulletproof vests?"

"No, bullet-resistant, high-velocity sniper fire can penetrate any vest, especially with repeated fire in the same area, but, my brothers, you will have the best protection available." Fakhir gazed from warrior to warrior, demanding their attention, determined to forge ahead before any understood the costs that would be exacted. "Sadiq, Nadim, the vests and helmets."

Fakhir's helpers went to the wooden crates and began placing vests and helmets on the tables.

"If you will come forward when your name is called, Sadiq and Nadim will show you how to put the equipment on that was ordered for each of you."

Sadiq took control, calling out, "Nasir." Fakhir exited the room. Three hours passed before the last vest and helmet made their way onto the last mujahid and their novelty had run its course, everyone feeling properly a warrior.

"Let us rest. In a few hours we begin anew," Sadiq said. Tired but elated warriors welcomed the coming rest few could embrace.

CHAPTER

39

United States Embassy, Consular Section 71 Ha-Yarkon Street, Tel Aviv

Day Three
Wednesday March 19, 2008

Looking down, Keane re-read the posting.

Dated: 19 March 2008.

Israel Standard Time (UTC+2): 0301 hours.

Posting URL: http://www.palestinianliberation/dar/alharb.sy

Body of Text: American dollars ready for liberation?

Click link for instructions.

Link page: Time is near. Everything in order. If tracking device discovered, immediate execution. Return to site in twenty-four hours for final instructions.

Link page URL identification: www.pmij.sy

Keane knew a ransom—even bait money that led to enemies getting neutralized—wouldn't help Deverell. Assets couldn't cover an entire PA town, and he doubted it would give Deverell much comfort that the Bowieite coating would help track his killers. Deverell would be executed or used in whatever sick manner his captors had in mind and it would all fall back on him, when he had been against the ransom all along. *I hate my job*. Of course, whether Deverell survived or not was a moot point: Several State people had been killed over the years. The issue was what would happen to his killers, and those even peripherally involved and whether that would send the right message. His phone rang. “Yes, Alice.”

“Mr. Cantwell to see you.”

“Send him in.”

“You didn’t come by,” Sid said, entering the room.

“Just trying to figure the game PMIJ is playing before I laid it in your lap. Here,” Keane said, handing the newest post to him.

Reading it, Sid’s face soured. “Game is right. They’re vying for time.”

“But why, we’re not the key player; Israel is. A major biological attack has more weight than a missing FSO on anybody’s scale, Sid.”

“Maybe one of the mujahideen is branching out, looking for a little retirement money, hoping the boss is too busy to notice.”

“Pretty dangerous game. Ready for the other hot topic of the day? Yesterday at 1500 hours, exactly twenty-four hours after the first four Arab countries showed up on Israel’s borders, Saudi Arabia, Kuwait, Libya, and Sudan joined the War Games. That brings the count to eight countries playing war on Israel’s borders. Something is going down, and we’re right in the middle of it. All safe rooms have been checked and are stocked, so we’ll be good until they can get us out of here should Washington decide it’s time to evacuate.”

“My people are ready, Keane.”

“They may need to be. Remember our missing link—the connection between our missing consulate officer and the bad guys?”

“You found one?”

“Janitor by name of Yasmina cleans your section.”

“My section?”

“She stopped at her cousin’s house on the way home from work the day Deverell arrived.”

"And you know this how?"

"Routine check, she left work early. We noticed it and followed up, just like in all the training films about how good we are."

"And?"

"My guy decided to hang around to check any movement at her cousin's house. Right after Yasmina left, her cousin's husband went out to the 'Anā jā'i' Café."

"So maybe he was hungry."

"Anybody ever mention you'd make a lousy covert operative? The 'Anā jā'i' is a known PMIJ meeting place."

"Even Palestinians get hungry."

"Must have been a hell of an appetite."

"Because?"

"Seems to have cost Yasmina's pregnant cousin her husband. Watched him enter the café, but he never came back out."

"So what did you find when you searched the place?"

"We ran infrared scans after the place was closed. He wasn't there. We don't physically search every insurgent meeting place unless our electronic scans give us a reason to go in. Tends to make them collect their marbles and find new places to play."

"What do you need from me?"

"Nothing, when we have the time one of my guys will get a statement from Lynda since she supervises the janitor. The husband will show up and we'll figure out how important he is. My guess, he picked up a few bucks for the information and is already back home with mama."

"So what's next?"

"I'll be in touch throughout the day as events unfold. I won't leave you or your people hanging until the last minute."

"Appreciate it, friend."

C H A P T E R

40

Wednesday March 19 2008

Wilsonville School District
Wilsonville, Oregon

Monday's postponed staff meeting crawled along at its usual pace, approximating molasses flowing down Mt. Hood. Crises were first up, but the plodding standardization of educating the next generation seldom brought calamity with the exception of an occasional student fight, which happened all too infrequently to be relied on. It was during a prolonged dearth of crises that this morning's meeting was taking place, in which some department heads attempted to obfuscate the fact everything was running smoothly and nothing needed fixing. Dr. Kasnow appeared relieved when Stanley knocked on the door. When he'd been waved in, Stanley approached the superintendent, bent down, and whispered intrigue, then handed him a slip of paper.

The interruption was a godsend for the bored department heads around the table. Janelle's concern raced to her assistant and his family. That was her Stanley interrupting.

"If everyone will excuse me for a moment, it seems a call cannot wait. Please continue, I'll be back momentarily," Dr. Kasnow said. Standing up, he looked at Janelle. "Dr. Henning, would you join me?"

"Should I take my papers?" Janelle asked.

"A good idea."

Gathering her documents, she followed the superintendent from the room. Catching up to him, she asked, "What's this about, Leonek?"

"You know as much as I do."

"Stanley?"

"Reception called and said they had the FBI on hold for Dr. Kasnow."

"Why call you?"

"Evidently the FBI was insistent in talking to your accountable supervisor—"

"Accountable supervisor?"

"That's what reception said and since phones are verboten during staff meetings, and it was the FBI calling, they punted the ball my direction. So I took the call, gave up Dr. Kasnow as the superintendent, and a lady was insistent I get him right away, immediately, as in right now—"

"I get it."

"So here I am."

"We'll know what this is about as soon as I call. Mind if we use your office, Janelle?"

"I'd prefer it."

Entering Janelle's outer office, Drs. Kasnow and Henning proceeded into her inner office. Stanley stopped at his desk. "You waiting for an invitation?" Janelle shouted from her office.

Coming in, Stanley sat in a chair adjacent to Janelle. Dr. Kasnow was seated behind Janelle's desk dialing the phone, receiver to his ear, waiting silently. "This is Dr. Leonek Kasnow, Superintendent of Wilsonville School District in Wilsonville, Oregon. Dr. Janelle Henning's executive assistant provided me your number and said it was imperative I phone." Nodding his head intermittently, he listened. "Yes . . . okay, I see . . . right in front of me in fact."

Janelle and Stanley exchanged puzzled glances as they listened.

"Of course, yes, of course I can, whatever time it takes. Just a moment, I'll ask." Looking at Janelle, he said, "Do you have a valid passport?"

"Yes."

"Yes, she has one. Okay, it's waiting at PDX. Electronic? First Class?" Looking across the desk he said, "I need something to write on."

Stanley went around the desk to the credenza and grabbed a notepad from a letter tray then handed it to the superintendent.

"Thanks." Speaking into the phone, "Now what's that information?" He started writing. "Hold it, what was that again? Good, just a little slower, I don't want to miss anything." He kept writing. "Okay, now let me read everything back to you. Departure 7:30 P.M. tonight, Alaska flight 2478 to Seattle. Leaving Seattle on Continental 234 at 10:15 P.M., arriving Newark 6:17 A.M. tomorrow. Out of Newark on Continental 1216 at 7:20 A.M., arriving Dulles 8:42 A.M., that it?"

"What's going on?" Janelle muttered under her breath.

Stanley shrugged.

Dr. Kasnow nodded his head as he listened. "You'll have someone there to meet her? Good. I'll inform Dr. Henning everything will be ready for her. Thank you so much. What's that? Of course I'll call when I drop her at the airport. This same number? Another? Okay, go ahead." He continued writing. "Great, I've got it. A grey suit? Janelle?"

"Yes, Leonek."

"You have a grey suit?"

"Of course."

"Yes, she has a grey suit." He continued to listen. "No, that should about do it. Thank you, goodbye." He started to hang up. Jerking the receiver back to his ear, he shouted, "Wait, you still there? Good, one final question, why was I called? Dr. Henning is a department head. Oh, I see, bureau policy considering the circumstances, just wondering, not that I mind helping. Thanks again." He hung up the phone. Looking at Janelle, he said, "Life is about to get interesting."

"Exactly what's going on?"

"I don't have the slightest idea."

"We just heard your half of a detailed conversation about my flying out of PDX tonight. How can you not know?"

"Here's what I learned. The number I dialed was FBI headquarters in Washington, D.C. A one-way, First Class, ticket has been electronically sent to the Alaska Airlines ticket counter and will be waiting for you. You are to take your passport and pack enough clothes for approximately two weeks."

"You need a passport for Washington now?"

"Might be just for identification. I wouldn't assume it's for out of country travel yet."

"Yet?"

"Someone will meet you at Dulles in Washington."

"So what happens if thirty of us are wearing grey suits?"

"I don't think that will matter. It appears whoever is meeting you has a file and knows most everything about you."

"That's comforting. So who was this person you were talking to?"

"She gave me her name but it was before I had paper to write it down."

"Let's see if I have this right. I am to fly out of Portland airport tonight to Washington, D.C., where I will be met by a complete stranger, at which point I may or may not leave the country, for an undetermined length of time, and you didn't get the name of the person you were talking to. Does that about cover it?"

"You were paying attention."

"Leonek, let's assess the situation for a moment. We both know you don't get on a plane because someone on the phone suggests it."

"Have you ever had anyone else trying to spirit you away to Washington?"

"Let's see what the internet turns up. What's the FBI number you called?" Janelle asked. Going over to the workstation on her side desk she pulled out her chair and sat down. Opening her home page search engine she typed FBI headquarters then clicked on http://www.fbi.gov, when it came up. She clicked on *Contact Us* then on FBI Headquarters. (202) 324 greeted her; the last four digits of the phone number were different. But since the listed number was probably reception, it could be valid. None of the other links on the page applied.

"I'm not getting on a plane just because someone called and interrupted my day."

"Our day, Janelle," Dr. Kasnow said. 'Do you know anyone who would pull a prank like this?"

"Well, no."

"Then call the airline. Either they have a ticket for you or they don't."

She called.

They did.

"Guess I should get home and pack, but still Leonek a call isn't much to go on."

"Then phone the FBI."

"You phone. You spoke to them."

Lifting the receiver, he dialed the numbers he was given to call when he dropped Janelle at PDX then put the call on speaker. It was answered after the second ring. "F.B.I., how may I direct your call?"

"Yes, this is Dr. Kasnow, Wilsonville School District."

"How may I help you, Dr. Kasnow?"

"I received a call earlier today about one of my administrators and a trip to Washington, D.C. I am calling to verify."

"What state, doctor?"

"Oregon."

"Thank you. I'll transfer your call. Please stand by."

The phone rang four times then went to voicemail. Everyone listened.

"Well, Leonek, was that the voice you talked to earlier?"

"If not, she's got a voice double working for the FBI, time to pack, Janelle. Since this has national security written all over it, your time will be covered. You have someone to take care of things at home?"

"Mom and Dad, but, there's only one person this could involve and—"

"Don't go there, you'll find out soon enough. If the government is indulging in a First Class ticket, your presence is important. Call if you can, either here or at home, no matter the time. If you can't, don't worry."

"All reports are current, Janelle, and I know the routine so I'll make sure everything is filed in a timely manner. Any authorizations I need, I'll go to Dr. Kasnow," Stanley said.

"No problem," Leonek said. "We'll take care of things here. Just get home. I'll pick you up 4:30 on the dot."

"Leonek, you don't have to do that. I'll take the shuttle."

"Not on your life. You didn't hear the FBI telling me to take you to the airport myself."

"They did?"

"I'll buzz your gate at 4:15. Be ready. Now get out of here."

Late morning was spent making calls. Mom had more questions than Janelle had answers. Dad calmed things down enough for her to get off the phone and pack. She showered, applied makeup, and dressed in her grey suit. When Leonek buzzed the gate at 4:15, she was ready. The only unanswered question was, ready for what?

CHAPTER

41

Thursday 20 March 2008, 0400 hours

al-Ubeidiya Formation Cistern

Breakfast for the tired mujahideen was hot, plentiful, and delicious. Morning prayers—along with all other daily prayers—were strangely absent for warriors carrying out god's will. Twenty-five full but bleary-eyed souls, back in the central meeting alcove, awaited their teacher.

Throwing open the back curtains, Fakhir strutted toward the center of the dais, pulsing with zeal. He waited to speak, allowing all eyes to converge on him, then waited one moment longer.

"The tasks you perform will inscribe our names above the stars. Generations to come will bless one another by their mere mention. Streets, parks, and cities will bear your names and that of your humble servant who leads you in all knowledge and wisdom. It is upon our bravery, in the face of all that evil can throw at us, that Palestine will be born into the community of nations."

Backs straightened as air filled reinvigorated lungs. "Where our resolve was born in commitment and forged in the heat of training camps in Syria, fervor has kindled a flame death itself cannot extinguish.

"We will review yesterday's instructions then drill until I see that your execution of each element brings the glory of our calling."

Alternating between providing inspiration and cramming more information than all but Nasir had ever encountered, Fakhir, Sadiq, and Nadim taught, badgered, encouraged, yelled at, cajoled, and, in the end, inculcated these nascent apprentices of death with the knowledge and skill required to surmount initial Israeli defenses. The plan: a lightning strike, at an unexpected hour, before the enemy could marshal its satanic power.

Each tactic was developed out of decades of observation: hundreds of eyes watching, always surveiling, making notes on the evolution of combat strategy, how and when enemy troops were deployed, above all the deployments of small numbers of troops. Eyes observed the ground conditions that preceded each deployment, how to turn the briefest hesitation to advantage, and the opportune moment for each type of incursion. Watching . . . gathering . . . waiting.

There was no more anthrax, not of this strain, not for this generation. It had taken a lifetime to locate, months to smuggle—in small balloons swallowed for concealment, a few ounces here, a pitiful few there. The moment was at hand.

Hour after hour they absorbed and practiced and soaked up yet more information.

After a too-short break for lunch, devoured in the meeting alcove, training resumed until growling bellies demanded dinner, but dinner came only after mastery.

Just as rebellion born of bone-weary tiredness was threatening to invade the unity of the tired mujahideen, nine unknown mujahideen barged into the rear of the alcove, blocking the exit. The biggest one spoke. "Little brothers, we are here to test skills under fire. Who is man enough to challenge us?"

Defiance burst into flames within the mujahideen:

"You came into our web; the spider's poison is bitter and strong."

"Let us deal with these intruders now."

"Our knives are honed and numbers strong."

"No, brothers, it is Zionist we annihilate," Fakhir said. "Our brothers are here to test us. Follow them to the back of the alcove. A mock tower, as will be faced at Burg Daūd, has been erected to execute an assault."

"Warriors of destiny," the biggest invader spoke, "let us proceed so my men and I can show you what is waiting from the enemy of peace." The invading team moved as one toward the back tower.

Chairs were toppled in haste as mujahideen swarmed after the intruders.

"Wait, helmets, vests, and rifles," Fakhir said, "your equipment."

Standing in front of the tower, the invaders gave the mujahideen time to look over the thirty-one foot edifice. "Four of my team will serve as hostages so that all elements will be as you will find them on the Burg Daūd minaret. Your Kalashnikovs and extra magazines have been loaded with rubber bullets, as have our rifles."

Whooping with glee at the chance to show these outsiders what mujahideen could do, hunger was forgotten. Testosterone and euphoria quickly sobered as rubber bullets raised welts on legs and torsos, from expert marksmen placing rounds in places unprotected by the new vests and helmets while deflecting counterfire behind strategically placed barriers.

Afterward, twenty-four exhausted mujahideen limped to dinner. The assault on the tower had demanded two hours of violent struggle, four times the allotted thirty minutes. Bruises and welts from the unrelenting rubber bullets mottled each warrior's extremities, but through the crucible of conflict, their will had been tested.

Nasir walked up to the dining table. "*Kef Halak*, How are you? Was training filled with surprise?"

"It was filled with pain. Memory had laid aside the sting of rubber bullets as peaceful demonstrations brought Israeli brutality when I was no more than a child."

"Does this not speak to the seriousness of our calling?"

"It speaks to the number of places a vest and helmet do not protect."

"Zero, what are your words?"

"It is good this day passes, but I have a question."

"Please."

"Why do Saghir and I take part in the tower capture exercise when our skill in marksmanship will be called upon to guard the door to the exhibition hall while you merely observe?"

"Each of us must understand all aspects of the mission, so no single brother can bring defeat. Each of you is skilled with the rifle. Though you and Saghir excel and have been chosen for your task, remember, you are but one of many, and should there be a need, you may take another's place. I observe to see where changes need to be made. Tiredness makes us forget things already known."

"Na'am, Yes, we are to know all things. But if Saghir and I are at the hall entrance, distance and obstacles to the minaret would prevent—"

"This is not mine to say; Nuri has decided which is why I have come. Today's training took more time than planned. We were to capture the tower twice over in the span of one hour and then our training to secure the exhibition hall would follow. This did not happen, so we must report to Nadim in the alcove when dinner is finished. Much learning waits to ensure your rapid access into the exhibition hall, where all will be protected from enemy fire. I know you are tired, but tomorrow's rest and prayers will heal battered limbs. Tonight we breach the exhibition hall door. It is your glory to have been chosen for this honorable task."

Tearing a corner from his pita bread, Zero speared a hunk of marinated lamb and placed it in the middle of his bread with a dollop of seasoned rice and a spritz of olive oil. Defiantly folding its edges until satisfied, he eased the oversized bite into his mouth. Chewing slowly, he gazed at Saghir who, coward that he was, had stopped eating. Defeated, Zero finished chewing and took a drink of juice. "Okay, I'm done." Pushing his chair from the table, he stood up and headed for the alcove.

A brightly lit room greeted Zero. Sitting on the left end of the dais, Nadim waited in silence. Chairs had been stacked and pushed to the side of the room and a table moved down onto the floor, its back legs against the front of the dais. A rubber mat placed under it extended two feet into the room. A four by eight sheet of plywood stood upright against the leading edge of this table. A five by three foot tubular steel metal frame leaned against the plywood held by the rubber mat. On the floor by the frame, two canvas bags sat both zippered shut.

Nadim made no effort to greet or interrupt Zero as he inspected the strange aggregation before him. Saghir, coming up beside him, took in the collection of items in silence as well. On closer inspection, Zero saw that the front of the steel frame, leaning against the plywood, had a small gash cut into the entire frame in the middle of the square tubing. Clay appeared to line the inside of the gash. Pulling the top of the frame away from the plywood, he saw no other cuts. "I put finger inside?" Zero said.

"Touch—inspect—see."

He placed the tip of his pinkie inside the tube in several places, feeling the hardened clay. "This is clay?"

"Is clay."

"Kiln-fired?"

"Na'am."

"In steel tube?"

"Is steel."

Zero wondered why they would line a square steel tube frame with kiln-fired clay. No answers came to mind. He glanced at Saghir, then Nasir; puzzled faces stared back. Was that a grin on Nadim's face? "What am I looking at?"

Nadim continued to sit in silence.

"Sometime before I'm too old to understand."

"Look closer."

Zero inspected the frame assembly again, wondering what it had to do with getting through the exhibition hall door. A square brace bar, the same width as the frame tubing, bisected the middle of the rectangular frame horizontally, its surface uncut. It appeared to stabilize the frame and keep it from racking. On the back of this brace bar, in its middle, a hinge had been welded. A round pipe was welded to this hinge which ran vertically to the ground. Inside the bottom end of this round pipe a second, smaller pipe was inset, held in place by a thumbscrew that had been threaded through the outer pipe. A rubber foot capped the inset pipe.

Rising from the dais, Nadim walked to the frame assembly and placed his left hand on an edge. "This is a charge frame. It will burn through the exhibition hall's metal door."

"How is this possible?" Zero said.

"You see the cut in tubing?"

"Yes, of course. I asked about this, stuck my finger inside."

"By tomorrow night the gash will be filled with thermite mixed with barium nitrate and just enough soft clay so everything stays in the frame."

"What is the burn temperature?" Nasir asked.

"Thermite with barium nitrate combusts near 4532°F.

"And the steel door?"

"Melts around 2400°F."

"So the frame must hold while the metal door burns?"

"That's the kiln-dried clay's part. It keeps the steel tubing from melting as it directs the heat."

"I thought we got to blow the door up," Zero said.

"And bring stones around the entrance down?"

"Oh, I never thought about that."

"Any more questions?" Nadim asked.

"Will clay change the temperature thermite burns at?"

"A degree, maybe two. Thermite, by itself, is granular and would fall from the frame. By mixing with soft clay it becomes moldable while retaining its performance."

"This is good."

"A magnesium ribbon will be embedded into the thermite at both top corners of the frame. These ribbons will reach from the charge frame to where you and Saghir are, on each side of the door far enough away so you won't get burned. When you ignite the magnesium ribbon; the magnesium ribbon will ignite the thermite."

Going to the bag, Nadim unzipped it and pulled out two butane micro-torches. "Pull the trigger and they start. The flame has been adjusted, do not change it. There are two torches in each bag in case the first torch misfires."

"You both know how to use a micro-torch?" Nasir asked.

"Nadim just said pull trigger, it lights, flame comes out," Saghir said. "Not like we need college to trigger torch."

Zero tested a torch by pulling its trigger; flame leapt out.

"Since you have energy from dinner, Zero, lift the charge frame around you and walk to the back of the room. The frame will feel awkward at first as it fights you. When you reach the back of the room, place the frame on its end against the plywood I set up against the tower, then pick it back up and put it around you again, balancing it as you walk back here. As you begin to feel the frame's movement while walking, speed will increase. After you master this I will show you how to set it up so the door will be breached before the Zionists can stop you. Saghir, take both bags with torches inside and follow Zero to the back of the room. You've both walked this route and know the terrain. Picture this in your mind: the ambulance has just stopped near the exhibition hall door. The exhibition hall door is just feet away and is yours to conquer.

Three hours later, exhausted from trekking back and forth across the room, Saghir and Zero, having traded places carrying the frame, were able to run with the frame and set it up to breach the door.

"Zero, Saghir, though tomorrow is a day of rest, I will call you down so you can see the charge frame filled with thermite and with the magnesium strips attached."

"Any final questions that come in the night, I will answer before Fakhir, Sadiq, and I take our leave tomorrow."

"You're not going with us? I was hoping you'd join us in al-Quds," Zero said.

Nadim smiled.

After one final run-through, Nadim, satisfied, released them to limp their way to bed.

CHAPTER

42

Thursday March 20 2008

Washington Dulles International Airport Dulles, Virginia

Janelle followed the crowd toward ground floor baggage claim. Having drifted off somewhere east of Wyoming, she was holding her own. *Now where is that escort?* Not that it mattered, caught as she was in the stream of humanity flowing through the concourse. She'd concern herself with that after claiming her suitcase. Janelle was content to follow the crowd and found herself next to someone mom would refer to as a big-boned farm girl. At nearly six foot tall and, she guessed, two hundred pounds, this gal could milk cows all day long. Just then the farm gal turned to Janelle.

"Hello Dr. Henning, my name is Diandre."

"Oh my, aren't you the surprising one. How long—"

"Identified you when you exited the plane, just waiting for the right moment."

Janelle claimed her bag and Diandre had no trouble carrying it to the parking lot, where they got in a black four door sedan, "Where to, Diandre?"

"Sit back and relax. We're twenty-six miles from Washington. I'll have you there before you know it."

"Are you going to tell me what this is all about?"

"Naw, don't know much more than that they gave me a couple of pictures and told me to hustle out to Dulles and pick you up. I did, and here we are. Best to do what you're told and not ask questions, if you know what I mean."

"Since my employment won't be jeopardized by asking questions, I have 3,000 mile's worth of them."

"Well, good luck with that, but I'm just your driver. You want we should take the grand tour once we get in the city? Boss never said I had to get you right there."

"A rain check? There are other matters on my mind at the moment."

"Right. I'm so dense."

"You're delightful, I appreciate the offer; maybe some other time."

"Son on your mind?"

"What about my son?"

"Isn't he the one in the West Bank?"

"The West Bank, he's in Tel Aviv."

"Aw jeez, I always do that. Shoot off my mouth about something I don't know nothing about. Besides, you just can't trust rumors. I'm sure they'll set things straight when I get you to headquarters."

"Diandre what do you know about my son?"

"Look I've said too much. We're going to 935 Pennsylvania Avenue, and you'll know more than I do in a jiffy."

Janelle decided it wasn't worth interrogating Diandre; she'd be to her destination in a moment and would be told the reason for her journey. She tried to stop thinking and concentrate on the passing spring blossoms budding on the trees. Their beauty did little for the churning in her soul.

"Here we are, Dr. Henning," Diandre said after about thirty minutes, pulling to a stop in the underground garage. She got out and grabbed Janelle's suitcase. "Follow me, Doc. By the way, I've got this pain in my neck that drives me nuts when I turn my head sharply to the right."

"Sorry, I'm not a medical doctor. I'm an educator."

"What the hay, don't hurt to ask."

"Though I might recommend you solve the problem by not turning your head sharply to the right."

"Now why didn't I think of that?"

"You're not a doctor."

Walking past the receptionist, Diandre led Janelle to her boss's office. "Hey, Lizzie, got the Doc from Oregon."

"Dr. Henning, welcome to Washington. I hope your flight was pleasant. Please have a seat. Mr. Theime will be with you shortly."

"Thank you."

Lizzie picked up the phone's receiver. "Yes sir, Dr. Henning is here. Yes, of course, sir."

"Dr. Henning, would you like some coffee or tea? We also have juice if you'd prefer."

"Thank you, but no. I had more than my quota on the plane."

Five minutes later the door opened and a diminutive, stooping, male came out. He walked over to Janelle and offered a limp hand. In an effeminate voice, he said, "Dr. Henning, Ray Theime."

Janelle tried to quash a smile as his prepubescent demeanor caught her by surprise.

Shaking her hand, he said, "I know, not your typical FBI type. I get that all the time. They hired me for computers, and then transferred me."

"No, I'm sorry. I'm just tired and on edge."

"Diandre and I will be escorting you to another location. I just need to verify your identification."

"Pardon?"

"Any photo I.D. A driver's license, passport will do nicely, Dr. Henning."

Janelle pulled out her license and handed it to the tiny man.

He studied it. "Everything looks okay," he said, handing it back to her. "We're just your friendly taxi service. Gotta get you over to State."

"My son works for the State Department."

"I know."

"Why didn't I go directly to the State Department?"

"Just how the government runs, Dr. Henning, inside the country we're the go-to guys."

"Does that mean I'm leaving the country?"

"We were just your taxi service. It's a need to know situation and all we were told is to get you to State when you arrived. Just a few more minutes and you'll talk to the people with the answers."

On their drive to the State Department, Janelle looked at Ray Theime sitting beside her in the back seat, "Between you and Diandre, I haven't had one question answered. You have to know they attack my every thought."

"Dr. Henning, I understand we haven't been a fount of information. Would my having told you one more time I don't know anything have helped or even have been believed? Contrary to urban legend, the different branches of government do not share information unless someone a lot higher up the food chain than me says to share. All I can tell you is that you weren't brought from Oregon to be kept in the dark. After I drop you off, ask away. You'll get answers; that's the way things work here, sometimes."

"Can you at least tell me where I'm being led?"

"That I can, Diplomatic Security."

Janelle wanted to stop, turn around. She didn't want to learn the reason she'd been flown across the country from Diplomatic Security which could only mean Addison was in trouble or worse.

The car pulled into an underground parking lot. Everyone got out and too soon they came to a sign, 'Bureau of Diplomatic Security.' Janelle felt the color drain from her face as her stomach threatened to empty itself of food it no longer contained.

"Dr. Henning, don't jump to conclusions just yet. Diplomatic Security has proven itself the world over. Wait until you're briefed."

She did not want to be briefed. She wanted to go home. Go anywhere. She did not want to hear what anyone at Diplomatic Security had to say about the one person she loved more than life itself. *Wait, think Janelle, if he were dead then why all this? There would be a call, maybe a telegram. Do they still send telegrams?* She wondered. *And then a body would be flown home, all official, all cut, all dried, with appropriate expressions of a proud and grateful nation when no words could bridge the void of such loss. There would be no reason to be flown across the country, or picked up at any airport. No reason for a trip to the FBI or State Department Diplomatic Security. Addison must be alive.*

"All the best, Dr. Henning," Ray Theime said as Diandre opened the door

Exhaling, Janelle entered the room and turned to her guides, forcing a smile. "Thanks, I think."

"They'll take good care of you," Diandre said, stepping forward awkwardly and hugging her. Stepping back, she watched as Janelle continued into the jaws of the reception area.

A woman Janelle's age was waiting; professionally dressed, every item projecting control, confidence. Immaculate makeup, enhancing while not drawing attention to itself. Hair, graying or dyed—for affect? It worked. Walking up to this stranger, Janelle stood there searching her face. It gave away no secrets.

"Dr. Henning, I'm Galena Orey. Was your flight agreeable?" she asked, extending both hands. Janelle put forth her right hand which Galena enclosed in hers.

Continuing to assess this stranger, Janelle considered the position she found herself in and guessed who this might be. "Pleasure was not the reason for my flight. Considering the circumstances, it went well. You're the psychologist."

"Very good Dr. Henning, while that is my field I'm here to help you understand everything. Please trust all is not as forlorn as might be imagined."

"My son is alive or I would not be here. Everything else I can handle. Is your office nearby? You have much to share, I hope."

Sitting on the polished cherry and leather chair across the circular table from Galena Orey, Janelle recognized the care with which an interior designer had chosen every item surrounding her, from the hand-embroidered French knot table linen to the antique brass alabaster urn table lamp. The lighting, inset in a low ceiling, was a subdued, warm yellow hue, creating the feeling of being embraced. No office noises invaded the confines of this haven.

"Now, Janelle, let me tell you everything we know and why you're here."

CHAPTER

43

Thursday 20 March 2008

Yechida Meyuchedet Le'Lochama Be'Terror (Ya'Ma'M) Headquarters Office of Colonel Aaron Samech, Henza Military Detachment Commander North Tel Aviv

The phone rang in Michael Ashtor's office. He answered it on the first ring. "Captain Ashtor."

"My office, now," demanded the familiar voice.

He was out of his chair before Colonel Samech could hang up his phone. Knocking once on the Colonel's door, Ashtor awaited the familiar bark before entering the Colonel's office. He snapped to attention and saluted.

"Sit," Colonel Samech said, ignoring the salute. "Your doctor from Hadassah did okay. I need to talk again, bring him."

"Now, sir?"

"Of course, now. If I wanted to talk later I'd ask later. You remember where Mount Scopus is, so get him."

"If he's there, sir."

"You want me to call someone else for a simple errand, Captain?"

"No sir, as you know, the doctor travels abroad and—"

"And get going before he leaves, dismissed."

Jumping up, Ashtor saluted and waited the requisite five seconds for a return salute. When none came, he pivoted sharply and marched out the door, making sure to close it behind him. He had made the mistake of leaving it open once when first assigned to the Colonel and had been amazed that one man had such an extensive vocabulary of profanities.

Returning to his office, he looked up Dr. Yochanan's number then called Hadassah, to be told the doctor was out and wouldn't be back until 16:30 hours. At 16:30 hours, Michael was waiting outside Dr. Yochanan's office. Afternoon turned into evening. Michael Ashtor didn't budge.

"Hello, if it isn't Captain Ashtor, if I remember correctly, from that nice Colonel's office," Dr. Yochanan said when he found Captain Ashtor on the verge of dozing outside his office at 6:17 P.M. "What can I do for you, Captain?"

"That nice Colonel would like to talk to you, sir."

"Do you have his number? I'm afraid I didn't keep it."

"He would like to see you in person, sir."

"Sounds important, how does first thing tomorrow morning sound?"

"With all respect, doctor, I believe the Colonel had tonight in mind. My car is outside."

"And so the intrigue continues. Let me put a couple of things in my office and I'll be right with you, Captain."

"I'm at your service, sir."

Forty-seven minutes later, Dr. Yochanan walked through Colonel Samech's door. "Colonel, how pleasant to see you, now what's this all about?"

"Please sit, doctor." Opening a file, Colonel Samech glanced at the information inside. Looking up, he began, "In 1950, you were born to Liba and Yossel Yochanan in Odessa Ukraine SSR. In point of fact, you were born in the village of Gvozdavka, but the birth record shows Odessa. In 1954, a sister, Shayndel Laila, was also born in Gvozdavka to the same parents. In 1957, Shayndel Laila was removed from your parent's guardianship. The matter was adjudicated under the Soviet Socialists Republic Politick Adoption Medical Services Authority. The reason for placement: politick insurrection. Assigned to Dom Rebyonka, Odessa Ukraine SSR."

"Colonel, so far you've said nothing that wasn't disclosed on immigration forms when making aliyah into Eretz Yisra'el in 1980."

"Doctor, there are no accusations. Everything will be made clear." Looking back at the file, he continued. "After aliyah, it was determined you are a Messianic believer."

"And?"

"It's not a concern for me, just reading information, though I suspect the Chief Rabbinate wasn't overjoyed."

"The Rabbinate and I do fine. My expertise appears to compensate for a lack of Jewish orthodoxy in embracing traditional beliefs. Colonel, I'm having a little difficulty figuring out why you'd be involved with immigration issues nearly three decades old. Certainly my parents are not implicated in a plot against a country they were never allowed aliyah to by the Russian authorities."

"If you could just be patient a moment more."

"Since it's apparent you have a prescribed agenda, Colonel, please proceed."

"Thank you. I was chosen for this assignment because my involvement with the anthrax vaccine brought me in contact with you. I always fulfill my duty. What I'm about to say must not be revealed to anyone not directly involved in this situation."

"You know, Colonel, conspiracy seems to follow you. I will, of course, treat everything discussed as confidential."

"Due to our investigation, which was a part of the anthrax vaccine incident, your attempts to locate your sister were brought to our attention. You already know French adoption records are strictly guarded, so your efforts weren't successful."

"How well I know that. Are you saying—"

"What if I said that an investigation at the highest level in Eretz Yisra'el found, through sources in France, the identity and location of your sister? Would this interest you?"

Asa shifted in his chair. As he leaned forward, his gaze bored into his inquisitor. "I have spent half a lifetime searching, but what could Shayndel have to do with anthrax? Colonel, please tell me what you know."

Colonel Samech smiled. Asa was reminded of a cat the split-second before its prey is pounced on, *he's enjoying this*.

Looking down on his notes, Samech scanned several pages before he stopped and looked up. "Doctor it's not your sister who's involved, but her son—your nephew—Addison Deverell. Mr. Deverell has become the guest of the *Palestine Mujahideen Islamic Jihad*."

"I have a nephew?"

"Somewhere in Judea or Samaria as we speak, intelligence forces are out in number, and, doctor."

"Yes Colonel."

"He's in great danger."

Over the next few hours, Asa discovered compassion in the Colonel. He explained and reviewed information Asa had spent a lifetime seeking, answering repetitive questions when Asa went back over every item, struggling to understand. It was a glimpse into a man Asa was certain few had seen.

"Two things, doctor," the Colonel said as he finished his account.

"Yes."

Aaron Samech wrote a number on a pad, he tore the sheet off and handed it to Asa. "This is my private number; I don't give it out, only for you. Call any time, it doesn't matter; I'll answer."

"Why—"

"I have a brother. If I am tough, he was tougher. Dov was smarter and he was always there. Then one day he wasn't."

"What happened?"

"Not a conversation for now, maybe some other day. I understand what it must be like to have family taken away, no matter who is doing the taking. You are being given a chance I never was, so I'll help. Much of our lives have been lived, we're both getting old, but there's still time for you."

"And the second thing, Aaron?"

"Your sister is being flown into Yisra'el and will be taken to your office in two days. You are to stay with her through everything, not that I need to tell you that but it came from above and is official policy. We are committed to victory, our survival depends on it, but when hasn't that been the case? We don't expect this to end well for your nephew, so maybe now would be a good time to pray to that God of yours."

"Aaron, I already am."

CHAPTER

44

United States Embassy, Diplomatic Security
71 Ha-Yarkon Street, Tel Aviv

Day Four
Thursday March 20, 2008

The posting went online at 0715 hours. Keane's first reading was for content, the second, memorization.

Dated: 20 March 2008.

Israel Standard Time (UTC+2): 0715 hours.

Posting URL: http://www.palestinianliberation/dar/alharb.sy

Body of Text: Blank

Click link for instructions.

Link page: Proceed to al-Eizariya. Only two people, both from embassy. Any Israelis seen, American not live. No weapons. Many eyes watching. Proceed main park to food cart. Be there 9:00 A.M. No sooner, no later. Arrive 9:01 A.M., goodbye to American. Wait instructions when arrive.

Link page URL identification: www.pmij.sy

Keane picked up the phone and hit the intercom button. "Alice, is everyone assembled?"

"Yes sir."

"Send them in."

They filed in.

"Don't sit, no one is staying. We've got to move fast. It's 0731 hours and we have a 0900 hours date in al-Eizariya. Josiah, get me road maps between this location and al-Eizariya. I want every known route plotted, including helo flight paths from the heliport to the nearest checkpoint. And, people, be aware that al-Eizariya is also known as Bethany."

"Where Lazarus was raised?"

"Yep, and if we're lucky we might end up resurrecting one foolish American. Hannah?"

"Yes, boss."

"Get drone surveillance photos for the same area. I need real time images from this morning."

"On it boss."

"Josiah, Hannah, why are you still here? Go!"

"Ellis, I want satellite images of the route and town. Then we need to start plotting everything out."

"On it, boss."

"Brandon."

"Yes."

"Sit. We've got a five million dollar drop to make in our target city, or at least that's where we're going to start. No telling where we'll end up. The money will be delivered here no later than 0800 hours, which will give us sixty minutes to acquire the target the PMIJ posted they want us at this morning. Here," Keane said, handing him the printout.

Reading it, Brandon handed it back to his boss. "You know terrorists can't be trusted. Even money Deverell is dead."

"It's also highly likely they plan on taking out whoever shows up for the drop. That's why it's going to be you and me."

"I agree with the me part, but you're the AIC. This needs to be handled by the troops. How about Hannah? She's as good as it gets, and we're a great team."

"Is there an acoustic problem in this room?"

"I heard you, but I just—"

"You think I run this show so I can sit this one out? The money has been prepared so that our satellites can follow it in real time and no bug will be found. The money and banding were treated and respond to a frequency no one else has, including our friends the Russians, who seem to have an interest in this. Anyone breaks the money packets apart and stuffs them in a well, we'll know where and how deep. They put it with other money, and we'll pick ours out. Needless to say, the money's not getting away from us."

"What about weapons?"

"None, we'll give the PMIJ credit they could find any weapons we carry, so we're going in unarmed."

"Not even drop weapons?"

"Brandon, it's Area A, full Palestinian control. If covert ops had the time to stash weapons the chances of getting caught would still be too great. That's why they kept us waiting for the drop location, not enough time for site countermeasures. We do anything they can detect and Deverell is gone, and that's not going on my resume. Relax, we're going to be covered. We have a new wardrobe courtesy of Uncle Sam. We'll be visible every step we take."

"Boss, I'm a believer. We've both had fun with some of the toys, but you know what al-Eizariya is like and what if we're inside a stone building? Even if we can be seen, what good would it do?"

"Let's put it this way: We both know how to extract from compromised conditions. Which reminds me," he said, opening his desk drawer and pulling out two envelopes and handing one to Brandon, "take this."

"And this is?"

"Open the envelope and swallow the pill if you want to join me for the fun."

Brandon tore open the envelope; a horse-sized capsule fell onto his palm. "RFID chip?"

"More sophisticated, but until you shit I'd avoid going anywhere you don't want to be tracked."

Sixty-eight minutes later

The Israeli Border Police cleared them through the checkpoint. Palestinians were absent from the normally crowded machsom. "Let's hope they want money and not American blood," Brandon said.

Leaving their car at the checkpoint, Keane and Brandon began walking. The twenty-two pound weight of the five million dollars pulled on Keane's hand. They had plotted and memorized the route. They were on target and on time. Before they left the embassy, Ambassador Walker hugged him, wishing god's speed. He hated being hugged, and it wasn't speed but being on time that mattered.

"Boss."

"Go."

"We need to take this alley."

"You sure, blasted streets are never marked."

"Got it on my lens," Brandon said, referring to the street map projected on his eyeglasses."

"Lead the way, Magoo."

As they passed between the backs of two rows of shops, garbage and oil drums lined the dirty lane.

"Stop!" A staccato command came from amongst the buildings. They kept walking as if deaf, covertly searching for the source of the voice. None could be seen. "Stop now, Americans!" They stopped. Adrenaline coursed through their veins, steeling them for action. They waited, motionless, an ability perfected over years.

"American with glasses, look on friend's forehead. What you see?"

Brandon looked at Keane's forehead. A pale red dot danced around its center. He remained silent.

"I said what do you see, American."

"Dot."

"And what do you suppose causes such dot?"

Brandon remained silent.

"American, you try my patience. Perhaps I decide you're not worthy to return to family this night. What means red dot?"

"Could be anything."

"Truly is something. What is guess? And do not tire me; I already know friend has money in briefcase so is no point to anger me."

"A laser."

"And what would laser be attached to, American?"

"Rifle?"

"American with briefcase, same question, what do you see on friend's forehead, and don't waste my time."

"Red dot—my guess—rifle laser."

"Is good, but time closes in on 9:00 A.M. and town square is many meters away. If you pay strict attention, maybe American Addison lives. If not, maybe he will be buried with stinking Jew. You choose."

"You want to keep us from delivering the money on time, it's your show, pal."

"Americans are so impatient. There enough time if you listen."

Under his breath, Keane said, "Brandon, you ready?"

In a whisper, he replied, "Ready, boss."

"Americans, stop with the whispering. You think we don't hear everything? Besides, where is place to run? You're in our home now. Look to left. See box on top of 55 gallon drum?"

"See it."

"Is gift. Glasses go over and pull gift from box, bring back. Briefcase, don't move."

Brandon went to the drum and pulled a briefcase from the box, bringing it back to Keane."

"Is good. Now, put on ground and open, not locked." Brandon placed it on the dirt and opened it. It was empty.

"Now, briefcase, open your case and also place on ground." Keane did as instructed.

"Very good, take gift for people of Palestine and put in new briefcase and make sure nothing but money is transferred. Our argument is not with America this day, so you decide—live or die."

Finishing the transfer, Keane caught sight of a prone male, indeterminate age, on an adjacent roof, rifle pointed at Brandon's head. Around his neck a checkered scarf stood out from his camouflage clothing.

"Now close and lock briefcase. Glasses put American case in box on 55 gallon drum." Both complied.

"There was no tracking equipment," Keane said.

"It no longer matters. Time to hurry, is getting close to 9:00 A.M. and Addison American needs you to make appointment. Next to food cart is little girl. Note attached to coat. Read and follow instructions."

"What if she's not there? Children don't stay put."

"She remains. Is daughter of Allāh, not like spoiled American brats."

"Let's go, Brandon," Keane said. "Take the lead; I'll follow, got to make that deadline."

As they wove their way through side streets, the town was empty. All shops were closed at the busiest time for shoppers and merchants. "How many mujahideen did you see, Brandon?"

"Two—diagonal roof corners—rifles on us."

"Same number I picked up."

"Town square's around the next turn, boss."

As they turned the corner, a grassless dirt patch where even the weeds were anemic greeted them. A single bench lay on its back.

"You sure, Brandon?"

"There's the food cart boss."

On the far side of the area, a green and orange cart stood, the lone occupant of the area, shut tight, its proprietor absent. Sitting within a fenced-off area, six feet in front of the cart, a waif of a child was playing with a rag doll in the dirt. They checked their watches; it was 0858 hours. As they scanned the surrounding area, none of the 17,000 residents could be seen, save the girl. They approached the fence.

"Brandon, I'll go in alone." Keane went toward the child and saw the reason she had not run off. A harness was attached to her upper body underneath her coat. From the harness a plastic-coated cable ran into a blue barrel attached to the food stand with a padlock. An envelope hung from the child's coat lapel, fastened with a safety pin.

Going up to the dirt-encrusted child of no more than five, Keane got down on one knee, setting the briefcase on the ground. "Marhaba, hello, do you have a note for me?"

Almond eyes returned his gaze. A lump lodged in Keane's throat as he looked down at this precious soul imprisoned in such ugliness. Gently, he reached out and unpinned the note. She watched him, interested in this new person in her world. Opening the note, he read:

'Congratulation on pilgrimage to town where prophet 'Īsā raised Lazarus from death. The briefcase is special. If you take it outside of fenced area, you will become a part of Palestine forever. Look to the food stand and see one of the gifts we have left. If the briefcase is left with the child, you will return home and live for many years to tell grandchildren of this moment when wisdom saved life.'

"Brandon."

"Boss."

"Check under the stand for explosives."

"Boss, the blue plastic barrel is nearly filled with what looks like fertilizer—picking up a strong smell of ammonia. I also detect diesel. Didn't want it camouflaged either."

"What about a fuse, Brandon?"

"It's here boss and I can see a battery at the base of the barrel."

Looking down on at the child, Keane swallowed hard. He wanted to scoop her up in his arms and take this beautiful waif from such evil, but knew he couldn't. Remembering something, he patted his pockets, coming up empty. "Brandon."

"Yeah, boss."

"Did I give you that cow chocolate bar I had?"

"Sure did."

"Tell me you still have it."

Brandon reached in his pocket and retrieved the *Shokolad Para*. "Catch," he said, tossing the bar across the fence.

He caught it, and the child's smiling eyes followed his hand with the bar. "Not a suitable gift for a princess, but it's all I have." She took it from him, tearing open the cover while beaming a smile as she began devouring the treat.

Reluctantly, he arose. "Let's go, Brandon."

"The briefcase?"

"It stays." Walking away from the child, he couldn't look back.

"Boss, what about Deverell?"

"Ask the child. She knows as much as I do."

CHAPTER

45

Friday 21 March 2008, 0510 hours

al-Ubeidiya Formation Cistern

Morning prayers came unbearably early for the aching, exhausted warriors. Each mujahid looked forward to breakfast and then bed afterward that would welcome their embrace.

Scooping *labneh* on a spoon, Nasir slathered the cream cheese yogurt onto his pita bread and took a generous bite. Sweet tea washed his mouthful down. The curtain surrounding the dining area parted, and Nuri entered the room with a man Nasir hadn't seen before. He watched as Nuri scanned the faces of the mujahideen focused on filling their bellies. On spotting Nasir, Nuri motioned him over.

"*Sabah Al-Khair*, good morning, Nuri."

"Sabah Al-Khair. This is Imam Marwan," Nuri said, indicating the salt and pepper bearded cleric standing next to him.

"Blessings, imam."

"Blessings upon you and our noble cause, my son."

"Last night's exercise must not stand," Nuri said.

"All were tired. I am filled with hope when the moment comes, all will succeed with Allāh's help."

"While Allāh grants those that do his bidding success it took four times the allotted thirty minutes to complete your mission, and this was with just five warriors providing a challenge," Nuri said. "Do you think the Jews will limit their numbers to five and also give us two hours before reserves show up? Success lives in accomplishing all within thirty minutes."

"But today is for rest— "

"My son," Imam Marwan said, "today was for rest and seeking Allāh, but we must ensure all can be accomplished in the time given. We proceed to the practice tower where all has been put in order. I will observe as you prove the skill of your training."

"What would you have us do imam?"

"Let our warriors finish their meal, then assemble them in the alcove. I will speak Allāh's blessings and we will improve our performance, for tomorrow a new nation will be born."

"As you say."

Five hours later, the tower had been taken three times. Their best time, with the constant fusillade of rubber bullets challenging every step, was thirteen seconds above the maximum time allowed. Mujahideen limped, bruised and exhausted, to their rooms. Scrambling across the finish line would wait the morrow, the weight of the next morning already taking residence in tired hearts.

CHAPTER

46

United States Embassy, Diplomatic Security 71 Ha-Yarkon Street, Tel Aviv

Day Five
Friday March 21, 2008

Scanning the internet, the last twenty-four hours had been among the worst of Keane's life. Being called to explain why a ransom produced nothing by the people who insisted their harebrained idea—which he repeatedly and loudly opposed—would work, was enough for him to consider retirement . . . again. What else could dampen his already sunny day? Then the intercom buzzed. "Yes, Alice."

"Mr. Bodine, Deputy Chief of Missions requests your presence in his office at your earliest possible convenience."

"Any clues?"

"Only that he wants to see you, according to Mary."

Great, it was Mary. Now he had to go. If the deputy's executive assistant called, there was no way to get out of it. He was up and out the door.

Walking into the Deputy's outer office, he was surprised to see Mary waiting for him. "Boss wants to see me?"

"Let's go in my office, Keane."

"Sounds serious."

Mary took a seat next to Keane's. Now he was nervous.

"Bad day?"

"Just wondering how it could get worse, then you called."

"Thanks."

"Mary, this isn't social, and if you're handling it yourself it's got to be something I won't like."

"But you're a big boy, Keane, and always choose what's best for the mission."

"Yeah, yeah. You know your pep talks are beginning to fall off lately."

"Could be what's happening with our missing consular officer."

"Look, Mary—"

"Relax, Keane, I got it. You were opposed to the ransom. So was Deputy Chief Mason. You know Dr. Janelle Henning?"

"Nope, should I?"

"She's Addison Deverell's mother."

"No, don't go there. I don't have anything to say to the woman."

"Much easier to kill 'em than comfort 'em."

"Funny."

"Look, Keane, she's flown from Oregon and has been kept from meaningful information."

"And you think I have any?"

"None of us do, but someone needs to talk with her."

"Gee thanks. How long do I have to prepare for this ordeal?"

"You notice the woman sitting in the outer office when you came in?"

"No."

"And you're Mission Agent in Charge for security?"

"I was focusing on you."

"That'd be a first. Take her to your office. Do whatever guys do when they're with an attractive woman, I don't care, just give the embassy a face that cares. Her son is god knows where, and at this moment, we're her only link. Give her something to hang onto, but prepare her. She's got a doctorate in education, so that should help some."

"A mother is a mother."

"I know, this is tough, but she asked to speak to the person in charge of finding her son. That's why you were chosen so blame her but it's the least the United States government owes the woman."

"I hate it when you're logical. I'll think of something."

"Of course you will, and Keane thanks."

Leaving Mary's office, he walked to the seating area and paused, looking down. "Dr. Henning?"

The woman looked up and nodded her head.

"I'm Keane Bodine, head of State Department security for the Missions in Israel. Shalom and welcome to Tel Aviv. Why don't we go to my office where we can talk?"

After time with Addison's mother, Keane knew he'd misjudged the woman. While she was fearful she had a mother's hope and was grateful for all that was being done which, at the moment, was pitifully little; an assessment he opted not to share. He ended up caring for the woman's son if for no other reason than because of her. He put his team to work checking with Shabak and local sources while he called Middle Eastern contacts. Maybe something would turn up.

CHAPTER

47

United States Embassy, Consular Section
71 Ha-Yarkon Street, Tel Aviv

Day Six
Saturday March 22, 2008

"Morning, boss."

"Hannah, what are you doing here so early?"

"I couldn't sleep, so I logged onto the net. Been on yet?"

"Just doing paperwork. Why is it there's twice as much when you're right?"

"You may want to see this," she said, handing him a single page.

Dated: 22 March 2008.

Israel Standard Time (UTC+2): 0300 hours.

Posting URL: http://www.palestinianliberation/dar/alharb.sy

Body of Text: America contributes to Palestinian people.

Click link for instructions.

Link page: As honorable servants of Allāh, we keep word. American Addison breathes. Whether he continues to live is for Zionist occupiers and enabling Americans to decide. Many have sought that which gives hope to the downtrodden. When the American fulfills his destiny, the oppressed will rise in glorious victory.

Link page URL identification: www.pmij.sy

"Well, one way or the other, boss, looks like it's about to end."
"Or get interesting, Hannah."

CHAPTER

48

Saturday 22 March 2008, 0325 hours

Outside al-Ubeidiya Formation Cistern

Turning right onto Highway 398, the convoy's armored 16,005 pound lead vehicle, a Palestinian Red Crescent Society Ford F-450 ambulance, accelerated as three modified PRCS Ford E-350 ambulances, carrying twenty-five PMIJ warriors and four hostages, pulled into line one hundred yards behind each other.

The lead ambulance's twelve-person capacity interior held two lone occupants along with five pounds of Semtex, from Czechoslovakia by way of Syria, strategically positioned inside its front bumper.

Quaseem Hadad, behind the wheel, and Azim Malouf, riding shotgun, both holstered Tokarev TT-33 pistols on their hips. A dozen fragmentation grenades, in an open wood crate, rested between two micro-Kalashnikov rifles in vertical mounting racks beside each seat, with ample magazines crammed among the grenades for the small war to be fought from their rolling bomb.

All doors had been welded shut in case a change of heart befell either mujahid before they met with destiny. Nuri understood bravery sometimes required encouragement. He kept the welding of the doors from Quaseem and Azim until they found themselves entering the ambulance through the passenger side's open window just after three that morning.

The pièce de résistance in this masterful creation, the apex of three generations of bomb-maker's art, Fakhir Saleem al-Din assured Nuri, was the inclusion of C-4 bricks that had been molded to the interior cavity of each door with explosive detonator caps wired to pressure switches set to trigger at 150 kilopascals—around 1½ times atmospheric pressure at sea level. The blast overpressure, when coupled with the Semtex, would pay homage to the genius of Arab bomb-making capabilities. A message would be sent, a legacy established.

The roads were dark and deserted in the hour before Arabs working in al-Quds began their customary trek to Israeli checkpoints, making their way through self-imposed daily bondage. The ambulances made good time. They kept their lights off—no need to attract roaming Israeli patrols with an offer of an escort or questions.

Unknown to the twenty-seven terrorists speeding toward the Old City in stolen ambulances, all four emergency vehicles had been picked up by *Zik*, a lone Hermes 450s Unmanned Aerial Vehicle 15,500 feet above them, navigating its normal flight path on auto-pilot in the cold pre-dawn air. Since Zik's feed to Palmachim Airbase drew no response from Ground Control, it continued its circuit.

At the precise moment the feed came through to his ground control console at 166 Squadron, 2nd Lt. Izaak Finkel awaited the emptying of his bladder. Finishing his business with a cleansing spritz of water on his hands, Izaak meandered by the snack drawer that contained his favorite, chocolate *rugulach*, which made long nights bearable. Who would be out at this hour? He made it a point to time breaks when it was safest, knowing from nine months experience at his post when to be vigilant and when to yield to a tantalizing pastry or nature's call. Let others radio for a relief; when the racehorse had to pee, it had to pee. His growing pile of accommodations proved the wisdom of his choices.

Approaching the control console, his *rugulach* one bite from extinction, Izaak saw the blinking amber light with its corresponding illuminated numbers signifying beacon contact and wondered what it could mean. Easing into the console chair, he chomped the remaining morsel of pastry, brushed his icing-laced fingers against his pant leg, and pulled the code book from its shelf, flipping to beacon codes. Hmm, 1-7-9-6—PRCS ambulance. *Some Arab in trouble, no doubt.* He looked at the UAV's live-feed monitor; dark rushing ground stared back at him, as Zik, Spark, had continued its circuit. He scanned the hard drive, looking for a visual on the ambulance just to be safe. Adjusting the rewind speed, he spotted it. He paused, studying the stored images. *Oh no, hell no—there's four ambulances down there. That much movement I would have been notified.* Grabbing the radio, he punched transmit. "Command, this is Lieutenant Finkel, just picked up a visua—"

"Stand by Finkel we've got priority traffic from Machsom 4170."

He knew the ambulances would have to clear 4170. *Please don't let the traffic be my ambulances. I'll never take a pee break again, I swear.*

~

The call to the infidel's checkpoint outside al-Eizariya just ahead played through Azim's mind as he rehearsed words committed to memory. His Hebrew, spoken with an Israeli accent, was flawless from years of practice. Provided the codes he learned two days ago and the cell's programming worked, they should be waved through. "Ready, Quaseem?"

Quaseem, color drained from his face, stared straight ahead. In a monotone whisper, he repeated "Allāuh Akbar, Allāuh Akbar."

Azim hit speed dial, and numbers raced past his ears as the phone connected to the enemy checkpoint.

CHAPTER

49

Saturday 22 March 2008, 0345 hours

Machsom 4170
Outside al-Eizariya, West Bank

Machsom 4170 is nondescript as checkpoints go: a single-story, desert tan, twenty by twenty-five foot building with windows on every side for visibility, sitting like a hen on her clutch of eggs beside Highway 398, where modified concrete Jersey barriers direct traffic off the highway for inspection. A rock-strewn field borders 398, which passing wildlife appear to prefer to the roosting hen's human occupants.

The phone vibrated on Mara's hip. Glancing at Caller ID, she saw District Command's number. "Shalom, Sgt. Palut, Machsom 4170, passcode."

"Ahasuerus," Azim said.

Sgt. Palut responded with one word, "Esther."

Azim replied, "Purim was blessed."

Mara enjoyed the intrigue. Most nights dragged on without much to pass the time. An occasional hedgehog scurrying past on nightly patrol for insects, available vegetation, or other small animals that would make a tasty meal barely provided a moment's respite from the stupefying boredom of standing watch on graveyard shift. Three months into her tour, she knew more than she could stomach about her three other Border Guards' sexual appetites and conquests, which she made clear didn't interest her when she was first assigned. Mara waited for the caller's identification and reason for calling, as if she hadn't been expecting the inevitable call to test her responses.

"This Captain HaLevi, Yerushaláyim District Command."

"Yes sir, what can I do for you, Captain?"

"We received a report on insurgent fighting outside Hizme. There are forty-one injuries requiring medical assistance Arabs can't provide in Judea or Samaria. Colonel Bialik cleared them for immediate treatment at Al-Makassed Hospital. Four PRCS ambulances will be coming through your machsom. Pass them on my direct authority, Sergeant. Is that understood?" Azim's heart raced as he waited for word that the traffic barrier would be lifted and the ambulances waved through.

"Of course, sir, they will be cleared immediately—"

Azim couldn't believe it. With one call they would live to fight at the tower.

"—right after you provide the secondary."

Secondary? What is this secondary? Covering the phone's microphone, he turned to Quaseem. "You know of a secondary?" Quaseem, lost in chanting, stared straight ahead.

"Sergeant, I don't have a secondary. Check instructions. I repeat, ambulances are carrying injured men. They must be allowed through."

Multiple arrays of metal halide floodlights burst through the morning air, turning night into day. Blaring sirens shattered the brittle morning calm. Quaseem stomped the accelerator to the floor as they bore down on the checkpoint. Border Guards started firing toward the approaching ambulance; its armoring held. Foam-filled tires convulsively jerked the ambulance while ensuring it would not be denied its mission.

Azim cranked down the passenger window with his right hand while keeping the dead man's switch in his left from triggering. He grabbed and pointed the barrel of his Kalashnikov toward the checkpoint, shooting wildly, trying to take out anything Israeli. His shots from the bouncing ambulance landed harmlessly in the dirt;

the grenade crate's back edge bounced over the L-bracket meant to hold it, careening unnoticed out of reach.

The three trailing ambulances stopped, distancing themselves from their shield, waiting for a way through.

Quaseem's fingers, now tight steel bands, strangled the steering wheel; his foot crushing the accelerator as the ambulance was hit by Israeli fire. Close to a trance, he held his course as he zeroed in on the checkpoint. Hitting the modified Jersey concrete barrier at an angle the ambulance, closing on seventy mph, shot up and over the barrier, becoming airborne, its front arching skyward. Its bottom rear slammed on the barrier, wrenching it back into a horizontal plane as the vehicle, more plane now than ambulance, closed on the checkpoint. Five feet from the machsom, a 50-caliber bullet infiltrated the ballistic windshield in front of Azim. The bullet's fury spent, it was unable to penetrate the multiple layers of tempered glass, polyurethane, polycarbonate, and spall shield. Just over one tenth of a second later, a second 50-caliber slug, faithful to its predecessor's trajectory, blasted its way through the now weakened shield, hurling its intended target against his seat. As Azim's torso quivered, blood spurted from the carotid artery of his nearly severed neck. The dead man's switch, attached by wires to Semtex in the front bumper, involuntarily released. The ambulance, thirty-six inches from the checkpoint shack, disintegrated in a deafening roar, obliterating the shack in its expanding gasses of utter destruction. The writhing aggregate of incoherent particles vaporized a ten-foot-deep, eighteen-foot-wide, crater in the ground, with ambulance, machsom, Israeli, and Arab remains hurled over a quarter mile.

The three trailing ambulances, rocked from blast pressure, resumed their journey, snaking their way around the destruction and crippled Jersey barriers on their way to destiny at Burg Daūd. Cheering exploded from within.

CHAPTER

50

Saturday 22 March 2008, 0352 hours

Magav (Border Guard)
Yerushaláyim District Command
Old City Yerushaláyim

As Corporal Danae Yadin took a sip of scalding coffee, the concave bank of monitors around her displayed the sleepy morning calm of the Old City. Caffeine began its circuitous route, kick-starting dozing neurons tilting toward somnolence in the monotony of the pre-dawn city. Danae was all too aware of the efforts of specific officers looking to gain points by catching anyone with normal REM cycles at District Command doing what nature itself demanded at this time of night. Rotating shifts were a killer, but constant infusion of caffeine, coupled with the sporadic sleep she was able to steal from a daytime world, kept Danae from minor disciplinary infractions. With less than a week before rotation, she was determined one specific dweezle Captain wouldn't catch her dozing.

A pair of ground sensors started chirping just as she felt a slight tremor. She could hear Adena in the adjoining cubicle. "You feel that, Danae? Nothing's up on any of my monitors. You got anything?"

When she checked her bank of monitors, everything looked peaceful. "Nothing here Adena. I'm rechecking mine; check yours again."

Captain Tzadok HaLevi burst around the corner. "Was someone going to call me?"

"When we have something, Captain," Corporal Yadin said.

"Well, what is it?"

"Captain, you felt what we felt and see everything we can. With all due respect, sir, I need a minute to determine the source of the alarms. And, while you're waiting, sir, I could use another set of eyes."

Both *magavnikyot* kept studying their monitors as phones started ringing. Danae hit the intercom button. "Dispatch, you sleeping?"

"More lines ringing than dispatchers. Feel free to jump in."

Danae took the first call, Adena the second.

Grabbing the third line, the Captain barked, "This is Captain HaLevi. We're busy—yeah, I know, alarm's going off. If I get free from this call I'll determine its source . . . . No, we'll radio field units when we find out." Hanging up the phone, he looked at Danae but kept silent.

Adena stayed busy with incoming calls; Danae began searching. Nothing caught her eye. The sensors continued their incessant chirping over the loudspeakers. Leaving her area, she went to the main control room. Swing and graveyard shifts were not allowed into the rarified confines of the day shift's bastion, lest a pencil be moved. The day shift's OIC was a Major; Danae's was a Captain: Rank brought privileges. The bank of monitors showed what they were supposed to: nothing unusual. Everything appeared normal except for those blasted sensors. Turning to leave, Danae's eye caught a faint red pulsing. It came from a nearby cabinet on the side wall. Swinging its door open, she was greeted by two flashing sensors. *This cabinet wasn't here yesterday and none of these sensors are tagged.* Grabbing the master log, she flipped to *sensors*. "Captain," Danae called out, "found the activated sensors."

Tzadok HaLevi hurried into the room. He looked at the flashing lights. "What are their identifiers?"

"Tags are missing."

"Tags were supposed to remain until the changeover is complete."

"Changeover?"

"All sensors are being consolidated for centralized access."

"When were we going to learn this information?"

"Everyone will be briefed when the changeover is complete."

"We need the identity of the two screaming sensors, Captain. Can you verify sensor numbers while I finish checking the log?"

Looking over the rows, Captain HaLevi counted. "Seventh row down, fifth and sixth sensors over—sensors seventy-five and -six."

Continuing her search in the master log, Danae found them. "They're from Machsom 4170, Captain."

Grabbing his cell phone, Captain HaLevi punched the code for al-Eizariya Machsom. No answer. Hanging up, he tried again. Nothing.

Pressing direct connect on his cell, he said, "Sergeant Malki'el, this is Captain HaLevi, copy."

The cell's speaker crackled. "Sergeant Malki'el, over."

"Sergeant, a couple of sensors may be malfunctioning."

"They have anything to do with the tremor, Captain?"

"That's what you need to check on. We have warning sensors triggering from Machsom 4170. We attempted contact, but no response. Proceed to the machsom, check status, over."

"Got a UAV on the way, Captain?"

"Don't want to bother Palmachim. By the time I get someone to divert a Zik, you'll be there and back. My bet, it's electrical interference."

"Does electrical interference cause tremors these days?"

"Sergeant, you have your orders, over."

"Your call, Captain, on my way, over and out."

Stepping on the accelerator of his Storm Commander, Hershel Malki'el figured it'd be ten minutes to the machsom, ten back. False alarms were more an irritant than anything else.

Scanning the road ahead with his binoculars, Ya'qub, riding shotgun in the lead ambulance, spotted a black dot that appeared to be growing. "Might have something, Nasir."

"Distance?"

"Too far. Can't tell what I'm looking at yet."

Turning on the ambulance's headlights, Nasir shouted, "Qadir."

No one budged.

"Qadir, you asleep back there?"

Curses could be heard as someone made his way to the front of the ambulance. "I'm coming." A bony hand jutted around the panel just behind Nasir, steadying its owner in the moving ambulance.

"What's the dot look like now, Ya'qub?"

"Israeli Jeep."

"How many inside?"

"Looks like one."

"RPG's ready, Qadir?"

"They're ready."

"Good, remember your training. Get to position; you know what to do."

Hitting his talk button, Nasir said, "Riyad, Dabir, copy."

"Go ahead we're listening."

"Israeli Jeep ahead."

"Copy."

"On it, over."

Both ambulances pulled off the road and shut their engines down.

Looking toward al-Eizariya, Sgt. Malki'el made out an ambulance in the distance heading his way, its emergency lights off. Opening the center console, he felt for his binoculars as he continued to close in on the vehicle. Adjusting the focus, he verified it was a PRCS ambulance. *Thanks for the heads-up, Captain.* The ambulance slowed to a stop; its doors remained closed per Magav regulation. Stopping, he put the Jeep into park facing the ambulance. Sgt. Malki'el broadcast over his loudspeaker, "PRCS ambulance, do not open any doors. Do not exit your vehicle."

He hit speed dial for District Command; the line was busy. He tried a secondary number and was routed to voicemail. Great, now what? If there's an injury and the ambulance is cleared, it'll be my head if I hold it up. Without authorization can't know. Pulling his

Galil SAR from the rack behind the console, he opened his door just enough to plant his outside foot on the ground. Resting the rifle's barrel on the door frame, he half crouched, leveling his rifle on the ambulance. He flipped off the rifle's safety then grabbed the microphone and pressed transmit, broadcasting to the ambulance over the Jeep's loudspeaker. "PRCS ambulance driver, you are to exit the vehicle alone."

The driver's door opened. An Arab, appearing to be in his mid-twenties, stepped from the ambulance, a sheaf of papers in his right hand. No other doors opened.

"Walk towards me, slowly. Do not make any sudden moves." The driver stepped toward the Jeep.

As Nasir slowly walked in the direction of the enemy soldier, the back door of the ambulance opened a crack. Qadir squeezed from the ambulance, away from the jeep's field of vision. An RPG-7, Rocket Propelled Grenade launcher, with red dot reflex sights, was passed down to him. Slipping to the ground, he crawled toward the front of the ambulance.

"What is your destination, driver?"

Nasir stopped, "Al-Makassed Hospital," he shouted. "We have injured—"

"Do not answer more than I ask, driver."

"Yes sir."

"The papers in your hand?"

"Medical records, sir."

"I have to clear your ambulance. Stay where you are." Sgt. Malki'el hit speed dial; it began ringing.

Herschel Malki'el didn't see the laser dot on his chest. His last image was a telltale flash of light from the front left side of the ambulance.

The phone rang. "Shalom, Yerushaláyim District Command, Corporal Yadin." No one was there. Caller ID showed Sgt. Malki'el's number. Danae pressed *Talk* on her phone. It dialed. No answer. She hit speed dial. "Captain HaLevi, we might have a problem."

~

"Addison," Elizabeth labored to whisper. "Addison."

A guttural moan reached her ears.

Elizabeth strained to hear Addison, bound next to her on the ambulance floor, her feet by his head. "What . . . was that?"

Her words were met by silence.

"Addison, you hear?"

The toe of a boot slammed into Addison's ribs. The sound of ribs snapping assaulted her ears.

"What is with talk? Did I, Ommar, give permission for talk?"

A choking groan escaped Addison's still form.

"You came to our land to learn truth, American. Your wishes are answered. Does this not much please you?"

"What was the celebration?" Elizabeth asked.

"Soon we will be to destination. Then covering removed from head and is seen most beautiful of beautiful: Noble Sanctuary, from a distance of course, infidel."

"The celebration?"

"Ommar feels generous, even to Jew, so I answer. Rejoicing was for Zionist machsom that is no more. Hole in ground greets those passing now."

"But what about the second explosion?"

"Silence. I grow weary with talk. My boot begs to caress Jewish head. More words and I give it permission."

Clear of the infidel border guards who tried to stop them, Nasir, behind the wheel in the lead ambulance, had eight minutes to make it to Burg Daūd.

The chaos of their precious machsom disappearing should keep the Jews busy long enough for him to avoid the enemy's UAV. The satellite wouldn't overpass until they made the tower complex, and Nuri swore the Zionists would divert Zik to their precious machsom. If the Jews wanted to photograph smoke rising from an abyss, fine by him. By the time they could launch a second UAV, all three ambulances would be to their destination. Everything hung on these next eight minutes and his ability to keep a green light flashing on a timer, which Nuri had shown him just before he left that morning. He floored it, unleashing all 359 horses as he led their way toward victory.

Coming up on Highway 417, Nasir slowed, turning left onto Derekh Yerikho. Two and a half minutes later, another left brought them onto Derekh Ha-Ofel. Winding around the Old City walls, closing on their destination, they faced no resistance. Surely Allāh was going before them, just like the imam said.

~

"Dispatch, Private Cha'it, Lions' Gate. Three PRCS ambulances heading southbound past my post turning Derekh Yerikho onto Derekh Ha-Ofel, over."

"Copy, Cha'it. Stand by, over."

"Dispatch, you copy three PRCS ambulances heading towards the Old City, over."

"Copy, Cha'it. Three PRCS ambulances southbound, status undetermined. Observe only, over."

"Captain HaLevi to Dispatch, Captain HaLevi."

Now what? Tzadok HaLevi thought. Walking into Dispatch, his only concern had been the status of the machsom Sgt. Malki'el hadn't reported on, and now Yadin was squawking about his phone not working. *Great, another thing to deal with.* He would not jump to conclusions, in spite of that anal fissure of a Corporal; that's how careers were ruined.

"Captain, we have three PRCS ambulances headed south on Derekh Ha-Ofel. I don't have clearance on file. You have anything from Tel Aviv?"

"Nothing, Sergeant."

"Then we intercept."

"What if they're just trying to get to a hospital? Have you radioed them yet?"

"There's no response, Captain."

"Dispatch, Corporal Nachman, Dung Gate. Three PRCS ambulances heading southwest. Ma'Ale Ha-Shalom. Lights out, emergency flashers off. Advise, over."

"Nachman, this is Dispatch. We are aware of the ambulances. Stand by."

~

The road turned into Ma'Ale Ha-Shalom. Nasir executed a right onto Khativat Etsyoni, which made a ninety-degree bend to the left then another to the right as it began running parallel to the Old City walls ascending to the *migdal* complex. *Where are the Jews? They've got to know we're here.*

~

The radio came alive.

"Dispatch, this is Corporal Nachman, still standing by. If there's any interest, the lead ambulance just turned from Ma'Ale Ha-Shalom onto Khativat Etsyoni."

"Nachman, continue to observe."

"They just passed my position. Nachman out."

~

Easing right, Nasir was on Kikar Omar Ben el-Khatab. "Everyone, thirty seconds," he broadcast on his walkie-talkie. His side window was hit by enemy fire, bullets bounced off the ballistic glass as he spotted the turn into *Gan David*. Glancing back, he barked, "Hamal, locate the shooter; take him out. We need sixty seconds from drop off to get inside the exhibition hall."

Hamal slid open the door window. The earsplitting anger of his AK-104 assaulted defenseless ears in the ambulance.

"Pretty good," Hamal yelled to Nasir. He pulled his earplugs out. "Able to butcher swine from moving ambulance."

"You'll get a medal later," Nasir shot back as he continued to close in on the exhibition hall. He pressed and locked the transmit button on his walkie-talkie, slipping it into the Velcro straps on his bullet-resistant vest's collar.

Rapid-fire prayers were lifted in whispers and shouts from each ambulance as souls made their final plea with fate.

Slowing to a near stop, Nasir took a hard right, edging onto the ancient cobblestones of Gan David, David's Gardens, then threading through the narrow entrance between the Ottoman Period stone building and the barrier gate arm set in front of a rock sidewall. The sound of tortured metal shrieked through the ambulance as its sides scraped stone and metal, snapping the gate barrier post and traffic arm off. "Watch the opening, barely wide enough to get through," Nasir warned.

"Yeah, we heard," a mujahid voice shouted. The ambulances started bouncing as foam-engorged tires chattered over the cobblestones. Hitting their brakes in succession, all three ambulances came to a stop ten feet apart, Nasir's ambulance inches from the stairs leading down to the exhibition hall's locked entrance. Side doors were opened. Mujahideen scanned adjacent walls, walks, and buildings from the protection of their armored boxes. Israelis, inexplicably, were absent, but they could be anywhere, waiting.

~

"Dispatch, this is Private Rapkin, on the wall adjacent to exhibition hall. Three PRCS ambulances . . . being fired on . . . setting up at . . ."

"Rapkin, dispatch, repeat. You're breaking up, over."

Listening, Captain HaLevi awaited the private's response.

"Private Rapkin, this is Sergeant Yaakov, Dispatch. Repeat transmission, over."

The radio remained silent.

"Rapkin, this is Yaakov, over."

"Rapkin."

Still silent.

"Captain, they're closing on the Old City and have engaged."

"Do we have additional boots on the ground, Sergeant?"

"I'll send two *magavnikim* to check on Rapkin, sir."

"Good. Let's get their report before we start a war. In the meantime, keep trying to raise Sgt. Malki'el. And continue to radio those PRCS ambulances. We don't have enough information for a proper assessment yet. When our assets reconnoiter the scene, we'll be able to see if the sky's falling in."

"Yes sir, Captain."

"I need to contact command, keep me appraised of new developments." Taking his phone from its belt clip, Captain HaLevi walked toward his office as he hit the speed dial number he normally hated calling. This time he didn't mind; in fact, the call should work to his advantage. His ass-kissing classmate, Shimon Cohen, had weaseled his way into Tel Aviv Command and was Officer in Charge this morning. Though better at passing the buck than he was, with the machsom's status unknown and three PRCS ambulances approaching the migdal without clearance, or radio contact, it wouldn't be so easy for old Shimon to pass the buck on this one, especially if Rapkin was taking fire. The sweetest part: HaLevi was following directives, so once he made the call, this mess would be off his back and permanently, not to mention officially, on Shimon's. He knew that with possible gunfire, Shimon would have to inform the commander. *Oh, to be there when he wakes a field grade officer from a dead sleep*, thought HaLevi. *That should start his day off right.* He had to be careful though considering the recent gossip about anthrax, but Shabak had combed the Old City for two weeks, and if they couldn't find anything it didn't exist.

"Magav Command, Tel Aviv."

"This is Captain Tzadok HaLevi, OIC, Magav Command Yerushaláyim District. Captain Cohen, top priority."

Ten seconds later: "This is Captain Cohen . . . ."

Chuckling to himself, Tzadok could picture beads of sweat forming on Shimon's forehead after this news had been dumped in his lap. He was solicitous and professional, a true friend, knowing Shimon's fate was sealed. When he learned the commander was Colonel Samech, he nearly went out of his mind with glee; the man was certifiably insane. Shit, he reminded his good buddy, with just the right inflection of concern, runs downhill, and Tzadok prided himself on knowing the massive amount of hill between a full-bird Colonel and a Captain. Whistling softly, Tzadok strode back to dispatch.

"Sergeant."

"Yes, Captain."

"Command has assumed incident control and orders us to track the ambulances without intervening, and yes, I told them about the possible live fire and no radio contact. Captain Cohen, Tel Aviv OIC, is contacting Colonel Samech. Continue surveillance, and increase the number of eyes on the ground. We need to know what the ambulances are doing. How many roving magavnikim are assigned this morning?"

Removing a clipboard, Sgt. Yaakov started counting, "Let's see, there's ten, no, wait, Liebowitz called in sick, Malki'el is out to the machsom, and Ofra's at home for lunch, so make that seven. But with another two out to check on Malki'el we're down to five roving in addition to the normal sentry posts sir."

"Activate twelve more. That's four per ambulance plus our existing nine when everyone shows back up, it should be enough. As to command's instruction not to intervene, if there's a shot it's not officially intervening to return fire. Rules of Engagement allow return fire, but no all-out war, got it? Should Captain Cohen call, inform me before implementing any order unless it's priority one. Understood, Sergeant?"

"Boots on ground, observe, don't intervene unless it's return fire, and contact you before implementing anything short of priority one from Tel Aviv. Got it, sir."

"I'll be in my office."

CHAPTER

51

Migdal David
Old City Yerushaláyim

The complex of buildings referred to as *Migdal David* does not actually contain a tower known to have been built by, or for, King David after he conquered the city then known as Jebus and renamed it Jerusalem around 1005 B.C.

Flavius Josephus, (37 A.D.–100 A.D.) is the first acknowledged Jewish historian (having lived some eleven hundred years after David) to name this complex the Citadel of King David. With no known contemporary Jewish chroniclers to disagree, the name, with all respect to the good king's many accomplishments, was set in historical stone.

Since Jerusalem was central to controlling the land bridge between Asia and Africa as a major trade route, conquerors through the centuries destroyed, rebuilt, and expanded Jerusalem, using the ruins their conquests caused.

The Tower of David, known as the Migdal David by Jews and Burg Daūd by Arabs, is a citadel complex of assorted towers, buildings, arches, and ruins on the western side of the Old City south of the Jaffa Gate.

The citadel's minaret is the highest point in the Old City and was built by Muhammad Pasha in the middle of the seventeenth century. Contemporary Jewish rule has subordinated Migdal David for use as a tourist and cultural center. The PMIJ had other ideas.

CHAPTER

52

Saturday 22 March 2008, 0412 hours

Gan David (David's Gardens)
Old City Yerushaláyim

"Saghir, Zero, is everything ready?" Nasir said.

"It's ready," Zero said.

"You checked the frame charge? Explosives—magnesium ribbons?"

"Everything is checked along with C-4. Everything gone over time and times again," Zero said. "Snipers ready? Keep enemy from blowing our heads off the moment we leave the ambulance."

"Shooters commence firing," Nasir ordered. Cacophonous automatic fire strafed walls, walks, and open areas unremittingly, ten . . . twelve . . . fifteen seconds.

Silence, instantaneous, tangible, penetrated the ancient ramparts.

"Go," Nasir said.

Scanning the area, Zero Hasan stepped outside the ambulance, lifting the five by three foot frame-charge over his head. It wrestled his rifle, claiming its spot on his back, as he lowered the rectangular frame around his torso.

Saghir Yaseen grabbed two canvas bags from the ambulance, heavier with C-4 bricks and netting, and stood as close to Zero as the frame would allow. With a quick nod, Saghir sprinted toward the exhibition hall as mujahideen rifles blasted the ancient stones.

Bending to control the frame as continuing fire snarled from the ambulances, Zero was on Saghir's heels. Clearing the first flight of stairs two at a time, he jogged to his right, powering past the entryway's ten-foot landing, while the frame, fighting to balance itself, haphazardly responded to Zero's unceasing motion. Zero and Saghir soared in tandem over the final two steps, coming to a stop eighteen inches from the exhibition hall's inset entrance, with its stone porch that promised more protection than it provided.

Zero shed the frame charge, leaning it against the door. "Saghir, cutter, ties."

Digging into his bag, Saghir found the cable cutter and plastic cable ties under a C-4 brick and handed them to Zero.

The ties secured the coiled magnesium ribbons to the frame's two upper corners. Cutting the first tie, Zero ordered, "Uncoil ribbon. Be gentle, not break."

As Saghir uncoiled the one-eighth inch wide ribbon, Zero wrapped a tie around the frame where the ribbon was imbedded in thermite, snugging it tight before moving to the opposite side with Saghir.

Spotting an enemy sniper bobbing up then down on the wall overlooking the exhibition hall entrance, Hamal steadied his rifle against the ambulance's side door.

Moving reflexively, from scores of mind-numbing trial runs, Zero held the frame assembly flush to the steel door's face.

Saghir pulled the pipe welded to the frame's center beam back forming a tripod, then he yanked the inset end pipe to the ground, wrenching tight on the thumbscrew. "Okay, is secure."

Zero checked.

Saghir pulled two butane micro-torches from the bag and clicked both triggers. A small blue flame leapt from each. Releasing the triggers, he handed one to Zero then grabbed his bag and went to the end of the magnesium ribbon, three feet from the door's stone archway. Zero grabbed his bag and went to the opposite side.

"Door ready for breaching, Nasir," Zero reported into his walkie-talkie.

"Light the ribbon."

Zero began counting down from three.

Hamal's breathing was slow, relaxed. He caught what he could of the enemy sniper and waited.

The triggers on both micro-torches clicked. Blue flame leapt onto the magnesium ribbon. A brilliant blue light from the exothermic reaction between the flame and magnesium shot toward the thermite. As they turned from the intense light, the magnesium ribbon ignited the thermite. A crackling sound arose into the air while the frame blazed red from the intense inferno burning through the door's metal skin and frame.

The Israeli's head cleared the top of the wall one last time. Hamal squeezed his trigger as the Israeli found his mark. Hamal watched the enemy head jerk from view, another Zionist sent to Jahannam where he belongs.

Saghir looked up at the sound of rifle fire.

"Get the door," Nasir shouted.

Zero was slumped against the wall.

"Zero, we check door."

Zero didn't answer.

Saghir got up. Taking his bag, he scanned the area as he ran to the door. Radiating heat greeted him.

"Saghir, Zero is down. Remove frame, kick door in," Nasir said.

Saghir didn't budge.

"Saghir, move now or I'll take you out."

Grabbing the frame's back leg, he yanked the smoldering assembly out of the way. The door, with rectangular bars covering its face, had been torched cleanly. It stayed upright simply because that was the only position it had ever known. Two angry kicks sent cut metal crashing onto the exhibition hall floor.

"Let's go, let's go, let's go," Nasir shouted at the mujahideen in the ambulances.

All four hostages were thrown over shoulders and used as shields.

Yazid jerked and slid the eighteen by thirty-six inch ballistic glass panel out the side door of the ambulance. He hefted the panel's eighty-seven pound weight into his gloved hands, locking his fingers under its canvas straps. Balancing the unwieldy panel, he was ready for the exhibition hall. Samien, with shorter arms, struggled with the second panel.

Cover-fire spat from three mujahideen snipers while the remaining nineteen PMIJ pressed their way down through the door opening into the safety of the exhibition hall.

"Hamal," Nasir said, "replace Zero."

"We leave Zero?" Saghir said.

"He's dead. You and Hamal cover the snipers." He pressed 1-5-9 on his cell, and a single staccato tone sounded on all three snipers' phones. Rehan, Adnan, and Ghassan sprinted to join their fellow warriors. Israeli fire continued its marked silence.

CHAPTER

53

Saturday 22 March 2008, 0414 hours

Magav Command Yerushaláyim District
Old City Yerushaláyim

"What's shakin', sarge," Corporal Orpaz said, coming around the corner into dispatch from lunch break.

"Got three unauthorized PRCS ambulances at Gan David, live fire has been reported, and everyone we've sent to reconnoiter drops off the earth, no radio contact. All the while the Captain's hiding in his office waiting on Tel Aviv. Is that enough shaking for you, Orpaz?"

"You tried calling the big guy to see what's stirrin'?"

"Not after he slammed me on whom the OIC is. We need to move. Try the intercom, Orpaz, won't be like I called him."

"Captain HaLevi, Dispatch. Your response would be righteous, Captain."

Charging around the corner, Tzadok HaLevi rushed into dispatch. "I'm here, but not for long; things are breaking. Just received confirmation from Palmachim that Zik shows there's a crater in the ground where Machsom 4170 stood. IDF's on the way. Feed didn't show survivors. Needless to say, we're on elevated alert.

"Continue ROE's Captain?"

"As per Tel Aviv, Sergeant. You recall Tel Aviv has operational control. Be in my office."

"Captain, with all respect, we've got three enemy ambulances at Gan David, a machsom destroyed, a *magavnik* fired on, and every magavnikim we've sent to reconnoiter disappears, and we can't engage?"

"Good, we understand one another, so I won't need to repeat that Tel Aviv's in command. They have reason to believe the mujahideen have an American consular officer hostage."

"So? We take him out."

"You recall the anthrax Shabak was trying to locate the past couple of weeks?"

"You mean by deploying everyone who's worked for them the last twenty years?"

"They think it's with the American, but thinking is not knowing and court-martials focus on knowing. I will apprise you when facts present themselves."

"Yes sir!"

"Roger that, great leader."

"Orpaz, one of these days," Tzadok HaLevi said. He headed for his office, concentrating on what was expected of him. Subordinates never understood the art of command. He lifted the phone from its cradle and dialed the familiar number. "Tel Aviv Command—OIC Cohen," came the recognizable voice when the call was answered.

"Shimon, this is Tzadok."

"Tzadok, you rotten bastard, what'd you pull me into?"

"My good friend, I am hurt by your words. I would've been happy to get assigned to Tel Aviv, but you beat me to it by dating the General's niece. Classic move, by the way. How is the porcine beauty?"

"Eating her weight in chocolates and pastries."

"Well good buddy, it's the heart that counts. Besides, I followed rules precisely as you would."

"Keep in mind I've got a good memory and I'm still at command while you're down at the quaint Old City."

"For now, but—" a distinct click was heard on the line. "Are you messing with the phone, Shimon?"

"Was just about to ask you the—"

"If you ladies are through gossiping in the middle of a crisis, I've got a mission to conduct."

"Excuse me, this is Captain HaLevi. You have interrupted an official conversation."

"And this is Colonel Samech. I'll do more than interrupt conversation, Priscilla. Shut your mouth and listen."

"Yes sir. Sorry sir, didn't recognize yo—"

"I say shut up and you talk more?"

"Yes sir, I mean no sir Colonel, shutting up sir."

"Good. I'm on my way from Tel Aviv with Captain Ashtor. You will have an office set up for me, and I don't want your office."

"When will that be, sir?"

"Interrupt one more time, Captain, and Hadassah will need their best proctologist to find your flapping lips. When I'm done, *then* talk, understand?"

"Captain?"

"Priscilla, you answer when I ask direct question."

"Sir, yes sir."

"PMIJ are breaking into the Migdal's exhibition hall. You know this, Captain?"

"Sir, we've been tracking three PRCS ambulances. Tel Aviv Command assumed incident control, sir."

"You managed to do one thing right, Captain. Magavnikim are to observe unless attacked, am I clear?"

"Yes sir."

"Good. Your visitors might have brought anthrax to the party along with an American FSO, and I don't want either hit by one of your hotshots."

"All bullets, defense only, sir."

"I need two secure level-one phones and lines. Call Major Alon Lotem, Telecommunication and Information Technology Unit. He'll have them installed within thirty minutes. Captain Ashtor will fill you in on everything else we need."

"Yes sir, I'll contact Major Alo—"

"HaLevi, this is Ashtor. "We need some general office supplies and a few specialized items. Ready? A dozen notepads, legal size;

a ream 8½ by 11 copy paper; box of pens, black, fine point. Two folding tables, one minimum six feet long; and two coffeemakers along with ground coffee, brand doesn't matter just make it strong. Also mugs, not cups. No cream, no sugar, Colonel likes his black. Get both pots brewing, hot and thick as mud or whoever made it might be wearing the first cup; the Colonel is particular. Get a network gateway, a hundred foot spool of cat 5e cable with connectors and a crimping tool; we'll make our own lengths. A copier-printer with USB cables. Make it fast, and also color. We're bringing laptops plus a secure server. Make sure there are eleven chairs. The room must be secure, one way in, one way out, and an adjoining bathroom would come in handy. Oh yeah, might need a couple of cots and bedding depending on incident duration. Final item," Captain Ashtor continued, "get two of the biggest bad-assed Neanderthals you got. Don't have to be rocket scientists, just have to keep everyone out till we want 'em in. If there's a problem, call. We can work through anything, but I need to have a heads-up so the Colonel won't feel compelled to get involved. If you have questions before we arrive, call my secure line. I'll send the number since the Colonel's line I'm on is blocked. Anything else you want to know?"

"Not that I can think of."

The phone went dead.

"You still there, Shimon?"

"Just taking it all in, good buddy. Seems a shame, with all the expertise we have here, for incident command to be moved back to your stomping ground, but hey, that's where the terrorists are. What was it you mentioned earlier about crap running downhill? I've run into the Colonel a few times, and over the phone, he's a real sweetheart. Tends to be a tad more gruff when subordinates don't please him in person, though, but you can handle a Colonel. Good luck, and watch out for the brown stuff."

Tzadok wanted to puke; instead he hit disconnect and raced to pull in favors, scrambling for the eclectic mix that he would have waiting for the Colonel within the next half hour. Twenty-seven minutes later, the last item was in the office and being set up as the first pot of mud finished brewing.

Three minutes to the second after that, Colonel Samech and Captain Ashtor walked into their new office and looked around. Colonel Samech said, "Everything ready?"

"Yes sir."

"Now, tell me about the incident."

For the next two hundred and forty-seven seconds, Captain Tzadok HaLevi used every skill he possessed to brief the Colonel thoroughly and professionally without repeating one unnecessary syllable.

"Terrorists are inside the exhibition hall, Captain?"

"*Mehablim* were photo-captured entering and have not exited, sir."

"Who's watching them?"

"Magavnikim that are assigned to each wall gate, where they have line of sight on the exhibition hall, and sixteen roving magavnikim are set up in proximity to the hall covering all access and egress points, sir."

"Firing orders?"

"Defensive only while awaiting your instructions, Colonel."

"So you let mehablim enter the exhibition hall, Captain?"

"Colonel, when the three PRCS ambulances did not respond to radio calls for identification, I contacted Tel Aviv command for further instructions. Tel Aviv command took operational control and you were contacted, sir. During that process the mehablim made entry into the exhibition hall. With all due respect, Colonel, no one has ever broken into the Old City that didn't have an army behind them. I was faced with starting a war in the Old City or going to my appropriate authority. I chose to go by the book."

Trying not to scowl, the Colonel said, "I didn't say your actions were inappropriate. I just need to understand, Captain. My men will report any minute; it's important none of them be held up.

"Michael," the Colonel continued, "get two helos, close support around exhibition hall. Make presence known, defensive measures only and make sure they know magavnikim are in the area."

"On it, Colonel."

"HaLevi, redeploy roving magavnikim so mehablim know they've got company."

"Defensive force only, Colonel?"

"Unless fired on, keep mehablim confined to the hall until our welcome committee is in place."

"Yes sir." Grabbing his cell phone, he punched speed dial. "Sgt. Yaakov, HaLevi here, redeploy all roving magavnikim around the exhibition hall, defensive only. Make sure the mehablim know they have company."

"Right away, Captain."

"Michael call Har-Paz, have his troops evacuate everyone within 750 yards of the migdal complex, no exceptions."

"On it Colonel."

"Captain HaLevi, on our way in I didn't see guards for the door. Did you forget?"

"Pulled from their sleep sir, they'll be here within minutes."

"That's all for now Captain. I have bad guys to deal with. Let Michael know if you leave your office, understood?"

"Yes sir."

Nine incoming Ya'Ma'M commandos bulled past Tzadok as he left, each one more unnerving than the one before.

Safe in his office, HaLevi set about typing an incident report he knew would be dissected letter by letter.

Finishing his call to Major Har-Paz, Captain Ashtor waited until the commandoes were seated. "We've run this drill before," Captain Ashtor said and turned to Colonel Samech. "We're ready sir."

Standing near the rear of the table, Colonel Samech took a final gulp of swill and put the mug down. Advancing to the table's front, he planted himself ramrod straight. "This operation is coming together on the fly, as usual. Old City's been shut down from 2100 hours to 0530 hours for last two weeks while Shabak looked for anthrax rumored to be in Yisra'el. They didn't find it. While they searched this morning, PMIJ showed up at Gan David, gaining possession of the migdal exhibition hall. I deployed magavnikim snipers and two 124 Squadron helos to surveil access and egress points to keep the mehablim inside the hall until you could be deployed." He looked at Captain Ashtor. "How many mehablim were identified entering the hall, Michael?

"Twenty-five PMIJ were photo-captured, sir. Shabak is transmitting identifications as they're made."

"I just ordered the IDF to evacuate all areas within 750 yards of the migdal. With the Old City being shut down in Shabak's search for anthrax the past two weeks, Major Har-Paz will be able to evacuate the few that remained in the Old City so we won't have that to contend with. Sergeant-Major Peled?"

"Colonel."

"Station your team using the magavnikim to locate strategic intervention points: They know this area intimately. Coordinate with Captain HaLevi so all magavnikim understand what's needed."

"Yes sir. How did we identify the mehablim as PMIJ?"

"Michael."

"The cell's tactical leader was picked up on an infrared illuminator goading mehablim into the exhibition hall. Shabak checked their database, got a hit, and transmitted the information. He graduated from a university in Nablus last year. Came up on Shabak's radar when intel indicated he was recruited by the Palestine Mujahideen Islamic Jihad. Thing is, until today, we didn't know what he was recruited for. His name is Nasir Ghafour. We now think we understand why he would break into the Old City."

"And that would be?"

"If you have inhalational anthrax—and that's what Shabak's been looking for—you need elevation for optimal dispersal. Either you have a small plane fly a grid and release the spores at altitude, which the IAF might object to, or you need a missile to attain elevation. Lacking both of those, you find the tallest tower you can and use a fireworks shell to gain the elevation needed for dispersal.

"I didn't think Shabak had pinned anthrax on anyone."

"They didn't."

"Why look at PMIJ?"

"Ephraim, we search for patterns. Anthrax is rumored to be around and it's Shabak's operation, but we also take a look-see. None of the local wannabe jihadists have been able to get their hands on bioweapons, thanks in part to Shabak's ongoing efforts. They also lack connections and cash to deal at that level, but we picked up noise on connected Russians willing to shop inventory if price was right. So we look to see what we can."

"So it's presumption based on guess?"

"Educated guess Ephraim, in searching for patterns we began tracking from the Russian's involvement in the MMR vaccinations when we learned their inoculations included a vaccine for a strain of anthrax that officially doesn't exist. An imam in Syria kept popping up in places most imams don't. He nearly slipped under the radar, but Mossad dug a little. They noticed a few heavyweight connections. Why have connections you never use? We plug this imam into the equation and, all of a sudden, the picture begins to clear up. Any guesses where this Syrian imam was born?"

No one spoke up.

"Anybody want to pick Iran? Now, that doesn't mean he needs to worry about a visit from Mossad yet—no crime in being born in Iran—but let's say he became a lot more interesting. Then, too, Mossad's not finished looking either."

"So where does that leave us Colonel?"

"Intel indicates a PMIJ leader had an incident with the IDF when he was a kid twenty years or so back near Khān Yūnis. Shabak looked, and while this guy was everywhere the past few weeks, showing up in photo-surveillance multiple times with none other than Nasir Ghafour, now he's nowhere to be seen."

"How'd we paint a kid from twenty years ago in the picture?"

"No longer a kid of course, name is . . . he shuffled through some pages in the folder, locating it, "IbnMansur, Nur-Rami IbnMansur. He moved to Syria at sixteen after IDF demolished his paternal home on a court order for terrorist activity, took the name Nuri. Wouldn't even be a footnote, except his father's deceased first wife was part Jewish and a son from that marriage ended up in Shabak, so in the ramp up to find the anthrax, he came forward and refreshed them on the original events and his concerns. Shabak's man being Nur's half-brother, Mossad had a look-see. Any guesses where young Nur showed up in Syria?"

"A certain mosque?"

"Small world isn't it. Any notion where the imam of that mosque likes to vacation?"

"Russia?"

"Close but no, the Russians' bioweapons development facility is in northern Kazakhstan. Satellite identified the imam along with his bodyguard getting in a Russian plane in Syria. After stopping in Iran, it continued the next day through Turkmenistan then into Uzbekistan, which borders Kazakhstan. Unfortunately, we lost the plane after it passed into Kazakhstan."

"How'd we pick up a flight from Iran? Their airspace is closed."

"Not when you assign an identifier to a specific plane and tell the satellite to pay attention, but even satellites can hiccup every once in a while and they lost tracking of the plane."

"So connections through Syria, link to Russia, and rumors of anthrax take on weight. Mossad wasn't able to conduct an inspection of the mosque, but they managed a look inside. It's surrounded by poverty, no surprise there, but the mosque just finished construction of new facilities with hand-carved reliefs, plenty of quarried stone, along with hanging leaded crystal lamps, imported tapestries and rugs, silver and gold appointments, not to mention an ivory inlaid chair."

"Guess no one told them ivory is banned. Still, extravagance in mosques is par for the course, Captain."

"True, but the level of lavishness is beyond the norm, Ephraim. Deep pockets are involved, and this time the money leads back to Iran."

"So today's incursion gives weight to the argument they have anthrax. You don't go near the lion till you're ready to kill him."

"Or be killed."

"But we need actionable intel specific to the anthrax before we allow these sons of Ishmael passage to the virgins."

"While avoiding being hung out to dry for helping them along their way," Peled added.

"If PMIJ had a missile, they wouldn't be here. Political statements aside, they'd choose to launch and scurry away. A missile from Gaza or Area A and there's a chance they fight another day. The migdal is a one-way trip and they know it. If they head towards the minaret it confirms they need its elevation for dispersion."

"Not to mention the statement to the Arab Street launching from the Old City would make."

"I'm convinced," Colonel Samech said, "our adversaries are risking everything for the symbolism launching from the Old City signifies. We're too good to be taken on head to head. We've proven ourselves time and again. What they need, perhaps even more than a tactical victory itself, is a victory to inspire hearts and souls that their god has finally bestowed favor which could lead to mass radicalized fervor. The migdal attack could be the catalyst to energize not only those along our borders but every son and daughter of Ishmael in every country his lineage lives."

"So why not deploy our team and end this? Leave the Arabs conducting war games to stare at the IDF and our armament while we mop up the operation at the migdal?"

"Ephraim," Michael said, "PMIJ's command isn't local. All intel indicates the hub that turns the wheel is in Syria, but we need actionable proof for the international community."

"Satellite pictures," Colonel Samech said, "like the ones showing the imam from Syria flying into and out of Iran, expose operational elements but can't be used for international support."

"Why is that, Colonel?"

"They're classified. I was only allowed to view specific satellite photos for our counter-ops, but officially they don't exist; if they were released our capabilities would be exposed."

"So they can't be used in any court proceeding to justify actions taken."

"How could they since they don't exist?"

"Shabak has been running massive undercover ops to locate the anthrax or even a single cell member with dirty hands—they've turned up nothing," Michael said. "Which again indicates roots outside Yisra'el. If the anthrax were in Eretz Yisra'el, with every resource we've thrown at it, something would have surfaced."

"Our camera network is everywhere except Area A, PALFA full control, and Gaza," Colonel Samech said. "Shabak links individuals photographed in proximity over time. Our surveillance cameras are so omnipresent people forget we're watching, recording. Software factors in family members, employment, and friends. Even with family and friends, we ask why specific people go places others don't. Individual profiles are often unlinked until we see identifiable faces in action."

"You mean like breaking into the exhibition hall?" Ephraim said.

"Obviously that's one. Another is a college graduate who abruptly gets religion and starts showing up at the mosque. Along with his newfound faith he begins to frequent different cafés all over Judea and Samaria, eating alone without meeting anyone, repeating that pattern week in and week out. Then one day he begins hanging out with grade school dropouts for no discernible reason. Or when a new face shows up at a known insurgent house then is photo-captured heading towards the Syrian border. Incidents arrange themselves. But all this will be gone through by the appropriate agencies and committees. We have a job to do. Are there any final operational questions?"

No one spoke.

"It's time, Michael," Colonel Samech said.

Heard before every operation, Michael Ashtor's next words were expected; each commando knew what came next never varied. "This concludes all off-the record discussion." Captain Ashtor said. "Colonel Samech will now brief us, Colonel."

Searching each face, Aaron Samech understood he must convey the weight of the challenge faced. In a near whisper he began as the men around him strained to follow words that would result in life or death.

"We face a strategic attack aimed at the soul of Yisra'el. This is not just to inflict damage, although damage will be inflicted. It's not to test strength, though strength will be tested. It's not to continue the evil campaign of Jewish death by a thousand cuts, though blood will be spilled. This moment has its life in our nation's death. Migdal David was chosen by those whose hatred drives their every move. Enemies are aligned against us with preparation, commitment, and belief in final victory. Unless we remember this, we will lose."

Gazing upon each warrior, he saw commitment etched on hardened faces. "We are confronted with an assault unlike any other in our history. Though this encounter appears as previous battles have, at stake is life and breath for Yisra'el. We ask questions after each battle to find answers and learn strategies for future attacks. Today we must ask them before the battle. Why destroy a checkpoint as an opening move, thereby ensuring forces are marshaled, forces known to have no equal in the Middle East? Why follow the machsom's destruction by boxing yourself into a stone tomb of an exhibition hall unless to draw adversaries to you? They've fortified themselves in an ancient maze where superior firepower has few advantages and where anthrax can be launched in a moment's time, or an errant bullet could release a plague that brings down a city. The mehablim you'll face are sacrificial lambs sent to honor bloodlust that demands the destruction of Yisra'el. They wage jihad that has changed its face over each generation, but has, as its heart, the same goal: the eradication of Jews from our ancient homeland.

"If possible, preserve life—interrogations return a harvest—but expect no survivors. Don't believe the mehablim, in the heart of our Old City with anthrax and four hostages are reckless, suicidal; they're not. It's Yisra'el's death, not just yours, they seek to exchange for their lives. Captain Ashtor will now brief you on mission-specific rules of engagement. Heed his words; Yisra'el's future may depend on your doing so."

"All actions fall under operation-specific ROE. Armaments consist of Tavor TAR-21 assault rifles, Glock 17 pistols, and commando knives. Kolokol grenades will also be issued; if we can isolate and contain the mehablim, they could prove effective.

"Carry sufficient ammunition. Resupplying inside the migdal complex could compromise tactical positions; therefore no full automatic or burst mode firing. Place each round carefully. Do not fire until cleared by Sergeant Peled, unless you need to extract yourself from a direct attack. We're familiar with the migdal complex, but magavnikim scouts know every pebble in the migdal and will lead you to optimal tactical positions. You'll face urban conditions at their worst, so the magavnikim's knowledge will save lives.

"Photo surveillance from the exhibition hall's entrance showed mortar tubes strapped on two hostages' torsos, which gives us two targets to remain situationally aware of. If the mehablim begin to separate the hostages with the mortar tubes into different directions, neutralize the mortar tubes. Deliver multiple rounds to the end of the mortar tubes to disable the tubes and prevent launch. Even if your action releases anthrax, ground release is better than, G-d forbid, a launch at elevation and dispersal into Yerusháláyim's atmosphere."

"So there is no misunderstanding, we are authorized to target the mortar tubes if the hostages carrying them are separated," Sgt. Peled said.

"Affirmative, after you're in position rounds will be introduced to the exhibition hall to encourage the mehablim to come out and play. Give the mehablim unimpeded egress from the rear of the hall. Ephraim, assign someone to cover the hall exit, but make sure he's invisible. He'll be our point man on mehablim leaving the hall. There are some bushes in the area that should provide cover. The mehablim didn't come all this way to be pinned down, so we'll oblige them by not using overwhelming firepower until they're committed and out in the migdal. The courtyard's layout, as well as their efforts to minimize the size of the target on their backs, should keep them single file as they move toward their destination. When you are cleared to fire, confine fire to the last mehablim in a given group. It's our opinion the mehablim will deploy several squads and risk losing a squad rather than chance a full-out assault on every mehablim. The exception, as covered earlier, is if the two mortars head in different directions. Then neutralize the launch tubes without regard to the hostages, since everyone in the migdal will be dead anyway. It won't take long to see how things shake out, so, as always, adjust your tactics to conditions. This is too big to avoid hearings. Plan on our actions being studied for the next quarter century by those looking to place blame, or celebrate our success, just remember when firing, cameras are everywhere, any questions?"

"Captain, why take out the launch tubes if the mehablim start to go in different directions?"

"The minaret catwalk is optimal for launch or there'd be no reason to be in the migdal. If the hostages separate, that means launching from the minaret is compromised and they'll launch before reaching it. We can't let that happen . . . anyone else?"

No one spoke.

Grabbing a handful of copies he had run off on the copy machine, containing four images of Nasir Ghafour on each sheet, Captain Ashtor handed them to Sgt-Major Peled, who took one and passed the rest around. "Study these. It's important that Nasir Ghafour outlives his brothers; if the mehablim think they are succeeding they will stay on plan. We take Ghafour out, they could panic and launch."

Looking at his team, Colonel Samech said, "A magavnik sniper sterilized one *mehabel* outside the exhibition hall, bringing their numbers down to twenty-four." He paused feeling his age as the weight of Israel's future pressed upon him. "Not only is the minaret the tallest tower in the Old City and optimal for launch trajectory to altitude, symbolically, a successful attack from the minaret's catwalk would drive a stake in the heart of a Jewish Yerushaláyim we might never recover from. This moment is like no other. All our history comes down to the seven of you and, when you do your duty, how Shavlev and Bar-On meet the challenges of this day."

Looking from man to man, each one nodded his head in assent.

"We're ready Colonel," Sgt. Major Peled said.

"Michael, contact 124 Squadron. Tell them to disengage and return to base. If mehablim don't see our helos leave, they could abort and attempt to launch. Any final questions, Peled?"

"You're still Daniel for this one, Colonel?"

"Affirmative Lion, same code names."

"Michael, get HaLevi."

Michael Ashtor dialed the Captain's number. After a moment's pause, he said, "Captain the Colonel requests your presence . . . yes now."

Within seconds the door opened and Tzadok HaLevi stepped inside.

"Close the door, Captain."

"Yes sir."

"Our jumping off point is imminent. We need magavnikim to escort Peled's team into position, how long to get them?"

"I anticipated additional resources, sir. Seven magavnikim are standing by in my office."

"That is good Captain. Have them report here."

"Yes sir."

"Assign three snipers to the exhibition hall. As soon as these snipers are in place have them report in then commence sporadic fire against the outside of the hall but limit fire, we just want the mehablim to know we're there. Then your seven escorts will guide our team to strategic positions in the migdal complex, but ensure the sniper fire from the exhibition hall is carefully placed; I don't want my team hit by friendly fire. As soon as we've received confirmation our team is in place your escorts are to withdraw from the complex. Have your team leader radio when they've cleared the complex. Once the message is received your exhibition hall snipers are to commence firing in burst mode into the front, back, and south side of the exhibition hall leaving the northeast exit open. Maintain fire while holding positions but don't target the mehablim, or the explosives they've placed at the hall's entrance. Do you understand all this Captain?"

"Yes sir."

"Good. The snipers will encourage the mujahideen to leave the hall. If your men do their job, Peled's team will be waiting for the mehablim. That's all, dismissed."

"Yes sir."

Ninety seconds later, seven magavnikim were in the Colonel's office. Two minutes after that they led Peled's squad to Migdal David as the exhibition hall began to receive sporadic fire.

Looking at the two remaining members of his team, Captain Gurion Shavlev and Sergeant Major Eban Bar-On, Colonel Samech asked, "Feel lucky today?"

"Feel prepared," Gurion responded.

Colonel Samech's phone rang. Glancing at the display, he saw Caller ID was blocked. Only one person could get through with a blocked number. "This is Samech."

"Samech this is Oz, how are things looking there?"

For the next few minutes, Aaron Samech gave a status report to his superior.

"Sounds like everything is in control."

"Always General. I'll call when things change."

"Not this time, Aaron."

"What do you mean?"

"Just got off the phone with Vice Prime Minister Dobrin. Written directives are on their way. The Prime Minister's office wants the operation run from Lod. Aaron, we're both hunters and know the easiest prey is a scapegoat. With the word coming direct from Dobrin, our vaunted politicians are already lining up to deny culpability. We prevail, the politicians will do battle to see who comes out the most prescient and bold, which should get you your first star. It's been your show to this point, and any victory will build on your foundation. If the mehablim and those waiting on our borders prevail, Yisra'el will need all the senior commanders we have. Colonel Aaron Samech, I am assuming logistical command of operation *Birat Hanezah*."

Samech's jaw could be heard grinding in Tel Aviv. "Yes sir, General."

"I won't step on your toes, Aaron. It's your show up to the catwalk; I'll assume direct command from there. Who's going in?"

A Cheshire grin made its way across Aaron Samech's face. "Have them in front of me right now."

"Who are they?"

"Old friends, Gurion Shavlev and Eban Bar-On."

"No, don't do this to me."

"You're the General. We can send for others. Maybe they'll be here in three or four hours, after we locate them. Who knows, could be Dannie won't care. Or maybe the mehablim will come back tomorrow if we ask nice."

"Damn it, Aaron, Shavlev and Bar-On are more bull-headed than you."

"Is this possible, Sagiv?"

"You remember November 04? Their orders were explicit: Only arrest Mohammed Rassan Sheikh, and three—not one, not two, but three—PALFA militants ended up dead."

"Could be that for Yisra'el we can't have less."

"I'll make do. Let me know if ground conditions change. One final thing."

"Yes?"

"Remind those two I'm the General."

"I'll do that." Aaron Samech hung up, smiling. Looking at Shavlev and Bar-On, he said, "Oz sends his love."

"Don't recall him sharing the love after our last mission," Gurion said.

"The General has future politics on mind."

"Colonel, Eban and I need time to prepare. Got a place we can be alone?"

"Michael, let's go visit that nice Captain."

CHAPTER

54

Saturday 22 March 2008, 0439 hours

Sherut ha-Bitachon ha-Klali (Shabak) Headquarters Office of Yerushaláyim District Commander Ira Ramot Yerushaláyim

Clearing security, Hafiz made his way into Commander Ira Ramot 's office, chasing cobwebs from his still drowsy mind. Seated behind the desk to the right of his area commander, First Lt. Doran, Brigadier General Oz's Executive Deputy Assistant, sat at attention. Observing Ira's posture, Hafiz understood the seriousness of this meeting and sat down at attention facing them.

"Mr. IbnMansur," Commander Ramot began, "since your assignment to locate your brother's involvement with the anthrax, what have you found?"

"Contacts point to Nuri being rolled up in the anthrax and Deverell's disappearance, but I haven't found any direct connections. Everyone in the family is wild with fear that this will bleed all over them. Commander, I've called in every favor owed along with a few that weren't; no one is talking."

"Then this meeting should prove illuminating. All available intel points to one Nuri al-Massalha, your half-brother, not only being involved in the American's disappearance but in command of the operation that effected his kidnapping. It appears, though it has not yet been corroborated, that the anthrax, so assiduously being sought by our organization, has turned up with your American. That is, if photo surveillance from Gan David showing the American and the female escort you left him with, now as hostages of the mehablim breaking into the exhibition hall, are to be believed."

"Photos show Addison and Elizabeth?"

"I am not finished. When I am, questions will be dealt with."

"Yes sir," Hafiz said.

"At this precise moment, terrorists, believed to be Palestine Mujahideen Islamic Jihad, are in the Old City, and it appears have either taken over the exhibition hall or are damn close to it."

"Elizabeth with—"

"This is the same Elizabeth Daniels you left Mr. Deverell in the care of when you were recalled in our futile search for the anthrax. The necessity of providing an escort is not in question Mr. IbnMansur, you were recalled to duty, but if your specific choice of this woman, who shares a messianic fetish with you, was responsible for an American diplomat's abduction, when the rest of us would like to live out our days in the greatest semblance of peace we can, the least that will happen is your career with Shabak will be over. That is for another day, for the moment attention must be focused on more pressing matters if we are to be afforded the opportunity to embrace those days."

"Yes sir," Hafiz said.

"Either the PMIJ learned of our concern that anthrax was inside Yisra'el and is capitalizing on those concerns—and I would be at a complete loss to explain the purpose of any attempt to occupy Migdal David if they don't have anthrax other than for the sheer joy of mass suicide—or the American has found himself face to face with the hatred of one of our so-called partners in peace who, in fact, possesses a lethal bioweapon that has the capacity to destroy damn near every Yisraeli Jew in Yerushaláyim. In addition, it appears there are two other individuals, yet to be identified, who have found their way into the middle of all this and are also being held hostage."

Hafiz sat stone still, his face an impenetrable mask. The volcano had not finished erupting.

"Yisra'el is now faced with four hostages, one of whom is an American FSO, along with the unimaginable possibility of an unknown quantity of anthrax in Migdal David, which, you may remember, is not only the tallest structure in the Old City but happens to be a mere 1600 feet away from the Dome of the Rock—and over one billion Muslims who live and breathe with a hair trigger when it comes to their precious dome."

Hafiz remained silent, let whatever it was play out until he learned his fate.

"Brigadier General Oz has assumed direct operational control of this incident. He is meeting with senior commanders as we speak. His chief of staff called this morning and issued direct orders from the General, thus the presence of First Lt. Doran, who should be with the General. You are, for the duration of this operation, to stand down. You are not to become involved in any aspect of this operation. You will remain available should any information be needed, but for this one you are a citizen, do you read me?"

"Yes sir."

"Any questions?"

"No, sir," Hafiz said.

Turning to his left, Commander Ramot said, "Lt. Doran, please assure General Oz that his orders will be carried out. I have undertaken many missions with Mr. IbnMansur and trust him."

Silently, the Lieutenant arose and exited the room. Turning back to Hafiz, Ira Ramot relaxed in his chair. "Hafiz, the Lieutenant wanted you relieved of duty. The General doesn't know you, but you're tied to this by too many strings for command to allow your continued involvement. For the record, it would have been the same if it were a Yisraeli born sibling who has his hands in all this."

"What about the message of Addison with anthrax?"

"The geeks are parsing the latest communication from the mehablim and found a line in it about hope for the downtrodden and your American fulfilling his destiny."

"Why connect those dots?"

"Adding two and two, we know anthrax is close, and the latest communication from the PMIJ is that the American would surface."

"Permission to observe from a distance, sir."

"I did not hear that, Hafiz. My career isn't going down with yours. You heard the Lieutenant."

"The Lieutenant didn't say one word."

"Well he said plenty to me, and his message for you is to go home. Let others be heroes for this one."

Rising, Hafiz headed for the stairway and the Hamsa gallery to pick up his backpack with everything required. He wouldn't even need to go home.

Ira Ramot picked up the receiver on his phone. "Send in Kolatch."

CHAPTER

55

Saturday 22 March 2008, 0439 hours

Exhibition Hall, Migdal David
Yerushaláyim

Yanking on the thick polypropylene netting attached to the expansion bolt rock anchors embedded in the stone jambs, sill, and lintel of the entrance, Nasir was satisfied. Two 1½ inch thick, clear ballistic panels, sitting on top each other with their ends secured to the jambs' rock anchors, protected the bottom three feet of the opening. Vertical steel rods joined the top and bottom panels, completing the defensive shield for Saghir and Hamal.

"Remember, wire C-4 so Israelis can see it," Nasir said. "And keep below the shield to the sides of the doorway. You're our rear guard."

"Don't worry, we're ready for target practice," Hamal said as he and Saghir inserted blasting caps into the C-4 bricks.

Inspecting their handiwork everything looked in order, the training had paid off. He led the group of fighters through a cavernous room and toward the rear stairs. The sound of their footsteps bounced off the smooth asymmetrical floor tiles and rough stone walls, echoing into the soaring Gothic arched ceiling above. Tense eyes probed the unfamiliar expanse, expecting the unexpected, while fingers hung over triggers poised to unleash lethal fury.

Ten feet from the back of the sixty-foot hall, they climbed five steps to a narrow landing. Forced left by an abutting stone wall on the end of the landing, they advanced toward an open archway five feet away on their right. Going under the archway's flat lintel, they walked ten feet into a craggy rectangular limestone block room, where an arched doorway ominously waited to swallow the unwary three steps up on their left. To their right a locked gated stairway discouraged entry to another part of this unknown labyrinth.

Turning to Musad, Nasir motioned him over. "Go up the passageway to the end; ensure Israelis do not wait in ambush."

"But if they wait will I not be the first to experience their presence?"

"Keep down and to the side."

"But why—"

"Do you wish another to take your glory?"

"No, but have others cover me so I can reside with the living should there be a welcoming committee. You know the end opens to the migdal courtyard."

"Look around; all eyes are upon us. You will be between your brothers and the Zionists; would wisdom invite their gunfire?"

"Suddenly I feel better, blessings to Nuri for noticing my skill with the rifle and assigning me as a sniper."

"Each has their part."

Musad approached the opened metal and glass door, the lone sentinel to the tunnel's entrance. Looking up the rising corridor, he entered the maw of the shaft. Hair prickled the back of his neck as the raw stone walls and ceiling throbbed its constricting welcome.

Crouching, heart pounding in his ears, he climbed the five flights of three stone steps, each separated by a deep stone landing, aware that he was a single Israeli marksman's shot from eternity but determined not to go alone. Just below the final landing, he lay down, pressing himself against the side wall as he scanned what could be seen of the courtyard beyond. Glancing back to the entrance he'd just come through, he froze; eighteen rifles were pointed in his direction, then—rotors. First a single helo; the sound, heard so many times, was a part of him. As he strained his ears, a second could be heard in the distance. Looking down the stairway, he saw mujahideen climbing toward him, oblivious to encroaching danger. Raising his arm, he waved them back. In confusion, some continued, others stopped, a few retreated to the landing.

Nasir pointed to his walkie-talkie. Musad shook his head, the Israelis could be listening. Motioning toward himself, and then tapping his index finger on his lips, he pointed back to Nasir then to himself. Three repetitions later Nasir started up the stairs. Near the top, he sank to his knees, crawling the last few steps to Musad's side. Nasir tried to whisper. Musad shook his head, pointing to his ear. Nasir listened.

It was quiet save for the sound of a helo—a helo? Nasir's heart started racing. Looking down the passageway at his confused warriors, he knew he had to come up with a plan. But there was no plan. They weren't supposed to be pinned down, not now, not here. A helicopter could destroy the stairway with a single laser guided missile but held off, why? *Is the American that strategic of an asset he would keep the Israelis from firing? Or is the Jews' precious tourist attraction too valuable to destroy?*

He signaled everyone back down the stairs. Whispering into Musad's ear, he climbed down to the mujahideen. Near the bottom he beckoned Qadir. When Qadir came to him, Nasir gestured while speaking close to his ear. Qadir trudged up the stairs, grenade launcher firmly in hand. He kneeled next to Musad.

Taking a look at the RPG, Musad fled down the stairs as mujahideen poured through the entrance room and converged on the landing. An explosion thundered, blasting ears as smoke shot back through the passageway.

Pushing through the dissipating smoke to the top of the stairs, Nasir warily checked the edge of the courtyard. No downed helo. The sounds of helos were absent, but he would have heard the impact as the RPG tore through its soft underbelly; instead the helo's high-pitched evasive screams were lost to the RPG's firing blast.

Nasir needed to locate another entrance onto the courtyard. There was no telling what the Zionists would have waiting now that they'd announced their position. "Everyone stay," he yelled, the need for stealth gone. "Musad, relieve Qadir. Talaal, come with me."

As they neared the entrance, sporadic Israeli fire could be heard. "Hamal, Saghir," Nasir broadcast on his walkie-talkie, "we're behind you. Status, over."

"Outside wall is taking fire, but the entrance hasn't been hit."

"How secure is your position, over."

"If the Zionists come knocking, they'll need a dozer and excavator to get through the rubble from the C-4, over."

"Affirmative, advise if status changes, over."

"Let's check other exits, Talaal," Nasir said. Turning, Talaal fell a step behind. Something struck the back of Nasir's scarf. His hand shot to his neck. Wet warmth clung to his fingers. Odd, his fingertips were streaked with crimson stickiness. Looking back, he saw Talaal, turning violently on the hard stone tiles in an absurd circle. Sounds of struggle were absent as he thrashed in silence. His black and white checkered scarf, against the darkness of the tiles, turning scarlet. Transfixed—was it three, four minutes—unable to intervene in this macabre dance, Nasir watched the choreography play out. Finally, all movements slowed, then stopped. Incapable of turning away, Nasir watched the heaving chest expand a final time. Then eerie whistling escaped the mortal wound, Talaal's chest at last still. Gelatinous crimson oozed past his scarf as serum and red blood cells fled this body of death.

He wanted to take Talaal's rifle, Talaal's ammunition. He knew he should. He could not. Nasir returned to his men.

"Where's Talaal?" Ommar said.

"In Paradise," Nasir looked at the faces before him. "I have words from Nuri. Two from our numbers, along with the machsom martyrs, have gone to their reward. This morning, just before leaving, Nuri told me to speak to you when two from our numbers were called to glory. He allowed no words be spoken until this moment. The equipment we carry has explosives to launch the fireworks' shell. All have been trained and will act honorably. Nuri knew life would be exchanged for a nation where Zionists no longer torment the sons and daughters of god as they have for the past sixty years. He spoke that at times, in the heat of struggle, noble warriors sometimes forget duty and act ignobly. His joy was to ensure all will present themselves victorious, no matter the challenge. The bomb-maker and his assistants embedded explosives in more than one place in all we carry. Should any decide to embrace failure, the explosives can be detonated and those who choose to dishonor their calling will fall to Jahannam."

"What is this you say, my brother? How do explosives trigger themselves unless you have been charged with killing those who do not please you?"

"I do not have this ability. I face the same challenge. The one who controls is not with us."

"How do we know he will not set explosives off even as we rise to glorious victory?"

"We are not like the infidels, Ya'qub. Our lives are a sacred trust, and upon victory all will be honored throughout Palestine. There exists remote technology. The one controlling it is aware of what we do. If we act honorably, our objective will be attained. If we do not, shame will be our eternal garment."

"Did you find another exit?" Ommar asked Nasir.

"Time and every opening passed proved not a friend; our plan remains. If Allāh wills, we prevail; if not, who can fight god?"

Turning, Nasir lead the way; mujahideen closed ranks behind him as they scaled the stairs in the passageway, stopping below the top step. He turned, facing his army of twenty. "You know this route. When you step into the courtyard, you will all recognize having been here; it's the same path we ran time after time in Syria."

"But this day we destroy infidels."

"Yes, Basim, death stalks the camp of the infidels, but it has also ushered four of our brothers into Paradise. Keep our calling before you; our destiny is the minaret. We must not become distracted; nothing must keep us from victory.

"Remember your training; all know we go in order by teams. Each mujahid with their hostage leads off, then equipment carriers, followed by team leaders, and snipers as we make our way to the tower. I will be in the first team; every other team will have four members in that exact order. If you encounter resistance you cannot overcome, signal. Snipers and team leaders will look for signals. If you are shot, you alone must arise. To stop, to gather in one place, is to become a target or be taken captive. All know what is required to avoid capture. If you are hit, this does not mean you're injured. A direct hit on our vests will feel like you've been shot, but you remain protected. These are level four vests with ballistic plates."

Looking from the American to the Jew, he continued. "Remember, hostages are shields; they go first in each team. If the American dies, let Israeli bullets be found in him then see how the infidels speak to his killing. Ensure our traitors are targets for their friends the Jews before their eternal torment."

"What about the Jew, Nasir?" Dabir said

"The Zionists may withhold fire as you carry her to the catwalk. If they prove weak, a bullet with her name inscribed awaits. She will not see the sun set this day. Are all ready?"

"You are sure the helos are gone?"

"Their silence remains, Jalil. If they again choose mujahideen company, our RPGs will welcome them."

~

Having been deployed at strategic points the magavnikim scouts laid out, the scouts retreated.

The Pride consisted of seven parts of a whole, each guided by intuitive knowledge, as operational awareness had been forged under fire until innate knowledge of every part of the team drove the seven as one. Yisra'el's survival demanded no less.

"Pride, this is Lion, acknowledge by op name," Sgt. Major Peled ordered into his walkie-talkie. Each sniper had a wireless ear bud in place and lavalier microphone clipped to his collar.

"Lion, this is Tiger, copy."

"Copy, Tiger."

"Jaguar here, reading you loud and clear."

"Copy, Jaguar."

"Cheetah here, over."

"Puma, waiting for lambs."

"Copy Cheetah, and Puma."

"Leopard here, I'm surveiling the exhibition hall exit. One of the scouts told me he thought the lambs were headed from the exhibition hall ten minutes ago. One popped out as the helos were withdrawing, fired his RPG so fast it's a wonder he hit air."

"Roger that Leopard. Sounds like some mehablim's nerves are fraying, should make our jobs easier, over."

"Lynx here."

"Copy, Lynx. Pride, keep in mind everything's recorded and you can bet the Americans will clamor for a copy."

"Got it Lion, work quietly."

"And remember these sheep aren't alone, someone may be listening so radio silence unless you have something I haven't heard today."

Eating dust at the back of the west wall arch behind a wild boxwood shrub, Leopard, concealed by the shrub, was fixed on the hall's exit, his belly taut, like it invariably was before a firefight. After every battle, faces he never chose for death would claim his dreams. He forced himself to exhale in one slow, deep, breath. "Lambs are moving, Pride."

"Roger that, Leopard, lambs on the path."

"Leopard hold fire until the last lamb clears the hall, easier to shear them in the courtyard, copy."

"Loud and clear Lion. Pride, American is draped over the lead mujahid's shoulders, pistol digging in his guts, a mortar tube strapped to his back."

"How many are heading our way, Leopard?"

"Total of six, Lion, including the American. Looks to be a couple of feet between them, might want to make the third one a priority, Lion."

"Why's that, Leopard?"

"He's shouldering an RPG."

Makeen the Ox was as stout and strong as the nickname he'd picked up when seven. First out of the exhibition hall, he balanced the American with ease on his shoulder in a modified fireman's carry. His right hand, over the infidel's right leg at the knee, gripped the hostage's shackled wrist with fingers that could separate tendon from bone should the inclination strike him. He grasped a cocked

Tokarev TT-33 pistol in his left hand—one round in the chamber, seven in the magazine—jerking it between the infidel's stomach and groin. He hated Americans, all Americans, and was tempted to blow this one's guts out, but if his bullet deflected and hit the mortar tube strapped on the hostage's back, everything might be lost. Besides, in and out of consciousness, the infidel wouldn't scream in terror. Maybe he'd wake at the tower, and then Makeen would have satisfaction.

Behind him, Umar wore an equipment-filled poncho. Two fitted canvas bags, one on his front the other on his back, hung from straps over his shoulders with a belt wrapped around his waist. Each team carried identical equipment save the awkward ballistic plates. If any carrier was taken out, others would have mission critical equipment down to the black powder and wireless igniters Fakhir had concealed within each poncho bag. Third in line, Hashim, rifle sweeping from side to side, RPG on his back, was ahead of Nasir with Rehan the sniper bringing up the rear.

Turning right after bursting from the hall, Makeen banged Addison's legs along the rough protruding stone wall. Hurdling three wood steps onto the age-worn stone landing—the place smelled of Jews—he bounded down the stairs, hitting the cobblestone walk headed for the stairway that would take him to the second level and then the minaret.

Scanning the ancient stone and crevice-filled inner courtyard, Umar, closing on Makeen's heels, drove himself forward as invading sounds screamed threats.

Nasir scrambled toward the flight of steps that would take him to the second level and reveal more of the complex. It would also expose him; he tightened his grip on his AK-104. At the base of the stairs he knelt, giving Umar a chance to scale the stairway while he checked the courtyard for enemy snipers; none announced their presence. Getting up he climbed the stairs.

"Pride, this Lion, let the American pass then let's see who can deliver the first round to the tail."

"Lion, this is Puma. Got the tail in my sights," he said, squeezing his Tavor's trigger.

A bullet slammed Rehan against the stone wall. "Nasir," he radioed, "been hit."

"Where?"

"My shoulder, bullet's lodged deeply."

"Check for blood."

He checked. "None yet but bullet stings, it's hot in my flesh."

"You have a hole through vest?"

"There's hole."

"Check, is it all the way through? Don't make me come down the steps; I can cover you better from here. Ceramic disks in vest were made to shatter on direct hits. There'll be an outside hole, but if no blood it's not all the way through."

Probing his throbbing shoulder, Rehan felt the vest's shoulder pad, feeling none of the blood he expected to greet his fingertips. "Shoulder is trembling."

"It hurts. You are mujahid. We've got a tower to take."

He felt his shoulder a final time; no blood grasped his probing fingers. "It feels like being shot."

"You were shot; your vest did its job. Now get up the stairs so you can cover us on the walkway, then I'll cover you from the wall, over." Sporadic mujahideen fire interrupted his words. Aiming blindly, Rehan added to the fire then climbed the stairs.

"Your sight need adjusting Puma?"

"Shoulder still belongs to the body."

"Wait, Puma, your lamb's getting up. You use an air gun?"

"Hit was solid, but there's more where that came from. Soon as he's up we'll see how he likes one down his pie hole."

"Gotta give it to your lamb Puma he runs pretty good. Looks to be beyond your range which is bad for you but good for me since he's just cleared the stairs into my cross hairs." He squeezed off a single shot. The mujahid spun around and slammed against the wooden walkway, screaming. An iron railing kept him from plunging to the cobblestones below. "That, in case you were wondering, Puma, is how it's done."

"Really Jaguar?"

"By the book."

"Mind telling me how he pulled himself up on the railing and is now running toward the wall?"

"I hit him dead-on."

"Must be tough, most dead guys can't run that fast."

"This is Leopard. Four more lambs exiting the hall, out in the courtyard. Lion, the lead mujahid's the biggest Arab I've ever seen and he's carrying an Arab big as he is. The imbecile has a pistol to his gut just like the first mujahid with the American."

"An Arab, you sure?"

"Lion, hostage's face is bruised and swollen but definitely Arab."

"Pride, this one's not in the books, so watch hostage, might be a trick."

"Lion, hostage's too badly beaten. Who'd volunteer for that?"

"Copy Leopard, observe as he comes past, over."

"No bullets anywhere near the American or Arab."

"Loud and clear Pride leader."

"Lion, third group's exiting the hall, same lineup as the last group with another Arab hostage."

"Gun to his middle?"

"More like his groin, Cheetah."

"Things are getting nasty. Let's see if they form a circle and start shooting."

"Could be divine retribution, *Shi'as* and *Sunnis* whack each other more than us."

"Only because there are more of them than us."

"Let's focus. I want to see firepower being delivered."

"Got my sights on the next lamb headed for eternity," Tiger said, squeezing his trigger. "Moment of silence if you will. One demented soul passes from this life."

"I'll be," Cheetah said, "another resurrection."

"Not possible. I watched him drop like a bug."

"Must be a cockroach, he's scurrying around like someone just flipped on the lights."

"Lion, bullets should be dropping these guys," said Puma. "We're making our mark."

"About to get more practice," Leopard said. "Fourth team is leaving the hall, headed your way."

"Breaking news Pride, another four, hot on their heels, are leaving the hall."

"Wait, do we have two groups of four or one group of eight?"

"That's two groups of four. The magic number mentioned in briefing was twenty-five. Three were left at the hall entrance, two as guards, and one a magavnik took out. There's also the unconfirmed hit in the hall itself, which brings it down to twenty-one," Lion said.

"Well, if twenty-one's the magic number, everyone has punched their card."

"What about hostages, Leopard?"

"One Arab hostage in the previous group of four, and a hostage in the last group, but we need to be careful."

"Come again, Leopard," Lion said.

"Hostage is female and a mortar tube is strapped to her back. They don't seem to play favorites with their beatdowns: Someone didn't like her."

"So one American hostage, three Arabs."

"*Hee Mishelanu,* she is one of us."

"One of our women—hostage?" Cheetah said.

"Stay on task Cheetah. Lose focus, someone gets tagged, maybe me. You know mehablim's tactics. Our women have been dying beside us for the past sixty years; why would this day be different?"

"Lion, bullets aren't getting through and I've made solid hits."

"Daniel, every hit is being shaken off, you tracking with us?"

"Affirmative, Lion."

"We need 99s to end the discussion, over."

"'Checking into delivery Lion, stand by."

"Pride, till we get 99s, avoid trunk shots, target limbs. We need to reduce numbers before the mehablim make it inside the minaret."

Hitting speed dial on his phone to talk privately with Colonel Samech, Lion covered his lavalier mike and waited.

"Go."

"We're losing time we can't get back, Colonel. Mehablim are closing on the minaret and no one we've tagged stays down with confirmed direct hits. We need SR-99s."

"The Magavnikim who took you to your positions will bring the Galils. I'll call when they're on their way."

"Affirmative, Daniel."

"Pride, this is Lion. 99s are in the pipeline. When they arrive ROEs remain: Confine hits to stragglers."

"Michael, we need magavnikim to take 99s to the migdal. Get HaLevi," the Colonel ordered.

Twenty-seven seconds later, Michael Ashtor hung up. "Colonel, magavnikim are on their way. Shavlev, Bar-On, and I will have the rifles and ammunition ready."

Charging as hard as his legs would carry him to avoid enemy fire and errant mujahideen bullets, Nasir passed Hashim, Umar, and Makeen. Turning right at the end of the wood walkway, he scaled the ancient limestone steps to his left two at a time. Reaching the landing, he veered left up a single stone step then scrambled up the remaining ten steps as fast as he could. To his left the minaret beckoned in the distance. Turning toward the walkway below, he saw his staggered squads making their way forward while the Zionists, from their infernal hidden positions, increased their fire. Kneeling behind the short iron railing, breath burning in his lungs, he bellowed into his walkie-talkie, "Let's go, move, move, move. Umar, close ranks. Your equipment is the first needed."

Umar stopped just beneath the wall and bent over, chest heaving, hands on his knees. Hashim passed him as Makeen, lost in his world, increased his distance while balancing the American on his shoulders, Tokarev jammed into his stomach.

"Coming fast as I can," Umar said, struggling to catch his breath. "Feels like I've been hit twenty times," he huffed into his walkie-talkie.

"We're all under fire. Get moving."

Going around Nasir, Makeen headed for the minaret tower. Nasir took off after him with Hashim in close pursuit.

Clearing the last of the steps, Umar turned toward Nasir's disappearing form—his right knee exploded. Going down hard on the cobblestones, shrieking in agony, he turned from side to side in the three foot wide walkway, struggling to grab his knee. The equipment-laden poncho and cramped walk between an iron railing and the stone parapet defeated every attempt.

Turning, Nasir yelled, "Shake it off; we need your equipment."

Umar continued to thrash.

Racing back past Hashim, Nasir slung his rifle on his back. He fought to release the poncho's straps and pull the equipment bags over Umar's head as Umar continued to flail.

Nasir, adrenaline fueling every thought, screamed, "Lay still. I can't help if you keep moving." He tried again to rip the bags from the violently twisting form. Grasping Umar by the shoulders, he bellowed, "Get up. Get up now! Move, you hear!"

Guttural moaning and spasmodic contortions were Umar's only response.

Nasir knew what came next but couldn't move.

Rehan, off the stairs, was unable to get past the writhing form. He looked down on Umar then over at his leader.

Nasir met his gaze, unable to speak.

Fixing on the struggling form, Rehan lifted his AK-104 to his shoulder and pointed it at Umar's jerking head. "Umar."

Umar stopped, looking up at the barrel pointed at his head, eyes wide, frozen.

The rifle's discharge exploded in their ears. Umar's face no longer recognizable.

"Get equipment," Rehan ordered.

Nasir froze, unable to pull himself from the moment.

"We couldn't leave him," Rehan's words echoed as through a tunnel. "Zionists would take him captive. Now get his bags."

Nasir struggled to find reality, the methodical plan practiced times without number. In a fog he found the knife sheathed on his leg. Jerking it free, he bent over Umar's still-warm body and cut the straps holding the equipment bag. He sheathed the alien blade. Grabbing the top of the poncho as the cadaver's head hemorrhaged, he pulled. The corpse slid toward him. "Grab his legs," Nasir more pleaded than ordered. He jerked hard as blood spurted over his chest and chin; the cadaver released its burden. "Others must get past; Aziz arrives next. Tell him the walk needs to be cleared."

Seventeen seconds later, Umar, in the city of peace, made no sound as his body hit the cobblestones two stories below, less than twenty-five feet from where he had left his safe haven in the exhibition hall.

Clutching Umar's equipment bags, Nasir struggled toward the minaret. Nearing the Old City's south wall, he hugged its edge and turned left across the cobblestone plaza. As he took the first of five stairs on his right into the base of the minaret tower, his tension abated—he'd made it—his confidence began to soar. A bullet slammed his helmet against the open archway, snapping his head hard against the stone jamb. Circles rolled across his vision, punishing him in their dizziness. Shaking them off, he thrust one foot after the other up the stone steps. As he turned right, still reeling, his refuge enclosed him. Feeling no blood between his helmet and the back of his head, he forced himself up into the minaret's inside stairs and found himself two feet from the minaret's iron gate, the lone barrier to the catwalk. Makeen awaited, the American crumpled on the cobblestones. A raised stone sill beneath the minaret gate bordered the end of the stone walkway attached to the inside corner of the Old City Wall. A three-foot iron railing enclosed the walkway that opened to a courtyard below. Away from the stinging bullets, the putrescence of death hung over him, but their position was still vulnerable from below. He needed to deploy mujahideen before the enemy inserted themselves to exploit their weakness. Samien and Jalil would secure the minaret base entrance with C-4, netting, and ballistic glass, effectively cutting off the tower. As he caught his breath, the teams began arriving. Nasir labored to open the equipment bag; blood covering his hands caused them to slip from the hook and loop straps. He let the bags slide to the cobblestone. "Get this vest off," he ordered, back in control.

Mujahideen hands pulled his rifle from his back, setting it against the railing. They released his vest then unstrapped his helmet; both tumbled over the railing to the courtyard below. The remaining teams made their way into the protection of the tower base.

"Jalil, Samien," Nasir yelled, "secure the lower base archway. Remember your training. Ya'qub," he said, pointing his bloody finger, "set up cover fire at the corner of the walkway over there." He grabbed his shirt, ripping off a bottom corner, and began wiping the blood's stickiness from his hands. Then grasping the hook and loop strips, he opened the equipment bag and removed a pair of bolt cutters. Approaching the iron gate, divided into thirty-six squares of welded square bars, Nasir snugged the blades near the end of a padlocked rod where it entered a stone pocket chiseled into the abutting sidewall. Biceps, triceps, and delts flexed. A loud crack resonated, and the end of the rod shot off and ricocheted across the stone walkway. Nasir handed the cutter to Makeen then yanked on the gate; it held fast. Looking down, he saw the gate handle had an inset lock that blended into the iron bars halfway down the gate. When he wriggled it, the lock held fast, "Kateb!"

Kateb pushed past the massed mujahideen. Kneeling in front of the gate, he opened a rolled-up cloth on the stone pavers. Selecting two picks, he inserted them into the lock. Adding a torsion wrench, he twisted them, and a triumphant look came on his face. He pulled the tools from the lock, "Nasir?"

Stepping to the gate, Nasir grabbed the handle and gave it a fierce twist. The handle turned but the gate held fast. Putting his shoulder into the gate, Nasir adjusted his stance, readying his shoulders and back. Leaning into the gate, he released coiled muscles. The gate's rusting hinges shrieked in protest then gave way while continuing their high-pitched disapproval; shouts erupted as the fledgling warriors looked upon the open doorway. Then silence assailed joy as the imminence of destiny confronted apprehensive souls.

Nasir rebuked the foreboding he saw on too many faces. "We've received the best training. We are brothers united in a just cause. Today is for those who cannot share in our glory. Today is for Palestine. Fulfill your duty."

Makeen was first through the gate. Dust and bird droppings competed for space on the steep spiral limestone steps. A black cable snaked its way up the left side of the circular stairway. He climbed to the top of the minaret spire just inside the catwalk. Ommar and Mifsud, each carrying an equipment bag, came behind, inhaling the dust and bird dung Makeen's ascent dislodged.

"Adnan, Ghassan, set up on the lower arrow slits. It's time to silence enemies of peace. Rehan, Musad, the upper slits await."

Retrieving a rope from Ommar's equipment bag, Makeen tied a carabiner to one end and lowered it to mujahideen along the narrow steps, who in turn passed it down.

"Dabir, Aziz, get American in tower," Nasir said. "Grab him by his arms, face down. Don't damage the launch tube."

They grabbed Addison's arms and dragged him inside the tower.

"Good, now careful, protect launch tube, sit him up. Stand behind him so he doesn't topple over. I don't—"

"Yeah, I know, you don't want launch tube damaged."

"Aziz, connect him to the carabiner."

Aziz took the carabiner, pulling the rope under Addison's arms and over the launch tube encircling his torso, then clipped the carabiner back onto the rope. Testing his handiwork, he yelled, "Makeen, load of infidel's ready."

Putting his muscles into it, Makeen lifted while mujahideen passed the comatose American up the steep circular steps. Each was careful not to let him twist and damage the launch tube as he was pulled up the stairs. When he arrived in the spire the rope was sent back down the stairway. Then the launch tube was carefully removed and set aside.

The Arab hostages made the same journey.

As Elizabeth was lifted to the spire, Nasir motioned to Ya'qub in the corner of the walkway. "Time to secure the gate, into the tower." Ya'qub hurried into the minaret tower.

Wrestling the ballistic glass inside the tower, Basim and Shafiq leaned both panels against the steps. Grabbing cordless drills from the equipment bag they drilled holes in the side jambs, then the lintel, and finally the sill below.

"Shafiq, hammer, rock anchors." Grabbing a small cloth bag of D-ring anchors and a four-pound sledge, Basim drove the expansion anchors into the holes. "Wire, pliers."

After handing Basim a spool of wire and pliers with a wire cutter, Shafiq closed the gate and wired it to the embedded anchors. Pulling three C-4 bricks from the bag, he laid them on the stone floor then strung wire through the bars and secured one brick on the middle top bar of the gate then inserted a wired blasting cap.

Grabbing a ballistic panel, they placed its long edge on the floor, spanning the gate, and then wired it, through pre-drilled holes along both panel ends, to the rock anchors on the jambs and sill. Setting the second panel's edge atop the first, Basim held them while Shafiq aligned pre-drilled holes in two steel bars to those in the panels, attaching them with screws. Then they wired the panel's ends as they had the bottom panel.

Basim took the remaining C-4 bricks and, inserting blasting caps, wired one brick on each side of the gate just above the ballistic glass to contact switches wired to trigger if the gate opened more than a quarter of an inch. Checking connections a final time, both were satisfied. They sat down, crossed-legged, behind their protective shield, a canvas bag beside each holding thirty-round magazines and a gas mask. Resting their AK-104's across their laps—they were ready.

"Daniel, this Lion. Where's our delivery?"

"Coming your way, Lion."

"Roger that, Lion, 99s in route."

Eleven mujahideen jostled one other in the claustrophobic limitations of the spire. The sweat of their confinement fused with intermittent prayers wafting heavenward as warriors scrambled to complete final preparations while Nasir looked on from the top of the stairs.

"Careful, my brothers, explosives live everywhere," Nasir yelled. "Makeen, Hashim, be mindful of the launch tube. We don't want fireworks before the catwalk."

"Come, show how it's done," Makeen bellowed back across the din.

"Just be careful. Today all is live."

Taking his knife from its sheath, Kateb cut the polypropylene rope binding the puny Arab, then freed the Jew. Unstrapping the empty tube from the Jew's torso, he tossed it aside.

Four diaphanous metallic mesh vests were eased from the equipment bags and carefully secured on each hostage. Two timers were placed in pockets on the American's vest.

Mifsud took two pairs of handcuffs and ratcheted one bracelet from each pair on the wrists of the Jew. Yazid did the same with two pairs of handcuffs snugging one bracelet on each wrist of the pint-sized Arab.

Taking another pair of handcuffs Mifsud attempted to shackle Aadil's wrist. "Handcuffs are not big enough, we got bigger?"

"You even look?" Yazid said, reaching into Mifsud's equipment bag. He pulled out two pairs of leg irons and handed one to Mifsud. "Place one cuff on his right wrist, I'll get the left."

"Aziz," Nasir shouted, "grab two pairs of cuffs and put one bracelet from each pair on the American's wrists."

Crested Larks normally found the Old City an ideal home. Their grayish-brown coloring blending into the walls and walkways in their daily search for weeds, insects, and seeds, as they nested in the many refuges the Old City provided. This day their routine upset the migdal's visitors as their movement and warbling brought automatic bursts of 104s as Adnan and Ghassan blasted anything that made a sound or threatened to move through the lower arrow slits. As the warriors' nerves began to fray, Rehan and Musad did their best to keep pace from the upper slits.

Ghassan's excited voice squawked over Nasir's walkie-talkie. "They're popping up like weasels, taking a shot then disappearing."

"This was expected."

"Didn't expect tower would be demolished."

"Nothing's demolished, over."

"Every shot blasts tower. Nuri said Zionists wouldn't destroy their precious tower. They're sure as hell trying."

"You can't even see the outside of the tower, Ghassan. Minaret was built by Arabs; it's solid enough to withstand occupier's rifles. Until you see the inside of the tower spalling, stay off the radio." Nasir heard incipient panic in Ghassan's voice; mujahideen were listening. He spoke before doubt could decay into surrender. "We all knew the occupiers would attempt to defeat us. Does their fire surprise? Snipers, when you get on the catwalk your firepower will unite with shooters in the arrow slits, overwhelming the Zionist infidels. Hostage teams, focus on your tasks; snipers will keep the enemy occupied."

"How will we get on catwalk with so many rounds incoming, Nasir?" Dabir demanded.

"Enemy fires to keep us from catwalk. When coming through the courtyard they hit as many as they could, yet we lost only one warrior. Our equipment protected us on our way to tower; the catwalk is no different," Nasir said.

The mujahideen inspected their hostages' wiring harnesses one final time, the connection seared into each mujahid's memory from the bomb-maker's training.

"Makeen, Aziz, Ommar, Dabir, open cell phones, fasten onto hostage."

"We know, in pocket on vest. Training just day before yesterday," Ommar said.

"And make sure hostage covers you as you go to positions; give Zionists a target. Qadir, Kateb, Tawil—weapons ready?"

"Rifles thirst for Zionist blood."

"Warriors in arrow slits," Nasir broadcast into his walkie-talkie, "remember slits are vulnerable, minimize your exposure. Occupiers' snipers wait to pick you off; maintain vigilance. When Israelis show themselves, make regret follow that decision."

Turning to the warriors in the spire, Nasir said, "My brothers, we are ready. The tower, catwalk—Palestine's future—is ours. Each of you knows what is needed; the fate that awaits the enemies of god. No force on earth can stop our cause; this is our supreme moment: Allāuh Akbar."

Silence hung over Nasir's words as they worked their way into hearts prepared for this moment. Then one voice joined another as, one by one, their crescendo built into unifying thunder: "Allāuh Akbar, Allāuh Akbar . . . ."

Reviewing images from the fiberscope cameras concealed inside the minaret, Oz's advisors, forced on him by the Vice Prime

Minister, opposed breeching the gate. The migdal could be taken, but political will had rendered its judgment. Civilians had no place with old warriors, but these were new times. If they were wrong there was a backup but timing would be crucial. If they proved right, he'd add a final medal to his uniform, retire and launch his political career. But it was time to transfer ops from Samech; the mehablim's next move was the catwalk.

The SR 99s were delivered along with fresh ammunition without a hiccup. Settling into position, the Pride heard "Allāuh Akbar." Dialing in their SR-99s, seven cross hairs centered on the catwalk.

"Allāuh Akbar, Allāuh Akbar," continued to pierce the morning air.

The catwalk gate jerked open.

Lion, prone beside the south parapet wall, snugged his index finger against the trigger. He could feel blood throbbing through his hand to his trigger finger. Addison's form filled his rifle's scope. "Pride, hold fire, American is shield."

"We don't have another catwalk to deliver firepower to, Lion."

"Puma, catwalk's open on all sides. We'll have shots. We don't fire on hostages."

CHAPTER

56

Saturday 22 March 2008, 0452 hours

Old City Walls, Yerushaláyim

Making his way through the Dung Gate, Hafiz presented identification papers, affecting disinterest. The young soldier waved him through after a careful check of his expertly forged credentials. Using known routes he avoided ubiquitous cameras set to catch or track the unwary. The Old City's perimeter was locked down tight and would stay that way for the duration of the siege, making it easier to spot Nuri—provided one knew where to look.

A three-story workshop with rooftop storage that had served well in the past would shield him from being observed by the few skilled enough to pick him out on satellite or drone scans. His sanctuary provided power for his equipment along with a view of the migdal minaret and surrounding area. The workshop, where craftsmen prepared souvenirs tourists demanded they return home with, was empty owing to the crisis. If Nuri was involved, this was where he needed to be. He had not joined Shabak to sit on the sidelines, General or no.

Hafiz tucked a wireless earbud in place. He adjusted the volume on his radio scanner so he could track the action on the tower.

Unzipping his backpack, he pulled out a laptop then retrieved the dual band digital receiver-scanner, next came an antenna. He set the elements at right angles to the boom and secured the assembly to the mast. Unfolding the tripod legs, he fastened them to the roof edge. Connecting the cable to the antenna, he ran it to the receiver-scanner and plugged it in. He grabbed a cable from the bag, plugging one end into a USB port on the receiver-scanner and the other end into the laptop, he rechecked connections. Satisfied, Hafiz fired up the computer and waited as it booted. Clicking on the receiver software icon, he watched as it loaded, and then he clicked on the DTMF button. He was ready. Phones, not radios, emitted dual-tone multi-frequency signals, so any cell call in the immediate area would be captured. Since the Old City was evacuated, save for select IDF, and the majority of their communications were by radio transceivers, Hafiz reasoned that cell traffic would be from those crashing the party, which meant Nuri. Hafiz knew he needed two things: line of sight to the minaret to see what was happening and a way to communicate, or as he suspected, a way to trigger the anthrax if the operation went south.

Pulling out binoculars, Hafiz brought the tower into focus then popped the tab on his second energy drink of the morning, settling down to watch the action. The radio squawked with action. Sporadic sounds of sniper fire appeared to be increasing as they echoed off the surrounding stone walls and buildings. A solitary shot could be heard, followed by rapid return fire as the sheep tried to tag snipers whose sole purpose in life was to kill them left, right, and center. Considering an all-out counter-assault hadn't launched yet, maybe Nuri had the anthrax. *Doesn't sound like it's stopping Ya'Ma'M marksmen from picking his sheep off when the opportunity presents itself though,* Hafiz thought. *I would absorb damage if I wanted to detonate a bioweapon, but they better have brought enough bodies to the party. We don't miss.* From his vantage point, only part of the tower's catwalk was visible. No sheep had grazed into view yet.

Hafiz scanned alcoves and crevices Nuri might choose. All were empty save scattered IDF patrolling in pairs, weapons drawn, surveiling the same ground again and again. He and Nuri used to play in the nearby streets when dad came for business in the days before the separation fence, running through store stalls while old men shooed them away. That was before father was killed. Before Nur took the name he now bore. But, Hafiz knew, it started with mother.

No memory lingered of this woman who had given him life. He searched for a remnant, a single thread, to connect him to this enigma that was always beyond reach, refusing to be found.

He pressed for the cause of her death; no one knew or would say. Records were scarce, revealing little. He had learned of mother's lineage, his lineage, as a man. Reluctantly, under his prodding, silent uncles had revealed secrets long held. Why their brother would marry this half-Jewish woman they could not say, in a land where such things mattered, only that a heart wants what a heart wants and father was deeply in love.

He'd been a babe of twelve months when father remarried, far too young to know. This time family approved, she, a daughter of Ishmael. Father never allowed two things: one, mention of his mother; and two, Nur's mother to treat him differently than his brothers. He had been embraced, but he understood why eternal words spoke of life being in the blood. His stepmother could not mask the love she bore for those from her womb. How could it be different?

Everyone knew the Israelis were coming; they always announced it. Unfailingly, it was the same for families of those whose sons and daughters chose the path of *shaheed*. Hafiz thought back to that hateful time.

The home next door would be demolished, under Israeli court order, the price for killing sons and daughters of Israel. There was no stopping the D-9R Cat, strangely called Teddy Bear, as its fifteen foot wide blade bore down on the house. Only later did he learn father had tried to tell the soldiers that his neighbors, friends, were inside. But they had fled out the back staying just long enough to finish rigging explosives to greet Teddy Bear when it demolished their home. Did the dozer even see father? There was no slowing its ponderous progress as it pushed concrete block walls down. Father was able to step aside; then the explosion.

He couldn't escape the annihilating blast as concrete tore through his body. He was dead, PRCS medics said, before his body hit the ground. How could they know this? How could anyone? The dozer was disabled, one track blown off, on the edge of the chasm, armor plating sparing the life of the driver but not the Arab or Jewish blood of those standing too close.

Three days later another Teddy Bear came, this time to their home. Someone said father was part of the evil. How could such a gentle man hate so deeply? His was tender compassion for all, standing against his family to marry a woman with Jewish blood. His sons had not been raised to understand this brutality. They lost their father, then all he had worked for was destroyed, in an instant.

Nur-Rami spiraled into Nuri, fire, as hate kindled and burned within.

Nur-Rami, haven't thought of that name for a long time, Hafiz reflected while scanning the tower. No mehablim had broken through to the catwalk, though radio traffic indicated they were close.

He was eighteen, Nur sixteen when Teddy Bear had come. *"How could you not hate these swine? Will father ever live again?" Nur spat out.*

"These are not the words he would choose for us."

"He's gone. What did his words bring? Death? There will be no rest until those who shed innocent blood are themselves dead." Nur left that day for Syria.

Letters always returned undeliverable. On hearing Nur had come back from Syria, Hafiz went to an uncle's house looking for his brother. He found him in Khān Yūnis at a cousin's home. "Nur, is good to see you," Hafiz said, going to kiss his brother.

Grasping Hafiz's shoulders in his hands while holding him away, his brother said, "Nur died over three years ago. I no longer claim Nur-Rami. I am now known as Nuri al-Massalha. A name given in Syria so family will not suffer if I am ever taken driving the son of pigs from Arab land. So what is it you have found to dedicate your life to, my brother?" Nuri said.

"I am just finishing my service—"

"You serve those who killed our father?"

"I serve my country. To make a future for all Yisraelis, Arab and Jew."

"Spoken like a Jew," Nuri said. "We do not leave our mothers."

"You speak like an enemy."

"Act like a brother, come join me, and you will not be one."

"This is not father's way," Hafiz said.

"Father is dead."

"As we now seem to be to one another."

"You have spoken the imam's truth," Nuri said.

"Truth does not live with hate—"

"Be careful, my brother, this is dangerous ground. Truth resides with the imam."

The memory lived as yesterday. The passage of time could not blunt the moment in which hate accused him of being a traitor. Hafiz knew this day would come. He kept looking for signs of a brother he might be forced to kill.

He listened to Ya'Ma'M's chatter as they constricted the firing zone—hits on stragglers only, a strange way to fight. Radio traffic increased as the sheep made their move onto the catwalk. It was just a matter of time now.

CHAPTER

57

Saturday 22 March 2008, 0503 hours

The Old City & Lod Command & Control

Colonel Samech pressed Instant Connect on his cell phone, "Lion, this is Daniel." There was no response. Trying again, "Lion, this is Daniel." Silence, he tossed the worthless technology on the table. "Michael, give me your phone; this one's broken."

Michael Ashtor handed the Colonel his phone.

"Lion, this is Daniel, copy." No response. Aaron Samech's ever-present scowl took a nasty turn.

His cell phone rang. He grabbed it from the table. "This is Samech," he barked.

"Colonel this is General Oz. Don't call Peled. The line is blocked."

"What do you mean blocked?"

"I don't want you calling Peled, Colonel. I am the General and in charge, so don't call. You call; you could mix signals and cause confusion."

"Then why did I come down to Yerushaláyim and set up a command center?"

"Because I needed you to get an op team in place. They're in place, you did your job. Now don't call them."

"I didn't do my job if I don't finish what I started. These are my men."

"I am a General; all are my men, Colonel, including you. You know the drill, Aaron. You were needed to get things up and running. You did—so good job. I need to take command of the operation. You'll get another commendation and before long you'll be a General, doing the same thing to some other Colonel. Besides, I already told you I was taking command of the operation on the catwalk, and the lambs are entering the catwalk, so don't take it personally. That's an order."

Guttural sounds came from the other end.

"Good. I like it when we agree. Now is time for me to be a hero."

"Cheetah, have you reconnoitered the minaret's base as ordered?"

"Affirmative, Lion."

"Report."

"Two mehablim all tucked in, ballistic glass across the bottom third of the entry. Net covers entrance, attached to rock anchors in all four corners. Behind the net looks to be explosive bricks, C-4 my guess, wired on both side jambs with a third brick centered just below the lintel. Each brick has an insertion point, got to be a blasting cap wired to some kind of switch. They don't appear to want company."

"Pride, remain aware of everything, think through each move. The enemies' position in migdal speaks to their training, preparation. Small details bring opportunity or catastrophe. See anything unusual, speak up. Worst case, we do it the old-fashioned way, one mehablim at a time; easy or hard they're ours."

"Works for me Lion."

"Lion, this is Command & Control, over."

"Roger, Command, go ahead."

"Operational control for Birat Hanezah, Eternal Capital, is transferred to Lod under my direct command. Copy, Lion."

"Say again, Command."

"Operational control has been transferred to Lod under Belteshazzar."

"Roger that, Command & Control. Welcome aboard, Belteshazzar. Haven't heard from you for awhile. Pride, everyone copy?"

"Copy, Lion."

"Affirmative on Lod, over."

"Pride, maintain distance. Stragglers only until fire zone changes."

"Belteshazzar this is Puma. How about we acoustically jam everything from Beit Shemish to Ma'ale Adumim, commence blasting mehablim, and not stop till they're dead, dead, dead. Then bomb disposal, standing by with Daniel, takes tower and disarms whatever they find."

"Four things, Puma: First, the strategic cell leader, Nuri al-Massalha, isn't part of the assault team. Every mehablim was photo-captured in Gan David; he's not among them. Second, we believe he, independent of the mehablim on the minaret, has an override switch. Third, we believe al-Massalha is in proximity to the minaret but not under our control. Boots on the ground are searching, but the target has not been neutralized. Fourth, we've yet to identify operational frequencies of enemy armaments. As of two minutes seventeen seconds ago, we've pinged ninety-seven separate devices, all are in proximity to the migdal. Physical contact could trip any triggering device. Each receives and transmits a four billion roving code signal. Our electronics ping them and record the detection, but before we can identify exact frequencies the device identifies our ping and changes its coding in real time. Signals are self-generating but also controllable, again in real time. If we commence our final assault before isolating and jamming their frequencies, they win, we lose."

"So we stay with stragglers, Belteshazzar?" Lion said.

"Long as sheep make progress and we stick to stragglers, Lion, we believe al-Massalha's locked into his game. Launching from the catwalk is the only platform for maximal anthrax airburst left." We'll stay on plan and see who's standing when this has run its course."

~

Grabbing Addison from behind, Makeen pulled him to his feet, encircling the American's neck with his left arm. Gurgling was the sole evidence of life. "You want Makeen to snug arm a bit more, infidel? Maybe stop gurgling before you make Makeen sick." Coming up under Addison's knees, Makeen's right arm jammed the infidel's legs against the launch plate separated from the thin metallic vest by a cotton pad. It had the advantage of giving the appearance of a clear target if the Zionists wanted to shoot through the half-dead hostage while the base plate shielded Makeen. Protected by his vest, helmet, and the American with the launch plate, Makeen stepped through the gate opening. Turning right, he hesitated; this was many times the size of the practice tower.

"Makeen," Nasir shouted from inside the spire, "move."

He headed for the west side of the catwalk where one of the fool bomb-maker's assistants said his tactical position would be strongest and enemy fire weakest, away from most of the courtyard. It was obvious though, that where he had entered the catwalk on the south provided the best advantage.

Behind him, Kateb, crawling on his belly, with the launch tube strapped to his back, bloodied his elbows and knees on the rough stones trying to keep up.

"Pride, lambs are on the catwalk. Remember, no bullets near the hostages.'

"Not even the Arabs?"

"Tiger, you want to spend next year before commissions, end up in a cell in Gilbo'a?"

"For an Arab?"

"Wouldn't be first time."

"Lion, this is Lynx. I've got a bead on a target. First mehablim through the gate has a hostage, target following is on his belly. I think I can tag him."

"Lynx, is there a tube on your target's back?"

"Looks like—"

"Resembles a mortar tube?"

"Could—"

"This is Belteshazzar. Launch tube has anthrax shell inside. No bullets near the mortar tube. Copy, Lynx?"

"Yes sir."

"Lynx, hold all fire until you clear it with me, copy?"

"Copy, Lion."

Makeen released his hold, and Addison slumped against the spire. Makeen shouted, "What happened to cover fire Nasir?"

Nasir responded, "Arrow slits commence cover fire."

Rifle fire began spewing in bursts from the slits.

"Need drill, Hashim," Makeen barked.

"Hold on, it's not like there's lots of room to get around with this stinking equipment." Coming up behind Kateb, Hashim half stood to maneuver around him. Straddling Kateb's prone form, Hashim inched his way past the mortar tube then, setting his equipment bags against the spire, pulled out the cordless drill.

"I'm waiting here," Makeen growled.

"Working fast as I can. Drill doesn't make holes without a bit, and bit doesn't put itself into drill." Hashim found the pack of 10 mm rock bits. Pulling one from the group, he pushed it into the drill's keyless chuck then squeezed the trigger; the sound of the revving drill filled the air between the rifle bursts. He handed the drill to Makeen.

Makeen set the point of the bit on the spire two feet above the catwalk and started to drill. Hashim, rock bit loaded into his Makdeha, began drilling four feet away; the stone yielded.

"Need anchors and hammer, little man."

"Just a few more seconds." Judging his hole deep enough, Hashim rummaged through the equipment bag and grabbed two–four-pound sledges, handing one to Makeen. Then his hand stabbed back into the bag, retrieving two burlap bags of D-ring expansion anchors.

"What causes such delay? Hammer waits for anchors. We have a job to do."

Listening, Nasir knew he needed to intervene. Leaving the security of the spire, he made his way around the catwalk. "Makeen, Hashim, this is a moment for brothers."

"Why not just order us to carry out commands or explosives will finish our work," Makeen said.

"I told you the bomb-maker planted explosives. I too live under such a device to ensure allegiance. Our calling is not man's but god's. Now finish what was learned at al-Ubeidiya or you won't need explosives to join Umar." Nasir chambered a round, his face hardening as he stared at Makeen.

"I am fulfilling my calling, my brother," Makeen said quickly.

"See that you do." Nasir worked his way back to the spire, keeping an eye on Makeen for sudden moves until he got inside. "Okay, Aziz, you know what's required. Lead your team to glory."

Lifting Aadil from the stone floor, Aziz slung him over powerful shoulders into a modified fireman's carry. Pulling his pistol from its holster, he brought his left arm across his chest and jammed the Tokarev's barrel into Aadil's groin. *This traitor might keep him alive, until Zionists saw he was Arab*. Bending low through the open gate, Aziz turned left. With his Tokarev useless beyond fifty feet, he knew his time was near.

Mifsud followed with the equipment bags.

"Tawil."

"What, Nasir?"

"Scan for the enemy. They pop up and down, so stay alert."

"If the cowards would rise and fight like men—"

"Men? They're Jews."

Standing just clear of the gate inside the spire, Nasir herded the next team onto the catwalk. "Quickly close in on Aziz's team, Dabir. Your hostage protects you unless Zionists shoot one of their own."

"And they cannot hit—"

"Go, go, go."

Grabbing Elizabeth from behind, Dabir wrapped his right arm around her waist and pulled her up into him. Elizabeth struggled against her captor. "Don't fight, Jew. The ground is a long way from catwalk; wouldn't want to drop you." Her scrawny frame provided little cover.

Ya'qub, next in line, had to pack equipment so the college boy could watch from the safety of the spire.

"Ommar, you're next."

"When I'm ready."

Turning back inside the spire, Nasir brought his rifle down, leveling its barrel at Ommar's face. "I told you move—now."

"I'm going. Enemies are outside, not here." Bending over, he brought his right arm around Khalil's neck then grabbed the back of the tiny Arab's belt with his left hand, easily lifting him. He moved his right arm down around the traitor's chest. Khalil, barely conscious, didn't resist. "I'm going to pull pistol. Don't go crazy on me, Nasir."

"Stop with talk. Get out there. The closer you get to the last team, the greater chance for victory."

Yazid followed with Qadir crouched just behind Yazid's equipment bag. His rifle swept the surrounding courtyard as he sniffed for Jews, craving to inhale their stench.

"Nasir."

"Go, Hashim."

"American's ready for wire harnesses."

"Launch plate and tube?"

"Done."

"I'm there." Looking past the open gate, Nasir surveilled what could be seen of the courtyard and walls. Satisfied, he bolted from the spire, emptying his magazine into the courtyard. Silence greeted his effort, lost in the cacophony of his drive to complete the short journey.

Checking the American, all appeared in order: butt on the catwalk, back against the spire. Each wrist handcuffed on the spire just like 'Īsā on the crucifix the meddlesome Catholics in al-Quds seemed so fond of. He yanked on the American's handcuffs, the rock anchors held. Legs, splayed around the launch tube, both feet hanging over the catwalk's edge under the iron rail. Nasir nudged the triangular launch plate; all three rock anchors held the catwalk with a singular will. The fireworks tube was stationary on the launch plate, its base a threaded pipe nipple welded to the plate. Getting on his knees, he saw that the bulls-eye level was dead-on center. The cell phone, on the American's chest, was flipped open, ready for its wiring harness. As he checked a final time, his radio squawked. "Nasir."

"Go, Ya'qub."

"We're ready."

"For what?"

"Hostages secured, wiring harnesses ready for connection."

"I'll be there. I need few more seconds to finish here."

"How much longer will Allāh bless our efforts?"

"I said I'll be there. Words delay. Nothing gets attached until I say, got it?" Returning to his inspection, Nasir examined both timers sheltered on the hostage's chest by the diaphanous metallic vest. The primary timer was stationary, displaying twenty minutes zero seconds. The secondary timer was static at 05:00 minutes. A wire was plugged into the launch tube. Nasir pointed to it. "Why is this plugged in?"

"It's the antenna cable. I attached antenna to iron railing, then plugged wire into antenna. Bomb-maker says to plug in before wiring harnesses. This is before wiring harness," Makeen said.

"I was to give instructions."

"It's done," Makeen said. "We followed training. Is there a problem?"

Nasir tugged, it held. All that remained was stringing and connecting wiring harnesses from the hostages on the opposite side of the catwalk.

He radioed Aziz. "Attach wiring harness to cell's accessory connector. Phone must remain open, and check that the plug is locked into the connector. Do it now."

"It's done."

"What do you mean, it's done? I just told you—"

"All were there for the assaults on the tower with rubber bullets stinging every part the vests and helmets didn't protect while you, with Nuri, watched."

"I trained."

"Once."

"Do I need to come over?"

"Others have rifles. Do your own job brother. Then we'll make connection calls."

Nuri had warned him of this moment, born when they learned a college graduate, a school boy, some thought, would be their leader. If he confronted Aziz, Nasir knew he would be fair game, and failure, for any reason, would not happen. "Dabir."

"Go ahead, Nasir."

"Is wiring harness from Aziz attached to Jew's cell yet?"

"Waiting your word."

"Attach it to the accessory connector. Don't connect secondary wire plug."

"Hold on . . . .Okay, wire from Aziz's traitor is plugged in and locked to Jew's cell phone."

"Good. Plug single wire into cell's audio jack."

"Done."

"Okay. Is it locked?"

"Yes, yes, it's locked. It's all locked. I trained, too."

"I am charged to check. Wire from cell's audio jack comes to launch tube. Ommar."

"Go."

"Plug wiring harness to little traitor's accessory connector and single wire to audio jack, then lock in."

"Done."

"Dabir, Ommar, unspool wires to my position, handle with gentleness of bride on wedding night."

"On our way."

~

Looking on the mehablim's progress Lion hit speed-dial, "Belteshazzar, this is Lion."

"This is Belteshazzar."

"Hostages are nearly secured to the migdal, sir. Mehablim are running wires between hostages. Request operational control, sir, we need to execute."

"Stand by, Lion." Turning to his Executive Officer, Major Weiss, Oz said, "Get Vice Prime Minister Dobrin on the phone."

"Yes sir," Chanan Weiss said, dialing the unlisted number. On the third ring it answered. "Major Weiss calling Vice Prime Minister Dobrin for General Oz." Nodding into the phone, he said, "I'm calling from Command Control. General Oz needs to speak with the Vice Prime Minister immediately." Weiss' countenance gave no hint of inner thoughts, a practice long mastered by command officers, which he intended to be. "He'll need to be available in the next thirty seconds. That's right, even if the Vice Prime Minister is in bed riding the beast . . . good. I'll inform the General." Hitting *End,* he returned the phone to his pocket.

"I say get Dobrin and you hang up?"

"The Vice Prime Minister will call on your line within thirty seconds. He appeared to be indisposed."

General Oz's pocket vibrated. Removing the phone, he hit *Talk.* "We need to change fire zone Mr. Vice Prime Minister. Mehablim are getting close; they will finish connections within minutes." Sagiv Oz was silent, listening. "No, not finished but close." The corners of his mouth turned downward. "No, we don't have triggering frequency. The geniuses you assigned haven't located it yet." Oz became silent, slowly moving his head from side to side. "You know what this means? If the mehablim finish, anthrax gets launched. You want that as your epitaph?" His face flushed, an artery on his neck pulsed. "We have narrowed the search . . . can block majority of frequencies . . . no not all, but pretty damn close to all, Mr. Vice Prime Minister. I request permission to neutralize minaret. It's my professional advice you allow me to do my job, considering what happens next if I don't." Sagiv's right heel started to hit the floor, *thump . . . thump . . . thump*, a habit those closest to him hoped never to see again. Harder and harder it smashed into the flooring as his face went from florid to beet red. "Vice Prime Minister Dobrin, this is on your head . . . .What, you can't make a decision without calling Prime Minister? I just told you what needs to be done. You won't make the call?" *Thump, thump, thump* . . "No, sir, I will not subvert authority by making the decision. I am a soldier, and you are the Vice Prime Minister. This day one of us will do their duty. Now, sir, do yours, we need to move." Sagiv shoved his phone in his pocket. "Weiss, tell Lion the politician's decision. I don't want to talk right now."

"Lion, this is Command."

"Go ahead, Command."

"Maintain fire-zone restrictions."

"Command, does Belteshazzar know what this means?"

"He knows, Lion. Order came from above. We'll keep you advised."

"Roger, Command. Pride, you heard the man. Maintain firing zone. We might just have the best seat in Yerushaláyim for the fireworks."

"Like hell we will."

"Pride, we are Ya'Ma'M. We do our duty, always. Is there anyone who cannot follow every order . . . anyone?"

"Sorry, Lion—"

"Can't identify who's talking . . . and no one else could either. Am I clear?"

"Affirmative, Lion."

"Just do our duty, Pride."

~

Unwinding the lone wire locked into Elizabeth's cell phone, Dabir preceded Ommar, who was uncoiling wires attached to Khalil's cell phone as they made their way to the launch tube.

A single shot rang out. Mujahideen threw themselves on the catwalk, cowering from shards of tower stone that never arrived. Qadir emptied his magazine in the direction he swore the shot came from. Trouble was figuring out where, surrounded by canyons of stone, echoes, and chaos.

"Finish wires before returning fire," Nasir yelled, a slight quaver in his words. He got up on his knees near the American. "Run wires around iron balusters to keep from being unplugged."

"Where's Dabir?" Ommar called out.

"What do you mean? He's in front of you," Nasir called back.

"Dabir's wire is; Dabir isn't."

Hugging the catwalk, Nasir forced himself past three mujahideen and the American while he searched for his sniper. Covering the endless distance, he looked around the spire: no Dabir. A wire dangled from the catwalk, swaying in the morning air. Crawling to the catwalk's edge, he peered over. Following the wire, he saw Dabir's body twisted on the rocks below. As he turned away, the stench of blood assaulted his nostrils. He started to back up then felt eyes upon him. He grabbed the wire, pulling it to himself as he made his way past Ommar, to the American. He handed the end to Makeen. "Plug this into the top launch tube port."

A few Crested Larks, with their grayish-brown plumage, made their way through the migdal, attempting to find their usual menu of crickets, ants, and spiders. Hunting wasn't easy as mujahideen snipers emptied their magazines while the tiny birds hopped along the walls and walks, alternately diving for cover and warbling their evocative songs as they hunted for food.

"Hashim, get the wires from bag," Nasir said.

Hashim went through the bag, looking for the cloth bag containing the wiring bundles.

"Quickly, your wire harness, Ommar," Nasir said.

Ommar handed the three-wire cable to him and Nasir plugged it into the American's cell phone; it locked into place. He gave it a tug; it held. "Good. Yazid, let's have your wire."

Yazid handed him his single wire. Opening a flap in the vest, Nasir plugged the wire into the top port in the primary timer. A solid click declared it seated. "Hashim, you have wires?"

"Here," Hashim handed the cloth bag to him.

Opening the bag, Nasir extracted three single wires. He plugged the first wire into the right side of the primary timer and the second wire into the right side of the secondary timer. One end of the third wire was plugged into the left side of the primary timer, the other end into an adjacent port on the secondary timer. Nasir verified all plugs were locked in place. Taking the free ends of the two timer wires, he ran them to a port on the bottom of the launch tube and clicked them into place. All was ready.

Lion tried hitting speed dial one final time.

"Go ahead, Lion."

"Are Command's cameras down?"

"Negative, Lion. Equipment is online and recording."

"Then you can see our lunch is being handed to us, and we can't open fire? Mehablim are finishing connections, permission to fully engage sir."

"Lion, stand by, I'm checking for orders."

"Belteshazzar, Yerushaláyim's near the end of its life support."

"Lion I know, stand by."

"Weiss—"

"Number's ringing, General."

"Give me the phone, time for politics is over."

Major Weiss handed General Oz his phone. As he hit *Speaker*, all activity around him ceased. Ears in the cavernous room strained to listen as the phone continued to ring. The bottom of Sagiv's heel began to throb. Each ring soured his disposition. The ringing stopped, and tones of connection filled the room. "Dobrin, this is Oz. The fire zone must change. Mehablim—"

"Shalom, I am unavailable. If you'll leave your name, number, and a brief message I, or one of my staff, will return your call at our earliest possible opportunity. Wait for the beep."

Sagiv Oz slammed the phone to the floor, driving his heel into the few pieces left. "Now he hides behind voicemail so I'll make the call. Damn right I'll make the call." Grabbing the phone from his pocket, he bellowed, "Lion."

"You're breaking up, Belteshazzar."

"Neutralize the area. Repeat, neutralize the area."

"Copy, Belteshazzar: Neutralize the minaret."

~

Hitting *Direct Connect* on his cell, Nasir said, "Tawil, Qadir, make the calls."

~

"Puma, feel like practicing Crested Lark call?

"You want my birdcall, Lion?"

"Affirmative, Puma. Click twice with your tongue so we'll cue that it's you and not one of our feathered friends out for a meal. Stand by to engage. Cheetah, Tiger, positioned for the south arrow slit?"

"Roger that Lion."

"Cheetah, you're the sniper. Tiger, after Cheetah fires, stuff a kolokol though the upper arrow slit."

"Roger, Lion. Locked and loaded."

"Jaguar, Leopard, ready to execute?"

"Roger that Lion."

"Jaguar, you're the sniper, Leopard, place a kolokol in the lower arrow slit."

"Lynx."

"Go ahead Lion."

"Fire a kolokol inside the lower minaret entrance between the mehablim. Ensure it gets past the netting."

"I can drive a truck through the open mesh in the netting, Lion."

"Pride, gas masks must be sealed, masks on now."

"Done boss,"

"Roger that."

"Affirmative Lion."

"Roger Lion."

"All secure."

"Pride, I'll insert a kolokol through the minaret gate. Timing is critical; execution must be simultaneous with Puma's birdcall."

Roger that Lion, came a chorus of replies.

"Cheetah, Jaguar, hit the arrow slit sides to send stone shards inside to clear any mehablim from opening. Tiger, Leopard, Lynx, introduce kolokol grenades on the heels of the rifle fire. Enemy sleeps and tower to catwalk is secure, with spire and catwalk for next phase of operation. Wait for my clearance before proceeding to secondary coordinates, then we'll neutralize catwalk, any questions?"

No one spoke.

"Pride," Lion said, "after we deliver the kolokols we begin earning our money. Avoid hostages if possible, but do your duty. If you don't have a clear shot, keep mehablim cowering on the catwalk. They can't execute plans if forced to crawl. Take your time and neutralize threat. One final thing, situation is dynamic. Watch every round: We don't shoot our own."

Brigadier General Sagiv Oz and Command & Control listened in silence as final instructions reverberated from the migdal. Some hearts carried prayers, others curses. None spoke; words distract—Judgment was at hand.

Puma's tongue clicked twice then he brought his right thumb and middle finger into his mouth and pinched them against the tip of his tongue.

A Crested Lark's sweet call made its way into the tense morning air.

Behind two separate arrow slits, four mujahideen heard the irritating whistle. Adnan and Musad rushed to shove their rifle barrels out their arrow slit—the sounds were too pronounced, had to be fake. Stone shards blasted in, cutting their faces, driving each from the opening as kolokol grenades flew into the tower. All four felt instantaneous pressure, and then a whiff of something pleasant as halothane gave a telltale hint of its presence. It was the last perception they experienced.

Four mujahideen, sitting cross-legged behind protective barriers in the lower and upper minaret entrances, slumped to their sides, unconscious, as the incapacitating agent proved worthy of its cost.

"Command, this is Lion. Grenades launched. Verify targets neutralized."

"Pride scans already running. Stand by."

"Standing by."

"Pride, scans identify eight separate breathing and respiration patterns consistent with slow wave sleep. Cameras show four mehablim slumped over at both minaret gates."

"We can see the gates, what about the arrow slits, Command?"

"We don't have acceptable visual in the arrow slits, but vital signs indicate it's nap time."

"Roger that, command. Pride, looks like everyone's sleeping. Remain vigilant in case anyone stirs."

"Lion, this is Dr. Abigail Ben-Meir. Multiple indicators attest all eight mehablim being tracked are in stage three and four deep sleep with brain activity transitioning to delta waves. None will be waking anytime soon. Considering the amount of fentanyl used and the mehablim's proximity to exposure, it's anyone's guess if they'll wake at all."

"Roger that, command. Can masks be removed now?"

"The fentanyl has had sufficient time to dissipate. Masks can be removed."

"Thanks doc."

Shedding their masks, the team members deploying in pairs pounded the catwalk with SR-99 fire. The cacophonous sound of their bullets ricocheted off stone as snipers dialed their Galils in.

Kalashnikov bursts attempted to answer as mehablim shot blindly in the direction their torment seemed to come from.

"Pride, everyone to secondary coordinates."

Increased gunfire preceded their move.

"Anyone not to their coordinate?" Lion's earbud remained silent. "If anyone leaves the secondary coordinates, broadcast before you move; no one gets tagged by friendly fire."

Keeping his head low to the catwalk, Yazid felt the ricocheting stone tear at the back of his neck. *Damn that stings.* On his belly, he pushed and pulled his way toward the Jew. *Why doesn't Nasir launch the anthrax? Only chance to break clear of minaret as sons of pigs watch fireworks explode over their precious capital, then scurry for life itself.*

"Make way," Hashim said. "I need to get a bead on the enemy. Yazid how do you kill the enemy while hugging the catwalk?" Hashim started crawling over him.

"Hey, I'm down here."

"Think maybe you're rug lying there with no bullets for Zionists. They won't commit suicide if that's what you wait for."

"I'm getting positioned, Hashim; I've fired many shots at infidels."

"How many have you killed, my brother?"

"I'm not one who says I can't get a bead on the enemy," Yazid said.

"I go to Jew, fire from there. Sons of monkeys maybe shoot their own, but better chance than here."

"Get off, you're heavy," Yazid said as he tried to push him off and roll back toward the spire.

"Hey, I'm only—"

Yazid felt Hashim's body, still lying across him, shudder and then go limp; its weight pressed him into the catwalk.

"Hashim . . . ?" There was no response, as dead weight bore down on him. Working his knees up under Hashim's lower body, he used his hands to force the motionless torso a few inches off him. Hashim's throat and larynx were worms of shredded muscle and soft tissue as blood pumped from his heart to where his carotid artery had been. Yazid's stomach convulsed. *Do not get sick.* He had to free himself. He forced his hands and arms forward. Hashim lifted just enough, and Yazid brought his legs and feet under the cumbersome weight and rammed them, piston like, into Hashim's torso and pelvis. Hashim appeared to half stand, head more hanging than attached, before gravity forced his carcass against the catwalk's railing baluster. Automatic fire exploded into Hashim's back, splintering ceramic discs while shredding his bullet resistant vest.

Hashim's corpse slid down the baluster falling diagonally on the catwalk his feet touching its edge.

Yazid, now on his knees, had to clear this rotting corpse out of his way to escape inside the spire, away from the unrelenting barrage. Confused, he tried to shove against Hashim's dead weight in the first half of a split second.

In the second half of that dismembered second Yazid's world-class vest yielded to the 7.62×51mm NATO rounds fired dead center into his tungsten ceramic discs.

Nasir hugged the spire as bursts of Israeli fire menaced every movement as he crawled toward Hashim and Yazid. Arriving, only blood and scattered bits of flesh and muscle greeted him. Easing toward the catwalk's edge, he peered at the ground, grasped the danger he was in, and rolled back toward the spire one motion. A shot rang out; the edge of the catwalk exploded. *I have just entered the gates of* Jahannam.

"Pride no shots on Ghafour."

"Just keeping him from the catwalk's edge Lion."

All eyes were focused on the catwalk. "Puma, see those two crawling toward the spire gate."

"Barely."

"Use your birdcall and see if we get movement."

"What are we after?"

"What else? They poke heads up, we shoot, they die."

"Challenge is getting the cowards to surface. For mujahideen that came for a fight, they spend most of their time hiding."

"That's where your birdcall comes in, either they don't like birds or your calls annoy them; whenever your birdie sings, they shoot."

Puma put his fingers in his mouth, and his birdcall warbled up to the catwalk.

Ya'qub stuck his rifle over the catwalk's edge, emptying a magazine in the direction of the sound.

"One more time Puma, I wasn't ready," Leopard said.

The Crested Larks were silent.

The mehablim stayed clear of the catwalk's edge.

"Try another call, Puma, I'm ready now." There was no answer. "Hey, Puma, you sleeping over there? Try another call."

"Puma, this is Lion, respond." Puma was silent. "Pride, anyone have a visual on Puma?"

"Negative, Lion."

"Not from here, Lion. I'm all tucked in."

"Command, need a locate on Puma's position."

"Negative, Lion. He's not on any cameras. Have to do it the old-fashioned way."

"On my way Command. Pride, I'm tracking Puma; exercise caution. Don't want to be mistaken for a mehabel."

"Tracking your position, Lion. Puma's still not in view."

"Roger that, Command. Using last known coordinates so I should know in a minute. Pride, keep the catwalk buttoned down. Don't need anyone spoiling the reunion."

SR-99 fire increased, chipping away at the catwalk's edge and upper spire. Seconds bled into minutes. Enemy fire was silent; no one challenged the onslaught.

"Belteshazzar."

"Go ahead, Lion."

"Found Puma."

"Status?"

"Rabinowitz is out of service."

"Repeat, Lion."

"Corporal Rabinowitz is out of service, sir."

"Roger that, Lion. Corporal Rabinowitz out of service, time noted."

"Pride, time to end this, if you get a shot near anyone other than the American take it."

"I can't do birdcalls, but I sure as hell can be heard," Leopard said. Charging from the south parapet wall, he hugged its edge while spraying all twenty-five rounds from his magazine into the catwalk. Releasing the empty clip, he grabbed another and slammed it home.

Two mehablim appeared above the catwalk's edge. Crouching, they began lowering their 104 barrels. Target in sight, Kateb and Qadir steadied themselves by placing a knee on the catwalk by the railing. A lone bullet slammed Kateb against the spire. A second bullet, coming in on the tail of the first, entered Qadir's torso, shattering his tungsten vest, hurling him against Kateb's legs, knocking them from under him.

Rolling onto the lower railing Qadir grabbed Kateb to keep from going over.

Launched into motion by Qadir's sudden grasp, Kateb started rolling over his friend. Terror seized his face; his fingers locked onto Qadir's shredded vest as blood flowed from his rapidly succumbing body.

Each frantically struggled to free himself as gravity compelled its own obedience. Qadir and Kateb, in their death grip, continued their merciless drop to the unyielding stones below.

Unaware of Qadir and Kateb in the chaos of battle, Nasir focused on the timer. *Why hadn't Nuri activated it?* He had listened for the distinctive chirps, two short, one long, but none came. Nasir was ready for glory, but senseless slaughter without infidel deaths, how did such dishonor exalt Allāh? Watching from near the American, he knew it was up to him. Slipping his fingers into his pocket, he felt the thin remote with its single button. Pulling it out, he began crawling toward the Yagi. The launch, it had been drilled into him, must be triggered through the Yagi antenna. Ahead,

Ya'qub was lying on his back, head propped against the spire, the soles of his shoes against the lower railing. "Ya'qub, pull your feet back. Infidels will see." Ya'qub appeared confused, disorientated. Sweat ran down his clammy face as he snorted air in shallow chugs. He did not respond. Nasir called again . . . nothing. Putting the remote back in his pocket, he crawled toward his brother.

Nasir's elbows felt savaged and bloody from the uneven stones. Catching his breath—crawling was so exhausting—he fumbled for his water bottle. He pulled it from his hip and yanked the nipple open with his teeth. His chest was so tight. Lifting his head, dizziness was now a part of him. He heard an enemy round as shards of stone battered him. The water bottle skittered across the catwalk and tumbled over the edge. Another shot rang out, hitting the catwalk's edge inches from the first. *Are shots closing in on Ya'qub?* A third shot, not more than a second from the last, tightened in on his friend. "Ya'qub, pull feet from edge; enemy fires for you." Ya'qub didn't move, lost in his world. A fourth shot rang out just inches from Ya'qub now.

"Ya'qub, move fee—"

A fifth shot chased the heels of the fourth. Ya'qub's face distorted in pain as blood shot from his foot, his shoe blown off. Ya'qub reared up from the spire.

"NO!" Shots ripped though him, the automatic fire incapable of mercy. Lifting against the force of the violence, Ya'qub's body pitched forward as unrelenting fire continued to batter the now dead mujahid. It seemed to come from two directions. Nasir couldn't tell; his world had become a solitary pursuit of hugging the spire of the catwalk as he retreated from the carnage. *The Yagi must get to the antenna.* Looking up, he saw Ya'qub half on, half off the catwalk, suspended on the railing. A final burst of gun fire dislodged him; without protest, his body surrendered to gravity. Focusing on the antenna, Nasir grabbed his rifle and began crawling.

As he looked at the spot where Ya'qub had been, Nasir's stomach churned. Coming in waves, saliva spewed from his mouth. Spitting acrid slime, he felt his warrior's breakfast crawling up his throat. In one blast it rushed to free itself from his stomach on the rough stones inches below his chin. Eyes watering, nose leaking, his stomach continued to convulse and explode. He tried turning his head from the putrid stench but jerked it back as the heaving continued. His body trembled as he lay there waiting for the purging to end.

Looking on, Makeen took in the disgusting betrayal of bodily functions. "Is this our glorious leader?" he asked, his rifle cradled across his arms.

Bits of food lodged in his throat, Nasir couldn't answer. Hacking, he disgorged the fetid remnants while Makeen's eyes stayed on him. "We need to fire the anthrax shell."

"You need to be a man."

Nasir had to crawl over his vomit, toward Makeen, to reach the antenna. "Makeen, the shell must be launched now."

"You're not a leader; you have never been leader. The weakness of those who fail to see have put a weakling in charge. All changes now."

Dragging his rifle under him, Nasir started forward. "You know how to launch the anthrax? You have the remote trigger?"

"You cannot fool me; all is controlled by others. Nuri wouldn't let a schoolboy control the most important part of all the operation."

"Makeen, listen, you can be the leader; I will follow, but let us move toward the traitors and the Jew. The shell must be launched." Nasir continued to crawl forward, away from the launch tube, toward his crouching nemesis.

"Silence, Makeen decides what to do."

Nasir stopped, his right hand sliding down the barrel of the AK-104 lying under him. His eyes locked onto Makeen's demanding attention as his fingers crept closer to the rifle's trigger. Touching the outer edge of the curved magazine, he was close. *How many rounds left?* He couldn't remember. *Think Nasir!* At last his fingers found the trigger guard, then crawled to the trigger.

Makeen's eyes hardened.

As he rolled onto his side, Nasir's rifle was exposed. His heart tried to jump through his chest, as his lungs gasped for air.

Makeen jerked his rifle to his shoulder. The sudden move threw him off balance, his right knee slammed on the catwalk as the end of his rifle barrel pointed skyward.

Jerking his rifle from beside him, Nasir jammed its butt plate against his shoulder.

Makeen brought his rifle's barrel down.

Crushing the 104's trigger, Nasir disgorged its bowels into the usurper. Makeen's shock registered the savage agony as the bullets' violence tore into him.

Have to move. Push through. Get to the Yagi. Leaving his empty rifle, Nasir advanced toward Makeen, who was somehow still breathing. He grabbed his foe's rifle and flung it from the catwalk. Reaching to his adversary's hip, he yanked the pistol from its holster tossing it behind him. Makeen's lungs continued to rise and fall as his death rattle grew louder. Closing in, Nasir spotted the knife on Makeen's leg. He unsheathed it and dropped it behind him on the catwalk. To drag himself over this dying traitor would expose him to enemy fire. He began to wedge himself between Makeen and the spire, crawling beside the ponderous obstacle. Reaching the half way point, Nasir turned on his side, back to the spire. He put hands and feet against the impediment, and pushed. Makeen moved. Regrouping, Nasir shoved again. Several more inches surrendered to his effort. Makeen's shallow breathing was labored now; no challenges issued from this ox of a man. Once more, Nasir pressed his back against the spire and pushed. Makeen was near the catwalk's edge. Nasir lodged his head and neck against the bottom of the spire, feet on Makeen's torso and hips. The man refused to stop breathing. With every reserve, Nasir shoved, his head and neck screaming in pain from the brutality of the rough stones. He shoved yet again. The lower railing snared Makeen, refusing to release him. *Oh god, do not let enemies stay our victory.* Crawling to Makeen, Nasir got on his knees and, with strength he didn't know he possessed, lifted. The ox's balance shifted as Nasir's effort recoiled through the muscles and bones of the dying beast. In silence the ox slipped past the railing's constraining bonds and plummeted to the stones below.

Pulling the remote switch from his pocket, Nasir resumed his crawl for the Yagi.

"That's far enough."

He craned his neck to look, but no one came into view. He continued.

"I said stop."

Scanning his confined prison, he searched for the source of the commands.

"Try looking left, the barrel against the spire just above the catwalk. Want to guess where it's pointed?"

"The voice is Ommar's. Why do you hold weapon on a brother, Ommar?"

"Murderers are not brothers."

"What is this you say?"

"I heard strange words. Could brother be against brother at such a time? I made my way around the spire to watch you shoot Makeen. He trusted his life in your hands and now has joined the dead."

"You did not see Makeen about to take my life? It was defense. For the mission to be accomplished, I had to act. To not do so would have brought defeat, eternal shame."

"What is this you say, leader?"

"We must launch the anthrax; I have the remote switch. Nuri himself gave it to me with a command to set it off if this moment came, and he was prevented from triggering our glorious fireworks launch."

"Was that the remote you just pulled from your pocket?

"Yes, yes." Holding the remote in his right hand toward Ommar's rifle barrel, He waved it back and forth. "Look, see, I live to get to the Jew by the antenna so I can launch this—"

"Why not act now if this is Nuri's charge to you, leader?"

"Because I was told by the master bomb-maker, in Nuri's presence, the remote must be triggered through the Yagi antenna. It demands line of sight of the antenna which lives behind the spire. If I fail to act, victory turns to defeat. We do not know if Nuri still embraces life."

"With my own eyes I saw you shoot a brother."

I told you I acted in defense of my own life, which Makeen could have claimed. It was to carry out a sacred responsibility I, and no other, have been given that forced me to defend myself. A responsibility Makeen would have taken from all those that await Palestine becoming a free nation. My life is in your hands, but first, I beg you, let me pass so I can trigger the shell."

"Pass you may, but first reach your left hand over to your right side and open the holster that is on your hip. Do it with care; I will not hesitate to usher you to Jahannam."

"Brother, we must not delay; I—"

"Silence! The next word will be your last. Do as I say and trust may build. Disobey, and your blood will not be on my hands."

"I need to roll on my side to reach pistol."

"*Nam*, yes, but a sudden move will not end well."

Rolling on his side, Nasir guided his left hand to his right hip, pulling the flap of his holster open.

Nasir looked at Ommar. He was now crouched, rifle still pointed at him.

"Take your pistol with your index finger and thumb and pull it from the holster. If any other part of your body touches the pistol you will not rise from where you lie."

Nasir pulled the pistol from its holster.

"Is good, my trust in you builds, leader. Now toss the pistol over the catwalk's edge."

"But I—"

"Did college take your hearing? Throw the pistol before my patience is forever lost."

Nasir did as he was told.

Ommar's face was hard, unyielding. "One last thing and my trust in you may be restored. With the same hand, pull your knife from its sheath. Your pistol cries out for company. I don't need to remind you that an AK-104 is faster than a knife."

Nasir reached his hand across his stomach and pulled the knife from its sheath, pitching it over the catwalk's edge.

Arising from his crouched stance, Ommar half stood against the spire but kept low to avoid enemy fire. He advanced slowly, stopping two feet from Nasir. "Get up."

Nasir arose.

"Hand over the remote, my brother."

"This was given for me to do."

"I will not speak—"

"You have taken my weapons; now you want the remote. What is in your heart?"

"Are you less than a murderer? I saw this with my own eyes."

"But I spoke of my reason for defense. When the anthrax launches there will be confusion in the enemy camp. There are but two of us. Alone we cannot prevail but together—"

"Give . . . the . . . remote."

Nasir tossed it behind him on the catwalk.

"Was this wise, leader?" Ommar stabbed Nasir's chest with his rifle.

Spotting Ommar's index finger on the trigger guard, Nasir lurched, grabbing Ommar's rifle; rolling to his side he shoved the barrel from him.

Ommar was pulled to the catwalk. Nasir's fingers shot out, jerking the rifle as they struggled between spire and railing.

The Pride, weapons at the ready, watched the drama unfolding above them. "Pride, hold your fire. They may finish our fight for us."

"Looks like hostages are safer from the mehablim than the mehablim are from each other, Lion."

"This is good, Leopard."

Twisting the rifle furiously, Ommar wrenched it loose with his left hand. His right elbow exploded into Nasir's chest, slamming him against the railing.

Launching himself back at his adversary, Nasir grasped Ommar's rifle with his right hand, jerking, wrenching.

Ommar flew toward him.

At that perfect moment Nasir unleashed a devastating left uppercut.

Ommar's head snapped back, stunned by the force of the blow, and then fell forward.

Seizing the moment, Nasir locked his fingers on the rifle, bent low, and came up hard with his head under Ommar's exposed chin. Staggered by his own blow, head spinning, Nasir hung onto the rifle by sheer will. He shook his head, as tiny flecks staggered across his vision. Ommar, pulled off balance, wavered.

Then, grasping the rifle with his right hand, Ommar cocked his left arm back and followed through with a hardened fist aimed at Nasir's face.

Nasir deflected the punch with his right arm. His hand, thrust backward by the impact, landed behind him on the catwalk. Something nicked a finger: Makeen's knife. Grabbing it, he brought the blade around, slashing at his adversary's face.

Ommar tried to back up.

Raking his helmet, the tip of the pointed blade caught forehead, slicing a gash above Ommar's eyes. Blood poured down over his face and washed over the blade.

Ommar's grip tightened on his rifle as he tried to yank it from Nasir—blood clouded his sight.

Wrestling to their knees, Nasir grabbed for the rifle as Ommar battled to knock the blade from Nasir's hand cutting himself with each attempt. Adrenaline coursed through each warrior.

Seething with fearful rage, Nasir held onto the rifle with his left hand and, using it as a fulcrum, swung the knife around, nearly lifting himself from the catwalk. The blade, exploding with pent up fury, buried itself into the side of Ommar's shoulder

A primordial scream arose from the deepest part of Ommar; his fingers flew from the rifle as he struggled to his feet, throwing himself back from Nasir.

Nasir dove for the rifle, but his thumb wouldn't close on it. Looking down, he saw a grotesque gash separating his motionless thumb from his palm. His upper palm, where his fingers intersected, was cut along its width. Blood pulsed from the deep laceration. Hand throbbing, Nasir's final vestige of humanity abandoned, he advanced on Ommar.

Agonizing pain radiated from his shoulder, driving Ommar from Nasir's advance. He backed against the iron railing encircling the catwalk.

Nasir closed on his quarry. Ommar's pathetic screams betrayed a weakling's cowardice.

Sweating rivers of pain, Ommar grabbed the knife's handle to free the tormenting blade from his shoulder. It was stuck fast; he couldn't budge it. As he thrashed about in desperate panic, the knife wedged behind an iron baluster trapped by an antenna cable which ran above his head to an intersecting iron ring that encircled the catwalk's edge six feet above. More animal than human now, he wrestled the inanimate metal beast, jamming, twisting, then trapping his right foot under the low horizontal rail that circled the catwalk's edge.

Nearly insane with rage, Nasir closed in, to grab then twist—slowly—the knife in Ommar's shoulder, to send this animal who dared turn on him to the stones below. He looked directly in Ommar's eyes. "Your terror, my brother, is good." He wrapped the fingers of his good hand on Ommar's windpipe and began to squeeze.

Ommar's head blasted forward, his helmet slamming into Nasir's forehead, knocking him back against the spire. Dazed, Nasir folded in two as he sank to the catwalk. Shaking his head to keep from passing out, he forced his eyes back on Ommar, imprisoned by the railing, dead as automatic fire tore into the cadaver. He watched Ommar's dance on his impalement pike as bullets in short bursts, tore into his body. The enemy bullets now through the vest, chipping stone from the spire, as Nasir hugged the catwalk. Then, silence; his mind lost in the violence he was a part of. He tried to remember—he needed to retrieve something. Then the second assault—round after incoming round, tearing, destroying that which was already torn and destroyed. Ommar, unrecognizable, seemed to sway. Nasir watched, lost in a world where sound itself had fled. The wind, was there wind? Some force imprisoned Ommar as he twisted slowly, grotesquely, arching backward. The knife handle still wedged between cable and iron baluster, postponing the hideous descent. Then a final burst, and Nasir saw but could not hear the body shudder and break free. He followed the body's descent, and then he looked back and saw an arm that had belonged to Ommar until the moment before still hanging on its knife anchor. Its handle, red with blood, wedged between the black iron rod and the cable running to an antenna, his antenna, on the far side of the spire. Then the cable slackened from its lightened burden and the iron baluster disgorged its prisoner as the knife and arm slipped free on their way to Ommar.

Nasir didn't move. Searching the sky, there was no place to put this moment. Quiet, hemmed in, alone—there was no comfort in the morning's embrace, no victory for the taking. His eyes gazed into the distance, whites growing large, fixed, corneas bulging . . . .

I've forgotten my lessons. Without study there will be no good job. Where is my book? Professor Khoury will be angry if I've not prepared. Looking around nothing was familiar. Nowhere for reading, so narrow, no desk even to sit like at An-Najah.

A Crested Lark began its warbling song. Nasir stood, hearing the piercing resonance. *So pretty.* Walking toward the spire gate, he paused then turned toward the mesmerizing call.

CHAPTER

58

Saturday 22 March 2008, 0535 hours

Jewish Quarter
Old City Yerushaláyim

Looking down on the old streets, Hafiz began thinking about the lifetime of years between then and now. *Wait, that's it. These streets were ours growing up before the separation fence. Father would bring them when he came to town. It's here, in front of him . . . somewhere. All three of them would come, so many times over the years, but what child knows of a father's business? There were too many distractions, until the day when going with father no longer brought adventure. When friends and teenage years were exciting and a father's trip into a dusty old town was to be avoided, so father continued alone, Nur abandoning the trips because he had.*

What could have caught a brother's heart to remain a part of a memory all these years later? Going back, he searched thirty years for a moment, a place, and a person that tied two brothers to these unchangeable streets. Something Nuri would remember, some place with a view of the minaret.

There was a man, forever old, with a flowing white beard and a gigantic glass jar filled with bars of chocolate. Each time they came to the Old City, father had taken them to his shop. Beaded curtains emerged from Hafiz's memory—curtains with too few strands of plastic beads that covered little, serving as a demarcation line between the public and private in his shop. But right behind the curtains, on its own shelf of honor, stood a tremendous jar of cow chocolate, Shokolad Para. There must have been a hundred bars always waiting for Nur and him inside this glass treasure, all in shiny wrappers with a cow on the front and rich wonderful chocolate inside.

Hafiz remembered how the old man made a production of stopping at the curtains, looking down at them and asking father if they had been good. On father's profession of their obedience, the old man took the next step in their accustomed ritual. He would ask each of them if the cow chocolate looked good. Nur and Hafiz vied to outshine each other in their descriptions of how wonderful the Shokolad Para looked. They would exclaim how long it had been since last they enjoyed the largess of his benevolence.

Then father would do his part and ask, "What do you say, sons?"

To which, in unison, they would both squeal, "please."

The old man's eyes would twinkle, and then his hand would dip into that immense jar and come away with a bar for each of them, at which point they showered this kind ancient man with their deepest thanks and eternal gratitude. If it were an auspicious day, his hand would return to the jar a second time and retrieve yet another bar for each of them, which they would consume with immense satisfaction and delight while they waited for father and white-beard to discuss whatever it was that brought them together. A lump came to Hafiz's throat as he relived the joy of moments rescued from memory.

But it wasn't here; there was no memory of coming to the Jewish Quarter. He scanned the little he could see, of the different Quarters with his binoculars. As he peered from his vantage point, nothing looked familiar; it was the inside of a shop that lived in his memory.

He had to walk the streets, gaze inside shops. A memory awaited that held him captive. Was it a memory that also linked Nuri to a hiding spot? Gathering his equipment, he left his sanctuary, surveilling the area as he made his way through each Quarter, dismissing streets that evoked no recollection. Finally entering the Christian Quarter, he stopped. This was it, where father had brought them so many years ago. He saw a familiar panorama through the eyes of a child. But why this place, a setting so foreign to an identity he was raised with? He knew he couldn't find the answer in the iron bars and locked shutters that secured each shop, he needed to see inside.

He passed a building and was three doors away when he stopped. He turned, came back, there was something about the shop. Yoram–Bookseller of Renown. Shining his flashlight inside he dissected what could be seen of the interior. There were no beads, but the bones of the shop whispered to his memory. Sensing movement inside, he slipped to the side of the entrance. There had been no specific sound, more a presence. His heart settled into slow rhythmic beating, every part of him focused on the interior of the shop.

Hearing the metallic sound of a rifle bolt chambering a round behind him, he froze.

"Keep your hands where I can see them," came the nervous voice of a female.

Turning his head, he saw the barrel of a Tavor assault rifle aimed at him. The eighteen-year-old eyes of its holder were wide with fear.

With quiet equanimity, Hafiz spoke. "I am officer Hafiz IbnMansur, Shabak. I have identification. Remain calm; you don't want to accidentally discharge your weapon."

"If I lower my weapon to check your identification, you could—Ariel, where are you?"

"What is your name, private?"

"Don't speak. Just give me a minute to think. Where did Ariel go?"

"Your friend is not here, but we can do this together. I am Yisraeli. Let's you and I do this. In front right pocket is the identification you need. I'll reach in with my left hand and pull it out."

"How do I know you won't pull a weapon and shoot me?"

"If I wanted to shoot, we wouldn't be talking now."

"Okay, so let's say you have a point, but what are you doing here? No one's supposed to be in the Old City. The Lieutenant told me everything was locked down."

"I am Shabak, think what this means. Your Lieutenant cannot speak for Shabak." Slowly, Hafiz took his left hand and inserted his index finger and thumb into his upper left coat pocket and pulled out identification. He knew the name didn't match his own. He tossed the papers in front of the frightened soldier.

"What did you do that for? How am I supposed to pick it up without looking away from you?"

"Pick up identification; we both have our duty to perform."

The private edged toward the identification papers, eyes jumping from Hafiz to the papers then back again. She bent over the papers. As her fingers closed on the papers, she glanced down. Taking two quick steps, Hafiz wrenched the rifle from the startled teenager.

"Hey, this doesn't say Hafiz IbnMansur," she said, looking at the papers that cost her rifle.

"Keep silent. You may have compromised a critical operation. I already told you I'm Shabak. I have many papers with different names. Go, find Ariel. Leave me to find the bad guys."

"What about my rifle, whoever you are?"

He retracted the charging handle, and the chambered round flew out of the rifle. "Go pick it up," Hafiz said.

After she retrieved the cartridge, Hafiz said, "Put it in your pocket."

"But I—"

"Put it in your uniform pocket, or I'll leave you handcuffed to the post for others to find."

After she put the round into her breast pocket, Hafiz handed her the ammunition magazine he had removed from the rifle.

"Now put magazine in back pocket."

She did as ordered.

"Is good you listen. Now I'll give you the rifle, but don't put the magazine in until you find your friend. If you make a move to arm weapon, you will be shot. Do you understand?"

"Look, I'm just doing my—"

"Do you understand?"

"Yes sir."

"That's good." He handed her the rifle, barrel first, and she turned to leave. It was then Hafiz felt cold steel on the back of his neck.

"On your knees Arab, I don't need any reason to end this now," growled a voice to his rear.

Hafiz went to his knees.

"Ariel, where have you been?"

"Not now, Tivona."

Hafiz tried to glance back at his captor. The rifle barrel jabbed into his neck. "I told you, Arab; I don't need a reason to shoot. Make one more move I don't direct and it will be your last," Ariel said. "Tivona, load your magazine and chamber a round."

Tivona complied then leveled her weapon at Hafiz.

"What's the story, Tivona?"

"Came across him looking into the bookseller's store. I drew down on him, but he got my rifle. He was sending me to find you when you came across us. Says he's Shabak, but the I.D. he showed doesn't match the name he gave."

"What name was that?"

"Hafiz IbnMansur."

Looking back to Hafiz, Ariel said, "You may be Shabak, you might not be Shabak, but if you don't follow every direction exactly, you won't live long enough for it to matter. Place your hands, one at a time, on the back of your head and interlace your fingers, now!"

Hafiz did as ordered.

"You just might live to prove you're Shabak. Tivona, take your handcuffs and secure the prisoner one hand at a time, just like you learned in basic training. Son of Mansur or whatever your name is, you might want to know if you attempt to overpower my friend, the least that will happen is you will have twenty rounds emptied into you."

After handcuffing their prisoner, Tivona looked at Ariel. "Now what?"

Hafiz remained on his knees, hands cuffed behind him.

"Now take your flex cuffs and secure the prisoner's legs, and don't be afraid to cinch them down. Today is not a good day to die, so I don't want him getting loose."

"But he's already handcuffed, Ariel."

"Yeah, and if he's trained, he could kill with a single kick. The sooner we neutralize him, the sooner we get to find out who he really is."

CHAPTER

59

Saturday 22 March 2008, 0547 hours

Kishle Police Station
Old City Yerushaláyim

When the call came from Kishle police station that Hafiz had been apprehended in the Old City, Commander Ramot scrambled to secure his release. Normally a call would suffice; today the world was anything but normal.

"Enjoy your morning in the Old City?" Ramot asked his insubordinate subordinate.

"I was careless. Did the number help?"

"Hafiz, trying to get through to a commanding General in the middle of an incident was impossible. I turned it over to one person who might help, but haven't heard back since your actions bought me a trip to Kishle."

"So you don't know?"

"What part of your ass is in it deep don't you understand? Believe it or not, there are other heroes out there, and somehow we manage to get through the day."

"I think Nuri is close."

"You and the entire command staff, we'll find your terrorist brother. Let's concentrate on where you're going to remain today.

As soon as I finish collecting your personal effects, I am taking you home. Understand this: You leave your residence for any reason I do not authorize in advance, other than to go to the store for groceries and return and I will not cover for you no matter where you turn up. Do you read me?"

"Yes, I read, but—"

"No—No exceptions, none. Hafiz, your intel may prove to be exceptional and you might even end up with a medal out of this, but I must know you are not going to draw the attention of a Brigadier General who has made it clear you were to stand down."

"Commander when I move it's because to not move would bring harm to Eretz Yisra'el."

"Nobody's disputing your patriotism, but I need you to stay put until this thing shakes itself out, then you can go back to old tricks."

Dropping Hafiz off with a final warning, Commander Ramot returned to his office and the unfolding crises on the minaret.

Pretending to clean up his condominium, Hafiz covertly searched his home and located the cameras Ramot had to know he'd find, monitoring the outside doors. Cameras or no he couldn't stay put, too much was at stake. He rigged a continual loop of the cameras showing the doors closed, noshed on a week-old bagel, and grabbed identification along with a replacement Glock hidden behind the baseboard in a wall cavity. Going to a chest with a partial false back panel, he retrieved a backup weapon, a Barak SP-21, with its ankle holster. He wouldn't get caught unprepared again. Finally he pulled out an RF detector donated by a mehablim who had met an unfortunate demise. He powered it up and removed seven sensors from his clothing. A final scan proved his thoroughness.

As he made his way back to the Old City walls, an infrared controller sewn into his collar triggered a vehicle response code that soldiers had to respond to within the prescribed thirty seconds which was all the distraction he needed to avoid detection. He entered the Christian Quarter through the New Gate, proceeding through locked buildings and deserted back alleys until he stood outside the shop where he had been too preoccupied to cover his perimeter, a novice mistake he wouldn't repeat. Yoram—Bookseller of Renown stared down at him from above the front door. The presence detected earlier was gone. Going to the back door, he picked the lock and made his way into the interior of the building. Nothing seemed familiar but there would be no surprises this time. He checked each alcove, niche, recess. Reaching the barred front door, he turned back toward the shop, exhaling slowly, clearing conscious thought. Inhaling deeply, he opened his mind's eye. Images spiraled through his memory. Beneath its surface, the shop father had taken them to a lifetime ago stared back at him.

Searching for signs of trespass, he spotted a cigarette butt on the floor. As he looked around, others presented themselves. They had been discarded in the hours the Old City had been closed down. No owner would have left their shop littered with cigarette butts. He picked one up, and its light orange paper and red lettering, *Na:ranj,* gave Hafiz all he needed. *I see you're still smoking, brother,* he thought to himself. *How careless.* Nur had taken up smoking after going to Syria, a stupid habit for a kid of sixteen. His brand—Na:ranj.

Ramot had been right; other heroes would face the anthrax he couldn't disarm if given the chance. Nur would be gone, after activating his handiwork, the odds of capture too great as the morning unfolded. If old habits die a hard death, Hafiz knew where he must go to spare a life and put an end to what no one else could. He made his way from the Jewish Quarter and out through the Dung Gate.

Returning home, he knew the journey ahead couldn't be made during daylight when he wouldn't make it out of his neighborhood before being stopped. Closing the drapes in the bedroom, he set the alarm, took off his shoes and placed his weapons in the nightstand drawer, then settled on top of the blankets. He knew there was one hope, and to prevail he would need sleep for the approaching night.

~

Lilith Kolatch, working under the cover of the Israel Antiquities Authority, had long been one of Ira Ramot's most enigmatic agents. Thanks to Hafiz's Kishle visit, Commander Ramot needed little convincing someone should keep an eye on him when she showed up to see if there was an assignment with all the excitement at the migdal. *Male commanders could be so receptive to the right demeanor and words,* Lilith mused. Ramot had nearly jumped in his chair when she let slip she often used her friend's spare room in Ma'aleh Adumim whenever she couldn't get back to the kibbutz—wasn't that near Hafiz's condo? A quick check of addresses showed what a small world it was.

Lilith assured the commander she understood the need for discretion. Even a commander couldn't surveil a Shabak officer unless going through the chain of command—a request—Lilith reminded the Commander, a certain Brigadier General would no doubt see. She happened to be in the same area as Hafiz and could be the soul of discretion. Who wants to ruin the career of a fellow Shabak officer based on suspicion and innuendo? Of course she would track Hafiz, if it would help the agency, but merely, she assured Commander Ramot, to verify his loyalty to Shabak and Israel, of which there could be no doubt.

Lilith knew Hafiz wouldn't stay put with his terrorist brother on the loose, and, predictable male that he was, she wasn't disappointed when she observed him leave for his morning jaunt. Lilith didn't care where Hafiz was going. She had no intention of being caught following him, knowing any rendezvous planned would be under the cover of darkness; vermin always surface at night. There must be no reprieve, no jail sentence; as brothers embraced their destiny.

With hidden microphones set, while he was occupied at Kishle, Hafiz returned home and Lilith watched as he closed his bedroom curtains. *All the better to rest for the night when a country would be betrayed,* Lilith thought. The sounds of light snoring soon filled her earbud. The coming night would be a great one for Yisra'el and a spectacular one for Lilith Kolatch. Lilith allowed herself sleep.

CHAPTER

60

Saturday 22 March 2008, 0601 hours

Migdal David
Old City Yerushaláyim

The last sound Nasir never heard was the 7.62×51mm round bullet hurtling toward his head at 2,800 feet per second. Flesh, blood, and bone exploded outward, spattering catwalk, spire, and railing, obliterating any semblance to a living, sentient, human being.

Hafiz scanned the catwalk with his binoculars as the motionless body hung over its edge. He couldn't see the blood drip, drip, dripping down, down, onto ancient stones where the bodies of intended subjugators made their final stand, forming a grotesque sculpture of twisted and broken forms bidding farewell to a world they neither understood nor made peace with; these lords of choices and slaves of consequences.

Yanshuf, Owl, made its way to the tower, hovering eighty feet above the catwalk. Rotor downwash from the helicopter nudged Nasir's upper body. In one slow motion his shoulder sagged as gravity released the lifeless torso from the confines of the catwalk to join fallen comrades below. No triumphal sounds heralded his passing, only the droning of rotors beating above. This son of commitment joined those in death he had pledged to in life.

DTMF tones sounded in one short burst across the roof. Confused, Hafiz's caffeine-saturated mind pulled back from the tower as he struggled to identify the sound. He surveilled the area, searching for its source. His eyes stopped on the laptop. Millions of simultaneously firing neurons connected. "Call," was nearly shouted. He rushed to the computer and there in aqua on a black screen blinked a fourteen-digit number.

With the evacuation of the Old City, normal cell traffic has been suspended and radio traffic doesn't transmit DTMF tones. What does this mean? Nuri would call the lambs, with changes to plans, to light fire under them for not dying fast enough, but after the last shot, no lambs are left to call. Yet those were cell tones; someone called or it wouldn't have been captured, but why fourteen? All mobiles are ten digits—think Hafiz. He counted the numbers again, still fourteen. *Is it a code and for what?*

Looking back at the catwalk, he saw two commandos fast-roping down the helo's dangling umbilical, descending to the catwalk.

Owl transmitted that it was jamming-pulse detonation signals. Going back to the roof's edge, Hafiz swung his binoculars toward the ground, scanning quadrants, working his way outward in an ever-widening circle. There was no visible sign of Nuri, but he knew his brother was there; the DTMF tones could have no other source. He'd figure the DTMF tones out, but the pulse detonator was brilliant. Steady-stream signals could be tracked and located, but a pulse detonator with over four billion codes could switch codes mid-pulse, making tracking virtually impossible. *Nice touch, little brother. I knew you wouldn't make this easy, but just like when we were young I will win.*

With the mehablim dead and sporadic radio communications obscured by intermittent chatter, there was little to hang around for as caffeine, from a six-pack of energy drinks, triggered nerve endings, taking turns spasmodically twitching. Surrendering to their demand for movement and nature's call, Hafiz inched onto the outside edge of the roof, and relieved himself. Scanning the area below, he checked for anything out of place, realizing it had been too long since he'd walked these streets, fitting all the pieces of daily life into the puzzle that would have told him if something was out of place, different.

The radio started squawking while the tower commandos talked back and forth with the General who had tried to remove him from the action. He needed quiet to think. Reaching to turn the volume down, he heard one of them ask the other about mobiles. *Mobiles, what is this mobiles?* He listened. Silence assailed the airwaves. *Talk mobile phones*, he mentally screamed. *There's a timer? There's always a timer. Get back to the phones. Maybe they're not so busy; I could call. Wait, I'm at home like the General's lapdog insisted. How would I know to call from home? Did either commando have a phone? Okay, of course they did. Information wouldn't have their number. Ramot—Ramot might get through. He had to know I couldn't sit by while Nuri tries to unleash anthrax on Yerushaláyim; he'll take my call.* Hafiz dialed.

"Commander Ramot."

"Commander, this is Hafiz."

"Tell me you're home."

"Is that what your GPS on my phone tells you?"

"You think I'm going to look so I have to answer to the General? What grief you trying to lay on my doorstep?"

"I heard Ya'Ma'M mention mobile phones, you got anything?"

"I'm not bringing you into this, Hafiz. You know Doran's orders from the General."

"I picked up something, maybe it's critical, but I need to know about phones and tomorrow's too late or I wouldn't have called."

"Tell me something solid or this phone's going dead. I'm not risking my career on your hunch."

"If my heart were set on a family reunion, I would position myself in Old City overlooking the minaret with equipment to track cell phone transmissions."

"Do you even begin to understand the coverage we have in place?"

"You got anything?"

"You're the one who called."

"If Nuri's around, he has to be in proximity to see the minaret, but not so close to get caught. If he needs to communicate with mehablim, he radios them, we'd pick up the transmission and track his location before he says goodbye, which leaves a cell phone call. He uses our cell tower antennas, not so hard to figure, we track his call, maybe block it, so he configures his own cell frequencies with roving codes and brings his own antenna. We have the best equipment in the world but I picked up a number on a scanner. Did anyone else pick it up?"

"Your point?"

"If I didn't look for my brother, like little General Doran wanted, what happens to the anthrax?"

"If your information proves itself, you might avoid charges of disobeying a direct order. What do you have?"

"I captured a fourteen-digit number. Mobiles are ten numbers, always ten, so this has to be mobile call with four additional digits."

"Got to be a passcode."

"Thing is, the numbers were intercepted after the last mehabel was killed."

"You sure of that?"

"Watched his face get blown off, what I could see of it. Pretty much means no life. Besides, as Owl hovered, mehabel, on the edge of the catwalk, dropped like a sack of terrorist to buddies below."

"You might have something; maybe Oz's geniuses can verify it. What's the prefix?"

"054."

"Give me the rest and anything else I need to know."

CHAPTER

61

Saturday 22 March 2008

Hadassah Medical Center, Mount Scopus, Yerushaláyim

Someone, it seemed, had paid for a 6900-mile trip for her to be left alone in a science lab. At least Janelle assumed it was a lab, with its laboratory table, Bunsen burners, rack of test tubes, and centrifuge apparatuses in repose. What did a lab have to do with Addison? After being dismissed by Keane Bodine, a driver had appeared from nowhere; he might have been helpful, if she'd been able to understand Hebrew. Had they done that on purpose? He had managed to articulate "Wait here," before ending his soliloquy, uttering the one Hebrew word she understood—shalom—as he too abandoned her.

Drawn to the oversized windows, she gazed across an emerald lawn and manicured low-lying bushes toward what looked to be the Old City walls. In the distance two helicopters hovered, so much for the panoramic view.

She thought of Keane Bodine with his calm assurances, every question answered with multiple conjectures. She understood nothing was scripted, that answers were as fleeting as hope. Bit by bit, he had relented, as truth had found its way to the surface when he'd been assured her persistence wouldn't subside until he revealed the little truth he could. Addison was in mortal danger—period—and, for the present, alive. That it seemed, was everything he knew. Was she happy with the facts? She would have settled for believable lies.

Her son, her only son, was in peril, and she didn't know where, and neither did the experts, though he must be close, the country was so tiny. Was it too late to acknowledge fear? What other sentiment was there to embrace since hope was so sparingly dispensed in this land, at least to outsiders.

As she walked around her prison, wasting tiredness gnawed at every fiber. She looked at the gray vinyl couch sitting opposite the lab table against the wall, but her nerves forbade sitting. She must not chance falling asleep, if sleep were possible. Phentobarbital had been offered. That should do the trick, a small dose and euphoric sedation; a larger one and no sensation. It was the drug of choice for assisted suicide at home. But she needed to feel, to apprehend, not short-circuit, no matter what happened. When Mom and Dad Layton died, she remembered the brutal numbness. When Blade betrayed his commitment, she felt its ugly presence again. Both times others had been there. Now she understood what it meant to be alone.

Was that a door opening? Turning, she looked to see. Would it be another person to encounter, deal with? A man entered the room, and then just stood there, a Jewish custom? Strange, no words in any language. She was good with people, but what was expected here? He appeared harmless, but why the staring? At least she was being acknowledged. Was it acceptable for a woman to speak first in Israel, or do all Jewish men stare?

Something about his face drew her, demanding notice, but what? He appeared to have the standard Jewish male face swallowed by a salt and pepper beard. His eyes were gentle; she didn't want to look away. Moving her head at an angle, she tried for a different perspective. A surprised look came over his face. Then tears trickled down this stranger's face from which she could not turn, unexpectedly a part of her.

Softly, as if carried on a breeze that could be swallowed by the tiniest sound, he whispered, "Shayndel Laila."

Tears clouded her vision as Shayndel Laila resonated through her soul. There was no place to turn, escape to; captured by a name only one other human being could know. The name Y'shua softly parted his lips as words she couldn't understand somehow brought comfort.

Looking into newly familiar eyes, she heard her voice say "Tevel." His shaking arms embraced her as weeping overcame brother and sister.

Finally, looking up at her brother, Shayndel said, "So much to ask—"

"We have time."

"But first let us speak of my son."

CHAPTER

62

Saturday 22 March 2008, 0615 hours

Migdal David Minaret
Old City Yerushaláyim

Three thousand horses from the Sikorsky UH-60 Black Hawk's twin engines assaulted the momentary calm that ensued after the death of the last mehabel. Ya'Ma'M marksmen left no breath of life in those pledged to annihilate Israel's sons and daughters in their beloved eternal capital.

Closing on the Migdal David minaret from the west at 300 feet per second, *Yanshuf*, Owl, to those whose lives are taken into and out of danger, slowed. Captain Gurion Shavlev and Sergeant Major Eban Bar-On, sitting at the ready by the open cabin door, waited to fast-rope onto the tower catwalk while adrenaline coursed their veins, heightening senses life would depend on. The tower, growing in size as they approached, was their universe; every fiber surrendered to one singular point of convergence. No thoughts of victory, or defeat, only the knowledge that nothing else in existence had meaning.

Listening to his wireless earbud, Gurion heard the familiar voice. "Shavlev, this is Oz, copy."

"Read you loud and clear, General."

"I'm in operational command, copy."

"Yes sir. Colonel Samech mentioned that, General," Captain Shavlev said.

"Roger that, General," Sergeant Major Eban Bar-On said.

"Traffic's been assigned alternate frequencies, so it's just the three of us. You will keep me in the loop on this one, Gurion," Brigadier General Oz said. "You too, Bar-On."

The helo beat air as it hovered eighty feet above the minaret's catwalk; any closer and rotor downwash might set off the gift the PMIJ had left.

"Time to execute, General," Shavlev reported, making a mental note to keep in touch, at least until things got intense. He tapped Eban's arm once and gave a thumbs-up, which Eban returned. Grabbing the 40mm thick rope hanging in front of him, Gurion swung his feet out the helo's door. A crewman unhooked the cabin tether from his harness ring and slapped once on his upper back. Clamping down on the braided rope with gloved hands, he pulled out from the cabin and plunged from the belly of the helo.

Five seconds later Bar-On followed. The pilot, triangulating precisely, positioned the bottom of the rope thirty inches from the top of the catwalk between the railing and tower spire away from the hostages.

The moment after Bar-On's boots hit the catwalk, the helicopter jettisoned its rope. Silently, the undulating snake caught on, then slithered over the tower's upper railing, continuing its descent onto ancient stones and fresh remains below. A smaller line swung from the cabin and shot downward, containing two equipment bags separated by three feet of rope. Unhooking the lead bag, Shavlev stepped back, stripped his gloves, and thrust them into the bag's side pocket, while Bar-On retrieved his equipment. As Yanshuf retreated five hundred yards, Bar-On removed and stowed his gloves. Tactile sensation was mission critical.

Gurion rounded the catwalk. He assessed the American before him: chin dislocated, eyes swollen shut. Red spittle dribbling between bruised swollen lips. Right cheek concave, raw, septic, with inflamed striations. Right shoulder at an odd angle, dislocated. Both wrists handcuffed, waist high, to metal D-ring expansion anchors embedded on each side of him into the tower's stone spire. A three-foot mortar tube jutted skyward between the hostage's thighs. His legs were under a low horizontal iron railing that encircled the catwalk mere inches above it. The railing was separated by short vertical iron balusters, spaced every eighteen inches, welded at their top to an iron railing that mirrored the lower railing. Both of the hostage's feet hung over the catwalk's edge a hundred feet in the air.

His left leg, twisted at an ugly angle, appeared broken. What Gurion could see was gashed and swollen. Two timers, one on top of the other, hid behind a thin metallic mesh vest on his upper torso. The first displayed nineteen minutes, thirty-one seconds, and was ticking off the seconds. Its companion timer, just below, rested at five minutes, zero seconds.

"What did you find, Captain?" Oz intruded.

"Still looking, General, cameras see more than I have. What do they show?

"Bar-On?"

"Wires connecting hostages loop to the other side of catwalk, General. Connections are professional. I'll know more when I finish my assessment."

Gurion observed an opened flip phone tucked into a pocket in the vest above the timers on the American's chest. "Eban, pick up mobiles yet?"

"Affirmative, Captain, three flip phones, one on each hostage. All are powered, open, and connected."

"Maybe they want us to close the phones, avoid overtime charges."

"And break the loop they went to so much effort to establish?"

"Would be rude, six-pack says I'm looking at the termination point in the mortar tube between the American's legs."

"Don't suppose they forgot to attach the launch base to the catwalk so we could just move this party."

"Got three rock anchors securing a triangular base plate to the catwalk, best not to dislodge."

"What'd you encounter Shavlev?" Oz asked.

"Bull's-eye level, welded onto two horizontal bars just below the top of the launch tube, General. Two mercury switches are attached beneath at right angles to each other with wires running from the mercury switches inside the tube."

"Bubble remains centered, mercury doesn't trigger launch."

"Simple but effective, General, allows for leveling of planes in two dimensions which sets up firing trajectory while keeping us from taking everything to the *Negev* for disposal. We bump or tilt it, mercury flows to either end and triggers firing of whatever surprise they have for us. How things look on your side, Eban?"

"Got what could have been a decent-looking daughter of Zion between two male Arabs."

"Could have been?"

"Her face has been battered."

Following every wire, searching branching and termination points, Gurion avoided physical contact, as did Eban—standard Ya'Ma'M procedure. "Eban, you remember the American's name?"

"It's Addison Deverell," General Oz volunteered.

"Roger, Addison Deverell, Eban, you listening?"

"Go ahead, Gurion."

"Addison has a primary and secondary timer, one on top of the other, under a metallic vest on his torso. The timers have jacks on two sides. On the left side a single wire runs from the primary to the secondary timer."

"What other wires you have coming my way, Gurion?"

"How many wire bundles you got leaving?"

"Three."

"None got lost but I need to see everything I have," Gurion said. He extracted the Wireless Induction Array Biosensor, from his equipment bag and attached its carbon fiber tripod.

Sixteen high-definition cameras with hyperzoom lenses and parabolic microphones were aimed at the minaret. The operation would be pored over by every political faction and military command for the next quarter century, provided Yisra'el made it through this latest crisis. There were always more fingers pointing blame than hands to contain them and no end to court-martials that could be brought for the smallest mistake committed in the heat of battle.

Sagiv Oz felt the heat in his air-conditioned command bunker at Lod. Every facet of the operation was displayed on oversized screens providing a live feed of his headstrong extraction team, into whose hands his fate was tied. Subordinates were locked on twenty-four standby screens viewing the feed from cameras tactically positioned around the tower.

Powering up the WIAB, Gurion aimed its air sampler at the mortar tube attached to the catwalk thirty-six inches in front of him, set to register trace spore emissions above background levels. Waiting for the detector to initialize, he dissected and committed to memory the precise positioning of the American. The timer attempted to seize his attention as each second ticked toward defeat. "Games," he snorted under his breath, as if this ploy could cause deviation from methodical procedures worked out through more crises than he could remember. Focus and intensity. Nothing went unnoticed, nothing undone.

When the WIAB's familiar beep sounded, he hit Scan, knowing five minutes would be demanded for results. Gurion used the time to pore over every inch on and around the motionless hostage with an optics scanner that separated the light spectrum to reveal differentials between adjoining materials.

As he worked his way over the area, a black-jacketed wire caught and held his attention. It ran from the side of the launch tube across the launch base plate, covered in electrical tape, to the outside lower railing that circled the catwalk's edge. *Why did they try to cover you, little wire? Didn't think we'd see?* Black cable ties held the wire as it climbed several feet to the top of a vertical baluster. From there it hitched a ride on one of four crudely spaced horizontal iron spokes which were inset into the spire's stone center on one end and a circular iron rail on the outside edge of the minaret that roughly mirrored the lower two rails several feet below. The cable continued around the spire to another inset spoke finally terminating at an antenna that was attached to the spoke where it intersected the circular horizontal rail on the far side, above the three hostages.

"The antenna above your position is attached to the launch tube Eban."

"Roger that."

Gurion returned his gaze to the American and continued to assimilate and catalog the minutest detail. After five minutes, the

WIAB's high-low warbling told him all he needed to know. "Eban, you copy?" Gurion said.

"I hear warbling."

Thirty-six miles away, Brigadier General Oz, intensity etched on his aging face, listened to the scanner's unmistakable condemnation. All eyes were fixed on monitors displaying the action playing out on the highest point in the Old City.

The three hostages before Eban sat on the catwalk, backs against the spire. Their legs hung under the low horizontal iron railing, all three mouths were duct-taped.

The woman, positioned between the Arabs, had her nose broken. Her left cheek, blackish-purple, was inflamed in palpable trauma, yet a fiery gaze demanded attention as she labored to breathe.

Both Arabs were comatose. Their outside wrists were handcuffed to D-ring rock anchors embedded in the spire waist high. Blood beaded under the cuffs. Their opposite wrists were shackled to one handcuff bracelet, on each side of the woman, the other bracelet was secured to the woman's wrists.

The hostages were girded in what appeared to be metallic mesh vests covering their upper torsos. On their chests, near their right shoulders, pockets held open flip phones. Wire bundles connected the hostages' phones then disappeared around the catwalk. Memorizing the wiring schematic, Eban focused on the hostages while maintaining a safe distance.

Black-crimson encrusted scabs deformed the upper arm of the large Arab, who hovered more out of consciousness than in. Blood outlined the edges of his pallid grayish-green wound. A bone, jagged and ugly, protruded through necrosing flesh.

The smaller Arab appeared to have been on the wrong end of an old-fashioned ass-whipping. The pattern of a boot sole clearly imprinted on his cheek and forehead, his right eye swollen shut. The duct taped mouths ensured silence while Eban set up the anthrax detector. Compassion, like everything else in Yisra'el, waited its turn. Powering up the detector, he grabbed his optics scanner and scanned everything on the catwalk that didn't belong while the WIAB initialized, then, with the push of a button, began its sample. Training ensured nothing was overlooked. Missing the smallest deviation cost lives; that would not happen on his watch. Five minutes later, clicking told him it was safe to approach. "General, anthrax scan negative, going closer for the explosives scan."

"Roger that, easy does it, son," General Oz said, observing the action on multiple monitors.

Pulling the explosives detector from the bag, Eban removed its nozzle cap and turned it on. Sixty seconds later it was ready to sample. As he moved to the hostages, the woman's eyes bored into him. He grunted, "Keep still."

He kept the trace detector six inches from each hostage while its nozzle sampled for vapors and particulates. Finally, certain of the results, Eban spoke. "Explosives scan positive for trace particulates."

"Roger that Eban, positive on trace particulates and vapors," said General Oz.

"Copy, Eban," Gurion said. "I'll get more than particulates, got a mortar tube with a positive for anthrax. My bet, black powder numbers will be off the chart."

Glancing down at Aadil, Eban said, "Marhaba, hello, you with me?"

A huge head rolled toward the sound of his voice.

Kneeling, Eban looked into eyes that didn't focus, a sign he knew all too well—he needed to act fast. "I remove tape, don't move. You have a connecting wire; if you move maybe it disconnects, everyone dies—understand?" Seeing Aadil's eyes flicker, Eban whispered in Arabic, "This will sting. Don't even twitch until I find all that binds you to minaret and one another. Best for one strong pull, less pain." He grabbed the end of the tape in his right hand and placed his left hand on Aadil's face by the edge of the tape and pressed—then yanked—hard. Blood beaded on Aadil's lips and cheeks. The hostage gulped air as pain radiated across his face. *Is good,* Eban thought. He saw the eyes react, bringing him closer to consciousness. *Shock kills if not treated, but a doctor has to wait.*

Eban turned his attention to the smaller man. When he went to move over the woman, her rapid eye movement telegraphed a demand for attention. Growing up the only boy in a house of three sisters, he thought better of noticing the muffled sounds emanating from under her duct tape. No matter how battered she was, there was far too much spirit in her eyes for him to hope she would remain silent if the tape was removed.

Looking at Khalil he saw eyes that were responsive. Eban said, "You see how tape released from friend? Ready?"

Widening, the little man's lone visible eye seemed to beg for an alternative.

"I know your cheeks are swollen, maybe broken, but must remove tape. It's the first step in getting you from tower. Can your thumbnail reach your index finger?"

Khalil shook his head no.

"Good, now listen, this takes mind from pain when I pull tape. Place your thumbnail against the flesh of your index finger. When I say ready, press thumbnail into finger with all your strength. It hurts, but not as much as tape pulling from your face. Ready?"

Khalil jammed his thumbnail into the soft flesh of his index finger. The pain from his finger, he would recount later in sorrowful detail, was overwhelmed by the tidal swell of pain that drowned his face. Pain never before experienced when his bruised, swollen cheek and jaw responded to the tape being ripped from his unshaven face.

"Good, worst part over. Now we talk," Eban said.

Looking up, Khalil said, "I . . . got . . . to . . . pee."

"Pee then," Eban said.

"Here?"

"Yeah, sure."

"What about privacy?"

"You want privacy?"

"Be nice."

"Then close eyes. Till I figure out how to get you from handcuffs and wiring, it's all the privacy you get."

"Eban, you copy?"

"Loud and clear."

"Going for explosives scan."

"Affirmative, Captain."

"Looks good from here," General Oz volunteered.

"Of course it's good; we're still alive," Gurion said.

Pulling the explosives detector from its case, Gurion removed its nozzle cap and turned it on. Sixty seconds later it was ready to sample. He approached the American and aimed the explosives detector at the mortar tube, taking care not to brush against anything. Five seconds later an oscillating tone signaled detection. A quick flip of the mode switch and there it was on the screen. "General, picking up a positive on potassium nitrate, charcoal, and sulfur vapors, over."

"Roger that, positive on black powder particulates," Oz said.

Gurion searched one final time for the smallest detail out of place, any of the myriad ways explosives could be triggered, running his optical scanner through its paces. A mehablim favorite was to arm the primary explosive they knew would be found then conceal a secondary trigger and charge to explode as the primary was disabled.

"Captain Shavlev, this is Captain Sagal, Night Bird."

"Go ahead, Sagal," Gurion said.

"We've been jamming incoming pulse signals. Someone's trying to light up your package. Signals are intermittent but coming from different directions. We've got your back, but you might want to proceed with guarded speed."

"Roger that, Night Bird, no coffee breaks, appreciate the heads-up."

"You'll trace the wire-map from your end, Captain," Eban said.

"Affirmative," Gurion said, retrieving the TDR scanner and turning it on. "Beginning wire-map scan, injecting signal into wire one, now." Correlating the signal with reflections in the neighboring wires, the Time Domain Reflectometer generated a map of the wiring loop, along with the distances of terminating and branch points. Lod Command was dialed into the results. Tracing the wiring in front of him, Gurion spotted an anomaly. "General."

"Go."

"Wire-map shows the loop between mobiles, primary timer, and the launch tube but doesn't identify the secondary timer. Eban, verify wiring on your side."

"Roger that, Captain. Mobiles are open and secured to each hostage's torso in a metallic vest. Thing is, when I checked, vests are not magnetic, some type of polymer."

"Maybe bad guys don't want mobile signal interfered with."

"Captain Shavlev, this is Captain Sagal, Night Bird."

"What's your pleasure, Night Bird?"

"We electronically tracked markers, in real time, the mehablim set up on the catwalk as well as visually scanning their activity."

"What do you have?"

"Four mobiles were powered up inside the spire, connecting them to the network and creating an open loop. Call in call out, regular mobile service. After the hostages were positioned on catwalk, all mobiles and both timers were physically connected, creating a closed mechanical loop. The final stage is a closed electronic loop. It was created when two mobiles made connection calls to the other two mobiles. Those connections remain active. We captured each IMSI number when the individual mobiles connected to the network."

"Those the numbers for mobiles?" Gurion said.

"International Mobile Subscriber Identity is the fifteen-digit number transmitted when logging onto the network, Captain. It goes out one time then switches to a randomly assigned, changing, TMSI number. Eliminate the first five digits and we have our number—as long as you're listening when the mobile powers up, and we were. Just transmitted the numbers to Command & Control, General."

"Maybe the mehablim didn't think we were listening."

"Maybe they wanted us to, General," Gurion said.

"Explain."

"Let us know they're dialed in. We're not dealing with amateurs. They put up enough roadblocks maybe we don't get through or try Plan B, which triggers the launch."

"No Arab works at that level, Gurion."

"Plenty of Arabs are smart, General. They just don't get what Eretz Yisra'el means to us."

"Night Bird, you capture IMSI on fifth mobile?" Gurion said.

"There's a fifth mobile?"

"Would be the alarm mobile," Gurion said.

"Only four numbers were transmitted, Captain Sagal."

"Had to be powered up and connected when PMIJ took the tower, Night Bird. Any way to know number unless we caught it when it powered on the network?"

"Negative on that Captain."

"General, the primary timer's counting down, the secondary timer is stationary, but it still needs to be traced."

"Why two timers, Gurion?" Oz said.

"Consider what we've got—connections are professional, design is elegant. Whoever configured this knows their stuff, with mobiles in a loop to trigger a firework's shell in the heart of the Old City. They didn't need to launch from the migdal; could have used a building in Area A, under full PALFA control, but someone wants us to see it coming. This isn't just for the greater glory of Allah; this is personal. A message to dead men: Nothing we can do. There's a bigger Jewish population in Tel Aviv and the Gush Dan area if they wanted to launch from Jewish-controlled land, but the Migdal David, in the heart of the Old City, is symbolic, personal. They're sending a message beyond Yerushaláyim. I'm not a *Tanakh* expert, but I know it says Yerushaláyim is where HaShem, G-d, put his name. Maybe someone wants to kick HaShem out."

"Eban, a single wire from the right side of each timer runs to a connector plugged into the mortar tube, but the wire from secondary timer didn't show up on the wire-map scan. I'm checking it with an RF detector. If there's no oscillation on the line, it's not part of the loop; it's got to be a dummy line to throw us off."

"Gurion, what do you see?"

"One minute, General . . . got it. There's oscillation on line from the secondary timer to the mortar tube."

"It's part of loop," Eban said.

"Why didn't it show up?"

"It can't be powered, General," Eban said. "The secondary timer is the fail-safe for the loop. We defeat the primary timer, the secondary powers up and we've got five minutes to stop launch or extract hostages."

"Just enough time to get us to commit but not enough to execute, my guess. Like I said, it's personal," Gurion said. "They don't care if the loop is defeated. Once we stop the primary timer, they want us to think the launch is defeated so we begin neutralizing the launch tube which would take a minimum of fifteen minutes to get in if we had an access code."

"Scan for it."

"General, if I programmed a passcode, I'd rig failed authorizations to cause timed lockout then wait until timer triggers launch, or launch with the first failed passcode. Could be any number. So, unless your geniuses come up with some way to disarm the loop without the passcode it may be time for Plan B. What do your geniuses say?"

Dead air filled the space between Lod and the Migdal.

"General?"

"You'll get an answer in a minute, Captain. Stand by."

"General, we don't have spare time here. The timer won't wait. If your experts draw blanks, we need to know."

"Captain, our experts may not be in time."

"Primary timer is at eight minutes, thirty seconds, and counting, General."

"Then I need to call *Beit Rosh HaMemshala.*"

CHAPTER

63

AGM-114TBI Kardum (Hatchet) missile

In 2002, Israeli arms manufacturer Gideon Military Industries (GMI) entered into a purchase agreement with Lockheed-Martin of the United States for the purchase of seventy-five Hellfire II missiles. The agreement was reviewed under the Arms Export Control Act (AECA) and was tabled for the standard thirty-day waiting period, pending Congressional review. Citing an emergency requiring the sale in national interests, the President of the United States, the honorable George Walker Bush, exercised his legal authority to proceed with the sale, notifying Congress per Section 614(a) of the Foreign Assistance Act of 1961 (FAA). What was withheld from all but one Senate Select Sub-Committee was the understanding that the purchasing country retained all rights to modify these missiles for specific theater needs. Due to the classified nature of these modifications, all specifications for changes were withheld by the acquiring country.

On receiving the missiles, GMI modified all seventy-five Heliborne, Laser, Fire, and Forget missiles into multiple platform and operational needs systems. Out of that modification process the AGM-114TBI Kardum (Hatchet) missile was born. The Hellfire

AGM-114TBI Kardum was the first laser-guided thermobaric implosion missile configured to perform in the limited geographical areas the Israeli Air Force is mandated to defend. Three Hatchets were tested in an isolated region of the Negev, south desert, to ensure the missile's modification parameters were met. All design specifications were exceeded. Israeli authorities guarded the existence of the AGM-114TBI Kardum (Hatchet), as is customary for all classified tactical weapons.

Near the fourth-largest city in Israel, Rishon LeZion, Base 25, also known as Palmachim Air Base, the 166 Squadron flies the workhorse of the IDF Unmanned Aerial Vehicles, the Hermes 450s. With its 52-hp rotary UEL engine, the Hermes, nicknamed Zik, is capable of staying aloft for more than twenty hours with a maximum speed of 109 miles per hour and a ceiling of 18,000 feet. It can carry two Rafael missiles, but specific Ziks were modified to carry a single 100.75-pound missile, the precise weight of the Hellfire AGM-114TBI Kardum.

On March 22, 2008, a call was made on a secure line from Lod Air Base Command & Control to Yerushaláyim. Immediately afterward, a call was placed from the Prime Minister's residence, Beit Rosh HaMemshala, to Base 25.

CHAPTER

64

Saturday 22 March 2008, 0626 hours

Sherut ha-Bitachon ha-Klali (Shabak) Headquarters Office of Yerushaláyim District Commander Ira Ramot Yerushaláyim

Dialing the number a third time, Ira's stomach churned while acid worked its way up his esophagus. His first call to General Oz had elicited "Are you out of your mind, Commander?" from one of Oz's underlings he had never heard of when he'd refused to divulge the specifics of his call to anyone except the General, the last words he heard were "Good luck" as the phone went dead.

The second call hadn't even lasted that long, and the third went through to Lt. Doran. The little punk forgot he was a Lieutenant and talking to a Commander. He would be reminded of that fact when this was over.

Shabak is never defeated, he reminded himself. Who owed favors, who could help? Smiling, he remembered Hod . . . Hod Heber, the geek he lived next door to a few years back who had gotten himself picked up with a certain lady of the evening. Such things were frowned upon but often overlooked by male commanders. His fiancée, out on Border Police duties, might not have shared his prostitutes don't count philosophy, should a memorandum have come to her attention with the help of other, less than understanding, female Border Police who made it their business to watch each other's backs. Ira had intervened, nothing more than a call, but that call, he pointed out to Hod at the time, saved untold grief, especially since Hod ended up marrying his fiancée, the Rabbi's daughter.

It had been a couple of years. He typed Hod Heber into Shabak's database, and there he was, Logistical Control IAF, Lod Air Base. Calling the number, he got voicemail; there was no time for a message. Trying again, he got voicemail a second time. Waiting for the beep, he gave it his best shot, delivering a plea for a return call that ricocheted between intrigue and begging. Hanging up, he raced through his options. No time to drive to Lod; he needed someone with connections to get through to General Oz and to get through now. The someone who came to mind would be at the Knesset in a couple of hours on a normal business day, but this wasn't a normal day and two hours might as well be two years. There had to be a home number if he could just dig it up—his phone rang. It was Heber's number. "Hod, do not hang up. Whatever you do, don't hang up."

"Ira, we're up to our eyeballs in a situation at the Migdal. Don't have time to talk."

"I know about the Migdal. Are you in Command & Control with General Oz? Please tell me you're in Command & Control.

"The General's in an adjacent building."

"What are you looking at right now?"

"We have a feed to what's happening over at Command & Control along with all the feeds they have on their system. It all ties into the network. What's up?"

"I have a number obtained in the last few minutes from someone next to Migdal David."

"What kind of number, Ira?"

"I don't know what kind; the information just came in. I mean I know it's a mobile number, but there are four extra digits."

"Ira, I'm computers, remember? Networks, fiber-optic, Ethernet, wireless. The situation on Migdal David's so far out of bounds I don't have a way to understand the basics, but the best talent in Yisra'el's on it and so I get to stand by in case something goes down or they need something else booted up."

"Just tell me what you know."

"You've got clearance, right?"

"Higher than yours."

"It doesn't come higher than mine, Ira."

"We'll discuss that later. What do you have?"

"The wonks seem to agree we're facing more than one system. Four hostages all dialed into each other on four mobiles hardwired together. Everything's looped into an alarm assembly—delta r trigger comes to mind, but don't quote me on that—attached to a fireworks shell filled with anthrax sitting in a launch tube between one of the hostage's legs."

"You have mobile numbers?"

"Yeah, sure, they were picked up on scanners before the terrorists started exchanging their lives to play on the catwalk. Did I mention a timer is also counting down? One other thing they're looking into."

"What's that?"

"The launch tube has a cable from a Yagi antenna running into it."

"That's the second time I've heard of that antenna."

"What's the first?"

"From a subordinate who fished the mobile number out of the air. What are your four numbers?"

"Let me look." He read them off.

"None of them are my number."

"And?"

"Heber, you said there's an alarm. Alarms have to be set. The number was picked up by my operative near the migdal after the last terrorist was eliminated."

"After?"

"Yeah, after. Hafiz, my guy, was sure, after. He watched the last mujahid get whacked."

"So if a call was made after everyone checked out, the only reason would be to arm the system. Unless the caller wanted to wish the mujahideen bon voyage to the virgins, and you don't need fourteen numbers to say goodbye."

"I can say it in ten."

"What's that number, we may just become heroes."

"054 . . ."

Hod hit speed dial and waited for his boss to pick up. After two rings voicemail kicked in. His building, he found after hanging up with Ira Ramot, was locked down for the duration. Command & Control, normally impenetrable, was now a fortress. Sitting at his network node, he pulled up surveillance cameras. He didn't need additional convincing of the impossibility he faced. Beyond his inability to get out of the building and negotiate the 1200 feet to Command & Control, there were physical barriers set up he'd never seen before, and he doubted his computer expertise would sway the Yeti guarding access to Command & Control to let him through. Staring at the monitor, he knew, if the information Ramot had given him was correct, there were only moments to act. His monitor, irritatingly, started blinking on and off. "Now what?" He opened Task Manager to check performance: Resources were good, everything looked fine. Observing CPU usage oscillating, it hit him. Closing Task Manager, he went to the *Run* dialog box, typed *cmd,* and hit *Enter,* bringing up *Command Prompt.* Typing a *Remote Procedure Call* to launch *Word*, he was satisfied. "Ignore this, General," he said to no one in particular, hitting *Enter.*

Sagiv Oz felt the weight of choices no politician would have been willing to make. The worst were former military commanders who knew what needed to be done but, having completed their evolution into politicians, forgot what it was like to sit where he was with the future of a country on your shoulders. One of his monitors had its camera on the timer as it continued to constrict its stranglehold on the breath of Yerushaláyim, but it was this monitor his eyes returned to time and again. He forced himself to focus on his extraction team on the tower.

"General, if experts have anything, now is the time. We've got four hostages on the catwalk with Owl and Night Bird hovering."

"Captain, execute countermeasures. This is not first time to face mehablim."

"General, has command been listening? Mobiles aren't wired for simple detonation. Both closed mechanical and closed electronic loops have been wire-mapped. We authenticated every connection of the mechanical loop. It can't be breached in the time left."

"Then—"

All monitors started flashing in unison. "What is with the monitors?"

"Sir, we're checking."

"So check. Without monitors we're blind."

All screen backgrounds turned blue.

"What's going on?" Sagiv Oz roared.

One second later a fourteen-digit number in 52 point white font replicated itself across each screen.

"What is this number?"

"We're on it, General. We don't know yet."

"Someone knows. Numbers don't put themselves on screen."

"General, there's a name just below the bottom number in a tiny font. Who's Hod Heber?"

"Logistical Control Network Administrator," a nearby lieutenant volunteered.

"Why is he not here?"

"We'll have him here ASAP, General."

"Get him: Now!"

CHAPTER

65

Saturday 22 March 2008, 0632 hours

Migdal David
Old City Yerushaláyim

"Shavlev, this is Oz. We have alarm code, copy. Passcode obtained."

"Roger that, General, alarm code has been acquired."

"Dr. Ben-Meir, one of the geniuses you asked about before, will brief you."

"Captain Shavlev, this is Abigail Ben-Meir. I transmitted a mobile number to your cell phone. It would prove efficacious if you would turn your phone on and confirm its receipt."

Shavlev grabbed his mobile from his pocket and turned it on. The radio was annoying enough without being interrupted by a cell phone. Seventeen seconds later, it acquired the network. "Got the number."

"My instructions are specific; they must be followed without deviation. Do not proceed until I finish and communicate final authorization, do you understand, Captain?"

"Affirmative, listen and don't act until cleared."

"Excellent. Dial the number just transmitted to your mobile. When it answers you will hear a single DTMF tone comprising the frequencies 1336 and 770 hertz. Wait at least two seconds, no less, and key in 0-8-1-9. Repeat 0-8-1-9."

"Copy, 0-8-1-9.

"You'll then hear two combined frequencies; 1336 and 770 hertz, repeated four times. That's four separate #5 keypad tones, Captain, which will indicate the loop has been deactivated. Repeat instructions, over."

"Call the number, when it answers, a single #5 keypad tone will sound. Wait two seconds, key in 0-8-1-9. Four #5 keypad tones will then sound which confirms the loop has been deactivated and we're ready to rumble."

"I suppose that's one way to put it, Captain, any other questions?"

"One."

"Which is?"

"There is a wire bridging the primary timer to the secondary timer, and a wire from the secondary timer to the launch tube. We stop the primary timer and the secondary will come to life faster than Lazarus."

"And you know this because?"

"I know the playing field I'm on—this guy is good. There won't be a dummy secondary, and he won't allow one passcode to defeat his system."

"While I understand your visceral response, Captain, I must base my determination on observable facts. We have the passcode to shut the system down, and the secondary timer is part of that system. If we don't act on available information, the alternative is, in less than sixty seconds, we will have launch. We'll do it my way unless you have an alternative that can be immediately implemented."

Entering the numbers Dr. Ben-Meir had transmitted, Gurion snorted in a short breath and hit *Talk*. Parabolic microphones picked up the cell's ringing while amplifiers routed the ring tones to speakers as hundreds of ears strained to listen. On the fourth ring the call answered with a clear tone.

"1,001–1,002."

He depressed 0-8-1-9. Silence assaulted every ear, milliseconds took on the weight of hours, then four crisp tones echoed from Yerushaláyim to Lod.

"Eban."

"Go."

"Disconnect wires on the smallest Arab's mobile. I need to watch the timers, and then I'll come around," Gurion instructed.

"Copy, pulling the connector in 3-2-1. The mobile's disconnected."

"Maybe geniuses know something after all. Primary's timer's stopped, secondary is stationary. Be right there." Grasping the chromium-steel bolt cutter and the tripod high-intensity laser beam he circled the catwalk.

While he made his way to the other side, the secondary timer's integrated circuit triggered an access delay, keeping its display stationary for thirty, two-second cycles. At the end of sixty seconds, with Shavlev and Bar-On freeing hostages, the quartz clock flashed 05:00 three times then initiated countdown.

Leaning over Khalil, Eban pulled the connecter from Elizabeth's mobile.

Handing the cutters to Eban, Gurion extended the laser beam's tripod legs then removed the tabs exposing its adhesive feet. He placed the device on the inside edge of the catwalk next to the spire and turned it on. The laser beam waited to be remotely activated while its self-leveling mechanism pointed ninety degrees above the horizon.

Eban snugged the cutters on the handcuff chain. With two forceful snapping motions, one on each side of the hardened steel chain, Elizabeth's right wrist was freed. Jockeying for position, he made two more snapping cuts, releasing her remaining wrist from its confinement.

Elizabeth stared at her emancipator. The duct tape remained. She made no move for it.

Eban looked into Elizabeth's eyes, he grabbed one end of the duct tape. "This is going to hurt, you ready?"

She nodded, bracing herself.

He yanked.

Tears welled in Elizabeth's eyes, running down swollen cheeks; no words escaped.

"Anything I missed that keeps Yanshuf from extracting you?"

Nodding her head no she remained silent.

"Yanshuf, this is Sergeant Major Bar-On. Need a rescue stretcher, over."

"Sergeant Major, this is Lieutenant Katz, Yanshuf. Upper tower railing makes stretcher too dangerous for extraction. You bring a rescue harness in your equipment?"

"Haven't done triage; injuries may increase unless we use stretcher, Lieutenant."

"Sergeant Major, there's no discussion—better injured than left on the catwalk."

Eban's jaw tensed. "Yes sir." He grabbed the harness from his bag and placed it over Elizabeth's upper body, securing straps with camlock buckles between her legs. "Yanshuf, where's our line?"

A woman's head and upper torso leaned out the side of the helicopter guiding the rope's rapid descent toward the catwalk while the helo steadied itself over the tower. As it closed in on Eban, it slowed its descent the last eighteen inches.

The rope stopped. He snapped the carabiner into the harness ring. "Slowly lift, avoid top rail," Eban said. Elizabeth rose toward the helo. When she had cleared the upper railing, the helo pulley's rpms screamed as they increased their speed, wrenching her upward. Elizabeth shot toward the cabin doorway.

Khalil was freed and in the Owl's cabin fifty-seven seconds later.

"Yanshuf, remaining hostage has extensive arm injury. Can't get rescue harness on, send the rescue stretcher down," Gurion said.

"Sergeant Major, this is Lieutenant Katz. I repeat, the rescue stretcher is too dangerous. You will secure hostage in the harness."

"Lieutenant Katz, this Captain Shavlev. I just told you the rescue harness won't work. Deploy the rescue stretcher."

"On its way, Captain."

He pulled the connecter from Aadil's phone. The twenty-four inch-long cutter handles provided scant leverage to bite through the hardened leg-iron chains. Uncoiling power within Gurion wouldn't be denied as he overcame each steel link. Secured in the rescue stretcher the hostage rose to the helo as Gurion watched. He radioed, "Owl, redeploy rope when stretcher is on board."

"Why do we need the rope?" Eban said.

"You're going, I need room to work."

The rope shot back down, its end coiling a few inches on the catwalk.

Eban searched Gurion's eyes: duty over friendship, a reality battle demanded from warriors; ingrained discipline kicked in. Eban seized the rope and attached an ascender tied into a two foot rope chest high. Yanking hard, he set its locking mechanism then looped it around his chest and attached it onto itself. Fastening a foot-loop sling just below ankle level, he inserted his right foot and jammed it down with his weight—it held.

Looking at his friend, Gurion barked into his lavalier, "Retract the line." Lifting its wings Owl reeled the rope into its cabin, rising slowly at first, then gathering speed racing into the morning sky, heading for Hadassah.

Returning to Addison, Gurion heard the General.

"Night Bird, position over the tower, lower rope."

"Copy, minaret acquired, deploying the rope."

Looking down at the timers, Gurion saw the secondary timer was active at 3:28 and counting. "General, is doctor genius looking at the secondary timer?"

"This is Abigail Ben-Meir, Captain. I'm looking at the wire map. We've located two inline nine-volt batteries, a primary and a backup, in the launch tube beneath the fireworks shell. It appears its power activated when the primary timer mechanically initiated the secondary timer."

"So the batteries didn't show up on scans?"

"They did not."

"Of course, you need power to spark an electrical igniter, which isn't news; even if we could disconnect the first battery, the second would launch the fireworks shell." As Gurion talked, he bent over the American's nearly comatose form and placed the chromium-steel cutter on his right handcuff chain. Snap . . . Snap!

"Captain, are you releasing the hostage?" General Oz asked while subordinates scrambled for a camera angle to zoom in on his specific actions, as Gurion's back blocked their view.

He moved to the other handcuff.

"Gurion, abort the mission, we're out of time."

"I came for an American and don't plan on staying long."

"Shavlev, look at the timer."

"Words only delay." Gurion leaned over Addison's left wrist. Snap . . . Snap!

"Captain, this is Dr. Ben-Meir. Look at the secondary timer."

He looked down; its display read 2:54. "Yeah, I can see it better than you."

"When the timer reaches two minutes, there's not enough time to extract. Captain, we're seconds from two minutes to launch."

"What do you mean launch?"

"Shavlev, this is Oz. Abort, repeat, abort the rescue."

Gurion ignored his commander.

"Don't you ignore me, Shavlev. This is the same shit you always pull—not this time. The stakes are too high; it's out of my hands. You will not imperil Yerushaláyim to be a hero. Gurion—acknowledge—Gurion!"

Hitting transmit, the General broadcast: "This is General Oz. All troops in proximity of Migdal David minaret fall back 1,000 feet, NOW! Leave any equipment you can't carry. This is your only warning." Turning to Weiss, he said, "Initiate the spire laser."

"Laser is activated sir."

Flying 18,000 feet above sea level toward Yerushaláyim at one hundred and eight miles per hour, Zik lifted its nose twenty degrees above the horizon, preparing to release its payload.

A computer voice overrode communications, broadcasting system-wide. "TARGET HAS BEEN ACQUIRED. MARK TWO MINUTES TO LAUNCH."

"Gurion, the firing sequence has been initiated. Abort the rescue. Evacuate now."

"What in hell is coming at me, General?"

"There's no time, Captain. Night Bird, where's that line?"

"This is Night Bird. The line is deployed and on the catwalk, General."

"MARK ONE MINUTE FIFTY SECONDS TO LAUNCH."

"Shavlev, extract NOW!"

Gurion yanked his knife from its sheath, nosing its razor-sharp tip into the vest beside the timers. A thin line of blood arose from Addison's chest as the nearly diaphanous polymer cut too easily. He lifted both timers as one; ensuring the bridging wire held. Setting both timers down gently, Gurion made sure the connection to the launch tube remained intact.

"MARK ONE MINUTES FORTY SECONDS TO LAUNCH."

He spread the American's legs; the sound of bones snapping assailed his ears. Grabbing under his arms he pulled the American clear of the launch assembly. Gurion straightened his back, lifting the hostage to a standing position. He swung him around, back to the spire. "AMERICA, OPEN EYES!"

Gurion jammed his knee just above Addison's groin, pinning his limp body to the spire. His left hand pushed Addison's torso against the spire. Pulling back his right hand, he unleashed its fury, slapping Addison's damaged face. Addison's head snapped against the spire.

Needles of pain stabbed Gurion's hand.

"MARK ONE MINUTES THIRTY SECONDS TO LAUNCH."

Addison moaned; his head jerked to the side. Putting pressure on his legs, Addison winced, semiconsciously shifting his weight to his right leg as he pushed against the pressure on his lower abdomen and chest, standing enough for Gurion to release his knee.

Addison weakly groaned, "Get out—leave me." The raw pain every syllable demanded unbearable.

"We're going together, America." Gurion hoisted Addison over his shoulder. Turning toward the waiting helo, he drove his legs for the rope.

"MARK ONE MINUTES TWENTY SECONDS TO LAUNCH."

Reaching the rope, Gurion shouldered Addison into a standing position against the spire, screaming, "STAY!"

Body trembling, leaning against the spire, Addison stayed.

Reaching into his cargo pocket, Gurion withdrew two locking ascenders attached to loops. He slammed one on the rope at shoulder height, yanking to lock it in position. He set the second near his foot. He pulled a static line with a carabiner attached to each end from his other cargo pocket. Grabbing and hugging Addison, he pivoted and jammed his boot into the lower ascender loop—it held. He pulled Addison between his body and the helo rope. He clipped one of the static line's carabiner to the upper ascender loop, whipping the rope around his back and securing it under their armpits before snapping it back into the ascender loop. He leaned back, testing its hold. Before he could lift his arm to signal, Night Bird began rising. Wrapping his forearm in the upper loop he awaited the jerk he knew would hammer him with the inertial stress of lift when both their weights and upward velocity attempted to pull him off the rope as Night Bird rose.

"Mark one minute ten seconds to launch."

"Hold on, Shavlev," Captain Sagal said. "Got a missile coming our way I'd rather not meet."

Three thousand horses shrieked their way from the tower in a combat take-off. Night Bird banked away from the Old City walls, rising at a sixty-degree angle. The main rotor's four blades screamed, accelerating rpms thrashed the suspended hitchhikers in a maelstrom of wind and speed as g-forces tore at Gurion's hands and fingers, clawing to separate them from their salvation. Fighting mind-numbing agony tearing at his hands and arms, Gurion entered a zone where the violence's demand for release was silenced.

"Mark one minute to launch."

Night Bird flew for her life. Hatchet's initial explosion would instantaneously send unimaginable pressure waves radiating outward, immediately followed by a vacuum that would pull anything flying within 500 feet into its destructive vortex.

"Mark 30 seconds to launch."

"Mark 15 seconds to launch."

One half of one second after hitting 31°30'0" N latitude by 34°45'0" E longitude, Hatchet, released from its flying taxi, roused from slumber, its Alliant solid-fuel rocket motor roared to life.

Grabbing hold of the morning sky and catapulting from 108 mph to 989.5 mph, Hatchet's nose lifted, twenty degrees from the thrust of its rocket motor, on its way to a rendezvous with Migdal David, 1600 feet shy of the Temple Mount.

Rocket fuel burned for three seconds, which gained Hatchet an additional 1800 feet of altitude. Gravity exerted its pull on the speeding missile as its nose was drawn earthward, slowing to 490 miles per hour. Its nose dipped to ninety degrees below horizontal as it fell 9,000 feet over the next five seconds. Gravity increased its velocity as photo diodes in Hatchet's nose picked up the high-intensity laser beam Shavlev had left on the spire. At 2,634 feet above sea level, Hatchet detonated, heating the tower to 5,400° Fahrenheit within three one hundreds of a second. The fireworks shell, filled with anthrax and its gunpowder lifting charge, along with the catwalk and the top two thirds of Muhammad Pasha's minaret were instantaneously vaporized as its rubble was reduced to $^{1}/_{205}{}^{th}$ its original mass in less than one second.

The hemorrhaging rotors, 1,700 feet from where the tower had stood for hundreds of years, were drowned out by the cacophonous immolation of the vanquished minaret as the helo sped toward Hadassah. Looking at the American, a smile passed Gurion's lips as their lifeline completed its upward journey into Night Bird.

CHAPTER

66

Saturday 22 March 2008, 0653 hours

HaMossad leModi'in uleTafkidim Meyuchadim (Mossad) Headquarters Office of Deputy Director Yonaton Aharoni, Special Operations Division (Metsada) North Tel Aviv

Yonaton Aharoni gazed around the oval conference table at his subordinates in their ergonomic chairs. On his orders, black coffee, scalding and plentiful, was poured into any empty cup by aides. It did its job; the alpha assemblage was ready to chew spikes. Yonaton stood and waited for silence, which seemed easier than demanding his strong-willed subordinates shut up and listen. "Sorry for the early wake-up, but things are coming to a head, so you get coffee—"

"That's what we've been here an hour for?"

"It worked. Coming through the door everyone's ass was dragging. Instead of a full night's sleep you get my personal blend of java and the opportunity to earn some of the shekels taxpayers keep paying you. Now pay attention, what follows is important.

"Since Yisra'el's founding, enemies never tire of challenging our existence. While that ensures job security, this time it's different, we've all been briefed on the anthrax. The latest intel, and by latest I mean I was pulled from a good night's sleep this morning, is that the anthrax Shabak has been scouring the country for surfaced this morning in Migdal David. Less than ten minute before I stepped into this room I received information, not yet verified, that it was just incinerated and no, I don't know any of the details. As might be expected, due to circumstances and time frame involved, information is sketchy but we'll hear through channels as Yerushaláyim works through crisis mode. With that in mind, we need to focus. If the anthrax surfaced and was incinerated it only adds urgency to our tasks. This briefing is to get you up to speed on recent events, so you can then initiate deep-cover action."

Conversation stopped, every ear seizing on the mention of deep-cover action.

"I thought that might get your attention. This morning, Ya'Ma'M snipers and magavnikim were at Migdal David where PMIJ terrorists, according to the information filtering down, seized the minaret. Boots on the ground reported four hostages including one American consular officer."

"Yonaton, how in hell did they get their hands on an American? Diplomatic Security is all over their people."

"Here's news, DS is close-mouthed. Especially since a ransom was involved and the grief Americans dish out when we bargain with mehablim. Fun thing is, they walked into a trap and lost a briefcase of money. This morning, Keane Bodine, DS's mission agent in charge, called my home. He wasted a half hour of my time and, being awoken at 0400 hours to listen to his obfuscatory crap, I was not in my happy place. I explained the finer details of what existence could be if Mossad shut down on them, because it won't be the Americans going in to get their guy if he needs getting—"

"Won't be us either. It's—"

"Hével at 4:00 in the morning he didn't know it's Ya'Ma'M and I wasn't about to tell him so he'd wake somebody else up. Besides, I didn't tell him Mossad would go in," Yonaton said, a grin flashing across his face. "Bottom line is the details are still playing out. All I could get out of Bodine was that the American was assigned to their mission in Tel Aviv but hadn't officially reported for duty. Which we already knew since it was Shabak's undercover who escorted him when he first arrived in country."

"Maybe the Americans will eventually realize we're both on the same side," Hével Eshkol said.

"Jonathan Pollard would welcome that epiphany," Yoel Ben-Zvi said.

"Let's get back on track. I had to pull a couple of teeth, but Bodine finally coughed up they went in with a five million dollar ransom which he claimed was pushed on him. There's more to it than I heard, but Bodine wasn't dispensing information; he was trying to get it. Who knows, Palestinians could have surprised the Americans and delivered the hostage unscathed since their different factions get enough money without kidnapping American State Department people."

"So, all the Americans had to do was go to the migdal and collect him," Yoel Ben Zvi said. Laughter erupted.

"How'd they get into the migdal complex? The place is crawling with our guys, everyone from Border Police to IDF. Hell, Kishle Police Station is by the Jaffa gate."

"Who knows, they got inside the migdal exhibition hall before any guardians of the Old City could get a sufficient presence to prevent access. They didn't advertise their destination or stop for directions. Besides, who breaks into the Old City?"

"You mean buck is being passed from one group to the other," Boas said.

"Way it looks to me."

"Okay, so the tower is involved and Ya'Ma'M gets to take out their aggression by neutralizing them. This isn't Mossad's operation. What's our involvement, Yonaton?"

"Matter of addition; one, the tower looks to be the target, two, it's too bold a move just to beat tourists for the morning tour, three, looks as if they were armed for battle and running a plan none of the local jihadists have the brains or funds to execute, and four we all are aware of the war games our neighbors are conducting on every border. Half the IDF's there along with most of the reservists. Rumor is after a successful launch of the anthrax and the confusion it would unleash, our neighbors planned on paying us a visit."

"Are they out of their minds? Everyone knows our firepower. Besides, Yonaton, the Old City is a high-value asset. PMIJ knows we'll defend it," Sarai said.

"Yeah, why would PMIJ want to suffer the losses required to take Migdal David?" Boas asked.

Yonaton waited to see who would jump in; no voice met the question.

"Come on, people, stay with me; think, Migdal David is within 1600 feet of the Temple Mount. It's far enough away that if PMIJ launched a mortar shell from the minaret catwalk the Temple Mount would be safe—"

"But since it's in the Old City near the Muslim's Noble Sanctuary, every Arab government would jump on the wagon if it were moving."

"Now you're thinking, especially if mutual action had been planned. Anyone remember the phrase casus belli from Latin class?"

"I remember a little, boss; means a provoking event."

"Close, Sabra. It means an event provoking war, in this case a pretext for war. So while events unfold at the migdal, our troops, on the border are a pledge to our enemies. Intelligence reports show none of the opposing combatants are first-line troops. They're sacrificial lambs, though I doubt they were told of their fate. Anthrax is fired above Yerushaláyim to infect the majority of our population in initial and collateral damage. Hospitals and clinics would be overwhelmed by massive causalities—"

Bringing the side of his fist down on the table, Hével Eshkol shouted, "The bastards were all immunized. The aerosol vaccinations the Russians brought in. A nozzle turned up with anthrax vaccine on it, and tests of a couple of Shabak undercover operatives receiving the vaccination showed the Palestinian no longer needed to worry about measles, mumps, rubella, or anthrax. Which set off the search for anthrax that evidently surfaced this morning."

The Director picked up where he left off. "War Games turn serious when enemy troops attack our positions on the border while word speeds to every enemy government in the Middle East where first-line troops are waiting. All that must be alleged is casus belli: their Noble Sanctuary has been attacked. No one will stop to check its veracity with the resulting chaos an atmospheric dispersal of anthrax in Yerushaláyim would bring. Besides, they could doctor a video of the Temple Mount showing anything they want, and El-Hamabi would do a running loop of it around the world, no questions asked. By the time the United States got through debating whether to assist or not, it would be too late. Our job—your sole responsibility—is to activate all deep contacts and provide them with specific high-value targets to neutralize. When neutralized, these targets will be prevented from bringing other countries with grievances against Eretz Yisra'el into an action that could have catastrophic results. We know the operatives, and those up the food chain they are assigned to contact. We break the chain then let the IDF and IAF take care of the border."

Yonaton had seven file folders on the desk before him. "I have a file for each of you with specific targets that must be neutralized. The list has been divided so that none of our operatives has more than one target. Even so, there may be losses. Completion is not negotiable; targets will be neutralized the first time out. And by that I mean every name on the list will be eliminated, no exceptions. Don't ask for clarification or explanation; the lists have been carefully prepared. I will hand you your file on your way out."

The room was silent; each mind focused. Steps taken in the next minutes would be scrutinized by every half-informed national leader with access to Yisra'el's internal affairs. "There's no way to contain the edges on this action. That's what the bosses in the corner offices have jobs for. Two final things," the Deputy Director said. "One, no one leaves this building until final word is received that all field operatives have neutralized their targets and been extracted, and that means their corpse if necessary. Two, my door is open until this is concluded. Got a question, I want to hear it. We each know what the next few hours mean. Now get out of my sight."

Grabbing their files, every Agent In Charge sped for their offices. Support personnel were geared up and ready for the coming storm, having been awakened along with their bosses.

Calls and coded messages went out on secure lines. Radio stations began playing golden-oldies. Interspersed among the requests, Breindel and Zemirah dedicated songs to Herschel and Ebril. Few ears paid attention. The ones who did knew what to do.

In the following twenty-seven hours, sixty-four men and women from fifteen sovereign nations took their final breaths.

Tragic automobile accidents, heart attacks where the tiny dot of a needle's insertion was so expertly hidden it could not be detected even by those with the expertise to notice. Where air was not injected cyanide proved equally utilitarian. Three pacemakers were bombarded by electromagnetic pulse generators, causing the pacemakers to oscillate, sending weakened hearts into ventricular fibrillation and death.

One Iranian citizen, too close to a blast at an outdoor café, succumbed to injuries when an Assistant Deputy Foreign Minister and two body guards were surprised by C-4 hidden under a table where they took sweet tea every morning on their way to the Guardian Council.

No one on Yonaton Aharoni's lists lived to see 0930 hours the following day.

Mission-level Israeli diplomats contacted counterparts in every Western Nation by secure satellite link. Assurances given were verified by a live feed from the Temple Mount showing The Dome of the Rock sitting in all its golden glory.

CHAPTER

67

Saturday 22 March 2008, 0659 hours

Lod Command & Control, Lod Airbase

Sagiv Oz turned to his executive officer, "Weiss!"

"Yes, General."

"Get Gabriel Aran, Husmayad al Bana, and Yeghia Boodakian."

"Don't know if they can be reached by phone due to the—"

"Phone, did I say phone? I said to get. Have them all here within thirty minutes or you won't like your next assignment."

"What if they're busy? You know those three—"

"You want to start packing for the Negev, Major? I only accept yes then watch your dust as you carry out my order. You have twenty-nine and a half minutes; it's a bad idea to waste more time."

"On it General, leaving now."

"How did you make Major? You can't go three places at once."

"Sir, you just told me—"

"Subordinates, Major, even you have subordinates but make sure they listen better than you. Go, go, go, but stay here to coordinate."

"Got it sir, be right back, got men to bring in."

CHAPTER

68

Saturday 22 March 2008, 1005 hours

Kishle Police Station
Old City Yerushaláyim

Opening the conference room door and stepping inside the room, briefcase in hand, Major Weiss snapped to attention as he kept the door open with the back of his left heel. He looked at the conference table holding the three adversaries: Gabriel Aran, Israeli Antiquities Authority, Deputy Director of Archaeology Yerushaláyim District; Husmayad al Bana, Muslim Waqf Religious Authority, Temple Mount Chief Archaeologist; and Yeghia Boodakian, Armenian Orthodox Israel Antiquities Archaeologist in Residence, Jerusalem. Each sat as far from one another as possible, feigning disinterest as Chanan Weiss bellowed, "Brigadier General Sagiv Oz."

Marching into the conference room, Sagiv Oz relied on military bearing hardened from thirty-five years of service for the ordeal ahead. If it were up to him he'd just build the damn thing and be done with it. But it wasn't, so he confronted a ruin that must be put back together with the cooperation of three men who hated each other.

Each of the antagonists watched one another and General Oz for the boundaries of the game each sensed they were about to play.

Sagiv Oz came to a halt beside the only unoccupied chair. Its appearance seemed ordinary, but equipped with sophisticated electronics, it gave the advantage required, recording even whispers, and was built to provide General Oz authority of stature when seated next to taller men. He sat. Weiss took a seat by the entrance after conspicuously setting down his briefcase then closing and locking the door.

Looking over the untouched teas, halawa, and sweet cakes on the table, General Oz said, "Honored guests, I had hoped the refreshments would be pleasing, considering the brief period for their preparation and regrettable circumstances that occasioned our meeting. Before proceeding, all information today is classified. Revealing any part of it to those without clearance will result in sanctions, from permanent expulsion to trial and possible incarceration."

"Your thugs show up and allow me the opportunity to come with them as my only choice and now you march in and speak of refreshments and prison," Husmayad al Bana said.

"The closing and locking of our sacred sites, which seems to be the rule as of late, is a troubling concern, General," Yeghia Boodakian said. "Not to mention the clandestine manner of my transportation to this meeting, most concerning indeed for interfaith relations."

"Gabriel, does Israeli Antiquities want to weigh in?"

"Sagiv, we have enjoyed the best of relationships—"

"So Jews stick together to oppress everyone else what else is new?"

"Husmayad, if you'll allow me to finish. The cacophonous blast this morning has, I would peradventure, something to do with today's events. Since I don't know what happened, I am ready to hear Sagiv's words."

"Each will understand the reasons for today's meeting, and then all questions will be answered. Is that acceptable?"

"Barely."

"Good, we agree. Nightly lockdowns of the last several days from 9:00 P.M. until 5:30 A.M. were implemented when evidence was uncovered that a bioweapon was in proximity to the Old City.

This morning's specific lockdown was the result of a terrorist attack to deliver that bioweapon to the Migdal David minaret for detonation. You have my assurance that none of these were the choice of the Yisraeli government. Even with our differences in the past, Yerushaláyim's future, for each of us, was at stake. Your choice is whether you wish those you represent to have a voice as we move forward."

The men at the table remained silent.

"This is the moment to act in inter-faith cooperation for the good of Yerushaláyim. If anyone chooses not to they will be confined to their residences under armed guard until all is completed. I know my words appear harsh. If there were time, those more skilled with words would speak them, but time is not a friend."

"Few things are."

"Husmayad, do you wish to leave without hearing my words?"

"Do I forbid words?"

"Portions of the Old City remain cordoned off because of this morning's attack by the Palestine Mujahideen Islamic Jihad terror group. The blast heard was a single ordinance imploding a bioweapon aimed at the Jewish heart of Yisra'el. As a result of the implosion, the migdal minaret was destroyed, with collateral damage sustained by buildings within a five-hundred-foot radius of the minaret. As I speak, scaffolding is being collected for the migdal, which will be erected then tarped, concealing activity inside from surveillance. We will rebuild the migdal and restore the surrounding areas within a thirty-day period, and yes, I said thirty days. To accomplish this we need master stonemasons, welders, carpenters, and other trained specialists."

"Israel has such skills. Why call on the Waqf?"

"The migdal minaret was built by Muhammad Pasha. It has changed hands many times. Yesterday it held a museum, a gathering place to be celebrated by all: Jew, Christian, and Muslim. As overseers of this ancient site, Muslim history was preserved and honored by its caretakers. It is for this site, as well as other more important ones, that tourists come to Yisra'el; American dollars, German euros, Chinese yuans, and Japanese yens do not end in Jewish pockets alone. The migdal is a part of our identity. Those visiting are good for all. If we Jews rebuild, there will be accusations that the historical significance of the site was supplanted by Jewish influence. By including all three major faiths, all will know it was built with the integrity of its historical roots. Each of you has been brought here because you represent your communities and have the authority and expertise to commit to this project. Construction must begin within forty-eight hours, when, I am told, the site will be cleared, foundation dug, and scaffolding complete."

"I don't need to hear more, Sagiv. Israeli Antiquities Authority is in."

"Yeghia?"

"Count the Armenian Orthodox Israel Antiquities in, General."

"Husmayad?"

"Who will pay for this great undertaking?"

"A surprising number of stones needed were not destroyed. Blasted to hell and back, but not damaged beyond salvage. Others, outside the wall, can be claimed, and if needed Arab and Jewish stonemasons are skilled and can replicate any additional stones needed."

"But who will fund the workers? Skilled labor does not come without its costs."

"Each group will pay its workers."

"I cannot commit money that is not mine."

"Then you will be escorted back to your residence under guard until the construction is completed within the month. You are here because you have the authority to commit everything needed. If you choose not to participate, then, due to the trying times, you cannot be permitted to foment trouble while reconstruction is under way."

"You cannot incarcerate a legal citizen of Israel without trial."

Sagiv Oz smiled. He turned his head to the entrance. "Major."

"Yes General."

"Is transportation for Husmayad ready?"

"As per your instructions sir."

"Wait. For such a worthy cause, I might find benevolence somewhere."

"Be mindful, Husmayad, we live in a delicate balance. Should a change of heart come during construction, the results may not be to your pleasing. If the world sees Yisra'el, especially Yerushaláyim, as unsafe, it could take years to repair damage that will visit us all."

"Then who am I to burden others with such calamity; I choose to participate. But one question occurs to me. During this time, how will my people get to the Noble Sanctuary as well as worshippers to al-Aqsa Mosque?"

"The Temple Mount was not involved in the migdal's destruction. All Waqf authorities and Muslim worshippers will be allowed normal unrestrained access. The area around the construction zone will be cordoned off as will supply routes. To ensure safety we will deploy sufficient numbers of magavnikim to ensure no one wanders into dangerous areas but no one, as I said, will be denied access to normal sites away from the areas of reconstruction. Major Weiss will brief you on all specifics as well as provide maps so all will know which areas are open. If difficulties arise he will speak for me, but if any matter cannot be resolved, you will have access to me. All must work together. Are there questions?"

No one spoke.

Pushing back from the table, the General got up leaving the room through a door hidden behind a curtain. Major Weiss approached the three adversaries. Placing his briefcase on the table he sat in the General's chair, waiting until all attention was upon him. "Gentlemen, you have twenty-four hours to put your teams together. I understand our time frame seems impossible, but each of you, being a man of god, can petition for divine assistance, yes? Each team will have one chief supervisor and consist of five hundred workers. I will not specify the exact numbers from each trade, but common sense tells you our greatest need is stonemasons. I want the name of each chief supervisor and a face-to-face meeting as soon as they're chosen, no later than twenty-four hours from now. Everything will go through these chief supervisors so that your oversight can be committed to ensure all work is done to world-class standards. A word of caution: Select master builders; this project is not for training. We have an extensive picture library along with thousands of drawings of the migdal from every angle, both interior and exterior, as it's one of the most recorded sites in Yerushaláyim. When building has been completed, I don't want

General Oz, or any of you, to be able to tell where the existing walls and buildings join what has been rebuilt."

"So we're keeping this from the world?"

"My no Gabriel, how could that last? The scaffolding curtain is to limit gawkers without drawing attention to our task and to allow the workers to concentrate on their responsibilities without sightseers underfoot. That said there won't be a gala reopening.

What we end with will respect the ancient architecture. All stones, after all, are ancient. It is merely our placing them back together that will be recent, much in the spirit of the Old City itself after over three millennia of conquests and rebuilding. Our concern is authenticity, and to that end . . ." Chanan opened his briefcase and removed four thick folders then placed the briefcase on the floor. He passed a folder to each of the men, keeping one for himself. Opening his folder, he fanned its contents in front of him. "These pictures," he said, lifting several at random, "and measured diagrams you'll find in your folders, will give workers all they need. Study them. If you require additional photographs or drawings, ask. Each of you brings a lifetime of experience in archaeology, especially the archaeology of Yerushaláyim. Your participation will ensure the integrity of all that is done."

'The General said he would be available. How is this to be accomplished?"

"Well, Yeghia, I suppose if we come to an impasse, then I would contact him, but let me assure you, if you need to speak with the General, contact will be made. I trust all will find I am most agreeable to work with, but I have to caution: No work stoppages or strikes will be allowed and there will be a Jewish security presence everywhere. I know worker unrest sometimes arises, but anything that stops or impedes this work cannot be tolerated. All must be clear on that."

"How are we to contact you?" Husmayad said.

"My number is on my card stapled inside the front cover of each folder. I will also be on site daily, except *Shabbat*. If there are no other questions . . ." Chanan looked from face to face.

"If anthrax, as I have heard, was used then is rebuilding in this short of time wisdom?"

"Husmayad, while we all have been waiting for this meeting, biological experts have conducted a thorough search of the entire area followed by a second team that also scanned the area. Each team was equipped with sophisticated detection equipment that could detect trace elements down to parts per million. Neither team found evidence of biological weapons present; workers will be safe. But if you desire to walk around the migdal minaret I have been authorized to take you there immediately."

"Oh no, we will trust your word, right Yeghia and Gabriel?" Husmayad al Bana said.

"Please take your folder and follow me; transportation is waiting. We have a tower to rebuild."

Fifteen hundred Jewish, Arab, and Christian master craftsmen, equipment operators, and laborers were assembled as two hundred fifty robust IDF Reserves were reassigned from the borders for the demanding work of gathering chaotically scattered stones in the limited confines of the migdal. They cleared and sorted the snarled and broken stones, reclaiming all that could be dressed for use. Each had been promised two days at Ein Bokek by the Dead Sea where the hot springs, hotels, and restaurants would provide a soothing reward for their arduous work.

When the clearing was finished, two leviathans rising from sleep, purpose in their giant buckets, began filling the uneven chasm created by the *Hatchet.* Rubble from the blast joined large boulders brought by giant dump trucks in disregard of weight limits on Khativat Etsyoni and Gan David. Plywood, covered with thick steel plates, protected vulnerable cobblestones. Surveyors with transits and levels directed the placement of each bucket. The giant machines, working with raw power, moved boulders like marbles while they added jagged rock fill then retreated as twin behemoth hydraulic hammers began pounding, pounding, pounding boulders and rock fill, defeating empty spaces, battering crevices into submission.

Thirty-six hours in, scaffolding grew on itself, embracing the sky above Gan David. It was covered by tarps to surround work that all knew was taking place but none could mention, as if an injury in the family must be healed before it could be acknowledged, the pain too deep to be shared.

Then the workers, locust-like, descended in seeming confusion, organized anarchy orchestrated by chief supervisors who understood order in the chaos and watched, pleased, as ancient walls climbed ever upward, blending, interweaving seamlessly, with walls, walkways, and buildings that had endured their fiery trial unscathed.

Two days shy of four weeks, tarps began to be removed from the east and west ends of construction; scaffolding soon followed. The migdal brokered no ceremonies marking the occasion, but hearts that saw truth differently rejoiced.

The day the final tarp was removed, the final standards, ledgers, and transoms disassembled, Gabriel Aran, Husmayad al Bana, and Yeghia Boodakian each received an anonymous gift: a bottle of Muscat Alexandria from Sagiv Oz. Knowing Husmayad could not drink it, but would anyway, somehow pleased the General. Certain his last battle as a warrior had been fought and won pleased him more.

CHAPTER

69

Sunday 23 March 2008

Ma'aleh Adumim, Judea

Just past one A.M., unrelenting buzzing broke into Hafiz's sleep. Lying on the top of the blankets, he turned the clock's alarm off while his body struggled to find the rest he'd just given it. Stretching and yawning, he sat up and shook his head, trying to dispel the sluggishness. Going to the bathroom, he left the lights off while he splashed cold water on his face. The water, failing to invigorate, merely irritated him. He grabbed a towel and roughly dried himself.

Back in the bedroom he put on his shoes and retrieved his weapons from the nightstand. Going to the kitchen, he flipped on the espresso machine, put a cup under the spout, and punched up a triple espresso. Within minutes the steaming mix was scalding its way down his throat, administering sufficient caffeine to begin dispelling weariness he knew must be defeated.

A quick glance in the fridge reminded him he had forgotten to pick up groceries; the caffeine kicking in would have to do. Leaving the lights out—no telling who was watching—he grabbed his coat and gloves for the cold trip ahead and made his way to the garage. Inside the garage his Griso motorcycle awaited. Hafiz kept his tank topped-off, with extra plates in the saddlebags. He figured the motorcycle had been bugged, but scanning it would be a waste of time. *Let them track me; by the morning it won't matter.* After double-checking everything needed was stowed on board and both weapons were secured, he opened the garage's side door and pushed the motorcycle outside and down the road away from his place before firing it up.

Lilith, shrouded in black, silently awaited Hafiz. When she saw her nemesis stealthily rolling his motorcycle to the road she went to the garage and her cycle. She turned on the modified RFID locator between her handlebars and a blinking amber light on its illuminated map pinpointed Hafiz's position. A Galil Mar assault rifle with its Mepor 21 reflex sight was concealed on the side of her motorcycle along with sufficient ammunition in the motorcycle's saddlebags for tonight's battle. Her skin, what could be seen of it through the dark camouflage of a Ninja, was gothically radiant.

Heading east onto Highway 1, Hafiz made for Beit HaArava Junction. The cycle's throaty roar, announcing ownership of the road, sent a surge of adrenaline through him. At the junction he turned onto Route 90 and then onto Route 449.

Lilith followed far enough behind to avoid being seen but easily kept him in the crosshairs of her locator.

Coming to a stop at the Allenby Border Terminal, Hafiz pulled out his papers. While the Border Policeman checked them, Hafiz removed a Jordanian plate from his bag and attached it to the back of the cycle.

"Always the covert trips with you Shabak types. Where's it going to be tonight?"

"You know I can't tell you that."

"Have anything to do with the incident in the Old City?"

"Doesn't everything now?"

"Are you expecting to come back through here?"

"It wouldn't surprise me."

"Everything looks fine. Have a pleasant morning," the Border Guard said, handing Hafiz his papers.

"You as well," Hafiz responded, placing them in a side bag and removing other papers the Jordanians would find more acceptable. He sped toward the Jordanian checkpoint.

By the time Hafiz paid the Jordanian passage tax, the Israeli Border Officer had phoned his commander, who in turn called Commander Ramot to report Hafiz's position.

Heading northeast, Hafiz made his way toward his target. It was now time to see if Nuri carried within the habits of Nur-Rami; two futures depended on it.

Closing in on his destination fifty miles south of the Dead Sea, Hafiz pulled off the highway in territory once belonging to the ancient Edomites. Shutting down the guttural roar of his cycle, he coasted behind a dense cluster of desert shrubs. After looking around, he checked his weapons and chambered a round in each before placing them back in their holsters. He looked at his watch in the starry pre-dawn hour—0432 hours. *Good, time is still a friend.* He proceeded toward the *al-Siq*.

In their teenage years they had come to Petra whenever their world threatened to close in on them. Hafiz suspected father knew, but he never questioned them upon their return from the day-long trip. Serenely and eloquently, the rock carvings whispered to them, demanding they pause as they saw how life could be transcended by the majesty of ancient creativity. To their still-forming souls, these time-worn etchings were just plain cool. They wandered among the colossal ruins carved from solid rock by the Nabataens so many centuries before. As Hafiz thought about the past, he realized it had been a lifetime since their travels had taken them anywhere together.

This was no time to reflect. Hafiz knew Nur might not be here. A part of him wished it so, but this, his only link, drove him.

Walking from the bushes he skirted Wadi Musa—the town that had grown around Petra—Hafiz's training kept him in the shadows. Darkened tourist shops and hotels were quiet, at rest, awaiting rebirth at the new day's dawn when commerce would, once again, resume its relentless pursuit to move hard-cold cash from eager tourist's pockets for any type of artifacts, food, or drink that could be sold. Local artisans competed with mass-produced Chinese relics feigning authenticity. Everything was bartered for where everyone but the most simple-minded understood priceless artifacts couldn't be purchased from local bazaars.

The Bedouins with their horse-drawn carts, transporting those who eschewed walking any but the shortest of distances had yet to arrive for their day's business. Hafiz knew there was little time if he hoped to find his target and escape a Jordanian prison.

As he pressed through the al-Siq, Petra's entrance pass, rock cliffs ascended on both sides, scant meters wide in places, with carved niches testifying to ancient artistry. His heart slowed as every sense quickened.

Pausing, Hafiz opened the thermal imager's case on his side, extracted the binoculars, and turned them on. He adjusted the head and chin straps. Scanning rock formations on both sides, he checked the device's focus and convergence. Heat residue, when ambient temperatures were fifty degrees and below, remained from any warm-blooded mammal's contact with the cooler surfaces. The morning hour and massive rocks provided ideal conditions to reveal heat traces. Without thermal imaging, time would have compelled Hafiz to call for an assault and extraction team, providing the Jordanians allowed the operation. With Yisraeli national interests at stake, they could be good neighbors. Still, you never knew. Keeping to the rock walls, he systematically searched, aware that, while he had come as the hunter, he could just as easily become a fly closing in on a web.

Sensing movement across his leg, Hafiz glanced down. Lifting his binoculars, he saw the outline of a camel spider crawling toward his groin. Hafiz ruled out shooting the beast, whose legs spanned his thigh. He attempted to brush the uninvited trespasser from his pant leg using the back of his hand but only succeeded in detaching half its legs. Pulling his pistol, he used the side of the barrel to dislodge the remainder of the spider and watched as the nine-inch arachnid limped away.

After an hour's careful search, Hafiz approached the Urn Tomb. Its red, brown, and tan rock-cut architecture was glorious in the dawning morning light. A faint pattern appeared in his thermal imager. He'd encountered a previous hit only to find a self-absorbed goat stretching in the morning air. Climbing his way to the tomb's second level, he faced the front of the edifice but lost any heat residue. On his left, a colonnade of free-standing columns provided sanctuary in its recessed shadows, as did an entrance to the tomb in front of him whose facade, with four massive columns carved into the stone, soared above him with high reliefs ravaged from wind and age. Fifty feet below the edge he was standing on, huge stone slabs, twelve to fifteen feet in height, jutted up from the basin floor in silent welcome for the careless. Turning, he scanned the area, noting its strategic advantage of view was offset by no means of escape. He tried to come up with a reason for Nuri to place himself in such position. He did not like what came to him. Taking a step toward the colonnade, he heard a familiar voice.

"I wondered if you'd come," Nuri said, stepping out from behind a column, his gun conspicuous in a holster on his chest.

"Long time, brother," Hafiz said. He unbuckled his chin strap, removed the thermal imager, and let it slip to the ground beside him.

"And we could speak of family with tears in our eyes, but that is not why you're here," Nuri said.

"We both know—"

"You understand, brother, we cannot walk together in this."

"Is there a choice? You must come if your life is to be preserved. You know what happens with Mossad," Hafiz said, drawing his Glock and leveling it at Nuri's chest.

Half raising his hands, Nuri looked into his brother's eyes and began moving toward him. "Can you do this, my brother?" Stopping two feet away, he said, "I think you cannot kill your own flesh and blood."

Staring at his brother, every nerve alive, Hafiz's breaths were slow and deep.

Nuri lunged, smashing the side of Hafiz's hand, knocking his gun from him. It skittered across the smooth stones and stopped eight feet away.

Hafiz tackled Nuri. Hitting the stones hard, they rolled over the thermal imager and each other. Hafiz slammed his fist into Nuri's jaw; the sound of crunching bone pierced the morning air.

Nuri grabbed for his gun.

Clawing at his brother's hands, Hafiz pulled Nuri's fists, breath by explosive breath, from his chest.

Every muscle engorged with blood, Nuri struggled for his gun.

As they fought to their knees, Nuri launched an elbow into Hafiz's ribs, knocking both men backward. Searing white hot pain stabbed Hafiz's side.

Fueled by adrenaline, Hafiz shot an uppercut to Nuri's chest. Nuri's gun flew from his holster, careening in circles before landing inches from Hafiz's gun.

Struggling to catch his breath, Nuri backed away.

Raw, driven by instinct, Hafiz looked for an opening.

Nuri drove his fist into Hafiz's side; more ribs snapped.

Chugging air, agonizing pain overwhelming every sense, Hafiz threw his arm around his brother's neck and began squeezing. Nuri struggled to throw him off as they battled near the rock's edge.

A rabbit punch to Hafiz's ribs shot spasms of pain ripping through him, breaking Hafiz's hold on his brother.

Nearing collapse, Hafiz followed through from his shoulder, screaming inwardly from torn, broken ribs as his fist slammed into Nuri's already crushed jaw.

Nuri shrieked in raw animal pain. His feet flew out from under his body and began slipping over the stone edge.

Instinctively, Hafiz's right hand shot out and grabbed Nuri's forearm and wrist. Searing pain flooded every pore of his savaged ribs. "God, don't let me fail," he pleaded. Hafiz hung on.

Nuri's legs thrashed about, dangling in the top of the archway below, struggling to find a foothold, anything solid, but finding only air.

"Stop kicking; you'll pull us down," Hafiz screamed as he grappled for a foothold, something to pull against on the stone's smooth surface, as their combined weights dragged them toward the edge.

Looking at his brother, his jaw grinding, Nuri cried out, "Don't let go."

Hafiz's grip began to fail, his hand slipping from Nuri's forearm to his wrist, then to his fingers as he struggled to hang on. Angry veins in his neck pulsed, engorged; the agony from his ribs shrieked to compel surrender. Reaching within, he knew he would be pulled to his death before letting go. Strength began to infuse him as he refused surrender. It was then his right foot found a ridge in the stone as he continued to be dragged inexorably closer to the edge. He dug in, fighting the overwhelming weight, pulling, straining, his foot begging to be released from the tiny ridge as brothers eyes locked on one another. "We do this, you hear? You won't fall," Hafiz shouted his head swirling, dizzy, and disorientated, the pressure and pain incomprehensible. Unable to grab Nuri with his left hand, Hafiz would not let go. "Nur, grab my hand."

"I cannot reach."

"Swing over; I can't move."

"I'll fall."

"You'll fall if you don't grab on. I'll hold on; I'm stronger than you. I need your free hand to pull you up, so swing then cross arm over and grab my hand."

Swinging his legs to his left, his upper torso scarcely moved. Trying again, his arc increased.

"Good. Swing more, grab arm."

Nuri tried again . . . almost. Building momentum, he swung once more. At the top of the arc he clamped onto Hafiz's hand.

"Now use both hands and pull up and over me."

Nuri began pulling himself onto his brother, the open arch below still under his feet. First his fingers, then hand, finally, agonizingly, his brother's wrist, as seconds took on the weight of hours. They were together, brothers again, the world to conquer, with father waiting at home. Hafiz looked into his brother's eyes.

The irises of Nuri's eyes burst outward. His pupils imploded on themselves, becoming tiny dots, his face blanched. Then Hafiz heard the sound of the Galil as Nuri's hands went limp and began slipping from his grasp.

A scream tore itself from Hafiz. Refusing to let go, he felt a thud through his brother's arm, then heard a second shot slamming into Nuri's back.

In slow motion, his brother's hands continued slipping from his, the strength to hold gone in the agonizing comprehension of reality. Yet he held. Somehow, strength was given he did not possess, and he held.

It was then, in one final pain-ravaged moment, that shattering agony ripped through his right hand as the sound of the Galil, now sickeningly familiar, invaded his hearing once more. He watched, helpless, as his grip on his brother released and Nur's body bounced off the rock face, hitting again and again as he tumbled to the waiting stone below. His crushed and bleeding body curled into a fetal position on the huge boulder.

Head down, too numb to mourn, lying on the cold morning rocks, he scanned for the Galil. Three hundred feet away, a sniper dressed in black was coming his way. At the stone's edge, unable to move, he couldn't make out the shooter's identity.

Time left no markers in his world. Was it five minutes? An hour? Somewhere in that time he pushed back from the killing edge; how far he didn't know. Hafiz sensed someone's presence.

"Is this the way you treat an enemy of Yisra'el?" the dark voice asked.

He strained to look up through blinding pain, the face obscured by morning sun. As he squinted, Lilith Kolatch's features came into focus. It was then he saw the Galil's barrel pointed at him.

"You didn't think I'd let you attend your heart warming reunion without me, did you, Hafiz? Now kick those two guns to me."

"Ribs broken, hand shattered from you—"

"Remarkable shot if I do say so myself. Three hundred twenty-five feet and straight through your pathetic hand that was trying to save an enemy of Yisra'el. Not to mention the ones I put in your brother."

"I was bringing him to justice."

"If Yisra'el had the stomach to execute those who do not deserve life, I could trust the courts. The most that could be hoped for would be life in prison, provided some fool politician didn't let him go in a couple of years to appease our so-called peace partners."

"You kill the wounded fighting for life? He was unarmed."

"Come now, Hafiz. Enough talk about a terrorist. Could I deprive him of seventy-two virgins? You're relieved of duty yet somehow manage to show up where your brother is. By sheer deductive brilliance, you lead me straight to him. Why was it you didn't tell Ramot at Kishle about your dear brother? I mean, after he drove you all the way home and tucked you in. I still need both those guns, by the way, so you best kick them over here. I would be careful; we wouldn't want you to join your brother. You already know I can shoot."

Hafiz looked into reptilian eyes devoid of life. He struggled to get up on his knees; he could not. "I can't get up."

"Crawl then."

He pushed with his legs, inching his way to the guns. Reaching out, he placed his right foot against the Glock and nudged it by Nuri's gun.

"Very good Arab, now just kick both of them over to me."

"Why do you say Arab? I'm Jewish."

"Save it for the weak-minded. Your father was Arab."

"Mother was Jewish, so under law I am Jewish."

"So now's the point we both sing *Hatikva*. I still want those guns."

"Why do this?"

"You don't listen too well, Arab. I said kick . . . the . . . guns . . . over . . . here."

Dizzy from the throbbing pain, Hafiz put his foot against the guns. He jerked forward, sending both guns over the edge of the stone to the rocks below.

"Still not listening, Arab, but you did what I was going to. According to the locator Ramot provided, it appears you are now without a weapon. Oh, did I forget to mention transponder chips were placed in everything you own? Not to mention the personal effects you got back from Kishle when you were so kind to get arrested for sticking your nose where it didn't belong. This was too easy, and you are supposed to be so good. All I had to do was share misgivings about your visit to the dig with the American and your consorting with civilians in Yerushaláyim, but I forgot, you're both Christians—how tender. Then I just waited for your nose to become lodged where it didn't belong and Ramot, always one to go by the book, couldn't authorize your surveillance fast enough. Men are so stupid."

"I need help, call."

"Hafiz, Hafiz. For Shabak you're just not all that bright. You think two Shabak are going to walk from Petra alive? I've had to stomach you all these years. Allowed into Yisraeli state security instead of being hunted down for the traitor you are. There can be no place in Yisra'el for Arab traitors. Now scoot over here where I can see you better, I'm much too close to the edge, wouldn't want anyone to see me help you meet your maker."

"You're going to shoot, in cold blood?"

"Hafiz, have you seen your hand? Nasty, all that pulpy mess hemorrhaging; who knows how long it will be before you bleed out? Why, even if I wanted to call for help, how would anyone make it into Jordan in time? It's over. You were caught consorting with the enemy, and considering what he almost accomplished, you're about to make me a hero. Now be a man, unless, of course, you want to push off over the edge to join your brother. Makes no difference to me," Lilith said, scanning for arriving Bedouins.

Head throbbing, dizzy, his right hand shattered, Hafiz's left hand brushed the broken thermal imager. He struggled to his knees, trying to buy time, as large drops of sweat rolled down his brow.

Lilith surveilled the surrounding terrain through the scope on her rifle for any unfortunate soul who might have to be eliminated; there would be no witnesses.

Grabbing the imager, Hafiz forced himself into a crouch.

On hearing movement, Lilith swung in his direction.

Setting his jaw against the pain, Hafiz pushed off from the stone's edge and hurled the imager with the last of his waning strength.

The edge of the imager slammed into Lilith's nasal bone. Blood began filling her nasal cavity. Her eyes, flooding with tears and blood, tried to focus. She struggled to aim her rifle pulling the trigger before the rifle was set—an amateur move—and the rifle butt slammed into her shoulder, knocking her backward. The bullet, inches from its intended mark, tore into Hafiz's thigh. Instinctively, his left hand blasted to his ankle, pulling the SP21 from its holster. In one sweeping motion, he pointed the weapon at Lilith's chest and unloaded all fifteen rounds.

Lilith's visage shed its Gothic pallor as the shock of the violence registered. Her legs gave way as her upper torso collapsed onto the unforgiving stones.

Through a fog of unimaginable pain, Hafiz began the grueling journey of crawling past Kolatch toward the stone stairs, downward, away from death and Jordanian imprisonment. Each inch sent waves of pain surging through his body. He fought unconsciousness, knowing to give in was to die. *Must get home-e-e-e-e-e.* Unconsciousness claimed him.

Voices surrounded Hafiz, floating around and over him. Darkness shrouded him again.

"Who is he?"

"One of my best officers," Commander Ramot said.

"A little far afield."

"It's a long story."

"And you haven't heard the end yet, right?"

"But I will."

"Maybe, lost a lot of blood. His hand looks like mush. Leg isn't far behind. It'll take several transfusions and luck; even then it's anyone's guess," Mirel said, finding a vein. She started an IV drip.

"Surgeons will know more when we get him back to Hadassah. If anyone can save him they will," Commander Ramot said.

"Let's go, he needs aid stat," a second medic said, taking one end of the stretcher.

"See you at the inquiry in Tel Aviv, Commander," Mirel said.

Turning to a Mossad agent, Commander Ramot asked, "Everything wrapped up?"

"Officer Kolatch's body's is being loaded as we speak. We recovered one rifle, three pistols, and casings which are labeled and bagged. We got all the photos time allows. Word has it the Jordanians are heading our way so we've got a helo to catch."

"What about the terrorist?"

"His body has been loaded separately. Schlomo's team has it. It will be flown to Lod for an autopsy."

"Let's do it," Ira Ramot said. *Lousy way to see Petra for the first time*, he thought. He climbed aboard the Sikorsky.

CHAPTER

70

Sunday 23 March 2008, 0701 hours

Hadassah Medical Center
Mount Scopus, Yerushaláyim

The doctor walked into the darkened room where shades had been drawn to keep the sunlight at bay. She approached the patient. Muted pools of light illuminated the top of the hospital bed, which was elevated thirty degrees. "Shalom, Ms. Daniels, how are we feeling this morning?"

Elizabeth tried to lift her head, pain shot across her face; she collapsed back into the pillow.

"Still experiencing pain, I see."

"Who are you?"

"Isha Ya'alon. You don't remember?"

"No, but since we're both aware of my pain, how about something for it?"

"Ms. Daniels—"

"Elizabeth."

"X-rays reveal a great deal, Elizabeth, but not everything. Having examined yours, I need to manipulate your injuries to see what else the pain reveals that X-rays don't."

"You mean in addition to the agony experienced by trying to lift my head?"

"Something like that. This shouldn't take long, and then I can order an analgesic injection which will bring immediate relief."

"You're a doctor, right?

"In maxillofacial surgery, which is good for you."

"Let's get back to the pain part. How is it anything but bad?"

"I know, it can't seem good and we'd like to avoid making it worse. But its absence, in specific areas of your damaged cheek, could indicate nerve damage. Unless you want each side of your face responding to stimuli differently, pain—which indicates normative nerve function—is good. Yesterday, while you were sedated, we repositioned your fractured cheek bones into more or less their normal positions, sometimes it's difficult considering the trauma experienced and subsequent swelling. That outcome should prove more promising than implanting a metal plate, which was also considered. You'll appreciate my choice in the coming years, not to mention when going through airport security. Now let's start so we can get you some pain relief."

"I'm not going to like this, am I?"

"Probably not, but you're a big girl."

The examination Elizabeth thought, after regaining consciousness from the pain of probing injured flesh and bone, had gone well—after a pain shot was administered. The good news was her leg injury was more superficial than originally thought and was healing without complication.

The next day her pain medication was reduced and, just as Elizabeth was considering mutiny, Dr. Ya'alon promised no more probing or face manipulation. Her nerve synapses verified, facial X-rays would thereafter suffice.

CHAPTER

71

Sunday 30 March 2008, 0909 hours

Assaf Harofeh Medical Center, Institute of Hyperbaric Medicine Outside Tel Aviv

"Why can't Aadil have company? I'm not so big to take up much space," Khalil pointed out to the she-male nurse towering over him.

"Mr. Ahmad, as you've been told five times, only patients meeting the Institute's guidelines for hyperbaric oxygen therapy can be placed in a hyperbaric chamber."

"But I have many ribs broken. Won't this chamber help me heal quicker like it does Aadil?"

"If your injury were more traumatic you might, and I stress might, with the director's approval, receive treatment in one of our chambers. Your friend's surgery involved a rod being inserted in his humerus as well as skin and muscle surgery. Even then it took the joint decision of his team of doctors that healing would be enhanced by hyperbaric oxygen therapy."

"But my friend needs me. I saved him, you know."

"Yes, Mr. Ahmad, we are all aware of that fact, and what a brave thing to do—"

"But I—"

"Ah-ah-ahh, there are other patients who need me. Doesn't it hurt to talk with all that swelling and bruising on your face?"

"There is pain but Aadil needs me."

"Tell you what, if you behave and stay out of the way, and that means not bothering me every time I pass, I will bring you up at our staff meeting this afternoon and ask whether you can stay in one of the hyperbaric side rooms reserved for families while your friend heals. Would that please you?"

"It's a start."

"The other alternative is calling security to escort you out."

"I can't go out; people don't like me for saving Aadil. Was told Welfare and Social Services Ministry will come for me when I'm ready to leave."

"What a wonderful idea. I'll call and let them know you'll be ready within a few days since they're working with you. Now off to your room, I have other patients who need care and everything will be decided this afternoon."

"But I want to be where Aadil can be seen."

"You'll have a good view of Mr. Gamal's chamber if the doctor approves. Just remember our agreement."

CHAPTER

72

Late March 2008

Third Floor Restricted Room, Hadassah University Hospital Ein Kerem, Yerushaláyim

Commander Ramot stopped in front of the third floor nurses' station.

"May I help you?" the supervising nurse asked.

"Shalom. One of my officers has been transferred from Intensive Care."

"Name?"

"IbnMansur, Hafiz IbnMansur."

"And you are?"

"Ira Ramot.

"If you don't mind Mr. Ramot, identification card please, you understand."

"Perfectly," he said, handing his ID card to the nurse.

Examining it carefully, he said, "Looks fine." He handed it back. "Would you mind?" He motioned toward the fingerprint scanner on the nurses' station counter. "Procedure."

Familiar with the protocol, Ira Ramot inserted his index finger in the scanner and waited for the obligatory tone indicating his fingerprint had been matched to the database on every government employee.

"A little over a hundred feet down the hall you'll see a 'Restricted' sign on a double doorway. A fingerprint reader is on the right. Insert your index finger and remember to glance at the camera above the doorway. You will be automatically buzzed in. On any subsequent visits, after scanning your finger proceed through those doors to Mr. Ibn Mansur's room."

"I have questions about Hafiz's condition. Whom may I speak with?"

Looking down at the computer screen, hidden from Ramot's view, the nurse made a couple of quick keystrokes and continued to scan the monitor. "Here it is. You're authorized full disclosure. The floor nurse is attending another patient. I'll call; she'll answer any questions." He picked up the phone and whispered into it. Looking back at Ramot, he said, "Nurse Sivan will be right up."

Three minutes later a smiling, dark-skinned, Ethiopian nurse walked up. "Shalom aleichem, I am Desta Sivan. How may I help?"

"Shalom aleichem, can you tell me about Hafiz IbnMansur's condition?"

Over the next few minutes, Ira learned that Hafiz's taped ribs were the most painful of his injuries but were expected to heal without complication.

"A short stainless steel rod was inserted into his femur to replace damaged bone. Hafiz will walk without a limp provided he takes it easy when we remove his leg from the traction splint."

"That doesn't sound nice."

"It's a simple weight to keep the bone and rod aligned. Besides, it seemed the easiest way to keep him confined to his bed, and even then he unhooks it and we find him down the hall."

"What about his hand it appeared to be his most serious injury?"

"Two surgeries so far, but it's healing well, better than anticipated. Doctors are optimistic that, with continued rehabilitative exercises, his hand should be returned to a functional level."

"I don't understand. When I saw him his hand was shredded. A high-velocity bullet had shattered it. His fingers appeared attached by mere tendons and strands of muscle with bones not only broken but shattered from the impact."

"I've had many conversations with members of Hafiz's medical team, and on its surface your assessment is correct. But taking into account advancements in micro-surgery and reconstructive repair, the situation wasn't as bleak as it might have appeared. A few years back, yes, but today we are blessed to have leading specialists from orthopedics to neurologists to microsurgery. Besides," the smiling nurse said, "I think Hafiz is not alone in all this."

"I don't follow."

"He has deep faith in our creator, as do I. One of his names is Jehovah-Rapha, the Lord that healeth."

"Might have been nice if whatever you call god would have kept him from nearly losing his hand in the first place, but maybe your deity has bigger things to contend with."

"People are his biggest—"

"Thank you, nurse. I need to see Hafiz now." Leaving Desta Sivan standing there, Ira headed toward Hafiz's room. After passing through the restricted entry, he was greeted by a utility closet and three rooms. Two were empty; he entered the third. "Shalom," he said, taking in the room and the man he didn't expect to see alive. "You look better than the last time I saw you."

"Shalom," Hafiz said. "Last time was at Kishle, didn't think I looked so bad."

"Hafiz, I trailed Kolatch as she followed you in your unofficial visit to Jordan."

"Kolatch to Petra? You were there?"

"Good thing I was."

"Mind filling me in? Things are muddled."

"I was hoping you could do the filling."

For the next few minutes, Hafiz pieced together memories of tracking Nuri. "The last thing I remember is holding onto Nuri as he was hanging over the edge of landing, then someone shot."

"What about your hand?"

"I woke up in the hospital, nurse Sivan says four days later, with my hand and arm in a cast up to my shoulder, my leg wrapped and in traction, my side taped, and so sore I couldn't move. Figured if I was in pain I must not be dead, but no one told me anything. Can you tell doctors to talk with me?"

"I'll see what I can do. You remember anything else?"

"That's it."

"What about Kolatch?"

"I tried to piece it all together. Going to the Urn Tomb, struggling with Nuri, bullets hitting him but beyond that . . . nothing. Some Internal Affairs type came by yesterday, started asking questions. I didn't know her so my mind went blank. She didn't seem too pleased, but I don't discuss missions when I don't know who's asking questions. She said an inquiry would be conducted and my testimony would be taken from the hospital, didn't say when. Also told me Nuri was dead, Kolatch as well, but not how it happened. She was only interested in asking questions, not answering them."

"Nothing unexpected there, Internal Affairs keeps to themselves unless investigating. I'm surprised she told you about the deaths. For what it's worth, I'm sorry about your brother. Everything else aside, he was your brother."

"Commander, I understand Nuri was involved in an attack and what it would have meant if he'd succeeded. There is too much killing in our country, but if we're not willing to face enemies, no matter who they are, Yisra'el won't survive. Maybe later things will hit me, but for half of my life Nuri has been an enemy of all I believe. If Nuri had won then I may be gone. I appreciate your concern, but I never lost sight of what was at stake."

"Is there anything else you remember?"

"I've been lying here trying to dig out memories. Not much else to do but sleep. Nothing comes. I know I wasn't supposed to leave my house, I'll stand for that, but I thought I might find my brother and bring him in before Mossad found him. The intelligence gained would be worth his life."

"This is off the record, and that means completely off, but I'll tell you what I know—it might stir your memory. Some time back, Kolatch filed a report that ended up on my desk after it was suspected Nuri was involved with the anthrax. Wait, she tried to see me after you dropped by her dig with the American; she never seemed to tire of pointing out your Arabic father. Since that was vetted before you came on board Shabak, I had Lt. Koret talk with her but filed nothing. After we learned Nuri was involved with the anthrax, someone was assigned to keep an eye on you."

"You had me—"

"Don't go there. It came from above, and if it hadn't I would have assigned someone. Problem is, you kept losing your tail, so I assigned a second agent; you slipped her, too. When told to stand down you ended up in Kishle, so transponders were implanted everywhere possible including the personal effects you got back after being detained in the Old City, just in case you kept anything with you, standard procedure. Though you knew brass wanted you relieved of your duties and weapons, what you don't know is command wanted you confined but accepted the transponders on my recommendation. Since Kolatch was so committed to nailing you aiding and abetting your brother, we figured she might be able to keep track of you and provided her needed equipment."

"I knew she didn't like me but thought it was personal. I never thought she'd question my loyalty."

"Kolatch wasn't informed that when she was tracking you, I was behind her. Since I had to put my career on the line vouching for you, no way I wasn't going to be involved. There's also some background you didn't have the need to know. A few years back another of our officers, also of Arabic heredity, was involved in a shooting; Kolatch was there. The agent was grazed but didn't see where it came from, could have been from multiple locations since he wasn't exactly standing still. With no clear evidence of the specific caliber used, the bullet was never recovered, ballistics were useless. There was suspicion Kolatch could have been the shooter, but with no direct link command couldn't act. No one wanted to believe anyone in Shabak would shoot one of our own. Over the years her growing bitterness against Arabs kept the incident in the back of my mind, but she was a credible agent doing her job when I assigned her to track you."

"Maybe you didn't follow her close enough."

"I saved your life, didn't I? When I rolled up on Petra, both of you were already past the al-Siq. By the time I heard the first shots and started tracking in that stone basin, three had been fired. After tracking you to the Urn Tomb, I spotted you and Kolatch on the second level with Nuri on the rocks below. I saw her draw down on you as she continued to babble on—always had a mouth on her. I was dialing in on her with my rifle when she stepped back from the edge just enough to lose visual."

Nurse Sivan entered the room. "Time for an injection Hafiz."

"What's one more shot?"

"No worry," she said, wiping the clave port with alcohol. "No sticks this time. Just going to ease it into your IV line; you won't feel a thing." In seconds she was done. "Now you two can continue your talk."

"So you lost sight of Kolatch, but what of me?"

"You remained near the edge but pushed away from its periphery while flinging something at her, a thermal imager, according to the lab tests identifying her blood all over it. You must have a pretty fair arm, considering Kolatch's nose. Next thing I heard was a rifle then rapid small arms fire. My guess, the Barak SP-21 we found on the scene was yours since we found five .45ACP rounds in Kolatch. Not the tightest pattern I've ever seen, but all things considered, not bad."

"Then what?"

"I radioed the extraction team, which was waiting on the border, and ran up to the second level. You could have picked something closer to the ground—"

"It was Nuri's choice, not mine."

"After getting there I found Kolatch dead and you close to it. The extraction team was right behind me; one of the Bedouins was helpful."

"Maybe he didn't want to get shot," Hafiz said.

"He's one of Mossad's undercovers. Everyone was gone before Jordanian troops arrived, and here we are today."

"When will charges be filed?"

"Well, that's the thing, Hafiz. Seems the brass and politicians see this in pretty much the same light. There was discreet political contact between us and the Jordanians. Appears they want to distance themselves from the anthrax plot but don't want their Arab neighbors to think they assisted us—politics as usual. So, long story short, nothing happened in Petra; you weren't there.

I had a conversation with General Oz and with Kolatch's history toward Arabs and what happened at the Urn Tomb, he said *me go'el haddam* pretty much covered it for him."

"He said me go'el haddam?"

"The law of the blood avenger still undergirds Yisra'el, without which we would cease to be a nation."

"But many times we let enemies go from prison after politicians make deals."

"We remember . . . always. Of course we'll have to live with a plaque at headquarters extolling Kolatch's bravery and loyalty defending Yisra'el."

"She's a hero?"

"She is now. Story is the PMIJ got to her near Nahal Paran in the Negev, which, by the way, is where you were injured. She died fighting for Yisra'el. You're going to be recognized as the hero Oz intends to make you, bravery under fire and all that. Before you protest, this is the way it's going down, which is a sight better than dismissal or prison. Oh, one final thing, you never owned a Barak SP 21, since that's what killed Kolatch. Looks like it should work out okay, you might even consider running for political office one day. You'd be surprised how many members of the Knesset got a boost to their political aspirations with help from the military. I'd vote for your becoming a member of the Knesset."

"Not politics."

"Suit yourself. Just remember how it happened when questioned. Your debriefing just took place."

"So what's next?"

"I imagine you'll be here for awhile. I hear rehab is fun. Expect you'll be assigned station duties for the foreseeable future. The American consulate has been notified you will be taking a leave of absence, but providing your hand heals as expected, I anticipate you'll be back in the middle of things."

"My hand will heal."

CHAPTER

73

Sunday 30 March 2008, Mid-Afternoon

Assaf Harofeh Medical Center, Second Floor Conference Room Outside Tel Aviv

"All right, the final item this afternoon," Dr. Sidney Kossman said, "is Khalil Ahmad's request, through Nurse Rosengart, to be admitted to the hyperbaric institute while Mr. Aadil Gamal, undergoing hyperbaric oxygen therapy, completes treatment. I've gone over your memorandum, Odeda, but I'm at a loss to understand the request. I also see Welfare and Social Services Ministry is tied into this. Why don't you give me an overview."

"I'll try, doctor, though my request was for a side room where Mr. Ahmad could be closer to Mr. Gamal and I could remain focused on my patients. Exactly eight days ago, we received Aadil Gamal and Khalil Ahmad with injuries sustained in the attack on the Migdal David in the Old City. Ira Ramot, Shabak's Yerushaláyim District Commander, phoned an emergency admit into the medical director's office specifying neither patient be released without prior clearance from his office. Examinations revealed that Mr. Gamal's injuries required immediate surgery, which was performed while Mr. Ahmad's injuries consisted of several fractured ribs along with minor contusions and bruising to his face and head. An MRI scan indicated no intracranial swelling, or pressure, so his ribs were taped, he was prescribed an anti-inflammatory, advised to rest, and was assigned a private room per Commander Ramot's request, though his injuries didn't require hospitalization. Earlier today I caught Khalil attempting to enter the hyperbaric institute several times where Mr. Gamal's medical team had placed him for hyperbaric oxygen therapy. I explained treatment protocol to Mr. Ahmad more than once, but he seemed without the ability to understand. Not being apprised of Commander Ramot's medical admit through the director's office, I threatened to call security to remove Mr. Ahmad so I could meet the needs of my patients. Thereupon Mr. Ahmad claimed he would be in danger if released and informed me Welfare and Social Services Ministry was involved. I called them and Sele Weintraub agreed to come over because of the nature of this matter."

"She's here?"

"Waiting outside the conference room, I'll get her."

Entering the room, a trim professional woman in her thirties with clipped black hair and a masculine suit and tie followed the giant nurse. "Ms. Weintraub, this is Doctor Kossman."

"We appreciate your allowing us to break into your day like this, Ms.—"

"Please, just Sele."

"What is the status of Misters Ahmad and Gamal, Sele?"

"All I have been told is they're awaiting transport out of Eretz Yisra'el and until then they will be in one of two places. Here, and when medically stationary, Kibbutz Shefayim. Their families are now residing in Kibbutz Shefayim and receiving assistance while they're in country, and I'm told this comes from the Vice Prime Minister's office but that's not official."

"Can you transport Mr. Ahmad to the kibbutz then return for Mr. Gamal when he's ready?"

"Sorry doctor, my instructions are they must remain together, and no, I don't know why; I just do what I'm told."

"As we all do, Sele."

"Odeda, since they're both here, is there a problem with keeping them together? I don't see any."

"You mean other than the fact one doesn't need hospitalization and we can't have him running around the hospital, doctor?"

"Anything else you need from me, doctor?"

"Not that I can think of, Sele. Thank you for stopping by. We'll get this figured out, might be nice if you'd send me something official for the file."

"No problem, when they're ready to travel, call and we'll pick them up."

"Thank you, Ms. Weintraub, we'll do that."

She left the room.

"Ideas anyone? We can't have Mr. Ahmad roaming the halls."

Raya Muscovitz spoke up. "Sid, what's the big deal? We're treating Aadil Gamal in the monoplace chamber; we'll just move him into the multiplace chamber and stick Khalil Ahmad next to him. The treatments will speed recovery on his ribs and we can keep them in a security room when they're not in the chamber, problem solved, staff is free to do their jobs. When Mr. Gamal has completed therapy off they go to the kibbutz."

"That's why you're my assistant, Raya."

On Sunday, 20 April, Sele Weintraub drove up to Assaf Harofeh's front door. Aadil was waiting in a wheelchair while Khalil wondered if they'd still have lunch. Kibbutz Shefayim awaited.

CHAPTER

74

Yedi'oth Aharonot
Erelah Vered

Posted 25 March 2008

Three Unidentified Gazans Killed in Chemical Explosion

Gaza, al-Bureij Refugee Camp (*Palestine Times*) 24 March—A blast occurred yesterday at 4:07 A.M. local time. Three unidentified males were killed in what Gaza authorities reported was an accidental chemical explosion.

Unnamed Israeli sources said satellite photographs of the blast area showed an adjacent school untouched by the blast. According to one source, "The pinpoint blast area, more than eight feet deep, yet merely fifteen feet wide, is not indicative of any known chemical blast. The blast would have caused massive loss of life and property had it occurred during the day."

A source in Gaza, who wished to remain anonymous, reported activity over several months at the blast site. When questioned what caused him to notice this activity, he replied, "You know, coming and going at all hours, closing and locking doors each time in and out of the building. No words to neighbors or people passing by. The same three men together except for the time my wife and I saw a strange huge man that dwarfed the trio. He wasn't from here either, don't make them that big in Gaza."

He scoffed when questioned about a chemical plant next to a school.

"If chemicals are found beside a school it is someone making bombs to protect innocent Palestinians."

Asked for thoughts on who might be responsible, he replied, "One of them made the Zionists mad. This is the work of the Zionists, pure and simple. We are a peace-loving people and condemn all Zionists' acts of aggression."

When this reporter called Abd al Sami Halabī, PMIJ's press liaison in Gaza City, to determine when the identification of the three blast victims would be released, Mr. Halabī said there appeared to be insufficient remains to make identification and that unless building lease records could be located or relatives came forward, identities would likely remain unknown.

When asked about specific chemicals involved in the blast, he said a detailed analysis would not be completed for several weeks.

Israeli officials, when contacted, said it was an internal matter for the authorities in Gaza and no official statement would be issued.

C H A P T E R

75

Sunday 30 March 2008, Mid-Morning

Hadassah Medical Center
Mount Scopus, Yerushaláyim

Given the option of remaining in the hospital until the start of next week or bed rest at her apartment, Elizabeth jumped at the chance to go home. Dr. Ya'alon was scheduled to drop by one last time before her release to find out who was going to drive her home and look after her when she was released. Just her luck Naava picked up the phone when the hospital called the mission to get a ride to her apartment and provide any care needed. But she'd rather a mother-hen spring her and monitor her recovery than spend one more day in the hospital. Besides, with Bible study commitments and mission needs, Naava would be far too busy for more than an occasional visit. After a few days' rest she'd get a ride to the mission and ease herself back into Messianic Jews International activities, which Addison had interrupted with his incessant demands to talk with real Arabs.

The American had a way of invading her thoughts. It had to be his helplessness, which she learned of from nurses who knew of the efforts being made to save him. They induced therapeutic hypothermia to prevent brain swelling, along with other medical procedures she didn't want to understand. Besides, Elizabeth concluded, anyone would pass her mind occasionally, considering what they'd been through together.

She managed to get a call through to Khalil, whose focus was on remaining with Aadil and a trip to America of which he had no details. Not likely, but in saving her she knew they'd need help and also knew where to take her concerns; she bowed her head.

"Morning Elizabeth," Doctor Ya'alon said, walking into the room. "Am I interrupting?"

"Hi, doc, I'm always praying, helps with the craziness of the world, but I'm sure you came to see how your star patient is doing before I'm released."

"Kind of."

"What do you mean, kind of?"

"I haven't signed the release order yet. According to the Resident's report I just read your leg won't require further treatment but it's always best to check for signs of infection even with superficial wounds. One last examination, and if everything looks good the orderly can wheel you out the door."

"I've already called my friend, Naava, who is a bigger stickler for rules than you are."

"Just have to ensure I haven't missed anything. Sit in the chair by the window so I can look at you in the sunlight." She removed the bandages from Elizabeth's nose and cheek.

Five minutes later a knock came at the door. "Hello, may I come in?" Naava asked as she stepped in the room.

"Naava, be with you as soon as the doc is finished."

"Need me to come back?"

Looking up, Doctor Ya'alon said, "It's okay, we'll be done in a minute." Turning back to Elizabeth, she said, "Okay, looks like I still do good work." She bandaged Elizabeth's face. "Stay on the liquid diet until I see you next week. It wouldn't feel too good to try chewing anyway. Better stick with rinsing out your mouth with tepid water with one teaspoon of baking soda mixed in; a toothbrush would feel like it was made of wire. No removing the bandages. If you notice anything unusual, and I mean anything—a bump, hardening of an area, excessive sloughing of skin, or swelling—I want to see you immediately. Probe your face, through the bandages, several times daily. If you notice anything other than continued slow healing, I want to know."

Turning to Naava, she pulled a card from her lab coat and handed it to her. "Elizabeth needs to stay put until she sees me in seven days. She gives you any problems, or you have any concerns or questions—call."

"You can count on it."

"I'll be a good patient."

"See that you are. There's a chance there will be no residual scarring if you follow my advice. An orderly will be right in to take you downstairs."

"Naava, if you want I'll meet you at the discharge door, that way you can get the car."

"Good idea."

Sitting in the wheelchair, as she was being pushed toward the elevator, Elizabeth wondered if it was good that Addison kept going though her mind. After all, Khalil and Aadil were part of the kaleidoscope of events. These past days had changed her life, and three men had their part in that change, but none shared her faith in Y'shua.

Did everything happen to her because she was a Christian, or was it being Jewish? Maybe she'd never know, but if it was the Lord's will, she wanted to see how Addison's search for answers had changed him. She knew it would be toward or away from HaShem, and she needed to know.

CHAPTER

76

Last Week of March 2008

Medical Intensive Care Unit
Hadassah University Hospital
Ein Kerem, Yerushaláyim

Looking down upon Addison, Janelle whispered, "Son." There was no response. Janelle searched for a place to touch, caress, connect with, but found only invading tubes, and monitor leads that covered his shattered body. Five stacked metal rings surrounded the only part of him left uncovered—his left leg from his ankle to his calf—even here there were pins piercing skin and bone. She placed her fingers over his right hand, covering the artificial arteries with the delicacy of a mother's love as she willed his fight for survival. He felt cold, the chilled water running though the vest and leg wraps chilling him to a steady 91°F to contain intracranial swelling.

Silence pervaded the pungent antiseptic room, broken by the electronic beeping of machines charged with monitoring life. Steady, rhythmical, their sounds of promise the only comfort violence could afford.

Mom?

Addison? That voice, how many times had he called out, but now his head was covered in white gauze. Eyes wrapped by the mummified-looking bandages, obscuring recognition while they protected against germs that would destroy, kill. But there was no movement save for the steady rhythm of machines. No voice, just the echo of his presence from memories.

Three days later

It was bewildering how time lost its meaning in the shadow of intensive care. Doctors, nurses, came with professional efficiency, testing, probing, prodding, marking hieroglyphics she could neither read nor understand on Addison's growing chart.

Day by day the kindness of the staff renewed itself as she was allowed a bed in an adjoining room with a window so she could feel a part of Addison even when procedures or exhaustion drove her from his side. Oregon, such a part of all she was, rarely came to mind. There was enough vacation and sick leave for now. Stanley called a couple of times, but responsibilities and distance made it difficult. She called mom and dad on a hospital phone; hers didn't work in this distant land, and left brief messages. Her calls, coming in the small hours of the morning with the ten-hour time difference between Jerusalem and Milwaukie, routed to voicemail. She tried to sound encouraging, but how do you reassure when the only news is that their grandson barely clings to life? There were no answers, and certitude was a moment by moment illusion a nurse's frown could destroy. She watched her brother pray—what a strange thing, a brother, and one who prayed. She didn't understand the concept of a plea for healing to a being that allowed such violence, but Asa's whispered words somehow held the only thing left . . . hope.

CHAPTER

77

Tuesday 1 April 2008, 0835 hours

Office of Vice Prime Minister Dannie Dobrin Givat Ram, Yerushaláyim

Seated around the sixteen-foot-long polished mahogany conference table in padded, gray leather, graphite base chairs, seven men enjoyed the sumptuous rewards of their positions: bountiful pastries on Wedgewood bone china platters; individual carafes of steaming Arabica coffee; along with coordinating sugar and creamer sets; and silverware on French linen napkins arranged in front of each man. A lone woman sat on the front edge of her chair, the coffee and pastries before her untouched, at the far end of the table.

At the head of the table, after chewing the last third of a cherry turnover, Vice Prime Minister Dannie Dobrin wiped his lips and sugar-laced fingers on his linen napkin, took an inelegant slurp of doctored coffee, and began: "On behalf of Prime Minister Olmert I want to welcome our American friends. Each of us understands the order of today's business. Two housekeeping matters: one, the Prime Minister desires this matter be concluded, in its entirety, before this plenum permanently adjourns; two, this proceeding, including all documentation, is classified at the Secret level. While it can be debated whether disclosure would cause grave danger to

Eretz Yisra'el, release of any documents could result in the death or serious injury of innocent civilians in Yisra'el and the United States, as well as raise questions of other bilateral documents' existence. Its Secret classification is set at seventy-five years, well past the time any release could incur damage, now to the real business at hand. In consultation with Brigadier General Oz, Major Chanan Weiss, his Executive Officer, has been selected to conduct this meeting. I will remain as Chair while Major Weiss is better able to ensure all legal requirements are adhered to: Major Weiss."

Adjusting himself in his chair, Chanan Weiss began. "Thank you sir and good morning honored guests. My job is to act as facilitator and to clarify, as needed, previously negotiated documents relevant to Mr. Addison Edmond Deverell, a United States of America Department of State consular officer assigned to the U.S. Embassy in Tel Aviv, currently residing in the Medical Intensive Care Unit, Hadassah University Hospital, Ein Kerem, Yerushaláyim. I hope the refreshments I ordered are pleasing; they should tide us over until lunch, which will be served here to ensure everything is concluded by this afternoon. The Prime Minister, as Vice Prime Minister Dobrin said, is committed to our finishing so all necessary subsequent actions can be implemented. Our task, having come to agreement in principle and specific, is to ensure conformity with preliminary agreements between the State of Yisra'el and the United States of America as well as to deal with any remaining issues. Upon conclusion each of you will report to your commands, while all hard copies of today's proceedings, including signed agreements, will be stored within the intelligence hub of the Israeli Central Command. Yael Davids is recording today's meeting on stenotype. This complies with internal Israeli protocol requirements for Secret documents and guarantees accuracy should there be a future need to review pertinent materials. In front of you, with the exceptions of our guests, Dr. Janelle Henning of the United States, and Doctor Asa Yochanan, each has a file containing your original signed agreements plus all other relevant documents needed for today's discussion and implementation. Are there any questions so far?" Looking around the table, Major Weiss was met with pastries in mid-chew, coffee on its way to waiting lips, and silence. "Good, then let us proceed. We will go around the table, starting with the Vice Prime Minister. Please identify yourself for Ms. David's stenotype recording, along with your current position and any rank you may hold. Sir."

"You all know me. I'm Vice Prime Minister Dannie Dobrin. Sagiv."

"My name is Sagiv Oz. My rank is Brigadier General. I am the IDF's Deputy Liaison to Sherut haBitachon haKlali, Shabak."

"Thank you, sir. I am, of course, Major Chanan Weiss, General Oz's Executive Officer. Commander Ramot."

"Ira Ramot, Yerushaláyim District Commander, Sherut ha-Bitachon haKlali, Shabak."

"Sid Cantwell, Deputy Administrator, United States Embassy, Tel Aviv."

"Good. Next please."

"Keane Bodine, Bureau of Diplomatic Security, Regional Security Officer, United States Embassy, Tel Aviv."

"Doctor."

"Dr. Asa Yochanan. I am a medical doctor at Hadassah Medical Center, Yerushaláyim, and Addison Deverell's uncle."

"And lastly."

The woman sat, head down, hands in her lap, making no response.

Asa scooted his chair over and took her hands in his. She didn't look up, leaving her hands where Asa put them. "This is Dr. Janelle Henning. She is Addison's mother and my sister."

"Thank you, Dr. Yochanan. If you will open your folders and follow along with me."

Files were pulled around the pastries and opened. Eyeglasses came from several pockets as the aging warriors acknowledged the march of time.

"Whereas the State of Yisra'el has a policy of aliyah, the right of return for all Jewish people worldwide."

"Whereas Addison Edmond Deverell (hereafter referred to as AED) is Jewish by birth from his mother."

"Whereas verifiable foreign intelligence has shown AED is a continuing and ongoing terrorist target of the Palestine Mujahideen

Islamic Jihad (PMIJ) as well as the Palestinian Freedom Army (PALFA), which could endanger innocent civilian life."

"Whereas The United States Department of State will release AED from active U.S. Department of State service."

"Be it resolved to allow and facilitate emigration from the United States to the State of Israel for AED."

"Further, Sherut haBitachon haKlali, Shabak, will effect AED's official death, creating a new identity with natural birth and education in Eretz Yisra'el."

"Further, AED's background and training make him a suitable candidate for the Ministry of Foreign Affairs." Major Weiss looked around the table. "Questions?"

Looking down to the end of the table, Keane said, "Dr. Henning is there anything you need to ask?"

"Yes," Major Weiss broke in, "please forgive me, this may seem without compassion, but behind our decisions is your son's welfare, Dr. Henning. Is there anything, anything at all, you want to know or need to say?"

"You said if this agreement were made public people might die. I don't understand."

"Mind if I take this?" Keane asked.

"By all means."

"A little background, then your question. PMIJ terrorist cell members who carried out this attack were all killed, but the structure of terrorist groups are amorphous, with few geographical boundaries; they are nearly impossible to eradicate since they continually recruit new members.

"And this is what Addison ran afoul of?"

"Sort of, but here is where I have to speculate because assets are just beginning to dig through everything and the picture will continue to develop. The Palestine Mujahideen Islamic Jihad are punks. I mean, they were voted into power, after a fashion, in Gaza, but they're still low-life. They couldn't have pulled this operation off by themselves to save their souls, if they had any. Thing is, the PMIJ came damn close to winning the big one. This operation involved half a dozen bordering countries and a strain of anthrax no one knew existed. So somewhere PMIJ hooked up with some serious players. The bad guys are dead while millions were wasted on the hope of ridding Jerusalem of her Jewish residents. To top it off, their dreams of an Arab hegemony ruling so-called Palestine were postponed for at least a generation. Your son was the lightning rod in the middle of this. You don't need to hear how he broke every protocol of State Department training to become that lightning rod. The thing you need to understand and remember Doctor Henning, is that there are some bad people out there who don't just believe in the law of blood atonement, but believe your son's specific blood is the only acceptable price for Arab blood that was shed in their failure."

"Are we in the Middle Ages? What are you talking about—blood atonement?"

"The law of blood atonement, Doctor Henning, decrees that when someone in your tribe is slain—and you need to know the Arabs loosely define the word tribe—there can be no peace until the murderer is slain."

"Addison didn't kill anyone."

"That fact, like beauty, is in the eye of the Arab blood avenger. Historically, blood atonement began before nation-states as we know them came into being, and whatever law existed was practiced among tribes in a given area. You might say the legal system was rudimentary by today's standards but it worked in that era. So the Arab custom of blood calling for blood makes a lot of assumptions, and in this case, the word on the street is that Addison got all the credit for the jihadists being killed."

"But it was Israeli forces who stormed the tower."

"I know that, and you know that, and I'm even willing to bet the jihadists who are planning their next attack know that, but we are, and I'm speaking about Americans now, not too popular in some places. The thing you don't know is Addison, in his foray into the West Bank, essentially pulled himself from the masses of the Great Satan, by which we are affectionately known, and became a marked target by shouting to any malcontent willing to listen that he was an American. So the nice folks who just sent the jihadists to die on the tower have now taken a personal interest in assuring Addison the American joins their fallen comrades. Fair, no, but if they were all that interested in fairness they'd scoot to the surrounding countries and leave the Israelis alone."

"My head is spinning Mr. Bodine. I need time to assimilate all this."

"I understand this seems surreal, but most events in Israel have roots that go back thousands of years. So you have a tower built in the 1650s that was leveled, five million dollars paid in ransom, and the loss of an Israeli commando all on his resume, and he hasn't even started duty yet. That's why the United States government's decision not to dismiss him on the spot and ensure the only future he'll ever have is as a fry cook is the greatest gift your son will ever get from Uncle Sam. If Addison leaves the hospital looking even close to what he did, wherever he goes he's a target. And those nice folks looking for him won't just take your son out; they'll take fifteen, twenty, or more people around him just to ensure they get the poster child of those who defeated them. If they miss and he survives, there are hundreds more behind them, bereft of hope, waiting in line to please their god. Addison's hospital reports say that under all his bandages serious damage has been done and he'll never look the same again. Everything that happened might give him a chance at life. With the help of Israeli doctors, Addison will come though surgery with a new face as well as a new life. With what Shabak can do, he'll have a new identity and can live without having to look over his shoulder for the rest of his natural life as an Israeli citizen. What he won't be allowed to do is cause more death to innocent people who want life as much as he does. Your son has won the lottery. I hope you will help him to see that, as I hope that, if he makes it into the Ministry of Foreign Affairs, he'll see every rule is there for a reason, some you never break and walk away from."

"I . . . I didn't know."

"My instructions were to brief you. I could have been gentler. You've been thrown into a foreign world and are still trying to catch your breath in the middle of an ocean of events you didn't cause, but truth is the one thing that will help your son as he faces recovery. Nothing will be forced on him, but he will live with the consequences for the rest of his life."

"As will I, Mr. Bodine, and the rest of our family." Janelle looked at Asa, his face a curious mixture of sadness and peace. She had never encountered the two together. She reached out and placed her hands on each side of his beard. "You knew?"

"So much to know Shayndel, we have time to see what awaits."

"Vice Prime Minister," Major Weiss said.

"Thank you, Major. All has been agreed to by the government of Yisra'el. Sid, Keane, what does the United States government say?"

"We were in agreement coming in the door," Sid Cantwell said.

"Diplomatic Security just needed to officially know Israel would open the door for Mr. Deverell. With that done, we're in agreement," Keane said.

"General."

"Yes, Commander Ramot."

"There's one last matter: the exchange agreement sir—on the Arabs—between U.S. State and the Vice Prime Minister's office."

"Nearly forgot. Thank you, Commander. During the kidnapping, two Abu Dis residents got involved with Mr. Deverell's abduction. Reports show they were to receive inducements. What were those, commander?"

"One minute, sir." Ira Ramot shuffled through his file, locating the papers he wanted. "Aadil Gamal and Khalil Ahmad, both residents of Abu Dis, were contacted by a member of PMIJ, a former elementary school classmate, name of Nasir Ghafour, to facilitate the capture of Mr. Deverell. They were offered homes and a monetary stipend in Aleppo, Syria, for themselves and their families under the sponsorship of one Ra'id Marwan, a local Syrian imam. Preliminary reports indicate that after agreeing to the plan, under the guise of protecting Deverell, Aadil Gamal endeavored to talk AED from going into Abu Dis from Yerushaláyim and, after being unsuccessful, accompanied him with Khalil Ahmad and Elizabeth Daniels of Messianic Jews International. There was a question as to whether Gamal and Ahmad led them to where a contingent of PMIJ was waiting or if the PMIJ herded Deverell into a trap. What is known is that upon a rape attempt on Ms. Daniels, both Gamal and Ahmad sustained injuries in protecting

Ms. Daniels and rescuing AED from the PMIJ. Unfortunately, they were later recaptured due to the aid of a local grocer and subsequently taken to the minaret tower, where they were rescued.

"If these men or their families are left in Israel, Judea, or Samaria, their lives would be in grave danger. Operatives have already uncovered intel confirming there is a $10,000.00 bounty on each of their heads. This is an enormous amount for renegade Arabs which telegraphs the efforts PMIJ will put into locating and eliminating them. In addition to risks on their lives, there's a possibility of collateral loss of life any assassination attempt might occasion since PMIJ are not known for their pinpoint hits.

"All that taken into account" Vice Prime Minister Dobrin continued, "in conjunction with their actions risking their lives to assist Mr. Deverell in his escape attempt, the governments of the State of Israel and the United States of America have agreed to allow Aadil Gamal, Khalil Ahmad, and their families citizenship in the United States. The State of Israel will transport them to Kibbutz Shefayim when both are medically stationary and ready for travel. Further, the State of Yisra'el will provide air transportation to the United States as well as a monthly stipend for an aggregate of five years, after which time they will have assimilated into American society."

"Thank you, Vice Prime Minister. I've got copies for you of the agreement Immigration and Naturalization have signed off on. They will need new identities before being allowed in the U.S. as Homeland Security has expressed concern about jihadists trying to target them when they come to us," Keane Bodine said.

"That is in the works, Mr. Bodine. Have you decided where to settle them?" Dannie Dobrin asked.

"Since Deverell is from Oregon, why not send these fine folks their way. Portland has a vibrant Muslim community. I think they'll fit in fine, since a good portion already there are hiding from one mullah or another back home."

"Then we're all in agreement? What about you, Dr. Yochanan?" Vice Prime Minister Dobrin said.

"Mr. Vice Prime Minister, let the record show the gratitude I have for the benevolence the government of the State of Yisra'el is extending to my nephew, Shayndel?"

"Too many unknowns, too much yet to assimilate, but I know my son and he'll make the right decision."

"So we're all in agreement? And we're finished before lunch, a shame. I'll take it from here Chanan. Let the record show," Vice Prime Minister Dobrin said, "all plenum members have confirmed their acceptance of today's agreement. It is my deepest hope that not only Addison but you, Doctor Henning, will decide to make aliyah to Eretz Yisra'el. It is Zion's most basic tenet and, for each son and daughter of Abraham, the brightest hope for our future. On behalf of Prime Minister Olmert, I thank each of you. This meeting is adjourned."

CHAPTER

78

Wednesday 16 April 2008

Astana International Airport
Nine Miles outside Astana City, Kazakhstan

Three nondescript tourists, bundled against the cold, made their way into the private terminal for their flight to Austria aboard G. Clement Simmons' Hawker 800XPi. Walking to the counter, the silver-haired grandfather said, "Good day, we're bound for Austria."

"Morning, sir, which aircraft that would be with?" said the eager to please young service agent.

"Yes, of course, G. Clement Simmons."

Looking down at the monitor buried in her reception desk, she chased her computer's mouse around its pad, scanning for the needed information. "Ah yes, it's being fueled as we speak, passports please."

"Of course," said the patriarchal leader of the group. He turned to the middle-aged couple behind him, "passports."

After they'd handed their passports to the agent, she opened and inspected each, checking photos and authorizations before stamping them. "Headed for vacation?"

"A few days rest before heading back to the grind. Well, at least for my son and daughter-in-law. I am a retired man of leisure. No more salt mining for me."

"I hope you enjoyed your stay in Astana City."

"Most assuredly."

"Excellent. Now, if everyone will put your bags beside the desk I'll have them processed and placed aboard the aircraft. You can then proceed through the passageway to your right where you'll find refreshments and comfortable seating along with restrooms. Your aircraft should be ready for departure within the hour. Please stay within the seating area until your flight is called. If you need anything, just use one of the courtesy phones and I will endeavor to meet your every need. Any questions?"

Everyone shook their head no.

"Excellent. Then please to enjoy yourself and remember us for any future travel needs."

Within five hours they had passed over the border into Austria.

Two hours later they landed at Lamezia Terma International Airport, Italy.

The next three hours found the trio inside Israeli airspace headed for Lod.

Following a night's rest, they reported the success of their mission directly to Deputy Director of Covert Ops, Avi Peretz, Mossad headquarters, and promptly disappeared in different directions into the interior of Israel for the next month.

CHAPTER

79

Khabarstanskaya Pravda Newspaper
Rakhat Gorshkov, Khabarstanskaya Pravda Correspondent

Posted 17 April 2008
Two Stepnogorsk Scientists Found Dead

On 16 April, in the freezing early hours of morning, the bodies of two Scientific and Technical Institute for Microbiology research biologists were found just outside their home near the town of Petropavlovsk. They were identified as Dr. Vikesha Nikitin and Dr. Aleksandra Feedorov. Initial examination concluded both deaths were caused by acute myocardial infarction pending autopsies.

Due to nature of professional employment, in bio-technology sector, bodies were sealed within bio-hazard containment units and placed aboard a Russian military transport, for immediate transport to the Faculty of Basic Medicine, M.V. Lomonosov Moscow State University.

Local Militsiya police authorities voiced suspicions, due to age of both scientists, in mid-forties and seemingly good health according to neighbor and friend Taras Sorokin. Authorities were unwilling to comment how two unrelated, apparently healthy, persons could have died from heart attacks at same time. An unnamed Militsiya source told this reporter Russian authorities assumed immediate authority over matter and to not expect additional information since investigation would be handled from Moscow.

CHAPTER

80

ARUTZ SHEVA
ISRAEL INTERNATIONAL NEWS
SCHLOMO DAVIDS

POSTED 18 APRIL 2008

POPULAR RELIGIOUS LEADER KILLED IN BLAST

Aleppo, Syria (*Syria Times*) 17 April—Longtime spiritual leader to the people of Aleppo, Imam Ra'id Marwan, along with his driver Jaafar Fakhūrī, were killed in a car blast that left a deep crater and damaged the side of the mosque where the religious leader spent his life ministering to the needs of the area's residents.

The blast, occurring at 9:41 A.M. local time, 16 April, could be heard several miles away. The popular figure, famous for organizing food drives to eliminate hunger and providing clothing for impoverished worshippers of his mosque, will be missed, according to reports from members of his community bewailing the loss of this man of peace.

According to one mosque source wishing to remain anonymous, the imam had recently been in touch with the Gates Foundation of the United States in an attempt to bring a vaccination program to Aleppo for the many children of the area who have not received basic childhood immunizations.

There has been no official word from the Syrian government in Damascus. The crowd at the funeral, estimated to be five thousand strong, carried the popular imam on their shoulders to the cemetery, shouting Allāh hu Akbar interspersed with threats against the Zionists and the United States.

No group has claimed responsibility for the imam's death.

The Israeli government had no official comment on the deaths, stating they were an internal matter for the Syrian government. The United States government, with no embassy in Syria, did not respond to a telephone message left by Israel InterNational News.

CHAPTER

81

Mid-April 2008

Third Floor Restricted Room
Hadassah University Hospital
Ein Kerem, Yerushaláyim

After more than three weeks of restraint by sedation, threats, and pleading nurses, Hafiz badgered the doctors into releasing him to home bedrest before their combined wisdom divined he was ready. Admitting his physical healing might not have run its course, he agreed to their draconian decree to confine his existence to his bed and their offices. Rumor circulated around the third floor nurse's station that straws were drawn to see which physician would manage Hafiz's follow-up care, with the loser assigned his case. No doctor would confirm the veracity of the report.

The psychologist Shabak assigned, and Hafiz's last hurdle to freedom, gave up on counseling when, entrenched and more resolute than his strength should have allowed, Hafiz declared that the Bible, which he constantly read, contained all the help his soul required, beyond which nothing could be done to resurrect his brother. Since acceptance was the outcome the doctor sought, she signed off on Hafiz's release, without which he would have remained in the hospital even if it had required physical restraints.

For the first two and a half weeks, Hafiz's world consisted of his bedroom and the doctor's office. The concern was that any stress to his hand could result in permanent disability. His leg, in a full cast, continued healing as did his ribs.

When June began its entreaties, the weather and stifling confinement of home incarceration drove Hafiz to the Old City when he could talk friends into a ride. As the month's warmth and sunshine brought strength and recovery, along with a new walking cast, his excursions lengthened.

Memories crept from recesses in Hafiz's mind, forcing his thoughts to Nur, not in those last moments—life must never be defined by the evil it encounters—but when they'd been children and had gone with their father to the Christian Quarter to see an old man with gifts of chocolate. He didn't know what would be found, but he knew one thing: He had to begin at the bookseller's shop.

Meandering through side streets and alleys, he savored the sights and sounds in the different quarters of the Old City. He knew his destination but there was no hurry. Anything might evoke a memory buried in the travels of a child, hand in hand with a beloved father. He understood the quickest way to one's destination was not always the straightest route, but no recollection claimed his mind and all he saw remained in the present. When morning turned to afternoon, he at last set his course for the Christian Quarter.

Rounding a corner, he found the familiar sign—Yoram—Bookseller of Renown. He stepped up to the door, then hesitated and moved to the side, busying himself with the titles of tourist and Christian books displayed to attract notice from passersby. He had no interest in books, was this nervousness? Where from? He had no way to understand the unease in his stomach, too many years and conflicts had passed and his perceptions had been colored too long by the adrenaline of conflict for him to recognize nervousness. That the deepest part of him could be laid bare somewhere inside these simple walls was a thought foreign to him. Doubtful—his world uncertain—he startled at a sudden voice.

"May I be of assistance?" a tender voice said.

"I just . . . I need to talk with Yoram," Hafiz said.

"I think he might not be of much help," she said.

"Not to doubt your word, but perhaps it's something best discussed with Yoram."

"Then I would direct you to Har Hamenuchos cemetery. My husband has been there for three years now."

"Please forgive me. I didn't know your husband. It's information I seek."

"What information would an Arab seek in a bookstore owned by a Christian?"

"Though my appearance shows my father's heritage, my mother was Jewish."

"So what does a Jewish Arab want in a Christian bookseller's store?"

"This Jewish Arab follows Y'shua."

"My, aren't you the complicated one. I'm Miriam. Let's go inside and you can tell me how I may be of assistance."

Following her into the store, Hafiz walked past displays of books, through drapes where beaded curtains once hung, into the back. Miriam tied one side of the drapes back, permitting her to observe the front, and went around Hafiz to the kitchen area, which contained a round cafe table and two chairs. "Please have a seat. Would you like something cold to drink?"

Hafiz nodded.

"Ice tea okay?"

"That would be nice."

She took two glasses and put ice cubes into them from the freezer of a small fridge under the counter. Setting the glasses on the counter she removed a pitcher of ice tea from the fridge and filled the glasses finally setting them on the table. "Sugar?"

"If it's no trouble."

"It's not."

Placing a bowl of sugar on the table along with a napkin and spoon by each glass, Miriam sat down across from him. "Now, how may I be of help to an anxious brother's heart?"

Forgetting the sugar Hafiz took a sip of tea and began the story of childhood visits of an Arab father, brother, and himself to this store in the Christian Quarter. Hafiz pulled from memory the picture of an elusive old man he felt tied to who was a stranger in his memory. "The old man I remember from my earliest years, but I have so many questions. Why would father, a follower of Allāh, bring me here to the Christian Quarter? What's the connection? In my life's work, I ask questions and find answers, but if answers aren't here I may never know why my memories won't release me from this place."

"We," Miriam began, looking older than her years. Then she caught herself. "Forgive me, it hasn't been we for three years. It's so hard to be an I when all recollections are of we. I . . . I, have been here fifteen years. My parents purchased this shop when I was young. At fourteen I started working here. How long ago would you have come as a child?"

"Thirty years, maybe thirty-one. It's just a guess, all I remember."

"There was an old woman who worked here when father bought the store. Her name was Sabra, if memory serves. She worked for some time and retired, but I was young and paid little attention. She died some years back, but all may not be lost. There was a granddaughter who still lives nearby who might know something, as Sabra spent her last years living with her. I remember because she and I share the same name. If you give me a day, let's say two, I will inquire, and we shall see what we shall see."

Hafiz, anxious to return the next day but understanding the advantage of patience, resolved to wait forty-eight hours. Besides, he told himself, the chances of finding anything were not good. Sharing too much was also not good. Why had a lifetime of habits deserted him?

Forty-eight hours after he walked out of Miriam's bookstore, he strolled back through the front door, straining to keep himself from gasping from the near sprint he subjected his still-healing body to in the rush to discover what she had learned.

"*Shalom, ma koreh?* Hello, how are things?" Miriam said.

"*Hakol tov*, everything is good." *Just get to what you found*, he mentally demanded while smiling at this woman's loveliness he should have noticed two days before.

"Let us go back for tea; we can talk. Would that be good?"

"Yes," Hafiz said, wanting to jump on her and squeeze out all the information on the spot. He meekly followed her past the drapes she again tied back before going to the fridge for tea.

Setting down a napkin, spoon, and the sugar bowl on the table, Miriam turned back to the fridge and poured ice tea into a glass she had put ice into. Sitting down, she smiled.

"No tea for you?" Hafiz asked.

"I just had some. Thank you for asking."

Hafiz looked at her and took a sip of tea. It tasted bitter. He had forgotten the sugar again but refused to add any now that the woman was watching.

"You're a patient man, Hafiz. I would have thought you would be asking about what I found, but perhaps you've lost interest?"

Hafiz took another sip of the sugarless brew. "I wait for your words."

"I talked with Miriam the day you left; she didn't have any memory of the shop during the time you would have been brought here as a child."

Hafiz's jaw tightened; he said nothing.

"She did, however, provide another name."

"Another person?'

"Yes, her name is Brachah Tivka. She lives in Gedera at Herzfeld Medical Center in their nursing home. She lived in the neighborhood thirty years ago and was known as a tale bearer. When anything happened, she was aware of it."

"God condemns gossip."

"Yes, He does, but He doesn't condemn talking with an old woman to see what lies in memories when one of those recollections may unlock truth."

"Gedera between Rehovot and Ashdod? I'll talk with the woman."

"It might prove wise if I were to accompany you."

"Why do you think that?"

"In my conversation with Miriam I learned Brachah suffers from dementia. You might well waste a trip, not to mention frustrate yourself and her if you try to interrogate the poor confused woman. There are times a woman's touch can accomplish things a man's can't."

"I can talk."

"If I ever need protection I'll know where to go, but let's see if I can help."

He knew he had shared too much. Maybe his injuries had softened his brain.

"Do you have a car? I don't think a bus would be good for your leg."

"No car, but I have a motorcycle."

"Can you ride with your bandaged hand and cast?"

"It's fine. I'm careful with my hand and have been walking all over the Old City with the cast, so why not ride?"

"How does tomorrow sound?"

"I rode my motor cycle here today, how about now?"

"So you are interested. Let me lock up and we'll be on our way."

Sixty-seven minutes later, Hafiz and Miriam pulled up in front of the Herzfeld Medical Center in Gedera, a nondescript whitish-grey building with blue metal railings that rarely occasioned notice from those passing by. Hafiz got off his motorcycle and limped to the front door. Behind him a female voice called from the parking lot, "Hafiz! Wouldn't it be nice if we went in together?"

"Sorry, I forget you came."

"I would have thought my fingernails digging into your sides around some of the curves would have reminded you of my presence, especially with your broken ribs."

"The ribs heal fine; it's no problem through leather jacket. You have a woman's fingers: not so strong."

Walking through the door, Hafiz heard his name called in what sounded like a threatening manner. Going back, he held the door open. Miriam passed through. "Thank you, Hafiz."

After speaking with the floor nurse, they were escorted to *Bayit Ba'Kfar*, a home in the country, the nursing home wing of the medical center, and learned that, although Brachah's dementia sometimes distorted reality, she was harmless. A black cloud gathered over Hafiz as he followed Miriam up the stairs behind the nurse leading them to Brachah's room.

After knocking lightly, the nurse opened the door. "Brachah, you have guests." Turning to them she said, "If you need anything call." The nurse disappeared down the hallway. Hafiz noted she'd given no number to call.

Passing through the wide doorway, built to accommodate wheelchairs, they entered the sparsely appointed room and were greeted by two time-worn hospital beds, each against opposite walls in the tiny rectangular room. Quilted Turkish rose bedspreads gave evidence to their many washings. White cotton sheets could be seen peeking out from under the quilts' edges. Identical varnished maple two-drawer nightstands stood sentry beside the beds. Each had its own complement of salves and inhalers and a rainbow-colored plastic glass filled with what appeared to be water. A single flexible plastic straw hung out at an angle over each tumbler's rim. A box of tissues on the nearest nightstand and a partial roll of toilet paper on the other completed the picture that could have been seen anywhere the elderly are sent to live out their last days.

An unbroken expanse of vinyl tile gleamed under its daily washing. No throw rugs to trip feet that no longer walked with ease softened its antiseptic glaze. Standing closets of varnished maple graced each side of the room, by the foot of each bed, containing the vestige of a lifetime of clothing. Their doors closed; all must appear neat and tidy.

A glorious window caressed the end wall of this cubicle, where two lives spent their remaining days. Sunshine flooded the room, radiating hope and promise where dreams, when they touched reality, existed only to get through each day.

The air excreted odors common to such places: ammonia and disinfectant trying to mask the odor of bodily fluids from those who could no longer control themselves, where caretakers attended to personal, private needs.

Hafiz felt uneasy. If not for Miriam's presence, he would have turned and walked away. It seemed better not to know than to confront the promise that awaits all for the crime of living too long. Looking up at him, Miriam took his hand; he was grateful.

Near the window sat two simple wood chairs, with pads on their seats, armrests, and backs. Each was angled toward the window. A frail woman, appearing asleep, sat in one. The other was empty.

"*Boker tov*, good day, I am Miriam and this is Hafiz. How are you, Brachah?"

The frail woman gazed at them without speaking. Hafiz didn't know if she heard. Her white hair, the little there was, hung in scattered clumps, some to the top of her shoulders. Age spots covered her arms and palsied hands. A washed-out smock, once pink, appeared to be her only covering save the fluffy reddish slippers protecting decrepit ankles and feet. Her head turned at an odd angle as if asking who these strangers were, but still no sound came forth.

"Brachah, we have come from Yerushaláyim to speak with you. Would that please you?" Miriam said.

The woman sustained her silent vigil, as she continued to stare. No fear passed her face, just a curiosity to observe, in silence, this intrusion into her world.

"Maybe this is a bad idea," Hafiz said.

"Patience, some things take time." Looking at Brachah, Miriam said, "I own Yoram—Bookseller of Renown bookstore. It is in the Old City, Yerushaláyim. Do you remember Yerushaláyim?"

"Bookseller?" Brachah said. "Are you my auntie?"

"I am Miriam; the bookstore is where I work in the Old City. Do you remember?"

"I remember a bookseller where I used to live, but was Uzziah, not Yoram."

"Do you remember Uzziah?"

"Yes, of course, everybody remembers Uzziah."

"Do you know of an Arab who used to come to Uzziah's shop with his two young children? This was many years ago."

"Would come every month or so to visit Uzziah? Yes, every few weeks; came with two sons to visit."

"Yes, this is good. Do you know his name?"

"Whose name?"

"The name of the man who came to visit Uzziah every few weeks with two young sons."

"Name was Dabir, Uzziah told me. No, maybe Dāwūd. He was son, son-in-law, too long ago."

"You are doing well, so well. Do you remember a last name?"

"Last name was Mansur. Dāwūd Mansur. That's it, Dāwūd Mansur. Uzziah spoke name many times."

Hafiz felt unsteady. The seasoned interrogator remained silent while this peculiar old woman peeled back the years. He looked at Miriam, imploring her with his eyes to continue before this enfeebled woman lost touch with reality.

"These children, did they have names?"

"All children have names. How else would you call them?"

"Yes, but do you remember what they were called?"

"No, they came seldom, but Uzziah said one was grandson."

"One of the boys that came to Uzziah's shop was his grandson?" Hafiz burst in.

Brachah's eyes shot toward Hafiz, appearing confused by his intrusion. She stared, going over every part of his face, then finally looking back at Miriam continued. "A daughter's son—grandson to Uzziah. Other boy I don't know about. Uzziah's daughter died in childbirth . . . so many lost in bringing life. One day Uzziah said daughter got promise from husband to bring grandson to visit him. Uzziah told me he begged son-in-law, Dāwūd, to bring grandson. But son said the day he told grandson Uzziah was his grandpa would be Uzziah's last day to see him. Uzziah was Messianic—"

"He was Christian? Uzziah belonged to Y'shua?" Hafiz nearly shouted.

"He always with the praying, but I tell him I am a daughter of the Book, I do not need his prayers."

"But why would Dāwūd bring him?" Hafiz said.

"Uzziah gave money to help Dāwūd, insisting he bring children so he could see grandson. Money is needed for family so Dāwūd brought son to visit. Uzziah would pray for days after visit. He told me times without number one day grandson know Y'shua. Do you know Uzziah?"

Tears trickled down Hafiz's cheeks.

"Why sad? I did not want for you sadness."

"They are tears of joy, Brachah. You did good," Miriam said.

Words would not come. Hafiz went deep within to keep from surrendering to his emotions.

"Is there something you would like that I could bring to make you happy, Brachah?" Miriam said.

"Could you take me home? I have daughter who must be worried for where I am. I don't know where she went. Please, would you?"

"I will check with the nurse."

"Don't do that. She is mean and never lets me do anything. Just take me home. I promise to be good auntie."

"We have to go downstairs."

"Don't leave auntie. I'll be good."

"I'll pray for you if you'd like."

"No, it is only good if I pray, but now is not the time."

"May the Lord bless and keep you. *LeHitra'ot*, goodbye, Brachah."

"Goodbye, auntie. Remember you promised to take me home. I want to be there for Rosh Hashanah, to celebrate the New Year in Yerushaláyim."

Miriam looked up. Hafiz gazed into eyes he knew could be trusted. His hand enfolded hers. Together they walked to the door.

C H A P T E R

82

Saturday 12 April 2008, Early Evening.

Twenty-First Day of Hospitalization
Medical Intensive Care Unit
Hadassah University Hospital
Ein Kerem, Yerushaláyim

Each new day buried the one before. Progress was measured by inanimate equipment monitoring respiration, blood pressure, heartbeats per minute, like so many switches all in a row that must turn on simultaneously, while Addison was still lost to her. Bandages didn't come off; they shed girth and weight as progress was measured by infinitesimal reductions in the size of bandages until finally, in places, swollen and discolored skin began to appear.

Looking down on his nephew, Asa manipulated his purple, yellow, and black jaw. "Resistance is increasing. This is good, Shayndel."

"How is it good when he has yet to awaken? And when he does, how can I know if he'll be functional beyond an eighteen-month-old child?"

"Shayndel, it may seem a lifetime but it has just been three weeks, and with cerebral edema there are unknowns. This is not like movies where in the next scene all signs of injury are gone. Powerful steroids were administered along with hyperventilation to oxygenate his brain cells, as well as therapeutic hypothermia to keep his brain from swelling. Each procedure was undertaken only after careful consideration of its effect on full recovery. Our last MRI indicated swelling is reducing to expected parameters."

"Can you promise Addison will rise from that bed and know he's my son?"

"Addison will awake, but until he does we can't know, with medical certainty, what we will face. Even with reduced capacities great progress can be made, but we should know soon."

"What does that mean?"

"Yesterday at 1530 hours the medication that kept him in a coma was discontinued."

"He's going to wake?"

"He's going to awaken."

"But he's not awake."

"It takes time. Medications leave the body slowly, Shayndel. His breathing is stable, resting pulse rate steady and strong. Vital signs are within anticipated ranges."

"Asa, I don't want to sound ungrateful—"

"But he is your son. He is also my nephew, the one who ties us to the next generation. Medical science has done all it can; now we wait for the One that heals."

Two days later, 11:22 P.M.

Asa placed his hand on her shoulder. "Shayndel . . . Shayndel, it's late. Go to bed; I will sit a while."

"What?"

"You were sleeping. Go, lie down. I just finished work; my mind takes time to calm. I'll sit with Addison awhile, you get rest."

"I'm good."

"Yes, my sister, you are. Now go, get sleep while I pray for my nephew. You wouldn't deny an uncle prayer, would you?"

Rising, Janelle stumbled from the room to her cubicle. She was back to sleep before Asa could begin checking Addison's chart to see how his nephew was doing.

The next morning

Sibilant buzzing invaded her sleep. It continued its barrage as she took a shower. Walking into Addison's room, she observed the source of the concert. "Asa." Asa's snoring drowned out her voice. "Asa," this time a little louder. The snoring refused to be interrupted. Finally, putting her face close to his left ear, she shouted, "ASA!"

The sound of lips smacking together in an attempt to swallow drool that accompanied the sonorous concert greeted her ears. One eye popped open.

Janelle grabbed the tissue box. "Here!"

Ignoring her, he padded off to the bathroom. Usual male sounds could be heard, followed by running water. Coming out, he turned and tossed a towel into the hamper by the bathroom door then walked to the end of the bed to observe Addison and glance at the monitors. Janelle followed.

"Thought you were just going to stay awhile?"

"The nurse usually wakes me. Guess she wasn't on duty last night. But rest was good. Doctors are used to sleeping anywhere."

Addison's breathing was steady and deep. "How is he, Asa?"

"Vitals are solid. Just a matter of time. He'll know when he's ready to join us, Shayndel."

"Will he be in pain from that awful contraption on his leg, those vicious pins?"

"The Ilizarov apparatus may look like a medieval torture device, but its pins stabilized the alignment of his tibia. Hadassah's orthopedic surgeons are the best in all of Mediterranean. They'll remove the Ilizarov as soon as healing warrants, but first Addison must regain consciousness. Everything takes time, while Addison's tibia is growing stronger than before. With time and physical therapy he should walk without a limp.

"He will heal as he was?"

"The same question in so many ways, my sister. I am not HaShem to know all things, so who am I to say? We monitor and signs improve to normal ranges, but there are risks with traumatic brain injury. When he awakens we will know. Then words won't be needed."

"I would trade my life for his, Asa."

"It is good you do not have to, Shayndel. We have many years that were stolen to recapture."

"Mom?"

Did she hear . . . ?

"Mom."

Tears flooded Janelle's eyes.

"Do I look that bad?"

"Oh, my precious, you look beautiful."

"Who are you?" Addison said, looking at the salt-and-pepper bearded stranger just beyond.

"Addison, that's—"

"Your eyes . . . I've seen."

"Rest, my love," Janelle said softly. "There'll be time to talk."

Addison looked at Janelle. "Mom, those eyes . . . can't forget." He peered toward the stranger. "Yad VaShem, it was you."

"Son, this is your Uncle Asa."

"Uncle? No, a picture in Yad VaShem, as a boy."

Asa struggled to breathe. He knew Addison's words could only mean one thing.

Janelle looked at her brother, "Asa?"

He forced a breath. "Our words have not touched upon Yad VaShem. The Holocaust Museum is part of our people but must be seen only when ready. There was a picture, from an exhibit, that touches our family, Shayndel. It is pápa's brother, Uncle Meier. Just after his Bar Mitzvah he was taken; this was during the Second World War. No one ever knew where—no one to ask, disappearance for those that tried; it was a fearful time. We were not born yet, but a picture with *zaydeh*, grandpápa, pápa, and his brothers survived, coming from zaydeh, to pápa, to me."

"I don't understand."

"One day I walked through Yad VaShem and found a new wall with hundreds of pictures on it, pictures of those believed lost in the Holocaust. Many had names, some were a mystery. As I turned to leave, a waif of a child caught my attention; there was no name. The more I looked, the deeper his image pierced my heart. I asked, but no one could bestow a name for this face, among faces, on the wall."

Addison lay on the bed listening, the steady rhythm of monitors his only response.

"This boy's image burned into my mind, seized my thoughts. How does a face on an old photograph do this? One day, while getting ready for work, I was combing my beard. The waif's eyes stared back at me from the mirror. I was on call so had to go, but those eyes refused to leave my mind. It would have been easier to forget my own face than those eyes, but duty consumed my days. Finally, at week's end, I was back at the wall. Looking and not finding, ready to dismiss all as overactive imagination. Then I spotted my waif, and I pored over every feature. Pulling out a mirror, I must have appeared strange, looking first at my face, then back to the wall, then at the mirror. I was convinced I was staring at my eyes, but who was this child with eyes from my face?

A museum volunteer came up and asked if she could help.

"Look at my eyes."

"And why am I looking at your eyes, Mr . . . . ?"

"Asa, Dr. Asa Yochanan."

"Dr. Yochanan."

"See if the eyes in this picture," I said, pointing to the waif, "are my eyes."

"That's not likely, Doctor—"

"Just look, then tell."

She looked from my eyes to the picture then back again.

"I'll admit, from what I can see, your eyes look similar, but resemblance seldom proves anything. If you have other pictures then I would want to see. It's how many are identified."

I hurried home and pulled the box of photographs from old country off the shelf. Picture after picture was looked at expectantly, only to be set aside. Then, with a precious few left, I looked down—my waif was staring at me. But this child was healthy, with the pillowy fat of young adolescence. Gauntness had not yet taken over, yet his demeanor was intent, eyes piercing, as they bore into mine. Next to him pápa and two other brothers awkwardly smiled in the way of boys."

Janelle tried to understand. "Where would Addison see . . . how could he recognize—"

"Mom."

Addison's voice startled her. She looked down upon his bandaged face.

"I saw Yad VaShem. A wall inside, thousands of pictures, can't . . . forget."

"Sshh, rest my love. There will be time and I'll be here. I promise I'll be here."

Addison's eyes closed. He returned to dreams and healing.

CHAPTER

83

Thursday 22 May 2008

Sixty-First Day of Hospitalization
Third Floor Restricted Room
Hadassah University Hospital
Ein Kerem, Yerushaláyim

Walking into the room, the signs of her son's reemergence continued to amaze Janelle. Sitting up, pillows behind his back, fork on the attack, he speared a quarter of a waffle, loaded with butter and syrup, and hefted it into his mouth.

"Good morning, Addison."

"Muhmm," Addison answered in greeting.

"Chew, then talk," Janelle said.

He swallowed his mouthful of waffle then took a drink of milk. "Someone needs to inform my taskmasters that to complete the torture they refer to as physical therapy I need enough food to replenish the energy drained during their physical assaults."

She smiled a mother's smile.

"Mom, one measly waffle with three tiny pieces of fruit and a glass of colored water they call milk ain't helping me any. Must be a food shortage in Israel—lunch and dinner aren't any better."

"Okay, so you're starved. I'm still happy to see you."

"Hey, Uncle Asa, where you been? Thought you and Mom were joined at the hip."

"Addison Edmond Deverell, even though you're in the hospital, show respect."

"He meant no harm, Shayndel. It's good to see progress. I would have been here earlier but was stopped by a research matter on the way up."

"Your uncle has some good news."

"I get to leave the hospital?"

"Soon," Asa answered. "In half an hour Dr. Sidleman will be here. Your leg has healed sufficiently and you're ready for a full-leg cast so you can come home and just return to Hadassah for physical therapy."

"Unless I missed something, I don't have a home, Uncle Asa. Mr. Cantwell was pretty clear I no longer work for State, so I expect as soon as they kick me loose here I'll be heading back to the states that is if you'll have me mom, since I doubt I fit in with dad's plans."

"Addison, a lot has happened since your injury, and we didn't want to interfere with your healing process—"

"Shalom, everyone," Addison's nurse said, charging into the room with her normal exuberant demeanor.

"It's not time for physical therapy, is it, Gilia?" Addison said, eyeing his dominatrix suspiciously.

"Nope, today the Ilizarov comes off, but first there's an IV drip ordered especially for you so mommy here won't see her big brave boy cry like a little girl."

"Funny."

"Without the IV you don't even want to think about the pain. We free your leg, maybe put in a couple extra screws—"

"Screws?"

"Titanium."

"In my leg?"

"I didn't shatter your leg. Besides, it's not like you don't already have some."

"In my bones?"

"You sure you don't want to train for doctor? You're pretty good at this."

"That's going to hurt."

"Finally we're back to the IV. You won't feel a thing, and then I'll personally watch you like hawk for a couple of days just to make sure everything is good—"

"Good?"

"No infection. Then if Dr. Sidleman is as wonderful as we know he is, you'll be off and running with a cast for the next six to eight weeks, but try not to run into mehablim. Now unhand that fork so I can set breakfast tray aside and get you hooked up."

"I'm not done eating yet."

"Yep, you are."

"Hey."

"Like puking? Eat the rest of meal and with the drugs going through your system you'll get rid of breakfast faster than you ate it, that is if you don't choke to death first."

"Oh, never thought of that."

"Neither did the orderly who ignored your daily orders and gave you breakfast." With practiced efficiency Gilia had the IV bag hung from the drip pole and the hypodermic needle inserted so skillfully Addison didn't have time to complain. "Now just lay back and relax while we give the IV time to work. You'll be feeling real nice in no time." She turned to Dr. Yochanan. "You staying, doctor?"

"Thought I'd observe Dr. Sidleman's procedure, that way I'll know what to look for when we take Addison home. When will he be transported to the operating room?"

"Not going. Everything's booked up this morning, but Americans are tough. They'll roll in a sterile gurney and do it here. Haya should be here in about fifteen minutes to give his leg a wonderful povidone-iodine scrub then the doc will come in, we'll drape his leg, and the fun begins. By that time Mr. Wonderful will be loopy enough he won't feel a thing."

"Until after," Addison said.

"That's where our famous Yisraeli compassion comes in. He doesn't complain too much, he'll feel no pain for a day or so."

"Hey, I'm listening here."

"Then you understand if you're a good boy you'll save yourself lots of pain."

Three minutes, forty-seven seconds later the first wave of drowsiness began. Two minutes, seventeen seconds after that, light snoring could be heard. Ninety-seven seconds later Addison entered Eden.

Elizabeth walked into the room she had been visiting each day since being cleared by Dr. Ya'alon. The swelling in her nose had subsided with makeup covering traces of lingering bruising. "Boker tov, good morning, everyone."

"Elizabeth," Janelle said, going over to hug her friend.

"Boker tov," Asa said.

"And how are you today, Addison . . . Addison?" . . . Is he still asleep?"

"Sedated, the Ilizarov comes off today," Asa said.

"Do I need to leave?"

"No, when Dr. Sidleman and his team come we'll put on sterile gowns and stay out of the way."

Just then a nurse entered the room, pushing a cabinet on casters in front of her. "Good morning," she said. Closely behind her an orderly wheeled a plastic-covered gurney into the room.

"You're early," Gilia said.

"Lots to do." Going over to Addison's bed she took his chart to her cabinet and recorded the last three sets of vital signs. Going back to Addison, she began her own exam while humming an evocative tune. "Rashid, everything looks good. Let's get Mr. Deverell prepped for the gurney. Gilia, you help?"

"Don't know I want to be here for this, Asa," Janelle said.

"There's the waiting room if you want to go there," Asa said. "I'll come by when it's over."

"This floor?"

"Follow the signs."

"Thanks. Elizabeth, will you join me?" Elizabeth nodded and both women hurried from the room.

The darkened waiting room was empty. Elizabeth flipped the switch and indirect lighting bathed the walls, illuminating pastoral lithographic prints in the fourteen by twenty foot room. Synthetic flowers held positions of primacy on two end tables that confined a light gray faux leather sofa. Additional chairs, of the same material, and end tables comfortably filled the remainder of the room. A nineteen-inch television hung unnoticed on the wall.

They took seats on opposite ends of the six-foot sofa and turned toward each other.

"Coffee?"

"Not right now, dear. I've been hoping for a moment away from the men to chat."

"I figured that, what do we talk about?"

"Addison."

"What about Addison?"

"Elizabeth, I've watched as you came in to Addison's room week after week when you hadn't fully healed and were under no obligation; this isn't an interrogation. The few things I've managed to understand have shown your kindness to my headstrong son. So, as a friend . . . you are my friend?"

"I am."

"This is all so overwhelming and I have to be strong, but sometimes I'm just not. How did my responsible son end up here?"

"Can I speak forthrightly so you know what I would want to know as a mother?"

"Oh please. Above all I need truth."

"This land has known many tears. We look to understand why, and answers seem more elusive than before we asked. You know I'm a Christian. That word means so many things to different people; it's no wonder the world questions it. But Christian is a singular word defined by each person who holds the deity of Christ sacred. Our handbook is the Bible, but sadly too many claiming Christianity are illiterate and define faith based on feeling rather than HaShem's holy word."

"I understand the desire to connect your soul to truth, but—"

"But what does that have to do with anything? It's the reason I agreed to escort Addison."

"Forgive me, dear, I don't see the connection."

"The connection is Addison's motive for coming to Yisra'el early was to understand this land's conflicts. To do that you must see Yisra'el as the juxtaposition of four major faiths."

"Four? I'm familiar with your faith and, of course, the Jewish faith—this is after all Israel—along with the Muslims, but I didn't think the Buddhists or Mormons exerted enough influence here to be considered a fourth spiritual pillar in Israel."

"The forth is atheism, that sometimes hides under the umbrella of Zionism. While Zionism began as a Jewish political movement, today, in Yisra'el, it attempts to supplant HaShem in everyday life. Not on the surface—our ministry of tourism loves religion, but not faith's heart and soul, the part where HaShem directs lives for our good and His glory. This blindness renders us unable to understand all that happens in our land while enemies who surround us know what they are called to do."

"I understand the concept of faith, but my questions—and I have questioned—have not been answered as yours seem to have been."

"Yisra'el is of no strategic value to anyone were it not for the spiritual. That fact is important because all that happened in recent days resulted from Addison believing he was asking a secular question that was actually spiritual."

"Which was?"

"Why Arabs hate Jews."

"That's it?"

"Did you know Addison came to Eretz Yisra'el three weeks before he was scheduled to report for duty just to find the answer to that question?"

"I knew he came early. I didn't realize it would cause such a problem."

"Embassies function under specific rules and protocols. In arriving early Addison breached one of those rules and forced the Deputy Administrator to find him an escort until his reporting date."

"He just couldn't let him find a hotel and see the sights until he started work?"

"That was what Addison hoped for. But he had a specific reporting date and, until that date, did not exist as far as his reporting embassy was concerned. When he showed up early he had to be dealt with because when you enter State Department service, it's not just a job. You are a representative of your country every moment of every day. That's why Hafiz IbnMansur was called from the consulate in East Yerushaláyim, where he worked, to the embassy in Tel Aviv to be Addison's escort. I don't know the details, but something came up and Hafiz couldn't stay with Addison until his reporting date. Because Hafiz is a Christian, we knew each other and he was aware I had served as an escort for visitors to Yisra'el—it's part of my duties at the ministry—so he asked, I needed the money, and became Addison's escort. There were only a few days before Addison had to report and I think Hafiz felt, with Addison's age, I might be more amenable than some fifty-year-old with a falafel gut."

"Maybe I could use some coffee."

Elizabeth picked up a courtesy phone on the wall and spoke in Hebrew. "They have a wonderful volunteer staff here; we should have refreshments in a few minutes."

"More than coffee?"

"This is Yisra'el."

"Wonderful. Unlike Addison, I didn't have the opportunity to eat this morning. How did my son get outside Israel?"

"Pretty easily, actually, it's the reason he wanted to that will answer more questions. His dad is high up in some NGO in your nation's capital, is that right?"

"Yes, my ex-husband heads an organization known as TRFI, The Religious Freedom Institute. It's his way to schmooze with power brokers and legally extort money for his organization in the name of doing good."

"Addison didn't have that exact take, but he defined a quest he hoped would win his dad's respect. I don't know all his reasons, but he wanted to understand why many Arabs in Yisra'el hate Jews. He had a professor who was killed by extremists when leading a student group in Syria, and Addison was convinced if he could just talk to authentic Arabs, not the ones posturing for news cameras, he could figure everything out, and that knowledge would win the day with his dad and help his career."

"His dad abandoned him when he left me, and no amount of broken promises has been able to convince Addison the fault wasn't his. So he got into the West Bank—"

"Judea."

"Where's the West Bank?"

"The Arabs call ancient Judea and Samaria the West Bank. They try to cut the land from its Jewish history. It's like calling Egyptians, Persians, and Arabs, Palestinians only when they live in Judea or Samaria. There are no ethnic Palestinian people, but this takes much time to understand. It was one of Yasser Arafat's more successful lies."

The door opened and a smiling octogenarian walked into the room. "I've got some wonderful coffee and hot pastries. Do I have volunteers to take them from my cart?"

Within two minutes the waiting room was filled with the delightful aroma of steaming coffee, halva and phyllo pastry, sufganiyot, and burekas. Janelle tried to give the sainted angel twenty dollars; she left smiling and shaking her head no.

"Is that feta I detect?"

"Yes, the burekas are healthier than the sweets, so I usually have a couple of them before I get to what I truly want. Addison, after initially sticking his nose up at them, found them to be delightful."

"Mmm yum, I agree."

Addison's story waited as hunger flexed its ravenous will and then was sated.

Finishing her sufganiyot, Janelle took a sip of coffee then dabbed her lips with her napkin. "I just don't understand the hatred. There are many different races in America and, at times, deep differences, but somehow we manage to make it work. Why is that such a problem here?"

"Because those who seek answers never acknowledge its spiritual roots."

"So all this trouble, everything that happened, has some type of spiritual element?"

"When you see a majestic tree you understand its grandeur comes from the strength of its roots. To understand the issues Yisra'el faces, we must also look to our roots.

The door burst open and a smiling Asa entered the room. Looking down at the tray of goodies, he sat on a chair and filched a sugary sufganiyot, downing the custard-filled donut in two bites.

Janelle waited while her brother finished the last two sufganiyots, three halva, and one phyllo pastry.

"Sorry, we ate the burekas."

"Burekas, there were burekas?"

"So now that you have sufficient energy, care to tell me how my son is doing?"

"That's why I came."

"Hard to tell," Janelle said then smiled.

"Dr. Sidleman is a great surgeon, the Ilizarov came off without a hitch. If ever I injure my leg or arm, he's the man I want. I'm so used to dealing at the cellular level I forgot the joy of watching a skilled surgeon working with a real, live person."

"I am gratified Addison is among the living, how about pain?"

"Shayndel, Addison couldn't have felt pain if a hammer had been taken to his leg. Pain management isn't like in old days. He will be kept sedated until discomfort is just a reminder to treat his ankle with kindness. Now what were you talking about when I came in?"

"Addison."

"What part of Addison's fascinating life were you discussing?"

"Janelle wanted to know why Addison went to Samaria."

"And you said?"

"Because Addison wanted to know the reason Palestinian Arabs hate Israeli Jews, well, all Jews for that matter. We're just in closer proximity."

"Shayndel, this is a question neither Addison nor you can know the answer to."

"You remember I have my doctorate, right?"

"It's not a matter of education, but vision. There are many living inside Eretz Yisra'el who don't know this question has an answer."

"Then think how ahead of the curve I'll be when you tell me."

"You sure you want to know? Many don't like truth when it visits."

"Asa, I know where you're going with this, and even though I don't share your beliefs, I've searched for truth many times; I actually thought I'd found it before all this. Something is happening—you don't end up a half a world away by chance—and I don't have a clue as to what that something is, but I'm willing to listen. But, with all respect, brother, no come to Jesus moment please. I just need facts."

Asa took a well-worn Bible from his pocket. "This is an old friend. It gives hope in all the turmoil I see." Turning to the Eighty-Third Psalm, he handed it to Shayndel. "Read?"

"I thought we agreed no proselytizing."

"This is not what you think, Shayndel."

Looking at the small print, she reached into her purse for her glasses.

"Start here," he said, pointing, "and stop there."

"O God, do not remain quiet;
Do not be silent and, O God, do not be still.
For, behold, Thine enemies make an uproar;
And those who hate Thee have exalted themselves.
They make shrewd plans against Thy people,
And conspire together against Thy treasured ones.
They have said, "Come, and let us wipe them out as a nation,
That the name of Israel be remembered no more."
For they have conspired together with one mind;
Against Thee do they make a covenant: . . . "

"Shayndel, these words were written over three thousand years ago. The enemies who surrounded Yisra'el had different names then: Philistines; Ammonites; Jebusites; Moabites; and many others, but each was driven by the same spirit that drives hate today. Addison was looking for a behavior, a mindset that could be understood then changed, when he should have been looking for a spirit."

"I can't even begin to understand what that means."

"A war rages, but not on the battlefield most think. It began in antiquity when HaShem promised Abraham, the father of all Jews, an heir from his own body. Time passed and becoming pregnant seemed impossible for his wife Sarah at seventy-six. So Sarah gave her handmaiden, Hagar, to Abraham as a wife, a legal custom back then. Hagar conceived and her heart despised Sarah. She bore a son, Ishmael, and tormented Sarah with the deepest hurt one woman could bring against another in those days when an heir was life itself: being barren. But HaShem promised not only would Abraham's heir come from his own body but would come through Sarah. Thirteen long years later at eighty-nine years old, Sarah became pregnant, and the next year gave birth to Isaac."

Janelle tried to follow Asa's words but she needed a connection to her world and saw none.

Asa continued, "Hagar's heart remained hardened against Sarah. Her son was first-born; nothing could ever change that. The strife grew, and when Isaac was weaned, an important event in tribal life, Ishmael, now a teenager, mocked Isaac. Sarah saw the results of not trusting HaShem's promise. She went to Abraham and said, *'Drive out this maid and her son, for the son of this maid shall not be an heir with my son.'* Abraham was in anguish—Ishmael was his first-born son—but Sarah was relentless so he went to the Lord in faith and was told, *'Do not be distressed because of the lad and your maid; whatever Sarah tells you listen to her, for through Isaac your descendents shall be named. And of the son of the maid I will make a nation also because he is your descendent'.* The next day Abraham took bread and a skin of water and gave them to Hagar and sent her and Ishmael away—HaShem must be obeyed. They wandered into the wilderness of Beersheba. Everything I've told you has been recorded in the book of Genesis."

"Asa, I appreciate the Bible story and would guess there must be a point buried here somewhere; I just don't have a clue what it is or how it relates to Addison."

"Shayndel, truth rarely comes neatly packaged; it must be sought. You are near the beginning of understanding that takes a lifetime to know."

"Asa, to help students understand a subject we—and I'm talking as an educator—don't throw them an enigma wrapped in a quandary then ask, 'got it?' I don't mean to seem impolite but I need to powder my nose." Janelle found the nearest restroom and, when finished, sat on the lounge bench prolonging her return to a subject that only confused when she needed answers that made sense. Finally she made her way back to the waiting room. "Any coffee left, Elizabeth? I could use some."

Jiggling the carafe, Elizabeth nodded.

Janelle poured the lukewarm brew then sat down facing Asa. "Okay. Ishmael mocked baby Isaac, Hagar forgot she was wife number two, and Sarah got Abraham to boot Hagar and Ishmael from the camp, that about everything?"

"What was Addison searching for?"

"We both know."

"Maybe, but it's your understanding I seek Shayndel."

"The cause of the conflict."

"Which conflict?"

"Arabs and Jews."

"So he thought. The world over we are accused of hating the sons and daughters of Ishmael, of taking their land, but they are blood of our blood through Abraham, there can be no hate. But Eretz Yisra'el, the land of Israel, was given us by HaShem, not a U.N. resolution. When Ishmael was driven from his father's camp, Abraham's heart was torn apart. His words were, *'Oh HaShem that Ishmael would live before You.'* But Abraham, as we all must, sooner or later, had to submit; HaShem's ways cannot be hindered. HaShem gave Ishmael an expanse of land hundreds of times the size of Israel, land that to this day produces untold wealth. It wasn't until over four hundred years later that Joshua led the descendants of Isaac across the Jordan River to possess Eretz Yisra'el to fulfill the covenant HaShem had established with Abraham. HaShem's words were, *'I will make you a great nation, And I will bless you, And make your name great; And so you shall be a blessing; And I will bless those who bless you, And the one who curses you I will curse. And in you all the families of the earth shall be blessed.'* But in choosing Abraham, Isaac, and their descendents to be an oracle to all mankind of G-d's eternal presence, those blessings came with a condition of obedience to live righteously, according to His word which is embodied in the Ten Commandments with a warning that if we did not keep the way of the Lord we would come under His judgment, a story we have lived too many times."

"Am I missing something, Asa? I still don't see the connection to Addison."

"Ishmael's spiritual descendents covet our tiny land. Their great wealth, their massive numbers are not enough. They scheme to take HaShem's gift from Isaac's descendents. Our people are hated because Ishmael, in rejecting HaShem's covenant, rejected the covenant giver and his birthright, but HaShem is not a man that He should change His mind. When Mohammed came, so many centuries later, hatred for the people of the book was enshrined for future generations. Millions never ask why such a small number of people, on such a tiny piece of this vast world, are so hated. This was Addison's quest and why he could not find his answer. Hatred is borne in the unredeemed hearts of man, and until hearts are restored to the true and living God that caused the writing of the Psalms you read, there can be no peace."

"Asa I don't know I can believe that. Why aren't people shouting this from the rooftops?"

"Shayndel, some are, but most do not know the spirit that drives them. Ishmael's seed is taught we are enemies from childhood, and when they become adults the venom runs so deep it is easier to lose their breath than their hatred. Such a small thing, this land you are in. Its current boundaries aren't even all HaShem gave our people so long ago, but it is enough. How much room does a heart need?"

"Janelle," Elizabeth said, "Asa's words come from a lifetime of study. The one thing you need take from them is that the box Addison opened was created a long time ago and maybe both you and Addison will find the answers he sought. But answers, like healing, take time."

"Elizabeth?"

"Yes, Asa."

"Can your ministry spare you to stay in my nephew's life a while longer? I will help with expenses; I know bills must be paid. He trusts you and I cannot be there for *Ulpan* and all the coming changes if he chooses to make Yisra'el his home."

"Of course."

"What is Ulpan?"

"School for the study of Hebrew. I know Addison studied before he came here, but this is more intensive because to be Jewish in Yisra'el is to speak Hebrew," Elizabeth said.

"Shayndel, will you make aliyah?"

"How can I answer that, Asa? Questions and emotions race through my heart and mind. I can't know what the next weeks will bring, but I will stay long enough to find out.

CHAPTER

84

Thursday 28 August 2008, 0900 hours

Israel Ministry of Foreign Affairs Givat Ram, Yerushaláyim

Rapidly warming sunlight poured through the fourth floor windows of the Foreign Ministry building on its way to 84.2°. Nine people stood around the nondescript conference table in one of the smaller conference rooms, lost in conversation and private thoughts while Yael Davids set up her stenotype recorder.

Outside the meeting room, near the vending machines, Elizabeth sat in a comfortable chair, open Bible in her lap, reading ancient words.

As the clock on the end wall of the conference room reached 9:00, one of the nine said, "Boker tov, time to get started. For those who don't know me, my name is Chayim Myrtenbaum. I am the Consular Affairs Senior Officer for the Ministry of Foreign Affairs, and I'm pleased to greet you this morning. I want to welcome everyone, especially Mr. Bodine from the American Embassy and our three guests, Drs. Yochanan and Henning, and Mr. Addison Deverell. If everyone would please take your seats, we can get started."

Asa, Addison, and Janelle remained standing.

"Oh, forgive me. Thursdays are not my day. Please take whichever of the remaining seats you desire."

They sat down next to each other with Addison in the middle.

"As you have no doubt noted, today's proceedings are being recorded. Ms. Yael Davids, operating the stenotype recorder, also recorded the initial meeting on 1 April of this year. I will now turn the meeting over to Major Weiss, who conducted that meeting, Major Weiss."

"Thank you, Chayim. I would like to remind everyone today's meeting complies with internal Israeli protocol requirements for restricted meetings and remains classified at the Secret level. Let the record show that from the April 1, 2008, meeting we have General Oz, Commander Ramot, and myself representing Yisra'el along with Keane Bodine representing the U.S. Embassy and are joined in today's meeting by Chayim Myrtenbaum, Israel Ministry of Foreign Affairs, and Rachel Jacobi, Ministry of Immigrant Absorption, and of course Addison Deverell, Dr. Janelle Henning, and Dr. Asa Yochanan. General Oz."

"Today's meeting is for final status disposition of Addison Deverell relevant to immigration to Yisra'el and absorption in Eretz Yisra'el."

"Thank you, General. Mr. Bodine."

"I have been meeting with Ira Ramot and we are ready to implement one of two plans dependent on the choice Mr. Deverell makes today. I want to emphasize the choice is Mr. Deverell's alone."

Addison nodded toward Keane.

"We know there are three family members living in the United States who could impact Mr. Deverell's choice. Dr. Henning, at the Department of State's request, you and Addison spoke with two of these individuals. Would you tell us the results of your conversations?"

"The individuals referenced, Mr. Bodine, are my Mom, Rebecca Henning, and Dad, Edmond Henning, who are of course Addison's grandparents. Addison has no paternal grandparents alive. Mom, Dad, Addison, and I talked about the continuing threat to Addison and possibly other members in the family. Their concern, as is typical of them, was for Addison and me. They understand they would not be able to have any contact for the first eighteen months Addison would be in Israel should he immigrate here, and they were amenable to the sacrifice, hoping to come to Israel after that time to see their grandson. As to their ability to safeguard information about Addison, I can testify to my parent's ability to keep a secret because, as you know from our conversations, Mr. Bodine, they kept a huge secret over forty years."

"Thank you, doctor," Keane said. "The third relative involved is Mr. Blade Deverell. Addison, unlike your mother, your dad chose not to come to Israel when given the opportunity at the beginning of the incident. FBI Special Agent Zuberi, who interviewed him at that time, recently conducted a follow-up interview. Due to his public persona in the nation's capital as the head of The Religious Freedom Institute and his expressed attitude relevant to this incident and your involvement in it, a decision was made to release the story of your death without informing your dad of the facts on the ground. We knew, should you choose not to immigrate to Israel, the Israelis could claim they misidentified a deceased terrorist only to realize you were alive. In view of the fact of your coma, that seemed the most reasonable plan of action. Remember we, as well as the Israelis, had just begun our investigation and were scrambling to determine the PMIJ's capabilities. We didn't know what your decision would be but we had to get a cover story out so jihadists wouldn't blow up every American they thought was you. I have an article from the *Arlington Post* dated two days after your death was reported. It's one of dozens that ran in various papers across the United States and around the world. I chose it because it contains your dad's complete statement on the news of your reported demise." Walking to the front of the room, he positioned a rolling cart with an overhead viewer on it toward the end wall.

Chayim Myrtenbaum went to the wall, retrieved a long-handled hook, and pulled a projection screen down from the ceiling.

Turning the projector on, Keane grabbed a transparency from the top shelf of the cart and adjusted the projector's focus. "Chayim, would you hit the curtain switch?"

Blackout curtains closed.

"Addison, I'm sorry to have to show you this, but you need to know the truth as you make your decision." He replaced the transparency with an article dated April 4th, 2008.

ARLINGTON POST
ANDREA MCDOWELL
APRIL 4, 2008

SON OF WASHINGTON D.C. NGO FOUNDER DIES

Addison Deverell, son of Dr. Janelle Henning of Oregon and Mr. Blade Deverell, co-founder of The Religious Freedom Institute in Washington, D.C., died from unspecified injuries on April 2, 2008, at Hadassah Hospital in Jerusalem, Israel. Deverell was kidnapped several days earlier by a faction of the Palestine Mujahideen Islamic Jihad.

The PMIJ is the ruling political power in Gaza and is believed to operate several splinter groups from parts of the West Bank north through Jordan into Syria.

Deverell, newly assigned U.S. Embassy consular officer in Tel Aviv, Israel, out for a morning walk a few days before officially beginning work, was kidnapped and a reported five million dollar ransom demand was issued. U.S. Department of State's spokesperson, Elveta Hurunui, denied a ransom payment was paid by the government of the United States. An Israeli source, who wished to remain anonymous, claimed five million U.S. dollars had been paid for Deverell's release after a joint U.S/Israel team failed to locate the American.

Deverell's rescue came a few days later at the top of Jerusalem's Old City Tower of David minaret as terrorists attempted to destroy the tower with explosives.

Israeli commandos secured the tower and nascent diplomat. During the rescue, Deverell was critically wounded, according to Israeli spokesman Moshe Galitz. Taken to Hadassah Hospital (Jerusalem), Deverell slipped into a coma and died while awaiting surgery.

International sources requesting anonymity maintain biological weapons were involved in the attack. Israeli authorities denied knowledge of any biological weapons. Asked for comment, U.N. Middle Eastern monitoring agency Surveillance Biologique stated no airborne release of bioweapon chemical particles were recorded at any monitoring station during the month of March 2008.

Dr. Janelle Henning, in Israel during the incident, could not be reached for a statement. Mr. Blade Deverell released the following statement through TRFI's spokesperson Herma P. H. Rodite.

"The death of any man, woman, or child diminishes each of us. When that man is my son it compels me to understand the circumstances in which he became involved with the noble, peace-loving, Palestinian people. Preliminary reports, from trusted Palestinian friends, engender profound sorrow for Addison's interference in internal Palestinian affairs. My son knew the sovereignty of the Palestinian people. That he did not respect their rights will be a cloud over the love I hold for him. My life's efforts have been dedicated to engendering respect between people. That Addison, with such promise, abandoned all that I value fills my heart with deep regret. To any his actions have brought hurt or disrespect, I apologize for his disgraceful behavior and rededicate my efforts to help those whose voices cannot be heard, no matter where they live."

Keane walked to the switch and flipped it, the curtains opened. "The article has a concluding paragraph you can read later, but I wanted you to see your father's words." Returning to the projector, he turned it off then took his seat. The room was still. Janelle's lips began to tremble as tears filled her eyes.

"Addison," Keane said, "you had to know. Your decision must come from knowledge, as you will live with it the rest of your life."

"This is not right. A pápa does not speak this way to the world about his son when he does not know, does not understand. Don't take to heart such words, Addison; they embrace no wisdom. They hold no love," Uncle Asa said.

"Have you made your decision, Addison?" Keane asked.

"Mr. Bodine, your words sound so official, so devoid of emotion. It's not the voice I remember from the hospital. You were there five times."

"How could you know I came to your room?"

"Am I right five times?"

"I can live with that number, but you were in a coma."

"I don't know the medical terminology that defines what happened. I just know I came in and out of awareness and heard you, listened to your words, to those in the room. Though your voice was unfamiliar there was kindness, understanding. As you spoke, thoughts bore into me I had never confronted before. Uncle Asa, your presence seemed constant."

"You heard my words?"

"You were also confusing as I tried to place a voice I had never heard before. Yours seemed the backdrop for all else, comforting, encouraging mom, but most of all I remember moments when you cried out—there's no other way to express what I heard than someone crying out—in prayer, though I am no expert on the subject. Your words covered me, not every time, but I came to desire those words and in them I knew, no matter what tied me to my surreal realm in and out of awareness, I would be okay."

"Was I in your dreams?"

"Mom, they weren't dreams. The words were real but spoken outside a veil I couldn't break through. Yours was the voice I recognized, but I heard fear and uncertainty. I wanted to tell you everything was okay but I could not will myself to speak, then your words would fade as I was engulfed by sleep. There were others that intruded into my world; they came and left as I went in and out of consciousness. The coma, far from blotting out awareness, focused my thoughts as words made their way into my consciousness, confronting me. Not that I've figured life out, but I may finally be in a place to find the road. It's the reason I have spent time alone thinking since released from the hospital, to make sense of what I heard."

Addison sat quietly, selecting his next words, knowing they would live with him a lifetime. "No word has ever been spoken that can change the moment that preceded it, and yet each life can only be lived in the combined totality of all such moments. The events in Judea and the migdal were not of my design or will. I sought understanding; however naïve my quest may seem in the glaring light of events.

"Were there ways in which I would not have become bound with evil? Hindsight answers yes, but I am content to let the entirety of my life, when lived, to speak for itself. I caution any who choose to judge me to keep in mind that in judgment mercy has its being, for none are cut from perfect cloth.

"In truth, redemption can only be embraced by the life I now live from this moment, but my life can never replace that which was lost. I regret, profoundly and deeply, actions that allowed evil to destroy the life of Ephraim Rabinowitz, whose blood was given so Israel would endure. I will live with his loss for the rest of my life, no matter how well spent.

"While I have known dad's heart for a long time, I hoped a vestige of love would redeem all that was lost which compelled me to reach out time after time. His words confirmed the spark of a father's heart for a son was gone, if ever there, or his words could not have come to mind much less be spoken to the world.

"From the ashes of evil I discovered a heritage I could not have known existed, which leaves but one path if I am to redeem that which has been given me. If Israel wants me and will accept the offer of my life's service, then with will and purpose I ask to be allowed the honor of aliyah to the land whose blood and heritage I now know I share."

No one spoke as Addison's words resonated in the small room.

"I am sorry events kept us from working together, Addison," Keane said. "It's obvious there's more to you than revealed itself in the trial that occasioned our meeting. Major Weiss."

"Let the record show Mr. Deverell has accepted aliyah to Yisra'el. Rachel."

"Mr. Deverell, as was said when I was introduced earlier, I work for the Ministry of Immigrant Absorption and I will be delighted to welcome your application for citizenship to Eretz Yisra'el. If you will come to the District Office after Shabbat, say Sunday at 0800 hours. Normally the process is handled at ministry bureaus or branch offices, but due to the unusual nature of your immigration I will oversee your processing with Ira Ramot. Be sure to bring your Diplomatic VISA and Passport. You still have them?"

"My keepers never seemed interested in them after verifying who I was. Can Mom and Uncle Asa come with me?"

"Of course. Yisra'el loves families."

"I would like to remind you, Mr. Deverell," Ira Ramot said, "that at this moment your state is somewhat undefined since you are not officially alive. I can rectify that with a temporary identification card in case you're stopped." He slid an envelope across the table to Addison. "Go ahead, open it."

Addison extracted a plastic-coated card with a recent photograph of himself he didn't know had been taken. The name Yossel Yochanan stared back at him along with Uncle Asa's address under the strange face he had not yet grown to know. He studied it.

Ira waited. "As I said, Addison Deverell no longer lives, so today begins your metamorphose. My cell number is printed on the card's back. My phone is always on and with me at all times. If you're stopped and there are questions, I can be reached anytime. Just remember all Border Police and IDF are armed and authorized to use their weapons, so understand this specific identification may raise some questions before it's verified. Respond diplomatically and all will be well. That said, remember not to reveal the details of your former identity, no casual conversation, no slip-ups—life could depend on it. At the beginning of the week you will be enrolled in a special Ulpan school to take what you know of Hebrew, as well as the history of this country, and turn you into a native. You will be amazed how little your country has taught you of the truth of Yisra'el and her people. There are specific techniques to learning a new identity that have proven successful, so rest, and enjoy the next couple of days. Life is about to get more intense and interesting, Yossel Yochanan."

"I know Uncle Asa's last name is Yochanan, but why Yossel?"

"Dr. Yochanan, care to answer?"

"Yossel was your grandfather's name. You will choose the permanent name you bear, but your surname will remain Yochanan. When I emigrated I chose the name Asa, it means healer. How often does one get to choose a new first name? It must be Hebrew, but the choice will be yours within security limits."

"Security limits?"

"Yossel Yochanan cleared a security check, no hits on it, but on the off chance another Yochanan is on a wanted list you might need to choose another first name."

"Yeah, the idea of being handcuffed again has little appeal. Next subject, can I ask about the Ministry of Foreign Affairs?"

"Major, I'd like to handle that."

"Of course, Chayim."

"Mr. Deverell, as I said in the introductions, I am Chayim Myrtenbaum and I represent the Ministry of Foreign Affairs. It was not a given you would be recruited for the ministry—we are a small country and your recent experience was not the best résumé one could present—but from what I've heard today along with recently collected information on your academic studies and U.S. Department of State training records, I am encouraged you will be offered a spot as a Ministry of Foreign Affairs officer. That said, assimilation into Yisra'el is a long path. Your master's degree in Foreign Relations proves academic ability, but you will also need to undergo intense training until you think, act, and feel native-born, and until your new identity is so fully embraced it becomes who you are. All comes with time. When the time is right I will be in contact. One final note, our beleaguered nation knows all too well your experiences of these last few weeks. It is, unfortunately, too much a part of who we are. Yisra'el's strength comes not from forgetting such times but from embracing and learning from them. Gain knowledge from all around you whose wisdom has been hard won, then take your place in this nation G-d called into being. We have no greater quest or demanding challenge."

"I don't know how to put this, but since I'm no longer under the employ of the U.S. State Department, I seem to lack funds. Is there some job I can get right away?"

"Mr. Deverell, Yisra'el is used to immigrants arriving without funds from impoverished nations. When you begin processing Sunday you will receive a temporary stipend which will take care of immediate needs. You'll find yourself far too busy to hold even part-time employment."

"If our business is concluded, General Oz would you like to close the meeting?"

"Addison . . . Yossel, it's Yossel now. This operation was my final battle of thirty-five years of service to my country. For you a door is opening into a future. I now go on to politics, where the battles will merely change. You passed through the fire and your life was spared for a reason. I can't tell you why; it's yours to discover. If you are wise, you'll find the reason and Eretz Yisra'el, the land I love more than life itself, will be changed by that discovery. Your words give me hope that the life you live will help to take your adopted nation into the future. Many say they want peace for Yisra'el, our Yisra'el, but at a cost that would destroy our people's life in our land of a thousand tears and a million joys. Your life was spared under my watch, and I intend to see what you make of the days you have been given. Yossel Yochanan, make each day matter."

"This meeting," Major Chanan Weiss said, "is adjourned."

Chairs moved back as people got up to stretch. Conversations continued as, extraordinarily, no one left, even when the doors were opened.

Janelle turned to Addison. "Here's the deal, I encourage your passion. In fact, I was impressed. Just never undergird it with your dad's heart."

"Little chance of that, mom, it wasn't only you he abandoned. Uncle Asa, you know where I need to go on Sunday?"

"Of course it's only twenty minutes from home. What are your plans Shayndel?"

"Yeah, mom, if I'm Jewish, odds are they'd let you immigrate, too."

"How can I leave my home to start a new life at my age? There's my tenure with the school district. Friends I have known for a lifetime, mom, and dad."

"How about the blood that ties us together, mom, along with Uncle Asa and this land."

"The truth is I knew this conversation would come. When you were in the hospital I went over to the Hebrew University and Bar-Ilan. It seems if I were to immigrate there would be a position open in my field."

"And?"

"And I applied for it."

"Shayndel, pápa's and mama's hearts' sing."

"No promises, but I remember those days before Tatyana came into my world and the hope my life had abandoned that I've found here. An expectation like when I was a child. I want to find its source, and to do so I must stay."

"Does that mean you'll make aliyah, mom?"

"It means that on Sunday two people will be going to the Ministry of Immigrant Absorption, but I have to warn you both, if I find everything I've felt is just the emotion of recent events, well then, we might have another conversation."

"Fair enough, mom, even though my commitment won't change."

"Shayndel, there is so much to see and know."

"Could be that for the first time since Blade I am ready to listen to a man, Asa. Now," looking at her son, "isn't there someone you've forgotten?"

Addison looked quizzically, and then smiled. "I didn't forget."

A breeze from the corridor washed through the room. Addison's look told Janelle all she needed to know. Turning toward the door, he walked from the room, embracing the air swirling around him. Elizabeth was waiting.

The End

Glossary

Abba:	Father, Arabic transliteration
Ahlan wa sahlan:	Welcome, Arabic transliteration
AIC:	Agent in charge
al-Haram Ash-Sharif:	The Noble Sanctuary also known as the Temple Mount, Arabic transliteration. Legend has it as the site where Muhammad travelled to heaven and back
al-Quds:	Jerusalem, Arabic transliteration
Al-Siq:	Main entrance to Petra
Allāhu Akbar:	God (Allāh) is the greatest, Arabic transliteration
'Anā jā'i':	I'm hungry, Arabic transliteration
Analgesic:	Medication that reduces or eliminates pain
Arab Waqf:	Arabic Trust controlling the Temple Mount
Area A:	Palestinian Full Control
Area B:	Palestinian Civil Control and Israeli Security Control
Area C:	Israeli Full Control except over Palestinian citizens
As Salam a' alaykum:	Hello, Arabic transliteration
Bacillus anthracis:	The pathogen (infectious agent) of anthrax acute disease
Ben:	Son of, in Hebrew surnames
Basboosa:	Arabic syrup-soaked tart
Beit Rosh HaMemshala:	Official residence of the Prime Minister of Yisra'el

Bête noire:	A person or thing particularly disliked or dreaded
Biopreparat:	The Soviet Union's biological weapons agency
Birat Hanezah:	Eternal capital, Hebrew transliteration. Secret plan to preserve Yerushalayim as Yisra'el's capital
Boker Tov:	Good Day, Good Morning, Hebrew transliteration
Burekas:	Triangular Sephardic golden brown pastry
Burg Daũd:	Tower of David, Arabic transliteration
Cenotaph:	Empty tomb or monument
Cerebral edema:	Swelling of the brain
Dar al-Harb:	The house of war, which exists everywhere Dar al-Islam does not exist
Dar al-Islam:	The house of peace, where the Muslim faith exists or predominates
Dāwūd:	David, Arabic transliteration
Diaspora:	The scattering of Jews outside Israel beginning in the sixth century B.C. when they were exiled to Babylonia until 1948
Dom Rebyonka:	Baby House, Russian transliteration
Dome of the Rock:	Building on the Temple Mount where Allah was reported to have ascended to Heaven on his steed, Al-Burāq
Do svidaniya:	Good-bye, Russian transliteration
DTMF:	Dual-tone multi-frequency signaling used for telecommunication signaling
Dweezle:	Obsequious and petty
Eretz Yisra'el:	The land of Israel, Hebrew Transliteration
Eubacterial:	Bacterium, singular, Bacteria, plural
Excipient:	Inert substance used as a diluent or vehicle for a drug
Falafel:	Patty made with chickpeas and/or fava beans
Fentanyl:	An opoid used in making Kololol-1 gas grenades
G-d:	Orthodox Jewish reference to God to avoid taking His name in vain, in violation of the Third Commandment in the Bible
Gan David:	David's Garden in the Tower of David complex
Gilbo'a:	Israel prison
Hafuch:	Hebrew for espresso and frothed milk from cappuccinos to lattes. Also the name of a Café in Jerusalem a suicide bomber attacked

Haganah:	The Defense, Hebrew transliteration. A Jewish paramilitary organization from 1920–1948 that later became the core of the IDF
Hakol tov:	Everything is good, Hebrew transliteration
HaShem:	Hebrew word for God, literally The Name
Hatikva:	National anthem of Israel
Hee Mishelanu:	She is one of us, Hebrew transliteration
Helo:	Slang for helicopter
Hookah:	Water pipe for smoking tobacco
Hyperbaric Chamber:	Used with pure oxygen to treat various injuries and speed recovery
IAF:	Israeli Air Force
Ibn:	Son of, when attached to a last name, such as Hafiz IbnMansur
IDF:	Israel Defense Forces
IED:	Improvised Explosive Device. A homemade bomb deployed by terrorists (mehablim)
Imam:	A Muslim religious leader
'Īsā:	Jesus, Arabic transliteration
Isrā'īl:	Israel, Arabic transliteration
Jahannam:	Hell, Arabic transliteration
Jubbah:	Full-length, loose outer garment
Kafiyyeh:	Arab scarf or head covering
Kalb:	Dog, Arabic transliteration
Kardum:	Hatchet, Hebrew transliteration
Kataif:	Nut & cheese stuffed pancakes
Kef:	Stop, Arabic transliteration
Kef halak:	How are you, Arabic transliteration
Kilim:	Tapestry-woven Arabic carpet
Kippa:	See kippot
Kippot:	Plural of kippa, also known as yarmulke. A round head covering worn by men in obedience to the Talmud's admonition to cover one's head that the fear of heaven may be upon you
Knafeh Nabulsiyye:	Arabic sweet pastry
Knesset:	Legislature of Israel
Kolokol-1:	An incapacitating gas that brings unconsciousness in one to three seconds. Thought to be a derivative of fentanyl dissolved in halothane
Law of Blood Atonement:	The ancient law of killing a murderer by a

	blood avenger, usually carried out by the slain victim's nearest male relative
LeHitra'ot:	Goodbye, Hebrew transliteration
Leila sa'eeda:	Good night, Arabic transliteration
M203 Grenade Launcher:	Single-shot 400 mm grenade launcher attached to specific Israeli rifles
Ma'assalama:	Go in peace, Arabic transliteration
Magav:	(Israel Border Police) Abbreviation for Magavnikim, Hebrew transliteration
Magavnik:	Single Israel Border Guard, Hebrew transliteration
Magavnikim:	Colloquial for Israel Border Police
Magavnikyot:	Two or more female Israel Border Guards
Magen David Adom:	Israel's national emergency medical, disaster, ambulance, and blood bank service.
Makdeha:	Drill, Hebrew transliteration
Marhaba:	Hello, Arabic transliteration
Ma shelomkha:	How are you, Hebrew transliteration
Masaa'al-kheir:	Good evening, Arabic transliteration
Me go'el haddam:	Law of the blood avenger, Hebrew transliteration
Mehabel:	Terrorist, singular, masculine, Hebrew transliteration
Mehablim:	Terrorists, plural masculine, Hebrew transliteration
Messianic Jew:	A Jewish person who is a Christian
Metsada:	Mossad Special Operations Division
Migdal David:	Tower of David, Hebrew transliteration
Mihrab:	A semi-circular niche in the wall of a mosque indicating the direction toward Mecca all Muslims must face while praying
Mossad:	Institute for Intelligence and Special Tasks. Acronym for HaMossad leModi'in uleTafkidim Meyuchadim (Israel's CIA)
Mujahid:	A person involved in Jihad (struggle)
Mujahideen:	Plural. People involved in Jihad (struggle)
Mutaween:	Arabic religious police
Na'am:	Yes, Arabic transliteration
Negev:	South desert in Israel
Noble Sanctuary:	See al-Haram Ash-Sharif
OIC:	Officer In Charge

Owl:	Israeli reference for UH-60 Helicopter
PALFA:	Palestinian Freedom Army
Parapet:	A low wall used to screen troops from the enemy
PMIJ:	Palestine Mujahideen Islamic Jihad
Pogrom:	An organized, often officially abetted, massacre or persecution of a minority group, all too often the Jews
Polymerase chain reaction:	A technique to amplify a single or limited copies of a piece of DNA by generating copies of a DNA sequence
Rabbinate:	Chief Rabbinate of Israel. Supreme halakhic (Jewish law) spiritual authority in Israel
Rekel:	A type of coat worn mainly by Hasidic Jewish men
Rosh Hashanah:	Jewish New Year
RPG-7:	Rocket Propelled Grenades. A Russian-made weapon officially known as Ruchnoy Protivotankoviy Granatomet hand-held grenade launcher.
Salam:	Hi, Arabic transliteration
As Salam a' alaykum:	Peace be with you, Arabic transliteration
Secular:	Worldly or temporal rather than spiritual: not sacred
Shabak:	Acronym for Israel General Security Service
Shaheed:	Suicide bomber
Shalom:	Hello, goodbye, or peace, Hebrew transliteration
Shalom aleichem:	Peace be upon you, Hebrew transliteration
Shalom, ma koreh?:	Hello, how are things, Hebrew transliteration
Sherut haBitachon haKlali:	Israel's FBI
Shi'a:	Sect in Islam
Shokolad Para:	Israeli Chocolate bar known as Cow Chocolate
Spasibo:	Thank you, Russian transliteration
SSR:	Soviet Socialist Republic
Stepnogorsk:	Stepnogorsk Scientific and Technical Institute for Microbiology located in Kazakhstan. A biological weapons research and development facility where a super stain of anthrax is reported to have been developed
Sunni:	Sect in Islam
Tachrichim:	Jewish Burial Shroud

Tanakh:	Jewish Bible
TDR:	Time Domain Reflectometry is the analysis of a conductor (wire, cable, or fiber optic) by sending a pulsed signal into the conductor, and then examining the reflection of that pulse
Tell:	An ancient mound, especially in the Middle East, composed of remains of successive settlements
Torah:	Also known as the Pentateuch, the first five books in the Bible
Tower of David:	A complex of buildings in the Old City Jerusalem
Tzaddik:	A title bestowed upon righteous Jews
Ulpan:	School for the intensive study of Hebrew
Varenykey:	Ukrainian dish. Stuffed dumpling of unleavened dough with mashed potatoes and cheese mixed in, topped by sour cream with fried onions
West Bank:	Arab delineation of Judea & Samaria
WIAB:	Wireless Induction Array Biosensor. Registers trace biological anthrax spore emissions
Yad VaShem:	Holocaust museum
Yagi Antenna:	Sometimes referred to as a Yagi-Uda antenna. A directional high-gain antenna
Ya'Ma'M (also Yamam):	Hebrew acronym for Special autonomous Police Unit
Yanshuf:	Owl, Hebrew transliteration
Yarmulke:	See kippot
Yawm al-Jumu'ah:	'Yawm' means day in Arabic, 'Jumu'ah' is the weekly Muslim Day of Prayer which falls on Friday. 'Yawn al' Jumu'ah' is the Muslim weekly day of prayer and rest
Yedioth Ahronoth:	Daily Hebrew language newspaper, whose name means latest news
Yisra'el:	Israel, Hebrew transliteration
Yerushalayim:	Jerusalem, Hebrew transliteration
Y'shua:	Jesus, Hebrew transliteration
Zaydeh:	Grandpápa, Yiddish transliteration
Zdravstvuite:	Hello, Russian transliteration
Zik:	Spark, Hebrew transliteration